THE NIGHTMARE THRONE

THE
NIGHTMARE THRONE

AUSTIN LYNN CLARK

AEILIC PRESS
LLC

This is a work of fiction. All of the characters, organizations, and events portrayed in this novel are either products of the author's imagination or are used fictitiously.

THE NIGHTMARE THRONE

Edited by Jonathan Smith
Map by Austin Lynn Clark
Illustrations by Austin Lynn Clark

An Aeilic Press Book
Published by Aeilic Press LLC
El Paso, TX

www.austinlynnclark.com

ISBN 978-1-969055-02-7

First Paperback Edition: September 2025
Printed in the United States of America

0 9 8 7 6 5 4 3 2 1

For Erika.

CONTENTS

The Empire of
Navara
Brelfall
Dairu
Lanredol
Tasheroc
The City-State of
Carhein
Jaed Keep
Naconta
The Ruins Of
Lithia
Sorvadel

Merilon
Silverwater Castle
The Kingdom of
Seldor
THE WORLD OF ERLAN
CIRCA 318 AFTER THE RISE OF THE ABYSS
Chamela
The Capitol
Perandolen
Fontelis
New Ahman
Wern's Hold

Part 1

Of Gods and Shadows

Black curtains of smoke
Sting my eyes, and wet the tongue
With the hot, resinous sweetness
Of scorched, caramelized sugar.

Smoldering strawberry fields,
Restless, writhing vines
Tethered deep within the earth
To simmer red and dark.

I want to forget the world.
Let me sleep in this land forever,
Bury my face amidst these ashes,
Unhear their anguished prayers.
-Confessions of Irisea
(year unknown)

Chapter 1
AGAINST THE UNSEEN

The skies were thick with blood.

Warm and crimson, it showered through the canopy of dead branches, clinging and soaking into the blackened wood. It ran in rivulets down their trunks, merging into rancid streams. To later dry upon the mountainside in a coagulated crust.

It took a special kind of person to see the abyssal rain, and Kaycia, unfortunately, wasn't one of them. To her, it was as though the blood wasn't there. She had to picture it in her mind—the viscous globs pelting her leather hood and the warm humidity against her face.

It was damn unfair.

The problem wasn't that Kaycia wanted to see blood—she'd never been fascinated by the bleak and morbid. No, the real issue was that she'd wasted seven years of her life chasing a dream. She'd gone against her mother's will and given up a reputable apprenticeship in bone smithing. She'd put everything into her training, all with the expectation that her eyes would be opened—to not only see the rain but the abyssal current itself.

In the end, her vision remained unchanged. Instead of setting things right, she'd ended up like her father. Two weeks ago, her rites of ascendancy failed, and there were no second chances.

From beneath her leather hood, as she rode alongside the rocking, armored carriage, Kaycia saw nothing to distinguish this afternoon from any other. There was nothing unusual in the pale buttermilk sky or the crunch of autumn grass beneath the mounted mercenaries. The air itself wasn't scented with copper but sweet, dry cedar.

Were it not for Tenlen's warning—reminding her to keep her dark red hair safely tucked within her hood—it might've been easy to believe there was no rain at all.

Her mare's step faltered, giving a snort and shaking its mane with irritation.

"It's miserable, I know," said Kaycia, stroking the horse's neck. Its slick black hair felt strangely dry. She could feel how the rain made it clump together, though she couldn't feel the stickiness itself.

Still, it'd been her choice not to ride inside the carriage. Instead of relaxing with her sister and the other two women, she'd sought a different kind of peace. Outside, at least, she could pretend to be useful.

More than that, she wanted to observe the mercenaries. Like her, these men couldn't see the blood, either, and yet here they were, risking life and limb. Days away from the nearest populated village.

Perhaps she, too, could find new purpose as a sentry.

Urging her mare forward, she came up beside Tenlen, their group's ascendant, who was stooped forward, driving the carriage from beneath a black canvas overhang. Shoulder-length iron hair hung beneath the brim of his rawhide hat. Only his stern face was visible, with his body hidden beneath the folds of his cloak, or wrapped in cloth bandages.

She bit her lip. "I thought you checked the ropes."

Tenlen worked his mouth in distaste. "Wearing thin already? This damn corrosive weather..."

"They're not going to last," Kaycia insisted. "Perhaps, if we moved the heavier cookware inside—"

"Can't stop," he said with a deranged smile. "We're being followed—don't turn your head."

Without the warning, Kaycia might've done just that, and it took effort to keep her eyes forward on the six riders in front—a number far fewer than was typical these days. She felt a chill at the thought of something back there, watching through the trees. But looking back wouldn't have done her much good anyway. Whatever followed them would be as invisible as the rain.

All the same, she found herself straining to hear anything above the fall of hooves and the bump and jolt of the carriage. The faint scrape of claws against the hard-packed earth. A rustling through the grass. The held breath of anticipation. But the forest was as empty and dead as it'd been since leaving Wern's Hold two days ago.

Her hand almost went to her spear at her shoulder, but she stopped herself. These weren't mindless creatures, and she had to be careful of such absentminded gestures. At moments like these, she had to trust in her training. She'd practiced drawing her weapon on time in the event of an ambush. If needed, she also had knives at her waist and a loaded crossbow clasped to the saddlebag behind her.

"Now, I need you to stay calm," he continued. "Don't start anything out of the ordinary, you hear?"

She nodded and drew her mare closer to the wagon. She lowered her voice just enough to be heard above the horses. "Did you get a good look at it?"

Tenlen merely grunted. "Not really."

Kaycia hid her frustration. Here she was, trying to understand a threat only *he* could see, and he didn't seem to care.

Gingerly, she pressed further, "I mean, what if you only thought—?"

"Thought what?" he asked, with a scowl. "You think I would've said anything if I wasn't sure?"

"I meant no disrespect."

"I know you didn't," he said, softening his tone. "But look... This conduct might've worked with your professors—but out here, on the road, it's not your job to question your ascendant officer."

"Yes, sir," she said, feeling foolish. After years of speaking casually with ascendants, it was a habit she found difficult to break. Tenlen had reminded her, more than once on this trip, to act deferential—but, this time, he seemed less patient than usual. And she realized she'd never seen him quite so on edge.

The ivory, indirect sunlight deepened as the trees down the path grew closer together. The widest trunks were over six feet across, with crisscrossed branches that twisted like thorn bushes. It was beautiful, in a way—not at all like the world Tenlen saw. And it wasn't just the blood...or the monsters.

Within the abyssal current, it was *always* dark, as though the sun itself had cooled into ash. There was no moon, either. No stars. It was a wonder ascendants could see anything at all.

Kaycia couldn't deny she'd been terrified by the prospect of entering that nightmare world. There had been times these past years when she'd climbed onto her dormitory's roof to watch the sunset. It'd been her way of making peace with never seeing daylight again. Kaycia still remembered how sad she'd felt, and how a part of her had *hoped* her ceremony would fail.

But when that failure became a reality, Kaycia became even more confused. The relief she'd expected never came. And while she *was* glad to see the sun, it'd come to represent everything denied her.

She adjusted her grip on the reins. "I'll ride to the front and inform the captain."

"What did I tell you?" he asked. "Just sit tight. No sudden movements. The men will know soon enough."

His condescending tone sent heat through her face. A simple ride forward was unlikely to provoke an attack. If anything, the warning would make the men more alert. More primed to respond.

Besides, shouldn't Captain Veldt be making these decisions? While it was true Tenlen held seniority as their only ascendant, he'd chosen to defer his command to Veldt. She didn't completely understand the arrangement but sensed it was related to Tenlen's advanced age.

Her lips parted, preparing to argue, but she stopped herself.

There was something in Tenlen's poise—an unsteadiness in the way his bandaged hands gripped the reins. It was nothing so evident as sweaty skin or shaky palms. Outwardly, he appeared tired—bored, even—but it was likely a cover. An effort to conceal how tightly he was stretched.

Rather than take risks, he was delaying the attack as long as possible. Long enough, perhaps, to reach the abandoned village she'd heard the others mention earlier. They were supposed to get there by nightfall.

"You can tell me," she said, keeping her tone aloof. "I won't panic. How *many* did you see?"

He hesitated, meeting her gaze, before turning away.

Kaycia swallowed hard.

Traveling with such a small escort was a gamble, but they hadn't much choice. Neither Kaycia, her sister, nor Marien—her financial sponsor—could afford the more prestigious caravans. The Lady Marien had invested nearly all her wealth into Kaycia's schooling, and yet, she'd insisted on paying this final traveling expense. They'd take this carriage back to Carheim together before splitting ways. Unfortunately, with insurance premiums on the rise, they couldn't afford more than a single elderly ascendant.

This was not to say small companies were always bad. In many ways, small escorts had proven equally effective as larger ones, due to their speed and tendency to draw less attention. Kaycia herself had traveled with similar groups in the past without incident.

But the countryside was getting worse.

There was little point in deceiving herself. They might've fended off a single attacker—two, at most. Any more than that, and there'd be no battle. It'd be more of a chaotic retreat—a desperate struggle to keep ahead of the invisible onslaught.

Kaycia would end up dead like her father.

All because her ceremony had failed.

"Could you give me a guess?" she asked. "How many there are?"

His grimace was sober. "Hard to say... More than I'd like. If you keep asking questions, I won't hear them coming."

And with that, she said no more.

Not fifteen minutes later, the riders stopped in front.

"What's going on?" asked Kaycia.

Tenlen shook his head, clearly nervous. "Go ahead," he said. "Check it out."

She nodded and urged her horse into a canter.

Like most hunters or mercenaries, their group wore hoods and matching livery—faded black cloth embroidered with a golden seagull. But, unlike most companies, their assortment of armor was a mismatched array of shapes and shades. This was either an indication they saw combat frequently—with a continuous need to replace damaged gear—or their earnings weren't consistent enough to afford more than scraps. Out of sheer hope, Kaycia preferred to believe the former.

When she reached the front, the leading riders were in a heated debate.

"We can't just stand here," said Roke, one of the men near Kaycia's age.

"I'm well aware," hissed Captain Veldt, controlling his tone with difficulty.

Their eyes looked ahead as though searching for something.

As Kaycia brought her horse beside them, she found no obstructions. They weren't looking for a way around, as she might've expected, had the land been washed away by floodwater.

No. The dirt road was simply gone. Not destroyed, but more as though the road had never existed. The forest looked the same on all sides, with no discernible signs of which way to go.

"I say we keep straight," said Roke. "We've been going the right direction, so sooner or later, we'll find where it picks up, you think?"

The captain grimaced but didn't disagree. He appeared to be weighing their options.

"You're wrong," said another man. "We lost the road at the stream. I *told* you that wasn't no deer trail!"

"Give it a rest," said Roke. "You even stepped in deer shit. We all saw."

"And?"

None of this helped Kaycia feel better.

"Haven't you traveled through here before?" she asked, unwilling to believe Marien would've hired mercenaries with such poor experience.

"Not recently," said one. "Been what? Ten years?"

When a few others admitted this was their first time through Graywood Pass, Kaycia became increasingly appalled.

"I have," said Veldt. "But that's not the problem."

Everyone turned as the carriage rolled to a stop behind them.

Tenlen met the captain's eyes and, in a raised voice, confirmed his suspicion. "The forest is moving."

"The hell?" asked Roke.

Kaycia, however, understood. It was a possibility that'd worried her since learning of their route. The only reason she hadn't said anything was because she'd expected these men's experiences to outweigh her own.

The young man, too uncomfortable to look at the misshapen ascendant, directed his question at Kaycia. "What does he mean, moving?"

"More like changing," she clarified. "People don't talk about it much, but it's the risk you take the further you travel from civilization." She shook her head. "None of this would've happened if we'd taken the main thoroughfare."

"I agree," said the captain.

His reaction confused her because Veldt wasn't the sort to admit his mistakes. There wasn't, however, any remorse in his tone. If anything, he sounded angry.

Did she have it wrong, then? Until that moment, she'd assumed this was his idea. And he'd chosen Graywood Pass based on personal experience.

But Veldt wasn't really in charge, now, was he?

Marien was the one paying these men.

Kaycia frowned. She'd known Marien's family most of her life and couldn't think why the lady hadn't consulted her first.

"We need a plan, now!" said Tenlen.

Kaycia shot the ascendant a wide-eyed look, as though to ask if the creatures had finally caught up.

Tenlen shook his head. "The rain is making us difficult to see. They're holding back—waiting for the storm to pass."

At this, the men exchanged nervous glances.

Kaycia swallowed, wondering if it could be so simple. So it wasn't luck they hadn't yet been attacked, but poor visibility?

Everyone agreed something needed to be done, but no decisions were being made.

That's when a woman's shout came from the carriage. "One moment!"

The side panel had been opened. The shadows within made it difficult to see, but it seemed as though the lady was leafing through some notebooks.

"Yes, here!" shouted Marien. She then leaned her upper body out the window. Her dark brown hair was a mess—a loose bun surrounded by several strays. She didn't seem bothered by the exposure to the blood—at least, not as much as she cared to be understood.

Kaycia looked where the woman was pointing.

"That peak above us..." said Marien. "We're in the right place. All we need do is find the ravine between this peak...and that one there. You see it? Above those elms?"

"You're certain?" asked Veldt.

"Without a doubt."

At once, Kaycia felt both surprise and reassurance. This not only confirmed they'd been traveling the right way, but that Marien had planned for this. The lady was wise to use mountains as landmarks, as their size made them more resistant to changes in the forest.

"You heard her! Move!"

Captain Veldt turned to the man nearest him. "Not you, Roke. I want you to drive the carriage. I'll feel better if Tenlen has his hands free."

When the captain turned to the ascendant, the older man nodded in gratitude.

Only Roke seemed to think this a bad idea, but he handed his horse into another rider's care.

Tenlen slid to one side, a crossbow clutched between his hands, as the younger man took the reins and got them moving again.

For the first time, Kaycia felt some relief. Here was proof these men could behave like professionals, which made her willing to give Marien the benefit of the doubt. For all she knew, finding men more experienced with the region was impossible.

The problem was that no one traveled here anymore.

Kaycia rode silently beside the large wheels, listening carefully for anything unusual.

Once she felt reasonably certain an attack wasn't imminent—that the creatures were indeed waiting for the rain to subside—she leaned over and rapped her knuckles against the wooden panel.

No one answered.

She became insistent and shouted, "Marien!" before knocking a second time.

The panel slid open, not by the lady but by Kaycia's younger sister, Elyriel.

A girl of fifteen, she was nearing the age when Kaycia had begun her training—except Elyriel had no interest in becoming an ascendant. She'd been content to let that be Kaycia's thing, but was yet to decide what she'd rather do instead.

Deep shadows concealed most of the girl's face but not her sullen mood. "Marien doesn't want to talk right now."

Kaycia groaned. "Damn it, Marien!" She leaned over to bang on the wood once more. "This is no time to hide!"

From inside came an exasperated sigh.

"What is it, girl?"

There was movement as Elyriel switched places with the woman.

For her advanced age, she wasn't unattractive, with deep green eyes and a few streaks of silver hair. Her facial lines were faint and more suggestive of a cheerful demeanor than otherwise. Her body was thin and donned with the refined, ochre dress of someone accustomed to getting her way.

Kaycia grit her teeth. "Graywood Pass?" she asked, getting directly to the point. "You never mentioned this was *your* idea! What the hell are we doing here?"

"Watch your tone, young woman!"

"Or what?!"

It felt strange to yell at Marien, who, in many ways, had become like her second mother—one who appreciated Kaycia more than her birth mother had. For the past seven years, the woman hadn't only paid for Kaycia's tuition, food, and clothing—she'd also covered Elyriel's needs. This, alone, went far beyond the terms of their contract.

The woman had done more than enough to earn her loyalty and respect, and Kaycia felt guilty for speaking so forcefully. But Kaycia was furious. Not for the woman's secrets or her reckless planning, but the fact she'd included her sister in this danger.

"Look," said Marien. "I didn't want to come here. There wouldn't have been a need had you only—"

"Had I only, what?"

Kaycia knew exactly what Marien was going to say and was outraged the woman would pin this on her—on the failed ceremony that neither of them anticipated.

Marien said nothing.

Taking a deep breath, Kaycia realized this was a poor moment to take offense. Her failure, after all, hadn't only ruined her life but Marien's as well.

If it was desperation, however, that'd driven the lady into Graywood Pass, the important thing, now, was to find out why. And Kaycia would get no closer to those answers by behaving like a petulant child.

She swallowed. "Just tell me what we're doing. What's out here, Marien?"

The lady hesitated, then said, "We're almost there. Once we clear the ravine, you'll see Hebril. It's an old village nestled between these mountains."

Kaycia had never heard of a village by that name.

Undoubtedly, it was the place the others mentioned earlier—an abandoned ruin. Until now, Kaycia had assumed it was nothing more than a rest stop—a safe place to camp for the night before passing through.

"This village—is it defensible?"

Marien appeared surprised—then uncertain. "I'm not the right person to ask that question."

Kaycia clenched her teeth in frustration.

The lady frowned. "There was mention of a tower, I think…" Then, she shook her head. "To be honest, my only information is what my husband wrote down. This all comes from his notes. They were never meant to be comprehensive."

"So you look it up! Gods, Marien! Do you even realize how dangerous—?"

Marien raised a hand to stop her. "I tried. But there's nothing to research. When it comes to Hebril, there *are* no records."

Kaycia didn't know what to say.

"No charters," continued Marien. "No histories. Not even tax reports."

While Kaycia trusted the woman, she still found this difficult to believe. "Okay. But couldn't you have asked someone? I mean, Captain Veldt claims to have traveled here before. There have to be others!"

Marien nodded. "You're right. Memories don't disappear so easily as paperwork. But, even so, when it comes to places like Hebril…you can't just ask anyone. You never know who might be listening."

"Suppose you're right—and someone *is* hiding something. Please, don't tell me we came all this way to satisfy your curiosity!"

"That's not it at all," said the woman with a smile. "We're out here because we know what's here—and why. It's all in the notebook."

Kaycia hoped Marien would get to the point.

"Hebril might be small for a village, but it has one thing most these places don't… A *monastery*."

Kaycia remained quiet, waiting for more.

A monastery, after all, wasn't anything special. It provided sacred ground, of course—a location closer to the gods and the aeilic realms than any other. But monasteries were everywhere. In Carheim alone, there were half a dozen.

Marien, however, appeared to be finished.

For a second, Kaycia couldn't shake her disappointment—as if all this build-up had been for nothing. But then it dawned on her.

This wasn't just a monastery, but an *abandoned* monastery. Which meant no monks, no priests. No supervising clergy.

Marien was plotting something—the sort that shouldn't be discussed out loud.

Kaycia returned her attention to the terrain ahead.

During their conversation, the path had brought them down a gradual slope, converging into the ravine proper. Sheer rock walls rose on both sides, where ancient glaciers had carved through the bedrock between peaks.

Now, however, there was no water to be seen—leaving nothing more than a clear, dry path.

Except...it wasn't really dry, was it?

If the abyssal rain was as bad as Tenlen suggested, wouldn't the runoff from both mountains run straight through here? She imagined cascades of blood running down the cliffs in a continuous current against their horses' legs.

The ascendant, however, didn't appear concerned, and Kaycia was forced to conclude it wasn't deep.

Even so, she continued to watch him and was surprised when the man rose to his feet. He hastily took down the canvas overhang, removing the obstruction from his line of sight—and the aim of his crossbow.

"Shut the window," instructed Kaycia.

Tenlen shouted, "Let's pick up the pace!"

The riders responded immediately. There was no moment of confusion or need for clarification.

Kaycia pushed her mare forward, maintaining her position beside the carriage.

"What is it?" she asked, looking up at Tenlen.

"Roke!" he shouted. "Get us out of here—now!"

His voice was all wrong.

It was as though her ears had been stuffed with cotton. And it wasn't just his words that were muffled. Everything, from the creaking wheels to the fall of hooves—to the sound of Kaycia's breathing—was becoming increasingly difficult to make out.

Oh, gods...! she thought, as she drew her spear—without hearing so much as the scrape of leather. *They're here.*

In less than a heartbeat, Tenlen turned, stepped onto his seat, and leaped high above the carriage roof.

Kaycia craned her neck, keeping sight of his dark cloak as it trailed behind him, snapping soundlessly through the air.

The man flew up over fifteen feet—impossible for anyone without an ascendant's strength—before his trajectory lurched sideways.

At first, Kaycia thought he'd been hit as he was thrown against the ravine wall.

She was forced to turn away—her attention drawn to the rocks ahead—but just before she did, she saw him land on his feet. He'd landed sideways, high above the ground, to stand perpendicular against the stone.

Only then did she realize the truth.

Tenlen's abilities were not the same ones for which Kaycia had been training. The older man was bound to a different god, a different realm, and a different set of rules.

And while Kaycia had taken time to study each of the eight aspects and their branches of ascendancy, this was her first real chance to see this particular variety—known as Equilibrium—in action.

Kaycia looked back again and saw Tenlen running diagonally down the wall toward the invisible enemy. He was surprisingly agile for a man of his ungainly physique. He made it seem easy, as though the entire world had tilted sideways, and he was running along the ground. From beneath the folds of his cloak came a flash of bone as he produced some weapon.

At one instant, the blade trailed behind him, his right arm bent back—then, he was swinging in an upward arc.

Tenlen sprung off the wall, flying parallel to the ground. To her surprise, his trajectory didn't slow but sped up. There was a moment's resistance as his weapon contacted something. His orientation of gravity—one that affected only him—sent him through the enemy and falling toward the opposite wall.

She wanted to keep watching but was forced to turn away.

Up ahead, Veldt signaled some riders to fall back to help defend the rear of the carriage.

At the same time, however, she saw the wagon bounce, with the ropes in the back stretching dangerously. All their packs—including their rolled-up canvas tent, bedding, and cooking supplies—drooped closer to the ground, threatening to break loose at any moment.

Knowing this would pose a risk for the others, Kaycia spun her spear. She waited for Tenlen to reach the side of the path, and she struck the rope.

Her aim was sloppy—against strands moving every which way—but it did the trick.

At once, the bags fell free. Some broke open as they hit the ground, scattering utensils and pots across the road. The enormous canvas roll bounced, turned, then collided with an unseen force. One end bucked high into the air while the other skidded forward, pushed by the momentum of the invisible beast.

The other tumbling bags produced similar effects as the charging horde swerved and stumbled.

Amid the chaos, the creatures fell back—but didn't stop completely. It was enough distance, however, to weaken the silence. Enough for a small but noticeable improvement in her hearing.

Taking advantage of this, Captain Veldt began to shout—as though his voice were passing through a long tunnel.

"The village entrance is narrow, walled off by these cliffs. So tight, two carriages can't pass side by side. We'll take advantage of that! And block that space!"

"What?!" shouted Kaycia. "With what time?"

"It'll be enough," said Veldt with a devious smile. "There's an old watchtower above the entrance. With a single, well-placed munition, I'll collapse the structure right into the gap."

"And then?" asked Kaycia, shaking her head. "Even if that works—you're talking about a rock pile! They'll force their way through!"

"I never said it would stop them," said Veldt, his voice growing fainter by the second. "Keep ahead of the blast, and we'll—"

She didn't hear the rest. It was enough, however, to convey his intent. They wouldn't stop at the village but keep riding through the night.

Just like that, Marien's careful planning had amounted to nothing. After coming all this way to visit this monastery, they'd have no more than a handful of seconds before rushing off again, deeper into the mountains.

At this point, however, Kaycia didn't care. For the first time since the attack began, Veldt had presented a feasible solution. And though she didn't relish the idea of pushing on through the night—bringing their horses and themselves to exhaustion—it was their only option. The only way both she and her sister might safely reach home.

Even Marien would have to agree. The lady might be foolhardy, but she wasn't suicidal.

As Kaycia alternated her view between the road and craning her head back, she found Tenlen soaring above the ravine. His arc curved until he landed atop the cliff.

When he stopped near a large boulder protruding from the edge—over half as large as the carriage itself—the strangest thing occurred. The rock began to tremble, breaking loose from its position.

Then, both Tenlen and the rock fell toward the enemy.

While Kaycia knew this was possible—that Tenlen could extend his influence to the area surrounding him—she also knew it came at a significant cost. Draining his reserves at an exponential rate.

Tenlen curved his path upward, just before the boulder slammed into the ground.

Unexpectedly, sound returned—the thunderous boom too loud for her sensitized ears. Her mare staggered as the earth trembled. Loose dirt rained down on both sides.

There was more she could hear: shouts from the soldiers, the thundering echoes of hooves. An unearthly wail. It all mixed like a deafening flood.

"Are they dead?" a man yelled, unwilling to look back and check for himself.

When Kaycia turned, she could only see an immense cloud of dust filling the gorge.

But then...she saw shapes—outlines of figures where the dust was absent. There were spindly voids where limbs twisted and rose to their feet.

"Bloody heavens..." she said, without revealing what she'd seen.

The dust didn't cling to the creatures as one might expect. Anything that didn't penetrate their hides, including paints, powders, or tinctures, would slough off.

This left Kaycia barely a few seconds to count at least three shapes. But due to the fact she was riding a horse, and the billowing dust refused to stay still, there could've easily been twice that number.

"Keep moving!" she shouted—disheartened to hear her voice diminishing. The creatures were recovering too quickly.

"Are we almost there?" she asked while the captain could still hear.

"I don't understand!" he responded. "We should've seen it by now!"

His change in tone was unnerving—casting aside his mask of confidence.

Kaycia, however, refused to give up.

Even if the forest was moving—it couldn't have changed much, could it? The mountains were still here, right where they should be. This pass—this gorge—was still here. So, the tower must be, too. Perhaps not in the same place, but close, right?

Try as she might, she saw nothing up the mountain or hidden in the trees—nothing that resembled an artificial construct.

Up ahead, the ravine curved, and she couldn't see what was causing the riders to slow.

Bloody heavens! she thought, knowing the last thing they needed was one more obstacle. It wasn't until she'd rounded the corner that she realized the truth was much worse.

The problem *was* the tower, fallen to ruin.

With no other choice, she pulled her horse to a stop.

"Damn it!" she yelled.

Had the unattended structure collapsed by itself? Or had another group, perhaps, fled through here before and concocted a plan similar to Veldt's?

Either way, there was more rubble than a single building could account for. The lumber was intermingled with great sections of earth and rock, broken from the cliff and adding to the barrier.

Due to the narrow space, wooden supports jutted twelve feet into the air, sharp and jagged. Moreover, the wreckage had spilled in both directions, creating a distance of over a hundred feet between their group and the opposite side.

"What now?!" she shouted.

Veldt didn't seem to hear. He turned back the way they came—eyes wide and jaw rigid.

This time, the air thickened all at once, like an avalanche of silence crushing them in.

She brought her horse around and looked down a canyon that only appeared empty.

At the moment, even Tenlen seemed to have gone missing.

Clutching her spear, she struggled to keep her hands from shaking. Beads of sweat ran down her neck and back.

"Oh gods..." she breathed.

But, by then, she could not even hear herself.

Chapter 2
EQUILIBRIUM

Without a sound, the left cliff face exploded.

Her horse danced sideways, resisting Kaycia's attempts to regain control.

Dust filled the gorge as rocks and pebbles scattered like hail. But the worst of the blast was kept at a distance—over twenty feet out, as Veldt must've planned. Where there'd once been a vertical crevice, the small explosive tore a wedge from the wall, pushing outward to obstruct the narrow path.

A small gap remained on the opposite side, where a void in the dust tried to claw its way through. The shape was indistinct, but the size was suggestive of a giant panther or an average-sized bear. Large enough to make its progress difficult but not stop entirely.

Making a signal, the captain dismounted with three other men and raised a wall of shields to intercept the beast.

Kaycia's breath caught in her throat, thinking their best option was to wait for Tenlen. But try as she might, she couldn't find him anywhere.

Her training kicked in, and her free hand fumbled to retrieve her crossbow. She laid it over her opposite arm, holding her spear sideways, as she prepared to provide what support she could. The two men mounted beside her did the same.

As the dust settled, she didn't see when the creature cleared the gap. She only saw the impact as it crashed into the shields. A second blow was directed at the captain in the middle. It drove him back a step while the soldier on his right was thrown against the wall, lifted into the air by invisible limbs.

Kaycia loosed her bolt, using the man's position to direct her aim.

And missed.

She cursed in frustration, knowing an ascendant would've easily made the shot.

Luckily, the man beside her had better aim. His wooden shaft jerked midair, blunted by the impact, and the floating mercenary was dropped to the ground.

Kaycia staunched her embarrassment and forced her hands to reload.

The line of shields drove forward in unison.

The mounted rider on her left, named Dent, spun a net in the air. It was a risky maneuver in such a confined area, but his aim was impeccable above the men's heads.

At once, the mass of thick cords grew taut as it caught flailing limbs. Too many limbs—six, maybe more—stretching out with such ferocity, the ropes snapped in a few places.

The mercenaries closed in, thrusting spears into the gaps—but there wasn't enough time. The second creature had emerged from the crack.

Kaycia swallowed a pit of despair, knowing this might've been their only chance to finish one off. If these creatures were too much for Tenlen to handle, what hope did the rest of them have?

She glanced back at the carriage—not because she'd heard something but more from a feeling.

And, for a moment, she could do nothing but stare in shock.

The shattered beams and rubble were rising.

It wasn't fast, like when Tenlen's body fell upward or even when he'd shifted the boulder from before.

Individual rafters and struts floated up, one by one, to join a mass of debris. Loose gravel and even a few decrepit human corpses revolved slowly in a cloud above the ravine, like flotsam suspended in a churning river.

At once, she realized *this* was the solution. Everything else, including their defensive formation, wasn't intended to kill the enemy or even drive them back. They were buying Tenlen time to secure their escape.

Even after she understood, she was overwhelmed by the implications. The strength required for such a feat went beyond the capabilities of the average ascendant. She'd only met a few others who might've even gotten close.

The only certainty was that Tenlen couldn't maintain this exertion much longer.

"The way's been opened!" she yelled, though no one could hear.

Thus far, the shields were proving their worth—made even more effective by the narrow enclosure. It didn't matter that a third beast had joined the fray, as there wasn't enough space to attack all at once.

She waved her arms.

The soldier on her right was too focused on the battle, but Dent turned toward her.

Kaycia pointed back. "We need to go!" She exaggerated her lips, making them easier to read.

Dent nodded in understanding. He mouthed something like, "I'll let them know," before pointing Kaycia toward the carriage. He was telling her to leave—in a reminder that, above all else, its defense was their duty.

But, instead of feeling honored, she flushed in shame. Without him saying it, she knew how useless she'd been. Her training was intended for someone with inhuman strength and inhuman speed. And it was time she stopped pretending she could make it as a mercenary.

She walked her horse backward and made a break for the carriage.

The horses belonging to the dismounted men stamped the ground in unease. Fortunately, they possessed enough sense not to run. The only way out was beneath the floating rubble.

Kaycia was surprised to find her sister in the driver's seat—only then remembering Roke was needed for the fight.

In many ways, the girl was a younger version of Kaycia—but with pale golden hair rather than red. Her nose was sharper and her skin more clear—save for a light spray of freckles across her nose and cheeks.

Elyriel's eyes were wide as she watched the maelstrom. She appeared smaller and frailer than usual, with her long hair plastered to the contours of her neck and back. Her light green traveling dress, too, clung tight to her skin—a sight all the more odd as both her hair and clothing were completely dry. In appearance, anyway.

"Move over!" said Kaycia, stepping down from her horse and propping her spear by the seat. At this distance from the creatures, her voice was muted but just loud enough to hear.

She didn't doubt her sister could've driven the carriage. Elyriel was old enough to have learned help wouldn't always come. And she was noble enough to know when others were counting on her.

"It'll be all right," said Kaycia, grasping the reins.

Elyriel nodded silently.

The only problem was deciding *when* to start moving. Much of the wreckage was still waiting to rise—but the terrain might *never* become clear enough. Not before Tenlen ran out of strength.

She might've expected the ascendant to change his approach—to drift to one side and drop off some weight. But, considering the sheer number of fragments, even a single direction would consume his focus. Moreover, keeping the debris in one place was smart—to quickly close the pass once their group was safely through.

Kaycia decided to risk it.

The carriage jostled wildly as they crossed uneven ground. The path was too narrow to do much steering, but she did what she could to avoid complications. She hoped the horses' instincts would handle the rest.

Beside her, she could feel her sister's tension—as though every muscle in her body had gone rigid.

"Don't look up," said Kaycia.

The girl nodded quickly, still watching the sky.

This wasn't Elyriel's first trip through the countryside—but it *was* her first attack. Her mind, no doubt, would be filled with horror stories—the ones difficult to avoid and impossible to forget.

Most notably, the one that'd taken their father.

Kaycia pulled a long dagger, still in its sheath, from her belt. "You remember how to use this?"

Her sister nodded. "I think so... I mean, yes. Of course."

"I want you to have it."

Elyriel accepted the offering with awed reverence. She began to tuck it into her sash before she hesitated. "...But don't you need this?"

"I still have seven more."

The girl blinked before looking her up and down, attempting to discern where the rest were hidden.

Kaycia said nothing, satisfied with the distraction this provided her sister.

They were nearly a quarter way across before the carriage struck something solid and screeched to a stop.

In a panic, she wondered if a wheel was caught—or worse, had broken.

With a mixture of stubbornness and desperation, she tried to get the horses to push through—but, ultimately, it did no good.

"What is it?" asked Elyriel, clutching her arm.

"Let go!" demanded Kaycia, leaning away to search for the problem.

Suddenly, the carriage began to lift off the ground. She heard faint screams from the horses as they resisted—but only hurt themselves more.

"Oh no..." she said, looking up into the sky. "No, no, NO!"

But if Tenlen was to blame—pulling up on the carriage—she didn't know where to look. There were so many obstacles, she might not have seen him anyway.

She jumped down, hoping for a different explanation.

Suddenly, Elyriel pulled her back toward the carriage—and out of the path of a galloping horse.

It was the first rider to leave the battle—favoring his left arm that'd been wounded.

Her heart raced as she watched the man gallop away. He'd been so terrified of the debris overhead, he hadn't seen her step down. Even now, he went onward, oblivious to what his carelessness had nearly cost her.

"Thank you," she muttered, checking behind the carriage if the way was clear.

Crouching down, she found a large wooden beam jutting up from the dirt, caught beneath an axle. It'd been buried so deep it must've taken extra time to begin its ascent. But from its size alone, Kaycia knew it'd be impossible to extricate the carriage in time.

Their only choice was to leave it behind.

"Elle!" she shouted.

As her sister stepped down, Kaycia pointed to the dagger at her waist. "Cut the straps! Hurry!"

Elyriel turned to set the horses free.

Kaycia looked back, but no riders were coming.

She wasn't sure what to make of this. She was glad they weren't retreating all at once—with the enemy hot on their heels. Had that been the case, it would've eliminated all chances of getting away.

At the same time, she hoped they wouldn't wait too long. Once the first man died, the rest would soon follow.

Kaycia banged against the carriage.

"Marien!" she shouted.

She yanked the door open to find Marien's daughter, Chesandril, mouthing a fervent prayer. At twelve years of age, she had long black hair and a smooth, freckled face. Her dress was brown silk and embroidered in gold.

"We have to run!" yelled Kaycia.

Elyriel must've finished because the horses immediately broke into a gallop.

"No!" shouted the girl, chasing a few steps after them, but it was already too late.

She turned back to Kaycia, her expression apologetic. She'd known Kaycia had wanted those horses—not only for the ravine but for their escape afterward. In the end, however, it was wishful thinking—and Kaycia knew better than to blame her sister.

Chesandril stepped down and waited for instructions.

"Run!" shouted Kaycia.

The girl bolted like a frightened deer.

A second rider—Dent—had begun his retreat. Like the first, he was by himself.

Without awaiting an explanation, Kaycia grabbed her sister's wrist and waved the man down.

Elyriel protested, but Kaycia ignored her.

Dent understood, slowing enough to hoist the girl behind him and continue his escape.

"What the hell is going on?" Kaycia shouted into the carriage.

Marien was bent over, fumbling through the contents of a large open chest.

"Hold on!" said the woman. "This is important!"

"More than your life?! There's no time!"

There was a sudden shift in the sky above.

The collected mass dropped several inches before catching itself again and renewing its revolution.

"I'm sorry," said Kaycia. "But you're on your own!"

In her mind, she cursed Marien for making her do this. Then, she grabbed her spear from the driver's seat and broke into a sprint.

She'd only crossed half the distance before the sky dropped again—this time, several feet, before lurching to a stop.

Or rather...*most* of it stopped.

A small rock crashed into the back of her hood—the shock nearly causing her to drop her weapon. Something else struck her hand, drawing blood.

She pushed herself faster as the bits became a shower—small at first but growing larger. They pelted the ground in an incessant barrage.

At last, she was through.

She caught her first glimpse of the outskirts of a village. There was a stretch of land once used for gardening, with rectangular canvas frames to shield plants from the blood. Further ahead were scattered trees and dozens of decrepit buildings tucked neatly between the mountains on either side.

She took a few steps toward them before she turned, breathing heavily. She dropped her hands to her knees, still grasping her spear, and watched the final moments of the tower's descent.

The first figure to appear was a lone horse without a rider.

The second, to her amazement, had Marien seated behind him.

But the third...

As the rest of the avalanche came crashing down, spewing dust and gravel from the mouth of the gorge, the last had been running on foot. She hadn't seen him clearly, but she could've sworn, for a split-second, she'd seen his legs buckle as he was forced to the ground beneath stone, earth, and lumber.

His name had been Melev. Or Melvin. Or...dammit!

Numbly, she quickly counted in her head and noticed two others were absent. Had they been further back, too far to see? Or had they fallen earlier in the heat of battle?

She had trouble breathing—more than could be explained by her recent sprint. Her mind was reeling—from adrenaline and loss—but also with a fury that could've only been directed at Marien.

Were it not for the woman's plan, none of them would be here. And worse—her delay had cost precious seconds—time the last man could've used to escape.

As the three remaining riders regrouped outside the village, Kaycia saw it was Dent barking orders, with her sister still behind him. He was preparing to leave—in keeping with Veldt's original plan.

The captain was nowhere to be seen. Roke, too, was missing.

Her sister began to yell, "Kay... KAY!"

A man had caught the reins of the riderless horse, and both Dent and her sister were waving her toward it.

Kaycia hesitated.

"Has anyone seen Tenlen?" she demanded as she turned toward the rubble.

By then, the sun had disappeared entirely, and when combined with the billowing dust from the crash—it was near impossible to see anything.

"Last I saw, he was near the center," said Dent. "Everything was swirling around him. I don't see how he could've..."

He left the thought unfinished.

Kaycia herself didn't know what to think. She could only hope Tenlen hadn't overexerted himself—that he'd retained enough control to avoid getting crushed.

"Someone needs to find him!"

The men exchanged nervous glances—some appearing guilty. All were on edge, anxious to leave.

Kaycia groaned. "None of you? Really?"

"If we stay, we die," said Dent, lowering his eyes.

Kaycia was incredulous. "If we leave him, we die!"

And she ran toward the wreckage before anyone could argue.

Her sister called after her, "Kay! NO!"

But Kaycia had already made up her mind.

It wasn't about orders or a sense of duty. And it wasn't about honor to help an old man in need.

No. This was out of fear.

Because even if they escaped this pack of monsters—there'd no doubt be more. With days left to travel between these mountains and Carheim, it was a matter of time before they were attacked again.

And when that happened, they'd have zero chance of running or sneaking anywhere without an ascendant by their side.

"Tenlen?!" she shouted before coughing away dust. She ducked a leaning pillar and scrambled over gravel. She might've taken more care—worried about accidentally stepping on the man or creating a shift in the rubble that'd make things worse. But fear gave her speed—anticipating, at any moment, creatures to come crawling through the wreckage.

"Can you hear me?" she yelled again—not so much expecting an answer but more from the need to hear her voice. She needed to be sure her hearing didn't change, and the easiest way was to keep making noise.

Kaycia looked back. "See anything?!"

She was relieved to find the men still there, watching from below. They knew she was right—no one could leave until they learned Tenlen's fate.

"No," shouted Dent.

At that moment, she thought she heard a groan. She strained her ears, trying to discern where it came from.

All was quiet for several seconds. Then she heard it again.

The groan changed pitch, converting into short, shallow gasps.

Kaycia found the man wedged into a crevice beneath two beams, so obscured by dust and shadow, she might've easily passed him by.

It only took one glance, however, to see it wasn't good.

The enormous pillars had his legs pinned—so firmly, they were most certainly broken, ascendant or otherwise.

"Tenlen!" she shrieked. She scrambled toward him, overwhelmed by a mixture of hope and fear.

With his hat missing and his cloak in tatters, she caught a glimpse of his deformed, mangled body. His neck curved the wrong direction, and his arms were bent—but these weren't injuries caused by the fall.

It was how he was—why he felt compelled to hide his shape beneath cloth and bandages. It was the cost of twisting the world to his will—that, without the protection of the gods, had twisted himself, in turn.

Tenlen tried to speak, but his voice was faint.

"Stay still," she instructed, dropping her spear. "I'll get this off you."

The old man shook his head, with eyes out of focus. He grimaced in pain and lifted his good arm toward the wood above him.

The pillar began to move—but only an inch.

"Save your strength! Just let me—"

The ground trembled.

"No...!" he hissed, with widening eyes. He looked at Kaycia as though seeing her for the first time.

"You need...to go!" he choked with surprising ferocity.

Only then did Kaycia hear the other yells.

One was her sister, sounding very far away. "Kay!" she was shouting. "MOVE KAY! GET OUT OF THERE!"

"Oh shit..."

Feeling like an idiot, she lunged for her weapon—but the rock pile shifted, and she fell on her wrists.

With the dust still thick, she had a clear view of the empty shapes rising from the rubble—not in one place but several. Worse, one of the voids was climbing from behind, blocking her escape.

It was almost upon her before she reversed her grip and drove her weapon down like a harpoon.

But rather than feel the penetration of hide—an enormous strength latched onto her tip and tried to yank the spear from her hands.

In sudden desperation, she planted a foot against a large stone block and used her legs to pull backward and upward.

Then switched directions. Hoping to take it by surprise, she thrust downward and matched the creature's pull.

The tip pierced through flesh and bone. She put her weight above her target and pinned it to the ground.

Even so, it continued to rise.

With bestial strength, it pushed back, lifting Kaycia into the air.

At that moment, there was nothing she could do. Her efforts had only cost her time and allowed the other creatures to surround her.

Then, she heard Tenlen's voice—so loud, it overpowered the silencing aura.

"GO!" he commanded, stretching a hand toward her.

The world turned sideways.

Kaycia shrieked, feeling the ground slip away—no longer horizontal but rising to form an enormous cliff face. Tenlen was above her, and she fell away with increasing speed—losing her spear to its skewered target.

The ruined buildings rose fast to meet her. Beyond the village, there was nothing but endless sky.

Her heart raced so fast she feared it might leap from her chest. Was it always like this for Tenlen? How could he manage to not lose control, much less keep his wits about him?!

Her greater worry, however, was the realization her body wasn't built like his. And the moment she crashed through those walls, she'd break both legs.

Just as suddenly, the world flipped back to normal.

Kaycia tucked into a roll an instant before hitting the ground.

She was moving so fast, her deft reaction degenerated into an uncontrolled tumble, as dirt and rock rained around her.

Flailing like a doll, she was twisted, bounced, beaten, and battered—until, eventually, she skidded to a stop.

Kaycia tried to curse, but nothing came out. There was a tightness around her chest, wringing her out like an old rag.

She forced her head up—toward the place Tenlen had been—just in time to watch the old man die.

Kaycia felt sick.

From this distance, she couldn't see the blood—but as gravel flew and the pillars shattered, there could be no mistake. With tears in her eyes, she saw his body ripped apart.

At this signal, the men spurred into action.

The riders glanced at Kaycia—still lying on the ground—but none came to her aid. They had no way to gauge her injuries, and beyond that, there wasn't time.

The first took off—followed by the second—galloping through the village toward the pass on the other side. All of them were leaving.

All but one.

As Kaycia rose to her elbows, Dent was locked in a struggle with the girl behind him.

"No!" shrieked Elyriel. "I won't leave her!"

"Keep still!" he demanded. With one hand on the reins, he reached back with his other to bring her under control.

Kaycia's heart sank. "Elle!" she tried to shout—but could not put enough force into her voice. "Listen to him!"

The girl screamed and pounded Dent's back with her fists.

How could this be happening? The only thing Kaycia wanted was for her sister to be safe, but the girl was impossible!

Somehow, Elyriel forced a knee between her body and Dent's. With a mighty shove, she fell backward off the horse and landed heavily on her side.

Dent's face contorted with rage and frustration, turning back toward the girl before locking eyes with Kaycia.

He shook his head as though in apology before driving his horse away and racing after the others.

Elyriel was on her feet, her dress streaked with mud. She broke into a run, shouting,

"Kay... KAY!"

By then, Kaycia had risen to her knees.

She wanted to scream at the girl and call her a fool! She wanted to yell something that would force Dent to come back.

But instead, she said, "We h-have to hurry! This way!"

Elyriel got an arm under Kaycia and helped her to her feet. The girl's muscles were spindly but possessed a strength that took Kaycia by surprise.

Clearly, they couldn't run, and they certainly couldn't fight. Which left a single option—they needed to hide.

With Elyriel's help, they stumbled toward the buildings. As they got closer, it was easier to see the signs from earlier attacks. Claw marks gouged the walls, and there were occasional faded stains of dried blood.

At the first opportunity, they turned a corner and broke line of sight.

There was a slight chance the monsters hadn't noticed them—too engrossed in their momentary feast.

"Over here!" came a shout, quiet enough to avoid drawing the creatures' attention.

Kaycia was shocked to find Marien and her daughter near an old stone building.

For a moment, she paused, unable to understand. Why was the woman still here? Why hadn't either of them escaped with the men?

At this point, however, she chose not to care.

Marien was low to the ground and holding open a wooden cellar door—perhaps to the monastery they'd discussed earlier?

"Hurry!" the woman hissed.

Kaycia felt light-headed as they pushed into a run. But with help from her sister, they reached the doors without Kaycia passing out.

The darkness made it impossible to see down the steps—but this stopped no one from racing down and slamming the door behind them.

All went black.

Groping with her hands, Kaycia found a heavy bar and slid it into place.

She regretted the loss of her spear. To her best recollection, it must've still been lodged in that creature's body.

"That's *not* going to stop them!" whined Chesandril. "Even the wreckage didn't stop them!" And she invoked another prayer.

"Calm down, Chess!" said Elyriel. "Maybe they didn't see us."

"Maybe?" The girl's voice was nearly a shriek. "*Maybe*?!"

"Hush! They'll hear!"

This prompted a sharp intake of breath, followed by heavy breathing. Chesandril renewed her prayer, more quietly this time.

Kaycia spoke up. "It'll be all right. There's a chance they'll chase after the men instead."

This did little, however, to calm the girl, and she began to whimper.

No one wanted to think of being chased through the night. The men wouldn't have time to catch their breath.

"Won't they come back?" asked the girl. "The men can't leave us here... They can't!"

"Coming back would be suicide, Chess. You know that."

Chesandril paused. "But what are we to do? They'll send for help, won't they? The ones who—?"

The girl stopped.

All of them had heard it—the change in her voice, becoming weak and muffled.

Kaycia stifled a groan, realizing she should've kept Chesandril quiet.

Both girls pressed in at her sides, each taking hold of Kaycia's arms.

With her eyes more adjusted, she could now discern faint cracks of light from outside. They weren't much more than thin purple lines—the last visage of twilight.

The air thickened as though her head had been plunged underwater. As the girls squeezed tighter, she could feel—but not hear—the race of their hearts.

In fact, Kaycia could hear nothing at all, even when she saw the faint lines shudder—and dust peppered their upturned faces.

The impact sent vibrations through the steps beneath them—causing both girls to flinch—but it hadn't made a sound.

Though it was possible to breathe, Kaycia felt like she couldn't. The surrounding pressure nearly drove her into a panic, and it took all her strength to keep herself still—and stare unblinking at the lines above.

The following impact nearly forced them down a step.

No longer wanting the girls up here, Kaycia extricated her arms and pushed them down the steps. She might've screamed at them and told them to hide—but they wouldn't have heard.

Regardless, she found nothing nearby to reinforce the door.

Kaycia drew her knives.

When the lines ceased shivering, she couldn't help but notice that some had gotten wider.

The cracks splintered beneath the ferocity that followed. The doors jerked violently as the beast pried between the wood.

She drove a blade upward, hoping to catch between its claws.

Kaycia knew the doors wouldn't last—and was confused when she found Elyriel, once again, at her side.

This time, however, the girl clutched a dagger tight in her fist—the one Kaycia had given her.

Oddly, this brought a grin to Kaycia's face—a momentary pride that felt bittersweet.

But she never got the chance to see her sister in action.

As quickly as it started, the tension evaporated.

No one moved.

They sat there, quiet, fearing its return at any moment.

But as the seconds stretched into minutes, it became easier to believe the monster wasn't coming back.

"Must've gone with the others," Kaycia whispered.

She turned around and returned one knife to its sheath. She kept the other out, drawing comfort from the solid heft of its polished wooden handle.

Even now, her heart didn't slow—her mind too full of things to process.

It was hard to believe Tenlen was gone—among the others who'd died.

And though, somehow, both she and her sister were still breathing—blessedly so— she was keenly aware they were no closer to safety than before.

Extra light spilled in from outside—the result of widened cracks and rising moon- light.

A few steps down, she found Marien's dim shape.

In her hands was a wooden box, unnoticed until that moment.

More surprising was that Kaycia recognized the box—though the darkness made it difficult to see.

"Marien...is that...?"

Kaycia swallowed. Her eyes traced the engravings, with ornate inlays of pearlescent wood.

Out here, in the middle of nowhere, the box was entirely out of place. It was rare for anyone to risk taking something so valuable from the city—let alone under the protec- tion of such a small escort.

To her surprise, some of her anger dissipated. Though she couldn't agree with Marien's choices—she could, at least, understand why the woman hadn't left this with the carriage.

The only confusion was how she possessed it in the first place.

"What's going on?" asked Elyriel.

Kaycia shared a look with Marien before turning to her sister.

"You've heard me talk of these bones—the ones in the box. They're the reason I needed Marien as my sponsor. But even she couldn't get her hands on them without amassing crippling debt."

The woman said nothing.

"Which is why," continued Kaycia, "she *returned* them when my ceremony failed. I *witnessed* the exchange! Gods, Marien! If the clergy discovers what you've done—you won't only lose your estate, you'll be imprisoned!"

"Mother?" asked Chesandril, with confused despair. "What's she talking about?"

"There's nothing to worry about, dear."

By then, it wasn't difficult to piece the rest together. Why else would the woman have kept the bones—before traveling to the middle of nowhere in search of an abandoned monastery?

"Marien..." breathed Kaycia. "Do you mean to ascend?"

Chapter 3
THE BONES OF GOD

For the first time that evening, Kaycia dared to feel hope.

It appeared as though Marien had planned and built toward this exact contingency. It was so nearly perfect, Kaycia wanted to believe. She desperately needed to believe, except...

She suppressed a groan because she knew the truth. More than anyone here—including Marien—she was intimately familiar with the ceremonial requirements. There were reasons, after all, she'd spent years in preparation.

It hadn't just been her. There'd been clergymen involved. Sacred vows. A monastery that wasn't a rotting ruin. And even with all that—even under the most favorable circumstances—they'd failed to invoke the presence of her god.

Looking up through the darkness, Marien said, "I meant to tell you..."

Which, of course, was a lie.

They both knew Kaycia would've argued against it. At the very least, she would've refused to come along.

"Marien...?" asked Kaycia, trying to control her tone. "How long have you been planning this?"

"You misunderstand. It wasn't my idea."

"Oh? Who else stands to gain from any of this?"

"I mean, yes, this trip was my decision. That's on me. But the proposition—that the ritual can be done differently..."

"What?!" asked Kaycia, with growing concern.

The woman nodded. "Stripped down to the essentials. Simple enough, a small group could do it."

There was so much wrong with this statement, Kaycia didn't know where to begin. There were reasons the rites were performed as they were, unchanged since the time the gods had died. To suggest alterations wasn't only sacrilegious, it was downright dangerous.

And yet, Kaycia had to make herself pause. With their lives on the line, some risk was to be expected. They couldn't end up worse than they were right then, so...

Was it possible her reaction was personal? Was she offended by the notion of a simplified ceremony because she wished it could've been *her* instead?

Looming in the dark was a single 'what if.' What if *Kaycia's* ceremony had been modified the same way? Would she still have failed? Or would her dream have been that much easier to attain? That question, of course, could never be answered. She'd been given her chance and wouldn't have another.

So why was dropping this so damn hard?

Kaycia grit her teeth. "Do you think we can do it? Just the four of us?"

To her frustration, Marien hesitated. "I thought... I thought Tenlen would be here."

Oh... thought Kaycia. But she didn't have the strength to be angry or sad. At least not more than she was already.

"Are we wasting our time then?" she asked in a dry monotone. "Should we skip ahead and start planning our escape?"

"Actually, I was thinking—hoping, really—maybe *you* could figure it out. Most of the diagrams have already been completed."

"Me?!" asked Kaycia in alarm. "You think it's that simple?"

The woman took a calming breath. "These notebooks... The theories therein... Your father wrote them."

"Wait...what?" asked Elyriel, speaking up for the first time. The girl didn't have many memories of Gendal, who'd died when the sisters were relatively young.

Kaycia gaped and needed a moment to find her voice.

"Bullshit."

Marien gave a timid smile. "It's true."

"But—! Why haven't you—? How did this—?"

"I only found them recently. Honest. I didn't realize my husband held onto these. I thought they'd been burned."

Kaycia narrowed her gaze. "But you knew about them."

"Knew *of* them. Not what they contained."

"You must've known enough. To have reason to think they'd be destroyed."

"A hunch, maybe. Some off-handed remarks when Beludan was alive. You remember how the two of them were—your father and my husband—back when both were training for ascendancy?"

Kaycia remembered though she'd only been a young girl at the time. It was the beginning of a long relationship between families—though Beludan ascended and Gendal didn't. Instead of driving the families apart, even their deaths had paved the way for Marien to become Kaycia's sponsor.

At least, that's how she'd always thought of it.

If there were secrets involved... Heretical studies...

"Can...? Can I see them?" asked Elyriel.

Kaycia groaned. "Not now, Elle."

"But—!"

"First, we need to find a safer place. And if anyone's going to read them, it's going to be me."

Just speaking these words sent a thrill down her spine. It was more than the chance to redeem her father. The thought of the work itself piqued her interest. So much that it made her rethink her future.

If they ever made it out of this, perhaps she wasn't destined for the life of a mercenary. Perhaps she could be a ceremonial worker instead.

At the moment, however, it was far too dark to read anything. Even if a scrap of wood was dry enough to burn, she wasn't convinced they should risk the light. Not with the door in the shape it was.

The group needed to keep moving deeper into the cellar.

For the first time, Kaycia took note of their surroundings. She stood up, reaching blindly to avoid bumping her head. She then passed the girls and felt her way down the stairs.

A horrible smell was coming from below—like mold and mildew. The wooden steps were moist and flexed beneath her weight.

"Stay here," said Kaycia.

"Are we going to try it?" asked her sister, without daring to come down. "The ritual, I mean."

"We can't decide that yet. Maybe...if it's not too dangerous."

"Dangerous?"

"I'll explain later."

"If father thought it was okay, then—"

"Just drop it, Elle. There's no way he planned for this specific scenario. We might not even have the requisite tools."

The girl was undeterred. "I've heard it said that the particulars don't determine success. It isn't the words of the ceremony that matter. Most the details are for show—a way for men to demonstrate to the gods their conviction."

Kaycia snorted, feeling offended. "So what're you saying? That my ceremony failed because of *me*? That *I* was the one without sufficient determination?"

"I'm not saying you lacked anything," said Elyriel, with a pause. "But maybe it wasn't the right kind."

Kaycia shook her head, unable to believe it. She understood why her sister might want an explanation—some logic as to why their lives hadn't gone as planned. But, sometimes, there wasn't a reason. Sometimes, reality dealt you a bad hand.

Weren't the gods themselves—more specifically, their horrifying deaths—proof of that?

The further Kaycia went, the more difficult it became to see. The dim light from above didn't stretch very far, and she was soon staring down through complete and utter black.

Kaycia took an exploratory step downward, with one hand in front and the other to the side, still holding her knife. To her best estimate, she should've been near the bottom, and she groped the stone walls in search of a lantern or a torch.

Even as she did so, she felt foolish, realizing she'd find nothing flammable amid this moisture.

"I'm sorry..." said her sister from the top of the stairs. "I'm not judging you, Kay... I don't know why our god didn't choose you. But that's no reason to believe he won't hear us now."

Kaycia frowned but didn't respond. She didn't have the heart to speak her mind— that she didn't think the gods heard *anything*—at least, not anymore.

She knew better, though, than to destroy what hope her sister had left.

As Kaycia's fingers continued down the wall, the stones became increasingly moist and slimy. Sure enough, her next step plunged into water. She'd been expecting it but gave a low gasp nonetheless.

"What's wrong?" asked Elyriel.

Committing her weight onto that foot, Kaycia felt the dark liquid squeeze around her boot. The pressure was tight and uniform, and, for a moment, the leather seemed to keep the water out. The stitchings, however, weren't so tight as they'd once been, and water seeped through, cold as ice.

She groaned. "It's just water. Don't come down."

"You're leaving us?" moaned Chesandril.

"I'm taking a look is all."

Taking a breath, Kaycia proceeded down the next step and felt the water rise to her knee. She tried not to think where the rainwater might've come from. And how much was mixed with abyssal blood.

Her mind was wearing thin, and it was difficult not to imagine leathery hands beneath the surface—pawing at her legs. Pulling her under. This had more to do, she suspected, with the invisible terrors above than with any realistic expectation of danger. Even now, she felt pent-up energy coursing through her muscles like a dull throb.

She explored with the toe of her boot. Gingerly, she found where the step ended and the floor dipped again.

"It's getting deep," she announced. For all she knew, the stairs might keep going until the water passed her head.

After two more, the chilled water circled her hips, soaking completely through her stockings and breeches. She could feel her legs growing stiff as her heat and strength were sapped away. The cold didn't feel like a cellar at all but a subterranean vault.

From above came a sudden pounding, and the girls shrieked.

Kaycia swiveled in surprise and nearly slipped. Her stumble, however, confirmed she'd reached the bottom.

The wooden doors rattled and banged again. It wasn't the sound of a wild creature, but she couldn't be sure.

She gazed up at the thin cracks of light, broken by the faint silhouettes of Marien and the girls—and another figure, besides, just beyond the door.

"Is anyone down there?" yelled a man. His voice conveyed concern—but not desperation.

Kaycia took this as a good sign. The last thing they needed was for the men to have brought the creatures back to their location.

Still, the doors made it impossible for Kaycia to identify who it was.

She supposed it didn't matter. As she gazed up through the darkness, she felt as though a weight had been lifted. She didn't dare hope to find *all* the men—but, with even one, she'd no longer have to do this alone.

"Open it," she said, clutching her knife more tightly.

The girls hesitated.

"Can anyone hear me?" he yelled.

"Open it!" she repeated, debating if she should return up the stairs. "We can hear him. There aren't creatures nearby."

Not at the moment, she thought.

"It's stuck!" said Elyriel. "Chessie—help!"

The girls grunted in effort, wrenching the bar from the battered door. Not a second later, the latch was pulled from outside, and fresh moonlight cascaded down the steps.

A man peered down, regarding each of them in turn.

"Over here!" he said to someone else outside. As he turned, there was no mistaking Captain Veldt's armor.

"You came back!" exclaimed Chesandril.

"No," said Elyriel. "Veldt wasn't with them. He never left." Looking up, she added, "We thought you were dead."

"Wasn't with whom?" he asked, his voice growing stern. "The others left?"

A second man limped into view behind him. "I told you!" he said, wincing in pain. "Those were tracks back there, leaving the village."

"Roke...?" breathed Chesandril in recognition.

Veldt raised a hand to his forehead, trying to contain his disbelief and irritation. "They just abandoned you here? No horses or supplies?"

For an awkward moment, no one knew what to say. Kaycia was preparing to speak, but his patience ran out.

"Tenlen wouldn't leave! I don't believe it..."

"You should come down," said Marien, "so we can talk more quietly."

The suggestion made him furious, but he brought himself under control. He turned to Roke, slipped an arm under his, and helped him down the steps.

Elyriel remained up top, making sure there was no one else.

"Shut it," said Veldt. "But don't replace the bar. We can't stay long."

Kaycia came up the steps, no longer caring about the cold or the water sluicing down her legs. It was all she could do not to ask what he meant—if he thought running was their best option.

The door closed, casting everything into dark once again.

"From the beginning," demanded Veldt, his voice echoing down the staircase. "*Who* left? I want names!"

"All of them," said Chesandril, before Elyriel added, "The ones still alive."

The captain wasn't satisfied. "But *who*?! How many in the group?"

"Three?" guessed Elyriel, her voice frightened.

"Three," confirmed Marien. "The rest were dead... Tenlen included."

Kaycia wanted to say that it wasn't the men's fault. That more would've died had they'd stayed a moment longer. But she also couldn't blame Veldt for the mood he was in. He'd just learned his livelihood was gone—his business and the lives of his associates and friends.

He wasn't trying to *understand* the situation. He was working through a problem that couldn't be solved.

Veldt couldn't keep his hands still—something between fidgeting and trembling. "You're certain? You saw him die?"

"We all did," said Kaycia. "The men saw it, too. It's why they ran."

"That's no excuse," he muttered.

"It isn't—but it's the reason we're alive. The fleeing men made for better sport. I suspect it was much the same for you."

Veldt took a deep breath but didn't deny it. She might've pressed for details—to ask what he'd been doing that prevented him from being there. But he was in no mood to answer questions. She'd already guessed most of it, and the rest didn't matter.

"Damn it!" shouted Veldt, slamming a gauntleted fist against the wall.

"Keep it down!" hissed Marien.

The man scoffed. "I'm done taking orders from you!"

"Are you trying to get us killed?"

He paused in consideration and lowered his voice. "You'd like that, wouldn't you? To make this my fault, somehow?"

Marien didn't respond.

"That's what I thought," he grumbled. "*You* got us into this, and it's up to me to get us out."

Kaycia understood his frustration—and it made her wonder, why wasn't *she* more furious? She hadn't been close to the men who died—not like Veldt—but she was confused by her emotional response. She felt pained, yes, but she wasn't a wreck. So what did that say about her?

"We can make this work," continued Veldt with increasing stoicism. "You said *all* the creatures left—when the cowards fled?"

"I...think so," said Kaycia.

"Then it's settled. We leave now. Before they return."

"Out there?" asked Chesandril in a pained tone.

"The only way through this is to follow my instructions. We've got a long night ahead, and anyone who's not okay with that is free to stay behind. It's your choice."

"That's it?" asked Kaycia. "We can't discuss this?"

"It's not so complicated. We can't go to Carheim, so we go back the way we came—back to Wern's Hold. Just think about it—the roads were clear these past two days. No threats till recently. It's our safest bet."

Kaycia frowned in consideration. When he put it in those terms, the choice was nearly obvious. No matter which plan they chose, there would always be risk. At least this way, they'd be putting distance between themselves and the creatures they *knew* were out there. The ones already hunting them.

"Veldt's right," said Roke. "They haven't forgotten us. And if we're still here—"

Elyriel was incredulous. "Can you even walk?"

"Don't got much choice, now, do I?" said the young man with a grimace.

"Actually...before you arrived, we'd been discussing another option."

Kaycia jerked in alarm. "Elle. No."

Veldt turned, genuinely surprised.

The girl was confused and looked down at Kaycia. "What?" she asked. "I think Marien's right. It's a good idea."

"Not now," said Kaycia, shaking her head.

She couldn't, however, explain the problem. Her issue wasn't with the ceremony but with their present audience.

Unfortunately, it was already too late.

The man grunted before turning his scrutiny on the older woman. His eyes flicked to her satchel, where her notebooks were kept. "You know another path? A safer way?"

"Not quite..." she said and clamped her mouth shut.

Elyriel still didn't get the problem, and she wilted beneath the large man's glare.

"What plan?" he pressed.

She answered timidly. "To make an ascendant."

"It won't work," interrupted the lady.

"What?!" asked Roke. "Here?"

Marien said, "No," at the same time Elyriel said, "Yes!"

"Explain," demanded Veldt.

There wasn't a way for the girl to back out.

"Turns out," she continued, "this building we're under used to be a monastery. And the bones for the ritual—the bones of ascendancy—Marien's had them with her this entire time!"

Veldt didn't react to the girl's excitement. The man went quiet, his jaw rigid. More-over, he appeared genuinely disturbed.

"There's no guarantees," she continued. "Like always, the ceremony might fail. But we've got to try! I mean, think of the difference it'd make! We wouldn't have to *guess* which path was safest—she'd *see* for all of us!"

Veldt swallowed and faced Marien. "This true?"

The lady groaned. "I already explained—"

"The bones, Marien!" His flash of anger was startling. "You brought them with you?"

She nodded reluctantly.

"This is why we're here?" He shook a hand at the woman. "My men died because...?"

Marien tried to speak, but he shouted over her.

"You stupid, arrogant bitch!"

"That's enough!" shouted Kaycia. "You agreed to the contract! And you know the attack wasn't her fault."

He huffed and made efforts to regain his composure. Somewhat successfully.

"Those bones belong at the citadel. Do the elders know they've been taken? What the hell were you—?"

"S—so you're saying, what?" stammered Elyriel. "You'd rather die? Who cares if Marien crossed some law?! This might be our only way out!"

"That *law* is the reason Carheim has survived. The bones need to be safe—not just for us but for future generations. So few remain... Who are *we* to speak for the gods? To even think such a thing borders on blasphemy!"

"Just drop it," said Kaycia. "It's unlikely to work, even if we tried."

This made everyone pause.

Kaycia was worried Elyriel would keep arguing—but, instead, it was Marien who broke the silence.

"I'm sorry if I've offended you. If you're in such a hurry, we won't keep you any longer."

The captain gaped in disbelief.

Marien pushed on. "You said it was our choice, didn't you? So let's end it at that."

"I'm just to walk away? And overlook this...crime?"

"What crime? I've done nothing to—!"

"So you didn't steal the bones?"

"They were given to me! My name's on the lease!"

"Don't give me that shit. At no point have the bones ever been *yours*."

"Maybe not," she acceded. "But neither were the bones ever *given* to the clergy. So why should they retain ownership?"

"The church was founded by the gods. The organization's entire purpose was to champion them and ensure—"

"That doesn't make the bones theirs! *These* are Telarien's."

At this point, even Kaycia was shaking her head—feeling Marien had gone too far. While strictly speaking, her words weren't wrong, speaking a god's name so casually was highly disrespectful.

Telarien—to whom Kaycia, herself, had been intended to be bonded—had been dead for over three hundred years. Were it not for the legacy the eight gods left behind—there'd *be* no ascendants. And the world would've drowned before Kaycia was born.

Veldt's expression was horrified.

"All I'm asking," continued the woman, "is why not give Telarien, himself, the chance to refuse me? What's the worst that could happen? If the ritual fails, I'll gladly accept his judgment. I'll return the bones without complaint.

"However...if he *doesn't* refuse... If god himself grants me ascension, then who are *you* to question his authority?"

For a moment, no one spoke.

"That box," said Veldt. "Hand it over."

"Why?" asked Marien in a menacing tone.

Kaycia didn't like where this was going. "Why don't we—?"

"Look... I'll return it—you have my word, Marien! I don't want it for myself. When we reach the garrison, you'll get your money. All of it. I swear."

"You know it's not about the money." She shook her head. "This isn't your call. Just forget our agreement. Though you *failed* to protect us, I won't file an insurance claim. Just leave! No one will say you had a part in this."

The man shook his head. "If it were only that simple..."

He lunged forward, stretching a gauntleted hand—but Elyriel was faster.

She snatched the box from Marien and raced down the steps, two at a time.

"Damn it!" hissed Kaycia under her breath.

But as Veldt stormed downward, Kaycia had no choice but to let her sister pass. The girl splashed through the water, leaving Kaycia to stand before the angry captain.

"Move!" he demanded. His dark silhouette nearly filled her vision.

"You need to calm down," she said coolly, twisting her knife through the air between them.

It took effort to keep herself composed, knowing her blade didn't pose much threat against his armor. If she wanted to do something about this, she'd have to go for his face—and she wasn't convinced she wanted to kill.

Veldt was following his convictions—which wasn't the same as intending harm. It wasn't enough to merit death.

The captain paused, regarding her expression and her stance. He might've been wondering the same thing—how far was she willing to take this?

They stared at each other for a moment, listening to the splashing fade into the distance. The girl was groping blindly, unable to see much of anything. She was undoubtedly freezing, wearing little more than her thin dress.

Veldt leaped forward, catching Kaycia by surprise.

Her reaction sent her knife slicing forward—but lacking force.

He caught it with his glove—and she felt the blade slide partially through leather—but he ignored the gash, set it aside—

And sent his other fist crashing into her face.

The impact spun her backward, and she caught herself against the wall.

Chesandril shrieked.

The bastard hit her! He'd actually hit her!

"Stay down!" he growled.

She raised her knife—this time, prepared to do more than threats—but he grabbed her wrist and pinned it to the wall.

"Kay!" shouted Marien.

Her head was reeling. Her movements sluggish.

She raised her other arm to shield her face.

But the strike never fell.

Coming up from behind, Roke intercepted the punch and caught Veldt's arm and neck into a headlock. He held a knife in one hand, pressed against the captain's cheek.

"Roke?!" asked Veldt. "What the hell are you—?"

The younger man tightened his hold, and the captain's face darkened further.

Kaycia stepped away from the wall and probed her cheek with her fingers. The side of her face was throbbing, and keeping her left eye open was difficult.

Roke's hands were trembling.

"I..." the young soldier stammered. "I think...y—you should go!" After a moment's hesitation, he added, "Sir!"

"Think what you're doing, Roke!" said Veldt. "You know they can't do this."

"Maybe not, sir. But you're the one who resorted to violence."

"Damn it, boy! Do you really think—?"

He twisted, catching Roke's blade with his glove while shifting his balance forward and tossing the smaller man up and over his shoulder.

Kaycia screamed, jumping back as he crashed onto the steps.

In her haste, she, too, slipped backward. Her palms scraped the rock walls to catch herself, but it wasn't enough.

In an instant, her head went numb, surrounded by the churn of ice-cold water.

Just as quickly, she got her feet underneath her and rose, dripping wet.

Roke had landed on his back, the force causing the moist, wooden steps to split. He groaned loudly and made no move to stand.

Kaycia's hood had fallen back, leaving her hair plastered to her head and caught on her leather pauldrons.

At some point, she'd dropped her knife.

She looked up, expecting Veldt to come for her next—but she found him just standing there, staring at Roke with bewilderment. He harbored protective feelings for the boy and never wished for this outcome.

But while the fight appeared to have left him, she drew another blade just to be safe. She widened her stance and clenched her jaw—to make clear she wouldn't make this easy for him.

By then, Elyriel had either found a hiding place or gotten so far they could no longer hear her.

With each labored breath, Kaycia felt her shirt cling tight to her skin beneath her leather cuirass.

Despite her greatest efforts, she couldn't keep from shivering.

"I won't be part of this!" he bellowed. "You want to play with the abyss? You're going to mess with the gods—the dead, friggin' gods?! Then, fine! Go damn yourselves, for all I care!"

He turned and stormed up the stairs. Near the top, he paused. "Come on, Roke. Let's go!"

The young man groaned but didn't get up.

"You want to live, don't you?" Veldt exhaled in frustration. "I didn't want things to go this way—and I apologize if you're hurt."

Roke met Veldt's eyes and clenched his teeth.

The captain stormed down the steps and grabbed the boy's shirt. "I said, let's—"

"Get off me!" Roke shrieked, jerking the other way—and whimpering at the pain that followed.

Veldt let the boy drop, none too gently. He stomped back to the door and swung it open. His face was livid as he turned back one final time, settling his gaze on Marien and her speechless daughter.

"Whatever comes of this...it's on *you*, Marien—you hear me?! The boy's your responsibility—so you best think hard what you mean to do here!"

And, with that, he turned and let the door slam behind him.

Chapter 4
PATHWAYS TO MADNESS

Kaycia was glad to see him go but feared they were making a big mistake. It wasn't so important they agreed with Veldt as much as they did what was best for survival. They'd later regret he wasn't fighting at their side—as getting away from this place was their top priority.

Now, they were stuck. Marien would never change her mind, and things would only worsen if the captain returned. Even so, Kaycia wished to see him again, someday, alive and well under different circumstances.

A faint shout echoed down the hall.

"Kay...? KAY?!"

"Elle?! What's wrong?" Kaycia splashed into the darkness, heart hammering in her chest. "Where are you...? Answer me!"

There was a long pause, followed by a faint "Sorry! You need to come see this!"

She sighed in relief. "We're coming! Stay where you are!"

Floating objects bumped against her as she pushed forward—clumps of tangled weeds and drifting wood. She did her best to ignore them—but couldn't stop from jerking back when her hand brushed something small, squishy, and covered in hair.

From behind, Marien said, "Come on, Chess... Get on Roke's other side and help with these steps... Now, girl! Or would you rather be left behind?"

Down the hall, to one side, Kaycia reached an open doorway. Through dim cracks in the ceiling, there was just enough moonlight from the upper floors to see a blackened rocking chair and a mildewed crib. It was too dark to see much else, but the putrid smell was suggestive of a storeroom, as though containing barrels in various states of decay.

"Elle?"

"Over here!" came the response—not from the room but further down the hall. Chesandril shrieked.

Kaycia spun—to realize the girl had stepped into the ice-cold water.

"We're going through *here*?!" she moaned.

"If Elyriel could do it, so can you," said her mother.

Under different circumstances, Kaycia might've felt sorry for the girl—who didn't have leather but a dress to keep warm. She was shorter than Kaycia, and the water, no doubt, came up past her belly. At the moment, however, it was all Kaycia could do to keep moving the right direction.

Shadows drifted across her vision, more or less, where the walls were supposed to be. More than that, however, she was mostly guessing.

A blur coalesced—causing Kaycia to jerk back as it splashed toward her.

"Elle...? I told you to stay put!"

"You were taking too long... Just...follow me. It'll be faster if I show you."

"Show me what?"

"This way," said Elyriel, tugging her hand. "It's not far."

Kaycia allowed herself to be pulled into the dark. She wasn't worried about the others getting lost, as, thus far, the path had been straight. What troubled her was how far they kept walking despite what her sister said. From outside, the building hadn't appeared half this large.

They must've gone over fifty steps before Elyriel stopped.

"Something's wrong. It was *right here*!"

"Just tell me what we're looking for."

"I found the worship circle—for our ceremony—but it was incomplete. Telarien's statue wasn't there. Most the gods weren't."

Kaycia's heart sank. Telarien, after all, was the only god to which Marien had a claim. Her bloodline—like Kaycia's—was specifically aspected to his, and if his statue was absent, the ceremony became quite impossible.

"You're sure it was the right room? How many gods did you see?"

Distractedly, Elyriel said, "We must've passed it. Come on."

Far down the damp hall, from where the trio was catching up, Roke's voice echoed, "Could someone tell me what we're looking for?"

"The worship circle," said Chesandril through chattering teeth.

Kaycia was surprised by how well their voices carried. The others had clearly heard Elyriel despite being separated.

"I got that," said Roke. "But what does it look like?"

Chesandril gasped. "You don't know?!"

Elyriel stopped at the next doorway and slumped in defeat.

"I'm sorry," he responded. "But I've only been in one, maybe two, of these places my entire life. No one in my family is a believer."

"What?" asked the girl, in shock. "They just pretend the gods weren't real?"

"Chess!" scolded her mother. "Don't be disrespectful."

"Her question's valid," said Roke. "And no—we're fully aware the gods used to exist. But that's just it—they *used to*. My father sees no point in continued worship. Or even learning their names, for that matter."

"But that's—! What about *your* god's name? You know you're aspected, right? Everyone is."

"Hmmmm... Veshir? Vasher?"

"Vashek," the girl corrected without hiding her disdain.

"That's the one... Don't get me wrong, I've heard them before. It's not the sort of thing you can avoid. But I get them mixed up. Their teachings. Their stories."

"Here it is," said Elyriel, her voice flat and strangely confused. "I could've sworn... It was on the left before." She paused for a moment, less than convinced. "There's no way I got turned around."

Kaycia said nothing. Amid this darkness, it was easier to believe her sister made a mistake. It certainly beat the alternative—that the basement, like the forest outside, had started to change. She didn't want to imagine what that might mean—as such changes were supposed to be impossible while people were looking. Or even nearby.

The splashes from Marien and Chesandril, supporting Roke between them, had nearly caught up, and Kaycia followed her sister into the room.

Wide cracks in the ceiling let in more moonlight than the hallway outside. It illuminated a statue near the center—a stern-faced woman with billowing robes. She was entirely alone, with no other gods hiding in the shadows.

Kaycia shook her head. "It's not the right room."

"But...?" her sister protested. "Don't you see who that is?"

"I recognize that one," said Roke from the doorway. "Ashaira, right?"

Elyriel pulled Kaycia to the side. "Do you get it now? This place was *hers*. The clergy who lived here—they *worshiped* her."

Roke frowned, trying not to lean so much on Marien. "Why's that bad?"

"It isn't," said Kaycia, hoping everyone would calm down.

"Oh, wait," he continued. "Ashaira...? Wasn't she like their queen? The consort of Shaelis, himself?"

The name 'Shaelis,' of course, was known by everyone. He'd been king of the gods and the aspect of Stratum. If the legends could be believed, he'd lived the longest—since before the world of Erlan came into existence.

Ashaira, on the other hand...

"Their queen...? Sure," said Elyriel. "These days, most people call her the betrayer."

"Oh..." said Roke. "I didn't know they were the same."

"Only if you believe the rumors," said Kaycia, putting force into her tone so her sister would drop it.

Elyriel, however, didn't take the hint. "I think we should leave... This place is cursed."

"That's enough, Elle! She did nothing wrong. It's never been proven."

"Then why was she locked up before they died? Her own husband, Shaelis, put her on trial! Does that sound like someone free from guilt?"

Kaycia groaned. "No one understood what the problem was. If Shaelis had, he would've stopped it—you know he would've! The fact the world ended, regardless, proves something else was to blame."

Roke appeared confused. "This betrayer... Didn't her aspect disappear? There are people bonded to the gods—but not to her. Not anymore. There used to be thousands, but they all died or something."

"Not exactly," said Elyriel. "I mean...they're *probably* dead. The belief is that they were lost to the current. Torn from this world and forced to coexist among those god-awful creatures."

Kaycia sighed. "The most likely explanation."

"But that just proves my point!" her sister insisted. "Ashaira condemned her people with what she did!"

"It doesn't prove a thing. Only how desperate we are to cast blame on someone."

Elyriel threw up her hands. "If not her, then who? One of the other gods? Who else could've possibly created the current?"

Kaycia was losing her patience. "The abyssal current wasn't *made*! No one even saw it till the gods were gone. Something else killed them."

"Like what?"

Kaycia didn't answer. There *was* no answer.

"So it *might've* been her," the girl pressed stubbornly.

But Kaycia was already finished with the conversation. "Not now, Elle... We need to search the other rooms."

The girl paused. "You're sure this isn't it?"

"To establish contact with the aeilic realms, you'd, at least, need Shaelis. Probably even more. Ashaira, by herself, is inadequate. You'll have to trust me on this."

Roke sounded doubtful. "What if someone just moved the rest?"

"Who would do such a thing?" asked Chesandril, in shock.

"It's possible," admitted Kaycia, "but unlikely. Just look at this room—it's too small for a circle. We need to keep looking."

She moved back into the hall but didn't feel comfortable starting from there. "Let's go back to the stairs. We can take each room—each path—one by one. At the very least, we can hope to find someplace dry."

No one argued, eager to be free of this wretched cold.

The journey back, however, proved to be a problem.

Only minutes had passed since they'd left the stairs, and she was sure they were headed the right direction. But the hallway seemed different. She thought the ceiling was lower despite her inability to see anything clearly.

She wasn't sure at first, but the waterline, too, seemed to change. She had to lift her elbows to clear the surface, as though they were walking down from a shore. But the floor remained level, without the hint of a decline.

"We're going the wrong way," complained Chesandril—who soon would have water up to her neck.

"See?" asked Elyriel in nearly a whine. "I wasn't making it up!"

"Okay..." said Kaycia, taking a deep breath. "Everyone stay calm. It's possible the directions were only switched. We'll try the other way."

This wasn't logic but ill-disguised hope. If the place kept changing, then every direction could be equally wrong. Turning back could lead to even deeper water.

Luckily, it didn't. The waterline receded as quickly as it came—down to her waist. Then to her hips. As though the place itself was leading them somewhere.

This should've been concerning, but she wasn't yet worried about being trapped down here. There were holes in the ceiling, large enough to crawl through. They could still take their chances elsewhere if this strange phenomenon amounted to nothing.

The room with Ashaira never reappeared. The water dropped to their knees. Then their ankles. And when the hallway seemed like it would go on forever, it abruptly ended with a set of stairs.

Only these didn't go up. They were carved downward through the bedrock, disappearing into dark. Dim moonlight fell through a hole in the ceiling, revealing pale stone steps that were strangely dry. There was no explanation for the receded water or why the lower levels hadn't been flooded.

It was only as Elyriel neared the edge and peered cautiously downward that a new possibility occurred to Kaycia.

"Wait! Stop!"

She pushed past her sister and inspected the ceiling—at the cracks that'd easily allow rain inside.

Was that what this was? Was it possible they were now standing waist-deep in blood? So much of it, it was pushing the other water back?

But no... If that were true, she would've known. She would've felt pressure, making it difficult to walk. And besides, the scattered scraps of wood would be buoyant. They'd be floating in the air.

"What is it?" asked Elyriel.

Kaycia sighed and shook her head. She had no choice but to concede it was something else—a phenomenon she might never understand.

"Dark heavens..." breathed Marien, propping Roke against the wall. "Is that...?"

Kaycia nodded.

While every monastery wasn't built above a subterranean tomb, it was common enough, this couldn't be anything else. There wasn't a worship circle up on this level because the monks had discovered a better location.

Death, after all, was a doorway where multiple realms aligned. Gathered like this, in such concentration, it blurred the lines between worlds and facilitated access to the gods.

"Chess?" asked Marien, suddenly concerned. She took her daughter by the shoulders.

"I... I'm all r—right," said the girl, through chattering teeth.

Marien gave Kaycia a look of apology. "I'd hate to slow you down. We'll catch up in a moment."

Kaycia was torn. While she knew how important it was to push on—to complete the ceremony before the creatures returned—they couldn't afford to start making mistakes.

Chesandril wasn't the only one past her limits. Kaycia had done her best not to notice, but her aching muscles demanded attention. Her mind had gone sluggish.

And she didn't want to go down that hole by herself.

"I'd rather not split up," she decided. "This scrap seems dry enough. We should start a small fire."

"You're sure?" asked Marien, with more concern than relief.

"We'll keep it brief. I've been wanting an excuse to look at those notebooks. And this way, we can dry off. Recover some strength."

"I meant the fire. It's not too much light?"

Kaycia looked down the hall. "I'm unsure where this is, but we aren't near an exit. The only way we'll be seen is if they're right above us."

No one objected.

There was no lack of wood that'd fallen through the ceiling. There were broken bits of furniture and tangles of branches. Strangely enough, it wasn't just dry but free from slime. Most of it, anyway.

For kindling, they made use of Chesandril's ribbons. Marien contributed paper—either blank or expendable for the writing contained.

All in all, the process took longer than Kaycia would've liked. But after her flint coaxed the flames to life and her face began to tingle—all lingering regret melted away.

"No one falls asleep, understand?" she said as they sat against the walls, ringing water from their clothing. "We're performing the ceremony tonight."

Without waiting to be asked, Marien retrieved a worn journal from her bag. It was bound in a deep, blood-red leather and contained a block of pages close to an inch thick.

Beside her, Elyriel rose to a knee. She gathered Kaycia's hair and pulled it to the side, so no loose ends would drip water on the paper.

"Thanks," said Kaycia as she set the book on her lap.

It was surprisingly heavy—not only in content but in the degree of responsibility she felt on her shoulders. There was no possible way she could read this all. And it wasn't long before her doubts resurfaced.

"Here," said Marien, with a look of understanding. "I've marked which pages pertain to the ceremony."

Kaycia nodded but didn't immediately skip to the designated section. Instead, she flipped to a random page, hoping for a hint of who her father had been.

Something about it made her stomach uneasy. It was all in the penmanship—meticulously scripted with the occasional flourish. She knew it at once for her father's hand, though she had no specific memories reading it, even as a child.

She remembered to breathe, surprised by the weight of her reaction.

More than once, her eyes lingered on a passage.

Ascension is not what it used to be, he'd written. *With each passing year, the world sinks deeper. The monsters larger, while we grow weak. Our ceremonies fail, denying ascension to the ones most deserving. The ones destined to rival the ascendants of old.*

Kaycia held back a sigh, unsurprised. There was no question in her mind he was talking of himself. He didn't only blame his ritual, he had the audacity to insist he *deserved* ascension. And that he would've been superior to the rest of his colleagues.

She knew what that was like—the need to feel important. To deny your faults and pretend to have value. But it was also a trait she'd learned to despise.

It was this need to prove himself, after all, that'd torn Gendal's family apart. He'd spent less time at home, lying to himself he was doing it for them. Ultimately, he never came home again.

She found much of the same on the other pages, only in greater detail. He didn't just insist the ceremony was wrong; he went to great lengths to justify his reasons. He broke down the steps into their constituent parts, focusing on the safeguards involved.

Shortly after that, she began to feel sick. She flipped ahead, just to be sure, but there wasn't any doubt about the changes he intended.

"Marien..." she said, swallowing hard. "We can't perform this ceremony."

The woman groaned. "Keep reading."

"Will it make a difference? I won't stand back and let you kill yourself!"

Chesandril's voice was languid, as though fighting sleep. "...What's this, mama?"

"I'm not going to die," Marien insisted.

"No?" asked Kaycia. "Then it'll be even worse. You'll end up like *them*. It'll be just like the day when the gods were destroyed. Their *minds* were destroyed. And their ascendants', too."

"You're sure?" asked Elyriel, completely horrified. "...Father wrote that?"

"Of course, he didn't," said Marien.

"He didn't have to," said Kaycia. "Because everyone knows what the safeguards are for."

"Yes," agreed Marien. "Yes... But you have to look at the bigger picture. Don't you find it odd that our ascendants have become weak? That none come close to the ones from before?"

"Not really. The gods are...well...dead."

"The gods, yes, but not their power."

Kaycia shook her head. "What would my father know? He wrote these excuses so he could feel better!"

"You must've missed the part where he writes about you."

Kaycia froze. "...Me?" she asked.

"You were still a young girl, but even back then, he recognized the potential within you. And he knew if you ever aspired to ascendancy, your ceremony was doomed to fail."

Once again, this was completely unexpected.

"Her, too," said Marien, nodding toward Elyriel.

Kaycia looked at her sister with sudden alarm. "You don't mean...! I never agreed to put her through the ceremony."

"And I wouldn't want her to. She's underage, remember? She'd be reported to the church by anyone who saw her. No offense."

"Don't be sorry," said Elyriel. "I'm glad it's not me."

When everyone turned to the girl, she suppressed a laugh. "I'm *already* special, exactly how I am."

She sounded so sincere, Kaycia couldn't help but smile.

"Now hear me out," continued Marien. "Almost universally, people believe that when the ceremony goes sour, it's due to inadequacies found in the candidate. They lack certain qualities and *would've* achieved ascendancy had they only been more in tune with their god.

"Now, while this may be true in some cases, your father wasn't satisfied. In fact, he theorized the opposite was true. That the subject, at times, possessed *too much* aptitude."

Kaycia wanted to argue but was too distracted, remembering her ceremony.

"Just think about it, Kay. If there were such people—destined for greatness—wouldn't their bond bring them that much closer to their god...? But since the gods are dead, *that* is what kills them. And would've killed *you* if the protections weren't there to disrupt the ceremony."

An unsettling silence fell over the group.

Kaycia didn't know how to feel. Was this supposed to be comforting? There seemed little point in believing she had potential for greatness when, in the end, it'd been for nothing. If anything, what Marien said only made her feel worse.

"I'm confused," said Roke after a moment. "These safeguards sound like a good thing. I mean...you're not suggesting her death would be preferable, are you?"

"Don't be foolish. If Kaycia kept reading, she might consider other ways around the problem."

Kaycia closed her eyes in frustration. "Could you explain it, then? How my father found a solution, when no one else has for hundreds of years?"

"Gendal was the only one brave enough to stand against the church. He dug into their records, finding everything he could on those ancient ascendants—the ones who went insane and tore down society limb from limb."

"Records?" asked Kaycia. "Carheim was razed to the ground. It's a miracle anyone survived, but...paperwork, too?"

"A few transcripts. Copies of copies. Interviews. Autopsies."

Chesandril gasped. "You mean...from cutting them up?"

"Of course—now, hush! There were many, back then, who tried to figure it out. To know what went wrong...up here." Marien pointed a finger to her head. "And you know what they found?"

After a pause, she said, "Absolutely nothing. Their brains were as healthy as any regular human's."

"So?" asked Kaycia. "A lot of lunatics lack such abnormalities."

"It was enough for your father to keep searching. Though we lump all the crazies beneath one blanket term—as if all malfunctioned in the same way—nothing could be further from the truth. These ascendants didn't suffer from malignant disease. And they didn't break under mental duress."

"Wasn't it a backlash?" asked Roke. "A surge from the gods that fried their skulls?"

"That's just rumor," said Marien, and she raised a hand before Kaycia could protest. "Trust me... Most people prefer the simple explanation. But your father knew better.

"He hypothesized there wasn't any damage at all—not to the body and not to the soul. He surmised the person wasn't insane, but the problem lay entirely within the dead god's mind. An *external* complication. And as such, one that might be counteracted by a *second* external force."

"You lost me," said Roke.

"It's quite simple. The ascendant needs to be bound tightly to their god, as that is what gives their aspect power. But what we don't want is for their *mind* to form part of that bond, because that's what kills them."

"You're still not making sense," said Kaycia. "It's not like you can choose. The mind and soul are connected. How did he propose to separate—?"

"By simultaneously creating a second bond—connecting the mind to something else. Another person, in fact—someone healthy to serve as their anchor."

"But that sort of bond doesn't exist!" insisted Kaycia, only to pause to reconsider.

An anchor.

Someone to protect the ascendant and hold it all together.

Kaycia gaped in realization. "You don't mean...?" She paused again in confusion. "But, Marien—you're already married!"

"Doesn't matter. My husband would've provided a sufficient anchor were he still alive. But his isn't the only soul in alignment with my own."

Kaycia blinked, then turned to Chesandril.

The young girl withered beneath the extra attention.

"So...wait," continued Kaycia, flipping through the book. "In his diagrams—there are overlapping circles? One of ascendancy and one of devotion? Of...matrimony?" It felt strange to say the word outside its usual context. It wasn't as though the woman would *wed* her daughter.

"Two circles," confirmed Marien as Kaycia reached the page. "Two ceremonies taking hold as one."

The diagrams had been drawn with a steady hand. Two perfect circles, enlaced with lines and symbols. Everything measured and exactly to scale.

Of greatest interest was the area where the circles overlapped—where she expected their designs to conflict with each other. Gendal, however, had discovered an exact orientation and size for each one so that both were reconciled in elegant simplicity. In the end, he'd added a few markings she didn't recognize, but she knew, from context, they were for balance and stability.

It was the last thing Kaycia had expected to find. That her father, in a way, had been brilliant. Reckless, perhaps, but his ideas had the potential to change the world.

They deserved further research. To be analyzed by priests with sufficient resources. To be tested in a controlled environment.

Not performed in a waterlogged cave by a cast of amateurs.

She looked up from the book. "There's so much that could go wrong. What if you and your daughter *both* go insane?"

Marien shook her head. "The bindings are different."

"That's what you think, but how can you be sure? Like right here," she said, pointing to a symbol. "These margins have never been tested. Are you certain they'll handle the additional load?"

Marien, of course, didn't have a response.

"And what of the rest? You realize, don't you, once Chesandril takes part in that circle—she won't be able to marry. Anyone. Ever. Have you thought of that?"

"She will. After I'm dead."

"Are you listening to yourself? And let's not forget the biggest issue of all. Even after all this, it might still be insufficient. Even if Chesandril's safe, the risk remains you won't be!"

For a long moment, the woman said nothing. She took a deep breath. "Then, at least, we'll know."

Kaycia blinked.

"I never said there wasn't risk," said Marien. "That's why I'm not asking this of anyone. It's *my* life, Kaycia! *My* choice!"

"One that affects us all! When everything suddenly goes wrong, and we have an insane ascendant on our hands, what are we supposed to do? Kill you?"

"Yes," said Marien, with eerie finality.

"And if we can't?"

Kaycia couldn't imagine what it might be like to go toe to toe against an actual ascendant. An *insane* ascendant.

It was so frightening that she began to wonder if Veldt had been right. Maybe they should put a stop to this.

Marien took a deep breath.

And, in the end, left the question unanswered.

Chapter 5
THE RITES OF ASCENSION

Kaycia originally intended to spend five to ten minutes, at most, analyzing the tome and familiarizing herself with their upcoming ceremony.

It wasn't long, however, before she realized how foolish that intention was. Gendal's theories went far beyond what she'd learned in school, and she had to accept it'd be a grievous mistake to rush into anything so complex and dangerous.

So she changed the plan—telling the others to get some rest while she worked the calculations. She convinced herself the delay would be worth it, as everyone would need to be alert and ready.

A few minutes became an hour, and she was surprised when her sleepiness never came. If anything, her mind was so engaged with the father she'd barely known, she felt more awake now than she'd been on the road.

After a certain point, however, she forced herself to stop. It wasn't just the realization she'd never understand it fully—not without additional texts or consulting the ghost of Gendal himself. She hadn't forgotten that time was ticking away.

They were lucky the creatures weren't back already. Perhaps they'd been distracted by other prey? Or they were busy sleeping off their recent feast.

"Hey, Roke?" she whispered. He'd been lying down all this time, but his eyes were open and turned to meet hers.

"I hate to ask this—but would you mind staying up here?"

She expected an argument—for him to insist he felt fine and wanted to help. So, it surprised her when he nodded as though he'd expected this all along.

"It has nothing to do with your injuries," she said, explaining her reasons anyway. "In part, it has to do with the ceremony itself. We...women...will require some privacy.

But there's more to it than that."

Roke had already guessed where this was going. "You want me to stand guard—in case Veldt returns."

"Him...or anything else."

The young man seemed torn—his curiosity, perhaps, piqued by her mention of privacy. But, eventually, he nodded.

"Do you think you'll hear me if I yell a warning down the tunnel?"

"Hopefully," she responded. "We don't know how far down this goes. But we'll keep our ears open."

"I'll do the same."

"Thanks."

She felt better having someone watch the entrance. While it meant she'd have fewer hands to work with, it would be easier to concentrate and not worry about potential interruptions.

She then awoke the girls and prepared for their descent into the catacombs.

Unable to create a lasting torch—as their lantern oil was still back at the wagon and buried beneath tons of earth—they did the next best thing. They took the choicest pieces from their campfire—the ones least likely to fall apart—and as much additional wood as the girls could carry.

It was the best she could come up with, knowing they'd need multiple fires to see through the ritual.

Even so, the flickering, orange flames made for an eerie sight, as they descended the steps, twisting and curving, deep into the heart of the mountain.

To their astonishment, the catacombs went deeper than anyone expected, having been incorporated into a preexisting system of caverns. Rock formations dripped from the ceiling like melted topaz candles, casting jagged shadows that danced and wavered. But there were no bones—not within close proximity to the monastery.

No. The bones didn't appear until later. And when they did, they caused even Marien to freeze momentarily in her tracks.

The path opened to a cave so wide, there were gaping stretches their torchlight didn't penetrate. The ground they could see, however, was covered in bones—not in tall stacks, as was the custom in the city, but spread out so the bones of one corpse wouldn't mingle with another.

"I don't like this..." whined Chesandril.

"There are so many!" exclaimed Elyriel, with a tone closer to wonder than fear. "How is this possible—for such a small village?"

Kaycia, however, wasn't surprised by the number. Rather, she took interest in the trinkets adorning them. In the city, it was unusual to find decorations or inscriptions, as the caretakers were in a constant battle with limited space. But here, it'd been possible for the dead to be honored by their loved ones in a way that made Kaycia feel jealous.

She would've loved her father to be buried in such a place.

And yet, she couldn't shake the feeling that something was wrong.

The trinkets, she realized. Unlooted after all these years, despite the precious stones and gold they contained.

"What's that?" asked Chesandril, pointing to an unnatural rock formation.

"Some kind of ruin?" suggested Marien, looking around and finding similar worn blocks hidden throughout the chamber. "They must've already been here—long before Hebril was settled."

"How can you be sure?"

"Use your eyes. The village can't be older than a few hundred years, built before the mountains were lost to the current. By the architecture, the Hebrilians must've come from the south. Among those who made pilgrimage to draw nearer the gods and build their home on Ahman's footstep."

"Small good that did," said Elyriel. "The gods were already dead—their city, vanished."

"Even so."

At this point, the path split into multiple directions, spreading out to take advantage of the network of caves.

Kaycia had no choice but to stop and consider which way to go. She'd always found it easy to find the center of a crypt—back in the cities, where it was all man-made. In this place, however, the layout was less clear.

She made her best guess, which, in the end, turned out to be correct. But it still required them to walk over fifteen minutes, descending through chamber after chamber filled with bones. As the path continued deeper underground, it curved back around, returning to an area directly beneath the monastery.

Here, they encountered the largest cavern yet—so enormous and vast, their light didn't reach the opposite side. Their destination, however, was easy to spot—a rock formation rising from the center. The top was flat—like a natural plateau, perhaps ten feet higher than the rest of the ground. It gave the impression of an island engulfed by a sea of corpses.

As they closed the remaining distance, they saw the large stone statues erected upon its surface—without a single god missing. Their construction was as ancient as the ruins they'd found, but the Hebrilians had taken care to restore their appearance. The reconstructed gods had been left in a circle around a wide open space meant for public observance. Or similar gatherings of religious nature.

Near the base of the plateau, the skeletal remains came to an end. This wasn't only to keep the ramp unobstructed—next to that ramp was a shallow pool of water, threatening to accelerate the rot of bones.

"I'm impressed," said Kaycia when they reached the top. "I wonder if the settlers knew this was here. Or if they just got lucky."

Marien shrugged.

Kaycia stepped into the circle, surrounded by stone gods—each over eight feet tall. She stopped to brush her fingers along an iron sconce—and found it one of several, spread at intervals around the platform. Each was comprised of a small metal cradle atop an iron pole.

"Let's get some light," said Kaycia. "Elyriel, why not start with this one and do a few more around the room? Four should suffice and leave enough wood to keep them going."

It wasn't long, however, before Marien discovered a store of firewood left by the caretakers. "Why not light them all?" she suggested.

Elyriel was hesitant. "That wood must be ancient."

"It'll burn," said the lady in a confident tone. "Better than anything you're used to, dried out like this. Chess—give her a hand, won't you?"

"Is that...a storeroom?" asked Kaycia, approaching what'd appeared to be a depression in the floor, only to find a framed entrance. A small, barred window was built into the door.

"I'll check it out," said Marien. "Maybe there's something we can use."

Kaycia nodded, thoroughly pleased by these recent developments. It was undoubtedly better than drawing a circle on moistened wood or dealing with the disrepair they'd seen above.

All her worries, it seemed, had been for nothing. She could nearly sense the raw power exuding from the cavern's design. It reminded her of the feelings from her own ceremony—only stronger, somehow.

The light from Marien's fire disappeared behind the door, which hadn't been locked.

Kaycia walked into the circle and tried to visualize everything that needed to be done. As both Marien and Chesandril were the ritual's subjects, she hadn't yet decided which tasks to perform herself and which to entrust to her sister.

Almost instinctively, her eyes went to Shaelis, standing at the head of the pantheon, orange in the firelight. The God of Stratum, however, provided no answers. Nor did Ashaira, the sleek Goddess of Ordination, standing by his side.

With these two as a reference, Kaycia quickly identified the position of Telarien—the

God of Conviction—behind her and to the right. As her own sworn god—and Marien's—it was there, at his feet, where Kaycia would draw their circles.

"What about him?" asked Elyriel, pausing before a god on the left. The statue appeared younger than many of the others, with a sharp beard and a smug expression. "I thought I knew them all, but I don't recognize this one."

"That's Vashek," said Chesandril.

Elyriel shook her head and pointed to the side. "Vashek's over there."

The younger girl was confused. She began to turn, making a count of the statues.

Kaycia narrowed her brows, having identified the problem. "This place must be older than any of us thought."

"What do you mean?" asked her sister.

Chesandril completed her count. "Nine gods? But there should only be eight!"

"This," said Kaycia, raising a hand toward the statue, "has to be Aviathas."

She stepped closer to get a better look. "This is the first time, however, I've seen his face."

"Aviathas?" repeated Elyriel. "Why haven't I heard of him?"

"You have," said Kaycia, "though maybe not by name. It goes back to before the abyssal threat—before anyone feared invisible monsters or a dying world. Back then, while the gods yet lived, there'd been a ninth aspect—home to thousands upon thousands of people, just like ours. You remember now?"

"Are they the ones who died first?"

Kaycia nodded.

"I'm confused," said Chesandril. "I thought it was Ashaira's aspect—Ordination—that vanished?"

"That happened, too," Elyriel explained. "Hers and Shaelis'—but only at the end. This other one was gone long before the city of Ahman disappeared, and Ashaira betrayed—"

Kaycia stopped her with a hand, not wanting to have this argument again.

Chesandril, however, was still at a loss.

"No one's sure how it happened," said Kaycia. "The people of Innovation were alive one moment, and then something ripped them apart."

"You mean, like the abyssal creatures?"

"In a way...but different. You see, no one else could do anything about it. They couldn't see what was happening or fight off the attackers. If there were monsters, they could walk through anyone not bonded to Aviathas. You could've used your own body to shield them from danger, but they'd still be torn to shreds, wrapped within your arms."

Chesandril's expression grew horrified—and, just as suddenly, became thoughtful. "I heard something about this—only I thought it was a story. I mean...stuff like that doesn't happen anymore, right? Killings inside the city? Inside the safe areas?"

"You're right, and I know what you mean. It's not the sort of story you'd want to believe. Some think it was an act of justice—as punishment for something Aviathas did. Some people think it was a warning to prepare us for the threat yet to come.

"Eventually, Shaelis removed him from the pantheon. As if, by forgetting the problem, it wouldn't happen again."

They stood there, saying nothing. It was easy to wish Shaelis had done things differently—that, with all his power, he'd found a way to stop the world from ending. But wishing only led to further disappointment.

"There's not much down there," said Marien, emerging from the storeroom. From a shoulder, she let a coil of rope drop to the floor. "Tools for masonry and climbing."

Kaycia frowned. There were areas in the cave where the rope might be helpful. For the moment, however, she couldn't think of anything that needed tying up.

"I also found this."

Marien handed her an old clay jug. "There's quite a number of these. What do you suppose they are?"

Kaycia removed the stopper and took a careful whiff.

"Embalming fluid," she said flatly, returning it to Marien.

The lady groaned in disappointment—perhaps, having hoped it'd be flammable or help in some other way.

"We need to get started," said Kaycia. "I'll need those diagrams again. I assume you brought chalk."

Marien rummaged through her bag, before handing Kaycia a sizable chunk—large enough, running out wouldn't be a concern.

"We'll need the bones ready," continued Kaycia. "And a rock to grind them."

Marien blanched at the thought of destroying something so valuable.

"Don't worry," said Kaycia. "We won't do it now. That part is reserved for the end—only after success becomes a certainty."

Marien nodded in understanding. After all, were it not for this detail, the bones wouldn't have survived past Kaycia's ceremony. They'd have been wasted for nothing.

"I'll need some time for this," said Kaycia, opening the book to the right page. "The two of you should start preparing yourselves."

Chesandril looked at her mother. "What does she mean?"

"Come on," said Marien. "Remember the pool down below?"

"We need to wash?"

Marien nodded. "We'll take turns holding the light."

The girl grumbled something about freezing again.

"Remember," continued Kaycia, before they left. "You'll need to remove everything made from metal—don't forget hairpins. You can't wear leather or skin—anything from another living creature. Only simple fabrics—plant fiber or cotton. Understand?"

It was only then that Kaycia realized the girl's dress was silk. It wasn't a direct violation, strictly speaking, but it wasn't worth the risk. She didn't understand what silk was made of, but it might interfere with the girl's life signature.

"What're you wearing under that? Don't tell me it's *all* silk."

"I'll go with them," offered Elyriel. "My slip's cotton. We can switch."

Kaycia nodded and motioned them to hurry.

For the next half hour, Kaycia labored over the chalk design. While she wasn't exactly an artist, she'd practiced drawing circles over fifteen feet across as part of her training. The result wasn't perfect, considering her haste, but close enough to meet their needs.

In the end, it wasn't the chalk that possessed any power. In the same way, there was nothing special about the floor or the statues of the gods themselves.

What mattered was the meaning behind each component—that each statue could be identified and each symbol easily read. As long as the meaning remained unambiguous, her artistry didn't matter. It wasn't the details that drew the god's attention but intent.

The women were ready before Kaycia was finished, and they waited outside the circles for further instruction. This, too, was a good thing, as it wasn't just the body that needed purging from outside influences. The mind benefited from cleansing as well.

As Kaycia finished the final mark, she looked up at her audience.

Chesandril's arms were clutched tightly across her chest, trying to keep warm. Her white, sleeveless slip was too large for her frame, and her hair—usually wavy—hung straight down her back. Her feet were bare, with her left big toe pawing absentmindedly at the stone beneath her.

Kaycia motioned the girl forward. "I'm going to need you right here. Watch your step, and don't smudge the lines."

"Where should I leave the box?" asked Marien. She, too, was barefoot and wearing a light, faded shift.

"On the floor is fine. You'll be over here, Marien. And Elle, why don't you come around the outside? I'll need you to watch this closely."

"What should I focus on?"

Kaycia realized she should slow down so everyone was on the same page.

"Listen up. All these symbols need to remain intact. I'll need your help with this,

Elle. Keep an eye on their feet. If anyone missteps and smears a line, you'll have to redraw it exactly as it was. Got it?"

Elyriel looked uncertain. "I can enter the circle, then?"

"Only if necessary. Get out quickly, and it shouldn't pose a problem."

The girl nodded.

"Okay...the chalk's the easy part. The rest's not so simple."

Kaycia then drew a knife from her waist.

Without needing to be asked, Marien proffered her left arm.

Taking care to avoid veins and tendons, Kaycia made a small incision along the woman's forearm. She stepped closer and painted a symbol in blood across Marien's forehead. As she did so, she recited from memory the accompanying invocation.

"Beneath the eyes of the gods, I mark thee for service. Thy head that thou might receive understanding. And thine ears, to be opened to the voice of the eight...err, *nine...* realms."

At this, Kaycia dabbed each earlobe with blood.

Marien looked confused. "Nothing's happening."

"It's not supposed to," said Kaycia, under her breath. "Not yet. Turn around."

With more blood from her arm, Kaycia traced a larger design across Marien's back and her exposed shoulders. It was reminiscent of a story—depicting a man grieving over his loved ones. The man was Telarien.

"Watch close, Elle. These lines smudge more easily."

Her sister's face went white, uneager to paint with blood.

In a louder voice, Kaycia proceeded with the ceremony. "Marien ti Olesca, marked for service, daughter of Rikkan and Corintha, wilt thou heed the call of thine professed deity? Wilt thou swear thyself loyal, to be born anew, as a daughter of Telarien? Speak now with thine own voice. Swear it."

Marien's head turned slightly.

Under her breath, Kaycia added, "Say, 'I swear.'"

The woman nodded hastily. "I swear."

"Close your eyes."

As Marien did so, Kaycia produced a cloth blindfold she'd cut earlier from Elyriel's sash. She tied it carefully so as not to disturb the blood on Marien's face.

Kaycia turned and walked toward Chesandril. She then repeated a similar incantation. In this case, the girl wasn't marked for service but devotion. Moments later, the girl was given a blindfold as well.

"Okay, Elle. Stand here with Chess. Don't do anything unless I tell you. For the next bit, my entire focus will be on Marien."

Kaycia proceeded into the more complex invocations. This part was more tedious, as she was required to move Marien to another part of the circle, where she was marked for purity, and another where she was marked for discipline.

Through all this, nothing unusual was expected to happen. Most of these words were for Marien's benefit. They primed her mind, like readying a pump so water could flow.

From time to time, Kaycia would turn to her sister and provide her with words to repeat for Chesandril.

In actuality, there were only a few passages Kaycia couldn't recall verbatim. But, even as she blundered through the words, she wasn't dissatisfied with the result. They conveyed the impression of correctness, though they were not the ones from her own ceremony.

Half an hour later, she felt the signs of the circle responding. The surrounding air felt lighter, as though losing a part of its substance. Kaycia heard her voice as though through a trance. And she could almost feel reality waiting to be rewritten.

And then...something even stranger occurred.

Kaycia had been reciting a passage of binding, to invoke the presence of the deceased Telarien, when Marien stopped responding to Kaycia's instructions.

To her surprise, it was Chesandril who responded.

"Sorry... I don't think Mother can hear you anymore."

"What makes you say that?"

"Oh gods..." the girl breathed. "A—actually, it's more like she can hear you...but she's having difficulty joining the sounds into words...or the words into meaning."

"Are you just guessing this?"

"I... I don't know," the girl said as her brow tightened above the cloth of her blindfold. "It's like I can feel her... Like being in her head... O—or she's in mine? Does it make a difference?"

Kaycia couldn't decide which was more disturbing: the fact Marien was losing normal function—as they'd feared—or the fact it could be sensed through Chesandril's bond.

At this point, however, the woman lifted her chin and asked, "So what now?"

Blinking in surprise, Kaycia asked, "Marien?"

"No," said the woman. "I told you—she can't hear."

Kaycia's heart skipped a beat. "Chess?" she asked with measured trepidation.

"Yes?" responded Marien—seemingly oblivious anything was out of the ordinary. With the blindfold on, she hadn't noticed the change in her own voice.

Right then, however, the ceremony was nearing a critical juncture, and this interruption had gone too long already. Still, Kaycia thought it best to perform a quick experiment.

"Chess? Can I have you raise your left arm for me?"

"Like this?" asked the girl—speaking through Marien's lips and raising Marien's hand.

Elyriel's eyes widened in shock as she studied the girl beside her, who hadn't moved a muscle.

"Good..." continued Kaycia, realizing she could still use this development. "Here. Take my hand. I need you three steps forward."

The woman was momentarily confused about where she was, but she took a deep breath and accepted Kaycia's assistance.

"Elle...? Get the box. You need to crush the bones into a fine powder. Do it now."

"But what about mother?" asked Marien, as Elyriel scrambled to obey. "Shouldn't we be—?"

"Chess... Right now, I need you to focus."

"But what if she—?"

"If you want to help Mother, we *must* keep moving. Everything will be fine, but I need *you* to get through this. Can you do that for me?"

A few tears dampened the cloth of Marien's blindfold. Her lips trembled before she gave a sudden, vigorous nod.

"Good girl. Now turn. Face me."

With the statue of Telarien directly behind Kaycia, the woman turned to stand beneath the gaze of her god.

As Kaycia resumed summoning Telarien, the firelight from the scattered sconces wavered all at once—though no discernible breeze passed through the cavern.

Her sister looked up in fear but never stopped grinding the bones.

Moments later, the final words were spoken, and the firelight went still.

For Kaycia, nothing had changed—except maybe the room was a bit darker than before. Or was that just her imagination?

"Chess...?" she asked gingerly. "Without removing the blindfold—open your eyes."

The girl didn't respond.

"Listen to me, Chess! I know you're afraid, but—"

Marien shook her head. Her face squeezed into an expression of agony, and her hands trembled.

"N—no...! I can... Bloody heavens...! *I can hear him...!*"

"That's good!" exclaimed Kaycia, feeling a flood of relief. Despite the unexpected turns, they were still on track. And for the first time, she believed their plan might work.

"Now listen! Chess, you need to open your eyes."

"He's having difficulty breathing... His voice is all raspy!"

"That's okay! It's *Telarien*, remember?" she continued with more confidence than she felt.

"I know, but—!"

"Now, Chess!"

Marien lifted her chin and straightened her back.

And began to scream.

"You're okay!" said Kaycia, trying to calm her.

But the woman panicked. Stumbled backward.

"Stay in the circle!"

Elyriel dropped the box. She got behind the lady before she crossed the line.

"It's all right!" said Elyriel, holding her in place. "Breathe!"

The woman, however, was far from convinced. And as Elyriel held onto her, Marien pushed back with her feet—with the strength of an adult.

"Kay!" shouted Elyriel.

"I don't want to do this!" shouted the woman. "I don't want to do this!"

Kaycia felt something in her heart break.

"Let go of me! I'm sorry! I'm sorry!"

"You *can*!" insisted Elyriel. "You have to!"

And, to everyone's surprise, Marien went still.

It happened so quickly, Kaycia didn't believe for a second the girl had conquered her fears. This was something else.

The woman's muscles had gone rigid—paralyzed with terror. She wasn't even looking at Telarien. Instead, with the blindfold on, her gaze went further, beyond the plateau.

Her neck jerked back and forth as though trying to look in all directions at once.

"What is it?" asked Elyriel.

Her breathing was ragged, making the words difficult to understand. "...S—standing up... A—all of them..."

Kaycia felt a chill. She followed the girl's gaze but saw nothing different in the surrounding cavern. Just the same bones as before.

"They're looking right at me...!" continued the girl. "They're warning me of...!"

Kaycia tried to ignore this, pushing to the end.

"Don't look at them!" she said. "You're scared. They're not going to harm us!"

But she'd spoken too soon.

"G—G—Get— G—Get—!" The girl was hyperventilating. "G—Get b—b—ba—!"

Marien jerked backward again as her eyes locked on the top of the ramp. She tried to say something else, but her voice died away, as though she couldn't quite get out the words.

Or, thought Kaycia, with a deepening sense of dread, *the sound was being blocked...*

Kaycia stopped breathing as her eyes locked onto that dark, empty space.

It was difficult to make out clearly, but it was almost as though a crossbow bolt were hovering in midair.

Damn it all! she thought. *It can't be!*

As the bolt rose higher, it was soon accompanied by an entire spear—*Kaycia's* spear—lodged deep in its invisible hide.

Somehow, the creature hadn't only come back, it'd managed to find her. It'd tracked her all the way down here—motivated, no doubt, by thoughts of revenge.

The timing couldn't have been worse. Her mind raced for a way to deal with this intruder—and she hoped, with all her heart, it hadn't brought friends.

"Stay behind me!" she told Marien and Elyriel, as she dropped into a crouch and moved a hand to her knives.

... Only to change her mind a second later.

Her eyes locked onto her spear as it came closer. She bent her knees—not tensing but preparing to spring.

In the briefest of moments, Kaycia noticed the spear dip slightly lower than its previous steps.

And both she and the creature jumped at the same time.

Elyriel screamed—as though from far away.

With all her strength, Kaycia dove at a diagonal, evading the attack while stretching for the weapon.

The shaft came faster than her hands could move. The wood slipped between her arms, striking hard across her chest. Her legs were twisted out from under her, continuing forward while the rest of her tumbled back.

As the world turned over, she locked her arms, clutching the pole to her body. Her added weight dragged the creature down, causing it to swerve. It slammed through an iron sconce, scattering embers and sparks.

Still latched onto the spear, Kaycia tried to stand, only to have something—a leg, perhaps—slam hard into her chest.

After being embedded for so long, her weapon finally pried free, and she landed heavily on her back.

At this point, she would've almost preferred the spear *not* to come free, so she'd at least have a way to maintain some control.

"Come on!" she yelled as she regained her stance. The shout, of course, wasn't audible for her—but that didn't mean the creature wouldn't listen. "I'm right here! I'm the one you want!"

Kaycia didn't wait, unwilling to risk its attention on the girls, and she thrust with her spear. Right then, their best chance was to keep it distracted, so the ritual could proceed.

Luckily, the creature was more than willing to accept her challenge.

As it pounced, she dove to the side, swinging her tip in a wide arc.

The strike wasn't as effective as wielding a halberd. But it still made contact and gave a fleeting indication of the creature's direction.

As it recovered its momentum, Kaycia pointed at the bones, then thrust that same finger at Marien.

Without time to confirm her sister understood, she re-engaged the enemy.

Rather than thrust, she opted to keep swinging. With hands near the bottom of the shaft, she created wide, sweeping circles that weren't so much intended to inflict damage as to drive the creature back.

Her entire strategy was to maintain the offensive in the hopes of preventing a counterattack. And while she knew she couldn't possibly maintain this exertion, she could only hope, maybe—*maybe*, Marien would ascend and come to her aid.

In the next moment, the creature disengaged and pulled to one side.

Kaycia followed, fully expecting a feint—that it would renew its attack from a different direction.

In truth, however, it was chasing something else.

Kaycia turned and found that Marien was missing. Elyriel stood alone in the circle, box in hand and horror on her face.

Had they finished already?

But that wasn't it. The woman had removed her blindfold and was running away.

Her escape was pitiful—not quickened by unnatural strength or with the aid of the gods. It was the run of a frightened girl—taking advantage of the creature's distraction, to find a place to hide.

And just like that, in a single, gut-wrenching instant, the ceremony failed.

Kaycia wanted to scream! And while she knew it wasn't Marien, herself, who'd lost control but a twelve-year-old girl—this did nothing to quell her fury and frustration.

What were they supposed to do now?

With the creature no longer fighting Kaycia—the girl's run became frantic and desperate. After three steps, her feet slipped and sent her sprawling on hands and knees.

Kaycia knew she'd never reach her in time, but she started forward anyway.

 AUSTIN LYNN CLARK

Their plan might've failed, but she *wouldn't* give up—not while her sister lived.

She rushed at the creature, determined to drive it off Marien, toward the edge.

But the creature was too fast. It didn't simply tackle the other woman—in a single movement, it tore her head clean off her shoulders.

In shock, Kaycia nearly lost her step but managed to, instead, add her rage and despair into the strength of her charge.

Her spear slammed into the beast, and she felt the satisfying snap of bone.

It tumbled to the ground and sent Marien's head flying through the air.

Ignoring the shower of blood, Kaycia screamed—soundlessly—as she continued forward and pinned the creature against Shaelis's statue.

It flailed, striking Kaycia's arm and sent her stumbling sideways.

She recovered, ignoring the pain—and the gouges ripped through her armor—and she came at the beast again.

It deflected her next two attacks.

By sheer luck, she avoided getting clawed a second time.

Her next attack plunged deep into something soft, and she exulted in the hope she'd struck something vital.

Indeed, in the following moments, some sound returned. The creature continued to thrash—showing no signs of giving up—but it seemed, momentarily, weakened.

Enough she could hear Elyriel's shout.

But Kaycia couldn't turn—not just yet.

Feeling the creature's location, she centered her thrust and pushed it back against the statue.

This didn't provide much of an opening—perhaps less than a second—but Kaycia turned her head to see what was happening.

Her sister was still inside the circle—not under attack or in discernible danger.

Except...Elyriel had removed her shoes and cast aside her dress.

Instead, she stood in the silken slip that'd once been Chesandril's, and she'd hastily painted, with her own blood, what marks she could remember on her face and shoulders.

"NO!" screamed Kaycia as she thrust again with her spear, pinning the creature in place.

But when she turned back, she could only watch as her sister took her place in the circle, brought the box to her lips, and choked down its contents.

Chapter 6
CONVICTION

There were several reasons why the ritual shouldn't have worked.

The chalk circle hadn't only been disturbed once but multiple times during Marien's struggle. There were severed lines and symbols smeared beyond recognition—which should've been enough to unbind what they'd accomplished.

For the power to linger, past this point, could've only been the result of Telarien's presence. Once invoked, the god would not be dismissed so casually.

Still, she hadn't believed Telarien would accept Elyriel—or any replacement. But if the god noticed she was a different person, he didn't seem to care.

Kaycia watched in horror as her sister was lifted off the ground, arms hanging limp to her sides, and her face raised toward the heavens.

The undead god had accepted her immediately and without reservation. Perhaps he was reacting to the girl's determination—or maybe all that mattered were the ingested bones.

Either way, it was happening too quickly. If a blood relative didn't join Elyriel in the circle, the result would be too horrible to bear.

Without time to think—Kaycia released her spear.

The shaft twisted as the monster rose—but Kaycia was already committed to her sprint.

The beast followed close behind, sending a thrill through her veins. The creature's recovery was entirely unexpected—suggesting it wasn't so weak as she'd hoped.

"Damn it!" she screamed, overcome with dread. Kaycia had needed it to be weak, if only for a moment. But now... She'd reach the circle, only to be torn to shreds at the same instant.

As she closed the last few steps, however, she was taken by surprise.

Both her spear and the crossbow bolt clattered to the ground.

She'd seen this before, when the creatures left the countryside and strayed too close to a civilized area. The creatures didn't die but lost their connection with the physical world. They were left with no choice but to turn back around.

This was the result of Telarien's presence. Even dead, his influence was enough to push the abyssal current back and prevent this beast from entering the circle.

With this realization, tears sprang to her eyes—despite her keen awareness this relief would be temporary. Once the ceremony ended and Telarien withdrew, she had no doubt she and her sister would still be in danger.

Which made it all the more important for this moment to count.

As she stepped into position beside Chesandril's collapsed form, she wondered if the girl would ever wake again—before Kaycia's attention was yanked back to her sister.

All at once, surges of heat washed up through her muscles, beginning from her toes and rising through her head. Wave after wave gripped her in place, each pulse in sync with her beating heart.

Removing her armor or marking herself with blood hadn't been necessary. The design of the circles—whole or otherwise—was enough to determine the binding's outcome. Though this role was initially meant for Chesandril, it eagerly accepted a compatible substitute.

Her breathing slowed while her sweat cooled and hardened against her skin. All thoughts of battle were swept from mind, replaced by feelings of intense introspection. The world melted away, leaving Kaycia alone with her thoughts and memories.

Until she realized some of those thoughts were unfamiliar and not her own.

As she examined these memories—those of a young girl who'd looked up to Kaycia with the utmost admiration—she understood what this was.

Nothing was held back. In a single instant, Kaycia had access to her sister's most carefully guarded secrets—from her deepest fears to her moments of greatest shame.

She saw an argument with Esmera, their mother, back when Kaycia wasn't home. Esmera's anguish was surprising as she pleaded with Elyriel not to leave. This didn't match what Kaycia remembered—who'd been told it was Mother's idea to send Elyriel to the garrison.

There was an image of a boy Kaycia had never met, sitting beside her on the dock as they dangled their feet above a canal near their home. That boy had been Elyriel's first kiss.

Kaycia wanted to look away, ashamed by this invasion of her sister's privacy. It wasn't that Elyriel would want to hide this boy or that she'd feel embarrassed if Kaycia found out. If Kaycia had thought to ask, she felt confident the girl would've shared every detail.

But that never happened. When the sisters were together, chatting into the night, their talks usually revolved around events at Wern's Hold. They'd both been content with their time together, and she'd never realized how much Elyriel had sacrificed. In the end, Elyriel had been truly happy—Kaycia could see that now. But that didn't mean she didn't also feel loss.

There were too many memories—so many that her confusion outweighed her epiphanies. And before Kaycia could process the tiniest part, the feelings began to fade.

As her sister's narrative caught up to the present, each emotion became replaced until one remained: paralyzing fear.

The memories were gone, but Kaycia still saw the world through her sister's eyes. One was covered beneath an enormous, leathered hand; the other peered through the gap between index and thumb.

And though it was Elyriel's face within the hand's tight grip, stretching her neck until it screamed in pain—to Kaycia, it felt like it was happening to her.

Together, feet dangling, they stared into the eyes of an undead god.

No matter how horrible or inexplicable it was to finally see one, first hand—Kaycia had never considered how much worse it'd be for a god to look back at *her*.

Those eyes, a deep piercing blue, severed their minds as a sword through flesh. And while Kaycia could not fathom the entirety of her own life, let alone her sister's, she was left with the impression that Telarien saw them both. He saw their lives laid bare, raw and exposed.

His stern, elderly face was a blistering white, with cracks instead of wrinkles. His hair unkempt, withered, and dry.

It took no degree of faith to acknowledge if the god was real or not. This felt so strange, she felt compelled to reconsider what she knew of her religion.

This experience demanded a different sort of faith—faith in his divinity. Faith that she even *wanted* him to be real. That he continued to deserve her veneration.

Despite her own terror, she could only imagine how much worse this would be for Elyriel.

Hold on! she called out in her mind, hoping her sister would hear. *You're not alone! I'm here with you!*

Telarien didn't speak, but Kaycia felt something happen—an intense pressure shaking the world. Something inside her broke. Shattered. Searing pain threatened to consume her.

A warm trickle ran down her thigh—no, not hers. Elyriel's.

But despite all the pain, revulsion, and pity, it was nothing compared to her rising horror. For, at that same moment, her sister's mind grew distant. Her brightly colored thoughts darkened and spoiled, and the connection between them withered and died.

"No!!" she screamed, as tears clouded her vision—but it was Elyriel's voice she heard. Not her own.

Her head felt as though on fire.

"BRING HER BACK!" she demanded of the dispassionate god, who'd already begun to fade.

As she was released from his grip, her legs folded beneath her. Her knees crashed into stone.

She caught herself with her hands—with Elyriel's familiar, slender hands.

"You can't do this to her!" she screamed. "It was never meant to be her!"

Her cries, however, were completely ignored. The room went dark, leaving no sign Telarien had ever been there.

She screamed in rage—so loud, it overpowered the dampening aura and sent a trembling echo through the surrounding cavern.

What was worse, her anger wasn't directed at Telarien so much as herself. Though the result had been born of godly power—*she'd* been the one who'd conducted the ritual.

This, however... This was *not* what she'd wanted!

As her mind struggled to keep up—she was suddenly struck and thrown sideways. The world turned over as she sprawled over stone.

"Damn it!" she screamed as she rose on bare feet outside the chalk circle's edge.

Her knees burned, and she'd scraped her shoulder blade. It was a blow that would've broken bones—for a regular human. But, as her mind snapped into focus, she was keenly aware of specific changes.

Wearing nothing more than a silken slip—with no armor to think of—Kaycia was surprised she didn't feel vulnerable. In some ways, the light material felt liberating, with nothing to restrict her mobility or speed.

Everything was so different! Elyriel's body was thinner than she was used to. Shorter. But, oh...not nearly so frail as she'd imagined. Kaycia had never felt so strong in her life.

The pain from her scrapes had already begun to heal.

It was only then she let her eyes take in the abyssal current—the blood dripping from stalactites and the rancid, carmine pools. After so many years dreaming of this moment, it felt strange to have it thrust upon her so suddenly—and to see it through her sister's eyes, no less.

The first thing she noticed was that the cavern was darker—*much* darker, with only a cool sputtering from the pale fires. Somehow, though, there wasn't a single part of the chamber too difficult to see. With the aid of ascendancy, she could discern the most acute colors—more vividly than she'd thought possible—even in the most obscured and heavily shadowed recess.

Only a heartbeat had passed since rising to her feet, but her mind absorbed every detail at remarkable speed.

Most surprising was the hideous creature regarding her across the circle—appearing nothing at all like she'd been led to believe.

Knowing its many legs, she'd expected a segmented body more akin to an insect's. But, aside from its long, bulbous torso—reminiscent of a mantis—any similarities ended there.

Instead, she saw an amalgamation of what appeared to be spindly human parts.

This singular detail told her this was not the same variety that commonly attacked on the roads. It also explained why it was no longer with the pack—as nightmaidens were more than capable of hunting on their own.

Its anatomy was lithe and feminine, with pale white skin. Its hide wasn't soft or thin as its human physique might suggest—but hardened and rubbery, like an embalmed corpse. It bore the signs from its earlier struggle with Kaycia, displaying lacerations that oozed with gelatinous, blackened blood.

From the nightmaiden's ridged back sprouted four legs that didn't appear to serve a purpose. They pointed into the air like useless wings. From their slender, curved shapes—and smooth, hairless skin—they shared an uncanny resemblance with a human female. With one significant difference.

In place of blunted toenails, they had long, blackened claws.

Similar spines protruded from its hairless tail. Still more jutted out from its two pairs of legs and two pairs of arms.

Topping it off, its head was framed by long, black hair. Lanky strands hung past its shoulders to cling, matted and tangled, against slimy ribs.

It had a sleek, feminine face—but with uninterrupted skin where its eyes should be. From the corners of its mouth—with lips that appeared quite ordinary—were cuts extending that smile almost entirely to its ears.

This was all the more apparent when, in the next instant, it unhinged its jaw, splitting its face wide open to reveal a massive maw of black, drooling teeth.

Kaycia observed all this in a few seconds and, just as quickly, devised a plan.

She'd need time to acclimate to her new agility—and, more importantly, her limitations. And though her muscles tingled with anticipation, feeling confident she could move faster than the nightmaiden—it'd be foolish to attack it head-on.

For this reason, she made no move toward the spear it'd dropped, laying much too close to the creature's clammy feet. Instead, she tucked into a roll in the direction of her knives.

She tried hard not to look at herself, as she pulled the blades from her unconscious body, lying beside Chesandril's. She didn't have time to consider if this transfer was permanent, or if she might return to that body later.

"Come on, then!" she yelled, raising her blades in invitation.

The nightmaiden shrieked in response, arched its back, and clambered toward her on its varied limbs.

Kaycia leaped again, luring it away from the circle—and away from the vulnerable sleepers.

Through Elyriel's ascendancy, she couldn't change the orientation of the world or gravity, as Tenlen had done with his Equilibrium. In much the same way, without the skills of Transfiguration, she couldn't pass through the stone as though it were water.

Kaycia couldn't alter anything from the seven other realms, but through the rules of her own—on which she'd spent years of her life in careful study—she could change something else.

Through Conviction, she could transform *intent*.

Throwing her knife, she instilled it with purpose—to pierce the skin where the beast's eye was supposed to be and plunge deep into its brain.

With alarming speed, the nightmaiden twisted to evade—so quickly, Kaycia felt sure her blade would miss, regardless. But she needn't have worried.

The knife altered its trajectory and buried itself, hilt deep, with a sickening squelch.

The creature shrieked like a madwoman.

Kaycia could hardly believe it. She'd seen blades swerve before, but not nearly so fast. Was it possible Elyriel's Conviction was so superior to her teachers'?

Unfortunately, even a puncture to the brain wouldn't bring the creature down. It had also left her with one less knife. Her throw, however, hadn't been meant to stop the nightmaiden so much as to provide distraction.

While it wailed and moaned, she leaped to the side and took up the rope Marien had found in the storeroom.

It hurt to be reminded of her recent death—but Kaycia could've *blessed* the woman for bringing this out!

Already, the creature was lumbering toward her.

With nimble fingers, she looped an end around her knife's wooden handle. She made a knot with a singular purpose—to hold the knife secure, no matter what.

She rolled away from the nightmaiden's charge and threw—while never letting go of the rope's other end.

As before, her aim was flawless, sliding into the same bleeding eye socket beside the first she'd thrown.

Rolling up onto a knee, Kaycia whipped out her arm, sending a powerful undulation through the length of rope. This extracted the weapon from its lodged position, while simultaneously accomplishing its secondary purpose—to hook beneath the hilt of the other knife and pull it free.

Both metal blades returned through the air, still hooked together. She yanked again, curving the handles' path so they'd land perfectly into her outstretched, free hand.

She wasn't only thrilled this worked—but that she'd made it happen on her first try!

"Ha!" she taunted. "Didn't expect that, did you?"

The nightmaiden rounded on her, black blood oozing from its obliterated face.

Kaycia attacked again, cracking the rope like a whip.

The creature's head snapped back as her blade slammed through its windpipe.

Even this wasn't enough to kill, but it *did* stop the screaming.

As the knife slid free, Kaycia swung the blade in a wide arc. She targeted its vulnerable tendons in a few sweeping circles, lightning fast.

The problem with knife blades, however, was that they didn't cut deep. After half a dozen slashes, she knew this approach was taking too long.

The maiden tried to shriek—but it sounded more like a pained gargle as blood sputtered from its exposed throat. Then, it pounced.

Kaycia leaped aside and felt the ground tremble beneath the impact.

Her rope whirred through the air, never slowing its circular momentum, even as Kaycia came up from her roll.

Knowing she needed to increase her game, she redirected her blade, not toward the creature but off to one side.

The rope caught beneath the head of Meileen's statue, before wrapping around the neck and sending the knife whipping back at the creature.

Even from this precarious angle, the knife, once again, found the nightmaiden's eye socket. This time, however, she told the weapon to go deeper—and to rotate once inside. With the blade turned sideways, its ends became caught against the creature's skull.

When Kaycia pulled, the knife acted like an anchor—snapping the creature's head toward the top of Meileen's statue.

A moment later, however, the nightmaiden reared back. It bucked sideways and dragged Kaycia forward.

 AUSTIN LYNN CLARK

The rope cut through her palms, and it was all she could do to keep her feet beneath her, bare toes gripping stone.

"Damn it..." she hissed, realizing her plan wouldn't work.

In a pure contest of strength, the nightmaiden was more than Elyriel's match. Moreover, it was larger and heavier.

If she wanted to win, she'd have to get creative.

With a few rotations of her shoulder, she wrapped the rope around her arm—ensuring her grip—before she leaped toward a second statue.

The rope flew her in a circle around this new anchor and whipped her to the other side.

Before the nightmaiden could pull her back the way she came, she drove her foot against the stone and used its weight to hold herself in place.

For a moment, this seemed to work. With the creature's head stretched back, the rope secured it in place. And though its limbs clawed against the stone, and gouts of blood erupted from its throat, it was unable to come closer.

Unfortunately, it soon diverted its attention toward the rope, thrashing with its claws.

"Stop that!" she screamed, as she felt an enormous draw on her strength.

Ordinarily, the rope would've been torn to shreds. The only reason it held together was because of her ascendancy. She'd given it a purpose, and it was doing everything in its power to fulfill her demands.

But, even then, the ancient rope could only do so much.

The longer this went on, it would only get worse. The draw on her strength would increase exponentially, to the point she'd be too weak to continue the fight.

If she didn't think fast, she'd lose her advantage.

"Sorry for this!" she muttered, driving her foot against the statue and pushing with all her strength.

Nothing happened.

She'd wanted to use the stone's weight to hoist the nightmaiden upward—but the statue didn't budge.

"No!" she shrieked, only then realizing how much strength she'd lost. Moments earlier, this approach might've worked, but the statue was too heavy.

"Damn it..." she hissed as she searched for a new plan.

The obvious solution was to let go of the rope—to accept her mistake and salvage what strength she had left. As long as she avoided its attacks, with some luck, she might get the chance to recover from weakness.

...To hell with that!

Holding fast to the rope, Kaycia allowed herself to be pulled forward—whipping around the statue by the nightmaiden's strength.

Now that the rope only supported her weight, it had an easier time keeping together. It provided centripetal force and circled Kaycia around the creature and Meileen's statue.

This untethered the nightmaiden from its anchor—but only for a moment.

Giving her own body purpose, she redirected her flight. She tightened her revolution to rebind the creature to the statue more quickly.

The nightmaiden lashed out as she came within reach.

Kaycia contorted midair, twisting her trajectory through the mass of limbs—avoiding them entirely as she made her first revolution.

But after she wrapped around the statue and passed the creature a second time—there was less rope to work with, and she wasn't so lucky.

Claws raked her upper arm, and she felt a flash of searing pain. Somehow, she didn't let go while twisting enough to keep the cuts superficial.

Kaycia didn't stop until she was safely behind the statue. She stood against it with her feet, having bound the nightmaiden in place, with the rope caught squarely across its neck.

Then, with savage strength, she pulled.

The statue trembled as the creature bucked and thrashed.

But Kaycia held tight, knowing her life depended on it.

Her vision blurred as her strength took a dip. Even with the statue blocking her view, she knew the nightmaiden was clawing the rope again. Clawing its own neck.

"JUST DIE ALREADY!" she screamed, pulling even harder.

While she couldn't assign intent to another living creature—and couldn't command the nightmaiden, itself, to die—she could work with the rope.

With all her focus, she willed the fibers to dig deep—to saw back and forth across the previously-severed windpipe. And, once past that, to target the weakness between vertebrae.

Kaycia willed herself to stay awake—feeling both the rope and her sanity withering dangerously thin.

Almost there...!

There came a splintering crack.

Drained of strength, Kaycia collapsed backward, unable to stop her head from slamming the ground.

Pain flashed through her skull—but even this felt distant as she drifted toward unconsciousness.

No! she screamed in her mind. *Not yet!*

Opposite the statue, she saw limbs still writhing.

Kaycia could do nothing as the nightmaiden extracted itself from the rope.

This is it, she thought, as it crawled into view.

Its movements were sporadic, each step causing its muscles to spasm.

Kaycia tried to rise but couldn't.

Her second knife—the one not tied to the rope—was missing. It'd likely fallen when her strength gave out.

The nightmaiden was slow—but gods...! There was nothing she could do!

Until she realized its head was missing, and the beast wasn't crawling toward her at all.

She should've felt relieved, but she only felt numb.

Her head sunk back to the floor as though never to rise again. From the corner of her eye, she tracked the nightmaiden's progress away into the darkness—knowing it could take up to an hour before the twitching limbs realized it was dead.

Minutes passed, and Kaycia did little more than stare into the dark. She lacked the energy to think. More than that, she lacked the desire to *remember*.

As an ascendant, however, it wasn't long before her strength recovered—but even then, she rose to her feet in a mindless stupor.

She came around the statue and extracted her knife from the severed head—ignoring its jaw as it snapped and drooled. She found her other knife nearby.

Her mind was in a haze—until she realized she wasn't alone.

"Drop your weapons!" came the yell—almost frenzied in quality. "Put them down... or your sister dies!"

A lump rose in Kaycia's throat.

From the moment he spoke, she knew it was Veldt. He was supposed to be gone, but he was here, somehow, and holding a knife to her neck—more specifically, the neck of her unconscious body.

"No sudden movements, you hear?" he said. "Just set your knives down."

Kaycia stared in confusion, her mind still reeling. *Damn it all! She'd WON the fight—against the TRUE enemy, and now she had to deal with this?*

But despite what power she possessed—with all her strength and speed—nothing changed the fact she was now utterly helpless. She didn't understand what'd happened—or what Veldt was doing here—but she understood that blade.

There was a clatter as her knives and rope slid from her fingers.

"Good," said Veldt. "Now—I need you to listen carefully. Just listen, and nobody gets hurt."

Kaycia tried to understand her bond with her sister. If the transition, after all, was meant to be permanent and she'd remain inside Elyriel's body forever—then Veldt's threats would mean nothing. It'd mean her old body was nothing more than a lifeless memento, and she could attack him without regard for the consequences.

But, for some reason, that didn't feel right.

Though she no longer sensed a connection with herself, she felt one was there, and it was vitally important. If Veldt slit her throat, she might very well die.

"I know how this looks," he continued, "but I don't want to kill you. You're a good person, Elle. You're not to blame for what happened here."

Kaycia said nothing.

Veldt was mistaken over specific details. He'd witnessed enough of the action to know the ceremony was successful—but he had no way of knowing he wasn't speaking with Elyriel. He'd just assumed Kaycia had been knocked out in the fight.

And Kaycia couldn't blame him. Even she didn't fully understand what'd happened.

"But this?" he said, gesturing toward her with his free hand. "This...isn't natural. You can feel that, can't you? The...*wrongness* behind it all?"

"Look at me, Veldt." She raised both hands so he wouldn't feel threatened. "Listen to my voice and look into my eyes... Do I appear *insane* to you?"

The question took him by surprise. He looked down for a moment before doing as she'd suggested. He met her gaze and furrowed his brow in deep consideration.

But then he shook his head. "I want to believe you. I truly do. But even if *you* aren't aware of the problem, it's become a part of who you are. And it will never go away."

"What are you talking about?"

"Has it never occurred to you?" he asked. "The state of the world—the rise of the abyss? Is it too difficult to conceive it's all the *result* of ascendancy?"

Something about this statement gave Kaycia pause. It felt familiar, as though she'd heard this line of reasoning before. And she realized she had.

"Oh gods...." she breathed. "You're one of *them*..."

This prompted a dry chuckle from Veldt. "So quick to judge... Does that make this easier for you? To give me a label and brand me for my beliefs? Will you so quickly disregard the truth when it's right in front of you?"

Kaycia groaned, already certain they'd never reach an understanding.

Veldt frowned. "Don't you find it odd the creature came back?"

"Not really."

He pressed further. "What about the timing? Was it a coincidence it appeared as the ritual neared the end?"

Kaycia shook her head. "You weren't here."

"I wasn't," he admitted, "but you know I'm right. It was *ascendancy* that lured it here. As it always has."

His argument was an old one—the observation that there were more recorded appearances of abyssal threats while ascendants were nearby. But even though the creatures might be drawn to their power—like how the creatures had focused their efforts on Tenlen—it didn't imply causation. It only meant they prioritized threats.

In the end, it was an argument that didn't even matter. Even if some tie existed between the current and ascendancy, what were they supposed to do? Abandon ascendancy? Cease their only defense against a relentless foe?

While a few people were insane enough to believe this would solve the problem, Kaycia was sure it would not.

Besides, there was something else wrong with Veldt's argument.

"You're right about the timing," she said. "But do you expect me to believe its arrival wasn't a coincidence—while *yours*, somehow, was?"

Veldt tried to protest, but Kaycia pushed on. "Why should I listen to anything you say, when the most likely explanation was that *you* were the one to lead it here?"

"...That isn't—!" His sudden frustration confirmed the truth. And the realization filled her with an overpowering fury.

"WHY?!" she demanded, thinking back to the horror she'd endured and everyone who'd died.

Gods... Everything might've gone smoothly, were it not for his involvement. Even her sister might still—

"Stay back!" he yelled, readjusting his grip on the knife. "There's only one way we're doing this. Or I swear—I'll slit her throat!"

Kaycia froze.

"STEP BACK!" he said, pointing with his chin. "Go on!"

In her moment's hesitation, Veldt slid a shallow cut across her cheek.

Kaycia gasped and stumbled backward.

A red line blossomed across her skin—clear in her vision despite the distance. At the same time, she felt a twinge. It wasn't pain, exactly. She couldn't feel the cut on her face, but she felt...something, nonetheless.

It was almost like being trapped in a dream—that moment when she could feel someone shaking her, but waking up felt like an insurmountable challenge. Her mind was stuck, half asleep and unable to respond to the call of danger.

"What do you want?" she demanded, her anger rising. "The ceremony's done! Finished! Even if I wanted to reverse the outcome—it's impossible!"

"Come back with me," he said. "We'll figure something out. Like I said at the start,

I'd rather not kill anyone."

Kaycia knew better than to trust what he said.

Instead, she returned her attention to that feeling—the connection she'd felt when she'd been cut. It was as though a conduit tied the sisters together—but it was like searching for a muscle she'd never used.

If she could figure it out—and somehow switch to her own body—she could take him by surprise. Upon any resistance, she could always drive a knee into his groin.

"This is *bullshit!*" she said—hoping to keep him distracted. "You might not have a reason to kill Kaycia. But me?!" she asked, placing a hand on her chest. "You can't *fix this!*"

Veldt grit his teeth.

"But you've known that all along, haven't you? The only problem is you don't know how to kill me yet. So, rather than point that knife at *me* where it belongs, you take the coward's approach and threaten a helpless woman!"

At that moment, she found the right muscle.

And Kaycia let go.

She wasn't sure how she did it, but it was not unlike letting her knives fall free. In one instant, her mind clung to Elyriel, and, in the next, she'd slipped back and was lying on the floor—feeling the cold bite of steel.

But something was wrong.

When her arms sprang into action, they were sluggish. Her efforts to control his hands were weak and clumsy, ultimately doing nothing more than letting him know she was awake.

"Stop!" he demanded, with one hand overpowering her arm, while his other brought the knife even closer to her throat. "Don't move!"

Kaycia wanted to scream in frustration. After everything it'd cost to return to her body, she'd only given up her advantage of ascendancy.

More than that, this body was exhausted. It was her own mistake for not realizing it sooner. It wasn't just fatigue; this body had been awake for nearly twenty-four hours.

Her best option was to go back and try again with Elyriel.

Veldt's expression changed from confidence to confusion. His gaze alternated between Kaycia and her sister.

Only then did she realize the girl had collapsed.

Veldt's mind, no doubt, was racing to find the correlation—why Kaycia would wake at the moment her sister fainted.

"What's going on?!" he demanded. "What did you *do?*"

Kaycia refused to answer.

"Stand up!" he said without removing the knife.

Acutely aware of the blade's edge, it took a surprising amount of strength to speak. "...You don't have to do this."

"On your feet!"

Slowly, Kaycia propped herself up.

"You weren't here for Marien's solution," she said. "The method she proposed to counter insanity."

"What is this nonsense?" he demanded.

The clues, however, were already laid out. This was merely a continuation of his conversation with Elyriel.

"We've been bonded," she explained. "It's the reason this works."

"Explain!"

From the corner of her eye, she detected movement. As Veldt studied her gaze... Elyriel rose behind him.

Kaycia pretended not to see—her mind struggling to understand what this possibly meant. By some miracle, was this actually her sister, or what remained of a broken mind?

"Look at me!" she said, not wanting him to notice. "Even if you believe my sister's broken—I want you to look at *me* and tell me *I'm* insane!"

"This is..." Veldt's expression changed to bewilderment. "...We can still fix this!"

"No," she said. "We can't."

Veldt turned, finally sensing something amiss.

In panic, he shoved Kaycia back to the stone.

She scrambled to catch herself but only succeeded at reducing the blow to her head. Even so, she kept her eyes trained on Veldt as he raised his knife toward her sister.

Elyriel let out a savage cry.

His eyes flicked back to Kaycia. "But—! You're still... How are you—?"

Veldt was interrupted as Elyriel pounced—more akin to a panther than an adolescent girl. She crossed the ten-foot gap and was on him, digging her fingertips into his head. One bare foot was on his hip, and the other on his shoulder.

The impact sent Veldt stumbling back, and he cried out in surprise. Anyone weaker might've tripped and fallen, but Veldt regained his footing and fought back.

In sudden fear, Kaycia scrambled to her feet as she watched Veldt's hand seize Elyriel's throat. His other drove his knife, hilt deep, into her leg.

Elyriel let out a scream—not of pain but something more like rage.

Kaycia rushed forward and pounded fists into his back.

Weak as she was, this didn't accomplish much. In the end, when he toppled onto his back, it had more to do with the raving girl atop him.

Elyriel's knee struck the ground near his chest, while her other leg—the one that'd been on his shoulder—now stretched taut and planted her heel by his head.

Ignoring the knife buried in her thigh, Elyriel effortlessly grabbed Veldt's wrist and forced him to release her throat.

And in an impossible contortion, her head came down. The girl sank her teeth deep into the man's neck, before jerking upward and ripping up long strands of bright red flesh.

Chapter 7
THE COST

Kaycia screamed. "Elle? Oh, gods... Elle?!"

She could only stare in horror as the girl straddled Veldt's lifeless body. Again and again, she tore strips away with her teeth. And once, Kaycia thought she saw the girl swallow.

"Elle... Can you hear me?" Kaycia sat up—slowly, not wanting to startle this— Kaycia didn't even know what this was. "It's me, Elle... Your sister."

But the girl didn't look up, too engrossed in finishing—what exactly? For the most part, she didn't seem to be *eating* Veldt. Most bites she spat back onto the floor as blood spilled from her mouth.

Most but not all.

"He's dead, Elle. You don't need to...! Elle, stop it!"

The girl's head jerked up as if seeing Kaycia for the first time. It was a quick motion, more like a bird's than anything human. And when their eyes met, it was like looking into the eyes of a stranger. As if everything they'd shared was...gone.

Kaycia froze, uncertain what to do. She desperately wanted to believe something of her sister remained inside this girl—but those eyes...! They regarded her with suspicion as though she were a threat.

With a sudden chill, Kaycia backed away.

"It's all right, Elle. I'm not your enemy... It's me, Kaycia. You remember, don't you?"

A picture flashed through her mind—of that bloodied mouth curling into a snarl. Screaming the same way she'd screamed at Veldt. What then? If Elyriel pounced, she'd have little chance of fighting back—not against the speed and strength of a feral ascendant.

Unless...

Kaycia wondered what might happen if she tried again to possess Elyriel. With the bindings in place, would it be as simple as reaching out with her mind? Taking control of a willing sister was one thing—but now? This thing might not want her control.

Elyriel, fortunately, didn't attack. She watched Kaycia back away before ignoring her again. As she lowered her face to Veldt's—hovering a moment, with lips slightly parted—it was almost like returning her attention to a lover. The bite that followed, however, was anything but playful.

Kaycia's heart was hammering. For the moment, she was safe, but for how long?

She was only dimly aware she was still crawling backward. And when she hit a statue and could go no further, she pressed her back against the stone as if trying to disappear.

Her chest was heaving—but only partially from fear.

How could she possibly live with this? She'd only gone along with her father's plan—with its insane risks—because it'd been the only way to survive. For *Elyriel* to survive.

Now, it might've been better to have died along with her.

Just thinking this made Kaycia feel worse. Here, her sister had made this noble sacrifice, and Kaycia couldn't muster the decency to be grateful. To recognize the girl had made her choice, wanting Kaycia to live.

But had Elyriel known what she was offering?

Kaycia had imagined quite a different outcome—one in which Elyriel might've simply burned out. That she'd become catatonic, like some lifeless puppet.

That would've been horrible enough and yet...easier than this. Elyriel's body would've served as a painful reminder of everything they'd lost—but Kaycia could've accepted the fact that her sister was gone. She'd have closure knowing Elyriel was dead and had only left her body as a tragic parting gift.

This, however...

Kaycia couldn't look at this girl and determine with any certainty Elyriel *was* gone. She found herself torn between desires—one that selfishly hoped some part of her remained. And a conflicting despondency that wanted nothing more than for Elyriel to be spared this fate.

As Kaycia studied her, covered in blood, she wondered if some part of Elyriel was horrified by her actions. If some hidden recess of her mind was frightened of what she'd become.

It was this, more than anything, that prevented Kaycia from attempting to possess her. She *wanted* to, if only to know she could do it. So she wouldn't have to worry when the sudden, desperate need arose to stop Elyriel from doing something—well...something even *more* horrible than this.

But if Elyriel was already lost and confused... Wouldn't it be worse to have her mind invaded by another?

"Elyriel..." said Kaycia hesitantly. "I know you can hear me. Well...I know your ears are sensitive enough. I know my voice can reach you from here."

The girl didn't look up—which, by itself, meant nothing. It was much like talking to an animal, with no greater reason than getting it comfortable with your voice.

At the same time, Kaycia hoped it was more. That, in the same fashion as people in a coma—who couldn't respond, despite, sometimes, being able to hear—Elyriel *might* be listening. Deep down, Kaycia's words might be reaching her.

"You don't have to respond. Just listen. And even if you're not... If you're not in there anymore...or too broken to make sense of words or meanings..."

She paused, feeling her throat constrict.

"You know what?" she said through stifled sobs. "I'm going to talk anyway. If only to get myself through this. Call me crazy, but I don't know what else to do.

"Right now, I have to believe I still have you with me. A part of you, at least. That I'm not sitting alone, in the middle of gods-know-where...

"I can't do this by myself. I just...can't."

The girl, as before, made no response.

There wasn't, however, much remaining of Veldt's face.

"I'm going to stand up. So...whatever you do...don't be startled. I'm not going to hurt you. But I can't just sit here, you know? You and I need to figure this out, so we might as well start."

Using the statue for support, Kaycia rose to her feet.

The girl looked up with renewed suspicion.

It appeared, after all this talking, nothing had changed.

"It's all right. It's me, remember? You wouldn't eat your sister, would you?"

Elyriel regarded her with an icy glare.

"I'm just standing up. No need to be frightened. I can stay here if you want. Just making certain you won't attack or anything..."

Kaycia's heart hammered. It was hard to tell if she was taking the correct approach. At the same time, if this wasn't going to work—if the creature were beyond all reason— she'd rather learn this now.

A few seconds later, Elyriel turned away.

By then, she'd lost all interest in Veldt and, instead, eyed the other corners of the cavern. Her eyes lingered on Marien's corpse as though recognizing what she was. A moment later, she paused on Chesandril, who still hadn't woken up.

"Don't even think about it!" said Kaycia.

She had no idea what'd happened to Marien's daughter—if the young girl was sleeping, or if her connection to her mother had left her broken as well. One more casualty to this godsforsaken day.

Elyriel crawled on her hands and feet. As she turned, Kaycia saw the handle protruding from her leg. Somehow, she'd forgotten the knife was still there. Her sister was bleeding out, and no one was doing anything about it.

"You shouldn't move! Just wait, and we can—"

Elyriel spun to face her, eyes furious.

Kaycia, without thinking, had taken two steps from the statue.

"Sorry! But...that knife...!"

The girl hissed—bloodied teeth stretching wide to produce a rough, guttural screech.

Kaycia flinched, dismayed to be the target of such overwhelming fury. But this was her sister, dammit! And she was all the more determined not to back down.

Some wild animals were encouraged by fear. Sometimes, the only way was to use a firm hand and let them know—

With no further warning, Elyriel sprang forward—giving life to the nightmare Kaycia hoped to avoid. The knife did nothing to slow her down. And as she flew through the air—teeth barred and fingers stretched like claws—she lost all resemblance to the sister she knew.

"Elle...! Don't!"

The room shifted.

Pain flashed through her leg, inciting thoughts of, *Bloody heavens! She's tearing me apart, just like—!*

But that wasn't it.

No fingers were grasping Kaycia. Nothing dragged her or tossed her around. There was nothing on top of Kaycia at all.

When she looked down, Veldt's knife was stuck in her leg. The pain was so excruciating—her mind couldn't make sense of it.

Until she realized it wasn't *her* leg but Elyriel's. Somehow, without the conscious decision, she'd successfully transferred to her sister's body.

"Damn it!" she yelled and was surprised to hear her sister's voice. She should've expected this, but it still felt wrong. Horribly wrong. The familiarity of that voice was *supposed* to be comforting. It should've been proof they were still together and could talk this out as they always had.

"Elle..." she moaned. "I... I'm sorry."

For all she knew, she was still talking to herself.

Either way, what was done was done. And she might as well do some good while she was here.

Sitting back, Kaycia curled one leg underneath her, while slowly and carefully stretching the other in front.

Looking at the blade made the pain feel worse. Her entire leg was on fire, throbbing to the beat of her heart. But somehow, Kaycia managed not to pass out. No doubt, she would've done just that were it not for ascendancy.

A small blessing, that.

Beside her, on the floor, was her spear from earlier.

Steeling herself, she jammed the wooden shaft into her mouth, while clutching onto the knife handle with the other.

Biting down hard, she nearly yanked it out before she stopped herself.

What the hell was she doing?

Kaycia looked around, trying to find something to tie around her leg.

While she knew ascendancy would aid the healing process, this was no reason to test its limits. She needed to be smart. She needed to be careful.

Her leg, however, seemed to disagree. It throbbed with renewed ferocity, as if to say *To hell with being careful—GET THIS DAMNED THING OUT!!*

She tried to ignore this and groaned, realizing her best bet was to scoot back to the circle's center. Taking care to immobilize the injured leg, she did all the work with the other. Even the slightest movement, however, sent waves of agony through her body.

Reaching Veldt's corpse took longer than expected, but she needed his belt.

Unfortunately, this required her to look at his remains—and, this time, from much closer up. Even before reaching him, she was overwhelmed by the stench—made all the more acute by her enhanced senses. Its coppery tang was so overpowering she could almost taste it.

And she realized...she *did* taste it. Until that moment, she'd been so focused on her leg—and the shock of being attacked—she hadn't noticed what was in her mouth.

The thought of Veldt's blood nearly caused her to gag—but she couldn't let revulsion stop her now. She'd come this far—she *would* relieve her sister from this damned blade!

As Kaycia scooted the final distance, she felt lightheaded. She ignored the discarded flesh that surrounded her. Her fingers prised at the metal buckle, slippery with blood.

She let her mind turn off, forcing her hands through the motions—just wanting this to end.

Before she knew it, the belt was cinched around her leg.

She couldn't remember what she'd done with her spear, but she no longer cared to have anything between her teeth.

Taking a firm grasp of the knife's handle, she pulled with all her strength.

And, less than a second later, lost all consciousness.

When her senses returned, she was back in her own body. Lying on her back, she opened her eyes to stalactites overhead, dim in the light of the waning fires.

Strangely enough, she felt a residual pain in her leg—despite knowing this shouldn't have been possible. It seemed to reaffirm the reality of the experience—the trauma had, indeed, been hers, despite the body belonging to someone else.

She forced herself to sit up.

How long was she unconscious? In sudden panic, she feared Elyriel had woken up. That she was gone and wandering by herself.

But when she turned to the spot where she'd left her sister, the girl was still there.

She was even more relieved to see the knife discarded to one side. That was good. Her memories were distant and hazy near the end, and she hadn't been certain she'd finished the job.

Her sister wasn't moving, her body stretched out, no doubt needing time to recover. Her head had fallen back, making a pillow of Veldt's mutilated... Well, the specifics weren't important.

For a brief instant, Kaycia wondered if her sister might be dead—that she'd been expelled from her mind due to excessive blood loss.

But she needn't have worried. After a moment's focus, she could indeed discern the rise and fall of her sister's bloodied chest.

"I'm sorry, Elle..."

And then, she nearly laughed—for, right then, she knew her sister couldn't *possibly* be listening. The girl was knocked out and completely oblivious.

But Kaycia hadn't spoken for her sister's benefit, had she?

More than anything, the apology was for Kaycia—so she could hear the words. She *was* sorry. Not just for this but for everything.

"Now... Let's have a look at that wound."

Her mind found solace in having something to do. That despite not knowing what the future held in store, nothing was confusing about this present urgency.

The first step, however, was surprisingly difficult.

She kept remembering the crazed look in Elyriel's eyes. Wild with rage and uncontrollable hatred. Kaycia wasn't sure she could face that right now.

Of course, there *was* another way.

It'd be easier to inhabit Elyriel's body from the start. She could wrap the wound herself without fear of the girl waking up.

But Kaycia didn't like that idea, either—and she wasn't entirely sure why.

In small part, it was because Elyriel needed her rest and shouldn't move around, regardless of who did the moving. But there was more to it than that.

Kaycia felt a need, deep down, to come to terms with these developments. She couldn't keep avoiding her sister forever. After all, if she asserted control every time she was afraid, she'd never stop.

No matter how she looked at it—controlling Elyriel didn't solve the problem but only put it off until later. And since giving up was out of the question, she'd need to face these fears sooner or later.

"Please," she said. "Dear gods... Stay asleep."

In the end, she didn't have to move Elyriel's body all that much, and the girl didn't wake.

As she peeled aside Elyriel's previously-white slip, Kaycia was surprised to find the skin already knit together. It was red and tender—not fully healed—but enough that a bandage was no longer necessary.

The only thing left was to remove the belt.

With that done, she gave her sister some space—to drift freely among her bizarre, crazed dreams.

Kaycia, herself, was surprised she'd been able to stay awake this long, unable to believe how horribly dragged out this night had been.

Sleep, however, came with its own set of problems.

It wasn't that she had trouble letting her guard down. Kaycia knew she could be safe by closing herself and Chesandril away into the storeroom. Though the door wouldn't stop Elyriel for long—it'd provide enough warning for Kaycia to wake up.

No. What bothered her was the idea of Elyriel wandering off. Just the thought of the girl being ambushed by monsters or—gods forbid—coming into contact with other people...

How could Kaycia possibly sleep and allow that to happen?

Ultimately, she supposed there might not be a solution. Perhaps this was one of those risks she'd have to live with, as she certainly couldn't stay awake for the rest of her life.

She bent over Chesandril's body, and the young girl stirred.

Kaycia might've felt glad—were she not on the brink of exhaustion.

The girl's lips parted. "What's—?"

"Shhh..." said Kaycia. "We're safe for now. Just sleep."

The girl didn't argue, and luckily, she wasn't all that difficult to carry.

Upon reaching the room and finding a second long coil of rope on the floor, Kaycia formed an idea. Laying the girl on the ground, Kaycia snatched up the rope and returned to her sister.

Forming a loop, she fastened one end to her sister's ankle. The purpose wasn't to hold her sister here, as she didn't imagine anything would trap Elyriel for long. For this same reason, she didn't tie the other end to a stone statue or anything that might *seem* sturdy.

Instead, she attached it to her own leg.

"Don't let the light go out," said Chesandril when she reentered the storeroom.

Kaycia groaned, forcing herself to add more firewood to the nearest sconce.

Then, she closed the door, running the rope underneath.

She didn't have the strength even to cry herself to sleep.

The rope lurched, pulling Kaycia from her dreams and sliding across the floor.

In near darkness, she quickly reoriented herself, with less than a few seconds to catch her heels against the door. The rope dug into her foot, twisting her ankle so hard she thought it might break.

Then, just as suddenly, the rope went slack. She heard a faint smack followed by a growl.

Kaycia didn't think the rope snapped so much as it'd fouled her sister's footing. Elyriel might be strong, but she wasn't that heavy.

"Elle!" she shouted, hoping to get her attention before the pulling recommenced.

There was a moment of silence before Elyriel hissed.

"That's right. Over here."

Hearing the sounds of approach, she pulled some slack on the rope, rose to her feet, and backed away. She hadn't fully straightened before Elyriel was at the door, pressing her face against the bars.

Kaycia thought the girl might pound on the wood—throwing herself against the door to break it down. Or that she'd stretch a groping arm through the window mindlessly.

For the moment, however, Elyriel simply regarded her with eyes stretched a bit too wide.

Kaycia decided to try something different.

While Elyriel was possibly incapable of reason and wouldn't respond to social cues—who could say for sure? Kaycia would rather believe there remained a shred of humanity inside the girl. And the last thing she wanted was to drive that away through anger and threats.

"Good morning, Elyriel," she said in as bright a voice as she could muster—which, admittedly, was more tired than anything.

Through the bars, the girl's jaw clenched visibly, working her lips as though preparing a snarl.

"How's your leg?" Kaycia lowered her hands to her own leg, to help her understand. She wasn't worried Elyriel wouldn't see. Though Kaycia's eyes had trouble in this darkness, Elyriel's wouldn't.

The girl's gaze broke away, becoming distracted by the bars in front of her—almost as though trying to understand what they were or what held them together. Perhaps wondering how to remove this obstacle.

"Well, you look much better, so that's a relief... I'm also glad to see you acting... calmer. You haven't broken the door. That's good."

She half-expected the girl to attack the door in earnest—just to prove her wrong. But Elyriel didn't. For the moment, anyway.

"Why don't we start over? It seems you don't remember me, but that's okay. I don't mind introducing myself. My name's Kaycia," she said while motioning to herself with one hand. "Kaycia. Understand? I'm your sister."

When she disappeared from the window, Kaycia groaned in frustration.

"Elle? I wasn't finished."

She considered herself lucky, however, her sister stayed as long as she had.

"Elyriel, what are you—?"

With a hint of suspicion, she walked to the window.

And saw Elyriel facing her from the center of the circle. Reaching down, her sister took hold of the rope—the same rope still attached to Kaycia's leg.

Had the girl noticed this? Had she, perhaps, been looking *past* the bars?

"You wouldn't dare!"

Elyriel's face was expressionless, and for a brief instant, their eyes made contact.

Then, the girl twisted, preparing a ferocious pull.

She didn't finish the motion before Kaycia took control.

From the middle of the room, Kaycia looked up from her hands—now the ones holding the rope—and heard a loud thunk opposite the door.

"Damn it!" she hissed, knowing the sound had come from her own body crumpling against the wood. That thunk had been much louder than she would've liked and would probably leave a bruise.

A few bumps, however, were nothing compared to what'd almost happened to her leg. Considering Elyriel's strength, it wasn't difficult to imagine the door breaking into pieces.

Worst of all was the thought she would've actually done it. Elyriel didn't care what became of Kaycia.

She clenched her teeth, determined not to cry.

Letting the rope drop, she took a look around.

With the fires so close to burning out, the enormous cavern had become indistinct and devoid of color—but she could see, nonetheless. She could make perfect sense of where she was, along with everything around her, largely due to the embers that remained. It must've been similar to the vision of cats prowling the night through darkened alleys.

But without those embers...she wasn't confident Elyriel's senses would be enough. The abyssal current had a mind of its own, as if making a conscious effort to drown the world in darkness.

Kaycia would need time to experiment later and test her limits.

She wanted to explore, knowing how important it was she get used to this place, this realm, and the creatures that lived here. But even that would have to wait while she dealt with matters far more pressing—namely, her sister.

Walking forward, Kaycia took note of how the leg was healing. The knife had gone deep—sliding past bone—but the pain had nearly subsided, burning down to little more than a faint throb.

She reached the door and opened it—having never locked it in the first place. The indistinct shape of her body spilled through and onto the floor.

Leaning down, she lifted her body easily and laid it carefully beside Chesandril.

The girl's eyes were open, staring at the ceiling.

"Chess?" she asked in surprise.

A soft moan escaped the girl's lips, and, with only her head, she turned in the opposite direction.

Kaycia couldn't imagine what Chesandril was going through. It seemed unlikely the girl understood much of what happened. It was impossible to tell if she even remembered her mother's death.

Chesandril didn't respond to Kaycia's questions, displaying a complete lack of emotion. She didn't even seem bothered by the fires going out.

All of this left Kaycia feeling helpless, presenting a problem she could do nothing about. Ultimately, the best thing might be to give the girl some time. After that, if she didn't show improvement, Kaycia could think of something else.

For now, she untied the rope from her own sleeping body before leaving the room. She added more wood to the nearest fire, shut the door, and returned Elyriel to where she'd been standing.

She then released control.

In that same instant, Elyriel screeched.

Ignoring the flash of pain across her forehead, Kaycia scrambled to her feet and returned to the window.

She couldn't tell what Elyriel might be thinking or what her sister might remember from the last few minutes. Had her mind skipped from one moment to the next, wondering how she'd lost hold of the rope? Or, was her rage prompted because she *had* seen it all, and she'd watched her own hands open the door and untie the rope?

Elyriel turned and met her eyes again. Teeth bared, she spat in her direction—so forcefully, at this distance, Kaycia felt the spray.

"Now calm down," she said, swallowing in frustration. "We wouldn't have this problem if you'd just—"

Faster than her eyes could see, the girl reached down and yanked on the rope. The motion was so unlike her first attempt, it was as though she was hoping for the element of surprise. To finish the action before Kaycia could stop her.

The rope, no longer tied to Kaycia's foot, merely snagged beneath the door. It shot into the cavern and landed behind the bewildered girl.

Elyriel turned to the rope's free end, then back to the storeroom, clearly confused.

So she hadn't seen. Good to know.

With renewed determination, she swung its length as though brandishing a whip.

Kaycia jumped back as it smacked the door, faster than Kaycia could cover her ears. The reverberation lifted a layer of dust.

"Stop it, Elle! Do you hear—?"

The rope struck the door a second time. A third. There was a resounding crack as the wood split apart.

Chesandril didn't so much as flinch, oblivious to the ruckus.

Kaycia groaned, realizing she couldn't allow this to go on. She couldn't bear the thought of losing that door.

This time, she lowered herself to the ground before taking control.

Elyriel must've been midswing because, in the next moment, she felt the rope slip from her fingers and go flying across the circle. Her body continued to spin before she caught herself.

Kaycia took a calming breath and followed the rope to where it'd landed. Coiling it together, she hid it behind a statue where Elyriel wouldn't see.

She felt flustered by the need to take such measures, but she hadn't anticipated her sister being so impossible.

Once again, she returned Elyriel to the cavern's center and released control.

The girl cried out in fury.

"Don't like that, do you?" yelled Kaycia, directing her voice through the window.

"Let me tell you something. *I* don't appreciate being attacked. Understand?"

Kaycia didn't expect the girl to comprehend the words. But, perhaps, she'd see the correlation between attacking Kaycia and its consequences. Sooner or later, she'd realize she only had to stop.

There came another crash against the door—likely a rock.

Kaycia grit her teeth.

Retaking control, she found a second rock already clutched in her hand. She tossed it harmlessly to the side. Then proceeded to clear the central floor from anything her sister might have a mind to throw.

When Kaycia rereleased her, it took Elyriel a moment to regain her bearings. She was likely caught off guard by seeing her surroundings stripped clean.

Shouting in rage, Elyriel threw *herself* at the door.

Only for Kaycia to return her to the center of the room.

"Just stop already!" Kaycia groaned, wondering if she might have to do this all day.

Elyriel screamed before jumping again.

This time, Kaycia had to redirect her momentum, targeting the outer frame, to spare the wood further damage.

Elyriel tried this two more times. And was returned twice more to the same spot.

Then, finally, to Kaycia's bitter surprise, she broke into a wail.

"Nggghhh! Weehhh.."

Kaycia paused to listen, wondering if this was just another tactic—an attempt to distract.

For the moment, however, the girl had given up.

Kaycia should've been glad—justified the lesson had finally gotten through. But there was so much confusion in Elyriel's tone—so much anger and despair—it broke her heart.

Bloody heavens, she doesn't understand! Elyriel was *trying*, but this somehow made it worse. Because, in some ways, her sister wasn't entirely broken. Kaycia could see that now—how Elyriel demonstrated intelligence in her use of the rope. It was proof she possessed her own flavor of resourcefulness.

But Elyriel didn't know that. In her mind, she was trying her hardest *not* to feel insane. And despite her greatest efforts, the world refused to make sense.

Rocks disappearing? Her own body changing position without any warning?

Kaycia was no longer sure she'd done the right thing. She needed to prevent the girl from breaking things—but at what cost? She didn't know how long she could see her sister frightened like this, unable to trust even herself.

"Elle... How am I supposed to do this?"

The girl, of course, made no response.

Letting out a sigh, Kaycia got up and approached the window.

Elyriel still stood at the center of the room, but her bloodied face was streaked with tears. With a look of abject bewilderment, she was searching the room for anything she might've missed—something to explain her present difficulties.

Kaycia opened the door.

The sound turned Elyriel toward her, and, for a moment, she paused.

Her face changed from confusion to something like resentment. Her eyes went wide with mania and fear.

Kaycia hadn't wanted it to be this way. Her sister wasn't a wild horse that needed to be broken. No matter how far gone or how lost she'd become—she was, ultimately, still human.

Elyriel shrieked as her eyes, once again, turned cold and hateful.

"We've done enough for now."

Faster than she could blink, the girl attacked one last time.

But Kaycia took control, landed the jump, and simultaneously caught her limp body as it collapsed. Laying it carefully inside, she closed the door.

"I'm going to look around," she said, in case Chesandril was listening. "It's nothing to worry about. I'll be back, and I'll bring food."

Then, as an added precaution, she found an enormous slab of rock—larger than herself—at the base of the plateau. With a little effort, she placed it in front of the door.

Though it was unlikely more creatures were stalking these caverns—it was better to be safe. She couldn't afford for anything to stumble across her body, vulnerable as she was. She'd made that mistake with Veldt already.

Kaycia took a deep breath and prepared for her first excursion outside. Though she planned to be quick, she hadn't forgotten the monsters above. Treading carefully, she hoped to recover the wagon's supplies without provoking a fight.

As an extra benefit, it gave her a break from her sister. It provided time for herself and a chance to think.

She attempted the trip with no light at all—with the reasoning she could always go back for an ember, should the darkness prove impossible to navigate.

In the end, however, her eyes were enough. Her sight range was drastically reduced—to a radius of roughly ten feet—but she *could* make sense of her immediate surroundings. As though a faint light emanated from her own body.

The limitation was worrisome—and she imagined creatures closing around her—but she decided it was for the best. Even a dull ember, after all, would attract attention.

With her speed, it was easy to make her way through the caves. And, in less than a few minutes, she'd ascended the stone steps leading back into the monastery.

She wasn't surprised to find Roke dead—eviscerated by the same beast that'd found them below. In the back of her mind, she'd already accepted it and only regretted not throwing the heinous deed into Veldt's face.

Gods... Veldt must've passed through here—and seen what his treachery had caused—and, yet, he'd had the audacity to call *her* an abomination?!

Kaycia heard a howl far in the distance. It was a harmonious wail of two separate pitches, one high and one low—a sound from no animal she'd ever encountered. The cry trilled for three full seconds before dying off. It was beautiful. Haunting.

And far enough away, she needn't be concerned.

Rather than exiting the way they came, she leaped upward to climb through the hole in the ceiling.

Strangely, there were no visible indications she was headed outside. From above, there came no light at all—as though the sky was as dark as the caverns below.

Near the roof, her handholds became slippery and coated in an increasingly thick layer of—

Not muck, she realized. Blood.

Even so, Kaycia pushed herself forward. There was no point in cleaning it off, so she might as well get used to it.

Pulling herself onto the tiled roof, a faint breeze confirmed she'd made it outside. But, as before, she could only see about ten feet in front—not even to where the tiles ended.

Still, she straightened her back, turned a slow circle, and took in her first real glimpse of the abyssal realm.

She struggled to describe how she felt beneath that oppressive, endless sky. There was nothing above but the immensity of space—of the entire universe. A vastness without stars. Devoid of light. Or heat.

But it was worse than that because it wasn't empty.

Though she couldn't see them, there were dark planets that roamed above. And there were other things besides—unknown things, impossible to observe.

She felt a chill as the wind picked up. The monastery settled in a chorus of wooden groans.

Without seeing the trees, she heard them sway.

Kaycia had spent years preparing for this moment—imagining what it'd be like. But, now that it was here, she only felt sorrow.

It wasn't her, after all, trapped in this world. At any moment, Kaycia had an exit. When she started to feel overwhelmed, as if the darkness would drown her, it was simply a matter of returning to her body.

Not so for her sister.

In addition to Elyriel's broken state—with all its confusion and shapeless fears—this was a prison she'd never escape. As if going insane wasn't bad enough.

Kaycia swallowed hard, realizing that no matter what terrible things Elyriel might do... If it came to broken bones or even Kaycia's death—it'd pale in comparison to what Kaycia had done to her.

For the second time that day, tears clouded her vision.

A vision, not of the reality seen by regular people—the illusory landscape touched by sunlight.

This darkness was the world as it truly was.

Part 2
THE TRANSCENDENT

It often surprises me
That the world is still here,
That, despite the unlikelihood
Of coming into existence...
That, despite mankind's propensity
To be monumental screwups...
Somehow, we persist.
We live on.
And it occurs to me
That deserving
Has nothing to do with it.
                    -Confessions of Irisea
                    (year unknown)

Chapter 8
THE APPRAISAL

After remaining beneath the monastery the next five days, it took another four before they arrived at a small village named Perandolen.

Given the choice, Kaycia might've chosen to stay longer. But their food was limited to what'd survived the carriage. Several packs, including all the dried meats, had broken open and been exposed to the poisonous rain. And while it could be rinsed clean and wouldn't be deadly—it would invariably lead to stomach cramps that weren't worth the trouble.

In the end, they were left with a small box of apples, a few loaves of flat bread, some hardtack, turnips, and a bit of aged cheese. All in all, not the worst fare to keep them going, but spread across three people, it'd quickly run low. And since they couldn't count on finding anything edible in the forest, free from contamination, it was vitally important to save enough for their journey.

At first, Kaycia attempted to share her portions with Elyriel, but the girl refused to cooperate. When Kaycia handed her some bread—eating some herself to show it was food—Elyriel showed no interest. Over time, Kaycia became insistent, but this led to greater resistance. Elyriel reacted with disgust, spitting and hissing any time she was approached.

It wasn't until the girl accepted the bread and ground it into the dirt that Kaycia gave up.

She didn't understand what was wrong. Having been inside her sister's body, she knew Elyriel was hungry—famished, even—but it was a problem that'd have to wait until later. From then on, Kaycia fed her sister while in control.

As the days disappeared, she accepted that Elyriel wouldn't be ready. If Kaycia was being honest, her sister was unlikely to reach the point of being safe around people. Not in five days and maybe not in five years. Her moods were too unpredictable, and she tended to lash out at the slightest provocation. Even with Kaycia at her side and watching her every move—which certainly would be impossible—Elyriel was too fast. One mistake and a bloodbath would follow.

Kaycia's solution, then, wasn't to return to civilization but to come just close enough to meet their survival needs.

Initially, she'd wanted to travel by night, as it'd make no difference for her ascended vision. She'd strap her body onto Elyriel's back and then stand watch, with the aid of sunlight, while her sister slept.

It would've been a good idea, were it not for Chesandril. The girl was too afraid to be led through the dark. And even if she managed not to twist an ankle, they couldn't risk sudden noises.

So, instead, each evening, they looked for a cave. They covered the opening with branches and brush, and nothing disturbed them for the first two nights.

On the third, they were lucky to be aided by moonlight, or Kaycia might not have seen when the branches moved. She didn't hear them break under the abyssal silence, but it was just enough warning for Elyriel to intervene.

By the end of their journey, they encountered and killed a total of two. They were grotesque mutations—both of them different and both of them alone. None were as challenging as the nightmaiden, but the stress stacked up. The endless walking—waiting to be ambushed by an enormous pack or some other surprise they couldn't handle.

They were stiff and sore—both physically and mentally—that just being near Perandolen felt like a godsend. And the village was just small enough it was unlikely a passerby would stumble across their hiding spot.

"I'm going into town," she told Chesandril after they'd settled in. "Wait for me here."

The young girl said nothing. Resting an elbow on her knee, she laid back against the side of the earthen grotto with eyes unfocused.

She'd hardly said anything these past nine days—not even during the memorial service they'd held for the dead—but she *was* improving. Kaycia saw it in her eyes. Enough to suggest she was healing gradually.

"I need an answer. Did you hear what I said?"

The girl exhaled in weak frustration.

"Not good enough."

With a groan, Chesandril met her gaze. "Go ahead... I won't go anywhere."

After dealing with this indifference for so many miles, Kaycia, perhaps, should've gotten used to it. But she hadn't.

Kaycia hated guessing what the girl was thinking—wondering if she might be hungry. Wondering if Chesandril might *want* to see the town, or if she actually preferred having time to herself.

The girl made no demands and left Kaycia feeling helpless, with no clue how to set things right. Chesandril was obviously in pain—as she should be after losing her mother—but she seemed to lack, even, the desire to grieve.

Several seconds passed before the girl looked up and realized Kaycia was still there.

"I said I was fine! Just go already!"

Kaycia ignored the outburst, unwilling to be provoked by a twelve-year-old girl.

"I'll go. But I want to say some things first. It's important you understand what I'm doing and why I'm not taking you with me."

Chesandril looked away, disinterested.

"I know you hate it out here, and it'd be good for you to be around other people. I promise I *will* make that happen—just not today...

"The main problem is that I'm going as Elyriel. No one will trade with me if they think I'm a kid. If *you* come along, it'll only be worse."

"I get it," said Chesandril. "It's fine."

"What I'm saying is I don't want you feeling like a slave. I'm not just using you to watch my body."

The girl was silent.

Kaycia's sleeping form was propped against the opposite wall. There was no need to explain why she was leaving it here. It wasn't as though she could leave Elyriel with only Chesandril to supervise.

"If something *does* happen," continued Kaycia. "If you hear strangers, or you think you're in trouble... I want you to send me a signal. Look at me! You need to hear this."

As Chesandril looked up, Kaycia approached her own body.

It was still strapped into its makeshift harness—the one she'd stitched from leather belts to carry her body. The loops had, unfortunately, restricted blood flow to her unconscious legs, but they'd made the journey significantly easier.

"Take one of these knives," she continued. "It'll only take a small cut, right here on my shoulder. Not deep, mind you. They're very sharp. I'll feel it and come back as soon as possible. Can you handle that?"

Chesandril nodded.

"Okay, then... Anything else? Besides food, is there something you need? Some clothes, perhaps?"

No response.

"Come on, Chess! Please work with me here. How am I supposed to know if—?"

"JUST STOP ALREADY!" shouted the girl. "I don't need you taking care of me!"

The outburst was surprising but better than nothing. It was a momentary glimpse beneath her stone-cold exterior.

"I know that. I never said you couldn't take care of yourself. But while you might not need it, I *want* to help."

Once again, Chesandril closed up. She turned away with her face still red and her jaw tightly clenched.

"What is this, Chess?" she asked, nearing exasperation.

A moment later, Kaycia decided to calm down. The girl was sending clear signals she didn't want to be bothered—so maybe it was best to respect that decision.

Kaycia rose to her feet, stooping forward to avoid the dirt ceiling. She raised her leather hood, hoping it would hide Elyriel's age. Then, she slung Marien's bag over her shoulder.

"Like it or not, we're in this together. I know I'm not your mother—and I have no right to ask anything of you—but please, try to understand what *I* have to deal with."

Chesandril didn't bother to look up.

"We'll talk later," concluded Kaycia before walking out into the cool afternoon air.

In the pitch blackness outside, she identified the faint, smudged pillars as trees. And though she was near enough Perandolen to be safe from the current, it was all too easy to envision shapes that weren't there. To see leathery fingers wrap a nearby branch. Or something long and slender uncurl from the canopy above.

There was nothing, however, wrong with her hearing, allowing her to feel reasonably certain no one was around. Even so, she proceeded quietly, unwilling to risk anything noticing their hiding place.

Kaycia's concerns, however, never strayed far from Chesandril.

Ducking a low branch, she realized the biggest problem was that the girl denied all memory of the ritual and, worse, emphatically refused to talk about it.

There was nothing Kaycia could do—no words that would be adequate. She couldn't even confront her about it, as Chesandril would never admit to the lie. How could the girl say she remembered anything without simultaneously admitting to something far worse? Without facing the fact she'd caused her own mother's death?

Perhaps there was no solution.

Leaving the tall grass, she followed the main road. Out here, there were only a few rundown farms, and it wouldn't be long before she reached the town's center. When it came to pockets of civilization like these, it wasn't possible to maintain large stretches of farmland. And though it meant less food, people had no choice but to wisen up and avoid spreading themselves too thin.

The road was quiet and free from travelers. There were no sounds of birds or insects. Her ears perked at the slightest rustle in the branches. Or the sound of a distant brook burbling with blood.

She found this soothing in a way, and she was free to continue sorting her thoughts.

There was one final issue she didn't know how to bring up. More pressing, after all, than Chesandril's condition, was her future.

It wasn't that Kaycia wanted to be rid of the girl. A few insults weren't enough to turn her away or make her forget Chesandril's redeeming qualities. Kaycia could forgive insubordination and could even appreciate the girl's rough, preadolescent exterior.

But, after mulling it over the past several days, Kaycia realized she wasn't at a point in her life where she could take responsibility of a child. There was nothing shameful in admitting this truth. It was difficult enough to care for her broken sister—and learn the ropes of ascendancy—all while avoiding the eyes of the church.

With how dangerous her life had become, she saw no other choice but to contact the girl's relatives and delicately tell them what happened to Marien. In the long run, this wouldn't only be better for Kaycia, it'd undoubtedly be better for Chesandril.

It seemed perfectly logical, and she felt sure the girl would understand. And yet, she hesitated at every opportunity to bring it up. She'd open her mouth to speak, only to be overcome with guilt, as if the words represented some betrayal.

This inevitably led to confusion, as Chesandril was practically *begging* to be let go. It was clear the girl felt no love for Kaycia—she didn't want anything to *do* with Kaycia— and yet... Kaycia couldn't bring herself to abandon her. To put into words, after the girl had lost everything, she'd also be losing Kaycia.

By the time she reached Perandolen's center, her feelings were no less muddied than before.

At first, she seemed to be entering a ghost town, without a single light from any window. This was misleading, of course, as there was no need for lanterns in the middle of the afternoon. It was bright and clear for everyone else, giving them a view of Elyriel—while she, in turn, could not see them.

Kaycia did her best to ignore this feeling, knowing no one had reason to pay her mind. There was nothing odd to her appearance—marking her as nothing more than a common traveler. And, in the end, if anyone *did* mean harm, she'd have no trouble seeing once they drew close.

She heard the sounds of a nearby smithy and a grocer from around the corner. She heard the rhythmic sloshing coming from inside—which must've been their vats for filtering water, purging the blood from their drinking supply. Other than that, Perandolen was quiet, as if everyone was holed up, lacking reason to go outdoors.

There were fewer, perhaps, than ten buildings in all—dark, foreboding, and covered in blood—and it wasn't long before Kaycia found what she was looking for.

Near the central office was a trading post reserved for local hunters. It was easy to recognize due to the large board out in front, plastered with information on the most notorious local threats. For most people, these papers were a warning, informing of which areas they ought to avoid. For a select few, however, the board represented a source for bounties.

On any other occasion, Kaycia might've looked it over, as any of these creatures would offer practice and the chance to hone her skills. She didn't plan, however, to stay in the area long.

Stepping through the door, she entered a wooden vestibule—unlit by pitch-black windows. The air was musty and heavy with the scent of oil and leather.

Several large hides stretched across the walls as though intended for display—but, to her surprise, none were the hides of abyssal creatures. Most had the lightly tanned look of deer or large mountain cats. One was the shaggy fur of a regular black bear.

To Kaycia, this seemed strange, as most trading houses took pride in showcasing the materials they brought in. They'd use extravagant displays to attract new patrons and communicate that business was good.

She suspected, however, in a small place like this, it was more expedient to keep the real valuables under lock and key. Perandolen didn't have much in the way of security, and they'd be more worried about strangers nicking a piece of bone while the owners weren't looking.

It was a sentiment Kaycia could respect—but also one that worried her. It suggested they might not want to deal with her at all. They might not even have the funds to accept trades outside their usual clientèle.

"Excuse me?" she called out.

By then, she'd had the chance to get used to Elyriel's voice, but she wasn't quite prepared to confront another living person. It felt strange to be reminded there were regular people—living regular lives—who hadn't had to struggle the past week to survive.

"Oh!" said a woman, emerging through a side door. Her face was wrinkled and ghastly—though that was to be expected from within the current. "I thought you were someone else. Hold on. I'll get... Is Dezek expecting you?"

"Dezek?" asked Kaycia, hoping there was nothing unusual in her tone. "Is he the manager?"

"Oh, heaven's no!" said the woman with a smirk. "Dezek's my son. Don't tell me he's spreading stories of—"

"No," said Kaycia, not wanting to drag this out any longer. "I don't know your son.

And no one's expecting me. Are you the one in charge, then?"

The woman was taken aback. She hesitated and asked, "What can I help you with, dear?"

"I'm here to trade," she said as though it were obvious.

"Then I'm afraid you're in the wrong place. You'll find the market just across the square. Didn't you read the sign? Here, we only deal in—"

"Bones and hides, I know. It's not my first time."

The woman regarded Kaycia with a healthy dose of suspicion. "Is *that* the way of it?"

"Here," said Kaycia, lifting her bag. "Have a look."

She tried to exude an air of confidence, as if to make up for her poor first impression. Even in these shadows, however, with Kaycia's hood raised, the woman had seen right through her.

"Is this some joke? Did Dezek put you up to—?"

"Honestly," said Kaycia. "I know what you're thinking. And I get that all the time— how young I look."

The woman grew angry. "What do you take me for? You're nothing but a child!"

Kaycia bristled with the sudden urge to yell back—but that would get her nowhere. It was the sort of response to expect from a child, and Elyriel's youthful features were doing her no favors. Even at fifteen, Elyriel looked young for her age.

So, instead, Kaycia tried a different tact. "I apologize, ma'am."

She altered her lie into something easier to swallow. With an innocent smile, she said, "I should've explained myself better. I'm here on behalf of my sister. My *older* sister. She's the ascendant in our family."

The woman worked her jaw as she considered this carefully. She didn't seem the type of woman who enjoyed deception, and it'd turned her mood irreparably sour.

"Does your sister know you're here?" she asked, in a tone that brooked no nonsense.

"She does! She's the one who sent me. But she's busy—hot on the trail of the pack of this one here." Once more, Kaycia held up her bag. "That's why she couldn't come. She gets like that sometimes. So she suggested—well, more like demanded—I 'make myself useful.' Her words, not mine."

Kaycia tried to remember what it was like to be a teenager and do her best to act the part.

The woman sighed as though unsurprised by this behavior—the way ascendants thought they could get away with anything. But still, the woman shook her head. "I'm afraid you'll have to give her the bad news. It's not just us—there are *rules*. All dealings in abyssal commodities are under the government's jurisdiction—making it quite improper for us to deal with children."

Kaycia swallowed, feeling it was an exaggeration to call her sister a child.

"But she'll kill me if I come back empty-handed! Please? It'll only take a moment. Have a look at this nightmaiden, and I'll be out of your hair. I promise!"

The woman shook her head. "I'm afraid your sister will—" She gave a momentary pause. "A nightmaiden, you say?"

"That's right, ma'am. I only brought the head—us being in a hurry and all. It's right here, in my bag."

She'd thought this might work. Though Kaycia was unfamiliar with the going rate of resources, she felt reasonably sure something as rare as a nightmaiden would catch the woman's interest. It was the sort of trade typically aimed for larger cities, with most hunters skipping over small towns entirely.

The woman made a face, torn by indecision.

"The kill was recent," added Kaycia, for further appeal. "It's been...nine? Yes, nine days."

"Does anyone else know you're here? Did anyone see you on your way in?"

It was the sort of question Kaycia might've found concerning—as though the woman aimed to rob her. The lady, however, seemed harmless enough. And though it occurred to Kaycia she might get swindled, there was no chance of her being overpowered.

"The streets were empty, ma'am. And I promise not to tell."

After working her mouth another moment, the woman said, "All right, then. Come along."

"Thank you, ma'am! Oh! And by the way, I'm...Elyriel."

Kaycia decided this name would be best. It made more sense if the older sister in her story went by Kaycia—to match the records of her enlistment at the garrison. Besides, it added more weight to her lie if she stayed near the truth whenever possible.

"I'm Veralyn," said the woman, in a voice slightly more amiable than before.

Passing through a narrow, musty corridor, they made their way toward the back. After passing a few rooms, Kaycia was given the impression the place was not only a trading post but Veralyn's home.

Their destination was a room slightly larger than the lobby. The walls were lined with thick cabinets and storage containers, all sealed up. There weren't any windows to allow others a view inside.

Instead, there was a large hole in the ceiling, no doubt to ventilate the overpowering stench that permeated every surface.

Kaycia tried not to gag as she watched the woman—who appeared completely unaffected—light a lantern above a large operating table.

"Let's see it then," said Veralyn, waving the bag forward.

The woman pulled on a pair of thin leather gloves—marked by the stains of countless years.

Gingerly, she reached inside and placed it on the table.

The woman grimaced as she tried untangling the matted hair and set it to one side.

Through Elyriel's eyes, Kaycia saw the head in perfect detail.

Such was not the case for Veralyn.

At the moment of death, the nightmaiden didn't become visible immediately. Rather, it was a gradual process that took several months to complete. And, since this head was barely over a week old, it meant the woman was looking at an indeterminate, translucent blob.

This was to be expected, as specific qualities could only be extracted while the material was fresh. Veralyn, no doubt, had been specially trained to ascertain such virtues despite her limitations.

The woman turned a knob on the lantern, making it brighter.

Then, leaning forward, Veralyn began muttering as though to herself. "Severe damage to the right, ocular cavity, and frontal cortex. Abrasions to the scalp, right temple, and lower jaw. Several missing teeth..." At this, she paused a moment and took a specific count.

Without removing her gloves, she opened a ledger and began to write.

"Eight missing... Seventeen partials and... Thirty-three still intact."

With one hand on the page, Veralyn continued to regard the severed head. "Minimal damage to the upper skull. Small fracture to the glabella and nasal bone. Right, lower mandible...cracked."

At this, Kaycia felt compelled to interrupt. From her vantage, she had a clear view of the jaw and could see it was intact.

While Veralyn was possibly lying to reduce the appraised value, it could've easily been an innocent mistake. With the nightmaiden still partially invisible, it was inherently difficult to make an accurate assessment—even for younger traders, whose eyesight was yet to dim.

Herein, however, lie the problem.

Kaycia *couldn't* correct the woman. As far as Veralyn was concerned, Kaycia had no reason to know anything of the kill. Playing the part of a younger sister, she couldn't well suggest she saw more than a professional.

She swallowed and let the matter slide. She became determined, however, to observe Veralyn more closely for additional signs of deceit.

"Which company is she with?"

Startled from her thoughts, Kaycia said, "My sister works alone."

Considering this further, she might've spoken too soon. The more believable story had the nightmaiden taken down by a group of hunters rather than an individual.

At the same time, pretending to be part of a group might reveal her fraud. Kaycia, after all, knew next to nothing of local companies, while Veralyn, quite possibly, knew them all.

"You're telling me a lone woman killed a fully matured nightmaiden...all by herself?"

"I swear! I saw it with my own eyes!"

Veralyn was unconvinced, looking up from the severed head. "You were there, on the hunt?"

"Well...not *right* there. There was a hill, and I thought... I wasn't in the way! I just wanted to watch—you know—from a distance."

The woman frowned but had no reason to doubt her. "I should like to meet this sister of yours."

"I'll let her know the next time we're in the area."

"You'd better! As I said, this is a one-time deal. You can pass on the message—I don't broker with children."

The woman turned away, but Kaycia thought she glimpsed the corner of a smile.

Something about this pleased Kaycia immensely—not because she doubted Veralyn's warning, but because she'd begun to grow on the woman.

For several minutes, she continued taking measurements and jotting them quietly into her book.

When Veralyn finally finished, she said, "I'm prepared to offer...six hundred shales."

Kaycia blinked, trying to hide her surprise. Six hundred shales was a lot of money—far more than she'd hoped to receive. Rather than provide for a few short days, it'd be enough to last them several weeks. It was a reminder she was still new to the business side of hunting and knew very little of prices and rarities.

If she'd known, after all, the remains were so valuable, she might've made the effort to carry more back—regardless of how much it would've slowed them down. In the back of her mind, she even entertained the idea of *returning* to the cavern before the rest could spoil.

But, of course, she wouldn't. It'd take more than the promise of wealth to inspire her back to that horrid place.

She kept all these thoughts from appearing on her face—not wanting Veralyn to realize she'd been prepared to accept less.

The woman, however, misunderstood her hesitation.

"Six fifty," said Veralyn.

Kaycia realized she needed to say something—to start pretending she was in control of herself and the situation.

"Could you be honest with me?" asked Kaycia. "Would the value be different if I took this to Carheim? I don't want to meet up with my sister only to learn we could've gotten more. And...well, if you really want to meet her, I suppose that's one way to go about it—but you won't like her when she's upset."

"Is that a threat?" asked Veralyn—not angry but in a tone that suggested amusement.

Kaycia found this surprising, as if the woman were an entirely different person from the one in the lobby.

Veralyn went on. "Well... if you want my advice, let me first tell you how improper it is to ask such questions. You wouldn't want to insult my business practice—"

"Oh no!" she said in alarm. "I didn't mean—"

"Peace, girl. Just keep in mind, if you intend to continue in this line of business—*as an adult*—you might consider accompanying your sister and watching how *she* chooses her words."

"That's good advice."

"As to your question... It's a bit more complicated. You must consider the freshness of your goods, as even traveling a few more days will impact value. However, if you knew, beforehand, of a specific trader in Carheim in particular need of nightmaidens... Well, those extra days might be worth your trouble."

"I see what you mean."

"I'll offer you seven hundred shales," said Veralyn, "on the condition you heed my words. You're a sweet girl but still too young to involve yourself in these affairs. Give it another five years before attempting this again."

"Oh, I will. I promise!"

Kaycia couldn't believe her luck. This wasn't the first time she'd noticed how people treated Elyriel differently. People never commented that Kaycia was sweet—but she suspected this wasn't entirely due to her age but to how she acted. Ascendants were expected to be commanding, while Elyriel was free to be herself.

"It's a deal," she added.

"Just wait one moment," said Veralyn, smiling, "and I'll write up a note."

In an instant, Kaycia's delight evaporated.

A promissory note? From what she understood, these documents were a reimbursement from the government and needed to be cashed at an official treasury. And while they were worth every shale, it was not the sort of tender she could spend today.

She found herself torn, wondering if she should try something else. But could she really ask Veralyn to return the head, after all the exceptions already made?

"Is the note...because of my sister? To ensure I don't spend it before the money reaches her?"

"I hadn't considered that," said Veralyn with a frown. "But no. All our recent dealings have been this way, and I'd expect you'd find the same in all the smaller towns. I apologize... We could've paid you in full a year ago—but the economy's been in shambles since the trading routes closed down."

Kaycia opened her mouth, about to ask what she meant—only to realize Veralyn wasn't referring to local trade.

It'd been over six months since Kaycia had heard the news—of the moment when the Navaran Empire, to the northwest, had severed all ties with its neighboring nations. With the countryside growing ever more dangerous, the emperor had reached the decision his dwindling resources would be best spent on the care of his people—and the rest of the world be damned.

To Kaycia—who, at the time, had been engrossed with her studies—the full effects of the proclamation hadn't time to sink in. She'd felt so confident the city-state of Carheim would pull through, it hadn't occurred to her who else might be affected. She hadn't realized these shifts would be most deeply felt among these smaller, less stable villages.

Within moments, Veralyn had the paper written up and stamped with an official seal.

"What else has been going on?" asked Kaycia after checking the document. "Navara has us completely cut off, but what of Seldor? Is there still no word after the past few years?"

"You're asking me? If your sister's been by the garrison, she surely knows more than I."

The woman was right, of course. Kaycia *should* be more up-to-date on these affairs—but she'd been distracted by her ceremony. After her failure, she'd become disconnected from everything.

"I know. I guess we don't talk much of these things."

Veralyn frowned in suspicion but didn't press the matter. "There've been emissaries sent into Seldor's borders—but when they return, they say the kingdom proper is completely inaccessible."

"What does that mean?"

With a grimace, Veralyn said, "To hear men speak of it, it's as though Seldor were under siege. But not like any I've heard of."

"How so?"

"Well, there aren't signs of enemy approach... To be honest, I'm hazy on the details. I only know what my son tells me. I could get him if you'd like."

Kaycia shook her head. "Never mind that. Just tell me—what is my sister supposed to do with this?" she asked, holding up the sheet of paper.

"I give you my word—the seal is official. Just take it up to Carheim, and they'll take care of you."

Kaycia tried to hide her disappointment. There were several reasons she wanted to avoid Carheim. It wasn't only the risk of being identified by people who knew her or her sister. More than anything, she couldn't bear the thought of confronting their mother. Not yet, anyway. What would she even say?

"How about New Ahman?" she asked. "They've got a sizable treasury. Would they honor a script such as this?"

"Oh..." stammered Veralyn in genuine surprise. "I mean, yes. They'll pay you. New Ahman falls under the jurisdiction of Carheim—same as us—so they'd be obliged to accept all legal tender."

There was something about the woman's hesitation, however, that suggested Kaycia should be worried. "But...?" she encouraged.

Veralyn's cheeks went red. "It's not my place to give advice."

"I'm sure my sister would want to know. Just speak your mind."

With a sheepish nod, the woman said, "I wouldn't go to New Ahman if I were you. Word is, they've had to deal with more attacks of late... But what am I saying?" asked the woman, shaking her head. "A proven hunter, like your sister? It wouldn't surprise me if she wanted part of the action."

Kaycia bit her lip. "I'd have to ask. Maybe."

She hadn't taken the time to think it through. While avoiding Carheim was one thing, it was quite another to begin looking for work. Was that what she wanted? If she started going on hunts, after all, it'd increase the chances of Elyriel drawing notice, which was precisely what they needed to avoid.

On the other hand, what was the point of ascendancy if she went into hiding the rest of her life? How would she master her skills without situations that demanded her best?

"Is there anything else?" asked the woman.

Kaycia nearly laughed as she considered the several things she still needed. But it wasn't as though she could ask for food. Nor could she return the note in exchange for less money.

"You've been very kind," she said. "Is there another way out so no one sees me?"

Moments later, Kaycia was back on the road, making her way to the grotto.

It was earlier than expected, having skipped her shopping, but this was also a good thing. To her best estimation, a few hours of daylight remained, and her departure would be viewed with less suspicion.

She hoped Chesandril would understand. It wasn't like another day of hardtack would kill them. They were down to their last skin of clean cave water, but if they headed out at first light, they could reach New Ahman in a single day. And, once they had their money, it'd be easier to forget this momentary hardship.

With the right attitude, there was always a bright side. Perhaps, in New Ahman, they could find a physician or someone to make sense of Elyriel's state.

They could buy new weapons. Possibly, a new life.

More than ever, Kaycia was determined to stay positive.

Lest she run out of reasons to survive.

Chapter 9
CITY OF HUNTERS

Civilized areas were usually safe from the abyss. But as to every rule, there were always exceptions.

There were tales of a kingdom known as Lithia, whose protection seemingly vanished overnight. Its people fell to the abyss over thirty years back, with few survivors and no explanation. Kaycia feared something similar might be happening in Seldor—subjected to the siege Veralyn mentioned. The story might be different, but the moral was the same. No one truly understood how the mystical safety worked.

This didn't, of course, stop people from trying—from testing their limits and expanding their knowledge. New Ahman was ultimately built as an experiment—not to keep old territories safe but to see if new lands might be reclaimed. To see if the monsters might be made to disappear, recreating the effect of previously established, civilized areas.

For decades, they fought the creatures off, but the operation never worked as intended. The abyss always returned, with even greater numbers, and threatened to raze New Ahman to the ground. The city almost fell on several occasions, but the surviving hunters redoubled their efforts—relying solely on conventional means. And thus, they found success of a different sort, inspiring others to join their cause.

New Ahman became a symbol—the place for anyone with the burning desire to fight back.

For Kaycia, it seemed perfect, except for one problem.

Near Perandolen, it'd been easy to find a safe place outside the city. Here, that wasn't possible. She couldn't leave her sister or her own unconscious body in some random cave, where they'd still be vulnerable to the smallest abyssal insects. People who took such risks would wake up one morning missing a few toes.

They'd need to secure shelter within the walls—preferably in the form of a private inn room—which presented complications. First, the innkeeper would have to let them in on the promise of getting paid. And second, since Kaycia would have to get the money herself, it'd mean leaving her sister in that room with Chesandril.

Tying her up was out of the question, as there was no quicker way of provoking Elyriel to anger. She'd scream—attracting the attention of everyone within a square mile—and, moreover, she was strong enough to break out of anything.

Kaycia had briefly considered bringing the girl with her—so she'd, at least, be nearby if anything went wrong. But that approach also begged disaster. Not only was Elyriel unprepared for large crowds, it'd be impossible for Kaycia to switch bodies unnoticed.

Their best chance of keeping Elyriel calm was to keep her secluded from everyone else. And though this meant risking Chesandril's life—being the only person who could be trusted to watch over her—it seemed like their only option.

In truth, it was unlikely her sister would harm Chesandril. Elyriel had yet to lash out at the girl, even once, and the two friends seemed to get along just fine. The greatest cause for concern, then, was the possibility Elyriel might not *want* to stay put. She could easily wander off, and Chesandril would be powerless to stop her.

With so much that could go wrong, Kaycia had nearly given up. After examining the problem from every angle, it almost seemed better to avoid New Ahman. They didn't really need the money. Without it, food would be a problem, but what was that in comparison to their secrets coming out? One false move, and they'd face imprisonment. Worse, Elyriel—the abomination she was—would likely be executed. When compared to all that, starvation seemed easy.

But Kaycia wasn't the sort to be controlled by fear. No matter where they went, there'd always be risks, and she didn't feel like running the rest of her life.

So, instead, she came up with a new idea. While not guaranteed to forestall every problem, it would effectively reduce their probability. Her solution was to bring Elyriel so near exhaustion, she'd lack both the energy and desire for trouble.

As they made their final approach to New Ahman, Kaycia began to hunt.

The grimwolves snarled, without skin or lips to cover their blackened teeth. They also lacked eyelids, but this had more to do with their lack of eyes. Instead, they came at her with hollowed sockets, dark and emotionless.

She relished the feel of the rope's fibers against her palms as her blade spun in a whirlwind. The darkness chilled her sweating skin.

Not only did this relieve some stress, it also provided the opportunity to train.

These creatures were a more common variety and nowhere near as dangerous as the nightmaiden had been. Even so, she couldn't afford to be careless. There was no shortage of ascendants who'd been killed by grimwolves—even when facing one or two.

Kaycia faced three but had dispatched the first in their opening encounter. It'd committed the grievous error of stretching wide its jaws, thus earning itself a roped dagger down its throat.

That left only two—a more reasonable number—but both were quick not to repeat the mistake. The fight dragged on for several minutes as she weaved and twisted between slashing claws.

Each was armored with a blood-red carapace, a chitinous material more durable than metal. It was enough to withstand her weapons and forced her to play a waiting game.

The wolves were incapable, of course, of keeping their mouths shut forever.

Throughout the exercise, she never lost sight of Chesandril or her sleeping body. Though her intent was to push herself and experiment with new attacks, she never allowed herself to take unnecessary risks.

After finishing off the third and final creature, she was surprised to hear Chesandril shout, "Someone's coming!"

Kaycia quickly glanced around—confirming that none of the grimwolves were rising—before she slipped out from her sister.

She'd barely the chance to recover her senses and take the roped blade from Elyriel's hands, before a dozen men came over the ridge, each riding an armored horse.

The man in front made a signal for his comrades to spread out.

"You there!" he said as he singled out Kaycia. "Drop your weapon!"

She tensed and adjusted her grip on the hilt. "What are you? Thieves?"

As they formed a half-circle, blocking her path, he responded, "You misunderstand. We hunt monsters, not maidens. Now put your knife down before you hurt yourself."

"Hunters?" she asked, without backing down.

The group of men smiled, unimpressed by her belligerence.

Only one of their number didn't share their amusement.

Riding in the back, he was the last to appear. From the way he regarded the grassy field, he was different. He didn't see only the signs of battle, his eyes went directly to each abyssal corpse—exactly where Kaycia remembered each kill, though she could no longer see them herself.

"You...killed these wolves?" he asked.

"I did," she responded without hesitation.

The first man, with a sneer, looked her up and down. He seemed to think she couldn't possibly be an ascendant wearing such cheap, undecorated armor.

Kaycia didn't let this bother her, knowing how she acted was far more important. She looked past the man as though he wasn't there.

"What brings you to New Ahman?" asked the ascendant.

"Personal business," she said, hoping to avoid further questions. "We're close, then? I'd just as soon be on our way."

He was just about to answer before his gaze landed on Elyriel. The girl was just standing there, with eyes unfocused.

Chesandril rushed to her side and took the girl's hand in a protective gesture.

Kaycia wondered what the ascendant was seeing—or, worse, what he might be thinking. It seemed doubtful, though, he'd reach any conclusions, even with the invisible blood spattering the girl's dress.

"What's wrong with her?" asked the first man. "She looks about to piss herself!"

With a glare, Kaycia rounded on him. But, before she could say anything, the ascendant intervened.

"You must forgive my lieutenant, milady. I assure you, from now on—" His voice became harsh. "He will address you and your sister with the utmost respect."

He'd inferred they were family by appearance alone.

The first man bristled—more angry than penitent—but he held his tongue.

"Allow me to introduce myself. My name is Soril."

Streaks of silver ran through his hair, though he couldn't have been more than a dozen years her senior. He had a handsome face, a strong jawline, and a short, trimmed beard. His metal armor was smooth with black lacquer—designed to repel blood and make cleaning easier.

Most notable was the greatsword he carried on his back. It was nearly as long as Kaycia was tall. Running down the center of the glistening blade, was a core forged of a specialized, highly-conductive metal.

There could be no clearer indication of the ascendant's order. Within seconds, a transfigurer could heat such a weapon to extreme temperatures—enough that it would begin to glow. Or, if desired, they could do the opposite and drop the metal below freezing.

Unlike Tenlen, the transfigurer didn't need to hide a twisted, deformed body. Instead, Soril had gloves that reached his elbows—to conceal the scarred flesh from frequent burns.

Kaycia noticed all this but kept her awe in check—reminding herself she was also supposed to be an ascendant. Rather than gawking, it'd be in her best interest to start making friends.

Except...Elyriel was no longer calm. Her mind had caught up, and she was staring daggers at the rude lieutenant.

Kaycia raised her voice. "I apologize. But as I said, we're in a hurry."

Soril was puzzled but didn't lose a beat. "Of course. Shall we escort you, then? Our horses will—"

"My sister isn't fond of horses," she lied.

Before Elyriel could start anything, Kaycia took her hand and dragged her down the road.

Heat flashed through Kaycia's face as she felt the eyes of the men watching. She was leaving an impression, and not the sort that would earn her any favors.

The only good to all this was the fact Elyriel lacked the initiative to resist. She allowed herself to be pulled, more accustomed now to Kaycia's lead.

Chesandril had the sense to grab their packs and the leather harness.

None of the men seemed to know what to say.

"I don't mean to be rude," she said over her shoulder. "You can keep the carcasses. Sell them. It's all the same to me."

It irked her to leave the grimwolves behind. They weren't worth much, but, under different circumstances, she might've asked the men for some small remuneration—enough to pay for their inn room.

When Elyriel began to growl, she knew she'd made the right choice.

They crested the ridge and dropped below line of sight.

Only then did Kaycia allow herself to breathe.

She wondered if her life would always be like this—to never again interact with other people. It'd be similar to her friends who'd gotten pregnant too young, with a baby in the way of their social life.

Except, in Kaycia's case, the person in her care was far from harmless.

"It's all right, Elle. It's just us now. You can calm down."

Her sister didn't respond but gripped Kaycia's hand with tight ferocity.

Kaycia squeezed back as though returning affection.

"See what you're doing?" she asked. "Following along and not acting out? It's hard, I know, but I'll need you to stay like this for a while longer. You can manage that, can't you?"

"She doesn't understand," said Chesandril in irritation.

"I think she does. Maybe not my words but the tone of my voice. See? She's relaxing already."

Chesandril rolled her eyes.

"You should try it," suggested Kaycia. "Say something to her."

The girl blushed in embarrassment.

"Come on. See how she trusts you? You used to be an important part of her life, and deep down, I think she still remembers."

Chesandril was unconvinced, but her face became thoughtful. Over the past week, her dealings with Elyriel had been awkward—clumsy—but it was clear she still had feelings for her. She missed the friend Elyriel had been, and, like Kaycia, she had difficulty reconciling that version with this broken one.

"I've got nothing to say."

"Well... What did you talk about before? Try to remember how you used to feel. How *she* used to feel. It'd be good for her."

The girl hesitated. "I...can't."

It wasn't difficult to understand Chesandril's reasons. Even Kaycia sometimes felt uncomfortable talking to her sister—feeling it was a sham and she was talking to herself. But sometimes... She found she felt better afterward. And, maybe, it'd help Chesandril, as well.

"You don't have to do it now. But think about it. It'll be just the two of you at the inn for a while. I don't know... Maybe you can say a few things?"

The girl didn't agree to anything. But she'd stopped protesting.

"And you," she said, turning to Elyriel. "You be nice, you hear? No running off. And, whatever you do, don't mess with the furniture."

"You sound like an idiot," said Chesandril, though not in a rude tone. If anything, she seemed to be hiding a smile.

Acquiring an inn room proved easier than expected. She only needed to produce her promissory note long enough for the man to see it was official, and he readily agreed.

Unfortunately, having also read the sum of that note, he'd insisted she pay interest. The rate wasn't small, either. By then, however, Elyriel had begun to hiss at the other guests, and Kaycia accepted his terms without argument.

Their room—down in the basement—was a huge disappointment. It was about three times the space of a carriage interior, with two straw mattresses that reeked of old dust. There was a shabby wardrobe where they could stash their belongings and a half-door leading to a mildewed privy.

In his last words, the innkeeper had mentioned a bath was available for an additional fee, just down the hall. Kaycia had allowed herself to get excited for a moment—but that was before she'd seen their room. By the smell alone, she couldn't imagine a communal bath would receive greater care.

In the end, however, when compared to the nights they'd spent in the woods, she couldn't complain.

The room was theirs, and the thick walls meant Elyriel wouldn't be easily distracted. If anything could be said of New Ahman's design, the thickness of its walls offered great peace of mind. Even the small window, high near the ceiling, helped serve that purpose—being so narrow, it'd be impossible for anything to crawl inside unnoticed.

Before she left, she had Elyriel perform a few more exercises. Taking a cue from her fight with the nightmaiden, she used Elyriel's ascendancy to hold the rope together, while Chesandril attacked it with a knife. Not only did the effort put Elyriel to sleep, it gave Kaycia the chance to gauge her limits.

"You don't open this door for anyone, understand?"

Chesandril nodded, knowing their lives depended on their secrets staying safe.

"We'll eat good tonight. I promise."

The girl responded with a heartfelt smile. Her attitude was so surprising, Kaycia could only attribute the change to their sense of security. And, reluctantly, she acknowledged their room had been worth every shale.

The streets of New Ahman were always lit, with lanterns burning both night and day. This was entirely for the ascendants' benefit, who might be called upon to fight at any moment, in any of these neighborhoods.

There was evidence of such scuffles in every direction.

On the corner outside, a large chapel was in the process of reconstruction and not for the first time. She could see it in the craftsmanship—the way the oldest bell tower had been erected with pride, with each successive repair showing less and less effort. At some point, they'd stopped repainting the woodwork.

Unlike the hunters, these were regular people. Unaided by ascendancy, these workers subsisted off a sense of duty. They had no other choice—and by the time they were finished, five more projects would be waiting.

Kaycia knew it hadn't always been like this, but Veralyn had warned her—the attacks were getting worse. And when human aspirations were compromised by fear, they could only move forward off sheer obstinacy.

As she traversed the muddy streets, she was surprised to see how much the place had grown prior to these setbacks. It was much more than the armor crafters and weapons dealers she'd been expecting—there were also dress shops and spice merchants. On one corner, she saw a young girl in a shabby frock selling daisies. What had started as a hub for hunters, had slowly cultivated into a more complete expression of human society.

It was damn unfortunate, then, some human characteristics left something to be desired.

"Seven hundred shales?" asked the clerk as he inspected the note.

"Is there a problem?"

The man tightened his lips but said nothing more.

She'd hoped to get her money and leave, but first, she'd been forced to wait in line for an hour. And, now, this?

Back in Perandolen, the woman had no reason to doubt Kaycia's kill—but that was because she'd carried the head as proof. Here, on the other hand, she had nothing more than a slip of paper. So it made sense the man would be suspicious of forgery.

The man was bald, with a narrow set of spectacles. He wore the fine leather vest of someone who'd never wielded a sword.

Reaching into a stack of books, the clerk retrieved a ledger and opened to a blank page.

"Before I can give you anything, I require additional information. Let's start with your full name."

This made her worried. None of the other patrons she'd observed had been given this treatment. Perhaps the protocol was different when dealing with larger sums of money. Either that or all the others were established clients.

"Kaycia Eldren," she said before spelling it out. Like in Perandolen, she thought it best to stay close to the truth.

Her name, however, wasn't enough. The clerk asked for her parents' names, after which he asked if there were any other ascendants in her family.

There weren't.

Due to her young appearance, he asked for the name of her sponsor, the location where she'd trained, and the day of her ascension.

This was all answered easily, with Kaycia providing the date of her original ceremony—despite the fact that it had failed.

"All right," he said. "Please wait here while I verify this information."

"Verify? You mean, you have a register...here?"

She'd already known such a list existed—a catalog identifying all local ascendants—but she'd never thought it'd be used in a place like this.

"Yes," he said, stretching his patience.

"But that's not going to work. You didn't hear me? I was only raised three weeks ago. My name's not there."

The man shrugged. "I'm sorry, miss, but it's standard protocol."

Like hell it is! she thought.

"Perhaps there's someone with you whose credentials we can verify? Usually, in your situation, we'd make an exception for your sponsor. Why don't you ask—?" He consulted the notes he'd written. "...Marien ti Olesca come in and claim the funds on your behalf?"

"She...can't," said Kaycia, shaking her head in exasperation. "But her daughter's with me. She's waiting at the inn as we speak. Would she be eligible?"

While Kaycia wasn't thrilled by the prospect—and figuring out what to do with Elyriel in the meantime—it'd, at least, be better than walking away.

The man paused as though he'd never been asked that question.

He shared a look with the clerk beside him, but the woman merely shrugged.

"Which inn?" he asked.

"The Golden Terrace."

He began to nod slowly, as though grateful to have a solution within walking distance. Lifting his pen, he asked, "The daughter's name?"

"Chesandril." And she spelled it out.

For a moment, the matter seemed settled.

"Oh!" said the man, in afterthought. "Her age?"

Kaycia swallowed. "...Twelve."

The grimace that followed needed no explanation. His pen returned to the paper and scratched out the name.

"Sit tight," he said. "Before we do anything, let me go back and consult our records. You'd be surprised by how frequently updates arrive. Might be, you've already been registered, and all this ado has been for naught."

Kaycia, however, wasn't doubtful. Her name would never appear in that book.

She felt sure the bald man had reached the same conclusion. From the beginning, he'd made no effort to hide his suspicion. All this pretending was merely a courtesy.

"If it's not there," he continued, "we'll go over your options."

He stood up, forced a smile, and made his way to a back room.

The man, however, made a mistake.

In his haste, perhaps, to confirm her fraud—or, maybe, he was on his way to the authorities—he'd neglected to bring the promissory note with him. It was still on the desk in front of her.

While no one was watching, she tucked the note into her sleeve. She obviously wouldn't be getting money today, and there was no reason to await his return.

Kaycia went for the door before anyone could stop her.

I t wasn't until she'd escaped into an alley that she blinked away a tear.

More than the money, she was saddened by Chesandril—of the thought of facing her once more empty-handed. The girl would understand and even forgive her for breaking her promise—but it wouldn't be surprising if Chesandril retreated again into her shell.

Rather than sneak away from their unpaid room, it might be best to confront the innkeeper directly. She could explain what happened before searching for other means of payment. Gods... She hated being desperate—but it was better than running off and behaving like a criminal. Well...*more* a criminal than she was already.

For a few seconds, she stood there, running through the possibilities, before she realized she wasn't alone.

"Sorry," said the man. "I didn't mean to startle you."

To her surprise, she recognized the voice—quickly enough to remember she was supposed to be an ascendant.

"Dark heavens..." she said. "Have you been following me?"

"Not intentionally," said Soril.

Kaycia barked a laugh, surprising even herself by the change of mood. "Is that the way of it? You followed me *on accident*?" She raised a hand to dry her cheek.

"That's not what I meant," he said in a cool tone.

She would've preferred him to be flustered—to appear self-conscious like a regular person. At least, then, he wouldn't be wondering why she, as an ascendant, hadn't noticed his approach.

"I only saw you leaving the trade office. I thought I'd make an apology."

"I don't follow."

Soril frowned as though it should've been obvious. "For the disrespect of my lieutenant. For driving you off earlier on the road."

Was *that* what he thought? She supposed this was preferable to knowing the real reason she'd fled.

"How is she?" he asked.

"Elyriel? There's nothing to worry about. She's stronger than she looks."

"I'm not surprised, seeing where she gets it from."

This made Kaycia pause.

"Excuse me, but what is this, exactly?" She motioned at the air between them. "Was that a come-on?"

"That," he said, without losing a beat, "was a job offer."

"Oh," she said, surprised and...oddly...disappointed. She'd expected her question to catch him off guard, but Soril proved the type not to embarrass easily.

A moment later, her mind caught up to what he'd said.

"I'm confused. I mean... You don't even know my name. And yet, a job? A bit much for an apology, don't you think?"

Soril shrugged this off as unimportant. "What's your name?"

She considered not telling him, only to realize, at this point, it wouldn't only be rude, it'd be unprofessional. "Kaycia Eldren."

"Well...Miss Kaycia Eldren...how about it? Maybe I don't know much about you. I see you're new to this. Less than a year, perhaps, out of training. But as far as I'm concerned, the only detail that matters is how cleanly you dispatched those grimwolves."

"But you didn't even see—"

"You're right. I didn't. And, to be honest, I might've forgotten the whole thing were it not for the reactions when our skinners arrived."

From Kaycia's understanding, skinners were common among the larger companies. They cared for the remains and performed other menial tasks so the ascendants wouldn't have to. They were one of the many perks of traveling in a group.

Soril went on. "You left quite the impression—each kill, swift and precise. More surgical than even the best convictors. You should hear the hell I usually get—how my weapon shatters bone and leaves blackened sears... But the carcasses you left were perfectly intact."

"So what? A few grimwolf hides? I can't imagine they're worth much."

"True. They're not. But you're missing the point. My company specializes in larger game. If your talents are as good as my skinners were boasting, it would significantly affect our profit margins."

Kaycia nodded as she allowed this to sink in.

Under different circumstances, she would've been thrilled. For years, she'd been worried no companies would take her, and she'd have to work hard to gain their notice.

And yet... Recognition was the very thing she needed to avoid. In the end, Soril's praise wasn't meant for her but Elyriel. And if he knew the truth, a job would be the last thing on his mind.

"I'm sorry, but I work alone."

For the first time, she saw cracks in Soril's demeanor. He still wore a smile, but it'd lost a fraction of its genuine quality.

"Is this because of my lieutenant? I'll have him transferred at once."

"Oh, no! It's nothing like that. Please, don't take this personally."

Soril was still confused, but she didn't know what else to say.

A moment later, he regained his composure. "It's your sister," he concluded—not as a question but a statement of fact.

"What makes you—?"

"No need to explain. I get it. It's not my place to tell you what's good for your family. That's your vocation and deserving of my respect."

Kaycia bit her lip, uncertain of what Soril thought he knew. He'd unlikely guessed Elyriel's true nature, but he'd seen enough to know she wasn't normal. He'd only suspect she was special and required much of Kaycia's attention.

To her surprise, however, Soril changed the subject.

"It's none of my business, but might I ask what the trouble was?" He turned the way she came, in the direction of the office.

Kaycia sighed, frustrated by the memory. "It was nothing."

"It wasn't," he said in a serious tone. "Believe me, you're not the first to come out with that look."

"Their books are missing information. That's all. It'll sort itself out."

This, of course, was a lie, but she was reluctant to involve Soril in her personal affairs.

"You have to give me more than that. Perhaps I can do something? I know some people."

"I appreciate your kindness, but, really—I'll just wait for them to update their registry."

Soril's expression became thoughtful. "Hold on... You mean *your* records? You're that new?"

"A few weeks," she said, trying not to blush. In truth, her training was far from finished, as many lessons weren't taught until ascendancy was attained. "So, like I said, it can wait. There's no reason to concern yourself."

By his expression, Soril appeared more impressed than ever. And rather than be dissuaded, he seemed even more determined to land this recruitment.

"Let me see that," he said.

"See what?"

He pointed his chin toward her hand. "The note you've tucked away."

When she looked down, no part of the paper was peeking out, making her wonder how he knew it was there. Did it make a sound when she moved? Or did he sense something else—some protective way she favored that arm?

"This isn't a robbery," he soothed.

"What's it to you? It's just paper."

"I want to buy it."

"You what?!"

Until that moment, Kaycia had been anxious to return to the inn—but now, he had her full attention.

Of course, Soril still hadn't seen the note's value. He knew enough to ascertain her problems were financial, but his offer might've been premature.

In the end, though, did it matter? It seemed wise to accept any offer, even if he could only afford a fraction of its worth. Kaycia was painfully aware how much she needed that money. And she was left with little choice but to swallow her pride.

She placed the paper into his outstretched palm. Then, she looked away, unable to watch his eyes as he unfolded it.

"It's real," she promised.

"Oh, I can see that."

She heard the crinkling of paper.

For a moment, he said nothing, and Kaycia felt sure he'd changed his mind.

Instead, Soril asked, "How many grimwolves did you kill to earn all this?"

"They weren't grimwolves."

"That was a joke," he said without laughing.

Kaycia looked up but couldn't read his expression.

"What was this?" he asked, holding up the paper.

"Look... You don't have to give me anything. Just hand it back, and I'll be on my way."

"What makes you think I'm reconsidering?"

Kaycia swallowed, but she supposed this made sense. For someone like Soril, he'd face no trouble cashing the note at full value. So, for him, any offer was a guaranteed profit.

"I'm listening," she said. "No doubt you've got some takeaway in mind for yourself?"

"No doubt."

She saw no reason to drag this out. "How much?"

Soril made a show of running calculations—but when he finally responded, it was clearly an act.

"Seven hundred shales."

Kaycia blinked in surprise. Soril wasn't the sort to make mistakes—so if he wasn't after the money, he wanted something else.

"Five hundred," she said. "And we call it even. I won't be indebted to anyone—or commit myself to favors."

"Just hear me out. I want to offer the full amount—with one easy condition that won't cost you anything."

Kaycia nearly refused, but mostly out of pride. She couldn't shake the feeling he was toying with her. But, in the end, it wouldn't hurt to listen. If his request was reasonable, it wouldn't be beneath her to earn the difference of two hundred shales.

"It's simple. All I ask is that you make a brief visit to our camp. You'll be under no obligation to join us or even stay longer than a few minutes. But who knows? We can try some accommodations—a private carriage for your sister? Or—? You let me know what you come up with. In the end, if you still decide our company's not for you... Well, that's your prerogative."

This shouldn't have surprised her. She was learning that when Soril had his eye on something, he found it difficult to let go.

Of course, what Soril wanted didn't exist. He'd placed Kaycia on a pedestal, imagining her to be some marvel or prodigy, and it simply wasn't true.

She'd feel guilty walking into his camp, knowing her answer was predetermined—but discomfort was a small price if it fed her sister.

"Where's the camp?" she asked.

"Beyond the northern gate. Ask for Soril, and anyone can point the way."

From his waist, he produced a sack, seemingly from nowhere. Without waiting for a verbal agreement, he counted the coins. He set aside a small fraction and handed her the rest, still inside the pouch.

"A pleasure doing business with you," he said.

Feeling the weight in her hands, the reality sank in.

"Thank you! You don't know how much this means to us!"

He smiled in return.

"Would tomorrow be okay?" she asked. "Some time in the morning?"

After thinking a moment, he said, "I can make that work. Try not to be late, or you'll catch us while we're making preparations."

Kaycia paused, unsure what he meant.

"No one's told you?" he asked. "But I guess you just arrived... There's a reason I'm stationed here. They're expecting the next attack tomorrow, at sundown."

"Expecting? You make it sound as though the creatures have a schedule."

"Well, it *is* peculiar... There doesn't seem to be a cause, but I've seen it for myself."

"This is new?"

"Relatively speaking."

Kaycia was intrigued, having never heard of creatures behaving so organized, not even where the current was deeper.

She asked the first question that came to mind. "You think the abyssal lords might have something to do with it?"

Kaycia expected him to brush this off and say the lords were nothing but the product of fear. There were rumors of these generals stalking the darkness, but no proof they were real. The gods, themselves, had never acknowledged their existence—or they'd deliberately left such insights unspoken.

"You're not the first to make that suggestion. But no, I don't think so. What would they gain by making themselves predictable? While scheduled attacks might indicate intelligence, it's not the approach that helps win battles."

"Unless that's what they want you to think. To drop your guard."

"Perhaps," he conceded. "In our previous engagement, there were signs of a break-in. Of something snooping through our camp while we were distracted. So don't you fret. We're prepared for many possibilities."

Kaycia exhaled, more fascinated by this mystery than fearful. It'd always bothered her so little was known of the current or even where it came from. As a kid, she often dreamed of uncovering some new detail, to shed light on this horrifying darkness.

Unfortunately, her hands were tied. While she intended Elyriel to take part in the fight, her capacity would be limited. She'd contribute in ways to hone her talent—while avoiding the things that drew attention.

She needed to lie low and let other people do these investigations. She couldn't afford to join a company where she'd be surrounded by people watching her every move.

"Tomorrow, then," she said as she backed away.

Soril just nodded. His expression was pleased, believing he was finally getting through to her.

And she wondered if it might be better not to show up at all.

Chapter 10
OFF THE RECORD

Mere moments after leaving, a new fear took hold.

As a transfigurer, Soril had the power to rearrange matter. It was far more complex than converting energy, but he could reshape wood chips into fraudulent coins with enough incentive.

With sweating palms, she pulled out the bag—not to count the shales but to inspect them more closely. They certainly looked real—but, just to be sure, she bit one with her teeth.

Only then did she sigh in relief.

Aside from transfiguration, there was a second aspect notorious for swindling. A creator didn't even need to start with wood or other worthless tidbits. He could make the coins pop out of thin air, only to disappear after the ascendant was gone.

Such counterfeit coins, created or transfigured, were convincing but never perfect in their rendition. For this reason, it was customary for merchants to inspect all transactions before they were finalized—and Kaycia scolded herself for being too distracted to remember this precaution. After her years in school, it'd been a long while since she'd personally dealt with money. And in a few minutes, she could've lost everything. She needed to be more careful.

Fortunately for her, Soril seemed an honest man.

Which made it all the more difficult to turn down his offer.

Still, she couldn't help thinking it over. She was intrigued by his suggestion of a carriage. With the right arrangement and boundaries, it'd provide a safe place to leave Elyriel—or her own unconscious body—without anyone else growing the wiser. She couldn't deny the clear advantages of being part of a group—the most obvious being safety in numbers.

Yet, it didn't solve the problem of keeping their identity a secret. When it came time to fight, it'd be obvious to everyone it was Elyriel—not Kaycia—who emerged from that carriage. Even in the dark, with poor visibility, the sisters were too different.

Moreover, there was no telling when Elyriel might grow unhappy with the accommodations. And when she got loose, it'd be Kaycia's fault for not preventing the bloodbath.

She was reminded of her need to get back to the inn. Though she was sure her sister would still be recovering, there couldn't be a worse time to be proven wrong. Now that she had her money, it was in everyone's best interest she play her hand as safely as possible.

Keeping her eyes to herself, she started back to the Golden Terrace. She stuffed the coins into her clothing, deep enough to confound the most subtle pickpockets.

With the hour growing late, the streets were flooded with smoke of the most pleasant aromas. She heard the sizzle of meat skewers and glazed vegetables, as hunters took their families for a night on the town. Were she not in such a hurry, she might've scouted for locations to bring Chesandril—but she felt no regret. They *all* looked good.

She limited herself to buying a few overpriced apples and a jug of filtered water. Other than that, she made one more stop.

The quaint boutique might've been easy to miss, hidden between much larger and more fanciful establishments. It gave off the impression of a traveling performer, with knick-knacks and curios from far-off places. There were brightly colored costumes, strangely woven chairs, and even a stuffed bird covered in paint.

For the most part, the place seemed all decoration, without anything of practical function—the sort she usually disregarded without a second glance.

Except, in the window case, a dark metal mask caught her eye. It covered the whole face, with holes to see through, and a slit for the mouth. Shaped with feminine curves and hair woven from burnished wire, its neutral expression was as frightening as it was beautiful.

The mask was so exquisite it wouldn't be cheap—but it sparked an idea that wouldn't let go.

A sking advice from a twelve-year-old didn't prove her best idea.

"*Of course*, you should join!" said Chesandril, around a mouthful of apple. "Don't you know how *awesome* that'd be? You, in disguise, on a team of ascendants?"

Kaycia laughed, glad to see the girl in a talkative mood. "No one said anything of a team. Most of Soril's fighters are regular people. The typical company only employs a few ascendants. Seldom more than five."

"So few?" The girl looked confused. "But...in the stories, there's always—"

"That's because people like to talk of larger battles. In those cases, a militia is brought together, formed of multiple companies at once. But that hardly ever happens. Ascendants are so scarce, it's more important to spread us out."

Chesandril nodded thoughtfully. "I still think you should do it. Tomorrow, you should go as Elyriel—not yourself."

Kaycia wasn't so sure. "And if they ask me to remove the mask? When I came up with the idea, I was only thinking of battle—you know—as part of my ensemble. But, the whole time in camp? You don't think that would be weird?"

"Maybe... But it'd be worse to show up and not demonstrate a lick of ascendancy."

Kaycia frowned.

"That's what *I* would be worried about," continued the girl. "Stories only get you so far. You won't earn their respect by keeping to yourself. Are you going to make excuses? Say you're not in the *right mood*?"

Something crashed loudly against the wall.

"Elle... No!" said Kaycia as her sister prepared to throw a second metal buckle. While no one was looking, she'd plucked them from the harness, tearing completely through leather. "Put it down!"

"What was that?!" came a muffled voice from the other side of the wall. The thick wood made it difficult to make out clearly, even with the man yelling loudly. "Keep it down over there!"

"Sorry!" shouted Kaycia. Then, in a quieter tone, "I said no, Elle! Drop it!"

"Behhluaaghhh!" said Elyriel from where she sat on the mattress.

Faster than the first, the buckle flew across the room, striking so deep, the wood splintered.

Kaycia was surprised the attack hadn't prompted her to take control. If the buckle had been aimed at her, it would've been deadly.

But it *hadn't* been aimed at her—and wasn't that the point? Her sister had learned it was a mistake to attack Kaycia directly, so she'd intentionally missed.

"Damn it!" came the shout from the other room. "What the hell is going on?! Do I need to drag the innkeeper down here?"

"All taken care of!" shouted Kaycia, rushing to block her sister before she threw something else.

Chesandril added, "Sorry to bother you!"

"Gwaawwuugghh," said Elyriel.

"Come on, Elle. What's gotten into you?" she asked, keeping her voice gentle. Yelling at her sister only made her more difficult.

"Does she need a reason?" inquired Chesandril.

"There's always a reason—even if she doesn't know it."

Elyriel backed across the mattress, avoiding eye contact with anyone.

"Is it okay if I sit next to you?" Kaycia kept her approach slow.

Behind her, Chesandril inspected the wall for damage.

"How bad is it?" asked Kaycia

"Pretty bad. Good thing the wood's so thick. But maybe I can try something. Can I use your knife?"

Kaycia sat behind her sister and wrapped an arm around her. Elyriel didn't relax—but neither pulled away.

"Here," said Kaycia, unsheathing a blade with her free hand. "Still think she's fit for a company of people? I don't mean tomorrow or the times I'm in control—but all the days after."

Chesandril took the knife and shrugged.

"Can you imagine?" continued Kaycia. "Locked in a carriage, smaller than this room? Just the two of you? Are *you* prepared to watch her?"

"It wouldn't be *all* the time, would it?"

"What do you think? Even when I'm around...it's not like we can take her for walks. Someone's going to see. She's crazy strong."

Chesandril shrugged again. "So we stay inside. And if anything goes wrong...we make a run for it."

Kaycia sighed, wishing it were so simple. She'd learned the hard way, however, life rarely conformed to anyone's expectations—let alone those of a twelve-year-old.

Returning to the wall, Chesandril tried forcing the splinters back into place. When this didn't work, she pried the hole apart and dug out some shavings. She then folded the larger pieces in, flush with the surrounding planks...for the most part.

While the damage wasn't so apparent as before, it didn't take much to see it was there—even from the opposite side of the room.

"I don't know..." said Chesandril. "The innkeeper doesn't do anything to tidy up. Might be, he won't notice?"

"I wouldn't get my hopes up. If it involves money... He might not make the repairs, but he won't miss the chance to charge us for them."

Kaycia slumped in resignation. She didn't know what to expect—or how much she'd have to pay—but she suspected she'd soon become an expert. She'd need to start a habit of saving money—to cover all of Elyriel's surprises.

"I got an idea," said Chesandril, taking hold of the wardrobe.

It was so thin and flimsy, the small girl could slide it by herself, albeit with some difficulty. Fortunately, it didn't need to move far.

"Can't see it now."

Kaycia saw something on the floor, previously hidden by the furniture. "Is that...a hairbrush?"

Chesandril handed it to Kaycia.

Carved from bone, with each bristle stitched by hand, it was difficult to imagine anyone leaving it behind. Many bristles were split, and there were stains on the handle—but, even so, a brush was a keepsake meant to last a lifetime.

She beat it a few times against the mattress to shake away dust. Then tested it through Elyriel's hair.

The girl jerked forward, turning her head over her shoulder.

"Don't move," said Kaycia. "It's all right. You remember what this is?"

"Ggggghhh," said Elyriel, eying the brush with suspicion.

"It's okay. You can watch. But you'll have to turn your head when I do the back."

"So, this Soril guy..." said Chesandril. "Is he handsome?"

Kaycia nearly choked. "What? No! I... Don't you remember? You saw him on the road."

"Ohhh! Him? I didn't realize it was the same guy... I suppose he wasn't *bad*-looking..."

"Chess!"

The man was old enough to be the girl's father, but Kaycia chose not to say this. Chesandril, after all, didn't have a father. So, instead, she said, "Soril's an ascendant."

"So?"

"I made my decision when I started training. Relationships are complicated, even without the problems of aspects or ascendancy. You know how it works—when two ascendants get married?"

The girl made a face to hide her disappointment.

The trouble, once again, came from the ceremony. In one possible outcome, the woman's aspect would change to match the man's. But it was equally likely to go the other way, so his would match hers. In either case, irreversibly, one would cease to be an ascendant.

And there was still a third possibility—that the marriage would fail.

Such failures marked a permanent end to the relationship. The laws were specific, unbending, and created for a single reason: any child born outside a perfect alignment would be born without an aspect at all. The result was unavoidable, even when both parents originally came from the same god.

Those children, without exception, didn't live very long.

When confronted with such horrific possibilities, Kaycia had decided not to take the risk. It didn't make sense—yet people everywhere made such irrational decisions every day. All for the sake of following their hearts.

Chesandril shook her head. "No one said you'd have to get married."

"You're kidding, right? Not even old enough to kiss a boy, and you don't see the problem?"

"I am too old enough!"

Elyriel turned, perhaps wondering what was wrong.

"And besides," the girl continued, her face bright red, "we're not talking about me!"

"Good, because we're not talking about *this*, either. Like I said, it's not like that. If anything, when Soril offered help, he was like an older brother. He was looking after me."

At least, she hoped it was that way. There was no guarantee Soril shared her perspective, and, to be honest, she didn't know his motivations. She could only measure what she'd seen: a relationship bounded by professionalism.

If she doubted this now, it was only because Chesandril brought it up.

Momentarily distracted, she failed to prevent Elyriel from grabbing the brush.

"You want to try yourself?" asked Kaycia, still holding a handful of hair. "Wait! Don't!"

It cracked against the wall, just above the wardrobe.

"Damn it!" came the shout from the opposite side.

"Sorry again!"

Standing on her tip-toes, Chesandril fumbled at the top of the wardrobe. When she found the brush, however, it came away in two pieces. Half the bristles scattered across the floor.

Kaycia groaned. "Why did you—?! Not you, Chess. Well...just so you know, we're not going to stop. I've got fingers, see?"

And, with that, Elyriel turned her focus onto Kaycia's hands, running through her hair.

In some ways, this only added to the nostalgia. Their mother had rarely shared her comb, convinced her daughters were incapable of being careful. There'd been many times when Kaycia had sat behind her like this, picking at tangles with nothing but nails.

Even back then, it was just the two of them. Their mother lived in the same house but hardly spoke after Father died.

"Could you teach me how to fight?"

Kaycia smiled, looking up at Chesandril. "What brought this on? Eager to take revenge on the current?"

Her eyes bulged. "Oh no. Nothing so frightful! I'll leave that to the grown-ups."

"Smart," said Kaycia, glad to hear the girl's head was on straight. She was always saddened by the youth, so driven by passion they practically ran to their deaths. It took a fair bit of maturity to accept which problems were beyond your limitations.

"I just... I want to take care of myself, you know? What if I meet some thug on the street, and you're not there to help?"

Kaycia grimaced. "Then you run—I'm serious."

"What? No way! *You* wouldn't run!"

"If I were twelve, I most certainly would."

Chesandril looked displeased.

With a sigh, Kaycia tried to explain. "Some training wouldn't hurt, but don't forget, many thugs out there *also* know how to fight. No matter how much you've practiced, *they've* practiced more. And they're bigger and stronger, besides."

The girl shook her head. "But what if running's not an option? What if I'm cornered?"

Kaycia took a deep breath and looked her in the eye. She didn't have the heart, however, to tell her fighting was still the wrong choice. That lashing out would only infuriate her attackers and provoke them into inflicting worse harm. Sometimes, when you were so thoroughly trapped that injury was inescapable, the best path was the one that ensured the least pain—both to yourself and the ones closest to you.

"I can show you a few things," she said, working out a tangle with her fingers. "Ways you might surprise an attacker, after you've convinced them you're harmless."

Chesandril beamed. "You will?"

"But you have to promise you'll be smart about it. If someone wants your money, give it to them. Money can be replaced. Your life can't."

The girl looked confused.

"Fighting's a choice," explained Kaycia. "Make no mistake—there are some things in life that are worth fighting for—even for a twelve-year-old girl. Everything else? Just let them go. Don't be the fool who died fighting for a hairbrush."

This prompted a laugh. "But what if it was a *really nice* hairbrush?"

Kaycia rolled her eyes. "Well, in that case..."

Elyriel got up, dragging Kaycia with her.

"We're not done!" she protested.

But Elyriel would hear none of it and growled as Kaycia extricated her fingers.

"You know what would make this easier?" asked Kaycia, more for Chesandril's benefit. "Just wait a moment. I'll have a word with the innkeeper and get a bath drawn. Water would help with these tangles. And a change of scenery might help her calm down."

And, if not... she thought. *If I have to control her myself, a bath would, at least, be relaxing for me.*

"Don't let her destroy anything while I'm gone."

"Uhh...?"

Elyriel had approached the wardrobe with curious eyes.

"You're right," said Kaycia. There was no doubt, with her sister's energy returning, it'd be dangerous to leave her this way.

So she took a few minutes to expend her energy—enough to last for the next short while.

"Keep the door closed," she said, exiting into the hall.

Near the lobby, she heard voices.

One was the innkeeper's, and as she came around the corner, she saw him speaking with three armored men led by someone she recognized. It was the same bald clerk from the trade office who'd been the source of all her frustrations. The same clerk who'd heard her say she was staying at the Golden Terrace.

She might've ducked back, but it was already too late. By some streak of bad luck, the clerk was facing her direction as she appeared.

"That's her!" he shouted, pointing a finger.

It took all Kaycia's willpower not to run. While she wanted nothing more than to avoid confrontation, leaving now would only worsen things. In the eyes of the officers, it would confirm her wrongdoing. And, what started as a simple inquiry would quickly degenerate into the pursuit of a fugitive.

She had to force herself to believe, as far as these men were concerned, she wasn't guilty of anything. They shouldn't have enough on her to perform an arrest, so her best option was to pull herself together and handle their questions.

The hardest part was leaving Chesandril by herself. She'd need to deal with this quickly to avoid worse problems.

With measured dignity, Kaycia walked straight toward the men.

The clerk's expression of victory seemed to waver a moment. He appeared slightly unnerved by her calm composure but not enough to remove the smug look off his face.

Directing herself to the officer in charge, she asked, "Is there a problem, magistrate?"

The man greeted her with a smile, as though unaccustomed to people willing to cooperate. His uniform was red beneath his gleaming cuirass, emblazoned with the sigil of Carheim. "Well, that's what we're here to investigate, miss. This man," he said, turning toward the clerk, "has expressed some concerns about your person. You're Kaycia Eldren, are you not?"

"I am," she said, without fear or concern.

The innkeeper returned his attention to his desk, glad he was no longer needed.

"We've been informed of your visit to the trade office earlier this evening. Was this the man who helped you?"

"I was there. But saying he helped anyone would be an overstatement."

The bald man bristled, eyes bulging, but he held his tongue.

Ignoring this, the officer went on. "Did you or did you not attempt to cash a note in the amount of seven hundred shales."

"I did."

"May I see it?"

She gave a helpless shrug. "I don't have it anymore."

The clerk's eyes shot to the magistrate, trying to get his attention.

Wearily, the officer turned, and the clerk's eyes stared daggers at Kaycia's hands. Someone must've seen her tuck it away.

Without waiting to be asked, she raised both sleeves to show they were empty. "I don't have it."

She was reluctant, however, to admit she'd sold it. There were reasons—mostly tax-related—such transactions were restricted to specific channels, and any circumvention would be classified as a misdemeanor.

The clerk huffed loudly, his doubt unmistakable.

"Where is it, then?" asked the officer. "Explain."

At this point, Kaycia was forced to make a choice, realizing if she didn't have an adequate response, their next step would be to search her room.

"I sold it," she grumbled in a low voice. "To a man on the street."

The magistrate frowned. "You admit to this?"

Kaycia rounded on the clerk. "I wasn't left with many options!"

Before the bald man could react, the magistrate stepped between them. His expression, however, had become distant, losing its touch of sympathy. "It would seem I'm out of options as well. We'll need to take you in for questioning."

Damn it! thought Kaycia. "Now?" she asked. Her eyes flicked to the innkeeper—knowing he couldn't help, but hoping he'd, at least, tell Chesandril what was happening.

"I'm afraid so," said the magistrate. "You must also provide proof of the exchange. You were given money, I presume?"

With extreme reluctance, Kaycia produced the bag of coins.

"Give it here."

"Will I get it back?"

The man held out his hand with a look of impatience.

It occurred to her that running might still be an option. If she switched to Elyriel, she could have her sister here before these officers knew what hit them. She could pick up her body and flee the city.

She handed him the pouch.

Opening it, the magistrate inspected a few coins to ensure they were real.

"See?" she asked. "No one would've paid if the note was fake."

Ignoring her, he handed the pouch to his comrades. "For evidence."

"That's mine!"

Kaycia couldn't believe this was happening. Could they treat her this way for a simple misdemeanor? Or was this related to ascendancy? Even if it was, as far as they were concerned, she'd only *pretended* to be an ascendant. And the crime of false representation wasn't so severe as to warrant this abuse.

Perhaps she was overreacting. So far, no one had accused her of anything, and if she didn't control her emotions, she might provoke the very investigation she hoped to avoid. It'd be better to comply and worry about the money later.

"We'll take it from here, Handel," said the officer to the clerk.

The bald man hesitated as though confused by the dismissal.

They'd only taken a few steps before the officer turned back to the innkeeper. "Was she alone?" he asked. "Was anyone with her?'

No, no, no!! thought Kaycia. Her eyes locked with the innkeeper's so he'd see the nearly imperceptible shake of her head. *Come on!* she thought. *You got paid, didn't you?!*

To her relief, the man shrugged. "All my dealings have been with her."

With a nod, the officer let the matter drop.

"What of the girl?" demanded the clerk, making no move to leave. "Callie or Chessie or... The daughter!" To the innkeeper, he asked, "You didn't see a girl of about twelve?"

Kaycia wanted to punch the man—unsure what she'd done to deserve his hatred—but she was more angry at herself for providing him the information.

"That's enough!" said the officer. "We got what we came for. Or is this twelve-year-old guilty of wrongdoing?"

The clerk licked his lips but decided not to press the matter further.

"Go home, Handel."

Beyond the door, the sky had grown dim, settling the world into the bright orange glow of street lanterns.

Kaycia had no choice but to follow along. Luckily, none of the men found it necessary to restrain or drag her behind them. It was a reminder she hadn't been arrested. At least, not yet.

If she was clever, she might explain this was all a mistake. She'd been *given* the note—as a generous gift from a real ascendant. Who'd overlooked the difficulties she'd face.

Whatever her story, she'd make clear her claim to ascendancy had merely been an act. It was better they think her a fool and a liar than suspect her of crimes exponentially worse.

"What's the meaning of this?" demanded a loud voice.

The officers stopped as a man stepped into the street and blocked their path.

Seeing who it was, Kaycia wanted to scream in frustration.

She'd already run into him twice today, and right when she needed to distance herself from ascendancy, Soril shows up again?

"It's none of your concern," said the magistrate. "Just a person of interest. Nothing dangerous."

"I'm afraid she *is* my concern. What crime has Miss Eldren been charged with?"

A few passersby were gathering. Their eyes were on Kaycia—some suspicious or accusatory. Some merely curious.

The magistrate was puzzled. "You know this woman?"

"No!" declared Kaycia, locking eyes with Soril's.

"Poor girl. She thinks she's protecting me."

Kaycia grit her teeth, realizing there was little she could say to make Soril change his mind. She'd experienced firsthand how stubborn he could be.

At the same time, she didn't want to lose his admiration and respect. After everything he'd done, for him to discover it'd all been a lie...

"Is this what you were looking for?" Soril held up a sheet of paper.

The magistrate frowned as he stepped forward to examine the note.

"My guess was correct?" asked Soril. "See for yourself. No fraud has been done."

"So it was *you* who conducted this illegal trade?"

Kaycia groaned. Soril, like most ascendants, had jumped in headfirst without considering the consequences.

"Nonsense!" he declared, with too much bravado.

"With all due respect, our government takes its funding quite seriously. The policies are strict and enforced for *everyone*."

"And rightly so," continued Soril. "So you'll be pleased to hear our exchange was perfectly within the bounds of the law."

Kaycia was equally as confused as the officers.

It was the clerk, however, who broke the silence. "You *dare* insult these—?"

"I appreciate your concern, but Kaycia, here, has neglected to tell you that our transaction was entirely an internal affair. No government tender was transferred between separate, private parties—as prohibited by your laws. As the newest addition to my company, it is within her rights to receive pension without being subjected to your local tax."

"Is this true?" asked the magistrate.

Kaycia was at a loss for words. Addition to his company? On the one hand, she was furious Soril would turn this to his advantage—and yet, his intentions weren't entirely self-serving. There was no denying this arrangement would simplify her problem, although it didn't address the matter in its entirety.

Handel refused to back down. "That's not possible! She's *ineligible* for membership. She's not even an ascendant!"

"I assure you, she is."

Kaycia avoided eye contact with everyone, undecided on what to do. While Soril meant well, they were approaching dangerous ground.

"You know this for certain?" asked the magistrate.

"I do. I've seen her fight with my own eyes."

Oh gods...! thought Kaycia. But, to her dismay, she couldn't bring herself to contradict him. What would she even say? If she hadn't killed those grimwolves, then who had? Could she really suggest some other ascendant came along mere moments before?

The magistrate looked uncomfortable but kept his words directed at Soril. "Are you also aware no records exist whatsoever of an ascendant by her name?"

"Easily explained. She told me herself. Your records aren't up to date."

"Actually... They are."

Kaycia felt a lump rise in her chest as the worst of her fears were confirmed. As she'd suspected, this talk of money had only been a cover—an excuse to bring her in, hoping she'd make a mistake and condemn herself of their true concern.

This, by itself, might've been okay—as they had no reason to believe her ascendancy was real—at least, not until her *employer* arrived...

Soril, too, for the first time, was at a loss for words.

"A messenger arrived earlier today," explained the magistrate sorrowfully. "Some of his reports were as recent as last week—including the paperwork from Wern's Hold, the garrison Kaycia claims to have attended. I would've refrained from confrontation had I not checked it thoroughly."

Kaycia felt Soril's eyes on her but didn't look up.

"A mistake," he said. "A clerical error."

"Unlikely...but possible. I hope you're right, Soril, but you must understand. We *have* to bring her in. I'd be happy to submit a petition on her behalf. If the garrison has anything pertaining to Miss Eldren, it should take less than two weeks to receive her records."

"Two weeks?" asked Soril, clearly displeased.

For Kaycia, however, this news was much worse. Such records wouldn't only reveal her attendance—they'd explicitly state her ceremony had failed.

She needed to intervene. After Soril was gone, she'd confess her fraud—anything to ensure the papers weren't sent.

The only good part, at the moment, was that no one knew of Elyriel. As long as her sister remained free, Kaycia could switch to her body from the privacy of her cell. With regular access, she could prevent the girl from drawing attention. And, worst case scenario, she could break herself free.

"There's a caravan headed south tomorrow morning," continued the magistrate. "I'll see to it, personally, the request goes out. In the meantime, we'll refrain from passing judgment."

Soril sighed loudly. "What you say sounds reasonable. But I'm afraid I can't accept."

The officers exchanged nervous glances, averse to locking horns with an ascendant in public.

The bald clerk, however, held no such reservations. "Excuse me?" he demanded, face growing red. "Who do you think you are? When it comes to civil matters, you have no authority to interfere!"

Soril ignored the man, completely unconcerned.

Kaycia, on the other hand, *was* worried. What the hell was he doing?

"What is this, Soril?" asked the magistrate. "Handel's right. In the city, only a local judge can rule on these matters."

"I don't deny that. But you're forgetting one thing. As a member of my company, she falls under military law—not New Ahman's."

The magistrate sighed. "Don't do this, Soril. There's still time for you to release her. You might not want my advice, but you don't want to implicate your company in this, especially if her records aren't clean."

Kaycia wanted to agree, to beg Soril to worry about himself. She couldn't, however, bring herself to say anything. And she felt like a coward.

"You're right. I don't want your advice."

Handel, however, seemed to possess a personal vendetta against her. "We'll see how far this gets when I inform the Baron! Then *you'll* be in court!"

"Be my guest," said Soril. "He won't much care for your civic dispute when I have you arrested for interfering with the town's defense!"

"You'll what?!" shouted the clerk, perplexed by the reversal.

"You heard me. With the town in a state of emergency, preparing for tomorrow's attack, the Baron would love to hear how you deprived me of my most recent and most valuable asset."

Handel's eyes bulged, but, for once, he kept his mouth shut.

The magistrate sighed. "If you're certain of this decision, there are some legalities we must discuss. Would you be willing to come in and sign an affidavit on her behalf?"

"I don't see a problem with that."

"Just so you understand, the request for her records will still be submitted. Nothing can stop that. The only difference here is that we're entrusting Kaycia into your custody. In two weeks, in the event she's found guilty, you will be responsible for bringing her in."

"I understand."

"If, for any reason, she happens to escape or you are otherwise unable to deliver her to the court—*you* will be the one facing trial."

Once again, Kaycia felt Soril's eyes watching her. And, once again, she failed to meet them.

"These terms are agreeable."

"All right, then. Let's proceed to my office and get those papers signed."

Soril shook his head. "We're not finished."

The magistrate groaned and raised a brow.

"You've taken something that doesn't belong to you."

"Ah, yes." The magistrate turned to his fellow officer, who produced the bag of coins. Kaycia accepted it without a word.

"Lead the way."

As they took to the street again, Soril turned back to Kaycia. "I'm sure more pressing matters require your attention."

No doubt, he was referring to her sister. "You mean I can go?"

"It's only paperwork. We can manage without you."

At this, Kaycia was genuinely surprised. After everything he'd agreed to, she'd felt certain he'd want to keep a close eye on her. How else could he be sure she wouldn't make a run for it and leave him facing the law by himself?

Soril, however, was disinclined to believe she'd do such a thing—a belief, to her dismay, she didn't share. While she'd feel guilty if anything happened to his company, she couldn't sit back and let them take away her sister.

"I'll see you in the morning," he said before following the officers.

"Uh-huh..."

In utter bafflement, Kaycia watched them go—not knowing what she'd done to deserve such a powerful and foolish friend.

Chapter 11
THE CHILD GODDESS

The rest of the evening went as planned. The bath water was cold—and carried a peculiar, unfiltered odor—but it freed them from the grime of the past two weeks. And, once clean, they went out to sate their gnawing hunger.

However, what should've felt like a fresh start and a moment to relax, felt nothing of the sort.

If anything, Kaycia felt worse now than she had in the forest. This wasn't because the events of Graywood Pass weren't devastating—but back then, she'd been numb to many things. Her thoughts were so focused on making it out alive, she'd never really processed the grief she was feeling.

For several days, she'd felt like she was going through the motions. She tackled each problem, one by one, and developed a plan to get their life back on track. There hadn't been time or good reason to allow her heart to get in the way. It wasn't even hard to suppress her feelings because she saw the results.

Unfortunately, this changed the moment she was caught. Moreover, she had entangled other people in her mess.

While Soril wasn't entirely innocent—with his ignorance and pride, jumping to her rescue—she had no doubt it would've gone differently had she not lied from the start. If he'd known what was happening, he most certainly would've left her to her own devices.

For the entire night, she found it difficult to sleep.

Staring up at the ceiling, she cradled Elyriel's head in the crook of her arm.

Kaycia wanted to be angry with Soril—for lying on her behalf and providing his witness of her ascendancy. She'd never asked him to do that. He'd made everything worse, leaving the investigation with no room but to wonder *how* she'd managed to ascend. And once that was under scrutiny, there was nothing she, or even he, could do to save her.

But, of course, she couldn't be angry. She could act angry all she wanted, but, in the end, she couldn't deny he'd been trying to help. In some ways, he had helped—but only in granting her a scant two weeks. And those would disappear before she knew it.

It was becoming clear she shouldn't go as Elyriel into camp. It'd be a mistake to provide Soril—or anyone—with proof that could be used against her in court. At the same time, however, she wasn't yet willing to confess her fraud. Eventually, there'd come a time when she wouldn't have a choice, but a part of her wanted to hold that off.

As she listened to the cadence of her sister's breathing, her mind played through scenarios of their inevitable trial—dreading what might happen if their secret got out. But no matter how she phrased her story—making the two sisters blameless in Marien's crazy scheme—she couldn't imagine the judges being lenient.

The church couldn't allow such crimes to go unpunished. It wouldn't only encourage others to attempt the ritual themselves and cast doubt on the methods currently in use. People might start questioning the church, wondering if there were more effective ways to fight the current.

Elyriel was living proof ascendants *could* be stronger, which, by itself, presented a deeper issue. Could Kaycia bring herself to escape and go into hiding, when doing so would withhold this vital discovery from the people? How could she keep such information to herself, when choosing to stay might lead to reform—changes the world needed to survive the bitter night ahead?

By the time the sun rose, Kaycia had come no closer to reaching a decision.

As she dressed, she chose not to wear her leather armor. Instead, she adjusted the straps and fit the gear onto Elyriel's smaller frame.

"This stays on, you hear?" she said, lowering her head until her sister's eyes made contact. "That means no picking or pulling on the bindings. You leave it alone. It's important."

By the time she'd finished speaking, Elyriel's eyes were elsewhere. But rather than get frustrated, Kaycia was content that her sister hadn't argued. For the moment, at least, she wasn't making a fuss with the unfamiliar outfit.

The armor was only a precaution—not because Kaycia intended either to participate in the battle. Until she came up with a better plan, she'd rather avoid that risk while still being prepared for anything.

After finishing the breakfast brought to their room, she left Chesandril and her sister to themselves once again.

As she stepped out onto the street, the morning sky was overcast—a brilliant white that grew darker as it neared the horizon. If anything, this reaffirmed her desire to avoid combat—as nothing was more miserable than fighting in the rain.

The streets were far less crowded than the night before. She wanted to think this only due to the early hour, but she couldn't shake the sensation that an ominous blanket had fallen over town. It was as though everyone sensed what was coming and had made the unspoken agreement to stay inside for the day.

No one tried to speak with her, giving her time to think as she walked. She still didn't know what to tell Soril—her reasons why she'd be sitting this one out.

No matter what she said, he wouldn't be pleased. Even if she claimed her sister had fallen ill—he'd see it as an excuse. Considering the stakes, this would sour the beginning of their relationship and her career—but what else could she do? After everything he'd done for her, she, at least, owed him an explanation. Even if it was a lie.

"Pardon me...but you wouldn't be Kaycia, would you?"

She frowned, unnerved at being recognized by a stranger. Until that moment, as she passed outside the gate and stepped onto the northern road, she hadn't noticed he was there.

He was young, somewhat close to Kaycia's age—perhaps older by a year. His slick, black hair fell neatly around his ears, and his embroidered, black vest announced he was part of the upper class.

"Who's asking?"

"Sorry! Name's Agren. I was sent to come get you."

"You were?" While this was better than asking for directions, she couldn't dismiss her suspicions so easily. "Which company are you with?"

"Master Soril's, of course." The young man leaned sideways, scanning the road behind her. "Your sister's not coming, then?"

"No," she said, feeling her voice become hard. "So explain this to me. You've just been sitting here the past few hours—hoping I'd show up?"

Ordinarily, she might've been flattered by Soril's efforts to be accommodating, yet... It was also presumptuous, as she wasn't certain she'd come.

"Nah," said Agren with a dismissive wave. "I was sitting down to eat. I didn't come until I noticed you at the gate."

He said this casually, though she hadn't seen any food carts nearby. For the most part, the road was empty, with only two other men at the base of the hill, and the cloud of dust trailing them.

She could only assume he'd brought food, perhaps stuffed in a pocket.

"All the same," said Kaycia, shaking her head. "You've been waiting here—

"Nope," he said with a low chuckle. "Here, I'll show you."

When he stretched forth a hand, Kaycia stared at it. She didn't mean to be rude, but she had difficulty agreeing with his carefree attitude.

Unabashed, Agren waited two seconds before reaching up and taking her by the shoulder.

Her natural reaction was to flinch back, but before she could do so, she saw something.

In that split second, the world behind him changed. Rather than the open road, she caught a glimpse of the interior of a tent. To one side was a bedroll, unkempt from the night before. And, atop a large leather trunk, there was a loaf of bread and a few plump, sizzling sausages.

At the instant she broke contact, the portal disappeared.

"As I was saying," continued Agren, responding to her surprise triumphantly. "Breakfast! Doubt me now?"

Kaycia kept her awe in check and regarded the man more closely. Only one explanation made sense—one that had nothing to do with illusions or tricks of the light.

The tent had been real—as real as the dusty road beneath her boots. In much the same way, it existed in an actual location, uncharacterized by anything extraordinary. That location simply wasn't *here*.

If she had to guess, she'd place the tent near the heart of Soril's camp, a half mile distant. Which meant Agren had told the truth. He hadn't been waiting near the gate.

"You're a founder?" she asked.

Agren smiled. "Never met one before?"

"I have. It's just...you're so young." Which also explained why he wasn't yet deformed. Unlike other founders, he still possessed all his fingers. His body was still intact.

He raised a brow as though to remind her of her own age.

"You know what I mean. I was surprised Soril wanted...*me*. I didn't realize he had a type—that he was actively recruiting fresh blood."

"Oh, he's not. Trust me. You can't catch the commander's eye without earning it. For him, only your skill matters—not the number of battles you've faced. If anything, the other camps have it backward—who won't look at you until you've got ten years under your belt."

Kaycia made a face, not wanting to argue. Both sides had merit, and she would rather put her life in the hands of a seasoned veteran—someone like Tenlen. But she could hardly point this out without speaking against her inexperience.

"Shall we go?" he asked, offering his hand a second time.

Once again, she peered at him distrustfully—although, now, for different reasons.

"You're not taking me through your tent, are you?"

He hesitated. "I apologize... It's just what I'm used to, you know...? To be discreet?"

Kaycia knew what he meant. While some ascendants delighted in showing off, others were less prone to creating a spectacle. Agren could hardly avoid his men's attention by popping in and out of camp, seemingly from nowhere. And, so, to put them at ease, he'd restricted his movements to his personal space.

She raised an eyebrow. "Emerging from your quarters with a woman you barely met—does *that* match your definition of discreet?"

His smile became sheepish. "...I see your point."

She might've asked for another tent they could use, but he reached for her hand and pulled her behind him.

Before she could blink, there was smoke in her face. All around, she heard the crackle of cook fires, the clink of hammers, and the raucous conversations of infantrymen.

Only a few quieted down—the ones facing their direction. Their reactions, however, appeared positive—not at all put off by Agren's display but more interested in the person he'd brought along.

Kaycia was used to such looks. As a female, she'd been the minority at the garrison. This wasn't because of rules keeping women from the military, or because her gender lacked the courage, either. Rather, she suspected—and this was only her guess—it had more to do with the filth and vulgarity.

"Captain Agren!" came a shout.

"Yes?" he responded as a messenger ran toward them.

The boy was in his early teens, with scruffy hair and a single knife at his belt. Though his words were directed at the captain, his eyes lingered on Kaycia.

Agren snapped his fingers to regain the boy's attention. "Is Soril ready for us?"

"That's why I came," said the boy, shaking his head. "His meeting's running late. But since you're here, he thought you might show Miss Kaycia around camp. This is her, right?"

When she smiled at him, his eyes grew wide.

"That's right," she said, preparing to ask his name. But the boy dashed away as though behind on his errands. More likely, however, he was only shy.

"Don't mind him," said Agren. "That was Pots. One of Soril's trainees. Not very good around people, but he works hard."

"The commander trains them himself? Is that typical? I wouldn't think he'd have time between his other responsibilities."

"I had the same reaction. But Soril always makes time if something's important."

"It's just training, though. Anyone could do that."

"It's *people* he finds important... You'll see soon enough. He's set time aside for you, hasn't he?"

Kaycia didn't argue, though she preferred to believe her case was different. It made sense he'd make time for a fellow ascendant—but to think Soril *also* made time for everyone else? She couldn't tell if this was stupid or downright impressive.

Agren smiled. "Never short on energy—that commander of ours."

"That's a joke, right? Since he's a transfigurer?"

"Well...in Soril's case, it might be true. Come on, I'll show you around."

Without further warning, he took her hand and brought them to the northern edge of camp—near the watchtowers that, until a moment earlier, had appeared distant and tiny.

This was so disorienting; Kaycia might've asked him to slow it down, but she forced herself not to. She had to remind herself she was pretending to be an ascendant. Between her augmented vision and the light of the fires, it should be easy to turn around and see exactly how far they'd come. If she started acting lost, it'd only draw suspicion.

A little discomfort was, of course, to be expected. She pulled herself together and took in the vast field he wanted her to see.

The towers, spread out at even intervals, were much taller than she'd anticipated. The enormous timbers stretched up a good twenty feet, with ladders leading to a scaffold on top. Each platform was encompassed by a guard rail and was manned, at the moment, by only two archers. When it came time for battle, she expected that number to reach closer to eight, alongside a whole pile of munitions.

While this was all impressive, it wasn't nearly as remarkable as what lay below. The field had been completely cleared out. There wasn't a tree or bush to hide the enemies' approach for over three hundred feet.

Moreover, the field had been flooded—intentionally. Local irrigation had redirected a river to blanket acres upon acres of land. The result wasn't meant to be deep, leaving the field pockmarked with shallow pools.

"But how do you know they'll attack here?"

"We don't. That's where the other companies come in."

"I saw those camps—from a distance—and none of them have taken such extreme measures."

"They all have barricades—like those there." He pointed to a collection of spiked, wooden walls. They were only six feet high—which explained why she hadn't noticed them before. Each was fifteen feet long, with handholds along the back to allow for repositioning. A few larger ones were hitched behind horses in case they were needed more quickly.

These were tactics she was familiar with, and while slower than shield men, they provided more complete protection against invisible, flailing strikes.

"So...the only task for the other camps is to redirect the enemy?"

Agren nodded. "Only if the creatures attack elsewhere. There's a high probability it won't come to that. You'd understand what I mean if you'd seen the maps from prior battles."

"Hold on... Each time, they've attacked from the same place?"

"Oh, no. That's not what I meant. But there's been a pattern, you see. To most, it seems random—but Soril figured it out. Had he not presented such a compelling argument, I doubt the council would've approved such an undertaking."

Kaycia couldn't help but feel impressed. A muddy field, after all, was the perfect battleground against this kind of foe. It became less important for ascendants to mark each enemy, as everyone would see the approaching tracks. Most creatures would be riddled with arrows before any ascendants needed to get involved.

It was a good plan—although it came at a cost. She found it hard to imagine how many workers this would've taken—until she realized her mistake.

"The water from the river," she said. "*You* were the one who brought it here."

He smiled modestly.

This, of course, painted a different picture. As a founder, he'd only needed to connect the two locations—removing the distance between the river and this field. He would've only had to stand there while the river did the work, flowing out, as it were, through a portal in the air.

"How many ballistae?" she asked, observing the line beneath the towers. The war machines made an impressive sight, like oversized crossbows fifteen feet across. They were well suited for this application, each aimed toward the trees, waiting for the moment the first tracks appeared.

"Thirty-seven," he responded. It was not an estimate.

Most of the defenses appeared finished, with only a few men at work. Most of camp was back at their tents, sharpening weapons and conserving energy.

Of the groups still present, Kaycia saw one, a few towers away, receiving instructions from an austere woman. With her dark, curling hair and commanding appearance, she was undoubtedly an ascendant and, potentially, one of Kaycia's future peers.

"I'd watch yourself around her," said Agren. "That's Neranda."

"Okay...?"

He suppressed a chuckle. "For years, her relationship with Soril has been...shall we say...special? No one talks about it, but the two aren't good at pretending otherwise, you know?"

"That's got nothing to do with me."

"Oh, it wouldn't... Were it not for the way Soril's been talking about you."

She narrowed her eyes. "But I haven't done anything to—"

"Oh, no. Don't get me wrong. He hasn't insinuated anything. He's had only good things to share—which is precisely the problem."

"You mean she's jealous."

"In so many words...yeah."

"But that's stupid!"

"I agree. But my advice stands. Step lightly."

Kaycia shrugged, pretending indifference.

"Seen enough? There's one more thing Soril asked me to show you."

"Lead the way."

He did this, of course, by taking her hand.

They were suddenly in front of a large wooden carriage, unhitched from any animals. It was much larger than the wagons she was familiar with—over twice as large as Marien's. Considering the thickness of its walls, it must've weighed over a ton and would require a large team of horses to move anywhere. She could only assume this was done infrequently, as its size wasn't practical for travel.

While it wasn't new, the wood appeared recently varnished. This produced a shiny ochre finish and the lavish impression of vehicles reserved for the wealthy. Thick iron bars protected the windows. And, through those windows, she saw yellow linen drapes.

"What's this?" asked Kaycia.

Agren smiled. "Soril had it prepared...just in case."

"For me? But I never said I'd—"

"Relax. Nothing's been decided. You might consider this a gesture of good faith. An added incentive, if you will. By all means, you're free to walk away—no strings attached."

Kaycia nodded, feeling only somewhat relieved. She didn't like being pressured—or feeling guilty by the pains they'd gone through. If they'd asked her first, she might've spared them the trouble.

Still, she couldn't deny the effectiveness of the gesture. Though Soril had only seen her sister once, he knew she had special needs. And knowing how much the girl meant to Kaycia, he'd come up with a way to provide comfort and privacy—a place they could feel safe—not only from creatures but prying eyes.

Kaycia found herself tempted—wondering if maybe...just maybe...this might work. It offered exactly what she needed to make use of Elyriel's talents. She could privately switch places with her sister, put on the mask, and not worry about the body she'd be leaving behind.

Only then did she notice something else—a table set to one side. It would've seemed entirely out of place, were it not for the contents on display—all clearly meant for her.

Most were basic supplies—linen sheets, plush towels, combs, and knives. But these were all mere adornments to their exquisite centerpiece.

There, neatly coiled, were two hefty lengths of chain—not made from metal but glimmering bone. Each link had been carved from abyssal skeletons—stronger and heavier than steel, and far more expensive.

At the end of each chain was attached a two-edged blade, also made from bone, the length of her forearm. For a regular person, they'd be challenging to lift and impractical to wield. But in the hands of a convictor, nothing could be more durable. Or deadly.

"Go on," urged Agren. "Check their balance. I bet you'll find them to your liking."

"I... I couldn't," said Kaycia, feeling her heart accelerate.

"Don't worry. Even if you decide our camp's not for you, this is part of the experience. Feel free to test what you like."

"I understand, but... Right here? In the middle of camp?"

She said this, hoping to appeal to his modesty. Just as Agren was reluctant to show off, couldn't she act the same?

"I don't see a problem. If anything, the men would feel inspired by what you do—it'd help their confidence, you know?"

Kaycia traced a finger down the chain's length and nodded appreciatively.

She didn't, however, try to pick it up. At her slightest exertion, he'd know something was off.

"They look perfect," she said before redirecting the conversation. "Can I see inside?"

"Of course!" he said, without a hint of suspicion. "Please do."

Kaycia knew she was walking a fine line. It was a matter of time before she made a mistake or was backed into a corner. Her only reassurance was knowing, when that happened, it'd benefit her trial.

The man opened the door and waved her inside, only to be interrupted by a shout.

"Captain!" said Pots, the boy from before. "I thought you'd be here. The commander's ready."

"Ah... Well then." Turning to Kaycia, Agren said, "We'll continue this later."

He waved the boy toward the table. "If you wouldn't mind, could you get out a tarp? Feels like rain."

Pots nodded. "Yes, sir!"

Kaycia waved to the boy—and waited for her eyes to adjust as a dim tent appeared around her.

"Master Soril," said Agren, letting go of her shoulder.

The commander looked up from a stack of papers. "Ah, thank you, Captain."

With a nod, the young man stepped back and was gone.

"Hello...?" said Kaycia, uncomfortably. She wasn't used to moving around so quickly and wished she'd had time to prepare herself mentally.

"Glad you could make it."

She forced a smile, not wanting to reveal how close she'd been to choosing otherwise.

The tent's interior was spacious—not a room where Soril lived or slept—but a command tent with bookshelves, drafting tables, and thick fur rugs.

On the table at the center was a large, colorful map displaying New Ahman and the surrounding region. Thick lines had been drawn for rivers and roads, and stylized triangles in the place of mountains. Everything was drafted with a fine tip brush, with such care to detail, she wouldn't be surprised if it was all to scale.

Most curious, however, was the grid that divided the map into squares. She was accustomed to such lines and knew they helped with measuring distances. But these were...wrong. The grid wasn't straight in many areas but sloped inward, with progressively smaller squares.

She ignored this for now and didn't ask questions that'd make her look foolish.

Instead, she focused on the ancient dagger beside the map. It was engraved with aeilic runes as though its purpose were entirely ornamental.

"Go on," he encouraged. "Pick it up."

She frowned and took up the brass handle. Seeing it up close, she got a proper sense of the relic's age. And she realized she was holding a piece of history.

"Now, tell me," he said, "when you look down at this map, what do you feel?"

Only then did Kaycia realize her mistake. He wasn't asking her opinion but for something more profound. Something that could only be asked of a convictor. Not that she alter intent but *perceive* it.

She set the knife down as though she'd been burned. "What is this?" she asked. "Is this why you wanted me here?"

He held his expression in reserve. "Why? Did you feel something?"

She hadn't, of course, which was precisely the problem. "I... I didn't come here for a test."

The man grimaced. "That's not what this is. Please don't be upset."

Kaycia, however, was less than convinced. Nothing about this felt like an accident. Daggers, by their nature, were sinister objects. By gleaning their intent—by sensing the place they *wanted* to go—it became possible to thwart assassination attempts. Which, alone, was enough for Kaycia not to get involved.

Except...this relic wasn't sharp. And with so little to go on, she couldn't intuit what this was about. Any guess would reveal her deceit.

She took a deep breath and tried to smile. But she couldn't explain. Instead, she needed an excuse—a reason for keeping her ascendancy to herself.

"Is it me?" he pressed. "Or the dagger?"

"Stop," she said. "Just...stop. This is exactly the reason I didn't want to come. Because now, it feels like I owe you something—and I *do*, after your intervention last night..." An intervention, she didn't add, that she never asked for.

He nodded slowly as though trying to understand.

But Kaycia herself was floundering for sense. "Just...tell me what you're after. What you're *really* after. Because this doesn't look like a hunt for resources."

He blew out his breath. "This part, no... I just thought, since you were here, you might help with some answers."

She tried to calm down. "Answers about what?"

Soril placed his hands on the table and regarded the map. "It's probably nothing. But the thought keeps coming back to me. We dug up this blade over four months back. Only weeks before the attacks began."

Kaycia narrowed her brows. "You think there's a connection?"

He made another face. "I didn't at first. But then we found signs of someone searching our camp..." His eyes came up. "So, please, just tell me. Is this what he wants? Is it the real deal?"

"The real—?"

He cocked his head as though it were obvious. "For finding Ahman."

The pieces came together. By this, he wasn't referring to *New Ahman* but its namesake—the city of the gods that mysteriously disappeared. Which explained why the runes were so familiar.

At that moment, Kaycia *wanted* to help but felt utterly horrible because it wasn't possible. Not without Elyriel.

Soril searched her eyes, then took her hesitation as an answer in itself. "But you would've already known that," he concluded, his expression growing distant, "if the dagger was special."

She wanted to correct him and say he had it wrong, but she was more afraid of the questions that would follow.

"I'm sorry..." she said, hoping for a way to fix this. An excuse to bring her sister here. Or a way to borrow the dagger for a while.

Something told her, however, it was too late for that. "Does this mean you'll no longer need my assistance?"

He looked at her askance. "You so desperate to get away?"

Kaycia was surprised but even more embarrassed. "I... I thought—"

"I would just give up?"

She sighed in frustration.

"Look," he said, suppressing a laugh. "This isn't just about you. I've been wanting a convictor a while now. Finding this dagger wasn't an accident. When I locate more, you'll wish you were a part of this."

"I thought your duty was to protect the city."

"For the time being. It's not the reason I initially came."

She considered this a moment. "...You're serious? About Ahman, I mean? You think you can find it?"

His eyes locked with hers. "With your help."

Kaycia wasn't sure what to think. On the one hand, she found the prospect fascinating. And yet, she still had her doubts.

Soril was far from the first to take on this endeavor. For most people, the search had ended centuries ago. The region had been scoured from every direction—with each mile accounted for—and there wasn't a place to hide a city of such magnitude.

The commander worked his mouth. "What's your take on all this? What do *you* think happened?"

"To Ahman?"

He raised a brow in expectation.

If anything, Kaycia was grateful for the new direction—to talk about something without lying.

"It's all connected, isn't it?" she asked. "It was the same day the gods lost their minds. The same day they died. So that tells me the place was dependent on their existence."

"A common theory."

"But one you disagree with?"

Soril folded his arms. "Just think a moment. I mean, yes, they're dead, but their power isn't gone now, is it? Otherwise, how do you explain our ascendancy?"

"That's different," she insisted. "We're *people*. Our connection is more—how should I say—? More spiritual? A place, on the other hand—a city—doesn't have a life of its own. The same thing happens when a creator leaves. Any objects she's formed just up and vanish like they were never there."

"They disappear," he agreed, "but what of the space occupied? Is that destroyed as well?"

Kaycia frowned, unable to grasp the distinction. "The space...?"

"Exactly. If Ahman disappeared in the nature you describe, we should expect the landscape to remain unchanged. There should be a vast open field where the buildings once stood—somewhere near the places the old highways cut off—yet such a wasteland doesn't exist."

"Really...?" she asked, with a sense of wonder. She might've felt silly for overlooking the obvious, but she hadn't spent much time looking into Ahman.

"You've never seen the maps? From before, I mean?"

"Not enough to make a comparison."

Soril smirked. "They used to be bigger. And it's more than just scale. I'm not talking cartographic errors or even terrain changes made by the current. The land was *different* and doesn't add up."

Kaycia was confused.

He turned back to the map. "The distances have changed. Look here," he said, tracing a finger along the lines she'd noticed earlier. "These are based on the land's original shape. The grid used to be straight. It's *supposed* to be straight."

"But that...?" She came closer and squinted.

"We've measured and remeasured. It takes less time to travel across these," he said, pointing at the smaller squares, "than the others."

"That's the first I've heard of this."

"Most people are only concerned that they reach their destination. Whether they arrive one hour early—or one hour late—goes beneath their notice. There's worse things to worry about."

"All right. So the land's gone missing. That hardly proves the city's still there. It might be permanently gone—and the world's just...smaller."

"One possibility. But not enough for me. I have to keep looking because it *can't* be gone. Ahman's here. Somewhere."

She frowned. It was almost as though he'd abandoned logic for...hope?

Seeing her reaction, Soril turned away. "For me, this isn't just a mystery to unravel. It's more than the treasure or the artifacts we'd find."

Kaycia thought she understood. "You want an explanation. For what happened that day."

He shook his head. "I want a *solution*! To give our world another chance."

Kaycia was in no position to judge him, but she'd heard this line of reasoning before. "Wait... You don't mean...?"

When he didn't meet her gaze, she knew she was right.

This man, like many others, was pinning his hopes on a fairy tale. On the unsupported belief that Shaelis and Ashaira had begotten a daughter.

She exhaled softly, not knowing what to say. Having spoken with many believers in the past, she'd grown tired of the issue. Of the way she was expected to tiptoe around lest her arguments offend.

"Go on," said Soril. "I've heard it before. The lack of evidence. How no one's seen this child. That the gods, themselves, never mentioned her."

"I'd rather not," said Kaycia, hiding her discomfort.

He looked up, unafraid. "Don't worry. I have no intentions of changing your beliefs. Just as you shouldn't be worried about mine. But that's no reason to leave them unspoken. They're part of who we are. Too important to ignore."

To her surprise, she agreed with him—on this single point. If anything, she was impressed by his sincerity. The way he didn't back down from sensible conversation. It made her more likely to reciprocate his tolerance.

She licked her lips. "I understand the appeal—why people need something to believe. Some*one* to believe in. But when it comes to Irisea, it feels so...*naive*. Humanity has been hidden—overshadowed by the gods for far too long. Yes, they were real. And yes, they protected us—and provided us everything. But don't you see...? How they left us weak? Overly dependent?"

Rather than be put off, Soril seemed intrigued. "How so?"

"We're like children," she continued, "coddled into adulthood. With the gods always there, we never had the chance to stand on our own. And now... When we can finally take responsibility for our future... You're telling me we should give that up? We should stand back while this pretend goddess comes to our rescue?"

He took a deep breath. "You make a good point. But you err in presuming the gods were at fault. If man is weak, as you say, do we not share the blame?"

"Of course we do."

"Good. Because in my estimation, these points are not mutually exclusive. You're right in saying we need to do more. There are monsters that need killing. Cities that need rebuilding. While too many sit back and wait for others to do the work."

Kaycia nodded, glad he understood but sensing a rebuttal.

"Why not have it both ways?" he suggested. "So long as we're doing everything in our power, would it be so wrong to accept help? Why are you so adamant we fix the world ourselves?"

"Because the legend of Irisea is too much like false hope! It's the exact story you'd expect people to invent. They pretend the gods haven't abandoned them by conveniently claiming there's still one left? One, I might add, that came from *nowhere*?"

"So your primary concern is lack of proof?"

"It's not just me. I've discussed it with my instructors. You're the first intellectual type I've met who feels different."

"I'll take that as a compliment… But I'd invite you to take another look at your teachers. From Wern's hold, right? Considering their position, so close to the Taelish church, they'd hardly share their true beliefs with a student."

She shook her head, adamant. "They were all quite open. None were worried about hiding a thing."

"In my experience, those who *appear* to be hiding something are the ones who lack the skill to do it well. But enough about them. I want to know about *you*. Have you considered that your bias against Ashaira's child might, in truth, be against Ashaira herself?"

She shook her head again. "I've got nothing against her—for the same reason. If she betrayed anyone, there should be evidence."

"Ah… So we, at least, agree on something."

"But a child? After *millennia* of producing no offspring at all? You've read the accounts of how fast it happened! In less than a day, the gods' minds were destroyed. They were given no warning or chance to defend themselves. I know Ashaira was a goddess, but if you expect me to believe she endured a full pregnancy in a matter of hours—"

"I'm going to stop you right there. Precious few have had access to the original testimonies."

"Testimonies?" she asked, reminded of the reports her father had studied.

"That's right. From those who witnessed the pronouncement."

She grimaced again. "Those who *claimed* to witness the pronouncement."

Soril didn't argue.

The problem with the story was that it shouldn't have happened. The pronouncement of Irisea supposedly came from the city—*after* the place had already disappeared. After the gods were supposed to be dead.

No one could get inside, save for a few who claimed to be exceptions. A few Velthr, as they were called—those born without aspects. The rare breed never lived past infancy, and yet, a few pretended to have survived the apocalypse itself.

Soril wasn't bothered. "Have you read them?" he asked.

"They're forbidden," she said. "The church concluded that—"

"Is that what you want? For someone else to decide what you shouldn't believe?"

She fell silent a moment.

"Let me tell you," he continued. "No one wrote the child was *born*—only that she'd been conceived."

Kaycia shook her head incredulously. "A few hours later, Ashaira was *dead*! So what should I believe? Irisea was born to a corpse?"

"Not a corpse."

"You're not suggesting that—?"

"Let me finish. You mustn't forget Ashaira's body was immortal. Not alive. Not dead. But something in between."

Kaycia's eyes widened as fragments from her studies lent their support.

Early on, while it was bad enough the gods died, there'd been worse complications. In a few cases, the gods hadn't stayed dead. As their ascendants went insane—attacking innocent people with wild abandon—a few undead gods joined the fray.

The most notorious had been Meileen—the Goddess of Creation—who, despite being severed into multiple pieces, had inexplicably held herself together and gone on a rampage through the lands in the north. For some people, her refusal to die proved her divinity might be restored. But nothing worked. Just like the ascendants, her mind was gone.

Luckily, the problem was its own solution. Powerful though she was, Meileen lacked the intelligence to outthink the armies who brought her down. And, as the years went by, people had no choice but to redirect their attention toward the greater threat—the rise of the abyss.

"Okay..." said Kaycia, with some trepidation. "So her body lived on—trapped within the tombs of Ahman. Then what? Her baby's born with no one to care for it?"

"I wouldn't put it in quite those terms. But I neither claim to know the specifics."

"That was centuries ago! Even if Irisea didn't die immediately—what's to stop her mother from throttling the infant?"

"A valid concern, but I wouldn't be worried."

Kaycia shook her head in derision. "Why? Because of *faith*? How do you know Irisea would *want* to help us? That she's not deranged or beyond the point of being reasoned with? How do you know she won't wish us harm?"

She wanted to say more—realizing much of her frustration lay rooted in Telarien. His blistering visage was seared into her mind—his callous indifference as he destroyed Elyriel.

But she couldn't share this with Soril—not without revealing too much.

"All good questions," he said. "If anything, I'm glad to have provoked such a...heartfelt interest. Unfortunately, there's more to this discussion than we have time at the moment. Moreover, you don't strike me as a person whom mere words will persuade. Am I wrong?"

She shook her head.

"Good. Good," he said with a smile. "I'd be worried otherwise. It means you're honest and care about the truth. So here's the deal: I don't need to say anything. Because when I find Ahman—"

"*If* you find Ahman," she corrected.

"Either way. In the end, is this something you want to hear about later? Knowing you had the chance to be there yourself?"

Chapter 12
THE RAGING STORM

To her surprise, Kaycia found herself thinking it over.

It wasn't Irisea that held her attention but the kind of work the man suggested. Regardless of what they found, the operation would be small and, more importantly, private. One far removed from the eyes of the city.

Soril pushed ahead. "You've had time to see our camp and what we have to offer. Has it been enough, I wonder—or do you still need time?"

She smiled, both relieved and reluctant to get to the point. "I appreciate everything—the chain blades, the carriage—"

"I'm prepared to offer you five percent of our company's holdings. In addition, you'll have unlimited access to our resources, including smithies, culinarians, tailors—you name it."

Kaycia didn't grasp the extent of all this, but she got the impression five percent was quite generous—more than was typical for recruits. And yet, she was unable to make the leap.

Soril sensed this. "Why don't I stop talking? I want to hear what you have to say. What are *you* looking for?"

It was a good question, but one Kaycia wasn't prepared to answer. Although money was a necessity, it was far from her primary concern.

If she wanted to take his offer seriously, she supposed she needed Soril to trust her. To look the other way. To accept her 'as-is,' and *not* ask questions.

But how could she say this? Rather than deflect his suspicions, she'd only encourage them.

She supposed, however, there was no harm in asking. She'd do her best to lay it out, and if he didn't understand, she'd walk away.

Soril raised a hand. "Did you hear that?"

She tilted her head. With her unaided hearing, she didn't know what he meant—but that didn't stop her from pretending. "You should go," she said. "We can finish this later."

He studied her eyes, making her wonder if she'd made the wrong guess. But when he finally nodded, she was able to relax.

As he left the tent, she only partially followed. She stopped in the doorway, holding open the flap.

The sky had gone dark, and her heart leaped in her chest. How could it be so late? While their conversation had been lengthy, it couldn't account for the entire afternoon.

She forced herself to breathe and clear her mind. Only then did she notice it wasn't dark everywhere. South of the tents, she found patches of silver sky, bright as the noonday. As further clarification, rain began to pelt the canvas overhead.

The thunderheads were darker than the ones she was used to, but it still meant she had plenty of time. There was enough daylight to return to the inn long before the battle began.

Except something was wrong.

The fires popped and crackled uninterrupted, but she could no longer hear the scrape of whetstones or the sounds of work. Conversations died mid-sentence as the men looked up from whatever they were doing.

This wasn't in response to shouts of warning. There were no sounds of bells or horns blowing. Rather, the men, in almost perfect unison, reacted to more subtle signs.

Above the line of trees, a few birds appeared despite the inclement weather. They were followed by more until eventually, an entire flock took to the sky, filling the air with their raucous protests.

The trees, themselves, swayed ominously.

Above the chatter of birds, Kaycia heard the distant crack of branches. Even without augmented hearing, she detected a low, wooden shudder.

For a moment, she could do nothing but swallow in dread. Until now, everything had gone so smoothly; it hadn't occurred to her that she should've left sooner.

"Captains Tremol, Bravert, Yavin, Gemool!" shouted Soril. "Send your light infantry to the supply wagons. We need lanterns! As many as your men can carry!"

There was a cacophony of motion as soldiers rose to their feet.

Beneath the darkness of the current, Soril had no way of seeing the stormy sky—but he could hear the rain. He anticipated the fires dying out, making it difficult for his men to see clearly.

"Squads seven, eight, and fourteen—you know your positions. We need every tower manned, with your heavies on the ground. Has anyone seen Neranda?"

There came replies in the negative.

As her mind struggled to keep up, Kaycia just stood there. The fighting wasn't supposed to start for several hours. And though it was undoubtedly dark—the creatures couldn't know this. It wasn't as though they could see the daylight!

Men came and went as Soril barked orders. Amid the general confusion, no one looked in Kaycia's direction.

Using this to her advantage, she let the flap fall and slipped back inside. She held onto no illusions she'd be helpful in this fight. They all thought she could do things she couldn't, and it'd only get worse the longer she stayed.

There was a second exit on the opposite end, and she left the tent before anyone could see. Luckily, she met no guards outside and wasn't required to lie on the spot.

Without a moment's pause, she set a determined pace toward the nearest line of tents. More than anything, she needed to distance herself from Soril or anywhere he was likely to check. The ascendant hadn't forgotten her and would come looking. But while the lanterns might extend his vision, he couldn't see through walls. He also wouldn't have time to search everywhere.

Still, she forced herself not to run. Despite her mounting urgency, it'd be a mistake. It'd be a confession, to anyone who saw, she wasn't as fast as she was supposed to be.

But while she couldn't rely on the strength of an ascendant, she *could* project the confidence of one.

With a straight back, she took deliberate strides, wasting no effort to hide in the shadows or shield herself from rain. She made her gait appear effortless, with an expression entirely unconcerned for the cold or her safety. Her goal was to make herself look like she belonged and thus avoid needless suspicion.

For Kaycia, keeping a straight face was easy. What wasn't so easy was feeling good about her choices. Soril deserved an explanation, and she swore she'd give him one... just not right then. Not until things had the chance to die down.

She passed a dozen tents and was halfway out of camp before a voice stopped her.

"Your carriage is back that way."

Calmly, she turned to face Agren. Her face was slick from the worsening rain, and she peeled hair from her eyes.

She'd been afraid of this—knowing, of everyone here, it was Agren who presented the most significant threat. He couldn't just move anywhere, he could *see* anywhere.

That didn't mean he could find her instantly—he couldn't home in on her location without knowing where to look. But, once he set his mind to it, he covered ground more quickly than anyone else. He didn't need to cross distances or search behind walls. In the world where he lived, he could make those obstacles disappear as though they weren't there.

"I'm not going to the carriage," she said without avoiding his gaze. "I'll explain later."

As expected, his face tightened in confusion.

She hardened her tone. "There's no time right now! Did Soril send you? He ordered you to follow me?"

"Well, no, but—"

"Then you shouldn't be here! Please don't help me. Go help your men!"

By his face, he was struggling to make a decision.

"I'll go," he said. "You're right. But what of your blades?"

She shook her head.

"I can bring them to you! If you wait a moment—"

"I'll come back when I need them! Could you listen?!"

His face contorted, unable to grasp her reasons. But he heard the urgency plain in her voice.

At last, he nodded.

"Go!" she insisted.

And then he was gone.

She suppressed a shiver, rain dripping from her hair. It'd gotten through most of her clothing, and, turning back around, she walked faster to regain lost heat.

Kaycia knew she'd been lucky. Most men weren't inclined to be pushed by a woman, but Agren was still young. He was more worried about himself and what others thought of him. She hadn't given him the chance to look at her more closely.

Though her gambit might've worked, she changed her trajectory. With no way of knowing if Agren would come back, she couldn't afford to be predictable.

She descended the western slope, where the terrain would hide her movements. The rain served to her advantage, progressing to a downpour and making her difficult to recognize. With all the men moving north, she hardly saw anyone this side of camp. As she passed the final tent, she took a final glance back before breaking into a run.

The sky rumbled with thunder.

A hundred yards short of reaching the city gate, her boots slid out from under her, sending her skidding down the hill. In desperation, she reached out with her hands, but the path was too slick and coated her palms with black mud.

She slid to a stop and wiped them clean on her leg, before removing the hair that clung to her face.

Only then did she see the approaching void, deflecting raindrops in an outward spray.

Everything grew quiet as if the storm itself were holding its breath.

Kaycia rose to her feet and drew her knives.

She didn't understand how this beast was here. Soril had posted lookouts for this express purpose, so it seemed doubtful it'd stolen through his base. More likely, it'd slipped past another camp, away from the danger zone. In those areas, they'd be standing guard but saving their full strength for later in the day.

By the size of the dripping outline, it appeared to be a grimwolf, leaving tracks in the mud similar to a dog's—albeit with abnormally long claws.

She supposed she should count herself lucky as the rain stripped the creature of its greatest advantage. She was given a constant view of the beast's position, which helped balance the confrontation.

Until she realized it wasn't alone.

The watery, translucent shapes spread to surround her. She counted four...no...five of them! And, with bitterness, she realized she didn't stand a chance.

Damn it! she wanted to cry out—knowing she had no one to blame but herself.

She became determined, though, to kill at least one before she died.

A bellowing yell shook the sky as a glowing blur arced downward.

Soril crashed into the ground, his sword sundering through beast and earth alike. Curtains of mud sprayed to both sides. The impact was so powerful that it sent an outward concussion through the rain itself, pushing the drops away from his landing.

His flight wasn't high—more a jump through the air—as he couldn't alter gravity as Tenlen had. Rather, transfigurers manipulated energy itself—both thermal and kinetic.

Raindrops hissed into steam, as they pelted the glowing blade—so blistering hot, Kaycia felt the warm wind from fifteen feet away.

Almost immediately, the surrounding shapes closed in, attempting to overwhelm him.

With surprising grace, Soril ducked to the side. The tip of his blade curved behind him, slicing up through the wolf before it landed.

Though Soril needed no support, he was joined by a dozen soldiers. They emerged from the rain, spread out in a circle, and watched as their commander did what he did best.

One by one, he felled each attacker, dropping them to the mud in hazy piles of steam.

When her hearing had mostly returned, he said, "I insist. This one's yours."

Her heart hammered, realizing he hadn't killed them all but had left one standing.

The creature, undeterred, made a leap for Soril, which he easily deflected with the flat of his blade. It was sent flying back to thrash in the mud.

Kaycia shook her head, unable to find the words. The man had eyes, didn't he? Certainly, he saw the problem—did she need to spell it out?

"What's wrong?" he asked.

When she looked into his eyes, she wasn't met with confusion but something more akin to betrayal. He seemed an entirely different person—not at all like the man from inside the command tent.

It'd only taken one glance, and he'd figured it out.

Nevertheless, he awaited her response. He wanted her to speak out loud and confess her guilt. And, this time, she was trapped, with nowhere to go.

The grimwolf got up, only to dart away from Soril's brandished weapon. Encompassed on all sides, it turned its attention to Kaycia. It singled her out as the weakest link and its best chance for escape.

Kaycia readied her knives, wilting beneath the glares of the men surrounding her.

"I'm not who you think I am!" she said, her eyes locked on the approaching shape.

"What was that?" asked Soril. "Must be the rain. I couldn't hear."

This, of course, was utter bullshit.

Without warning, the creature pounced. It was all Kaycia could do to dodge sideways.

She wasn't fast enough. Something slammed against her shoulder. She brought her other hand around, slicing with her blade—but her attack went wild.

The creature followed her direction.

Kaycia slashed again in a desperate lunge, only to have her foot slide out and send her crashing into the mud.

It was her final mistake, but she suppressed the need to scream—unwilling to provide Soril the satisfaction.

A moment later, the creature was dead—impaled by a glowing sword as the man closed the distance and drove it to the ground.

The mud popped and hissed, heated to a boil.

Kaycia backed away from the oppressive heat, crawling with her hands in the mud.

"I'm a liar and a fake! Is that what you want? Like the magistrate said—I'm n— not..." Her voice cracked, and she found it difficult to breathe. "Just leave...! J—just... Go back!"

For a moment, he stood there, silent as a statue.

The rain concealed the tears on her face, but she looked downward so he wouldn't see the grief written there.

"A liar..." he repeated. "A spy, as well?"

She looked up in surprise—remembering the intruder. He couldn't possibly think it was her, could he?

"Take her away," he declared. "Keep her safe till I return."

"Wait, what?!"

She nearly told him why she needed to get away—that her *sister* could help. But she suppressed the urge to explain. No matter the vindication it might bring.

A man came forward. "Come on, then. Off we go."

She offered no resistance as she was dragged to her feet.

Soril was already gone in his haste to join the actual battle.

"Damn it!" she cried, not caring if the ascendant heard. Nothing she said would bring him back. And nothing she did would make these men disobey orders.

Her fate was sealed—and for what? For believing she had time before the battle began? It was clear, now, she should've stuck to her gut. She should've avoided the invitation and gotten away.

As the men dragged her through the camp, she didn't struggle. Not only would it be pointless—strangely, she felt she owed these men something. It was because of her, after all, they were stuck on guard duty, instead of taking their rightful place in battle.

Kaycia would rather save her anger for Soril and his suspicious nature. She wanted to blame him for everything—for preventing her return to the city—except...damn it! If he hadn't come, she'd be dead, now, wouldn't she?

She found this frustrating as hell. It was her own damn fault she'd run into the rain. In her desperation to keep her lies under wraps, she hadn't been thinking straight, and it'd nearly cost her her life. So no—no matter how much she wanted to cast Soril as the villain—she couldn't do it. She could lie to everyone but not to herself.

"Well, well..." said a woman, causing her to look up.

To her surprise, it was Neranda, the lady ascendant she'd seen near the towers. A man was with her—perhaps, a steward.

Kaycia knew next to nothing of this woman—only Agren's mention that she and Soril were close. None of this explained why Neranda was here rather than on the battlefield.

"Aren't you the pretty one—? Soaked to the skin and painted with mud."

Kaycia resisted the urge to look down. She clenched her jaw and met the woman's gaze.

Neranda appeared in her late twenties. However, as ascendants tended to age more slowly, this wasn't easy to ascertain reliably. She was wearing a cloak of dark red leather, keeping her face dry and mostly hidden beneath her hood. The little Kaycia could see were freckled cheekbones framed by lavish, brown curls—and an expression as smooth as it was austere.

One of the soldiers unlocked a door.

Only then did Kaycia realize where they were. It was one of the few areas she recognized—the carriage meant to be hers. Earlier, she'd been delighted by the thickness of its walls, thinking only of privacy. It hadn't occurred to her that they also made the perfect cell.

"Was it worth it?" asked the woman.

When Kaycia didn't answer, she made the question more specific. "I mean, you had him thoroughly convinced—not only of your ascendancy but that you were someone special."

"I don't need to explain myself to you."

Neranda smirked. "You'd best come up with something. Because the judges aren't going to wait two weeks. After tonight and these witnesses? You'd be lucky to get two days."

The steward looked confused. "I thought you wanted to question her now."

"So I did," said the woman. "But why waste time?"

He hissed beneath his breath. "What of the intruder?"

His words were an echo of Soril's—the outrageous suggestion that it might be her.

Neranda worked her mouth. "Don't be ridiculous…"

She stepped closer to Kaycia—uncomfortably close. "It couldn't have been you. During our last engagement?"

The man was insistent. "Soril named her a liar."

Neranda rounded on him. "Is that worse than a craven? You only wish it was her to put your fears to rest."

Her gaze returned to Kaycia. "But what would she gain, telling us of her ascendancy, before pretending otherwise…? No. I can see it in her eyes. She couldn't harm a soul. Much less a full contingent of men."

Kaycia swallowed. No one had mentioned the intruder killing anyone. "I don't know what you're talking about."

The woman studied her a moment, then forced a smile. "Of course you don't."

Kaycia merely frowned. While the jibe was meant to be offensive, it was nothing of the sort. If anything, it left her feeling relieved.

When it all came down to it, she wanted everyone to think her a fraud.

No, she hadn't wanted it to come out like this—and she would've given anything to avoid that look on Soril's face—but this worked in her favor.

She could handle humiliation. She could sit there while people branded her a liar.

So long as Elyriel stayed out of the picture, Kaycia could bear it all.

She'd make it through this—the jeers, the trial, the sentencing. When it was over, she'd leave with her sister. They'd go somewhere safe and avoid repeating these mistakes.

Without a word, Kaycia stepped into the carriage.

For the first time, she saw the details of Soril's generosity. The inside was clean, with polished wooden furniture. All of it—the cabinets, the tables, and the plush, cushioned couch—were affixed to the walls so as not to shift when the carriage was moved. On her right was a door to a closed-off area. The bedroom, she supposed.

Strangely, Kaycia didn't want to go further in. She couldn't stand the thought of tracking mud onto the carpets, even knowing they were no longer hers.

Hearing the door latch, Kaycia turned and looked out the window.

Through the glass, she heard the steward still arguing with Neranda. "We're just going to leave?"

Even with the woman's face turned away, Kaycia sensed an eye roll.

"It could be anyone!" he continued. "The intruder left no witnesses."

Neranda cocked her head. "You keep calling it that—why? To maintain this pretense we're searching for a human...? Let's go. We need to keep moving."

Kaycia found this curious and a little frightening. She couldn't help but be reminded of her initial impression—that the abyssal lords were behind these attacks. Some greater intelligence and darker purpose.

This was so intriguing that despite her imprisonment, she was tempted to ask details. To find out what else this stranger might've done. Whether he'd made off with anything or searched specific areas.

Instead, she crumpled down, with her back against the door.

All of these were things she could find out later, after the battle ended and her problems were resolved.

She considered, for a moment, reaching for her sister. With no one else inside the carriage, leaving for a minute or two should be safe—enough to tell Chesandril of the mess she'd made.

But she couldn't do it. She didn't have the strength to share more bad news. For now, her only plan was to wait this out. And hope her luck turned over soon.

When she emerged from her thoughts several minutes later, she was unnerved by how quiet the carriage had become.

It was almost as though the battle had ended—without a single survivor screaming in agony. But that was impossible. Though she couldn't determine how much time had passed, it couldn't have been longer than a quarter-hour.

With measured care, she peeked above the window sill.

The soldiers were gone.

Well—no—she found their shadows off to one side. But they were outside of view, even when she leaned as far as she could.

Their erratic movement suggested a fight or a momentary panic. And when she tested her voice...it was deadened and mute.

Any qualms she might've previously held against her prison were gone instantly. And she fervently hoped these men were good at their job.

Unfortunately, this wasn't the first attack to come out of nowhere. For the creatures to have made it this far into camp—or to have met her on the road only moments before—it suggested a massive hole in their defenses.

A soldier crashed into the mud ten feet from her window.

She covered her mouth, thinking he was dead—but he rose onto his hands and started crawling away.

Two armored men came to his defense, one on either side, swords raised. They were the same she'd seen guarding her door, and she had no desire to watch them die.

But, try as she might, she couldn't look away. Though her sense of preservation was screaming at her to hide—to duck down before the creatures saw her—she couldn't bring herself to move.

A clear set of tracks approached in the mud, circling the men. To her surprise, however, the creature froze. It turned to the side as an enormous spike skewered it in place.

Kaycia blinked, not knowing what she'd seen. No one would be crazy enough to fire a ballista into camp, and this spike appeared nothing like a bolt or javelin. It hadn't dropped from the sky at all.

It'd erupted from the ground at a low diagonal, straight through its target. It was easily over ten feet long and fashioned of dark brown stone.

As quickly as it appeared, the spike vanished.

The creature flopped onto the mud, spreading water away from a shallow crater. It thrashed a moment and then went still.

Kaycia saw it clearly—the indentation where the body lay, preventing the puddle from filling in.

As if in confirmation, some sound returned.

"Sir Ascendant!" shouted a soldier, lowering his sword.

Kaycia turned as a figure stepped into view. But the ascendant was one she couldn't possibly identify. In fact, with such overwhelming power, she was sure this ascendant shouldn't exist.

His black cloak did nothing to lighten the mystery. His hood was raised, overshadowing his face. And though he was smaller than the muscular soldiers, nothing was lost from his air of intimidation.

"We're in your debt, Lord sir! If you hadn't arrived—"

Kaycia didn't share the man's enthusiasm. Her mind was still racing to understand what she'd seen. The appearance of the spike was suggestive of Creation, except... The creators she knew were always slow in their formations, requiring minutes to fashion a shield or a small stepping stone.

That spike had been fast enough to penetrate armor.

The soldier licked his lips and tried to hide his discomfort. "I apologize, Lord Ascendant, for not knowing your name. We weren't told reinforcements would arrive."

At that moment, however, Neranda returned. "Because there are no reinforcements. You, sir! Name yourself!"

The stranger cocked his head as though taking her measure.

Neranda worked her mouth in consternation, but she refused to be cowed. "You've entered the camp of Master Soril! By law, you must answer and defer to our command!"

The soldiers exchanged nervous glances and gripped their swords.

The woman raised her chin. "Are you disfigured, Lord Sir? With an ailment that impedes your speech? If so, a hand signal will suffice."

Kaycia, too, had been wondering this. When it came to ascendancy, one could never keep track of the varied side effects.

When he raised a hand, however, he didn't motion to himself but to the space where the creature had recently fallen.

The space...slowly refilling with water.

Kaycia searched for new tracks, but there weren't any. She could only imagine it standing there, rising from the mud.

Neranda turned toward it and spread her feet. With a sideways glance, she gave the stranger a nod, to adjourn their discussion.

Once again, the man's attack seemed to come from nowhere. An enormous pillar materialized from the mud, pushing out with the force of a galloping horse.

...But not at the monster.

It drove Neranda against a stack of crates, splinters twirling, as she spasmed and went still.

Chapter 13
INTRUDER

Kaycia stifled a gasp and ducked even lower.

The soldiers gaped in soundless cries. One man turned his sword on the stranger, only to buckle as the tracks pounced from behind.

To her surprise, the creature's aggression didn't stop with him. It lunged at the intruder, unaware the two shared a common foe.

The cloaked figure held his ground without so much as a backstep. His spikes shot from the mud with almost surgical precision, disappearing again before Kaycia could blink.

The tracks skidded backward and dove to the side but failed to evade the following strikes. Even so, the creature fared better than the men, who never saw the stones barrage their backs.

In a scant few seconds, the contest was over.

The tracks fled into the darkness—only alive because the intruder wished it so.

Kaycia could only suspect that this man—if he was a man at all—wasn't just here to take advantage of the attack. After seeing how easily he'd toyed with the enemy, he was just as likely to have *caused* the attack.

Or was that too much? She tried to see it in her mind—him wandering the forest and inciting the creatures into a wild rage. Certainly, that was more than a lone person could handle.

If he was even a person...

Either way, she didn't have many options. It wasn't as though she could call for help. Or sneak away to send a message. She was locked in a cage and cut off from her ascendancy.

If she could stay hidden and alive, she'd have more to offer than these fallen men. Her accounting of events would make her useful—even indispensable—when Soril decided what to do next.

By then, however, the cloaked figure would've finished what he came for. He'd escape into the forest without any hope of reversing the deed.

Kaycia groaned, more determined than ever to stay put. This *wasn't* her fight. It was all she could do to keep her fears at bay. To convince herself he was just a man. Not an abyssal lord with actions harboring sinister intent.

She was powerless, however, to still her heart. To ignore that this carriage didn't guarantee safety. And the possibility her involvement might, once again, put her back into Soril's good graces.

In frustration, she went to the couch. No longer caring about the mud, she laid down and tried to get comfortable.

She took a deep breath...and the world shifted.

In the next instant, the carriage was ripped out from under her. She was no longer on her back but crouched low to the ground and...soaking wet?

In panic, she realized this wasn't their inn room. Kaycia didn't recognize this place at all. Somehow, her sister was outside, and—!

And there was blood in her mouth.

Kaycia spat in revulsion. She didn't know what this was, but it was happening at the worst possible time!

There was blood on her cheeks and running down her fingers—and there was something else besides. Something dark and coarse, and...! Were those knots of hair?

"Oh gods...!" she choked, stumbling backward. She spat in earnest, wanting nothing more than to be rid of the dead cat—a mangy thing with clumps of sodden fur.

This was an alleyway, she realized. There were discarded old crates and—thank the gods—no people to see what Elyriel had done.

She turned, searching for anything she might recognize, when an idea occurred to her.

Taking a deep breath, she focused on the grit sliding around her teeth and used Elyriel's conviction to give it purpose—to get the hell away from her! When she spat again, the bilge was forcibly expelled through her lips.

And yet, for some reason, the coppery taste didn't leave. She was positive it'd worked—that she'd rid herself of every last drop—but her mind refused to be cleansed so easily.

Kaycia rose, wanting nothing more than to worry about this later. She was keenly aware that time was short. And her recklessness would mean nothing if the stranger got away.

"Oh!" came a voice, splashing toward her. "Don't you dare rush off again! You hear me, Elle? You've any idea what you put me through?"

Kaycia turned to Chesandril. "How the hell did this happen?!"

The girl jerked back in surprise. "Kay?!" Her expression, however, wasn't one of relief. If anything, her fear had gotten worse.

"Bloody heavens!" she squeaked. "I'm so sorry! I had no idea she'd...! I was talking to her like you said, but...there were scratches at the window. I tried to stop her!"

"Where are we? I need my knives. I need them now!"

"Oh!" said the girl, struggling to keep up. "Ohhh... There! Over there!"

A window was broken, low against the wall. The ugly shards made it clear why Chesandril had come out a different way.

Having lost too much time, Kaycia dove headfirst through the opening. She twisted enough not to get cut, before tucking her head and rolling onto the wooden floor.

Her roped weapon was pitiful when compared to Soril's elegant chains. For now, however, it was better than nothing. Taking hold of the end, she whipped it into the air. It filled the surrounding space, uncoiling, then recoiling around her body and shoulders in an orderly fashion.

Only then did she notice other changes to the room. There were more nicks than she remembered. The flimsy wardrobe lay in fragments on the floor. The beds were untidy but still in one piece.

All of this confirmed how stupid she'd been. She'd been away for so long, these damages were as much her fault, as Elyriel's or Chesandril's.

Her armor, at least, remained undisturbed. And once she donned the ornate metal mask, the ensemble was complete.

Returning to the window, she heard voices outside.

"You there! Stop!" It was a man. Possibly, the innkeeper.

"I already told you," implored Chesandril, "We had nothing to do with that!"

"Do you think me daft? You're going to pay for—!" His voice died away, before coming back, full of anguish. "Bloody hell...! Puddles?"

So the cat had a name.

"*What did you do*?!" he bellowed. "You're...! What kind of sick—?!"

Through the window, Kaycia glimpsed the girl's feet. In her haste to back away, she'd led the man straight to their room.

Except, in the next moment, it became clear why. In a low voice, she muttered, "I'll keep him distracted."

She disappeared around a corner, and Kaycia could only hope the girl knew what she was doing.

"Damn it!" The man groaned loudly, reluctant to give chase but making the attempt anyway. He wasn't very fast and was soon breathing heavily, but his footfalls communicated a sense of resolve.

Ten seconds later, Kaycia leaped outside and rolled soundlessly across the pavement. Making sure no one was watching, she jumped into the night, using the walls to gain height.

The darkness of the current made it difficult to see, even with street lamps in every direction. The dim specks were so smothered they didn't illuminate the rain-slick rooftops. She only caught a glimpse of obstacles before ducking, sliding, or changing course.

It was even more dangerous at the end of each roof when she'd jump without seeing the opposite side. She'd meet resistance as the wind tried to sweep her off course, but none of these hurdles were a match for her will to reach the camp on time.

When the lamps in her periphery came to a stop, it was her only indication she'd reached the city's edge. With all her strength, she threw herself skyward. She never caught sight of the wall itself.

As she pierced the freezing gale, leaving the lights behind, she soared through total dark. Raindrops streaked past toward a ground that no longer seemed to exist.

Kaycia felt confident, however, she was going the right way. Though she'd never made the trip in person due to Agren's shortcut, she'd only lost her sense of distance, not direction.

She curved around a tree, rolled her landing, and frantically devised a plan.

More than anything, she needed to avoid getting caught—not just by Soril's men but by the cloaked trespasser. Her mask didn't offer any natural protection. And she wasn't about to start a fight she couldn't win.

But, perhaps, there were other ways she could stop him.

As she reached the tents, she convinced the mud to hold shape and leave no tracks. She made the air go still so no one heard her passing.

Her Conviction did everything but make her invisible, and for that, it wasn't long before she had to slow down. She stopped frequently to ensure no one was watching. But luckily, most of the men had gone north to the towers.

To her relief, the camp was much as she remembered. The sounds of battle could be heard in the distance, but there were no alarms. No indication of patrols scouring for criminals.

More importantly, there weren't any creatures nearby. The one at the carriage must've been an exception, deliberately meant to distract Neranda. To negate the largest threat to the stranger's movements.

This lull, however, wasn't bound to last.

Kaycia reached the carriage and immediately hid from the sounds of approach. The men were still distant but headed this direction. Where they'd see the bodies and call for reinforcements.

She stifled a curse, wanting to blame the innkeeper for her late arrival.

Instead, she observed what she could of the scene—the turned-up mud and shattered crates.

Neranda was laid out like a ragged doll—but Kaycia thought she could see her breathing. It was hard to be sure from so great a distance, but her chest seemed to rise at slow, uneven intervals.

Perhaps it was good the men were close.

Kaycia's eyes were drawn to the nearby table. Underneath the tarp, the weapons seemed to beckon her closer. Inviting her to take them before time ran out.

With those chains, she'd be unstoppable. Not only against the abyss, she might stand a chance against this unknown threat.

At the same time, her secret would be out.

Elyriel was too young for such power, and if anyone saw her—with the mask or not—she'd be forced to run. Even worse, they'd think she was the intruder all along.

Kaycia took a deep breath and left the weapons where they were. At least, this way, she could pretend to be normal.

"Is that...?" asked a man. "Sound the alarm!"

The sounds of running came sooner than expected.

But Kaycia had already found what she came for. Having seen the fight in person, she knew which tracks she needed, and followed them away before anyone noticed.

To her bitter consternation, they followed no pattern. They went in and out of unimportant tents. It was almost as though he didn't know where he was going. An outsider, in truth.

To make things worse, the horns began to blow, calling Soril's sensitive ears back from the field. A warning that'd spur the intruder to hurry.

Kaycia chose to take a risk. Instead of following the tracks and falling behind, she followed her instincts.

She'd confirmed he was searching for something, so she crossed the distance to Soril's tent. Even if the ancient dagger wasn't his target, it was a likely place for other valuables.

Unfortunately, she wasn't alone in this assumption.

A dozen guards had been posted at each entrance—more men than she'd seen in the past five minutes. They were unnerved by the blaring horns, but there were no dead bodies or signs the stranger had come this way.

It was good reason for Kaycia to leave, but she stuck to her gut.

Though the intruder could've easily destroyed these guards, it was in his best interest for the horns to blow elsewhere—while he took the effort to slip inside unnoticed.

Seconds passed as she debated what to do. With so little time, it might be best to withdraw. He might be anywhere. And the risks kept compounding, more than she'd anticipated.

Even if he was here, what then? In such a small space, she'd find it difficult to hide. And she didn't have a plan if she ran straight into him.

At that moment, however, her unerring eyes spotted movement behind the tent, sneaking away.

And against her better judgment, she increased her pace.

It was incredibly stupid. Her sense of preservation was screaming for her to stop.

But there was something about this stranger that didn't feel right. That lacked the malevolence she'd expect of an abyssal lord. It'd bothered her since learning Neranda was alive.

That had clearly been intentional, as spikes would've offered a much cleaner kill. Instead, he'd knowingly left her to recover.

It was enough to dilute most of Kaycia's concerns—though not enough to drop her stealth.

She kept to the shadows and followed from a distance.

No longer did the stranger wander aimlessly. He'd procured his objective and was using the tents to obscure his retreat.

Kaycia followed the same tents from the opposite side. She kept good pace and didn't make noise.

As far as she could tell, she didn't make a mistake.

Were it not for her conviction hiding her tracks, she might not have sensed when the mud was disturbed.

Her reflexes twisted her away from the pillar. Mud spattered the tents as the earth heaved again with a second attack.

She ducked and weaved—not perfectly, but enough to avoid more than glancing blows. She controlled her sliding and willed herself not to lose footing.

After nearly a dozen strikes, she saw the stranger. He'd stopped momentarily as though unaccustomed to missing his target.

For the briefest of seconds, they stared at each other.

The dagger was tucked into his belt, but she also saw details her natural eyes had missed.

She saw beneath his hood, where his head was bound in cloth. It covered everything except his eyes.

Deep, throbbing eyes. Lined with the same white scales she saw on his hands. For anyone else, he would've seemed like a monster. Kaycia, however, was used to such deformities.

"You're human..." she breathed.

The man faltered but turned away his hood, hiding his face.

Some of Kaycia's teachers had been warped and twisted like Tenlen. Others bore scars on their hands, like Soril. Some were blind. Others leprous.

And some...had bodies slowly turning to stone.

It was the mark of creation. Evidence of corruption introduced to the body, to mirror what creators introduced to the world.

The scales were usually small—sometimes unnoticeable—but this man wasn't like any creator she'd known. He was an aberration from the norm, exhibiting more power than was allegedly possible.

Which, in a sense, was not so different from Elyriel.

For a moment, Kaycia was unable to speak as she finally understood all her reckless decisions. Why she'd abandoned caution and thrown herself into this daring pursuit.

She'd seen his power and wasn't just amazed, she'd felt a sort of kinship. Not one of aspect but of sheer circumstance. The need to discover how he'd gotten this way and to further her understanding of Elyriel.

Without thinking, she made another stupid choice.

"Look!" she insisted, removing her mask. "I'm not with the others!"

She'd barely gotten out the words before she blushed in embarrassment. Elyriel's deformities, after all, couldn't yet be seen on the surface. And this stranger wasn't likely to get a sense of her mind.

He paused, however, seeing her youth. Unable to forget how she'd dodged his attacks.

She awaited a response—only to be interrupted by a nearby patrol.

"You there! Stop!"

Kaycia tried to run, but her leg was stuck.

She pulled harder, but it wasn't just an obstacle. A stone coil had wrapped around her boot, with roots extending deep into the ground.

"Damn it!" she hissed.

The stranger, however, had already slipped away.

She scanned the route to the forest but couldn't spot his tracks. Perhaps he'd made his shoes a different shape?

By then, however, there was nothing she could do. Near a dozen men formed a circle, and she couldn't escape.

"Did you see him?" she asked out of desperation. "A man, all in black?"

They hadn't, as none attempted pursuit.

"Name yourself!" demanded the lieutenant in charge.

"I can explain," she said, "but *he's* the one you want. He was headed for the forest!"

The men shared a look of doubt.

To her relief, one shrugged. "I can check it out."

Taking two others with him, he broke into a jog. A casual jog, showing that he wasn't quite convinced.

She looked down at her leg, but the coil was gone. Instead, there was nothing but a hole in the ground. Strange, yes, but nothing she could point to as actual evidence.

The lieutenant shook his head in dismay. "If they're walking into a trap, I swear to the gods..." He suddenly frowned and narrowed his gaze. "I remember you... You're that girl's sister."

To Kaycia's horror, the man was right. It was the lieutenant they'd met on the road to New Ahman. Who'd reacted to her ascendancy with open disdain.

He laughed and turned to the man beside him. "Get a load of this? Older sis gets caught, and the young one has the mind to finish the job?"

She bit her lip, suppressing a scream.

This man was nothing! She could break him like a twig before he took another breath! She could string up his feet from the nearest tent post!

But who was she kidding? A forced escape would only make things worse. She hadn't only been seen without her mask, she'd been identified. She'd become implicated in a theft she didn't commit. Did she need to give proof of her ascendancy as well?

Bloody heavens! She loathed the idea of submitting to these men. Of being trapped in a corner while the stranger walked free. But what else was she to do? She couldn't just kill them...

For a moment, her breath caught in her throat.

She regarded the sneer on the dirty man's face. The accumulated stains underneath his armpits.

This man was nothing. Worse than nothing. If he died on duty, confronting a rogue ascendant, he'd receive more honors than he'd earned in life. He might even be remembered with fondness.

She didn't know these others, but she knew their type. They took delight in her discomfort. And eyed her up and down as though intending much worse.

The lieutenant mistook her hesitation for fear.

"That's right," he said. "You're in deep shit now. Not just for trespassing but obstructing a military engagement. At a most *critical* moment of New Ahman's defense. You know what that means, don't you? We're not talking a few days lockup. But a full-blown conviction. You and your sister."

Kaycia clenched her jaw and resisted the urge to bash in his skull.

His lips curved into a smile. "So what's it going to be? You've surely heard of Carheim's dungeons. Pretty lass, like you? You'll be dead in two weeks—and that's if you're lucky."

Kaycia was familiar with these rumors and knew they were often believed by the ignorant. But while she wasn't afraid of his threats, she was increasingly troubled as to why he was making them.

"Or..." he continued. "We let you off easy... You'll be home by morning. Punishment reduced to a scant few hours." His gaze wandered to an empty tent.

Blood rushed into her face. The insinuation was so revolting, her hands balled into fists, and her body trembled. It wasn't just his words but her disappearing reasons not to commit murder.

Only the thought of Elyriel held her back—thinking how the crime would reflect on her. Knowing the judges wouldn't see her as the victim.

No. She needed to proceed with caution.

He worked his mouth. "You look old enough... Do this right, and it won't feel like punishment. You'll even have something to brag to your friends."

She bolted away at normal speed—allowing herself to be easily caught.

In a fashion.

She twisted and drove one man into another, as though the strength were his and not hers. She made it look clumsy and pretended to stumble.

By then, however, they had her surrounded. She whipped herself around, flicking mud from her fingers—which happened to land perfectly in two men's eyes.

This created an opening, and she charged into it.

But another man caught her stomach with an arm, and she couldn't break through without giving herself away.

She kicked a foot back and *incidentally* caught a man beneath his chin.

These accidents, however, didn't leave them discouraged. If anything, their mood took a turn for the worse.

With the man still holding her, another jammed his fist into her side. She wore leather, but the impact still drove the wind from her lungs.

The injury, of course, was nothing to an ascendant, but her cry of pain wasn't an act.

She had to swallow her frustration and convince herself this would all be worth it, as her escape would seem much more believable later.

"Keep her still!" said the lieutenant.

She twisted in the man's grasp and muttered something beneath her breath.

"What was that?" he asked, inching closer.

He held himself back at a safe distance—and was all the more surprised when she surged forward.

Her head rammed his nose in a sickening crunch.

He stumbled back, and she used the distraction to twist free from her captor. This required more force than she liked, but her size made it seem like his hands had slipped.

It was all she needed. She burst into a run and would've gotten away...were she not confronted by a familiar voice.

"Elyriel, wasn't it?"

Once again, it was Soril blocking her path. Only this time, he'd arrived too late to save her.

She froze in her tracks, debating what to do. With Soril, she'd, at least, have a chance at fairness—far more than she'd gotten from his degenerate men. At the same time, however, escape became impossible.

The lieutenant caught up, holding his bloodied nose with one hand. "It's her!" he bellowed. "We caught your thief!"

"No!" said Kaycia before he got the wrong idea. "I came for my sister! She didn't come back, and I thought, maybe... I'm sorry! I should've been more patient."

Soril's face tightened in confusion, likely remembering the Elyriel from before—the near-catatonic version, unlike what stood before him.

But it was far too late to change her approach. She'd hardly get anywhere if she played dumb.

He shook his head in frustration. "I don't have time. Lock her up, and I'll sort this out later."

"No!" she protested. "I'm telling you—!"

"What?" he asked, in clear distrust. "If you're so eager to talk, just tell me one thing. How did she do it?"

His question needed no clarification. He still felt betrayed and wanted to know how she'd feigned ascendancy.

But despite her predicament and her desire to be freed from these wretched men, she was *still* unwilling to tell the truth. To exchange these never-ending problems for another far worse.

"See?" asked the lieutenant. "We caught her fleeing camp. She's a thief, and I'll prove it!"

To her horror, he began to search her. He patted down her sides with his bloodied fingers and groped between the joints of her leather armor.

It was all she could do not to rip off his arms. She did, however, push him away with just enough force to regain some decency.

"What's the problem?" he growled. "Hiding something?"

"It wasn't her," said Soril.

The lieutenant made a face.

And Soril added, "Neranda caught sight of the real culprit."

Kaycia stifled a gasp, not only relieved to be free from implication but glad to know the woman was alive. More than alive but conscious at the time of Soril's return.

"I saw him, too!" she added. "Headed to the forest!"

Her words, however, achieved the opposite effect, as though she were speaking out of sheer desperation.

"She tried the same lie on us," said the lieutenant.

"It was him! I saw the dagger!"

Soril raised a hand and narrowed his gaze. "What dagger?"

"I—!" Kaycia stammered. "I just happened to see—!"

"A dangerous stranger...? So you followed him? Close enough, you saw what he was hiding?"

Once again, it'd been a mistake to say anything.

"I'll deal with you later," said Soril, gritting his teeth.

"I wasn't following—!"

"Like I said. Later."

"I won't go!" she shrieked. "Not with *him*!"

And she meant it, too. If she found herself back in the same situation, she wouldn't be responsible for what happened to these men.

Soril's anger rose, only to falter a moment later as he reevaluated the scene.

He took in the signs of their earlier struggle—the broken nose and the flecks of blood it'd left on her face. He saw the various injuries sustained by his men—while none were apparent on Elyriel herself.

His gaze paused on her the longest, as though seeing something he hadn't before. Something that narrowed his brows with suspicion.

"Lieutenant," he asked. "Did she do this to you?"

The man faltered, mostly from embarrassment.

Soril worked his mouth. "I'm not asking if you deserved it. Only if you might be in want of retribution."

These words came as a surprise to everyone.

The commander turned his attention to the group. "As repayment for Destin's years of service, he may take his justice in the form of his choosing. Off the record. Just this once."

"What?!" asked Kaycia in sudden alarm.

Even Destin was confused. "...Anything at all?"

The commander looked impatient. "Don't kill her, of course. It's only your nose."

For everyone present, this suggested a test—to see what justice his officer would choose.

But Kaycia knew better. She could see it in Soril's eyes. This test was for *her*, similar to the one she'd faced on the road. Similar but opposite. Instead of proving her ascendancy, she had to demonstrate otherwise.

"You're serious?" she asked. "What of your battle?"

Soril didn't waver. He was either confident the operation was going well, or he considered this mystery worth a few minutes.

The lieutenant took his time deciding what to do. He seemed to realize a wrong choice would reflect poorly on him. And he wasn't stupid enough to pursue his original, lecherous goals.

With a smile, he pounded a fist into a palm.

"Nose for a nose? Sounds fair to me."

He was trying to gloat and appear intimidating. The smeared blood on his face even helped a little.

She shook her head. "No...!"

"Stand still, and I'll make this quick."

For a moment, she debated letting him do it. She'd withstand the pain, crumple to the ground, and be done with the ordeal.

Except...she knew it wouldn't work. It'd buy a minute or two, but everyone would see how fast she recovered. Her traitorous nose would heal before their eyes.

So she turned her head and gave an ear instead.

"Arghh!!" she whined, falling to the ground.

"I said stand still!" He tried to grab her.

But Kaycia directed her conviction into the ground.

To the surrounding audience, he appeared to slip and dive into the mud.

She scrambled away with widening eyes. She made an act of being surprised herself and fearful of reprisal.

"You little bitch!" he yelled, wiping mud from his face. "Someone grab her!"

His companions turned to Soril, doubting such intervention would be permitted.

The commander said nothing. His eyes never strayed from Kaycia.

She needed to be more careful. To strike a balance and lose this fight in a believable way. No matter how painful. Or how humiliating.

"Get away from me!" she spat, backing away.

The man was reluctant to charge in again. Instead, he looked around and found a long wooden stick resting against a tent. It was roughly the size of a hiking staff.

"That's not fair!" she insisted.

Soril didn't intervene.

Without a choice, she ducked the swing and sidestepped another—but not by enough. She allowed herself to be struck, high against her leg, at a glancing angle that wouldn't break bone.

She moaned and dropped to her hands and knees—preparing to roll out of his next attack.

The man took his time, satisfied to have finally regained control.

She looked up at Soril, wondering how long he would let this last.

The commander spoke—so softly, only an ascendant would hear.

"Your sister was what? A cover? So no one would expect it was you?"

Kaycia swallowed in defeat, knowing it'd only been a matter of time.

She rose from the mud and didn't bother to turn as the lieutenant came up behind her. She could hear his approach and the staff gripped in his hands.

Pulling her shoulders back, she stood tall as his weapon cracked against her skull. It didn't just break—the loose end bounced back so perfectly that it knocked the lieutenant unconscious.

Kaycia didn't even wince. It hurt like hell, but it was a small price to pay for how good it felt! To put off this charade and give the man what he deserved.

If anything, she regretted it was over so soon.

The soldiers murmured, openly speculating what she was.

Only Soril was unfazed. "All right," he declared. "Show's over."

Kaycia turned, preparing herself for the commander's anger. For him to chastise her deceit and demand an explanation.

But his eyes weren't only filled with approval, he was practically exultant.

"How is this possible?" he asked. "I mean—! I can see why you'd hide it, but...! Just how old are you?"

"Old enough," she lied.

He seemed dissatisfied with the answer, but his excitement more than made up for it. "You're going to tell me everything, understand? I don't care about your reasons. We'll figure something out. I'll set aside some time to—"

"You're leaving?"

His lips turned down as though this were obvious.

"Let me help!" she blurted. "I saw your thief! I *faced* him! Let me prove myself to you!"

To Kaycia's surprise, she meant it. She was tired of the fear and surviving by herself. Moreover, she wanted the chance to make something of her life. Though there were difficult questions she'd still have to face, they'd all be easier with Soril on her side.

Right then, Agren appeared from thin air.

"We've caught the man's trail. He's tried covering his tracks but couldn't get them all. He's gone into the forest."

"See?" she asked. "Like I said!"

Agren was confused. "Who's this?"

Soril worked his mouth but couldn't keep the smile from appearing on his face.

"All right, then. Let's go."

Chapter 14

THE ANCIENT CITY

Within moments, the three were headed into the forest.

It felt...surreal. Considering the danger, it was the sort of mission that demanded preparation—performed with people who'd earned your trust.

But Soril hadn't taken more ascendants from battle. He wanted to move quickly and quietly and didn't need help to keep an eye on Kaycia. His only concern was to find their thief.

In the darkness, the trees didn't look like trees but scattered columns with blood-stained roots. They disappeared into the void above their heads, concealing leaves, branches, and anything hiding within.

This wasn't an excursion for the faint of heart or people unready to face an ambush.

But Kaycia had never felt so unburdened. She'd been given the opportunity to turn things around, and the abyss itself couldn't darken her mood.

The change was so sudden—and, moreover, undeserved. After all her lies, she'd expected to remain trapped. And yet, Soril had decided to withhold his judgment.

This didn't guarantee absolution. For the time being, however, she felt some hope. That he wouldn't only be accepting, he might offer solutions.

And even if he didn't, there was still this stranger. She couldn't help but think they'd met for a reason. That his timely appearance and unexpected mercy might lead to something meaningful.

It left her feeling giddy when she should've been afraid.

"There's nothing here," said Soril as they neared two miles. His voice was so low it was more a subvocalization than a whisper.

"Are you suggesting we stop?" she asked, mouthing the same way.

"No... But Agren should stay here."

At Kaycia's confusion, Agren explained, "My range isn't infinite. Any further, and I'll lose my direct connection to camp."

Kaycia nodded slowly. They couldn't afford delayed warnings or a staggered escape plan.

"Don't worry about me," he said. "I'll still be with you—my eyes and ears. You can talk as though I'm right beside you."

She raised a brow, impressed.

"So long as my attention isn't elsewhere," he added. "Just wait for my response to know I heard."

With no further comment, Soril and Kaycia kept going.

She wondered what might happen if they didn't find something soon. Eventually, they'd reach the point where they'd be just as far from Agren as he was from camp. After that, he'd be unable to keep track of both—at least not simultaneously.

Luckily, it wasn't half so long before they reached something of interest.

Throughout their journey, it'd been common to see broken branches and upturned soil from the rampaging creatures. But here, the damage was worse. Entire trees were pulverized, their trunks leaning at odd angles or fallen completely to the ground.

At the center of the wreckage, in the space ahead, stood a peculiar shape that couldn't have been natural. It was over ten feet tall and didn't appear to be moving. The frame, however, was distinctly humanoid.

"What the—?"

Soril raised a hand to silence her. He shook his head to suggest this might be a trap.

The thing appeared to have multiple limbs, but they were bent, broken, and sticking out at odd angles.

"It's dead," said Agren.

Unconsciously, Kaycia turned to his voice, but the young man wasn't there.

"Is it safe?" asked Soril. "See anything else?"

Agren took a moment to answer. "There are more to the west. I don't know what to make of them. You'll have to see for yourself."

Reluctantly, Soril nodded to Kaycia, and they both moved forward.

As they closed the distance, Kaycia wasn't sure what she was looking at. If it was dead, then why was it standing?

It wasn't until she saw the familiar spike rising from the ground that it began to make sense.

The cadaver's hands and feet were splayed out, pierced by thinner spikes. The design was roughly reminiscent of a scarecrow or some other devilish effigy.

"Was this meant for us?" she asked. "A kind of warning?"

Soril frowned, then shook his head. "Look at the blood—how it congeals. This beast has been dead a while. Before the attack began."

The thought was disturbing. It didn't only confirm the creator provoked the attack, but it provided evidence of his unusual power. These spikes should've disappeared over an hour ago. But they'd held together despite the man going as far as Soril's camp.

"If this was here before, are we on the wrong trail?"

"No," said Agren. "He's going back the way he came."

Blood was everywhere—not red but the black sickening muck that coursed abyssal veins. It decorated the trees and painted the monster's naked, male torso. An enormous pool had collected on the ground—more blood than would have been possible had the thing been human.

As there was no way around it, Soril strode straight in. He stood beneath the dead creature, his boots sinking past his ankles.

"This intruder..." he began. "You said you faced him? And managed to survive?"

Kaycia steered the conversation away from herself. "I don't believe he wanted us dead."

"Tell that to my soldiers."

She suppressed a groan. Secretly, she'd been hoping the men, too, had survived, but that'd been overly optimistic.

"Well..." she swallowed. "Ascendants are more important."

He looked at her sideways. "You truly believe that?"

"From *his* perspective. As a fellow human, he didn't want to leave us crippled. That's all I'm saying."

"Sounds like you're defending him."

"No. Just trying to understand."

Soril shrugged and raised a hand to the porous spike. "I've never heard of a creator capable of this. No one except..."

When his voice died away, she couldn't keep quiet. "You know what this is? Has someone been performing illegal experiments?"

Soril's expression became curious. "I was going to say Meileen."

"Oh," she said, hiding her embarrassment.

Meileen was the name of the goddess of creation. Naturally, such spikes wouldn't have presented her a challenge.

"She's dead," said Kaycia.

She remembered the silent stranger—his diminutive size, wrapped in cloth. And she was no longer confident he hadn't been female.

Soril watched her face and guessed what she was thinking. "It couldn't have been her."

Kaycia blushed again. "Of course... Wasn't she incapacitated? Her corpse, I mean, when the fighting was done."

"Utterly," he confirmed, working his mouth. "She couldn't have retained the intelligence to escape. Or the dexterity for anything like this." He gestured toward the effigy.

"Escape?" she asked, suddenly intrigued. "You know where she's held?"

His expression soured. "We need to get back. The council needs to hear this."

"But we just got here!" she said. "We knew he was powerful before we left!"

"You did, maybe. This changes things."

"What are you not telling me?"

"I'm sorry, Elyriel..." He appeared torn by an internal struggle. "These matters are... sensitive."

Kaycia couldn't believe this. "If you don't tell me, I'll figure it out myself." Without waiting for a response, she turned west to follow the trail of spiked corpses.

It was a bluff, of course. She wasn't eager to leave alone, but it seemed preposterous that Soril would withhold information.

"Elyriel!" he said. "It's dangerous."

"Is it? Because you just said this *wasn't* Meileen. It's not a god or even a monster. That makes him a person. An abnormally powerful one, granted, but as far as I'm concerned, he might be on our side. He's killed the creatures for us, hasn't he?"

"He's not on our side."

"So which is it? If it's the Navarans, say so! What interest do they have in the city of the gods?"

Soril took a deep breath and tried to hide his discomfort.

"I'm right, aren't I?" she pressed. "I can see how important this is for you. But it's not like I'm spreading government secrets!"

He began to nod. "You saw the dagger..."

She raised a brow, waiting for more.

"Yes. You're right," he conceded. "We've known about the Navarans a while now. Undisclosed facilities. Unusual behavior. But this isn't public knowledge. We'd rather people focus on the *real* problem."

Kaycia grimaced. "Did you know they were making aberrant ascendants?"

"Only suspected. We found some papers signed by Emperor Mahod, but we haven't seen proof. Not till now."

She mulled this over. "All the more reason to keep going. And see what he's after."

"Elyriel..."

"Don't you want to know? If he already has the dagger, he won't stop there. He might even know where Ahman is!"

At this, Soril paused—as she knew he would. It'd only been a guess, but, for him, it posed a threat against his life's work.

"Just a little further," he said solemnly. "If we don't find anything, we head back, understand?"

Kaycia agreed.

They made their way west and, after some fifty feet, came across a second desecrated corpse. This one was female, with silvery hair, indistinguishable from spiderwebs.

"Take care," said Agren. "I've seen her twitch once or twice."

They picked up their pace, not knowing how much a lead the creator had. At the moment of his choosing, these spikes would disappear. Which would be the wrong moment to discover which corpses were dead and which were not.

"The trail ends here," said Agren as they reached a lakeshore.

Kaycia assumed they'd arrived too late, and the man had already escaped across the water. Until she took in the enormous rift sundering the beach in two.

The soil had given way to erosion on both sides, exposing smooth, jagged rock tilted toward the middle. The result was more a fissure than a cave, as though an eruption had pushed the rock upward and outward.

"You think he went inside?" she asked, remembering to subvocalize and refrain from noise.

Soril narrowed his eyes in doubt. "I've been down there... Once."

At first, this surprised her, but then she remembered. If Soril had been searching for Ahman, he'd had plenty of time to wander these hills. It gave reason to check everything, especially a peculiar crevice.

He regarded the entrance with suspicion. "It's a dead end."

"You're sure? He might've gone underground to avoid being seen."

"No. I remember. After fifty feet, there's a drop-off. It's large—about thirty feet down—but after that, the passage ends. I checked the walls and ceilings. There's no way through."

"You're saying he's trapped?"

"Or he's set one for us."

Kaycia considered this but realized her mind hadn't changed. She'd come this far and wasn't going to walk away empty-handed.

Still, she froze upon reaching the opening. Holding her breath, she couldn't hear anything—not inside nor from the forest around them.

Her natural reaction was to make some noise—to be sure her senses were unaffected—but she exercised restraint and entered in silence.

The interior, of course, wasn't darker than outside. The ground was solid rock, washed clean by the rain, making it impossible to discern any tracks or prints. If the man was here and the place was as small as Soril described, there was no hurry to reach the bottom.

Except, minutes later, as they peered cautiously past the drop-off...they saw nothing. A shallow pool of water, leftover from the storm, an inch or so deep. Not nearly enough to hide anything beneath its surface.

Her first impression might've been right. He'd left by boat, and they were wasting time. But she wasn't so stupid to drop her guard or leave the cave without checking more closely.

It wasn't until they shimmied down the wall and searched every crag that they had no choice but to concede the place was empty.

"You positive the trail led here?" asked Soril quietly to Agren.

For whatever reason, the man didn't respond.

Soril turned to Kaycia. "Check the walls."

At first, this seemed an act of desperation, until she realized what he meant. They were searching for material that didn't belong—something the creator might've shaped himself.

Ignoring the squishing water in her boots, she worked her way counterclockwise. Everything appeared natural, even the submerged rock beneath their feet.

She was about to give up when something changed—and it had nothing to do with false surfaces. At the end, where there'd previously been nothing, a vertical line had appeared.

She traced it with her fingers and gasped when it sunk deeper, like a groove chiseled into stone. Not only that, the line extended to form part of a larger design.

"What's wrong?" asked Soril, splashing toward her.

The intricate pattern was revealed to be rectangular, not much larger than she was. At the center was an indentation in the form of a dagger. The same size and shape as the one she remembered.

"A door...?" she asked, with a hint of wonder.

"What? Where?"

"Come closer. It's right here."

As she reached forward, the door moved on its own. Slowly, the stone sank into the wall as if turning upon an invisible hinge. The air on the other side was completely dark, suggestive of a tunnel proceeding deeper into the earth.

Rather than dust, it gave off the scent of rich, moistened dirt.

"You didn't see this the first time you were here?" she asked, stepping inside.

Soril didn't follow.

For some reason, he was still unable to see the opening—but what did that mean? He'd seen her go somewhere, hadn't he? This alone would've shown him where to follow.

She reached out her hand, and Soril flinched back.

"What? Did I scare you?" she teased, stepping outside.

At last, he was able to see her again.

"How did you...do that?"

Without waiting for an answer, Soril walked closer, not looking at her but the doorway itself. Reaching forward, his hand stopped midair.

"Push harder," she suggested. "There's nothing there."

"Maybe not for you..."

To illustrate his point, he slammed his fist against the barrier. With both hands, he groped the contour of a surface she couldn't see. Even when he put his full weight against it, a force prevented him from going further.

"Why don't we try this...? I'll pull you through." She extended her hand.

His face became skeptical. "I don't think—"

"Won't hurt to try."

In some ways, it made her think of Agren's abilities—how he momentarily pulled others into his reality by merely touching them. Perhaps she could do the same, despite her aspect being nothing like Foundation.

A curious expression crossed his face, and he took her hand.

Slowly, Kaycia went through—increasing her caution as his fingers neared the threshold.

"Damn it!" he yelled, jerking his hand back.

Kaycia had felt it—the moment his fingers jammed into rock. The contact was solid and completely inflexible, with no indication anything had changed.

"What did you say? It wouldn't hurt?"

"Don't be such a baby!"

When he didn't react, she realized he hadn't heard. For him—and the reality he was a part of—there was enough rock between them to block her voice.

Coming back through the door, she asked, "You okay?"

He gave a half-hearted smile—but his thoughts had wandered elsewhere.

She, herself, had a few guesses as to what this was.

The simplest explanation stemmed from the fact both she and Soril were from different aspects. And while they might appear to inhabit the same world and the same geography, this wasn't the truth.

Reality was not one whole but divided into layers. It was the reason ascendants from one aspect were governed by different laws than those from another. In truth, people from different aspects existed in distinct, overlapping worlds.

In most situations, this didn't pose a problem. The physicality shared between layers was—usually—logical and free from inconsistencies.

But this passageway, miles outside of town, in the middle of nowhere...

"The door's aspected?" she asked. "It exists in some but not others?"

"I'm not so sure."

"Maybe I can see it because it's part of Conviction. Part of Creation, as well—if the Navaran's inside."

"I need to think," said Soril, taking a deep breath. He looked around the cave, lost in thought. A moment later, his gaze returned.

"Could you do something for me? The path... I want you to check if it leads to Ahman."

Kaycia blinked. She hadn't forgotten the city, but they were deep underground. A cave hardly seemed the place to hide something so vast.

"Just a quick look," he continued. "Do it quietly, and make sure he doesn't hear. When you reach the end, come straight back, understand?"

She nodded.

"I mean it," he continued. "I don't want you wandering around in there. There are things about Ahman you wouldn't understand. Dangerous things."

His insistence was getting on her nerves. Did he think she was that stupid?

Of course, he did. Throughout this excursion, she'd done nothing but press onward, even when it was unreasonable to do so.

She forced a smile. "I'll come back. I get it."

But before she could leave, something else worried her. Finding a large rock, she wedged it into the frame—to stop the door from closing as mysteriously as it opened.

Then she took a deep breath and plunged into the passage.

Within moments, though she hadn't thought it possible, the corridor became darker. She'd thought she'd gotten used to pitch black, because her eyes discerned shapes in her immediate vicinity.

This, however, was no longer the case.

Even when she waved a hand inches from her face, she couldn't see a thing.

This nearly compelled her to turn back—but what good would come of that?

So far, the path had revealed itself straight, as evidenced by the walls on either side. As long as her hands kept steady contact, there was no possibility of getting lost.

At least, so long as the geography didn't change.

Her thoughts returned to Hebril and the underground cellar. Was it possible this place shared a similar curse?

She hated feeling lost, but here, it was worse. Here, she was alone, with no one coming after her. Even if they wanted, they couldn't see the door.

Was she walking into a trap? Had the stranger lured them to this place so she'd never get out? The door would disappear, or the path would keep changing, until the moment she died?

Even so, she pressed onward. There was nothing to be gained by giving in to such fears. If anything, they only prevented a cool head and her from sensing details that might be important.

She walked straight for five minutes before noticing the walls felt...different. The rock had always been smooth and clammy due to subterranean moisture. But now, she had to ask herself if it'd always been so pliable. Early on, she hadn't pushed hard with her fingers, but now, the surface seemed to give, just a little, under pressure.

This wasn't ordinary rock.

Further on, she sensed additional abnormalities. Along the surface were thin, stringy extrusions. They ran along the wall, branching out in multiple directions like pulsing veins. Or softened roots, perhaps?

Suppressing a shudder, she forced herself onward.

The air became cool, like fog in the morning. As she allowed the sensation to fill her nostrils, it felt so familiar, some of her tension dissipated.

After a short while, she began to see things, but they were faint, as though wandering through fog. A dark, red light was coming from somewhere, but so diffused by mist, it might as well have come from everywhere.

She moved faster—not afraid but intrigued by what this meant.

And then...

Kaycia didn't know when the ceiling disappeared—or if one had even been there since she'd entered the darkness. But now, as the fog began to part, she gazed into a distant sky.

The colors were wrong—a deep scarlet, nearly black, with darker splotches that might've been clouds. But how was that possible? The darkness of the current was supposed to be absolute. There were no lights at all in the eternal void.

The place took on an almost dream-like quality.

Returning her attention to the walls, she found them, once again, to be plain, unremarkable stone. They weren't only solid but completely flat.

At some point, the path had turned into an alleyway.

The fog made it difficult to see very far, but she was clearly walking between large buildings, with occasional dark recesses cut into stone.

Kaycia strained her ears but could still hear nothing.

It was as though she'd entered a ghost town, and there was no doubt in her mind what place this was.

Her eyes were drawn to a dark window, and she thought something was staring back.

At first, she thought it was the Navaran—that he'd seen her—but that wasn't it. She got the same feeling from *all* the windows.

In fact, when she looked up, faint shadows were on the rooftops, and vague figures were turning to regard her arrival.

Kaycia slowly backed away, giving heed to Soril's instructions.

Her heart was hammering in her chest, but she forced herself to keep an even, soundless pace.

She waited for the world to disappear into fog, and when it did, she turned around and ran.

"You were right!" she said as she burst through the opening. "I saw it. The city's real!"

Soril looked up with a smile—but, even so, he lacked the enthusiasm she'd expected. And he wasn't alone.

Agren leaned against the opposite wall. At the mixed expression on his face, she guessed what might be wrong.

"Is it the same for you? The door's not there...? But that makes no sense! Can't you get past it...? With your Foundation? Have you tried?"

"Elyriel..." interrupted Soril. "We need to talk."

He made it sound as though someone died. At least, there was more to his solemnity than she'd initially realized.

She was bursting with things to tell them—of the glimmering sky!—but it'd have to wait.

"What's going on?" she asked.

"My guess was right. Your aspect has nothing to do with this pathway you've entered."

Kaycia opened her mouth but decided to wait for further explanation.

"It's been a concern of ours for years—that there might be a separate, more important reason we haven't found the city. It's because of the changes, you see. Now that the gods are dead, a few have speculated ascendancy, itself, is the problem."

"I don't follow."

"That ascendancy...isn't enough. I mean, think about what we've seen. The man we've been following—he's far more powerful than your average creator. I'm convinced he's not an ascendant at all."

Kaycia was at a loss until she remembered her lessons. Historically, a rank had been known to exceed ascendancy, reserved for the gods' most powerful adherents.

"Yes, but...! That might explain him...! You can't be suggesting *I'm* a transcendent!"

This should've been obvious, but, to her surprise, neither of the men spoke.

"What the hell is going on?" she demanded.

"I've tried being patient," said Soril, drawing a deep breath. "But this charade has gone on long enough. I want an explanation, Elyriel, and I want it now."

"What?!" How had this turned around on her so suddenly?

She'd seen this expression before. It was Soril's way of confronting the problem. And while it didn't make him a bad person, there were moments his zeal went a bit too far and crested on downright cruelty.

"I'm talking about you!" he said, shaking his head in exasperation. "And your sister—the both of you! I thought by disregarding your secrets, I was doing you a favor... You both seem like nice people—was I wrong?"

"Please don't do this," she said. "You weren't wrong! I appreciate everything you've done for us!"

She wanted to plead with him—to ask for his trust a little while longer—but she suspected it was already too late.

"You mean with the magistrate?" Soril asked. "You still haven't told me why your name's not registered."

She paused, feeling something was off, and it took her a moment to figure out what.

There were two ways to interpret this.

On the one hand, his words might be meant for Elyriel—that, since she was the ascendant, it was *her* name that should've been in the book.

There was, however, a second possibility—that he was referring to Kaycia. Had he figured it out? That *she* was the one he was speaking with?

Kaycia took a step back, not knowing what to say. None of this made sense, nor explained why they suspected *her* of transcendency. The mere thought was ridiculous!

Agren stepped away from the wall and immediately disappeared.

"Don't even think about it," he said from behind her.

She turned to find the young man between herself and the door. His intention was obvious—to block her escape. He'd done it before she'd considered it an option.

It was logical, wasn't it? It was the only place she could go where they couldn't follow. Of course, they'd be worried about her slipping away.

Kaycia took a different approach.

"The Navaran's already in there, right? I'll tell you everything, but isn't it more important we stop him?"

"I haven't forgotten. Don't you worry. If it's any consolation, my concerns regarding him are greater than those with you. But make no mistake—it's the only reason we're still talking."

"So you *do* want me to go after him?"

"We'll get to that. Right now, it seems you're our only option. But that doesn't mean I'll let a second person of questionable loyalties waltz into Ahman."

"I'm on your side! You know that!"

"I don't even know where you're from. So let's have it. You said you'd explain. Be quick about it."

When it became clear she didn't know where to start, he barraged her with questions. "Who are you, Elyriel? Who made you? Who do you work for?"

She stammered wordlessly.

The man groaned, unconvinced.

"I was born in Carheim! Same as my sister. You can ask anyone! I've never stepped foot outside our nation's borders!"

He raised a brow in disbelief. "And the clergymen who performed your ceremony? They were also from Carheim?"

"You only ask that because you think I'm a transcendent! But I'm not! I swear on my life! I have no idea what—"

"Cut the shit! You're far too young for the standard ritual! You have to know *something*!"

Agren turned toward the darkness, focused on something Kaycia couldn't see. His eyes weren't on the stone passage but crossed distances she could only imagine.

Reaching down, he grabbed hold of something. With effort, he dragged it into the cave.

"Why don't we start with this?" he said, looking up again.

There, in the shallow water, was her own unconscious body.

Soril closed his eyes, looking very tired. "Let's hear you swear again that you don't know anything."

Chapter 15
JUDGEMENT

For a moment, Kaycia considered feigning distress and acting the part of the concerned sister. *What's wrong with her*? she'd cry while falling to her knees.

But the time for lies had come to an end.

These men had their suspicions, or they wouldn't have presented the body in the first place. To persist in her denial would be deeply insulting.

"She was like this when they found her," said Agren. "They checked her for injuries but found none. Neranda believes there's more going on. And suggested you'd know exactly what this was."

"Neranda?" she asked, momentarily confused—but then it dawned on her. "She's a devoter, isn't she?"

No answer was necessary.

Devotion was the aspect that dealt with bindings. It was present at weddings when souls were realigned. It could move a person from their original layer to more perfectly coexist within the world of their mate. It was the part of the circle that linked Kaycia to her sister.

With a lump in her throat, she slumped to her knees.

So that was it. Even if she wanted to lie, she couldn't explain her way out of this. Her only choice was to confess. And hope Elyriel might be spared execution.

Through her vision, now clouded by tears, she was surprised when Soril's expression softened.

"Let's suppose we did this your way," he said in a gentler tone. "What if I did decide to trust you...? Trust goes both ways. Aren't you willing to place some trust in me?"

She didn't respond.

"I get that you're afraid—the both of you. I apologize for not seeing it sooner. But if I'm to put my career on the line, this is something I demand in return. I need to understand the risks. And you... You'll have to trust me to be the person you know me to be."

"Meaning what? If I tell you everything, you won't report us to the authorities?"

"Let me make the right choice—whatever that may be."

In this, the man's sense of honor did him no favors. If he was always intent on doing the right thing, didn't that guarantee he'd side with the law? What else could he do? The local magistrates were already on her trail. And he wasn't about to forget the affidavit he'd signed.

In the end, however, none of this was his fault. She'd brought him into this, and she was wrong to expect him to do anything differently.

"You're right," she said. "Of course, you're right. I just..."

How was she supposed to say this? Her throat constricted at the mere thought of Elyriel. And now, she was expected to confess what happened? To divulge her role in destroying the only person she'd ever loved?

"Take your time," said Soril. His tone was comforting but also underlined his conditions. Yes, she could take all the time she needed, so long as she eventually got to the point.

For over a minute, Kaycia said nothing. She could only imagine how confusing it might be to reveal she wasn't, in fact, Elyriel. But maybe the task would be easier if she referred to herself in the third person.

So that's what she did. Without making eye contact, she talked about her training—about *Kaycia's* training—as though it was her sister who'd been chosen and not herself. Though it felt strange to speak this way, it had the unintentional side-effect of detaching herself from the story. She felt less emotionally involved, and it loosened her tongue.

It was only awkward when she got to Elyriel. She'd have to say things like, 'Kaycia invited *me* to come with her to the garrison,' or '*I* took lodgings with my sister's sponsor.' So she kept these comments brief and quickly moved on.

Soril listened and didn't ask questions.

After recounting what happened at her first ceremony and subsequent failure, she soon arrived at the events of Graywood Pass. Fortunately, she'd built enough momentum by this point to push through. She addressed the creatures that killed Tenlen and their group's escape into the monastery as though these things had happened to someone else.

The impromptu ceremony, of course, was Marien's idea. Though they were all at fault—for not disagreeing or proposing another plan—Kaycia found it difficult to take full ownership.

Though Soril might've sensed this, he respected her right to share her story in her own way. When he asked his first question, it regarded the ceremony itself.

"Two overlapping circles—Stratum and Devotion? Do you still have this notebook? Can I see it?"

"It's in my bag. We left our stuff at the..."

Her voice died away, suddenly grateful she was here, and that she hadn't rushed off into the ancient city.

"I nearly forgot! I left her in the street, and...!" She wasn't sure how to explain the rest. She wasn't in a position to ask more from Soril, but what else could she do? The innkeeper might not accept remuneration after the incident with the cat.

"You mean Chesandril?" asked Soril before sharing a significant look with Agren. "She's by herself in New Ahman?"

Kaycia quickly described where she'd last seen the girl and the direction she'd been heading. It'd been hours since this happened, but she hoped it'd help.

"I'll find her," said Agren. "Shall I fetch your belongings as well?"

At a nod from Soril, he disappeared, and Kaycia reluctantly returned to her story.

This last part was the most difficult—making sense of how Chesandril had taken control of her mother's body. Recounting how Veldt's treachery had led to Marien's death. And how Elyriel had taken it upon herself to complete the ritual.

It was at this point Kaycia stopped pretending to be her sister.

By the time she was finished, the life had all but gone out of her voice. She couldn't meet Soril's eyes. It was the best she could do to force the words out, if only to be done with them—to be free of them. As though, by finishing her story, her problems, too, might find resolution.

Which, of course, was impossible. But she was surprised to feel Soril's gentle hand on her arm.

"Kaycia?" he asked, with a strange mixture of caution, confusion, and sympathy.

She nearly shoved him away, not wanting his pity. How could he possibly understand what she'd been through? What she was still going through? It made her angry to be forced to relive these problems.

"That's right," she confessed. "That's me on the floor...and here in this body. It's been me the whole time... N—no one else."

She realized this wasn't exactly true. On their way to the city, Soril had seen a glimpse of what was left of Elyriel.

Kaycia sensed him putting the pieces together, but she was no longer in the mood to talk about her sister.

"So what now?" she asked.

He paused a moment, then withdrew his hand.

"Now... I need to present this to my advisors."

"What?!" Kaycia climbed to her feet.

"Calm down. I'm not trying to be insensitive. This is your story, and if you'd prefer, I'd consent to let you share it yourself."

"Never mind who tells it!" she said, turning back to the doorway. "That stranger's still in there!"

"It'll be all right," said Soril, raising a hand. "A few hours will hardly make a difference in the long run. He has an entire city to explore. If anything, this works to our advantage—making him believe he got away. That he wasn't followed."

Kaycia narrowed her eyes, considering.

"Trust me, I've no intention of dragging this out longer than necessary. My people will understand, and we'll have a plan worked out before the night is through."

Only then did she nod. She liked the idea of having a plan. It'd also give her the chance to see Chesandril safe.

The only thing that worried her was the possibility of something else going wrong. It seemed overly optimistic to assume Soril's council would reach a quick agreement. After his own reservations trusting her story, why should he expect them to be any different?

S ure enough, in less than half an hour, things fell apart.

"Mind control?" asked Neranda. "So that's why they're bonded? You mean to tell me this is Kaycia? She's taken forcible possession of her own sister?!"

Soril drew a deep breath. "Not by choice. It's not nearly so dour as you make it out to be."

"Like hell it's not!"

Not only did Neranda appear healed from her injuries, her condescending tone had returned in full force.

Kaycia herself didn't disagree with the assessment. No matter how you looked at it, it *was* that bad... Elyriel's fate was undeniably horrific and shouldn't be made light of or softened in any way.

But since she couldn't bring herself to speak this out loud, she could only stand there once again and feel her face burn red.

"Neranda? Pumpkin?" said Soril, trying to smooth things over. "I must urge you not to draw conclusions. It's my fault for summarizing her story so quickly. I fear I glossed over critical details."

Her story, you say?" She raised an eyebrow. "The version she gave you, herself? Is this not the same woman whom you, master, branded publicly as a liar?!"

His face fell, having forgotten the weight of this mess.

Kaycia, however, had an idea. "Has Agren returned? If he's caught up to Chesandril, she can corroborate everything I've said."

"The witness of a child...?" intoned the lady with a sneer.

"We're still waiting to hear back from him," said Soril. "But listen, Neranda. We can't afford more delays."

"I heard you the first time. I haven't forgotten the Navaran or the problem he represents... But that doesn't make her any less of one! She's not one of us. She's a charlatan, a compulsive liar, and now...a *transcendent*? I can't stand back as—"

"You can, and you will!" declared Soril. "What's happened to your objective mind? We all know your feelings toward Kaycia, but the fact remains that while she can enter Ahman, you cannot!"

Neranda's eyes bulged. "Are you suggesting I'm...jealous of this girl?"

"I never said—" He swallowed his frustration. "All I'm saying is it shouldn't matter."

Kaycia wanted to disappear. She hated being at the center of this conflict. It wasn't as though she'd asked to be special. If there were any way to give these abilities to Neranda—and get her sister back in the process—she'd do it in a heartbeat.

The woman, once again, scrutinized Kaycia. "I'll have to perform an examination."

Soril creased his brow. "What do you mean?"

"Isn't that what you asked? My objective opinion?"

The man pressed his lips together.

Neranda went on. "What if her bond is not what she thinks it is? What if there are side effects? Unforeseen complications?" She raised her eyes at the older man. "I'll need to check their aspects for stability—each individually."

On the one hand, Kaycia was grateful for this shift in direction. These were legitimate concerns—even helpful ones. But, though she'd wanted such evaluations from the start, she wasn't certain she wanted them from Neranda.

Soril's face was concerned. "I hadn't considered that. Thus far, Kaycia has certainly seemed in control. At least, I've observed nothing to suggest... But, of course—it'd be best to be sure."

"Yes," agreed Kaycia. "But if I might ask... Is Neranda the only devoter available? Is there no one else who could—?"

"Who could what?" interrupted the woman with a scowl. "You think I'll be biased? Don't insult me..."

Soril raised his hands between both women. "I understand your anxiety, Kaycia, but there are other matters we must consider. Not only of time...but of discretion."

Kaycia took a deep breath, unable to argue.

"How long do you need?" he asked Neranda.

The woman groaned, thinking it over. "I wasn't suggesting anything comprehensive—that could take days. But a simple demonstration would suffice if only to alert us of immediate concerns. You could invite the other councilmen—so everyone can watch."

"A...demonstration?"

"A switch. Have her return to her body while we observe the transition in progress."

"Wait..." said Kaycia. "That's not a good idea."

"It isn't?"

Kaycia paused, reluctant to explain. Her main apprehension was how Elyriel might respond, surrounded by so many people and frenzied emotions.

She couldn't, however, come out and say this. Nor could she imagine any confession of Elyriel's delicate mental state—or her open hostility—to positively affect Neranda's opinion.

"Only if it's quick," said Kaycia, "A few seconds. No longer."

"A few—?!"

"That's fine," said Soril, placing a hand on Neranda's shoulder. "We've still much to discuss, and I fear we've lost too much time already."

Neranda grumbled but argued no further.

At Kaycia's insistence, they cleared out the area. Choosing an open space surrounded by wagons, only Soril's ascendants were permitted to stand audience. Everyone else was turned away, with a contingent of guards posted around the perimeter.

This helped somewhat ease Kaycia's nerves. It was a quiet part of camp—far enough from the injured and the sounds of overnight repairs—she should've felt more confident.

But she didn't.

"When you're ready," said Neranda.

"Could you, maybe, stand back?"

The woman shook her head. There was no need to explain what an examination entailed.

Kaycia groaned. "Just...be careful what you do. Try not to startle her."

Neranda exhaled in frustration.

"Okay," said Kaycia, closing her eyes.

When she opened them again, she was lying on a cot a few feet away. Her eyes were heavy and her head muddled.

The devoter took a step closer to Elyriel.

"By the gods..." she breathed, not with derision—nor compassion—but something that bordered on intrigue. She studied the girl as she would a laboratory animal. "This is quite the change."

Elyriel looked down at Kaycia, then back at the woman, with eyes a bit too wide. She kept her arms to her sides, exhibiting far more restraint than Kaycia would've imagined. Her fingers, however, were clenched tight. Every muscle in her body had gone rigid.

"It's all right, Elle," said Kaycia. "She's not going to hurt you."

Neranda looked puzzled. "She understands?" Without awaiting a response, she reached for the girl's hand. "Can you understand *me*?"

Elyriel snatched her arm back and began to hiss.

"No!" instructed Neranda with consternation. "Give it here!"

The girl spat in the woman's face.

"We're done," said Kaycia. But as she reached for her sister, she encountered some barrier.

"Neranda?" she asked, with sudden dread. "What did you—?"

In less than a second, Elyriel seized a fistful of the woman's hair.

"Stop it, Elle!" screamed Kaycia, to no avail.

The surrounding council stiffened, uncertain what to do.

Neranda caught hold of the girl's wrist and twisted. With such a move, it was no longer a contest of strength—in which Elyriel would be the clear winner. With a proper understanding of human physiology, there were ways to use an opponent's strength against them.

"You need to let me through!" Kaycia insisted.

Elyriel wailed as her arm was twisted behind her back, and she was shoved bodily to the dirt. The girl fought back, only to find the more she struggled, the more pain was redirected into her arm.

"Get off her!" shouted Kaycia, trying once more to assume control—but the woman's interference was insurmountable.

Elyriel's chest heaved against the earth, snarling like a ferocious animal.

There was an unsettling pop as her shoulder twisted free from its socket. Contorting madly, she escaped Neranda's lock, drove the woman off balance, and took hold of her leg.

The woman slipped, but even as she hit the ground, she landed a kick to Elyriel's face.

The girl didn't let go.

Rising, she swung Neranda in a circle before hurtling her toward the nearest wagon.

The wood splintered but didn't fully break. The carriage lurched a few feet before settling back and depositing the devoter onto the dirt.

Spurred into action, the ascendants closed in around the manic Elyriel.

"No!" screamed Kaycia. "Wait!"

Neranda's barrier had, at last, weakened. It hadn't disappeared, but Kaycia forced her way through with renewed determination.

"Stop!" she said—this time, through Elyriel's voice.

The council members faltered...but not Neranda.

She was back on her feet and more furious than ever.

"It's me!" shouted Kaycia, grimacing as she popped her arm back into place. "It's over now!"

The woman wouldn't see reason. She started forward and only stopped when Soril stepped in her way.

"That's enough!" roared the man, But rather than confronting Neranda, he jabbed a finger toward Kaycia. "You! Back in the carriage!"

"But I'm not the one who—!"

"You will *remain* in your carriage," he continued, as though he hadn't heard, "until our council has reached a decision. You won't contact anyone or ask questions. You won't do *anything* until someone gets you—is that clear?"

"Isn't that a bit—?"

"*Do you understand*?!" he demanded, eyes blazing.

Kaycia scowled but forced out the words, "Yes, sir..."

Soril took a deep breath, making his exhaustion clear.

"I suggest you get some rest," he muttered, still struggling with his temper. "This might...take a while."

For the next six hours, Kaycia sat beside her body on the couch, unable to sleep. How could she possibly rest while a group of ascendants argued her sister's fate?

She felt certain the council was doing precisely that—that it was no longer a question of investigating Ahman. They'd have completely forgotten the Navaran—too worked up by the display they'd witnessed.

If Kaycia fell asleep, she imagined waking up to the carriage being hauled away. They wouldn't even tell her anything. They'd send her off to be delivered to the courts of Carheim, without giving her the chance to defend herself.

There came a knock on the door, followed by the bolts sliding loose.

The soldiers, however, hadn't come for Kaycia but to admit an additional prisoner.

They locked the door behind her.

"You're okay!" said Kaycia, enveloping the girl in Elyriel's arms.

"What's going on?" asked Chesandril.

"They didn't tell you?"

"Only that you were here. I don't think they like me very much."

"Nothing else? No questions? About...what happened?"

She avoided specifics, not wanting to remind her of Graywood Pass. Chesandril's eyes, however, drew inward, knowing exactly what she'd meant.

"No," said the girl, without further elaboration.

Kaycia assumed the council hadn't wanted to be bothered, so Chesandril had been dropped off here.

Still, that was a good sign, wasn't it? If they'd been serious about treating Kaycia as a prisoner, they'd have made sure the two of them remained separate, wouldn't they?

Rather than press the issue, she helped Chesandril curl up by the couch, supported by a stack of cushions. There was likely a bed in the adjacent room, but the door was locked.

Letting her sleep, Kaycia pulled a chair to the window, and it wasn't long before her thoughts drifted off again. She felt relieved to know Chesandril was okay, but this did nothing to stop her thoughts from circling unproductively.

Her life was over... There was no coming back...

She tried to stop—to convince herself her future was out of her hands. But she found it impossible to think of anything else—even when the soldiers returned a half hour later.

"What about her?" she asked, tilting her head toward Chesandril.

"Let her sleep. Soril's instructions were for you and only you."

When Kaycia stepped down from the carriage, they locked the girl inside.

They then led Kaycia across camp into one of the larger tents.

Inside the lavishly decorated forum, the six council members were arranged in a half-circle, each with their own formidable desk.

No one but Agren greeted her arrival.

She mouthed a "Thank you" for what he'd done for Chesandril.

But the rest of the members bore dour expressions—perhaps, due to the late hour—getting close to sunrise. Kaycia couldn't help but feel surrounded and outnumbered. She felt the weight of their eyes watching her. Judging her.

Condemning her.

She ignored them all except Soril's. But his gaze remained subdued and told her nothing.

Rising to his feet, the Master Ascendant declared in a loud voice, "This council has decided to permit your entry into Ahman."

Kaycia breathed a sigh of relief—knowing this, at least, bought her more time.

Many of the others appeared uncomfortable, as though displeased by this outcome. Soril wasn't finished.

"This verdict is contingent upon your adherence to stringent protocols."

She narrowed her gaze in sudden concern.

"First," he continued, "the physical body of Miss Kaycia Eldren shall remain within this camp, under the watch and care of Master Soril himself."

Her face flushed red. "Are you sure that's—?"

She clamped her mouth shut, sensing she was in no position to argue.

Soril grimaced. "I assure you, Miss Eldren, every effort will be made to respect your privacy. There is nothing...indecent...behind this decision. You understand, don't you, why we can't allow you to proceed unsupervised?"

She took a deep breath. "Might I make a request?"

He raised a brow in disapproval.

"Only that Chesandril be present at all times."

"You stand before a tribunal," said a man on the left, whose name she didn't know. "And you make demands?"

Soril merely frowned. "It's quite all right." Looking at Kaycia, he said, "Agreed."

She was tempted to say more—that she wanted Chesandril to maintain line of sight and not be left on the other side of a door. But these were details they could work out later.

Soril sighed before moving on. "Second, you'll be required to return to that body, at the very least, twice daily and provide us with a comprehensive report. You'll respond completely and truthfully to every question asked. You're to leave nothing out. Everyone will share ownership of this investigation—not just you."

She nodded, having anticipated such a request. "I'll do my best—so long as I can find a safe place to leave my sister."

"Make sure that you do. Plan ahead if you have to. We won't have you rushing off at the expense of being thorough."

"Of course."

Neranda broke in. "Before we move on, might I add something?"

The woman's face had been cleaned and bore little trace of Elyriel's assault. "Your companion—Chesandril, was it?—can watch your body while you're not around, but she *won't* be permitted to sit on these meetings."

"I understand."

"Neranda makes an excellent point," said Soril. "All knowledge of this investigation is to remain strictly confidential—no exceptions. We cannot emphasize this enough. Everything that goes on here is to be limited to the people you see present—and a few others I'll name in a moment. Is that clear?"

She couldn't help but wonder what he meant—who these few others might be—but she nodded and said, "Perfectly."

Kaycia felt her attitude shift toward excitement. She was reminded that even though a prisoner, she was participating in something extraordinary.

"Anything else?" she asked.

"You'll stick to the areas we specify without deviation. We've determined which locations will provide the best insight on what happened that day, three hundred years ago."

She felt her heart leap. "But isn't the Navaran my objective? Has that changed?"

"You'll be doing both. Think of it this way—we've yet to identify the Navaran's goals in the ancient city. It's not unreasonable to assume he, too, is on a quest for answers. By having you do the same, you'll be more likely to cross paths."

"Okay... But you're just guessing. You don't know what he's after."

Once again, she felt the council's disapproval. "I'm not arguing!" she said, trying to recover. "I just didn't think there'd be time—you know—to indulge my curiosity."

Soril suppressed a grin. "This is a unique opportunity we'd be foolish to let slip by. But let's not get ahead of ourselves. We've yet to determine if anything useful has survived without succumbing to rot."

She nodded.

The man continued. "The stranger might be after something specific to aid the Navaran Empire."

Her eyes narrowed.

But Soril shook his head. "Exactly what, we don't know. You just need to be aware of the possibility. We want you to watch him. Should you encounter signs of the Navaran's activity, under no circumstances must you attempt communication or endanger our relationship with the empire."

"What? You're saying I shouldn't stop him?"

"Not at first. All we ask is that you avoid confrontation, at least, until we've determined his aims."

Kaycia couldn't deny this made sense. They all knew she was no match for the Navaran's abilities, and they'd decided to go with a safer approach.

She knew she'd be expected to go along with it. That she should shut her mouth and not ask questions. But she couldn't hold them back. "What if he approaches me? If he attacks me?"

"Then," said Soril, in a controlled tone, "we expect you to exercise appropriate caution. Please try not to be discovered. So long as he thinks he's alone, we hold the advantage."

"And if he notices right away?"

"Then use your best judgment! A strategic retreat might be in order. Either way, it'll be up to you to get into contact with us—as Elyriel or yourself—so we are all included in these decisions."

He made it sound so simple.

She realized, though, how frustrating this must be from his perspective. After years yearning to find Ahman, he could do little more than watch from the sidelines. His instructions couldn't be more specific, but they were his only means of active participation.

"In much the same way," he continued, "you're not to manipulate or interact with any artifacts or contraptions left behind by the gods. Many are considered delicate, and some extremely dangerous. It is vital you refrain from touching them. Rather, it'll be your job to observe and take note of any details for our group to identify the objects in question."

The man produced a comforting smile. "I'll be taking steps to assemble a team of scholars and historians before your first report. Through them, you'll have access to all the ancient knowledge that's survived to this day."

So that's what he'd meant—the few people who'd be 'in' on the secret.

"That...sounds helpful," she said, doing nothing to hide her concern. "Can I trust they'll be equally forthcoming with what they know?" Echoing the instructions he'd just given her, she added, "Will they respond truthfully to what I ask? Leaving nothing out?"

Soril nodded gravely, understanding what she was getting at. There was a lot of information—particularly regarding the deaths of the gods—that many people would feel compelled to control.

It wasn't unreasonable, then, to assume some alleged scholars might hide information. They'd want to prevent Kaycia from fully understanding what she saw. It was the sort of hand-tying, of course, that'd put Elyriel's life, needlessly, at risk.

After a few seconds, Soril was still forming a response.

So Kaycia followed with additional questions—ones she thought easier to answer. "How well do you know the people on this team? Who are they? How many are we talking about?"

"Not many. Three—maybe four? I apologize, but we're doing our best with limited time. Luckily, some of the greatest minds in respect to Ahman are living right here. Two are long colleagues of mine—and I'd trust them with my life."

"And the others?"

"That's what we're still looking into. Unfortunately, there are key documents that can only be accessed by Taelish sectarians."

Kaycia didn't like the sound of that, but she understood Soril's reasoning. None of those schematics were considered public knowledge, and it practically forced their group to get the church involved.

She was tempted to suggest an alternate course—to steal the papers in question—but she didn't think that would sit well before a council of judges.

"All right," she said, growing impatient. "Is that all your stipulations? Because there are still answers you haven't given me."

He worked his mouth, having no difficulty guessing what she meant.

Kaycia ignored the rest of the council. "I want to know what's to happen when the investigation's over. Specifically, what's been decided for my sister."

"I'm afraid the matter's still up for debate."

This was followed by uncomfortable silence.

"...Care to elaborate?"

"Centric to the problem is your ongoing involvement with local authorities. Even if we could, somehow, convince them to hold their silence—something I'd never attempt—the paperwork has been submitted."

She groaned. While she couldn't argue with what he said, she'd hoped they'd considered other solutions.

"In the end, you will stand trial. Of that, we have no control."

Kaycia swallowed.

"However, " he continued. "in light of whatever this operation unearths, we might convince the judges of your inherent value."

"What? You're not suggesting a *bribe*?"

He reddened in embarrassment. "Perhaps 'unearth' was the wrong word. I wasn't talking of treasure. But referring to *you*."

"Don't you mean Elyriel?" she asked dryly. "Being the transcendent and all?"

"She's certainly part of it. There might be ways to make you both...indispensable. So that even if you were to be executed, no judge could pass that sentence."

"That's not a solution."

He tossed up his hands in defeat. "What do you expect from me? I apologize, Kaycia, but I don't know what's going to happen. Everything you've done—everything that's happened to you—there's no precedent for this. I can't predict how Carheim's leaders will respond."

"But—!"

"One step at a time. There's too much ahead to worry about that now."

Kaycia shook her head, astonished by his lack of sympathy.

But with those words, the meeting adjourned. With a signal from Soril, the guards escorted Kaycia from the tent.

The night was icy cold, and the men's orders were to deliver her back to the carriage and make sure she got some sleep.

They didn't make it far before their group was stopped.

Kaycia turned and was surprised to find Soril had followed them.

"Give us a moment?" he asked the soldiers, motioning them away.

"What now?" she asked, doubtful he'd come because he'd changed his mind.

"Everything I said back there was true," he said in a low voice. "Right now, your best defense is to show the leaders how much they need you... But, there's one more thing— something I failed to mention in front of the others."

"I'm listening," she said, drawing her brows together.

"While you're in there—in Ahman—I want you to search for Irisea."

This again? She'd nearly forgotten their conversation of the child goddess. And after everything that'd happened, she wasn't in the mood to talk about it now.

"So that's it?" she asked. "The reason you persuaded the others? It had nothing to do with me—it boils down to your legends?"

"No! Well...both reasons are true. It's not what you think."

Kaycia shook her head. "I don't have the energy to argue this again."

"Then don't argue," he reasoned. "Just listen."

She groaned, feeling resentment he'd push this on her. If anything, she was less likely to consider what he said.

"Hear me out. Everything that's going on—dealing with this Navaran, the rediscovery of Ahman... These things are well and good, but they're not what we need. We can't reverse what happened to the gods. It'll do us good to know more, but it won't solve anything."

"But this mythical child will?" she asked incredulously. "That's what you're saying? You think she can help us?"

"Not just us. Think of what she might do for Elyriel."

Her mouth gaped. How could Irisea—who wasn't proven to exist—possibly help? Even if she was real, she'd been locked away for centuries! And for all that time, she hadn't proved capable of saving herself.

But there was something in Soril's expression that persuaded her to listen. This didn't sound like conjecture or hypothetical solutions. She sensed a deep feeling behind his voice—enough for her to think his intentions were sincere.

"Maybe Irisea won't fix Elyriel," he continued. "But any help at all might be just what we need. It might sway the judges—finding a way to make your sister less dangerous. More in control. Understand?"

"I don't. Why would Irisea have anything to do with—?"

Soril stopped her with a hand. "Don't you see? If *death* is the problem... Isn't it time we bound ourselves to the one god who's still alive?"

Part 3
The Silence of Flames

-Confessions of Irisea
(year unknown)

Chapter 16
UNEARTHLY SIEGE

As Prince Nesil left the schoolyard in the late afternoon, he was met by two priests bearing the news of his mother's death.

A few classmates overheard and stood unmoving by the weathered schoolhouse. Their uncertain stares made Nesil self-conscious, but he was grateful he didn't have to bear this alone.

Since he was little, he'd learned to keep a straight face around others. But though he'd mastered the art of hiding his feelings, he was not so adept at making them go away.

Nesil found this frustrating as hell. He'd thought he'd be prepared for this. He'd realized long ago that no one, not even his mother, could forever elude the death that'd brought the grand Kingdom of Seldor to its knees. So why was her passing so surprisingly difficult?

The elder of the priests—a bearded, gaunt, old man—bowed his head in respect. "It's our solemn duty to inform you, with Queen Kena's passing, you're to hereby take her place as the heir-apparent. At your grandfather's command, your anointing will take place this very evening."

"So soon?"

"Yes, the King was quite clear. He's insisted no abbreviations be made to the festivities. The event is to last the entire night. Preparations are already underway."

The old man raised bushy eyebrows. "The heralds have decreed, at sixteen years of age, you're to become the youngest heir-apparent in Seldoran history."

Nesil, however, didn't feel like celebrating. "And mother's funeral?"

Shaking his head, the priest was overcome by a fit of hacking coughs. He cleared his throat. "I'm afraid there won't be one."

"For the *queen*?! Tell me, which of the royal councilmen made that decision?"

"None, my dear prince. The mandate came from your sovereign grandfather, himself." The priest became sympathetic. "Like it or not, Her Majesty will be recognized alongside the rest of the dead at week's end."

Feeling a shortness of breath, Nesil closed his eyes. Whether his emotion was brought on by anger or sadness, he couldn't be certain.

The old man continued, "I believe the king's methods appropriate. The kingdom aches from lack of good news. You'd be wise to learn from his initiative when you, in time, take the throne." He spread his arms. "Instead of fueling more grief, he's elected to do something about it."

Nesil nodded, though he didn't consider a celebration the same as doing something. Not really. The people would come to the commemoration, if only for the wine. But cheeriness wouldn't stop people from dying. No one was doing anything for Seldor. They didn't know how.

The siege had gone on without interruption for three long years.

Remembering to be gracious, Nesil inclined his head. "You may inform the king I accept his invitation."

The priest cast his gaze on the nearby students. "Go! Tell your families!" He shooed them from the yard like pesky flies. "Or whomever you live with."

Reluctantly, they left. As they passed Nesil, some bowed their heads in commiseration, while others offered uneasy congratulations.

Nesil smiled appreciatively to assure them he was okay. It didn't matter how he felt.

Until he realized the opportunity this provided.

After months of deliberation, he didn't pretend he could lift the siege or make the enemy go away. But he'd thought about it often—far more than could be expected from a sixteen-year-old in school.

The problem with the aeisr was that nothing could harm them. Whether steel or fire, it'd pass through their bodies without effect—like a horrible dream that'd never go away.

Nesil's plan, then, was not to flee but to confront them directly. Rather than fight, he meant to get close and make them an offer they couldn't refuse.

With unfeigned solemnity, he dropped his gaze. "How did she die?" A part of him didn't want to know. Most of the recent deaths had been drawn out and gruesome, and it hurt to imagine his mother in pain.

The old man turned away. "...She leaped out a window."

"But...! There shouldn't be windows that high! It's the whole reason for relocating to this district!"

"One of the reasons...but you misunderstand. It didn't happen here. When word got out she was missing, they sent for a founder. But, by then, she'd already made it to the castle. There's good news in that. The queen died instantly—I assure you—and free from pain. The Northeast Tower is the tallest in Seldor."

That *was* good news. Not only the quick death but the fact it'd happened in a place free from people. Silverwater Castle had been abandoned for years, and Nesil could search for the high aeisr in absolute privacy.

"How recent was this? A few hours?"

"I suppose..." The old man furrowed his brow as if wondering why the prince would want to know.

Nesil, however, kept his eyes on his feet. Such details were a natural part of grieving. They weren't morbid. If anything, they provided a last connection between the living and deceased.

Seconds passed before the priests turned back to the main road, giving Nesil his space. Their final expressions were apologetic, as though the priests were remembering their own loved ones, recently lost.

But Nesil wasn't thinking about mother any longer.

To persuade these phantoms to his way of thinking, he'd need his mind to be sharp. He needed to stay focused, no matter how his heart ached.

Nesil waited a few minutes before heading north toward the forbidden districts. As long as he was quick, he'd only be gone a few short hours—leaving just enough time to prepare for his ceremony.

Discarding his princely vest, he took to the darkened alleys lest he be recognized. He'd already learned which ones were frequented by drunkards and which were left alone.

Even so, it took nearly fifteen minutes to walk up the hill, passing boarded-up buildings with blackened tile roofs. The further he went, the less often he had to hide, as scant few people ever traveled this way. And never because they wanted to.

It wasn't until he was completely alone that the first of many doubts began to surface. Did he truly believe he could outsmart the aeisr? It'd taken months to convince himself he could, but he'd also thought the same of his mother. Queen Kena had been the smartest person he knew—and even she'd been outmaneuvered.

No, he told himself. If his plan ever stood a chance, it had to be now. This wasn't recklessness or driven by vengeance. His motivation was simple—a sanguine confidence his plan would work.

At the crest of the hill, the old masonry was little more than a heap of rubble. It was high enough, however, that from atop the remains of a mildewed hearth, he had a clear view of what used to be Seldor.

The sight was pitiful as the sky of dust deepened into dusk. Gazing back down the hill, he saw the faint glow from windows and doorways, like a swarm of fireflies resting in the brush. The burning lanterns and candlelight, however, came from a single district. It seemed so small, surrounded by the burnt-out ruins that extended for miles in every direction.

A kingdom on the brink of drowning. Left alone by its allies, without so much as an ambassador from Carheim.

A year ago, it hadn't been uncommon to find a few scattered lights amid these remnants—signs of people who refused to leave their homes. *The aeisr don't frighten us,* they'd said. *They can't harm us—physically—so why should we flee?* No matter how much Nesil's grandfather pleaded, their minds were made up. *We won't die like the others...* They were wrong.

The air up here stank of the dead—of corpses old and recent, with some yet waiting to be recovered and burned. It was a sour smell, like fetid berries and putrefied bile, but Nesil had gotten used to it. This was the land to which he was heir. The memory of Seldor. Silenced to less than an eighth of what it was.

Somehow, it'd never seemed this small—not while Mother was around. And he knew, with time, it'd only get worse.

A sharp crack echoed from the masonry's back lot, and he jumped down behind the hearth.

He heard a giggle, sweet and melodic. Girlish. "You'll have to hide better than that."

His first thought was impossible—that his mother wasn't dead, and it was all a mistake. His second thought was more likely—that an aeisr was deceitfully using his mother's appearance. But, as he stepped out, neither was true.

Stepping gently across the rubble was a young, blond girl with pale white skin. Sefina wore a shiny white dress that hung closely but loosely to her delicate frame—the dress was small, but she was smaller. It was sleeveless, seemingly seamless, and ended past her knees.

Three years younger than he, her familiar face filled him with relief and trepidation. She was one of his closest friends—but he'd have to lie to her.

He couldn't let her know the reason he was here. If a word slipped out, the aeisr might overhear. Visible or not, the ethereal beings could be anywhere. And it'd always been necessary to devise his plans within the privacy of his mind.

"Do you like it?" Sefina smiled as she twirled once, showing off her dress. It was an odd sight, so pristinely white in contrast to the wastes.

"You're wearing *that*?" he asked, stepping forward.

She made a face. "I can be careful."

He wasn't in the mood to argue his point. "You shouldn't have come. I wasn't escaping."

"Silly boy," she said—one of the few people to address the prince in such fashion. "I didn't even know you'd be here."

So what was she doing? Nesil hoped she wouldn't wait for his own reasons. Fortunately, she continued with her own.

"You remember my parents, don't you?" She bit her lip and looked up at him through aqua-green eyes.

He nodded and sighed.

Sefina was a member of the marquessate—and it was thanks to her heritage that her family was at the castle when the attacks began.

Her smile disappeared. "Today's the day," she said, slumping her shoulders. "It's been three years since they died."

Nesil was reminded of his own loss—so recent and acute it was difficult to believe. But, right before him stood a girl who knew exactly how he felt. It was no longer necessary to explain his reasons—she'd assume he, too, meant to visit the dead.

It also meant he couldn't turn her away.

"You were going alone?" Nesil couldn't help from feeling impressed.

"I don't feel so brave." She laughed. "And, each year, It's not that I *want* to go alone. I just never get around to telling anyone."

"What are they going to do? Lock you in a room?"

"They might!" she said seriously. "But I'm more afraid if I speak the words, I'll convince myself of the danger. And hate myself afterward."

"You don't seem bothered telling me."

"Well..." She seemed about to smile but changed her mind. "I—I'm sorry. You probably don't want to talk about your mother."

"No... I get it."

Nesil wondered, in the future, if this might become a regular thing. Once the aeisr was gone, neither would have to make this trip alone.

He adopted a more jovial tone. "Let's be quick. No one will care if I miss the ceremony, but if *you* show up late, the whole court will be devastated."

She wrinkled her nose at his attempted humor but offered no objection.

As they left the masonry and carefully drew closer to aeisr territory, Nesil found where he'd stashed a long, slender pole. It was light, hollow, and made of burnished brass. He only had one, but it'd serve them both as they neared the castle, tapping the ground as blind people do.

As such, it took a few minutes to descend the hill, weaving past buildings decrepit and burnt.

Sefina bumped him when he stopped.

"There's a hole," he said. He dropped to a knee and stabbed the shaft further down. The length disappeared into illusory dirt, and he still felt no resistance.

"It's deep," he said, pulling the pole back up. "A well, perhaps?"

Dragging the tip sideways, he kept track of where the real earth ended and the fake ground began. "Stay close," he said, sliding the tip along the edge.

The aeisr had the bad habit of altering the world around them, as though weaving it from dreams. But no matter how lifelike these hallucinations might appear, they couldn't support your weight if you stepped onto them.

After one more block, his pole encountered an invisible structure—made imperceptible by phantom air. They worked their way around it without time to identify its shape. Nesil guessed it was an overturned wagon. Sefina thought it a stand for selling cakes and chocolates.

They soon reached the market outside the castle, where they encountered their first wandering aeisr. These particular ones were of the lesser variety—incapable of creating illusions or traps—but their presence was disturbing all the same.

Outwardly, they appeared quite ordinary. Their clothing hung in tatters, and their skin sagged—but they weren't real people. Not even real dead people. Not spirits but something else entirely.

An old lady in an apron was bent over, perusing the contents of an empty stall. Across the square, a washwoman was quietly reprimanding her daughter. They stepped aside as a man emerged from the alley, hauling a load of firewood.

None of it was real, of course. If Nesil touched the wood, he'd get a sense of its texture, but his hand would pass through. If it was added to a fire, Nesil might feel heat, but it wouldn't warm his body.

Leaving the market behind, they neared a wide ditch, which, in better days, had formed a defensive moat. A drawbridge was precariously suspended across the gap, as it'd been ever since the castle was abandoned.

The path, however, showed signs of erosion—enough for Nesil to slow their approach.

"Hand me a rock."

She did.

Feeling its weight, he attempted to crush it with his hands. Eerily, it gave way beneath the pressure, fell through his grasp, and landed in the dirt.

He shivered at the strange sensation. "No good," he said, smiling. "It has to be a real one."

Sefina made a face as though she'd chosen it on purpose.

After selecting one himself—and making sure it was solid—he hefted it at the drawbridge and listened for the thud.

"Let's go."

They slid down the slope and carefully went across.

As they passed beneath the gatehouse, Nesil continued to prod at the shadows with his pole. The heavy iron portcullis loomed overhead as though it might come crashing down at any moment.

Beyond the massive walls, the castle baileys was more a wild garden, with plants dried and withered beneath the open sky. Long grasses as high as his chest surrounded the stone path leading up to the keep.

He wondered if they might have to worry about coyotes—or other wild creatures. He was saddened to see his home in such ruin, but what bothered him the most were the castle's new tenants—dark figures lurking behind every corner.

While the aeisr outside had been content to ignore them, these were not.

As Nesil and Sefina walked by, old men turned their heads at odd angles. There was no contempt in their eyes—just empty stares. A few women, in silent conversation, suddenly stopped and followed from a distance.

"Nesil...?" Her voice was almost a whisper.

He had to force the words out. "They can't hurt you...remember?"

It was all he could do to believe this himself—and not think about what was waiting in the castle. Hoping the high aeisr hadn't noticed their arrival.

When Sefina didn't relax, he tried something else.

"You should've worn a different dress."

"Huh?"

"If you didn't want the attention."

She punched his shoulder. "That's not funny!"

"You're right," he said, holding back a chuckle. "...Sorry."

Her tension didn't leave, but it changed somewhat. Enough that he didn't feel sorry at all.

The great double doors groaned loudly, announcing their presence to everyone inside. With only a few windows, high near the vaulted ceiling, Nesil was surprised by how much light remained.

Rather than deep shadows, an almost imperceptible ambiance infused the castle walls, making torchlight unnecessary. A thin, steady glow seemed to permeate everything. An attempt, perhaps, to appear more inviting.

Nesil didn't mention this to Sefina, not wanting to add to her worries. He merely stayed by her side as she remembered the way—down the eastern passage, past the collapsed kitchens, and toward the north wing.

He imagined his mother walking these halls and passing these same dust-covered tapestries. Not too long ago, she had breathed this stale air.

Had she been aware of her actions up until the end? Or had she been free from cares, as someone walking in her sleep? If she'd thought it a dream, had it been a good one?

As they started up the stairs, Nesil increased his caution.

The castle had been constructed with high, spacious ceilings, raising the second floor twenty feet above the ground. There was no telling which floorboards might be loose, or which supports were so charred they were a hair from breaking.

At his insistence, they proceeded slowly, tapping with his pole.

It wasn't long before Sefina stopped at one of the doors. And he realized she never meant to visit a grave.

As he thought about it now, it was unlikely her parents had been given proper burials. They'd likely been burned by the first of the nightmares—as Seldor rose to confront the aeisr, and soldiers were tricked into fighting themselves.

Without a tombstone, she'd chosen the next best place—the room where they'd stayed during their visits to the castle.

The cracked windows gleamed—though no natural starlight could've penetrated the dust. Ignoring this detail, he was surprised to find the room largely untouched by the years. The burgundy curtains, billowing softly, were ragged and worn but refused to fall. The ornate bed was powdered with a sheen of dust and was still dressed with its lavishly embroidered canopy and faded bedding.

Wooden partitions were pushed against the walls, providing a yellow wallpapered backdrop for cabinets, bureaus, chests, and dressers. The drawers, however, were skewed and open—from the thieves who'd liberated the castle of its valuables.

This had only been Sefina's temporary home, but Nesil thought he saw a sense of peace come over her. Her real home had been in the province of Merilon—farther than Nesil had ever traveled and well outside reach after the coming of the aeisr. This room, then, was the closest connection she had left and, by the look on her face, one she deeply treasured.

"I need to check on something." He was reluctant to leave her alone, but he hadn't forgotten the reason he was there. "Just...stay in this room, okay? I'll return in a moment."

Beneath the light of the moon, her dress had turned a light shade of blue. Her aqua-green eyes were filled with questions, but she didn't stop him.

For a brief moment, he was tempted to forget the whole thing. Why did *he* have to be the one to deal with the aeisr instead of being free like a regular teenager? It'd be so easy to relax and share these precious moments, reminiscing of their past. Thinking of his mother.

But he backed away and closed the door behind him.

Making careful use of his pole, he navigated the north wing, ignoring the wide-eyed stares of lingering figures. He knew exactly where to go—the place most likely to produce the high aeisr. It was on the same floor and not too far from Sefina's room.

It was the only chamber in the castle not stripped of its assets—as any thief, fool enough to try, never came out alive.

Taking a deep breath, Nesil opened the door to a treasury filled with chests, display cases—and a single pedestal at its center.

Upon a cylindrical base, beneath a soft light that seemingly came from nowhere, was the statue of Ashaira—the betrayer—the goddess of Ordination.

...Or, at least, a fragment of her statue.

It was as though someone had broken this section from somewhere else and had only managed to take her head, her bare shoulders, and most her left arm. What remained of her long, flowing hair was spread out as though caught by a wind. The entirety was supported by metal struts, holding her straight in the absence of her body.

With Shaelis, Ashaira once stood at the head of the pantheon. They were the rulers of the gods and rumored to have produced a child yet still alive.

Broken though she was, the goddess' face was flawless. Her eyes seemed to follow him wherever he stood—lending to her beauty a malevolent quality.

His grandfather never explained where he got it, but it was shortly after this statue's arrival that the otherworldly beings began to manifest.

In response to the attacks, the King commanded men to take sledgehammers and reduce the bust to rubble. It'd seemed to work, with the physical stone crumbling away, pulverized by their blows. But the immaterial appearance of Ashaira remained—of some intangible material nothing could harm.

A new tactic was tried, believing if they chopped the wood from beneath the base, nothing would support it, and it'd break on the ground twenty feet below. This, too, was a failure—and all they gained was a large hole at the center of their treasury and a pedestal floating midair.

Nesil knew all this, so he was surprised to find the floor undamaged and intact. No jagged hole. No powder or debris.

Ashaira was the same as she'd appeared that day.

She seemed so harmless he started walking toward her.

It wasn't a compulsion so much as a longing she instilled within. Some darker purpose that exuded from her creation.

An incomprehensible restlessness.

Something not unlike insanity.

In an instant, Nesil planted his feet where they were. His heart thumped wildly in his chest.

Somehow, if only briefly, he'd been persuaded to believe the hole wasn't there. A few steps further, and...

He took hold of his thoughts. Despite what almost happened, he wasn't in danger yet. The solution was simple. He'd back away from the edge and continue with his plan.

"Is anyone here?" he asked.

He turned around and nearly stumbled in surprise.

The entire room seemed to shift, revolving with his movement. Somehow, the exit was *still* behind him. He was facing Ashaira as though he hadn't turned at all.

He turned his head back, wondering if she'd move again.

She didn't.

Nesil cursed, unwilling to be tricked. His eyes might be wrong, but his memory wasn't. If he turned back now to where the exit seemed to be, he'd only move closer to the actual drop-off.

So, instead, he took steps toward the statue before him.

Only for the floor to tilt downward and start sinking away.

"The hell?!" he stammered, planting his feet.

Great cracks jolted the ground so powerfully he was dropped to his knees. He caught himself, palms burning, as his pole clanged beside him.

The floor bent past its limit in an explosion of splinters. It tore away, disappearing into the darkness below. Followed by the sound of shattering glass.

A chill wind blew up from the abyss, so strong, he closed his eyes.

The torrent encircled him and ripped at his clothing.

Something hard struck his shoulder—the pain so real that he actually cried out and stumbled forward.

It took all his willpower to focus on the floor—the only thing he positively knew to be real. He tried not to lean, as this would only move his body the wrong direction.

The wind relented a little, and he opened his eyes. But he was no longer sure which direction he faced. Though it appeared unchanged, there were no guarantees.

In some ways, he was glad to have fallen. On his hands and knees, he had more leverage, making it more difficult to be tricked off the edge. As long as he stayed down, he could proceed slowly.

Except, right then, he remembered Sefina.

Alone in her parent's room.

What did it matter if *he* was safe when she, too, might be in danger?

With growing dread, he forced himself up. He could only hope he was still facing the exit, as he could no longer trust anything he saw.

So he closed his eyes.

Grasping his pole like a spear, he leaped forward into the abyss.

For a sickening moment, it felt like he was falling.

Except his feet were still on solid ground.

He wanted to shout in triumph, grateful for being right. But it wasn't enough for him to open his eyes. Better a blind man than a fool.

He forced himself forward, remembering where the hallway should be. When the rod slammed into stone and sent vibrations up his arms, it confirmed he'd finally left the treasury.

Pole still quavering, he turned left and began to run again. He anticipated this next stretch to be nearly twenty feet.

Still blind, his boot caught something solid, and he sprawled onto the ground. But he ignored the pain that shot through his shins and his burning palms.

He forced himself up and reached the next wall.

From here, I go right. It became easier as he ran, not caring if he veered into walls or bumped the occasional table or doorpost.

Once, his hand caught onto something, digging into skin.

But what did he care about bumps or scrapes? In this area, at least, he didn't remember any drop-offs. There were no ledges or balconies.

All the windows were in the rooms, like where—

"Sefina!" he yelled as he drew closer. "Sefina!"

Left turn down the hallway. Another left after that.

His hands found the latch, and he burst his way through.

Opening his eyes, he found the young girl kneeling on the floor, turned away from him. With a sigh of relief, he rushed toward her.

"Are you—?"

His moment's reprieve was yanked away.

He stumbled backward and fell onto his rear.

Sefina stared back through empty sockets.

Dark blood ran down her face and the front of her dress and the tips of her fingers— as if she, herself, had clawed out her eyes.

Limp as a rag doll, she crumpled sideways to the floor, her face still toward him, staring back through dark hollows.

It's a trick, he assured himself. *It has to be!* The aeisr was not capable of anything like this.

This wasn't the real Sefina. It was just a frightful doll—a perverse imitation to unsettle and terrify.

"There's no escape," whispered the doll.

And the room burst into flames.

Smoke filled his lungs—so hot, he couldn't breathe.

In loud pops and bursts, the wardrobe fell apart. Sparks dashed across the floor. Ash spun in the air. Wallpaper peeled away from partitions, and the bed flared up like a sacrificial altar.

The fire didn't touch him, but he could feel the heat searing into his flesh. There was sweat on his face and palms.

At the center of the room, the thing that was not Sefina also burned, caressed within the undulation of flames.

Nesil tried to close his eyes but found that he couldn't.

He tried to look away, but his vision was transfixed.

And the blood-covered thing that was not Sefina crawled toward him.

Through tear-filled eyes stinging from smoke, he could almost see her smile. And a new thought crossed his mind.

Was *this* the horrendous thing he'd sought to challenge? Could this doll-shaped apparition be the high aeisr itself?

It'd never occurred to him it would be like this.

Had his mother experienced a similar nightmare? Right before she died?

And what of the real Sefina? Was she off somewhere, in another part of the castle, helpless and afraid? The thought sickened him beyond belief.

The girl's head swayed to the side, limp across her shoulder. A fragile doll with no eyes. Embraced by fire.

"You'll not kill me!" Nesil hollered. "For you've not heard what I have to say. It's the reason I'm here! I came here *looking* for you!"

The girl didn't pause but drew ever closer.

The tips of her blond hair were dark and sticky. Flames licked her frail body and her withering dress.

"Why settle for me when I can give you more?" he asked, feeling more confident with his rehearsed speech. "I've seen how you try to kill who's left, but most manage to elude you. They're learning. We all are. And it's increasingly difficult for us to kill ourselves."

She swayed from side to side, trailing blood behind.

Nesil pushed himself back with his feet. Coughing away smoke, he spoke more quickly.

"These hands," he said, holding them aloft. "Here are corporeal means to accomplish your goals. Physical weapons you can dress in illusion. I give them to you to use as you wish—to make invisible so your enemies won't see them coming.

"I will be your assassin because we both want the same thing."

Nesil steeled himself for the worst of his lies. Knowing how important it was not to betray his intentions.

"You see," he continued, "I was glad today when you killed my mother—the happiest I've been for the longest time. This evening, I shall be named the heir-apparent of Seldor—positioned with access to the secrets of my kingdom. The people hide from you, but they cannot hide from me.

"I'm to be king, you see. So let us be allies, you and I."

Nesil watched the girl as she closed the distance.

Bending down, she brought her sightless face within inches of his own.

He remained resolute, though his heart was thumping madly in his chest.

This *had* to be done. All other attempts had failed. This was the only way to get close—to become part of their plans—so, someday, something might be done to stop them.

"I am Prince Nesil, heir to the throne, and I've come to offer you the head of my grandfather, King Renat Kirchem, the fourth of his name, Lord of the Silverwater, and Sovereign Ascendant of Seldor."

Chapter 17
WAKING NIGHTMARE

After several minutes searching the castle, Nesil had no choice but to leave Sefina behind.

His mind reeled at the idea, unable to believe he had to choose some meaningless social gathering over the prospect of saving his dear friend from death. It was absurd. It was perverse. And, worst of all, it was necessary.

As late as it was, he was already walking the fine edge of a knife, risking someone noticing his absence and raising the alarm. After his mother's recent murder, they wouldn't hesitate to call upon their founder again—and the castle would be the first place they'd check.

It'd ruin everything.

If Nesil were questioned or brought under the slightest suspicion, he'd have little chance of continuing his dealings with the aeisr. That plan, in the end, was all he had left. Nothing could be more important than that. Not even Sefina.

No one spoke a word as he arrived at the villa, crossed through the parlor, and headed to his room. This was likely due to his stern expression, emotionless and hard. He was in no mood to speak with anyone—his mind tormented by not knowing if his plan was working.

His only comfort was that he was still alive. The aeisr hadn't answered or provided clarification. The fire had disappeared, and he'd been allowed to leave.

If his temperament toward his attendants seemed harsher than usual, he could pretend it was due to his mother's passing. Nesil could always apologize later. As such, he didn't hesitate to dismiss them from his room, insisting he could dress himself.

He chose a black velvet tunic embroidered with fine silver thread.

To his bitter surprise, he found his hands were shaking. It was nearly enough to make him change his mind and call his servants back.

His problems, however, were ones he'd brought upon himself. His arrangement with the aeisr was a nightmare of his choosing. No one else could alleviate the thoughts and fears of his mind.

Images of fire and blood.

More than anything, Nesil hated feeling powerless—having been unable to look away from the aeisr's dark, hollowed eyes.

He'd always believed it'd be a matter of sheer willpower—that if he could only demonstrate mastery of himself and keep a level head, he'd recognize any influence enacted on his mind.

But that hadn't been the case at all. He'd never faced such overwhelming power in his life. His usual lucidity had been stripped clean away, and he'd been reduced to little more than a trembling child.

For a few seconds, he'd even lost control of his bowels.

Only now—a full half-hour later—he was finally regaining his sense of composure. He changed out of his breeches—only slightly damp—and convinced himself not to be ashamed.

There was nothing shameful in what he'd done. His only regret was losing track of Sefina.

Taking a moment by the washbasin, he cleaned his face and neck of dried sweat. Lacking the time for a full bath, it was the best he could do.

His dark hair was still straight, and he considered leaving it alone. But if his mother were there, she'd run a brush through it anyway.

He examined his reflection. Then combed his hair.

As he'd practiced so many times before, he produced a warm smile.

The boy in the mirror appeared genuinely happy and free from deceit. He was a bright young man who astounded the nobility—drawing attention as a bard with a crowd of children.

This fearless, pleasant boy would never hurt anyone—especially his friends. He was a normal boy—exceptional, even—and not worthy of loathing.

When Nesil arrived at the party, the music was in full sway—a sweet harmony of strings at a low, lively tempo. Without an adequate ballroom, a park pavilion had been cleared so the celebration could take place in the cool night air.

With the dusty sky hiding the stars, a team of transfigurers had strung countless glowing spheres of limestone in the air. Amid the roving gnats, the infused stones cast a steady incandescence upon the dancing couples and conversed pleasantries.

Everyone was dressed in their finest, which, in only a few cases, meant proper formal attire. For others, it meant wearing the last dress they owned. Or even threadbare work clothes for those who'd lost everything.

The dance floor was lined with tables of food—so much, Nesil couldn't guess where it'd all come from. The roast pigs and wild ducklings were small but well-seasoned. A generous assortment of flatbreads, nearly-ripened fruit, and fresh cheeses were carried around in wide baskets and trays.

Older men sat at tables, drinking and sharing stories of how things used to be. Children laughed as they played on the outskirts, creating a spirited racket that was not unpleasant.

In a way, Nesil was glad so many had come—at least a few hundred. It was a pleasant change to the sullen faces so common these days. He wished his mother could've seen this, knowing how much she'd worked to make her people happy.

Upon his approach, many rushed to greet him. They congratulated him on his recent test scores and said he'd grow up to be an excellent king. A few older women were more forward with their glances, insistent on mentioning how handsome he was becoming.

Only once did someone dare talk of his mother—saying how proud she would've been and how much she'd loved him. No one was eager to mention her death, as though desperate to preserve this festive facade. They evaded the topic with such surprising grace that it wasn't helpful. If anything, it made him more uncomfortable.

For Nesil, it was easy to remember their names and respond appropriately. He knew when to make jokes and when to express sincere concern—even while his mind was focused elsewhere.

When it all came down to it, social maneuvering was simple and petty—especially compared to the rest of his problems.

Only a single person suspected he was hiding something.

"You're rather morose this evening," said Terak after inexplicably extracting the prince to one side.

Before Nesil could respond, the older boy continued, "I know, I know. I'm not accusing you of anything—but your smiles are a bit too sincere. And that means you're lying."

Nesil expected this. But it was more a game than actual truth-telling—a game only fun because Nesil was difficult to read. If anything, the guesses were entertaining and evidence his friend cared.

There was no real worry of secrets coming out. Or feelings.

Terak shook his head. "You need to liven up—don't look at me like that. After my mum died, I wouldn't have been caught dead at an event like this. But that shows you're the better man, am I right?"

Nesil groaned. "I'm not in the mood for jokes."

"Good. I'm not joking."

With an arm around his neck, Terak pulled him close conspiratorially. "You're damn good at pretense—and I'm not saying that's a bad thing—but there's room for improvement. It's not a matter of fixing the surface, but what's in here." He jabbed Nesil's chest. "Dark thoughts don't leave on their own. You've got to *drive* them out. *Replace* them with something."

Nesil didn't deny this was good advice—for anyone but himself. His problems, unfortunately, weren't ones he could forget. While his mother's death might be a thing of the past—the very recent past—the aeisr was very much a problem of the present. A problem that would kill at any misstep.

But since Nesil couldn't say this, he decided to go along with it. "Replaced? Sounds to me you've got something in mind."

"A woman!" said Terak as though he were the first male to come up with the idea.

"Have you been drinking?"

The older boy waved his hand dismissively. "And I don't mean that scrawny stick you always spend time with. No disrespect but a girl that age doesn't count. Not for this."

Terak grasped his shoulder. "For such critical situations, I prescribe an older, more experienced—"

Nesil's mind, momentarily, disengaged from the conversation—convinced he'd never see that scrawny stick again.

"Take Alerisa, for example."

Terak was wise not to point—but clearly, he had no compunctions with staring.

Alerisa stood twenty feet away, against a table, sipping from a wine glass. Her satin dress was carmine red and stitched with black floral lace.

"There's a fine-looking doll. Glistening, dark hair. Perfect skin. Most important is the way she keeps looking at you."

Nesil scoffed. "You skipped the part she's married."

"Oh?" asked Terak with a grin. "Paying attention, after all?"

"To you. Not her."

"No matter. Master Jeros is too old—nearly enough to be her father. Everyone knows it. Their marriage was of convenience, not satisfaction."

"Don't care."

"*You* might not, but Alerisa does. Do you see Jeros anywhere? She's just standing there by herself, looking at *you*."

Nesil shook his head. "You're imagining things. If you haven't noticed, they're *all* looking at me."

"What are you so afraid of? Sure, Jeros might be an ascendant—but you're the gods-damned prince! He won't so much as pretend suspicion."

"Is that the way of it?" Nesil raised a brow. "As heir apparent, everyone will do as I say?"

Terak frowned, sensing a trap.

"Because even *you* refuse to listen. I'm *telling* you to drop it. ...You're the one who wants a girl, it'd seem."

"You're not wrong," said Terak, laughing at the reprimand. "But that was never the point. My only aim was to get your mind off things, if only for a moment. And since a girl wouldn't do it, I knew your obstinacy—to argue what's right—would."

"You're impossible," muttered Nesil. "That was never your plan."

"Wasn't it?"

"Seriously, though. You don't have to worry. I'm fine."

And he *was* fine once his gaze crossed the dance floor.

There stood Sefina, having just arrived.

Even at such distance, surrounded by the court, their eyes met almost instantly. Beneath the scattered limelight, her entire appearance, from her white sandals to her light blond hair, seemed to glisten and shine.

To Nesil, she was beautiful.

"Just like that, she gets a smile?" asked Terak. "I could've waited two minutes and spared myself the trouble."

Ignoring the protests of dancing couples, Nesil crossed the floor in a straight line. Needing to confirm she was real.

Sefina watched in amusement, hands on hips.

"Fashionably late," he said, returning her smile. And holding back his rush of questions.

She wrinkled her nose. "What's that supposed to mean?"

Unable to wait a second longer, he gathered her into his arms.

She cried in delight and offered no resistance. There were a few stifled gasps from people nearby, but he closed his eyes and held her close.

Her glossy hair was like silk against his cheek and filled him with the scent of strawberries and lavender. Beneath the straps of her dress, her shoulders were soft and smooth.

Delicately pressed against him, her tiny body felt real.

But as he tightened the embrace—in a movement so slight, no one else would notice—he knew she was not.

Nesil forced himself not to cry out. He'd only draw attention if he suddenly let go.

And so he held onto this little nightmare—wondering, in silent horror, if the real Sefina was still wandering the dark halls of Silverwater Castle.

He backed to arm's length and wanted to scream.

With a smile on his face, his mind returned to the blood-covered demon that'd so recently tried to kill him. There was no sign of blood now. Looking at her, it was impossible to tell the difference between the high aeisr and the real thing. Same cheekbones and sharp nose. Same delighted expression.

The thing that was not Sefina turned her head up, with aqua-green eyes sparkling at his reaction. She'd been perfectly willing to let him discover who she was. As though part of some test.

Nesil hated her from the start, but he pushed that hate to the back of his mind. Though he hadn't anticipated this exact situation, he'd been fully prepared to play this game.

Which meant, it was time to turn the game around and see if she'd uphold her side of the performance.

With a bow, he extended a hand toward her—an invitation to dance.

The strings were playing a waltz with a slow canter rhythm.

Sefina gave a wry, quizzical smile but didn't hesitate to accept and follow him onto the floor.

Nesil had danced with the real Sefina on a few occasions and wondered how different tonight's experience would be. Even among the most experienced partners, there were always subtle differences in posture and how well they followed his lead.

But, as he took Sefina's right hand in his left and placed his other high against her back, he found her warm touch weightless and provided no counterbalance. As he stepped across the floor, it was like practicing without a partner. Even so, he found the aeisr to be highly skilled, matching his movements with a grace so perfect, no one would see the difference. In the end, it wasn't difficult—only highly disconcerting.

With a peaceful expression, she said, "You're quiet this evening."

"You have questions, then? About my proposal?"

She looked him square in the eye, excited. "Why not start with Kena's death?" Her voice was soft enough no one else would hear.

But if this was an attempt to distract so he'd miss a step, it wouldn't work.

"As I said, I never cared for my mother." Those weren't his exact words, but the lie was the same.

"Want to know how she died?"

Nesil looked at her expectantly, wondering why she'd offer free information. A part of him did want to know. It was a long walk to the castle—more than enough time for his mother to suspect something was off.

Sefina licked her lips. "You'd be right to guess it wasn't easy. You see, I've been watching Kena for quite some time. She was smart. Very smart. She'd always catch on."

"Oh?"

A pair of dancers came close, and he steered Sefina in a different direction.

"...That's why I didn't lure her with tricks. For Kena, only something real would do."

"Another person, you mean? Someone she'd want to save?"

Sefina beamed. "You catch on quick."

"I'm impressed," he lied. "But how'd you know it'd work? Though mother had a weakness for those in need—to expect she'd risk her life for just anyone—"

She pressed a finger to his lips. "You're smarter than that."

Nesil didn't know what to make of this.

She gracefully spun as he led her through a turn. "But you're avoiding the real question. It's obvious I wouldn't have used just anyone. You're just too frightened to ask who it was."

Only then did he understand the purpose of this conversation. She wasn't merely providing information. This had little to do with his mother at all.

Once again, this was a test—to see how well he handled his emotions.

And he knew she was right. He *didn't* want to know who the other person was.

"No one found the body, of course. It's still there, at this moment, a short distance from where they found Kena." Her smile brightened. "Invisible. Small."

A sickening dread welled up inside.

"The queen was such a darling. She went to the castle to save a young orphan. A young *marchioness*. But it wasn't the girl she cared about—you see? Kena came because she cared about *you*. How *you* would feel to lose your childhood sweetheart."

Nesil didn't want to believe it, but still, he didn't miss a step. He felt something tear within him—but, somehow, he kept his face detached and nonchalant.

After all this time, agonizing over Sefina's safety—to suddenly hear, conclusively, she was gone... It wrenched at his chest and made it difficult to breathe.

Worst of all, he wasn't allowed to cry.

As far as everyone knew, the real Sefina couldn't possibly be dead. She was right here in Nesil's arms, smiling broadly as they whisked across the floor.

Additional pieces fell together in his head.

If what she said was accurate and the real Sefina had died with his mother—it must've all happened before Nesil left school. Which meant the girl who'd accompanied him—as incredible as it seemed—had been a fake all along.

It didn't seem possible.

But the more he thought about it, the more he realized the truth. The real Sefina would've shown more care. She'd have gone earlier, in broad daylight, and brought her own pole.

This fake, however, couldn't risk anything Nesil might touch.

She couldn't even hand him a real rock.

Was he such a bad friend, he couldn't tell the difference between the love of his life... and this heinous impostor?

Gods... What the hell was he doing? Here, he'd been testing the aeisr to see how well she could act—when her entire existence was founded upon deception!

Nesil found his voice. "I'll never forgive you for this."

He wasn't sure why he said it, aware Sefina had been dead before he'd gone to the castle—before he'd even made his proposition to the aeisr.

In any case, if he pretended to be pleased by the news, she'd know it for a lie.

The thing that was not Sefina, however, didn't look offended.

"I don't need your forgiveness." She jerked her head to the side, flinging hair from her face. "I need your understanding."

Nesil narrowed his eyes, stepped her lightly through a spin, and let her continue.

"Just as you loved this girl, I'm perfectly aware you also love your grandfather." She raised an eyebrow as though daring him to deny it. "The question that remains is if your love for him—or your love for anyone—will hinder your resolve to end his life."

Ever smiling, she continued in her light sweet voice, "If you come with an offer as bold and arrogant as what you're trying to pull—you'd damn well better be prepared to back it up."

He smiled back. "Don't insult me. I stand by my word. You mustn't mistake arrogance for confidence."

Sefina smiled thinly with satisfaction.

But Nesil wasn't finished. "So when I say I'll not forgive you, it's for one reason only. That marchioness you killed—my childhood sweetheart—was to be my queen."

The music stopped, and he spun her one last time, noticing—all too casually—the eyes of the entire pavilion on the two of them.

As he watched Sefina under the scattered limelight, it was not difficult to imagine her with eyeless sockets and blood running down her body.

"But don't you see?" she asked in a soft voice, nearly drowned by applause. "It is *I* who will be your bride." She wrinkled her nose playfully. "Who could possibly stand against us, with me as your queen?"

Chapter 18
KNOWING THE ENEMY

Nesil predicted the assassination would begin tonight.

At no other time could they anticipate the king's whereabouts with such certainty, due to the festivities and scheduled ceremony. More importantly, with so many hundreds of bystanders, it'd be difficult to narrow down suspects after the king was dead.

There were people everywhere. And Nesil was certain the aeisr would love nothing more than to kill the old man in view of his kingdom.

Sefina, however, was yet to confirm this. She clung onto his arm, seeming to all the world an affectionate girl, very much in love with Seldor's prince.

It could only mean she didn't yet trust him. If he knew her plan, after all, he might lose his nerve or find a way out of it.

This led him to assume her plan would be simple and wouldn't need his involvement until the last second. He'd be cornered and trapped, with no option but to do as he was told.

Nesil, of course, wasn't about to let that happen.

In a moment of meaningless pleasantries, he took Sefina's hands in his, leaned forward, and spoke gently in her ear, "Is there a place we could talk? In private?"

Her face became coy as she stepped back, looking directly into his eyes. *"As if I didn't know what boys and girls do alone together."*

Nesil blanched, horrified by how loudly she spoke. He glanced around to see how many overheard.

Until he realized...her lips hadn't moved. Her voice hadn't come from where she stood at all. It was an unearthly sensation.

Sefina laughed as she tugged at his hands playfully. *"You should see the look on your face!"*

He knew how he looked, but that was unimportant. This time, he was sure her mouth remained closed.

It confirmed something he'd always wondered. The girl at his side didn't possess real vocal chords. And since her words were illusion, nothing stopped her from placing the sound wherever she pleased.

If she kept her voice quiet and close enough to his ear, no one else would be the wiser. Not even the ascendants.

But even though he knew this, he didn't want to talk here. Instead, he led her to the outskirts of the pavilion. Even a prince couldn't be denied a moment to breathe.

As the crowd thinned out, he considered what to say. It was important not to reveal how intelligent he was lest she grow suspicious. At the same time, playing dumb wouldn't work. She was just as likely to drop the plan than confide her secrets to an incompetent fool. He needed to strike a balance—without letting on it was all just an act.

With much of the court watching them leave, the Taelish cathedral was the safest destination. It was the same place his anointing would be held, so it wouldn't seem odd. It would neither seem dangerous to any of the guards, with the black, stone walls so close by.

Most importantly, though, it housed enough niches and corridors to provide all the privacy he needed.

Before they even made it to the building, he pulled her around a corner and made a quick search for people. In the narrow space, there were only a few broken crates and a scattering of black leaves.

"Can you make us invisible?" he asked. While the precaution wasn't strictly necessary, he wasn't in the mood for random interruptions. Even the most unlikely stranger, it seemed, couldn't resist the chance to gain audience with the prince.

"Kinky," she said, making a face.*"I like it."*

He pressed his lips together, unamused.

"You're cute when you're upset."

"I'm not upset."

"Hard to believe. Forgotten your dead girlfriend so soon?"

He huffed in exasperation.

"Like I said. Cute."

In the next moment, they both disappeared.

It was a disquieting sensation to look down and find his body gone. His eyes were left floating midair, and, for a moment, he lost his train of thought.

"*Go on,*" she said. "*Say what you need to say.*"

"Can you hide my voice, as well?"

Nesil wasn't worried about anyone eavesdropping, but he was curious. Sound worked differently than sight and would likely not be so simple to hide.

"*No harm in that, I suppose. You won't be able to hear yourself but talk anyway. I'll know what you're saying.*"

"*You mean you can really—?*" It was even more bizarre than being invisible. He could feel the vibrations in his throat, but his ears were met with dead silence.

"*Damn…!*" he said inaudibly. It made him wonder at the mechanism behind it. Was it a dampening of sound—or something more specific? A calculated resonance to cancel the noise?

"*What if I tried to scream?*"

"*Don't,*" she replied.

"*Well, then,*" he said, forcing out the words despite how odd they felt. "*We need to discuss our plan.*"

For a moment, she hesitated. "*What about it?*"

"*You mean to do it tonight, don't you?*"

He knew this was a risk, but the longer he was left in the dark, the more difficult it would be to regain his leverage.

"*Now that you mention it,*" she said, taking on a devious tone, "*that's a good idea.*"

"*Enough bullshit. I'm not wrong.*"

"*Is that really what this is about?*" Her voice in his ear began to tickle, sounding amused. "*You needn't be concerned.*"

"*Let me be clear,*" he said, regretting not having a face to talk to. "*I don't trust you. And I refuse to take part in any plan that doesn't guarantee my survival. That was never part of our deal.*"

"*Relax, little boy. Your death would get me nowhere.*"

"*Not good enough,*" he said, holding his ground. "*You either tell me everything, or I'm calling it off. I'll walk back to the party and tell everyone you're here. Sure, it won't make me king any sooner, but at least I'll be alive.*"

To his chagrin, Sefina giggled. "*You think anyone will believe you?*" Her voice became threatening. "*Somehow, you just stumbled across me? Or will you explain what you were doing—your attempt to side with the enemy?*"

Undeterred, Nesil said, "*You're wasting time. You going to tell me or not?*"

Her second pause was longer than the first. "*It's going to be a lot of fun with you on the throne.*" She laughed. "*I love games.*"

He grinned as though he'd expected this response.

"Come on then," she said, taking his invisible hand in hers. *"I wasn't going to keep the secret much longer anyway. This puts us ahead of schedule. Certain preparations need to be made."*

Nesil allowed himself to be led from the alley, as there was little she could do to drag him along. As always, he kept his senses about him in the event he might be walking into a trap.

Such was the risk of their relationship—one that would never go away so long as she lived.

Shortly after entering the grounds of the towering cathedral, she led him to an open courtyard. The surrounding buildings created a wall on three sides, sheltering the garden from errant winds.

It was a place Nesil knew well, with its overgrown trees and untended, cracked stonework. He knew it as a place where they wouldn't be bothered, if only for the fountain at its center.

Amidst the dying garden, the white, sterile granite stood out in sharp contrast. The crystal, clear pool hadn't changed at all—not since its appearance three years earlier.

Back then, the only worry was the abyssal creatures outside the walls. No one knew about the aeisr. As long as everyone stayed inside, they thought they'd be safe.

So that's what they did. The garbage piled up, and it didn't take long before their supply of clean water became a serious problem.

Nesil still remembered the joy when, overnight, twenty of these fountains appeared out of nowhere. They were all identical, measuring fifteen feet across, and had been scattered throughout the kingdom, flowing with endless supply.

Most people, of course, approached them with caution—but others insisted they were an answer to prayer. People began to preach that the gods had returned. Or that they hadn't really died.

The water was tantalizing and sweet—a cool respite from their life of poverty and fear. Many drank nothing else for days.

Until they dropped dead from dehydration.

"Why here?" Nesil asked, unnerved by the memory.

All was quiet except for the steady splash of simulated water and the noise from the distant party.

She made their bodies visible again, confident no one was watching.

A ball of light appeared above her outstretched palm, scattering a berth of crooked shadows longer than they should've been.

Turning toward him, her porcelain face cast the darkest shadow of all.

"You made a good show of being fearless a moment ago. Don't ruin it."

"I just meant..." He paused, noting that his voice was back to normal. "How does this figure into our plan?"

Tilting her head in the glow, she teased a smile. "Get in the water, and you'll see."

"Can't you just tell me? Why do you have to be so cryptic all the time?"

"It's a damn surprise, okay?!" Her irritation faded, and she smirked. "Why do you have to be so distrustful all the time? You're so uptight."

Nesil decided further argument was pointless. He didn't think she'd kill him so soon.

As he approached the fountain, he couldn't guess what she wanted to show him. There was no way, after all, to trick his grandfather into coming here. Even if she put Nesil's life in danger—using him as a lure—the king would never come alone.

Sefina removed her sandals and stepped over the granite edge. She shrieked at the cold, though the rippling surface only passed her knees. The hem of her white dress began to float and sway.

With a flick of her toes, she kicked water at him. "Hurry up!"

Compared to most illusions—which only needed to deceive one or two senses—this fountain was an anomaly. The sensations it invoked were far more complex, with careful thought in every detail.

As Nesil stepped into the pool—making a point not to remove his leather boots—he was surprised by the convincing discomfort he felt. With each step, cool water squished through his socks. It even required effort to move despite the lack of real resistance.

"I'll be dry when I step out, won't I?"

Sefina ignored the question and splashed to the far side, taking the light and shadows with her.

"There's something down here," she said. "It's been lying here for years."

"What is it?"

"Oh... You know how men get. This guy got all upset when his wife and children died. He thought he'd come and smash the fountain to bits. You should've seen the bastard. He just dropped the thing and ran."

Curious, Nesil followed. "Dropped what? I don't see anything."

The next moment, a dark shape appeared, rippling beneath the surface.

"Surprise!" she exclaimed.

Reaching down, he lifted the ax from the pool, sending water down its haft and dripping from his sleeves.

This *was* a surprise—as everything that remotely resembled a weapon had long ago been locked away, far from the hands of the surviving populace. The decision was intended to prevent further accidents—the kind that weren't really accidents.

He'd assumed the murder would be done with a dinner knife—but this? It'd just been lying here all this time. The aeisr hadn't tricked anyone into using it—preferring to save it for something more special.

Its weight required the use of both hands. The grip was solid, and the blade looked sharp—and miraculously free from rust.

And though Nesil knew he'd never go through with it—determined to back out before axing his grandfather—the mere thought made him sick.

"I don't like this," he said. "There's too much risk. If my aim is off, even by a little, the king will have time to counter my attack."

"Aim for his face."

"With an invisible ax? You know I'm not a trained assassin!"

"No one thinks you are!" she said, laughing. "But you forget—Renat isn't like your other ascendants. Not anymore."

Nesil groaned.

"When he was younger," she continued, "I would've been worried about him healing through anything. He *used* to be powerful. He *used* to be the best. But all of that changed when he found his precious armband."

Nesil didn't need to be reminded. He remembered the person Renat had been— powerful, dangerous, and horribly unstable. It'd gotten so bad, the king had willingly sought a way to suppress his abilities.

He shook his head. "I still won't do it. You said it yourself: it's the *armband* that changed him. If his life is in danger, he'll take it off!"

"I don't think he will."

Nesil scoffed. "It doesn't matter what you *think*! I already told you I won't—!"

Sefina sighed. "This argument is pointless. If it makes you feel better, the plan was never to kill with the ax. That's not what it's for."

"It isn't?"

"No. Though it'd be certainly entertaining to watch you try."

She stepped out from the pool, dripping water onto the dirt. Her sandals reappeared on her feet.

Her ball of light winked out, dropping the garden into darkness.

"Come on. Our next stop is inside."

Moments later, Nesil got to experience firsthand the difficulty of aiming an invisible ax. His targets, fortunately, weren't people but a row of antique wooden balusters.

Beneath the high vaulted ceiling of the main chapel, the thick posts were part of a guardrail, where a large platform had been raised. The central dais was fifteen feet off the floor, so an audience on both sides could view the ceremony.

His goal was to weaken the railing, so merely leaning on it would send a person falling to his death—and it was his first real clue of Sefina's grand scheme.

Nesil was so relieved to finally learn something useful, the vandalism of ancient, religious property didn't bother him in comparison.

The primary difficulty, at the moment, didn't come from the ax but a secondary illusion. Since they couldn't afford witnesses to see the handrail chopped to bits, Sefina obscured all signs of his ongoing handiwork.

This meant, with each invisible and inaudible swing, he couldn't see so much as a scratch on the posts. This made it difficult to tell if he was close to finishing. Occasionally, he'd prod with his ax head to see if it was starting to give or flex.

"Someone's coming." Her invisible lips brushed lightly his ear.

When he turned his head, the cathedral was still vacant. With his platform positioned at the center, he had to look both ways, to the long rows of benches facing from the north and the matching set from the southern side.

It was an unusual design for a Taelish chapel, but it provided twice the audience with a closer view—never mind, half the time, the priest's back was turned to either direction.

This made the platform more like a raised bridge, splitting the chamber in half. As high up as he was, he should've easily seen if anyone had arrived.

"I didn't mean for you to stop," she added. *"Just be prepared. If he comes this way, it'll be through the guest doors—the eastern ones near Shaelis's portrait. And even then, he won't know you're here—so long as you don't let him step on you."*

"I know," he said silently.

When he returned his attention to the balusters, they all looked the same.

"Sorry, I've lost track. How many have I done?"

"Four. You're working on the fifth. Don't tell me you're tired already."

He resisted the urge to groan in frustration. What the hell did *she* know of manual labor? The aeisr, quite literally, hadn't lifted a hand to do work in her entire life.

But, as there was nothing to be gained from pointing this out, he chose to say, *"This ax isn't as sharp as it looks."*

"Want me to grab you something else?"

This was a joke, of course, and he chose to ignore it.

"You could look around, maybe? See if there are any gloves I could grab myself?"

"In a church?" Her voice bore the hints of an eye-roll.

"You found an ax, didn't you?"

With one more swing, he finished the post. The handle was warm, and he felt blisters forming.

"*How are we on time?*" he asked. "*Do you know?*"

"*I could take a look outside if you want.*"

"*That would be helpful. I mean, I'd hate for people to start showing up. It could ruin everything we've done so far.*"

He also felt he could use a short break.

"*Glad to assist,*" she said cheerfully.

Nesil didn't hear her go, but he didn't need to. He did, however, count the seconds in his head, to see how long she took to reach the party and back.

It was his first opportunity to measure her speed, and it couldn't go to waste. Much of his plan would depend upon moments like these, when he'd be free to do things behind her back. He'd need to start taking risks—but only after knowing, with some degree of certainty, how long she'd be gone at any given time.

At the very least, he'd confirmed one thing—the high aeisr couldn't be in two places at once. While Sefina might seem godlike with her ethereal body and extrasensory perceptions, she couldn't possibly watch the party and him simultaneously.

Were it not for this single limitation, his plan wouldn't stand a chance.

What he needed—more than anything—were ways to keep her occupied. If he could distract her elsewhere for a reliable amount of time, it'd give him a chance to warn his grandfather. A single message, without her knowledge, could mean the difference of Renat's survival through the night.

For the moment, this was all Nesil could hope for. He wasn't so foolish to think he could take her down in a single day. Right now, he only needed to get the king out of danger—making it seem like luck and not the result of his intervention.

If he could do that, he'd have more time to search for her weakness. Perhaps, a few days, while she planned their next assassination attempt.

Otherwise, if she suspected his treachery, he'd have no choice but to call off everything. He'd rather abandon his plan and put himself in danger than risk responsibility for his grandfather's death.

Without warning, Sefina came up behind him and wrapped thin, invisible arms across his shoulders. Soft hair tickled the back of his neck.

This was sooner than expected—105 seconds.

Not good. Had she run that distance? Or was she able to fly?

"*We've got plenty of time,*" she said, pressing herself against his back in a gentle embrace. "*They've only served the second course. Honey-glazed mutton, onions, and spiced mushrooms. The scent was to die for!*"

Aiming his ax at the next post, Nesil remembered not to chop all the way through.

They planned to weaken the handrail without it collapsing, so a few of the posts needed to remain partially intact.

If the railing fell early, it'd be too much hassle to hide the pieces.

"*Speaking of smells,*" he said, "*is there anything you can do about these wood chips? It's starting to feel like a forest in here. Someone will notice.*"

He swung the ax and felt it collide with the wood noiselessly.

"*Hmmm,*" she said, considering. "*I might be able to cover it up. With all these lanterns, I could increase the burning oil?*"

So aromas couldn't be made unsmellable. Perhaps insignificant, but good to know.

"*Do you need to eat?*" she asked. "*There might still be time if you hurry.*"

"*I... I've lost my appetite,*" he said, being perfectly honest. "*You can go on ahead if you want.*"

"*Oh, can I?*" she asked, tightening her embrace. "*What a thoughtful dear you are. I'll have you know, I can still taste food, believe it or not. I just skip the biting. And the chewing. The swallowing.*"

Nesil didn't care.

"*In all seriousness, though, the cooks prepared everything especially for you. Apparently, it's become common knowledge you love mutton.*"

"*I do?*" He moved on to the next post.

"*It's a matter of time before someone comes looking.*"

"*Have you ever chopped through hickory? This isn't easy.*"

Nesil's next swing went wide and clattered between balusters. Instead of a single sound for Sefina to silence, half the noise escaped and echoed through the room. Loudly.

"*Oh, damn!*" she said, suppressing a giggle. "*Don't miss!*"

Nesil looked warily around the room, but no one was around. No footsteps either.

"*It'd be easier if I could see what I was doing.*"

She giggled some more. "*This isn't fun for you? Most people would give anything for the chance to be invisible.*" She rested her chin on his shoulder in something like affection.

"*Stop,*" he said, extracting himself from her arms and stepping away. When he turned around, however, he lost track of where she was.

"*Stop what?*"

He waved an invisible hand in what he thought was her direction. "*This whole act of yours! No one's watching us here, so you can stop all this smiling and pretending. It's like you think we're best friends or something. But you're not really her, remember?*"

"*For all you know, this is just how I am,*" she said defensively.

"*Really?*" He did his best to be incredulous, without the help of facial expressions or vocal inflections. "*You actually enjoy being around me? There's no deceit behind this playfulness?*"

"*Is that so hard to believe?*"

"*What else could it be? People drop dead whenever they're around you! You can't expect me to think you care for anyone at all!*"

She paused a moment. Then said, "*Go to hell! You don't know a damn thing about me!*"

Nesil didn't think his point difficult to understand. But his patience had been dwindling thin for a while. "*So I'm wrong? You're not secretly plotting to have me killed someday when all this is finished?*"

She scoffed. "*This again?*" Her voice became diffident. "*It wouldn't be much a secret if I told you, now, would it?*"

"*Is that supposed to be a joke?*"

Her tone became exasperated. "*Of course, it is.*"

"*This isn't something we can ignore. Not if you expect me to keep working with you.*"

"*It's not something I regularly talk about, okay? Nothing about this is ordinary. Usually, I only pretend to talk to people. So you'll forgive me for not being good at it.*"

Nesil wasn't sure what to make of this confession. Did she feel bad because she wanted to kill him? Or because she couldn't *hide* the fact she wanted to kill him?

"*Ugh,*" she continued. "*And you're right. I'm not the most trustworthy person.*"

"*An understatement. The part about you being a person.*"

She ignored the jibe. "*But you knew this from the start. You're the one who came to me, remember?*"

"*Yes. I did. But that makes us accomplices. Not close friends.*"

"*What do you want me to say, Nesil? Even if I told you I wished you to be alive forever and ever, you'd never believe me.*"

"*I'm not asking you that.*" He grit his teeth. "*Just... Please, stop pretending you're her. You can do that much, can't you?*"

She didn't respond.

Nesil wasn't sure what she might be thinking. There were moments when he detected a semblance of emotion behind what she said—like a window into a real personality. Hurt. Vulnerable.

But even that could be made up, couldn't it? An attempt to seem more human than she was. He could never really tell. Talking with her was proving more difficult than swinging an invisible ax.

"If we want this to work," she began, her voice stiffening. *I suppose we could benefit from some base rules."*

"I agree."

"First of all, stop giving me shit about the way I act!"

"What?!"

"Just because I'm friendly does NOT mean I'm pretending to be her, got that?"

"What's so important about being friends?"

"You need a reason? Honestly, Nesil. Sometimes, I think you're less human than I am."

"Me? Less human than a psychopathic killer?"

She laughed, sounding very girlish and cheerful. *"I can't argue that."*

He shook his head, unsurprised. *"All right, then. So long as you're pretending to be honest, let me ask you this: Are you even female?"*

"As a matter of fact, I am. Do I need to prove it to you?" An invisible hand brushed his cheek.

"Stop that," he said, trying to push her hand away—only to pass through it like air.

"Look," her voice was annoyed again. *"I'm sorry. I don't often have real conversations—with people who know who I am."*

Nesil said nothing.

"Most times, I have to trick people into talking to me. I have to make them think I'm someone else. But not with you. You know what I've done and the disposition I have. Incidentally, I feel free to be myself. Play around. Act impulsively."

Her words took Nesil by surprise. Could her emotions boil down to something so ordinary? She was the high aeisr for gods' sake!

How could she possibly be interested in making friends while simultaneously killing them on a daily basis? It was such a contradiction, it strained belief.

And yet, a part of him suspected this wasn't an act. There was something deeper to this girl than he'd ever imagined. Something that left him intrigued. And terrified.

"But it doesn't work like that," he said. *"Knowing what you do and knowing who you are are two separate things."*

"Are they?"

"You want to pretend to be real? Then give me something real. Tell me something about you—something you've never told anyone."

"I..." Her voice actually sounded uncomfortable. *"I suppose I could... But what would be the point? It's not like you'd believe anything I say. How would you know I wasn't making it up?"*

"Oh, so you DO see the problem," he said dryly. *"The two of us are in no position to*

be friends. What we have between us is entirely one-sided. You can see me, my life— my ambitions and dreams—and you admit I can't learn the same about you. I can't even TRUST you."

Sefina was silent a long moment.

So long, Nesil began to feel worried. While he thought his point was fairly straight-forward, it was also possible he was making a mistake. By convincing her, after all, that they shouldn't be friends, what was the alternative? Was it really so important to make her think they were enemies?

But even as he thought this, he had no regrets. When it came to enemies, you always knew where you stood. You were never surprised when they stabbed you in the back, because the arrangement was honest. At the very least, there could be mutual respect.

"Ask me one question," she said at last.

It was the last thing he'd expected.

"I know it won't make us friends. But I want to try anyway."

Nesil didn't like this, and he was tempted to refuse. No matter the question, it'd only lead to more confusion. Most likely, she was only pretending to be vulnerable. She was toying with his mind to throw him off balance.

And yet... It was also an opportunity he couldn't pass up.

So long as he was careful—anticipating, from the start, that her response would be a lie—he could avoid real harm. He might even learn something useful by seeing which manner she targeted his sympathies.

"Anything?" he asked.

"Better make it quick. Before I change my mind."

The question, of course, needed to be about her—as he had suggested. If he were to go off-topic—and ask if she had a weakness—it'd only reveal his stupidity and prevent him from getting an answer at all.

"Please, try to be honest," he said, settling on something safe—far enough away from the things he wanted to know but that needed clarification, nonetheless. *"Can you name one thing—anything at all—in your entire life that you've valued more than yourself?"*

The aeisr didn't respond.

Nesil tried to imagine what she was thinking. It was a question that practically begged for a lie. It seemed unlikely this psycho could care about anything—but he was curious to see what she'd say. What lie she'd come up with that she thought he'd believe.

It took nearly a full minute before Sefina gave her answer.

"Honestly? No."

Nesil frowned. While her response was disappointing, he couldn't help but feel impressed she'd be open to the truth.

Until he realized she wasn't finished.

"There used to be something...however. Someone, who came close."

"Oh?" was all he could say, trying to hide his returning skepticism.

Sefina didn't continue immediately. She pretended to need time as though mustering the courage.

"It's been such a long time since I've spoken his name. Kadrek, if I recall correctly. And... I guess you could say he's the closest thing I've ever had to a friend."

It was a good act, Nesil thought. She made it believable.

"I thought you said you never had any friends."

"No..." Her voice became irritated. *"Are you going to listen? Because I'd be happy to stop."*

Nesil swallowed, realizing he'd been insensitive.

Thinking back, she'd only admitted to not having much experience—which wasn't the same as no experience at all.

"You're right," he said. *"I'm sorry."*

Even if her story was a lie, he could at least pretend, couldn't he?

"Where I come from," she continued, *"there aren't any people. I know that doesn't make sense—and you couldn't possibly understand what it was like. But Kadrek found me. He SAVED me. If that's not a friend, I don't know what is."*

Nesil was suddenly bursting with questions. To this day, no one knew where the aeisr had come from. Or why she was here.

But he bridled his curiosity.

No one knew those answers, of course, because she'd never been willing to say. For years, she'd avoided these fundamental issues, so if he thought she'd be suddenly open about everything—something had to be wrong.

She laughed softly.

"You can't tell if I'm lying. I see it in your face."

"Are you surprised?"

"Well...no. It's not your fault." Her voice seemed hurt. *"Not really."*

Nesil debated if he should go along with it. Even if her words were carefully calculated—she couldn't force him to believe anything he didn't want to. Not through a simple story, could she?

But before he could say anything, Sefina stopped him.

"Just forget it. We can try this again later."

"No, it's okay," he insisted. *"Tell me about Kadrek. I'll listen."*

Sefina, however, had lost her mood to talk.

AUSTIN LYNN CLARK

"We're wasting time. You've got eight balusters left."

He couldn't argue with that. He was grateful for this momentary breather, but these posts presented a true challenge. By the time he was finished, his hands would be raw. Maybe even bleeding.

As he took aim with his invisible ax, Sefina offered one last comment.

"If you want to learn about Kadrek, you should ask your grandfather.

"King Renat, after all, was the one who killed him."

Chapter 19
THE CRIMES OF SELDOR

These words couldn't be unheard.

His grandfather, a murderer?

It brought back memories of how Renat had been before he'd found the armband. Back then, he'd fly into a rage over the simplest thing.

But *murder*?

Nesil was desperate to find a reasonable explanation—that the king had been forced to defend himself and wasn't to blame.

But he also feared this wasn't the case. If it all boiled down to something so simple—something Renat could dismiss with his side of the story—then why would the aeisr bring it up?

Sefina's words were calculated—not only to unhinge but to strike deep at the underlying problem.

Because, now, there was a possibility he feared above all else:

The aeisr might not be to blame for the ongoing conflict. Despite what people claimed, she might not have even dealt the first blow.

He completed the remaining balusters in record time. With so much on his mind, he didn't need more rest. With frustration lending strength to every swing, he even enjoyed the ache in his arms.

It wasn't until he started back to the party, out of worry he'd been gone too long, that Sefina spoke again.

"*I think I'll stay here,*" she said. "*Someone might come in, and we can't afford anyone to bump this prematurely.*"

Nesil nodded and hid his relief. There was still a lot he wanted to ask, to know what came next in their plan, but he was also desperate to be free of her surveillance. He needed time alone, and he was glad the aeisr made the suggestion, herself. If it'd been him, it would've only drawn suspicion.

Nesil returned to the party—fully intent on keeping to himself—only to discover this wasn't what he wanted at all. Before he realized what he was doing, he was searching the pavilion for his grandfather's steward.

Because, in the end, Nesil's confusion didn't matter. The one thing he knew for sure was that he couldn't allow his grandfather to die—even if the old man deserved it.

Despite this certainty, he wasn't in the mood to explain himself to anyone. After finding the royal secretary, he didn't request an audience with the king—he *demanded* one. He nearly chased the steward away, telling him to be quick and, above all, to be discreet.

As Nesil sat down to await Renat's response, he feared he was losing control.

While saving the king's life was his highest priority, he knew better than to resort to threats or demands. If Nesil didn't start behaving appropriately, Renat would have no choice but to deny him altogether.

It was uncommon for Nesil to make such stupid mistakes. If he'd had a chance to rest and pull his thoughts together, he was confident he could get back to his usual, dispassionate clarity.

Nesil was too worn out—not because his day was stretching longer than expected. It wasn't from exertion or the heaviness of the ax. Or the stress of leaping through the aeisr's mental hoops.

No. This lassitude was wholly unfamiliar. It was the lack of support he needed from his mother. It was the absence of his dearest friend. And the emotional agony that made him want to quit everything and scream.

"The king will see you now," said the steward with a bow.

Nesil nodded, wondering if he should apologize for earlier. But even that required too much strength.

So he said nothing as he followed the man away from the pavilion. They went through an alley toward a more secluded area, away from the bustling activity of the kitchens.

It was well known King Renat never went to parties. Some said it was a sign of his passing years—that the wine and noise were wont to cause a heart attack. Others believed he was shouldering too many demands, up to and including the defense of Seldor.

Those were the two leading opinions, but others weren't spoken so openly. The king was hiding in fear for his life. Or he'd succumbed to madness, and it was all his council members could do to cover it up.

Nesil's belief was the simplest of all—that the king merely had a distaste for pleasantries and saw social maneuvering as wasted time.

In his heart, Nesil often criticized the man for his lack of effort. But, after tonight, he felt like he could almost understand.

No matter the true reason for the king's absence, he was grateful. A private audience was just what he needed. Not because he wanted to talk about Kadrek—as that would only lead to confusion and make his job more difficult. Nesil's only goal, at the moment, was to inform about the handrail and his developing theory it'd begin with fire. Not a *real* fire, but, due to the intangible nature of flames, it was always difficult to discern the difference.

Whatever the case, the ascendants should avoid all attempts to put the fire out, lest their displaced energy—and resultant gust of wind—produce enough lateral force to push Renat off the platform.

"Your grace," said the steward, bowing before the king's large desk. "I present your grandson."

Renat looked up from a stack of ledgers before removing his spectacles. He wiped his face with a palm. "I can see that," he said in his deep voice. "Leave us."

The heavy doors were pulled closed.

Rather than the king's traditional audience hall, this temporary study had been chosen for its proximity to the cathedral. The stone chamber had only been cleaned that day and smelled heavily of dust.

As the king didn't care for opulence, his servants had only brought in a wooden desk, two tables laden with books, four leather chairs, and a fire burning low in the hearth.

The impression it gave was utterly pragmatic. There were no retainers to wait upon Renat's every need. He kept on hand only what was necessary—what the king *deemed* to be necessary. Which, in Nesil's opinion, were *not* the things he needed at all.

"Going to just stand there?" barked Renat. "Out with it, then! What's so godsdamned important it couldn't wait until the ceremony?"

"I..."

Nesil was tempted to shout back—that the *king's life* was so important—but he held his tongue. If he didn't do this properly, the king wouldn't recognize the amount of thought he'd put into this. Renat wouldn't see a tactician but the dreamer he used to be. The headstrong romantic. The *child*.

"At the party, I took note of the dignitaries present—among them, the lords from the Kaern farmlands—and I realized... My mother won't be there to head up tomorrow's committee."

Renat leaned back in his chair, surprised.

"With your permission," continued Nesil, "I'd like to take charge of that meeting myself."

The king regarded Nesil in silence, with a single lantern illuminating his iron-bearded face. Beneath some cuts in his sleeve, his armband glinted from his muscled shoulder. Around him, on the desk, were stacks of parchment, a pot of ink, and a plate of forgotten, cold chicken.

There was no crown on Renat's bald head, but no one would doubt he looked the part of a king. There was confidence in his dark, steel eyes, his strong jawline, and the way he held himself. There was weariness, too. A creased face that didn't smile like it used to, back before his kingdom fell to ruin.

"Have a seat," said Renat.

Nesil did as he was told, hoping to create the right impression. If he could get Renat listening, the man would be more receptive to what came next.

"Give me one reason why I should trust you with our nation's largest providers."

Nesil swallowed. "To reinstate confidence in our family's name. After everything my mother did to keep the houses together, we can't afford for them to doubt us now. It is *our* name—the Royal House Kirchem—signed on every agreement. And we need to assure them her death has not made us weak."

"And we'd be showing that strength—how? By placing a child in front of them?"

Nesil struggled not to lose his composure. "I may be young, but I will show them I am worthy of their trust."

The king shook his head. "If you want their trust, taking charge before you're ready would be a mistake. They'll feel better if they see you gain experience *first*."

"I *am* ready," insisted Nesil. "And what better way can I gain that experience than active involvement? In our current state, the people *need* to see their prince in action, not sitting on the sidelines. They need assurance that we—"

"Yes. These are all good points. But we have to do this right. If it's strength they need—don't forget—they still have *me* to look to. I'm not dead yet."

Yes, thought Nesil, *but for how long?*

"I appreciate the thought, but the answer is no."

"What...? Why?"

"As prince, your attendance will, of course, be mandatory. But the task of conducting the meeting, I'm afraid, has already been delegated to Ascendant General Corvan. You'd be wise to watch. And learn."

There was nothing unreasonable about the king's words. Nesil didn't pretend to qualifications he hadn't earned, nor did he believe there was nothing to be gained by observing men of more experience.

But the words hurt all the same. If Renat couldn't trust him with a reasonable request, what were the odds he'd accept an unreasonable one?

"I'll keep an eye on your progress," continued the king. "It *might* be prudent you assume duties at an accelerated rate. We'll speak more on this when six months have passed."

"Six months?!"

"I've made my decision," said Renat, with growing irritation. "I'll hear no more on this tonight. There's a lot I need to do before the ceremony starts."

Nesil, however, made no move to leave. His eyes flicked to his grandfather's shoulder—where his sleeve revealed the band underneath.

"Did you not hear what I—?!"

"There's something else!" stammered Nesil. "*About* the ceremony. It needs to be changed."

He had to force the words out—knowing how much they needed to be said.

The king's glare became dangerous, making it difficult to speak.

The approval and judgment of this man—the most powerful person he'd ever known—had always been important to Nesil. And the source of much fear.

"This is most improper," said the king. "If you'd wanted to participate in the planning, you should have come to me hours ago. It is far too late for this discussion. We're done."

Nesil opened his mouth, ready to suggest the slightest change he could think of—that he wanted the Taelish High priest, *not* his grandfather, to conduct his coronation.

But no words came out.

Because, right then, he realized *another* problem. It wasn't just his grandfather's temperament but something more dire. Something he should've realized before pursuing this conversation.

It was the same reason Nesil never spoke of his plans with anyone.

The aeisr might've been lying.

Although Sefina told him she intended to stay behind—to watch over the handrail—there was no guarantee she'd done so. She might've only wanted him to *think* she was gone so she could watch what he'd do.

At this very moment, she might be somewhere in this room. Invisible. And growing more distrustful by the second.

There came a knock at the door.

Renat huffed in exasperation. "Enter."

The royal steward came in and bowed his head. "Your grace, it is time."

"Right, then," said Renat, rising from his chair. His face was angry—disgruntled, no doubt, by his inability to finish the things he'd planned.

"Wait!" said Nesil, as a new idea occurred to him—an idea so insane, if it worked, it'd take care of several problems at once. At the very least, it'd buy more time.

The steward frowned. "Is something wrong?"

The king stared Nesil down as though commanding him to keep quiet.

"If you'd just let me explain!" demanded Nesil, standing up so his eyes were near the king's level. "I promise you, the delay will be worth it! So much, the people won't mind waiting another hour."

"An *hour*?!" The king's face had gone red.

Nesil's only chance was to get through this quickly. "Just think what this night means for our people! That's the reason we're doing this, right? For *them*? So *they* can be happy and not lose faith?"

"Get to the point."

"Do you remember Sefina?" asked Nesil. "The orphan daughter of the Merilon marquessate?"

In that same instant, he heard the aeisr's voice in his ear, sounding very upset. "*What the hell are you doing*?!"

Inwardly, Nesil sighed in relief. He'd been right to suspect she'd be listening.

She'd waited to catch him at this moment—the moment she believed to be his betrayal. And that's exactly what would've happened had he not changed tactics mere seconds before.

"I know the girl," said the king.

"I mean to marry her."

Any respect that'd once been on the king's face was replaced by unmistakable skepticism. And disapproval.

To his steward, Renat asked, "Could you give us a moment?"

"Of course, your grace. I'll be right outside should you need me."

Once again, the heavy doors clicked shut.

"HAVE YOU LOST YOUR MIND?!"

"Just think about it!" Nesil held up a placating hand. "Imagine the joy she would bring! If a prince can be anointed, then why not a princess? The people would love her. Cherish her."

And watch her like a hawk, he thought.

From that time forward, were she to disappear or try anything suspicious, she'd risk having her identity discovered. And he was willing to bet the aeisr would do almost anything to keep her crown.

By itself, the idea wasn't enough to ensure victory—but it *would* provide some much-needed freedom. If he could never do anything, after all, without the certainty she wasn't looking—what options were left to him but failure?

"I think the people need something like this, don't you? With my mother gone, the throne is bereft of that comforting touch. That female grace."

These last words brought the king pause, though he was still far from convinced.

"And it's not just the people," he said, growing quiet. "*I* need her, too."

The king shook his head as though to remind that personal feelings should be left out of such decisions.

Which made it even more surprising when Renat said, "Your proposition has merit; I'll give you that. I'll need time to think on this. Some other night, perhaps. As I've already said, there's no time to prepare."

Nesil, however, wasn't about to let go. "The preparations are nearly identical to those already made! It's been done before, has it not? A dual ceremony? An anointed marriage?"

"Yes," Renat conceded. "But those nuptials were prearranged. And, every time, before the couple was born."

"So tell *that* to the people! Are you afraid her dead parents will object? Tell them Sefina was promised—in secret—long, long ago."

"I've heard enough of this foolishness," said Renat. "You'll not stain our family's name with a lie."

"Is that all you care about?" asked Nesil, dismayed. He wondered how many lies Renat himself had been hiding all these years. "Why can't you trust me?"

"Because trust needs to be earned!"

Nesil groaned in frustration as his brilliant idea crashed down around him.

He'd felt so sure he was onto something. He needed this! Couldn't his grandfather see that? It wouldn't only keep Sefina out of the way tonight but for all the days to come!

Why did his grandfather have to be so stubborn?

Renat tried to regain control of his temper. "It's good you're taking thought for the future. But you must realize—these are *not* decisions to be taken lightly. They don't only affect you and your future family but the entire kingdom."

"Do you think I only came up with this tonight?" Nesil groaned. "But, of course, you do! You still think I'm a stupid—"

"HOLD YOUR TONGUE!" shouted the king. "It's been a long day for everyone, and I'll hear no more—understand?! If you feel so strongly this path is correct, that's all the more reason to *do it properly*!"

Renat took a deep breath. "Look... It's not my intent to crush your dreams. It might feel that way, but there's more to being king than following your heart. You have to do things right, lest your reign be crippled by regret."

"Like yours, you mean?" asked Nesil, adding steel to his tone.

The king drew back. "Excuse me?"

Nesil hadn't wanted to go this direction, but if this was what it took to make his grandfather listen...

"What of *your* mistakes? The ones that, even now, are setting ruin to our kingdom?"

Renat dismissed the accusation with a wave. His expression, however, spoke volumes. As king, he was accustomed to possessing the upper hand. For it to be snatched away—by his grandson, no less—made his eyes light up with unspoken fury.

"Did you think no one would find out?" asked Nesil, unable to hold himself back. "About *Kadrek*?"

Renat's brows drew together, and his anger, at once, began to pale. It didn't leave but became diluted with uncertainty and fear.

"Where did you hear that name?"

Nesil stared back and saw the cracks begin to form. As though his grandfather had become an entirely different person.

"What is this, Nesil? Are you...threatening me?"

"I just want you to listen. To see I'm no longer a little boy. You can count on me to know what's best for the kingdom. That's why I've kept this to myself. I promise...I haven't told anyone!"

The insinuation of the word 'yet' hung in the air. Even without saying it out loud— this *was* a threat—no matter how gentle he made it out to be.

With a calmer expression, Nesil added, "This can stay between the two of us. But we *need* to talk."

"Right now?" Renat's tone was irritated, adverse to causing further delay. But he'd also begun to bend.

"The people can wait," said Nesil. "This doesn't need to take long. But, if I'm to be the future king of Seldor, don't you see how important this is?"

"But how—? Where did you—?" Renat began to ask before his anger returned—rekindled with suspicion. He'd begun to fear the aeisr was involved.

"*Tell him it was Hadrey,*" said Sefina.

Nesil had no choice but to trust her. She'd know, after all, which people were involved in Renat's secret—and who'd lend credence to Nesil's story.

"It's all in a letter," he lied. "Written by Hadrey a few days before he died."

Renat studied Nesil's eyes, searching for deceit. Then he shook his head. "Hadrey was loyal. He would've never—"

Nesil groaned. "He handed it to me, himself! It was weighing on him—I could see it in his face. But go ahead—*don't* believe me. Even if my intel came from elsewhere—even if the aeisr tampered with that letter—should it even matter? Here's your chance to set things right. To make sure I get *your* side of the story."

Renat clenched his teeth, unwilling to speak. He continued to take Nesil's measure.

Then he turned away and directed his voice to the open room. "Was this your plan?" he asked, as though certain the aeisr was listening. "To turn my grandson against me?"

Nesil tried not to feel uncomfortable. He'd seen this kind of paranoia before—though never from his grandfather.

When no response came, Nesil spoke for himself.

"I *haven't* turned against you. I just want to know the truth. ...*Please*?"

The king searched the room despite knowing he wouldn't spot a thing. Not unless the aeisr wanted him to.

"Take a seat."

Nesil was only dimly aware they'd been standing, arguing over the table, since the steward's interruption.

The two sat down at the same time.

Renat leaned forward and spoke in a whisper.

"To be clear...Kadrek's death was *not* my fault."

"*Bullshit!*" said Sefina.

Nesil ignored her and waited for his grandfather to explain.

This took some time.

"It was a stupid idea..." he said with a grumble. "From the get-go, I made my feelings clear. I told him it couldn't be found. He should forget the whole plan—but Kadrek... It's like the man had a death wish. Once he had his heart set on something, nothing in this world could stop him from trying."

"It'd help if you started at the beginning," said Nesil. "Just forget Hadrey's letter. I want to hear it in your own words. What was it, exactly, Kadrek wanted to do?"

Renat sighed. He looked at Nesil warily and licked his lips.

"Do you know how the world is comprised of layers?"

"Of course."

The king shook his head, suddenly upset. "The answer's not so simple. I'm not just talking about the aeilic realms—the layers to which we've all been aspected."

Rather than guess what his grandfather was getting at, Nesil waited patiently.

"It's been known for a long time the layers go much deeper than that. There are layers beyond our comprehension. And others we still know nothing about."

Nesil frowned. The topic of world theory was *not* one to cross his grandfather's lips lightly. When it came to anything associated with the deceased gods—or the abyssal threat, for that matter—the leaders tended to sidestep the issue. They'd move on to problems requiring more immediate and more practical solutions.

Early on, Nesil had thought much the same as everyone—that the government acted this way for the people's benefit. The leaders were hiding sensitive information, not wanting to cause unnecessary panic.

It wasn't until he was older—after witnessing many of these evasions for himself—that Nesil suspected a different explanation. That the king never talked of religion because he was as much in the dark as everyone else. And he only pretended to understand the state of the world so no one would lose confidence.

The problem with this approach, however, was moments like these—when Nesil wasn't sure how much to believe.

"So, what're you suggesting?" he asked. "The abyssal current, itself, is one more layer?"

Renat smirked as though his grandson's intuition was merely luck.

"Not just one. *Several.* In fact, the creatures we used to fight—the silencing ones outside our borders—only belonged to the *first* layer. The shallowest part."

Nesil swallowed, not wanting to think of what creatures might be worse than those.

Renat went on. "I didn't know Kadrek very long—only about a week—but he knew things I never thought possible. The way he spoke of the current—"

"But who *was* he? Where did he come from?"

Renat grimaced, wishing for fewer questions.

"Kadrek was... How should I put this? To be honest, I can't be certain of everything he said. But, from his own mouth—he descended from the aspect of Ordination."

Nesil knew this, at once, for Ashaira's aspect. The one that disappeared when the betrayer died.

"Is that even possible? The ordinators are dead."

"Not dead. According to Kadrek, his aspect had become part of the abyssal realms. He claimed to live *inside* the current—which seems plausible enough, considering what he knew."

Nesil was bursting with questions, wanting to learn everything Renat had gleaned from this encounter—but it wasn't a good time. They were already late for the ceremony, and if he meant to marry Sefina tonight, preparations still needed to be made.

"So what was it Kadrek asked you to do?"

"He wanted me to go with him—deeper into the current. He said it was important—that there was something we needed to get. A key—but to what, he didn't say. He only said he needed someone like me—someone from outside—to carry it out."

"He didn't say why?"

"He tried... But I don't think he understood it completely. He wasn't there when the gods died. Like us, he was working off stories passed down by his ancestors. He only knew it was important, and it was vital we get it."

"Okay... From where?"

"From the very bottom—the lowest depths of the current."

Nesil had never heard of such a thing. To even consider such a concept sent a shiver down his spine. It was no wonder his grandfather hadn't wanted to go.

Renat went on. "There, where the darkness is thicker than water—so thick, it becomes difficult to move or even see straight—there's a place he referred to as *Eyvian Kothel*. I thought it just a name, but Kadrek let slip, just once, it'd been passed down from some forgotten language."

"Eyvian Kothel?" echoed Nesil.

"Or—in his best interpretation...The Nightmare Throne."

For a moment, Nesil could only stand there in silence. If any of this was a lie, the aeisr made no objections.

"So I explained to him," continued Renat. "I told him all our people's troubles with just *one* layer. What chance could we possibly have going all the way down?"

Nesil could only nod.

"And yet... He convinced me to go."

"You went?" asked Nesil, leaning forward in his seat. "If you were so certain it couldn't be done, why would you—?"

Renat shrugged helplessly. "Because of what he offered in return."

There was a moment of silence as the king mustered the courage to go on.

"I wouldn't have done it—not at any price." Renat's tone became filled with sadness. "Except Kadrek claimed to possess the one thing I wanted most in the world. Something worth my own life—and I could have it, even if we didn't survive. Even if we never came back from our mission."

Nesil clung to every word, unable to guess what reward was worth such a price.

"An escape for our kingdom," continued Renat. "A way for Seldor to be safe from the current."

"What?"

"That's right. You didn't know this, but our defenses were beginning to falter. Invisible creatures were slipping through the walls—only a few at first, but more each passing day. So I *had* to accept. I didn't have a choice."

"But he was lying!" said Nesil. "You didn't think he could—"

"Kadrek was many things—a reckless fool, a visionary!—but he wasn't a liar."

"So it was true? He knew how to save us? You believe it would've worked?"

"Believe it? Nesil... It *did* work. Since that day, no abyssal creature has stepped foot within our borders."

Only then did he understand. "You mean... The gift he gave you... It was the aeisr?"

Renat nodded somberly. "You need to understand... What happened next was nobody's fault. If Kadrek had only made it out alive, I don't believe the aeisr would've turned out the way she did."

It was strange for the king to call her a 'she,' but to Nesil, it added a sense of realism.

"I've explained it to her multiple times. I told her I was sorry! That I did *everything* to help him escape!"

"*That's a lie!*" she shouted—but not out loud. Despite the anger in her voice, she was still aware of Nesil's situation and how important it was for her not to be seen with him. "*Renat only made it out because he STOLE something—a protective gemstone that belonged to Kadrek.*"

As Nesil looked into his grandfather's eyes, filled with grief, he thought he could almost see something else. Something not unlike guilt.

And it became clear he wasn't telling the whole story.

"*He's never even bothered to hide it!*" she continued. "*It's right there, on his arm-band!*"

Nesil's eyes flicked to the large, white stone glimmering in the firelight.

"You can't imagine what it was like," said Renat, with eyes unfocused, sorrowful, and haunted. "The things I saw... The things I had to do..."

Nesil couldn't bear to see his grandfather like this. The man was broken in a way he could almost understand.

It wasn't so different from his own sense of shame.

And he realized his grandfather would never confess. If something had happened down in the dark, it'd caused the man so much remorse, he'd carry the secret down to his grave.

So, instead, Nesil moved on to something else. "What of the key? Was it there?"

Renat let out a sigh and shook his head. "We never made it that far. What Kadrek meant to do... I don't think it's possible. That place... It isn't meant for people. It isn't meant...to exist."

Nesil struggled to understand.

He almost asked for details—for Renat to describe a single example... But doing so wouldn't get them closer to the ceremony. They'd lost too much time, and it wouldn't help anyone if Renat became *more* unfocused.

"I'm glad you told me," said Nesil, stretching a comforting hand toward his grandfather but placing his palm on the table instead.

Renat looked up. "I've answered your questions?"

Not really, thought Nesil, but he knew better than to keep pushing. "Enough for now," he said.

The king worked his mouth. "And you won't...share this with anyone?"

Nesil took a deep breath. "Of course, I won't. It was never my secret to tell."

He said this truthfully, knowing he was making a mistake. By giving up his leverage, he was no closer to his goals than he'd been from the start.

But something in Renat's eyes seemed to change. It was more than weariness, breaking him down. He now regarded Nesil with something like respect.

"My boy," said Renat, narrowing his brows. "Marriage is not a decision taken lightly. Nor made quickly. This choice remains with you the rest of your life."

"You mean...?" Nesil tried to suppress his hopes. With conviction, he added, "I'm sure about this! Sure about *her*. For me, it's never been a choice of whom. Only of when. I've familiarized myself with the responsibilities of a husband."

Renat nearly laughed. "Maybe you are getting older. But don't push it."

Despite the king's cynicism, Nesil was determined to play the role of a perfect, loving spouse. As the days went on, it'd be vital that nothing appear amiss. Not until after the aeisr was defeated.

Renat studied his face. "You love this girl?"

It was a difficult question, but not because Nesil wasn't sure of the answer. His love was the reason this hurt so much. Marrying the sad imitation of his friend.

Renat gave him a serious look. "You'll be taking full responsibility, you hear?" Coming around the desk, he spread out his arms.

Nesil entered the embrace, both relieved and troubled.

"I'll not have you mistreat this girl," said Renat. "You'll care for her as you do your own life. See to it that nothing ever happens to her."

Then, there were tears in Nesil's eyes. Unexpected tears that weren't part of any act. He forced himself to smile as though he hadn't already failed. As though nothing had already happened to Sefina.

After a long evening sifting through lies—both the aeisr's and his grandfather's—

Sometimes, the truth was far, far worse.

SWORN UNTO DEATH

Nesil's plan began to pay off immediately.

At the news of his engagement, the entire pavilion was struck dumb. Then erupted into cheers that echoed all the way to Silverwater Castle.

Sefina became the center of everyone's attention, smiling shyly on the stage and accepting their praise with dignified reservation.

At first, Nesil was worried they'd all rush forward, and the press of the crowd would expose her identity. But, with surprising grace, she managed to extricate herself in time before the crowd's enthusiasm reached that frenzied peak.

It was explained the princess needed time to get ready. And with Nesil's help, she exited the pavilion without more than brief physical contact from anyone.

Nesil wasn't entirely certain what happened next. Among her attendants, there were a few he suspected of being illusions themselves. It was the only thing that made sense—given the close intimacy of dressing the princess.

This was supervised by members of the royal entourage—whom Nesil knew to be real. And it provided him with some much-needed peace of mind to know Sefina's whereabouts would be accounted for down to the very last second.

It was done in a rush, as there was pressure for the ceremony to start as soon as possible. But though it didn't give him much time, it was better than nothing.

At the cathedral, Nesil didn't bother to go through Renat's steward but, instead, went to the king directly.

Pulling him aside in an empty corridor, he said, "This won't make sense at first, but I need your trust on one more thing."

Renat huffed in frustration, already back to his callous behavior.

"Don't tell me you're getting cold feet."

"Just listen! I have reason to suspect an attack from the aeisr."

The king blinked, startled. Only to replace his expression with disgust.

Nesil pushed forward. "I'm not sure on the details, but they'll try to stop the wedding. It'll start with a fire—at least, that's my best guess."

"You...guess?! Because you think the aeisr gives a damn about your marriage? Do you know how often people come to me because they suspect—?"

"I wouldn't have said anything if I didn't have a source."

Renat shook his head. "You know better than that. With the aeisr, the more reliable a source seems, the more suspect it becomes."

"I realize that, but..."

There was nothing he could say that would satisfy the king. Any traction he'd gained was swept away, and he was no longer worth Renat's time or trouble.

But Nesil no longer cared.

What was the worst that could happen? It wasn't as though the king would call off the wedding—not after the impassioned reaction from the crowd. Nesil only needed to plant the idea—the slightest notion an attack was imminent—so Renat would think twice when the time arrived.

"You have no reason to believe me—but, please, keep away from the handrail." He searched his grandfather's eyes to make sure he understood. "It might appear sturdy, but—"

Renat's hand was raised as though desperate for Nesil to stop talking. "You need to calm yourself. Even if there were an attack, we've dealt with them before."

Nesil refused to back down. "I'm telling you, something will drive you off the edge. So you need to stay still!"

The king paused and briefly studied his grandson. "You think I would've lived this long if I didn't know how to respond to an aeisric event?"

"Of course not..." said Nesil, realizing his mistake. "I never meant to tell you what to do. It's just important I warn you."

Renat worked his mouth as though tired of the whole thing.

"You've got a lot on your mind, boy. But right now, your chief concern should be your wedding. This was *your* idea, remember? So keep your head on straight!"

"I will, sir. I won't disappoint."

Still unconvinced, the man walked away.

The cathedral was packed.

It was apparent the news of Nesil's engagement had spread. Many party guests had gone home to wake up children, the sick, the elderly—and anyone else who'd opted out of the festivities.

For some, this meant showing up in their night clothes, with drooping eyes and irritated yawns. For most, however, the chance to witness a princess' coronation—the first Seldoran princess in over a decade—was enough to put them wide awake.

Besides, who could sleep amid all this racket?

From where Nesil stood, at the end of the raised platform, overlooking the crammed benches on either side, it took effort not to shout in frustration.

He understood why the mothers had to bring screaming babies—as there was no one left to watch them at home. But couldn't they, at least, have the decency to stay out of the main hall? If their children wouldn't shut up, they should be kept at a distance so everyone else could enjoy the ceremony!

If Nesil's mother were here, she'd have berated him for even thinking such a thing. She'd have told him these ceremonies belonged as much to the people as to the prince being crowned. In the years to come, those mothers could tell their children they were actually here. And wasn't that worth the price of a momentary headache?

Nesil, of course, would've nodded and told her she was right.

Kena had always been right.

So, instead, he stood tall with a smile on his face. He pretended not to be tired and waved down to the crowd as he'd done these many years... Only this time without his mother by his side.

Leaving the doors behind, he walked down the narrow bridge to where the priest stood with his grandfather. The wooden platform was much broader at the center, in the shape of a large circle. Over fifteen feet across, it was protected by the handrail Nesil, himself, had put out of commission.

The circular shape wasn't chosen for ascetics but to accommodate the intricate grooves chiseled into its wooden surface. Each line and symbol was carved with expert precision, coming together in a design much more permanent than chalk or paint.

If he remembered correctly, this circle of devotion had been here for over a hundred years. It was in this same circle his parents had been married. And his grandparents. And literally thousands upon thousands more couples, besides.

"As vagrants come we into this world!" declared the priest, holding out his hands so the people would quiet down.

Within moments, the commotion dropped to a murmur, a handful of shrieking children, and—surprisingly—a few snores.

Nesil, at least, on the edge of the circle, could make sense of the priest's every word.

For the people in back, there were no such guarantees.

"As shards do we grow." The man raised his hands towards the vaulted ceiling, some thirty feet above. "Mere fragments of our true selves. Incomplete. And in the dark."

The words were practiced and rehearsed—and ones Nesil had heard dozens of times before, at every marriage he'd attended. But, this time, they were different—not the words themselves but in the way they felt. This time, the words were meant for him.

It didn't matter that he hadn't prepared himself mentally. Or that this moment wasn't anything like the way he'd imagined. The marriage might be a sham and his fiancée an impostor, but nothing changed the fact that this ceremony was his. In all likelihood, it was the only ceremony he'd ever have.

So couldn't he, at least, pretend to enjoy it?

The priest stretched a hand toward him and bellowed, "Before us stands a young man. Untried, undeveloped, and incomplete. I still remember the day he was first carried through my doors. A beautiful baby boy. Our dear prince..."

All eyes were drawn to Nesil as the priest presented a brief sketch of his life.

Nesil didn't mind the attention. It felt good to listen and relax a short while. For the time being, he had no need to second-guess his actions. He only had to go through the motions and hope nothing went wrong with his plan.

"...and it is with great pride we see him before us today," the priest concluded. "Ready to take this last, final step. Let what was forgotten be remembered! Let what was broken be made whole!"

The priest turned to the opposite end of the bridge, where the doors were opening. The chamber became filled with stifled whisperings, gasps, and murmurs of adoration.

The small girl stepped into view, and—with sparkling eyes meant only for Nesil— she gracefully approached the priest and king.

Sefina's dress was of a style Nesil had never seen, with white layers of diaphanous fabric so pristine they nearly glowed. The material coiled first around her neck, in a diagonal across her chest, before circling her hips and fanning at her ankles. It gave the appearance of a spiraling flower, with soft petals brushing the ground with each step.

Her back and shoulders were bare, covered only by her loose spread of blond hair— left plain, straight, and unadorned. Rather than attempt to hide her youth, she wore no jewelry or makeup, leaving nothing to distract from her natural qualities.

This simplicity, however, was deceptive, as Nesil had no doubt her appearance was enhanced in ways only illusion could accomplish. Her thirteen-year-old face was shaped too perfectly—her smile too refined. Every inch of her pearlescent skin was smoother than silk and impossibly immaculate.

When the people looked at her, they saw something more than human. And very few would hesitate to venerate their princess.

"You can stop staring, you know," said Sefina's voice directly into his ear.

The priest continued the ritual, but Nesil already knew the words. He only needed to stand in place without anything expected of him for the next short while.

"If you want to say something, press your teeth together," she continued. *"No one will hear your voice or see your lips move."*

He kept his confusion from appearing on his face, keenly aware the audience was watching. He didn't think, however, she had reason to trick him. So he kept his teeth together and tried to speak.

"...You put an illusion over my mouth?"

"Yes. But it only activates when your jaw is closed. That way, you can still speak normally with everyone. Just don't talk to them through clenched teeth."

It would take conscious effort, but Nesil was confident he could remember the distinction.

"Trust me, though," she continued. *"No one will notice a thing. What they'll find odd is how much you keep staring."*

"That's not odd. They think we're in love."

Sefina groaned. *"Maybe. But you're not seeing the look on your face. You're smiling, sure, but it doesn't look like love."*

Nesil realized she was right. As his exhaustion mounted, he was making more and more mistakes. His only relief was that it'd soon be over. Once the ceremony was complete—and his grandfather safely home—the people would understand if their prince retired from the remainder of the festivities.

"So you're the expert now?" he asked. *"What would YOU know about love?"*

It surprised him when Sefina didn't answer. Rather than receive her usual retort, he was met with pained silence.

Did that mean he was right? And she regretted her deficiency of ordinary, human emotion? Or was it the other way around? Had her relationship with Kadrek gone deeper than expected? So deep, it hurt to think about?

Per tradition, the priest shared the tale of the First Ceremony. It was the oldest love story known to man, of how the god Shaelis had saved Ashaira from certain death and forged a relationship that spanned millennia.

Despite how it ended—with no explanation for Ashaira's trial—nothing could erase those thousands of years. It set the pattern for all marriages to come—the ideal that love was meant to endure.

It was a story Nesil had always taken seriously. He'd longed for the day he'd be united with his soul mate, for whom he'd strive to be a better person.

Some dreams, unfortunately, were not meant to be.

The king stood quietly to one side, his role in religious customs more akin to supervision than active participation. Lending authority to any observance. As such, he'd often stand there, looking very tired, inattentive, and impatient.

Tonight was no different, and Nesil wondered if he should be grateful for the old man's frown. It was better than appearing apprehensive, lest the aeisr suspect something was off.

At the same time, however, this wasn't just any ceremony. He could've, at least, pretended to care for his grandson.

"So how's this going to work?" asked Nesil. *"The ceremony isn't just words, you know. The devoter is going to activate the circle and inform everyone if our realignment is successful."*

Sefina didn't answer.

"Please, tell me you've thought this far!"

"Of course, I have." Her voice was irritated.

"And?"

"And... Just wait and see."

"So this IS something illusion can handle? It will APPEAR to activate? So convincingly, even the devoter will believe?"

"Well, maybe... But what would be the point?"

Nesil blinked. *"You understand, don't you? If our marriage fails, you WON'T be princess."*

"A possibility, yes. But an acceptable risk."

Nesil didn't understand what she was saying. He'd felt certain the aeisr would rig the ceremony and guarantee her coronation. He was worried, since she wasn't a real person, a successful wedding might not even be possible.

Did the aeisr *want* the ceremony to fail? Had she changed her mind after realizing how much it limited her freedom?

Or was this something else? Was it about exposing *him*? To make everyone doubt him, as he explained how he hadn't realized his bride was a fraud?

Too many possibilities rushed through his mind, he almost didn't catch what she said next.

"I suppose I'm not interested in a fake ceremony. What would that make me—a fake princess?"

"It's only a title." he contested. *"A few signatures on a certificate and a crowd of witnesses. They only need to SEE us get married. Isn't that what we're doing?"*

"Silly boy... Why would I want it to just be on paper? It's every girl's dream actually to BE a princess! And since I wasn't born one, my only option is to marry a prince."

Nesil laughed through his teeth. *"I'm just a regular person. Titles have power because we GIVE them power. If you took away my ancestral line, I wouldn't even—"*

"I'm not stupid, Nesil. I know how things work. But just because people invented a sentiment—with nothing that can be touched or measured—doesn't mean it isn't real."

Nesil shook his head in bewilderment, not caring that the audience saw him do it. It seemed absurd an aeisr, of all things, would lecture him on what was real!

Sefina went on. *"For me, it's not a matter of being princess for show. Hell, I've already been QUEEN a few times when I've impersonated your mother. But that wasn't real. SHE was still queen. There's a difference, you know."*

"How is it different? Back then, you masqueraded as my mother—and now, you're doing it as Sefina. It'll be SEFINA'S name on the paper. Not yours."

It was the aeisr's turn to laugh. *"But don't you see? YOU'RE the one who's confusing what's fake. It's not the PAPER that matters. You're not marrying Sefina because she's not here. I'M in the circle. You're marrying ME."*

Nesil paused, surprised her words actually made sense. There was just one problem. *"But how can I marry someone who isn't real?"*

"If I weren't real, how do you explain what happened to your kingdom? Just because you can't touch me—"

"That's not what I meant. I'm talking about the ceremony—of two people coming together and bringing harmony to their aspects. But you...? You don't HAVE an aspect. You don't even have a body!"

Sefina merely laughed and said nothing more.

The priest was looking at him and waving him forward, so it was possible she wanted him to focus. Or she was playing dumb.

With a nod, Nesil reorganized his thoughts and approached the priest.

In the man's left hand was a small, ivory chalice filled with dark, coppery blood—Sefina's blood. It'd been taken from her only moments before—or, at least, she'd made a show of it being taken.

Nesil had watched it happen—but he'd been so distracted by their conversation, he hadn't realized its significance. Luckily, he'd seen enough of these ceremonies that his inattention didn't disrupt the proper flow.

With deft precision, the priest painted a symbol across Nesil's forehead.

Her blood was still warm.

"Beneath the eyes of Jaesha, I mark thee for devotion. I touch thy head to receive understanding. I mark thine ears, to hearken unto the voice of thy bride to be."

Nesil turned to look at Sefina and saw there was, indeed, a small bandage on her forearm.

"Face me," said the priest, using the clean back of his hand to turn Nesil's head the right way.

"Nesil tel Kirchem, marked for devotion, son of Devaren and Kena ta Kirchem, wilt thou profess thy love for this woman, Sefina ti Dreyton, daughter of Taiwyn and Hania ta Dreyton? To be her guide and confidant? Her servant and dearest friend?

"Speak now with thine own voice. Swear it."

Without thinking twice, he said, "I swear." As he spoke, he made a point of opening his mouth wide so his teeth didn't touch.

The priest smiled before turning and setting down the cup.

When he returned, he held a different cup of similar design—this one empty and made of gold.

He was also holding a ceremonial dagger.

"With your permission," the priest said, indicating toward Nesil's arm.

For a moment, he stared at the blade. It hadn't even crossed his mind when seeing Sefina's bandage. And yet, now, he wondered—did it have some role in the assassination?

He nodded to the priest.

Knowing better than to watch, Nesil turned to face Sefina.

He winced at the sharp pain as the golden cup was filled.

"*Explain this to me,*" said Nesil. "*He's going to mark you with my blood—or try to, at least—but that's not even the difficult part. The man's a DEVOTER. He's expecting to join two aspects—but how can that work if you're a patch of air?*"

"*Relax. Though you don't want to believe it—I DO have an aspect. It'll work just fine.*"

As the priest cleaned his arm and bandaged the wound, Nesil tried to understand.

Which aspect could the aeisr possibly have?

His first impulse was that she had to be abyssal. Wasn't that the gist of his conversation with Renat? There were *more* layers than the traditional eight? With some that no one even knew about?

At the same time, however, his guess was probably wrong. The aeisr, after all, had been gifted to Seldor precisely because she worked *against* the current. She repelled it somehow, through means Nesil didn't understand.

The priest marked Sefina—more carefully than he'd done with Nesil, not wanting an errant drop to sully her dress. As his fingers crossed her skin, he went immediately into her vows without indication he'd sensed anything wrong.

Unable to wait, Nesil spoke over the priest. "*But what do you mean? Which aspect? Does it have a name?*"

It needed to be asked, though he fully expected her to avoid the question. Or outright refuse to answer.

Which surprised him all the more when she said, *"Come on, Nesil. I thought you'd have figured it out by now."*

What was that supposed to mean?!

For the past three years, no one had suspected the aeisr of having an aspect, much less made a guess as to which it might be.

Her words themselves, however, were a clue. If she claimed he could figure it out, it must've been listed among the aspects he knew.

Which meant he was right—she *wasn't* abyssal.

But, as he thought through the others—Foundation, Equilibrium, and all the rest—none described what the aeisr could do. Creation was the only one that came close, but even that felt wrong. She created objects, sure, but they weren't physical.

It was only then, he remembered there was still one more—a *ninth* aspect—from the god Aviathas. The problem, however, was that the aspect was destroyed. The world had watched as an entire people was torn to shreds.

What was its name?

"I swear," said Sefina as the priest completed her vows.

Nesil, however, wasn't paying attention.

Though he suspected this was her plan—that she'd teased this information to distract him from everything happening—the subject was too important to drop.

And then it hit him.

The ninth aspect had been named *Innovation.* The formation of ideas.

He had no doubt this was it. The aeisr didn't merely create floating projections but actual thoughts in people's minds. It explained why she fooled more senses than vision. She could make a person think he was actually touching something. So much so, he got a sense of weight and pressure.

Nesil was certain this distinction was important—yet he didn't know how the discovery helped him. How the hell did he *fight* an idea?

Moreover, he couldn't ignore the rest of the puzzle.

If Innovation was dead, what did that mean for her? Was Sefina *also* dead?

Moreover, the aeisr had arrived in conjunction with Ashaira's statue—the goddess of Ordination, *not* Innovation. Though the statue's shape might have been meaningless, and there wasn't a connection, what if there was?

All of this was giving Nesil a headache. But though none of it made sense, he refused to give up.

It was Sefina who dragged him away from his thoughts.

"So, how far do you plan to take this act of yours?"

Nesil was frustrated by the interruption but also noticed they were nearing the end of the ceremony. It seemed wise to put his thoughts aside before someone caught him staring into space—bored of his own wedding.

"What do you mean?" he asked.

"Well, are you going to start bringing me flowers? Jewelry?"

She'd distracted him for this?

In truth, Nesil was planning to give her a few guards to stay with her at all times. After his mother's recent death, the people would view this as an appropriate precaution.

The aeisr wasn't finished. *"Will we be spending the night in your room? Or did you have something more elaborate in mind?"*

"I haven't given it much thought." Nor did he want to. *"I'm making this up as we go."*

"Obviously..." She sighed. *"You must've thought of it before. Sleeping with your girlfriend."*

"She was never my—" He stopped. This felt awkward. *"You have no right to talk about her. And I don't want any discussions about..."* He drew a breath through his teeth. *"I've known you a whole six hours? Seven, tops? And you talk about sex?"*

"Calm down. I wasn't sure how seriously you were taking this marriage thing."

"This is an alliance," he said. *"Nothing more."*

Looking serenely into his eyes, her voice laughed in his ears. *"An alliance? With unspoken terms? I thought this was only about securing your crown."*

"It is. But if we take the throne together, then we rule together. Wouldn't that create a semblance of peace?"

"Is that how you imagined this?" She giggled. *"Once I'm your wife, I'd become submissive? And people would stop dying?"*

No, he hadn't thought that. But he was hopeful enough to ask, *"Why would you kill your own subjects?"*

"Why indeed..." she said without further explanation.

He decided to drop it.

"Nesil," she said, her tone condescending. *"You might be the prince. And very soon, you might be my husband. Hell, I might even make you MORE than that. But not for a second has this been about diplomacy."*

As the devoter completed the last part of the ritual, he waved the two of them forward.

Nesil stepped toward Sefina and took her weightless hand in his. Together, they faced the priest.

Sefina continued. *"I'll play the role of your doting sweetheart. But this was never, in any way, an equal relationship."*

"I know."

In a loud voice, the priest declared, "With the blessing of Shaelis, these young souls are brought together! Let them cleave to one another, secured in his light, as one complete whole, never to split asunder!"

To Nesil's surprise, the room was quiet. There was the sound of shifting movement—a few coughs from the crowd—but even the babies had gone still.

And he realized what they were waiting for.

Without overthinking it, he slipped a hand behind her back, while his other cupped her cheek.

Then he kissed her.

As he did so, he tried to imagine the real Sefina. But no matter how convincing it all felt—the sweet taste of her lips and the soft skin of her back—his heart wasn't in it.

Everything about this was wrong. He was marrying someone with which he shared *nothing* in common.

Which made it all the more surprising when something...happened.

Like sunlight refracted through a crystal window—a stream of memories flashed through his mind.

And they weren't his.

Usually, at the conclusion of the ceremony, the ritual simply ended, and the people went home. In the rarest of events, however, when a couple was perfectly matched, the realignment caused each person to experience a portion of his fiance's life story.

In Nesil's case, who was most *certainly* incompatible with his partner, it came in a few short, confused bursts.

The cathedral melted away, and he was standing in a city empty of people. It was a place he didn't recognize—there one second and gone the next.

He saw a man without knowing how much time had passed—possibly decades. Perhaps centuries. He had ear-length hair and a devilish grin.

And Nesil knew, without a doubt, who the man was—not because he'd met him but because *the aeisr* had met him. In that fleeting instant, Nesil felt what the aeisr felt.

Dark heavens... Sefina had been telling the truth.

To her, Kadrek had been the *only* person she'd known. His arrival in her wasteland had been nothing short of miraculous. He'd plucked her from oblivion and given her the chance to *be* someone.

From that moment forward, everything she came to love and appreciate was wrapped up in that single relationship. Kadrek, quite literally, was her entire world.

And for her to lose that... How could she possibly make Renat feel the same way? Upon her arrival in Seldor, Renat didn't have *one* person at his side—but hundreds. If she killed just one—no matter how dear to him—it wouldn't come near the total loss she'd experienced.

The vision ended as quickly as it began. Nesil stood there, stunned, wondering if he shared something in common with her after all.

When he opened his eyes, the crowd was in awe. And he could imagine what they'd seen.

It was always obvious when a married couple received the visions—because both participants froze at the same moment. Sometimes, they stood there for several seconds. At others, they collapsed or thrashed with seizures.

Fortunately, Nesil was still on his feet. A fortuitous sign to the surrounding crowd that the marriage was blessed by heaven.

They roared with approval—clapping, hollering, and whistling.

Nesil's face flushed red, and he saw tears in the eyes of the women below. But though the ritual was over, there was one last step to make everything complete.

When the priest stepped back, the king came forward, silencing the crowd.

Sefina spoke into his ear, sounding sly. *"I'm making you invisible now."*

Nesil tensed with sudden dread.

"Don't worry," she said. *"No one will notice. They'll see a version of you beside me. I'll even make him look believable."*

Through his teeth, he asked, *"Why?"*

"I need your hands free to catch my crown."

That wasn't unreasonable. All the same, the idea of being replaced by a puppet made him nervous. He'd have to watch carefully to ensure his double didn't do anything... unseemly.

"Right now?" he asked.

"Yes. Just take a step back."

Nesil did so and suddenly felt very odd. In front of him stood an exact copy of himself. As promised, it was utterly convincing.

His doppelganger had an arm around Sefina, gazing at the crowd with a beaming smile.

It was an out-of-body experience—only in reverse.

As the applause faded, the newlyweds knelt side by side.

The king came forward, holding two crowns.

It was the first Nesil had seen of his circlet—simple and wrought of pure gold. The crystal tiara in Renat's other hand, however, was easy enough to recognize. It'd belonged to his mother.

Renat stepped in front of Nesil first, raising the circlet high to the roar of applause. In a loud voice, he proclaimed, "I present to you Nesil, Prince of house Kirchem! The first of his name! Heir to the Silverwater and the realm of all Seldor!"

Nesil reached forward as his copy was crowned. Though the circlet appeared to remain in place, he felt the weight of the real one, invisible in his hands.

"I must apologize," the king announced to the crowd. "On the morrow, a new tiara shall be commissioned. But under present constraints, the queen's will have to do. I hope it fits."

He approached the small girl.

"I give to you Sefina, Princess of Merilon! My new granddaughter!"

Nesil carefully caught her crown.

Then, froze in shock, as the king lifted her to her feet.

And, undeterred by the blood that marked her forehead, pulled the girl into a loving embrace.

Chapter 21
CONFLAGRATION

"**O**h, shit..." said Sefina, within the king's arms. "*Push him off! Push him, NOW!*"

Nesil didn't move, unsure what to say or what to do. He certainly wasn't going to follow her demands.

Renat, too, was speechless, as if unable to make sense of it all. He took a cautious step away, his eyes wide and stunned. Perhaps searching for an easy explanation. One in which his grandson's bride was real but only elsewhere for the moment. A reason, at the very least, for Nesil not knowing of this treachery from the start.

"Has something gone wrong?" asked the priest.

"*He won't fight back,*" Sefina urged. "*Not if you're quick. Look at his face!*"

There was nothing Nesil could do. He stood there dumbly, clutching both crowns in his hands.

Strangely, a part of him *wanted* to do it. He understood why she wanted him dead—why she so desperately needed Renat to suffer. Nesil had *felt* what she felt, if only for a moment. A part of him agreed with the person she'd become.

But he held himself back. And it wouldn't be long before she realized it wasn't out of fear but refusal. Defiance.

"*NESIL!! He can't even see—!*"

In an abrupt change of tone, she said, "*Whatever...*"

And the stage caught fire.

Without so much as a lantern falling over, there was no plausible explanation of where the flames came from. They ignited from thin air, roared upwards, and circled the platform in an incandescent tide.

All havoc broke loose as people scrambled to their feet, pushed, shouted, and climbed over benches. Only a scant few remained calm, remembering previous attacks and suspecting the flames to be false.

Despite knowing the truth, Nesil found himself shielding his eyes and retreating down the length of the bridge. He coughed away smoke and tried to catch a view of his grandfather somewhere in the middle of the blinding inferno.

It now towered over eight feet high—its roar deafening.

There was a shrill cry as the priest, in hysterics, fell through the handrail and disappeared from view. More people screamed in response.

Renat turned, face aghast. Only then—watching the handrail break—did he seem to remember Nesil's warning. His face flooded with confusion as if no longer sure how to respond.

Nesil knew precisely how he felt, recalling the flames that'd trapped him at the castle. He could still remember the heat searing through his flesh—more intense than any real pain in his life. And, for his grandfather, it'd be even worse, standing closer to the firestorm than Nesil's experience.

The king's eyes were wide—his face glistening with sweat—resisting the urge to flee in terror.

It was all Nesil could do to keep from shouting, *That's it! You're doing it! Just stay planted, and DON'T MOVE!*

But no matter how much Nesil wanted to come to the rescue, doing so would only make things worse. It was one thing to freeze at a critical moment and quite another to blatantly act against her.

Somehow, he needed to salvage the situation. Once his grandfather got away, he'd convince the aeisr he was still on her side.

Nesil's back hit the door, and he stopped at the end of the bridge. He needed to squint to discern the wavering forms of his grandfather and the newlywed couple, staring across at each other with blank expressions.

Even at this distance, the tumultuous heat was unbearable.

Seeing Renat there, stalwart and undaunted, was nearly enough to bring Nesil to tears. The king had finally chosen this moment—when it mattered most—to listen. Against his every inclination, Renat was willing to trust his grandson's advice.

But even then, he faltered when the fire reached his clothing.

He spasmed violently as the flames intertwined upward, lighting him up like a torch. He reached for his armband but lacked the strength to pull it off.

As he fell to his knees, his howl was even louder than the flames.

The people turned at the sound. From congested doorways, all eyes looked up as the pillar of fire engulfed their sovereign lord.

A loud crack split the room, and the central platform broke apart in great splinters and flares, setting fire to the benches below.

Nesil stared in confusion as support beams exploded and sent shudders down the bridge. It brought back memories of the floor imploding at Silverwater Castle—but this felt different. A powerful force was behind the tremor that couldn't possibly have been—

NOOO!! he wanted to scream, as dread flooded over him. *This wasn't—! HOW THE HELL COULD THIS HAVE HAPPENED*?!

Sefina laughed—a shrill sound only he could hear. Standing amidst the blaze, her dress burned a scintillating white.

He couldn't figure it out. How could the flames possibly be real?

The crowns slipped from his fingers as he fumbled for the latch. He tried to get the door open, but his hands were clumsy and refused to cooperate.

Renat's screams withered into silence, marking the end of his misbegotten torment.

Burned alive because he'd listened. Because he hadn't removed the band sooner. Or risked the fall from the raised platform. Either of those choices would've increased his chances, but he'd chosen to stand there. All because of Nesil.

It didn't make sense. Where'd the fire come from? Had someone been lured too close to a candlestick?

The door finally complied, and he burst into the stairway—cool, dark, and empty.

"Come back!" yelled Sefina.

Realizing his body was visible again, he broke into a run.

"Nesil, wait!" she said, following after.

Without looking back, he raced down the steps, two at a time. He ignored the orange waver up above. The distant cries of panic. All of it attesting to what could never be undone.

He imagined every inch of his body afire. Skin peeling. Flesh broiling. Longing for that moment of sweet release.

"See?" she said when they reached the end of the long corridor. "All worked out, just like I said."

Her voice wasn't angry, but that didn't ease his fears.

Not only had Nesil refused her commands—she must surely be suspicious of the king's final moments. For Renat to do nothing and attempt no escape—it was the furthest thing from normal. No doubt she'd be wondering if Nesil was involved.

He couldn't control his breathing. He could barely control anything at all.

Not knowing how else to respond, he said, "Your dress is still burning."

She smiled seductively. "I know."

Black, wispy fragments curled, writhed, and drifted away. Underneath, her skin was smeared with ash but smooth and unscathed.

Her eyes danced as she wrinkled her nose. "Should I cover myself? We're married now. Don't you remember...my king?"

He ignored the distraction and regathered his thoughts. It was impossible to pretend that everything was normal. His heart was so fast, it pulsed through his vision.

"Why didn't you tell me?" he demanded, his voice cracking with emotion. "About the fire...? Everything? That wasn't the plan!"

Sefina smirked. "If I'd told you the plan, you would've never gone along with it."

That much was true. No one—not even his worst enemy—deserved such horrible cruelty. Except maybe the aeisr herself.

"We could've found another way! A way that didn't burn our kingdom to ash! He could've died painlessly when he was—"

"You're missing the point," she said flatly. "This was never just about taking his life. You realize, don't you, if I'd wanted him dead, I could've done it at any time?"

Nesil didn't want to believe it. But she'd somehow produced fire—an actual fire—without his help.

Her goal, all along, was to deprive the king of an ordinary death. After the pain she'd been through—the pain Nesil, in part, had relived through her memories—she'd been bent on a fate far, far worse.

"So why change your mind?" he asked. "You've waited this long. What's so special about today?"

"Because..." she said, as though explaining herself to a child. "Today, the king didn't only lose a daughter. In those final moments, he realized...he'd also lost *you*."

It took a few seconds to understand what she meant.

At the heart of the firestorm, those thoughts must've crossed Renat's mind—that Nesil had betrayed him. His own grandson had led him, by the hand, to be offered sacrifice to the cruelest of deities.

Except...that offering only happened *because* of Nesil's warning...

How much had Sefina figured out?

"You're frightened," she said, gazing up at him. By then, less than half her dress remained, with curling edges that glowed like cinder.

He no longer desired any part of this. He wanted to run and pretend none of it ever happened. Except, if he stopped, Renat's death would be for nothing.

"In fact," she continued, stroking his hair, "you seem uncertain."

"How did you start the fire?" he asked.

They were interrupted by the sound of running steps.

"Your grace!" came the shout from an adjacent corridor.

Sefina didn't seem to notice or care. "You hesitated," she said, with eyes unblinking. "You said you'd kill him—but you failed."

"What does it matter? He's dead now, isn't he?"

"We had an agreement!" she hissed. "You want to be king, don't you? So go on! Prove yourself to me!"

Though Nesil feared what she meant, he found himself nodding. "I want to, but how?"

"Easy," said Sefina, as the ascendant approached. "You can do it right now."

The man was someone Nesil recognized—Alerisa's new husband, Jeros.

Through clenched teeth, Nesil asked, "*You want me to kill him?*"

"We need to get you safe!" declared the ascendant before taking a second glance at Sefina. Covered in only rags and ash. "Dear gods...!"

"He's seen too much," said the aeisr, implacably, without bothering to hide her voice.

"*You should've turned invisible!*" he hissed through his teeth.

"Princess...! I'll send for help!" Jeros looked her up and down with wide-eyed concern.

"This is where you left your ax," she said. "Right behind you."

Nesil hadn't forgotten. It was the reason he'd run here—to have a chance at defending himself.

There was steel in her tone. "Win my heart, Nesil! Make me believe!"

Jeros looked confused, alternating his gaze between the two of them.

Nesil felt too weary to decide. He knew, however, that if he didn't do this, he'd lose all chance of neutralizing the aeisr.

What was one life in comparison to all he could save?

"Pick up the ax!" she commanded.

"Ax?" echoed Jeros, taking a wary step backward.

Wasn't Nesil prepared to go to any lengths? The decision was one he should've already made.

Sefina's patience, however, didn't last that long.

"Figures."

Jeros swallowed, his face gone ashen. But as he started to run, Sefina turned and swung an upward fist through his head.

The sharp impact lifted Jeros through the air, to collapse against the wall in a red smear.

There was no explanation. Somehow, his skull became severed at the jaw. As though her fist had opened a straight and sunken gash.

His body twitched once and, then, went still.

Nesil tried to understand—unsure if Jeros had ever been real.

He fumbled behind him, searching for his weapon.

...It wasn't there.

Which left only one conclusion that made any sense.

"It's time we rectify your indecision," said Sefina while rivulets of crimson streaked down her ashen body.

She was the embodiment of excess, with blood in her hair and on the crystals of her tiara. Nearly enough to distract him from her swinging fist.

He barely turned his face aside, but she was already spinning. The bottom of her bare foot caught him square in the chest.

The solid blow sent him flying back—but since he'd been expecting it, he was quick to recover.

"Who are you?" he asked—not to the aeisr but to the person helping her. The ally she'd used to start the fire.

He tried to block her next attack, but, this time, her arms passed through his like mist. For a split second, his gut twisted with dread.

Instead, the blow came from behind, as the invisible attacker threw him off balance.

His head slammed against the wall. And forward onto the ground.

The room began to spin.

In an instant, Sefina was atop him, holding him down. Her weight wasn't that of a thirteen-year-old girl but a grown man.

A beefy hand forced his face into the floor, scraping teeth against stone.

Instead of giving up, Nesil kicked with both feet and tried to throw the man off. When that didn't work, he swung an arm—to have it caught and twisted behind his back.

"Don't make this harder on yourself," said Sefina. "It'd be a pity if I had to kill my new husband."

Nesil tried to ask, "*Who the hell is it?*" but the stone got in the way of his lips.

She understood just fine. "You honestly didn't believe you were the first to come to me, did you?"

He didn't answer. If she'd already had an ally, why hadn't she used him? With such an advantage, she could've wiped out the kingdom long, long ago.

"There's no need to take this personally," she said. "It's not like you had time to meet all your subjects. Or understand their problems. My tireless assistant isn't anyone you know."

A pause. "Get him up."

Pain shot through his arm as he was hauled to his knees.

Sefina leaned over from behind him, with arms behind her back.

When Nesil caught sight of her face, he immediately recoiled and pulled away. But a sturdy hand gripped the back of his head and forced him to look.

Her eyes had reverted into sunken hollows. The skin surrounding the pits was loose and torn, and in the faint light, he saw the darkness in her skull.

The corners of her mouth pulled up in a smile.

"Perhaps I share the blame for this recalcitrant behavior. After all, it's difficult to command subservience and respect while taking on the appearance of someone so young."

The thing that wasn't Sefina tilted her head to one side. "But you mustn't, for one second, forget who I am."

Her bloody face drew close, and she kissed him.

Nesil resisted, but even squeezing his lips didn't hold her back. Her parted lips slipped around his—through his—and her taste entered his mouth anyway.

Ash, blood, and strawberries—soft and tender.

When she finally drew away, Nesil spat in her direction. It passed through her unnoticed.

Even so, it earned him a whack to his head—likely a cupped hand.

Nesil squeezed his eyes shut as his ears rang.

Sefina laughed. "If I were you, I wouldn't provoke him. He's already upset you're the one I married rather than him."

"You're serious?" Nesil asked, forming a smile. "You can have her!"

This earned his ear another clout, harder than the first.

"But don't worry," she said. "He knows you're our king. And won't kill you without my express permission."

As if in contradiction, something slammed Nesil's throat, hauling him backward while constricting his breathing.

His hands fumbled at his neck, feeling something like wood, and he realized he was being dragged by the ax handle.

Only when he twisted his head to one side, he managed to draw air. His feet scrambled, desperate for purchase, but it was a wasted effort.

They were soon outside, his feet sliding over dirt. He heard the shouts of other people but from far away. Oddly, above this noise came the sound of running water, which made it easier to guess where the man was taking him.

He was released suddenly and pitched forward. His hands hit the dirt, too weak to break his fall. He only managed a few short, ragged breaths before he was lifted again and carried a short distance.

When he opened his eyes, his face was mere inches above the illusory water.

Before he realized what was happening, his head was shoved down.

The world became a cold, sickening blur.

His hands tried to grasp something, but the stone rim wasn't real, and the man too strong. Nesil's exertions only earned him a mouthful of water and a horrible burning that entered his nose. His lungs heaved in agony and made him more frantic. But, for all his flailing, he could not get free.

He sputtered and spat as his head was pulled up. His skin prickled against the cool night air as water drenched his shirt and ran down his arms.

He'd felt himself drowning! How was that possible in an illusory pool? He'd never felt anything so horrible in his life!

A second plunge and it started all over again. That inundation of cold, suffocating darkness. He tried to twist his head free, only for a second hand to seize his chin and hold him like a vice. Nesil's head was slammed into the stone at the bottom, hard against his brow. Bubbles escaped past his face, and water was forced down his lungs.

"This shouldn't be necessary," said Sefina when he was pulled up again. She sat nearby, legs crossed, atop the white granite rim. "But I've had enough of your uncertainty. Your moments of hesitation. A lot of that is my fault, I know, for failing to spell out the nature of our relationship."

Her hand signaled, giving Nesil a split second to take a deep breath. This time, he entered the water without struggle, resigned to the fact the man was too strong.

He told himself he was saving his energy. Waiting for the moment the stranger dropped his guard. But it was difficult to relax amid the icy shallows, listening to the rhythmic pounding of the nearby cascade. His momentary surrender felt too much like failure.

And just when he suspected he'd be held down forever—despite Sefina's assurances—he was hauled up a third time.

"I don't give a damn if you're king. Understand? From now on, you'll *not* make decisions without my approval. You'll sit your throne and attend your meetings, but you will not so much as speak a word I don't give you. Is that simple enough?"

Nesil didn't respond.

She relaxed and gave him a sideways glance. "As time passes, you'll learn our marriage doesn't need to be all threats and fear. So long as you follow orders quickly and thoroughly, you may even be surprised by my unique generosity. It's quite easily in my power, you see, to make your life a rewarding one... Even pleasurable."

In that instant, the courtyard transformed into a lush garden, bathed in the light of a noonday sun. Nesil was suddenly dry, and his restraints loosened, allowing him to straighten and look around.

Everything was so bright it was difficult to imagine this was the same place at all. The cloudless sky was a brilliant blue, illuminating countless blossoms surrounding the stone rim and the sparkling water pouring from the fountainhead. There were more colors and flowers than Nesil could identify—more beauty than he thought possible to come from her mind.

He wondered how far he could run before the man could catch him.

Sefina was clean and her eyes back to normal—her wedding dress, white, wispy, and unburned. She smiled as she reclined in the warm sunlight.

"Anything you can dream—that is the true power of Innovation," she said. "I could be older if you wanted. Taller. You name it."

"But not real," said Nesil, lowering his eyes. Seeing her like this—so pristine and beautiful—brought pain to his heart. It drew his mind to the real Sefina. And feelings the aeisr couldn't possibly replicate.

"No one ever realizes how far indulgence can go," she said, her eyes turning mischievous. "I can make the spectrum of sensuality as real as any fire. Equally intense as drowning in water."

Nesil said nothing, trying hard not to think about it.

"And if that doesn't satisfy," she continued, "it's simply a matter of further accommodations... You remember that ascendant from the hallway? The one we killed?" Her voice didn't betray a hint of remorse. "Jeros, was it? It'd be easy to make you look like him. Your body's about the same height and build. Near enough, I guarantee his wife won't tell the difference, even after a whole night together."

It was a disturbing thought. Nesil had never heard of the aeisr doing such a thing. It stirred an odd, sickening sensation in his gut, followed by intrigue, and then self-reproach.

Compelled to argue, he insisted, "Even *that* wouldn't be real."

"Okay..." Sefina sighed. "Cling to your delusions of dignity a bit longer, if it makes you feel better. In the end, however, it's not exactly a difficult choice. You either take what I give or..."

At the snap of her fingers, the flowers shriveled and wilted.

The world plunged into darkness and didn't just revert to how things were. This time, there was something wrong with the smell. The stench was rancid and coppery. And humid.

The fountain no longer flowed with water. It spurted blood with dark clumps where

 AUSTIN LYNN CLARK

the surface had begun to coagulate.

To his horror, Sefina repeated the signal from before.

Abandoning his decision not to struggle, he lurched violently against the man's grasp, frantic in his scramble to get away. But once again, he was overpowered, and his head was forced down into the thick, tepid muck.

The pungency was so sharp and the warmth so oppressive it sent a churl through his stomach. Within moments, he was choking on his own bile—gaging while trying to keep his mouth closed. But there was nothing to keep the stickiness out of his ears and searing up his nose. The revulsion was overwhelming.

When he was finally let up, he began to retch, sucking in large gasps between heaves. He repeatedly shot air from his nose in an attempt to expel as much blood as he could. His eyes stung, even though they were closed. And when Sefina began to speak, her voice sounded strange through congested ears.

"It's not much of a decision," she said. "Especially once you realize I will *not* hesitate to kill you, should I ever find it necessary. As I said before, appearances can be disguised. It doesn't matter that my assistant here is so much larger than you. With some extra precautions, no one will notice him masquerading in your place."

She made it sound simpler than it was, but to Nesil, it hardly mattered. By the time things escalated to that point, he'd already be dead.

Sefina continued, "In fact, I'd bet my friend here is so eager to be king he's likely thought through dozens of scenarios, each leading to your death. All of them, of course, appearing like an accident."

Nesil felt her hand on his face, wiping illusory blood from his eyes. He opened them. Amid the sanguine flowers and pressing dark, her white skin seemed to shimmer and glow. As though she were a firefly.

"So, what's it going to be?" she asked. "Will you be a good husband?"

"Yes," Nesil choked. There was no point in refusing.

"When I tell you to kill someone, will you do it?"

"Yes," he said. His response made him sick—realizing that if that moment came soon, he might actually do it.

"I hope you realize—this hurts me as much as it hurts you."

He didn't believe that for a second.

"You *know* me, Nesil! Perhaps better than anyone. You know I don't have friends... If I lost you... That's not what I want."

"Okay..." he said, without feeling.

"I want to trust you," she said with a pained smile. "But I don't think I can. At least, not yet."

Nesil wasn't sure where she was going with this. He hoped she wasn't considering another godsdamned test.

She stood up, then, before traversing the railing and wading into the dark pool of blood. The crimson surface licked her calves, and smears of red seeped up her white dress.

Nesil forced himself to watch.

Sefina lowered herself, unbothered by the blood oozing up around her legs, her waist, and her stomach. Reaching her hands below the surface, she adjusted her skirt to sit cross-legged, as though sitting in a warm bath.

"Let me tell you something," she said, leaning forward, with the tips of her hair skimming the red, curdled surface. "It would be impossible for you to drown in this pool."

Not understanding, he stared dumbly back into her aqua-green eyes.

"Don't get me wrong," she said, smiling. "It certainly *feels* like drowning. What I mean to say, though, is that you won't die. Despite whatever asphyxiation you experience, it isn't real. And since you can't hold your breath forever, you either give up or eventually pass out. No matter the end, you get enough air to stay alive."

Nesil surged with panic as her words sank in.

Her sticky hands cradled the sides of his head. "Maybe after an hour of this, I might believe your promises." She kissed his forehead. "Your grace."

Then, the hands of both Sefina and her invisible ally forced Nesil's head down into the darkness.

Chapter 22

BENEATH THE BLOOD

Even in defeat, Nesil didn't give up easily.

He grabbed fingers. He feinted in different directions—but even both his legs around a single massive arm didn't give enough leverage. Not even a foot to the man's face. Nor an elbow between the legs. In the end, it was not unlike grappling an invisible bear.

And it only made the drownings worse.

He never knew his lungs could ache so much. They strained against his ribcage as though trying to wrench free, all the while stretching his throat like rubber. The involuntary spasms should've driven him unconscious—but despite his dizzying headache and queasy insides, he wasn't even able to black out properly.

In fact, rather than a gradual loss of feeling, the soreness in his chest only increased in acuity. He was so worn out and exhausted, dying would've been preferable.

There's no escape, the blood-covered doll had whispered the first time they met.

If struggling didn't work, what was next? Should he try bribing the man with riches? Servants? Women? Though Nesil was king, none of that seemed to matter. From the man's perspective, accepting such an offer would be the equivalent of switching to the losing side.

And he wouldn't be wrong.

Renat was dead. Mother was dead. And countless others besides. How many more needed to die before the kingdom became no longer worth saving?

Perhaps, rather than viewing defeat as some inevitable future, it might be better to admit this battle was lost long ago.

Would it really be so bad to submit to her commands? If they were all going to die anyway, what difference did it make? If anything, it'd be a mercy to help his people die quickly than suffer this prolonged, unnecessary torment.

Lightheaded and wheezing, Nesil almost didn't notice when the warmth around his mouth suddenly withdrew. It was like a bubble of air amid the shifting darkness had curiously formed around his lips.

It seemed too good to be true, but he spat out blood and drew an experimental breath.

The dusty air was cool and brought immeasurable relief. As the sweetness shuddered through his chest, the dry flavor was reminiscent of a stone walkway—a taste of the world beneath the facade.

It suggested the bubble wasn't part of the illusion but more akin to an oversight. A hole. A defect.

He took as many gulps as possible, but the moment ended as abruptly as it began. And since his mouth was still open, he was soon gagging on a large, salty clot.

Rather than be discouraged, his mind stirred with renewed interest—awakened by the strange miracle and his desire to know the cause.

Before he figured out anything, he was pulled back up.

"Had enough?" asked Sefina, unaware that anything odd had occurred. Maybe she didn't see everything after all. "Which do you suppose is worse? Drowning or burning?"

Nesil didn't bother to speak or even open his eyes. He didn't need to remember the mess of red bubbles piling around the geyser of thick, churning muck.

It was easier to relax, limp as a rag doll, and sink all his weight onto the bear's burly arm. He hoped the continuous exertion might take its toll, so those muscles would ache when all this was over.

He heard Sefina stand, and, for a moment, he was hopeful. Was she bored already?

As though guessing his thoughts, she laughed.

"Brach's just getting started," she said. "It's only been twenty minutes."

Nesil's first sluggish thought was that Sefina was right—he'd never heard the name Brach before. His second thought: *Only twenty minutes*? Followed by: *Shit*.

With a surge of energy, he tried to slip free. But, for what must've been the hundredth time, Brach anticipated the move. Nesil wasn't allowed breath and was engulfed, once again, by lukewarm stickiness.

Nauseating darkness swirled around him. Even the ground seemed to tilt, making it difficult to distinguish up from down. He was so dazed by his complete lack of respiration, he felt sure this would be the moment he passed out.

It took all his concentration to focus on his lips, longing for an echo of that air bubble.

He'd barely the strength to hold his breath anymore, and sometime soon, he'd deplete his reserves. But no air appeared. And even his expectation of blacking out was optimistic.

Nesil tried to understand, but he was too far gone to come up with explanations.

Should he pass off the phenomenon as a one-time occurrence? What were the odds? These illusions were unlikely to betray an imperfection—especially with the aeisr standing two feet away. And for the flaw to appear exactly around his lips? Was that simply coincidence?

He was pulled up sooner than usual.

As his ears cleared, Sefina's voice was further away than expected.

"Change of plans," she announced. "The fire's too close."

The fire? he thought. *The same from the wedding?*

Nesil shouldn't have been surprised. If it'd been burning all this time, how far had it spread? More importantly, did this mean they were leaving the fountain?

From above came the deep voice of a man—one Nesil didn't recognize.

"What should I do with our prince?"

The aeisr groaned. "We'll have to end this early."

Nesil couldn't believe his luck!

Until she added, "We've got five minutes. Hold him under till he passes out."

In sudden panic, he sucked a deep breath.

"Nuh-uh," she said. "Squeeze it all from his chest. We can't afford to—"

Nesil didn't hear the rest as he was muscled to the ground. Lying flat on his stomach, intersecting the stone rim, he couldn't avoid the bear's full weight. His chin mashed against the ground, clamping his jaw and straining his neck.

His lungs trembled beneath the load, and he wondered if it might be better to inhale. There was no chance of getting free. So why not get it over with and save himself the suffering?

The thought of drawing breath, however, was not the same as actually doing it. As much as he wanted to, his body wouldn't let him. He could only yearn, in desperation, for another bubble to magically appear.

But wishing got him nowhere. Neither did praying. He wasn't getting help from a mysterious outsider. And, unlike fairy tales, Nesil didn't have mystical powers of his own.

This last thought was so ridiculous that, despite himself, Nesil started to laugh. This, unfortunately, drove precious bubbles from his lips.

Except...the bubbles disappeared, and he could suddenly breathe through his teeth once more.

In a moment of lucidity, it made a strange sense.

He could only breathe while his teeth were clenched and his voice passed through them. Or, in other words, when he triggered the illusory mask over his mouth—the one Sefina had given him so they could speak in private.

He wasn't sure how it worked, only that it kept others from seeing his lips move. As such, it didn't involve an actual pocket of air—the fake mouth and fake blood simply couldn't coexist in the same location.

One illusion counteracted the other.

In that same instant, he knew his discovery needed to stay secret. If Sefina found out, she'd rescind the gift and his last remaining hope.

It was such a frightening thought, Nesil immediately forced himself to avoid deep breaths. Despite his debilitating lack of air, he only allowed himself the smallest of sips, not wanting Brach to notice.

He kept his voice low—the sound required to activate the mask—worried his wheezing might be felt through his chest.

A minute crawled by, and his plan seemed to work. Crushed and weak though he was, he managed just enough air to sustain a semblance of consciousness.

That minute, however, stretched into more, and he felt like he was only delaying the inevitable. It wasn't as though the mask offered any real advantage, and he wondered what he'd do when they lifted him back up.

Obviously, he'd pretend to be knocked out, but that was easier said than done. The human body was designed to react—to protect itself from injury. One mistake and Sefina would notice. It might be as simple as the sound of his breathing or the speed of his heart. She'd know he was awake and drown him all over again.

In the end, however, he wasn't left with much choice.

Forcing himself to relax completely, he lowered his breathing rate to something like sleeping. He only hoped Sefina wouldn't check his lungs for blood.

When the man got up, Nesil didn't move.

For a long time, nothing happened. He supposed they might be talking, and he couldn't hear.

Without warning, Nesil was dragged from the fountain, leaving less than a second for him to quiet his voice.

He was rolled onto his back as a slight breeze cooled the blood on his face—the sticky film becoming dry and stiff.

"Should I follow?" asked Brach.

The bear's voice came from directly above.

Without warning, Nesil's arm was lifted above his face. Then abruptly let go.

Recognizing the test, he didn't avoid hitting himself. Fortunately, his hand missed his nose by an inch, making it easier not to flinch or appear startled.

"Not this time, Brach. This is something I've got to do by myself."

Strangely, the voice was not Sefina's but an older woman's—perhaps in her early twenties. It was slightly deeper in pitch and breathy.

Nesil supposed this made sense, as the aeisr had only adopted her thirteen-year-old form earlier that evening—entirely for the prince's benefit.

So, was this her natural voice? Or someone else she used when dealing with Brach? Did the aeisr even have her own voice?

"I'll see you back at the stable," she continued. "Take care of my husband."

Nesil heard movement but couldn't see the man's response.

"I mean it, Brach," her voice became stern. "I've taken a liking to this boy. He keeps things...fun."

The man grumbled.

"Just stop," she said. "Don't give me that look. You're fun, too...in different ways. This isn't up for discussion. But fair warning—if anything happens to our king—even on accident—I'm holding *you* responsible, got that?"

Brach's attitude changed. "Of course, mistress..."

The aeisr huffed in frustration.

"Might I ask...?" began Brach. "I guess I'm just confused. Renat's dead, isn't he? You've got what you wanted...so what are we doing?"

No answer.

It was a fair question. As far as Nesil knew, the aeisr's entire motivation was rooted in revenge.

Brach seemed to hesitate. "I shouldn't have said anything."

"No," the aeisr agreed. "Just... Do your job. And let me do mine."

Nesil was surprised to hear a sadness in her voice. Something almost like regret.

What had she been expecting? That the king's death would somehow solve her problems? That his suffering would make up for the emptiness inside?

Under different circumstances, Nesil might've felt sorry for her. The aeisr didn't know what she wanted. At least, not anymore.

"How soon should I expect you?" asked Brach before amending, "...your Highness?"

It was easy to hear the smile in her voice. "Fires aren't quickly put out. Even if the ascendants make some headway, it'll be far too simple to undo what they've accomplished... Once the flames turn invisible."

Brach was intrigued. "I've never seen that trick."

Nesil couldn't imagine the chaos of an invisible fire. He tried not to think about it and keep his heart rate down.

"Not much to see, really," she said. "But that's kind of the point. Don't come watching. I need you at a safe distance. Even if I'm not back by morning."

Nesil was lifted off the ground and slung over Brach's shoulder as easily as a grain sack. Feeling the touch of both the man's hands, it registered that Brach had left the ax behind.

"That long, huh?"

Her tone became derisive. "Fires move, Brach. Not to mention the fake ones I'll use to keep them distracted. It could easily take longer than that."

"Go on," he said. "Have your fun."

"Oh, I will. And Brach?"

"Yes?"

"Use chains and manacles this time. Ropes aren't nearly so reliable."

"Nothing but the best for our king," the man agreed.

Nesil was turned and carried away—each step driving a brawny shoulder into his gut. Each step made him want to gasp. Or retch, if his stomach weren't already empty.

Despite his inability to move or change into a more comfortable position, his mind was racing.

Chains? If he didn't think of something soon, he wouldn't get another chance.

His body, however, was too feeble and sluggish to accomplish anything. Even if he could somehow get free of the man's clutches, how could he run without collapsing?

Without moving his head, Nesil opened his eyes—cautiously, at first, then wider.

There wasn't much to see. No soldiers were nearby or anyone else who could come to his rescue. For the most part, the dark alleyway was littered with garbage. Wind-blown papers. The rotting carcass of a dog.

But he couldn't see Brach. With the man still invisible, the ground passed by as though he were flying.

To Nesil's surprise, he, himself, was invisible. He didn't know for how long, but it made enough sense. They couldn't risk bystanders seeing a floating body.

In that same instant, he came to a realization. Earlier, Brach had always held the upper hand because he was invisible, and Nesil was not. No matter what Nesil tried, the man saw it coming.

Now, on the other hand...

He made his decision. If he ever hoped to take Brach by surprise, it had to be now, while he seemed unconscious.

There was no time to rest. No time to plan.

Atop the man's shoulder, Nesil twisted, grabbed the man's head, and used all his strength to drive a knee into his nose.

Brach turned his face at the last moment, but Nesil felt something smash—perhaps, the man's jaw. The contact was solid, using the combined strength of his leg and both arms—but to Nesil's horror, the man merely yelled.

"You little shit!"

Brach didn't fall. Or let go.

"Stay still, before I—"

Using his leg like a ram, Nesil kneed the man's face again and again.

He was sure something fractured beneath the impact—causing the man to bellow and roar—but before his fourth strike, Brach caught hold of an ankle. And before Nesil could switch knees, the man had his legs locked between massive arms.

"You're gonna pay for that!"

Nesil would've hammered the base of Brach's skull, but by this point, he'd been pulled too far forward. So, instead, he used the back of his elbow. The impact shot a tingle up his arm, but he ignored the pain, striking as hard as he could, as many times as he could.

He might as well have been striking a brick wall.

And he wondered: if illusions could create pain, perhaps there were ways to dull pain as well? Surely, no ordinary man was as stoic as this brute.

All of Nesil's exertions drove Brach into a frenzy. And, the next moment, Nesil was sent flying through the air.

He slammed against a wall, and everything flashed white.

"Now stop moving before I *make* you stop!"

Before Nesil knew it, he was on the ground—head throbbing with each heartbeat.

But he moved anyway, scrambling across the cobbles. No matter what happened, staying in one place wasn't an option. He'd make the man grope if he wanted to find him.

There was nothing Nesil could do, however, to hide the sound of his movements. Yielding a trail for Brach to follow.

"Get back here!"

His voice was close, and Nesil, on all fours, kicked his leg backward and upward like a horse.

He hit only air. A second kick, however, seemed to strike a hand.

Scrambling further, he kicked a third time—only to be grabbed and hauled backward.

Flipping onto his back, he slammed his other foot into the man's grip, aiming to break fingers.

Brach's other hand groped for Nesil's free foot and missed.

"Stop moving!"

Nesil was suddenly upside-down, dangling by an ankle.

The man searched for the other foot as Nesil flailed, doing everything he could to avoid those fingers.

"Put me down!" he yelled.

With his abdominal muscles, he twisted upward to free his captured leg.

And ended up kicking Brach's head instead.

The man let go, and Nesil's shoulders hammered the ground.

He rolled away, even as he landed—moving, this time, behind Brach, going back the way they came.

Somehow, he managed to regain his feet. He was too weak to run, but he achieved some distance.

The man wasted no time to follow. For all of Brach's injuries, his legs were just fine.

Nesil turned at the first intersection as quietly as he could. He searched for something to throw, to create a false trail, but there was nothing on hand. Nor was there time.

He didn't remember this neighborhood, so when he crawled through a window, it was entirely at random.

Perhaps he could hide and let the man run past. But that could be dangerous while he was breathing so hard.

So he crossed the room toward the nearest doorway. It was a tavern of sorts, abandoned for years. There were overturned tables and splintering chairs, making a straight path all but impossible.

Hearing Brach behind him, Nesil threw an empty bottle.

His aim fell short, and it shattered on the floor. The glistening shards crunched underfoot as the man came forward, much closer than expected.

Nesil stumbled for the door behind the bar. Finding it locked, he took the stairs instead.

With the help of his hands, he scrambled to the top—the exertion leaving him sick and lightheaded.

The first door was locked. As was the next.

The dark hallway turned a corner, leading to an open window—revealing a night sky glowing faintly orange.

That didn't seem right. The sun shouldn't rise for several hours.

Until he remembered—the city was on fire.

Nesil shuffled toward it and caught himself on the windowsill. It was only a short jump to the next building's roof.

He should've thought about it first.

Bone-weary, his legs didn't cooperate, and instead of landing on the tiles, they cramped. Then buckled.

Flailing to catch himself, he only skinned his fingers.

He tumbled. Felt momentarily weightless.

Then the ground drove all the air from his lungs.

The sky seemed to fade.

For a while, Nesil could do nothing but lay there, forcing his chest to suck in air.

He couldn't move. He couldn't run. The world was spinning.

But all too soon came the sound of steps.

By then, he'd regained the use of his neck, and he turned, expecting the road to be empty.

But no.

There was a soldier! Visible and armored.

"Help!" he called, but his voice was hoarse.

The man was walking the wrong direction.

It was all Nesil could do to turn onto his side.

"Come back!" he tried to say. "Over here!"

The soldier had almost reached the corner.

Nesil struggled to his knees.

Then watched in horror as—all by itself—the man's dagger slid free from his belt.

"The hell?" the soldier said, stumbling back from his own blade, now floating mid-air.

He threw up his hands, too late to defend himself.

It stabbed through his throat and caught on his spine.

His eyes bulged as his hands grappled at the air, finding the arm behind the thrust. He flailed and harmlessly beat his attacker. Before coughing up blood and slumping to the ground.

Nesil surged to his feet, but his legs were indisposed. He searched for the soldier's companions, but the man was alone.

The dagger rose into the air, dripping blood. It turned a full circle before moving decidedly in Nesil's direction.

No, no, no! Even his lungs refused to cooperate. His throat rasped with convulsive heaves.

Shit! BE QUIET! he yelled in his mind. But as the dagger drew closer, his gasping got louder.

The levitating blade wasn't ten feet away when Nesil remembered to clench his teeth. He renewed his mumbling, and, in that same instant, his breaths were canceled out.

The dagger paused as though in confusion.

It took all Nesil's strength to slowly crawl away—murmuring through his teeth, all the while.

The blade lurched forward, and there were scuffling sounds as Brach's boots searched the ground.

By then, Nesil had reached the side of the road. His coordination and strength were slow in coming, but they were returning nonetheless.

The dagger clattered to the ground.

The man had gotten smarter and no longer wanted to advertise his position. His shuffling became frantic as he ran in wide circles, hoping to stumble across Nesil's location.

At one point, he must've only missed by a few inches. But there wasn't a way for Brach to check everywhere. The street was too broad.

"You can't hide!" he threatened. "There's no place to go."

Nesil never stopped moving in case the man circled back. He paid extra attention to where he set his hands and knees, knowing a single loose stone or scrape of dirt could mean death.

But, slowly—gradually—he regained his feet, slipped into an alley, and left the road entirely.

"If you come out now, I'll go easy on you… You honestly can't believe the aeisr won't find you! She'll know exactly where you are. And, trust me, she can be one hell of a bitch!"

Nesil didn't disagree. He already dreaded Sefina's return.

For the moment, however, Nesil was free. Even if that moment wasn't bound to last.

He continued to push through the narrow side street—too scared to move quickly or risk any noise. For two entire blocks, he kept his cool.

Then, unable to stand it any longer, he broke into a run.

Chapter 23
SYMPHONY OF RUIN

Nesil couldn't go for help—not while invisible.

If he returned to the villa, it would likely be empty. And if he followed the survivors, they'd be too overanxious to believe it was him.

He could only imagine how the servants might respond, hearing his voice from thin air. They'd be wary of a trap and ignore any deception so clearly tied to the aeisr. Even if he tried written notes.

There was no doubt Sefina would be watching the survivors. That was her plan—to use the invisible flames to break his people. If he went to them for help, he'd only get caught.

So where did that leave him?

Should he flee to the abandoned districts and find a safe place to hide? A secluded corner, removed from the fire, where he could rest and recover his strength? While this didn't come close to a solution, he desperately needed a chance to pull himself together.

His muscles were bruised and sluggish, not only from his fight with Brach but from prolonged deprivation of oxygen. It hurt to move. It hurt to breathe... His thoughts were unresponsive, and he was becoming increasingly convinced every choice he made was wrong. No matter how much he learned, the aeisr seemed five steps ahead and determined to make his every move work against him.

After all his mistakes, was it worth the effort to keep going, only to make more? His grandfather was dead! Burned alive because Nesil had the arrogance to challenge a spectral goddess.

If he only had the chance to sleep, then maybe...maybe, he'd find the clarity to salvage what he could. Maybe he'd gain the sense—and the courage—to give up.

But Nesil didn't have time to sleep. Because, amid the chaos, he knew this opportunity would never come again.

The aeisr was distracted.

For the next hour—possibly, several—she'd be so caught up with the fire she wouldn't give a damn about what he was doing. As far as she was concerned, he was still held captive and not worth her attention.

While there was always the possibility Brach would find her and tell her of his escape, Nesil thought this unlikely. It went further than shame for the large man to confess his inability to overpower such a small boy. Brach would be terrified—aware of how his mistress responded to failure—and he'd first try to solve the problem himself.

This meant Nesil had some time. Time to try one last thing.

With eyes half closed and a pounding headache, he forced himself to move. Each step was a struggle to keep balance, but he slowly made his way to Silverwater Castle.

Unlike before, he didn't rely on the assistance of a brass pole or wooden stick. He was too afraid of anything Brach might see.

Instead, he was forced to rely on his memory—pinpointing holes or other obstacles. Having made the trip recently, this should've been easy.

But a blanket of clouds—or was that smoke?—blotted out the moon.

With the orange glow of the fires at his back, the way ahead was shrouded by night. His sense of distance became erratic, as if walking through an entirely different land.

What was more, as he made his way down the first few blocks, the darkness itself was moving. Evershifting.

At first, he ignored this, thinking it was in his head. He was seeing things. His lack of sleep was making him dizzy and preventing the shadows from keeping still.

But that wasn't it at all.

The shadows began to spread, keeping just enough distance for him not to see clearly. But he soon recognized them for what they were.

The mindless wanderers. The lesser aeisr.

Somehow, though he was invisible and couldn't see himself, they were drawn to his presence.

Maids in woolen dresses, shopkeepers, a few children. Though none of them stared at him directly, they seemed to know he was there. They'd collectively stop when he stopped and move when he moved.

They circled in the dark as though seduced by curiosity.

Like moths to an open flame.

Nesil tripped a few times, bruising his shins. But compared to the pain he already felt, a few scrapes—and a few wraiths—were hardly enough to discourage him now.

Nothing could prevent him from reaching the castle and the room where Ashaira held her eternal vigil. Though he didn't understand the statue's purpose, he had no doubt she was important. The fact the aeisr hadn't appeared until the statue arrived was enough to ensure a direct correlation.

Possibly, a dependency. One he could exploit.

Though he wasn't sure what would happen, he was determined not to rest until the goddess was destroyed.

The idea, of course, was far from new. Since the siege began, every effort had been made to pulverize the stone. They'd smashed it with sledgehammers and hacked away floorboards.

But, still, she stood—an illusory effigy, floating midair—that none of their tools could harm or touch.

They hadn't stopped there. They attacked her with wind. With energy. With fire.

They even tried attacking with illusion.

Nesil wasn't the first to have that idea. There were illusions everywhere—fake objects that could be picked up with your hands. It wasn't long before someone threw a fake rock at the statue, hoping it'd cause damage.

It didn't.

Sometimes, the high aeisr was there and would cause the rocks to disappear. But even when she was elsewhere, illusory projectiles simply bounced off.

People laid down boards, crossing the hole to walk up to the betrayer. Then, with all their strength, they'd bludgeon the goddess, thinking their hands would prevent their fake instruments from deflecting or changing course.

The results were more promising. The rocks would stop for a second, making momentary contact. Ultimately, they'd pass through their hands and drop to the floor. This was tried repeatedly, but each collision was still too brief and insignificant to have lasting results.

To have any hope at all, they needed to exert a continuous force against the statue. But they lacked access to anything, real or illusory, capable of doing so.

Until now.

It was Nesil's experience, drowning in the fountain of blood, that gave him the idea. It was in the way his fake lips repelled the muck to counteract the illusion already in place.

There was something profoundly different about having an illusion anchored to his body. Whatever Sefina had done, she'd made it a part of him. Not just his lips but an illusory invisibility that pervaded his entire person.

If he threw *himself* at the statue, one of two things would happen.

The illusion making him invisible would either stop in place and be forcibly removed from his body. Or it'd remain attached and go through Ashaira.

He sincerely hoped for the latter. And he convinced himself it'd work, since he was physical and she was not.

It was this determination that pushed him forward. To fight the urge to collapse or momentarily close his eyes.

He crossed the market and passed over the bridge. He crossed the castle gardens while ignoring the accumulating crowd around him. His only concern was to reach the treasury—and something was bound to happen.

And something did—just not what he expected.

As though an invisible barrier shielded the door, the crowd of aeisr stopped in their tracks and refused to go further.

They all still faced his direction—dozens upon dozens of them—but they didn't try to stop him. They simply stood there as though forming a wall of human bodies.

It was so dark, he found it hard to make out their faces. But he could feel them staring with unblinking eyes.

Undeterred, Nesil pushed his way through. He half-expected, at any moment, for them to turn on him. They'd suddenly become feral and attack all at once, doing everything in their power to wear him down.

But, instead, they watched. Breathing raggedly but, otherwise, not making noise.

They closed in behind him, not giving him space, until he finally reached the door.

Oddly, he felt something like an actual barrier—an outward pressure making it difficult to enter. As though the aeisr had anticipated his arrival.

Nesil shook his head, trying to convince himself there was nothing to be afraid of.

Except, when he finally pushed through the door, his fears were confirmed. The illusion was dispelled, and he could see himself again.

Once again, the aeisr was prepared. Even with the town in disarray, she hadn't left herself unguarded. She'd arranged contingencies to prevent any and all illusions from entering the chamber.

Even the false floor was no longer there, allowing him to see the gaping hole beneath the statue.

The Goddess of Ordination stood frozen as though trapped by a wind. As always, she was a mere fragment of her body—her shoulders and a single arm, encircled by the hair from her implacable head.

Condemned to stand sentinel over this hellish place.

Smiling as though mocking him.

In desperation, Nesil clenched his teeth together, hoping his mask would still work.

"Come on...!" he hissed.

But he heard himself clearly.

He slumped to the ground. "Damn it all."

So that was it.

He'd come all this way, pushing himself to the brink of exhaustion, and it amounted to nothing.

He shouldn't have been surprised. Even if he'd only just learned her weakness, the aeisr had known for years. She wasn't so stupid to leave herself vulnerable or provide her sworn enemy with the only weapon that might bring her down.

Out of sheer determination—or rather, stubbornness—Nesil forced himself up to one knee.

In front of him, two large planks spanned the gaping hole. They'd been nailed in place long ago during the attempted attacks on the statue.

It wasn't until the illusions were stripped away, however, that Nesil realized the boards had remained here all this time.

He didn't think they were a trick, but, all the same, he crawled toward them on hands and knees. Making sure the ground supported his weight.

The planks, too, were sturdy and allowed him to cross.

So long as he focused on the wood and not the twenty-foot drop, it was easy to prevent his head from swooning. He only needed to grasp the edges and keep his mass centered.

The only tricky part was near the middle, where the wood flexed beneath his weight. It wasn't only because the planks were old. He suspected exposure to the abyssal rain, which tended to corrupt anything, given enough time.

At the worst point, the bridge sagged several inches, and it took all his determination not to scramble backward.

But what more did he have to lose?

If he was going to die anyway, he wanted the courage to at least stare this demon in the face. Even if she was, in the end, just a statue.

He let go with his hands and climbed to his feet.

Nesil tried not to think of the aeisr showing up. Of the statue gaining movement. Or a strong gale rushing forth, like his first time here.

At full height, the betrayer was still taller than Nesil. Her stone face was tilted downward as though sneering right at him.

Had she always been that way? He couldn't remember.

Nesil touched the stone. He cupped her face in his palm, the cool texture so smooth, it might've been flesh.

Pushing harder, however, caused his hand to go through.

He tried a few things—slowly, to not disrupt his balance—but nothing made a difference. He even used his lips, on the off-chance a figment of his mask remained.

But nothing worked. He hadn't thought it would. The goddess stood there, taunting his failure—one more to the list, three years long.

He retreated from the planks onto solid floorboards. If he couldn't destroy it, what else was there to do?

He'd gained nothing by coming here.

Only knowledge of a room that stripped away illusion.

Was there a way he could use that?

He briefly entertained the idea of going after Brach. The man, after all, wasn't invulnerable like the aeisr. If he lured Brach here and made him visible again...

Nesil laughed at himself before dismissing the notion as wishful thinking. Not only was it doubtful he'd find the man—he felt certain it was a fight he couldn't win.

Having lost his invisibility, he'd be at a complete disadvantage. Brach would sneak up behind him before Nesil got the chance to return to the castle.

Still... Without a better plan, he entertained the idea. There was still a remote chance he could out-think Brach. It was more possible, at least, than controlling the fire. More possible than bringing his grandfather back to life.

But Nesil did nothing.

Too much of a coward to face that monster again.

Instead, he left the room and pushed his way back through the crowd of aeisr. Then, traversing the dark castle corridors, he found the private garden he'd been desperately avoiding.

Long misshapen brambles grew along the stone path. Even in the dark, beneath the sky of twisting smoke, it wasn't difficult to find the faint black smear—where the servants had unsuccessfully washed away his mother's blood. Her body wasn't here, of course, returned to the villa for a proper burial.

Nesil did his best not to look, having come to this place for a completely different reason. Dropping to hands and knees, he searched the withered flowers between the cracks in the stonework.

Sefina's body should be here. Overlooked. Cast aside.

He didn't think the aeisr had lied about that.

If he could just find the body—her *real* body—and carry it to the treasury, she'd be visible again. Incontestable proof their new princess was an impostor.

Nesil searched faster, scrambling over stone.

Perhaps, he couldn't take the aeisr's life or the life of her accomplice.

But he could take her crown. Her fame. Her adoration.

The idea seemed petty—a mere thorn in her side—but Nesil needed to do something. He hated feeling powerless. He couldn't sit back while others suffered for his mistakes.

Nesil was still searching when he heard the creak of an iron gate.

Looking up, he wasn't met with the meandering aeisr but was surprised to find a group of soldiers instead.

"Prince Nesil?" asked the man who seemed in charge, appearing in his mid-twenties. "Is it you?"

Nesil rose to his feet, wondering how to explain what he'd been doing. Or why he was here. Never mind that these men shouldn't be here, either.

"It's really me," he said, extending an arm in greeting.

They shook hands, physically confirming each was real.

"My lord!" exclaimed the man, suddenly worried. "You shouldn't be here! We'll take you somewhere safe! Follow me!" He signaled a few men to form a guard beside the prince.

But Nesil raised a hand to stop them.

"Your name, soldier."

He didn't seem to hear, looking back the way they came as though worried something had followed them here.

"Your name!" repeated Nesil.

The man's eyes snapped back as though the last thing he'd expected was orders from a teenager.

"Hawkern," he said, in sudden consternation. "Of house Melbadon." He signaled to the others behind the gate, making sure they held their current position.

"What are you doing here, Hawkern? Is something after you? Who is your commanding officer?"

"We..." the soldier paused, seeming at a loss. Ordinarily, these questions would be the other way around, with the older man asking why Nesil was alone.

But now that he was king, protocol had changed.

The man swallowed, looking nervous.

And Nesil guessed why.

There was only one reason to come this way: to procure weapons from the locked-up armory. And if the men needed those, they must be running away.

Abandoning their duty to take their chances outside the city.

"We had no choice, your majesty," Hawkern explained. "Our commanding officer... Gerieth. He... He's dead... We thought it was the fire. In some places, the flames have gone invisible. Without warning, people beat at their clothes...howling in agony! It's so horrible! I've never—"

"Skip to the end, Hawkern."

"We were escaping the flames," he continued. "Except... Just recently, when another man died—"

Nesil knew better than to trust a deserter, but he guessed where this was going. "There were slash marks on his body."

Hawkern blinked in surprise. "Well... Yes."

To Nesil, it made sense. Where else would Brach be if not out here? He'd want to avoid the more populated areas, so he wouldn't risk confronting the aeisr. Afraid of explaining his recent failures.

He'd be searching for Nesil and killing every man who might come to his rescue.

"I'll explain later. Right now, you need to do something for me. I'm taking command of this unit, understand?"

The soldier clearly didn't like this idea.

"You'll have to trust me," said Nesil, removing the signet ring from his hand.

The man squeezed it with his fingers, getting a feel of its shape and inscriptions. The royal family sigil would be easy to recognize and confirm that Nesil wasn't an impostor.

Hawkern nodded, satisfied, and handed back the ring.

"How many men do we have?" asked Nesil.

"Nine, at last count. Four back at the entrance, those three at the gate, Sergeant Sevi, and myself."

Nesil bit his lip, fearing their number was too high.

Earlier, Brach could pick them off one by one. In the castle, however, where their position was more defensible, he'd think twice before making his next move.

"If I might make a suggestion," said Hawkern. "If we retreat to the armory, nine men would be sufficient to—"

"No," said Nesil, making his decision. "...But we can make it look like we're headed to the armory... We need to split up."

"Sir?" The man was in obvious disagreement.

"You and two others are to come with me. No more, got that? Meanwhile, your sergeant will return to your men with orders to secure the armory and await our arrival."

Nesil turned and spoke to Sergeant Sevi directly. "You'll need to make clear—loudly—that you've found me. But that I've gone into hiding. I'm laying low until I'm confident you've secured the area."

Sevi nodded.

Hawkern narrowed his eyes. "You expect us to defend you with only three men?"

"That's an order, captain. I don't want a large group, or the trap won't work."

Only then did the man nod.

"And one more thing," said Nesil, with rising confidence. "Before we head up, we need to find something first."

A short while later, he was back in the treasury.

"Bloody hell..." said the man who'd been carrying the corpse. It was only from respect he didn't drop her on the spot.

"I'll take her from here," said Nesil with forced stoicism.

He didn't explain why she wasn't in her wedding dress. The real Sefina, after all, had never known about the party and wore a simple, blue frock he'd seen on several occasions.

As he lifted her broken body, he supported her head as though she were asleep.

Here was reality, with an imploded skull and a face he barely recognized. Meeting her cold, dead stare, he wiped tears from his eyes, not caring about the blood he smeared on his face.

"Be ready," he said, retreating deeper into the room. "This man's a monster. It'll take all of you to bring him down."

Hawkern nodded.

At first, he'd been hesitant, but his attitude changed upon seeing Sefina's body. It was proof of Nesil's claim—that the invisible assassin would be stripped of his advantage.

Except...that didn't happen.

When the door burst open a short while later, no one was there.

Hawkern was dead before Nesil could do anything. His sword clattered to the floor as he clutched the line that split his throat.

"Get back!" shouted a soldier, raising a hand toward Nesil.

Dual knives flew through the air, suspended over nothing, slicing with deadly precision.

The two soldiers circled, aiming their strikes between the dancing blades but hitting only air.

Nesil laid down Sefina's body and used his sight of the men to track Brach's location. Backing away, his heel found the edge of the wooden planks. They wobbled and flexed but remained strong.

A soldier landed a cut. His sword stopped midair at roughly neck height.

Brach let out a roar, and Nesil's heart lurched with hope.

Until the sword was wrenched from fingers, gave a sudden turn, and was shoved through its owner's face.

"I told you not to run!" the man bellowed. "I WARNED YOU!"

Nesil stumbled backward, doing his best to keep balance.

One soldier was left, but the dancing blades came after Nesil instead.

He turned—his vision going black as he passed through the goddess—but he was still too slow!

He tried to leap but lost his footing.

Something latched onto his ankle, and his chin slammed hard into the board.

Its length wobbled, driving splinters through his throat as he was dragged in reverse.

A blinding pain cut through his back, low between the ribs.

The stab of a knife, hotter than the sun.

"NO!!" yelled the final soldier.

Nesil didn't see the tackle but felt Brach topple forward over his head.

The plank snapped.

As they fell, Nesil turned his head upward.

The goddess shivered.

The world became a swash of color, lightwaves, and explosions.

Part 4
THE
FAR SIDE
OF
DREAMING

Who will glue her together?
This Princess of Ash
With mismatched pieces
Long scattered on the winds?

Her smile has begun to wilt—
The lost cadence who she was
Before her limbs grew thin as paper;
Her swollen heart burst into flame.

She's forgotten how to breathe,
Yet still, it is asked of her
To uphold the weight of mankind.
Does no one fear her breaking?
                    -Confessions of Irisea
                    (year unknown)

Chapter 24
BRIDGES IN THE SKY

Kaycia awoke to the sound of weeping.

The night was still dark, and the carriage swam in shadows.

She tossed in bed, tightening her heavy quilt around her body, as she gazed down at the mattress laid out for Chesandril.

The young girl, however, was fast asleep.

In the dark, Kaycia barely made out the rise and fall of her chest—slow and steady, and not at all congruous with the mournful sobbing that'd broken through her dreams.

Curious, she turned over to gaze at the ceiling.

Then she heard it again—the shuddering intake of breath, followed by a faint, pitiful whine.

"Elle?" she whispered in sudden alarm.

When she turned to her sister beside her on the bed, the girl's back was turned, hiding her face.

Kaycia didn't know what to do.

It broke her heart not knowing what Elyriel was going through. The confused girl wouldn't even know why she felt sad. Which made the pain worse, as no words could help her through it.

She stretched out a hand, about to place it on her back—when Elyriel moved and rolled toward her.

In a voice barely above a whisper came the words, *You did this.*

She shrieked.

"What?" asked Chesandril, coming awake behind her. "I'll get the light!"

Kaycia could only lay there, unmoving, as the girl coaxed the lantern's wick to life.

As the orange glow fell across her sister's face, Elyriel flinched away with her eyes clenched shut.

"What happened?" asked Chesandril.

Kaycia, however, was unable to make sense of it.

As her sister raised her hands to fend off the light, it became apparent her face was completely dry. There was no trace of tears—wet or otherwise—on her cheeks or pillow. Rather, Elyriel was her usual self, growling with irritation at being woken in the night.

"Is something wrong?" asked Chesandril, resting a hand on her shoulder.

"I..." Kaycia shut her mouth, not knowing what to say. "It was nothing," she said at last. "I must've been dreaming."

She spoke without confidence, feeling certain it wasn't a dream at all. She'd heard a voice—a wail that'd sounded like her sister—but she was reluctant to say this out loud.

"I'm sorry," she said. "You can go back to sleep."

Chesandril didn't look convinced, but she was too tired to argue. She set the light down without lowering the flame.

Kaycia closed her eyes, but sleep didn't come.

Even if the words had only been a dream, her sister's suffering was *not* imaginary. Nor was the guilt in Kaycia's heart.

Those feelings didn't leave when the sun came up. They stayed with her as she ate breakfast and crossed the camp for one last briefing.

It was only then, as she forced herself to focus on what the council had to say, that her doubts evaporated, if only for a time. She couldn't afford to miss a single detail as she was walked through ancient maps and told where to go.

Afterward, however, when she was taken back through the cave in Elyriel's body and she was on her own once again, her misgivings returned.

It was difficult to feel excited about exploring Ahman when she could only do so at her sister's expense.

Was this the only way to help Elyriel? Perhaps, with the right doctor, there might be ways to minimize the threat of her transcendency. With the proper facilities and care, they might convince the judges that Elyriel was harmless.

Of course, no one would be willing to pay for such treatments—not without a return on their investment. And with this thought, Kaycia came back full circle to what she was doing—using Elyriel as a tool to prove the girl's worth.

Ideally, such a thing shouldn't have been necessary. Kaycia shouldn't have to put her sister's life at risk when her only true goal was to save it. But here she was, sending Elyriel into a place beyond the reach of outside help. One wrong move, and it'd all be over. If Elyriel were to become lost or trapped, it was possible Kaycia would never see her again.

"I won't let that happen," she said out loud. "Your life is more important than this entire investigation. At the first sign of trouble—if Ahman rears its ugly head—I'm getting you out, you hear?"

Her words disappeared into the darkness of the tunnel without so much as an echo.

"It's just you and me now. Like old times. We'll take care of each other, won't we?"

This, unfortunately, didn't help her feel less alone. As she groped through the dark, she found it difficult to replicate the enthusiasm from her first time here. Somehow, the darkness had become more tangible. More...oppressive.

Her anxiety drove her to keep talking. "I suppose I should tell you what we're doing since you weren't at the meeting. Really, it was Soril's idea—that we first locate Ashaira's prison. You remember her, don't you? The goddess you, yourself, called the betrayer?

"Maybe you were right. I guess we'll see. The abyssal current might've been her fault—and led to the gods' downfall. Perhaps, you'll get to rub it in my face—you'd like that, wouldn't you?"

From the darkness, Kaycia thought she heard a response carried on the wind.

Fa—ult...

Your...fault...

It was so faint, she might've imagined it. In fact, she was sure she imagined it—as proof her mind was still unhinged. After this, however, she lost her nerve to speak. Instead, she focused on where she was going.

She was determined, this time, to identify the precise moment when the cave ceased to be a cave and was replaced by the alley beneath an open sky. However, even when she was waiting for it, the moment passed her by.

All at once, she was in Ahman, staring up at the dim sky as though it'd been there all along. Looking back the way she came, the alley was too dark. There was no cave mouth or opening where the ceiling had ended. Only impenetrable shadows.

She was tempted to walk back, to investigate further, but she'd been warned against such distractions. According to Soril and his council, she needed to avoid the urge to look into every mystery that crossed her path. The way they put it, there'd be phenomena she'd never understand, even if she spent years in careful study.

For that reason, she'd been given a list of priorities—of the questions that mattered most and were most likely to yield helpful discoveries. Finding Ashaira's prison was near the top of that list—just below making sure she didn't get lost.

Keeping track of the exit, however, proved difficult once she realized the old maps were wrong.

Leaving the alley, she emerged onto an enormous patio—so distinct, she knew exactly where she was. She recognized the area because of the rising stone steps, crested with a dried-up, old fountain. At the center were three naked stone women holding up cast iron pots, from which water had once flowed in abundance.

Multiple thin, stone arches crisscrossed overhead—their light brown stone stretching forty feet into the sky—even taller than the three-story buildings surrounding them. A few had collapsed, raining destruction upon the tiled walkways and porticoes. The remaining arches bore hairline fractures and were draped with so many vines, they seemed more like billowing, verdant sails.

This was Hin Gelnida—the patios of creation—built to welcome any pilgrim fortunate enough to gain admittance to the holy city.

But, instead of dividing into four major streets, as Kaycia had been told, the plaza forked into seven. And, more disturbing than that was the largest stone building overshadowing the fountain. There was no doubt in her mind it was Jaesha's library, famous for its multi-tiered balconies, and yet... The maps placed that library in an entirely different district, on the opposite side of town.

At the outset, this might not have been so bad. Though Kaycia didn't relish the idea of shifting geographies, it was a concept with which she was, at least, familiar. The streets were fairly straight, and, with Elyriel's eyes, she had a clear view of much of the city. She only needed to rearrange what she remembered and form a new map in her mind.

Except, after the first few hours, this, too, proved impractical.

Just as she started to feel comfortable with her bearings, she circled back to the fountain and discovered there were only six intersecting roads—not seven.

The place didn't just change, it managed to do so while her eyes were wide open— the acute, discerning eyes of an ascendant.

"You'll have to make for higher ground," said Soril when she returned to her body and consulted the council. "Find a tower or something large so the Navaran doesn't see you."

"I already did that," she said with a groan.

This earned a few looks of disapproval, which she ignored.

"...And?" he asked.

"If I may?" She made a gesture toward the maps on the table.

With their permission, she took a clean sheet of vellum and laid it on top of a city map. The thin material was semi-transparent by nature, allowing a partial view of the map underneath.

She then began to trace parts of the city, using a thin stylus to keep her lines precise and even. From time to time, however, she had to shift the paper elsewhere to trace the areas that deviated from their proper locations.

As the council members watched, their faces became worried.

"What's wrong?" asked Soril when Kaycia hesitated.

She moved the paper around, seeing it from different angles. At last, however, she could only say, "These neighborhoods here... They're backward."

"What?"

Kaycia searched the room, on the off-chance there might be a mirror nearby. There wasn't one, of course, but that didn't stop her from another idea.

She blew carefully on the ink—making sure it was dry—before she flipped the vellum over to draw on the opposite side. Like this, it was still possible to see the lines from before, but she could add the missing areas, reversed as she'd seen them.

Minutes passed as she reproduced the city from memory. But by the time she was finished, she was more discouraged than ever.

Not only was she aware the map would keep changing, she'd failed to identify a sensible pattern. That, after all, had been the point of all this, but, instead, it'd only given her a headache.

Soril breathed the words, "Like a hall of mirrors..."

Kaycia creased her brow, and the man continued.

"They have a way of messing with your mind. Just when you think you've got the maze figured out, you find yourself turned around and walking in circles."

Kaycia tried her best to envision reflections upon reflections all around her. She knew what it was like to be lost, but it was more difficult to imagine her own eyes responsible for leading her astray.

"This part's wrong," said Soril, pointing down at her map. "You've drawn the Palace of Shaelis here... And once again over here."

"I did?" she asked, lowering her face to the paper.

She closed her eyes and consulted her memories. The most likely explanation was that the building had moved between the first time she'd seen it and the second.

Unfortunately, however, that hadn't been the case.

"No," she said. "I saw them both at the same time. And it wasn't some trick of the light. Both were real."

"You're sure?" he asked gravely.

She nodded with confidence. "They weren't even identical."

With the stylus, she added new marks to the maps. "On this one, these towers were collapsed—here, here, and...here. But on the other palace, only the north one was broken. Even the moss and ivy didn't grow on the same walls."

Neranda raised a skeptical brow. "You're remembering it wrong."

Kaycia shrugged in resignation. "I'm just showing what I saw. It might be similar to a hall of mirrors, but it wasn't a reflection."

"Not in the literal sense, no," said Soril. "But, even in the absence of mirrors, that doesn't mean the tangled streets aren't a sort of maze."

"To throw me off path? You're worried I'll get lost?"

"You might not have a choice," he said with a sigh. "Just think... If you saw more than one palace, it suggests there might be more of everything. More than one prison. More than one exit."

Her heart skipped a beat. "But wouldn't that...be a good thing? More exits make it easier to leave, should anything go wrong."

Soril shook his head. "Only if all the exits lead to the same place..."

Over the next several hours, after Kaycia reconnected with her sister, she began to notice certain things she hadn't before.

Sometimes, after heading down a street, certain qualities of the city would transform. The sky would grow dim at an alarming rate as the sun descended, of all directions, toward the south.

It wasn't just the light. The weeds and vines became more withered. The cracks in the stone multiplied. As did the shadows.

Sometimes, turning around helped. After returning the way she came, the sun would ascend to its rightful place in the sky.

But not always.

Sometimes, the path grew even darker, and she'd have to find another way. At first, this worried her, as it took her down streets she wouldn't have chosen otherwise. It took her to districts she hadn't intended to go.

But, as long as she was looking for it, she could always stay in the light. And, as far as she was concerned, this was her only reassurance she wasn't truly lost.

These extended detours—in addition to moving cautiously so the Navaran wouldn't see her—likely kept her from finding the prison the first day.

Or the second.

The hours stretched into a blur as she wandered street after street—several more than once. Her only interruptions were her short breaks to feed and care for her body back in Soril's camp.

It wasn't long before she grew frustrated and suspected she was going about it all wrong. The prison should've been easy to find. And, maybe, it couldn't be found in this version of the city.

Perhaps it was time she searched the darker streets.

On the third day, however, she stumbled across it quite by accident.

By then, she felt more anger than relief. After searching for so long, she'd thought there'd be a good reason. She'd begun to think it was a matter of solving the puzzle, and it'd all make sense.

Instead, the solution appeared entirely at random. She'd only found the place out of sheer stubbornness, and her careful calculations had been wasted effort.

The enormous edifice had been built into the side of a cliff, using natural rock to fortify its thick, massive walls. As a result, it looked more like a tomb. And it hid in the shadows despite the sun's position directly overhead.

The interior was surprisingly bright. Skylights had been cut into the cliff face she hadn't noticed from outside. Shafts of golden light descended from fifty feet overhead, glittering with motes that drifted and spun.

Within moments, her irritation melted away, replaced with wonder and intense curiosity.

At the far end of the antechamber, a massive set of steel doors barred the entrance to the living chambers where Ashaira had been contained.

Everything was covered in a thick layer of dust, undisturbed for centuries.

Kaycia found this odd, as she'd felt certain the Navaran would've come here. She'd been prepared to turn around, as she'd been ordered to do, and avoid the possibility of crossing his path.

But, for whatever reason, the man had no interest in this place. Or, up to this point, he'd been unable to find it. Or, he *had* come, but he'd covered his tracks by creating a new, fresh layer of dust.

She felt she was worrying too much. The only thing she knew was that if he came by later, he'd know *she* had been here.

...Unless she provided the dust with the conviction to hide her tracks.

As though to guard the steel doors, there was a large wooden desk, and upon that desk, there were papers left behind after all these years. These, too, were caked with dust.

To her astonishment, however, as she took one by the corner and shook it clean, she found it was still readable. That didn't seem possible after so much time. She could only imagine it had something to do with the materials the gods used—an archival paper resistant to yellowing.

She gave a sudden sneeze—before looking around warily as the noise echoed loudly through the chamber.

Setting the paper down, she leaned forward to examine the precise, archaic script. The letters didn't match their modern forms, but luckily, she'd had experience deciphering texts from this era.

The first page appeared to be a rotating schedule, listing the times and names of those assigned to clean the cell and surrounding premises. A second document was a request for fresh linens to be brought in.

It took a while before Kaycia found anything of interest, and even then, she wasn't sure what to make of it.

> *I regret to inform you nothing has changed. From the moment our prisoner arrived, she has not eaten. Your suggestion to bring in her personal chef has failed to make a difference. The prisoner was grateful for the familiar company but wasn't moved by the best selection from our local gardens and bakeries. She touches none of it and only takes half a glass of water at breakfast, at midday, and before retiring to bed.*
>
> *Some have suggested she might be fearful of poison, but the introduction of food tasters has prompted no improvement. We've questioned her directly, but she merely shakes her head. The prisoner acknowledges our presence and thanks us for our efforts. Indeed, she's gone so far as pronouncing her blessing upon us. But, of food, she has no interest at all.*

As Kaycia looked the paper over, she found nothing to suggest a date or how much time might've passed since Ashaira's arrival. It could've been days. Weeks... Considering she was a goddess, it could've been years.

Judging by the writer's level of concern, however, it was doubtful to have been that long.

When Kaycia found nothing else useful atop the desk, she turned her attention to the drawers. At first, they refused to open, with the wood stuck firmly in place. With Elyriel's strength, she could've forced it out, but she didn't want to risk unnecessary damage. Instead, she found a flat piece of metal—a straight edge, perhaps, to aid in drafting—to pry the drawers open.

The first contained nothing more than a few ink pots, their insides stained with a fine, black powder. The following drawer had more papers stacked within, without discernible organization.

> *You must ask her again. We're nearing the limits of the council's patience and understanding. Though they're currently willing to exonerate her from this mess, the lady's silence is working against her. If she is truly innocent, then she MUST come forward and aid our investigation.*
>
> *We don't expect her to know everything—only that she tell us what she can. When did she first notice anything odd in her conservatory? Could she tell us what was there the last time she entered?*
>
> *If the lady truly knows nothing of Aviathas' whereabouts, then she MUST come forward and provide access to her property. It is not too late to claim she'd been used—that she was compelled, against her will, to do Avi-*

athas' bidding. Otherwise, her inaction will be seen as a deliberate attempt to keep us out of the chamber. She will be branded a traitor, in league with Aviathas, and convicted of harboring a known fugitive and felon.

Kaycia looked up from the paper in disbelief.

Aviathas?

The God of Innovation had been confirmed dead—for *hundreds of years*—prior to Ashaira's incarceration. His was one of the last names Kaycia expected to find, and she had to read the note again to ensure she wasn't mistaken.

Were the recorded histories wrong? Was it possible, perhaps, Aviathas' death had been faked? That he'd lived on, and the gods themselves had been none the wiser?

Or...was this suggestive of more formidable powers at work? Of forces capable of bringing back the dead?

Kaycia had the urge to get back and tell Soril what she'd found. He'd likely know more and would, at least, provide a more sensible hypothesis.

But before she could leave, she returned her attention to the drawer. She pulled out the remaining papers and searched for further mentions of Aviathas' name.

There weren't any.

She did, however, find a single handwritten note that offered additional insight into the strange occurrences surrounding Ashaira's conservatory.

> *There's no better answer I can give you. Due to unforeseen complications, our search of our lady's palace has failed to yield results. Until such matters can be resolved, her incarceration must remain indefinite.*
>
> *I understand your frustration, but it cannot compare to what we are dealing with. The conservatory continues to elude us. We know exactly where it is—where it SHOULD be—but the locale remains inaccessible from our world.*
>
> *The double doors to get inside lead only to a brick wall. We immediately, of course, broke down this wall—only to discover it to be none other than the wall OPPOSITE the chamber, some hundred feet distant!*
>
> *Every attempt to enter—through floor or walls—has been met with the same result. A person may enter these holes only to cross, in an instant, the intervening distance to the other side.*
>
> *And yet, despite all this, our Lord Shaelis appears unconcerned. He assures us this phenomenon is NOT the result of Foundation. He remains convinced we WILL get inside—but, for now, we must be patient. When asked, he only stated we're waiting for 'Lothren to make his move.' Do you have any idea what he means?*

The note ended without signature or response.

A shadow crossed overhead—giving Kaycia less than a second to look up and watch a figure disappear from the high window.

She groaned with the realization she'd been spotted. She set the papers down and was about to put everything back the way it was—dust and all—before she realized there was no longer a need.

Instead, she sprinted for the doorway, hoping to catch a glimpse of the departing stranger.

It didn't occur to her this might be a trap. Nor did it bother her that this went directly against her instructions.

All she knew was that the man was getting away—and, to her, this suggested he meant no harm.

As she emerged into the sunlight, she felt certain the rooftops would be empty. In a city this large, with ample places to hide, she hadn't been fast enough.

So when she *did* see something, it left her not only baffled but also in awe.

Without the means to fly or even jump away, the creator had used his natural talents.

Protruding from the cliff face was a thin bridge leading away into the ruins. Suspended fifty feet in the air, it was supported by tall, spindly strands that rose up from the city and buildings it crossed over. Each support was slim, no thicker than Elyriel's wrist, but they held firm and didn't wobble beneath the weight of the structure's occupant.

Kaycia could actually see the bridge growing as new supports stretched into the sky to meet its progress.

From her angle, however, underneath, she couldn't see the man himself.

She was tempted to chase after him if only to satisfy her curiosity. It would've been a simple matter of climbing to the top and using the man's own construct.

This, of course, would've been a mistake. As easily as the creator formed the bridge, he could cause it to disappear. And Kaycia wasn't eager to put herself at the stranger's mercy.

So, instead, she stood there and watched him go. She'd save her questions for a later time.

A s she settled back into her body and made her way to Soril's tent, she decided to keep this encounter to herself. At least until she learned something useful.

It wasn't so much that she was hiding information, she just didn't want the council distracted from the more pertinent conversation.

"I know where to head next," she announced as the ascendants settled into their seats. "But I need you to tell me what you know of Ashaira's palace."

The council members exchanged uneasy glances.

It was Soril, however, who took control of the discussion. "Let's back up a moment... You found the prison?"

Brimming with excitement, she spilled what she'd discovered. She reproduced the documents from memory—if not word for word, at least close enough that none of their meaning was lost.

Upon mention of Aviathas' name, she watched the council's eyes with eager anticipation. Their reactions varied from irritated skepticism to wide-eyed shock. Neranda sputtered from the cup she'd been holding to her lips.

Only Soril held his expression in reserve.

Kaycia went on. "The penmanship was clean and easy to decipher. It spelled Aviathas. Do you know anyone else who might've gone by that name? I mean, there's no question he was dead, right?"

Soril drew a deep breath and said nothing for several moments.

When he finally spoke, he did so slowly. "Even now, it's against custom to be named after the gods. This was even more the case back then. Their names are held sacred and mustn't be used lightly."

She nodded. "I thought you might've heard of an exception."

"I haven't," he said.

"So...what does this mean? His aspect disappeared. His death was a matter of public record! From my studies, it was clear there were witnesses!"

Soril gave a wry smile. "That's not just in your textbooks. I've had access to the original sources, and there's no room for doubt. Aviathas' body was ripped into shreds before the eyes of gods and men. If that wasn't enough, the...finality of his passing was confirmed by Lord Shaelis himself. And the gods don't lie."

Don't they? she wondered, without speaking this aloud. It was difficult to revere the gods as infallible beings when people didn't hesitate to brand Ashaira a traitor. Even the note had named Aviathas a fugitive and felon.

It was a matter, however, she was willing to drop, not wanting Soril to get sidetracked with his inexorable defense of the gods.

Instead, she moved on and shared the third note she'd found—the one concerning the missing conservatory.

As she went through it, however, she wasn't met with the same reactions as before.

"You're not surprised," she observed.

It was Agren who explained. "This part you wouldn't have found in your books. Ashaira's conservatory was where it all started. People aren't just suspicious of her because of her imprisonment. Her palace was at the center of what became of the city."

"What...became of the city?" she echoed.

"The way it disappeared," he said, as though this should've been obvious. "Many people have the impression it happened all at once—the city was there one second, then—poof!—gone. But it wasn't like that. It started at her property and expanded from there."

It was a disturbing thought and difficult to imagine. What would that even look like? It was one thing to picture a door to nowhere and another thing entirely for an open space to be forcibly removed from existence.

From what she'd read in the note, they weren't talking about an empty lot where the palace used to be. Rather, distance and space folded into itself. Whatever existed behind the palace—that'd once been distant—would now appear close.

Already, her head was beginning to hurt.

And she hadn't yet imagined that nonexistent space *growing*.

"There is, however, a silver lining," said Agren. "By occurring gradually, it gave everyone, including the gods, enough warning to escape."

"Now hold on," said Kaycia, trying to keep up. "Even if you didn't outrun the boundary, wouldn't you just be spit out on the opposite side?"

"That's one possibility," conceded Agren with a bitter smile. "But only if you were the only person or object passing through the center at the time. You have to remember, as the horizon grew, there'd be more walls—more obstacles—blocking your path on all sides. As everything converged, you were more likely to be crushed."

Her imagination took a dive into the grisly and horrifying.

"But the gods escaped, you said? That wasn't what killed them?"

"Correct," said Soril. "From that point, however, they found themselves cut off from the source of the problem. You see, whoever did this—be it Ashaira, Aviathas, or anyone else—this was only one part of a larger plan. From what we can determine, the culprit or culprits needed the city to themselves. They did this to prevent outside interference."

"Isn't that a bit...excessive? What were they trying to do?"

Soril shook his head. "At that, we can only guess. It really depends on who was behind this. For all these years, it was easy to point a finger and say Ashaira was to blame, but that explanation has always fallen short. No one could ever say why she did it. Not convincingly, at least. But Aviathas..."

The man took a deep breath, thinking it over. "If he was still alive, as your note suggests... Vengeance sounds reasonable."

Kaycia frowned. "You think he held them responsible? For his death? But I thought it was the abyssal current that..."

She left her thought unfinished. No one knew, after all, where the current had come from. Some people believed it was a force of nature—something that predated even the gods. Those same people claimed the current was there all along but was held at bay by divine protection.

So long as the gods were alive.

This, however, wasn't the only theory. There were whisperings the current was *created* by the gods. That it was designed as a weapon—an instrument of war. And, even if that wasn't its intended purpose, it wouldn't stop the gods from using it as such.

So was that the explanation? That the gods had secretly been at each other's throats? That this was all the product of an internal war? And Aviathas had been at the center of it all?

Kaycia wasn't so sure. It was too far removed from the picture of Taelish divinity—from the sublime beings whom Soril believed in and worshiped. Hadn't the gods been smarter than that?

The alternative, however, seemed worse. If the gods weren't to blame, it meant something else was. It suggested there was something else out there, even *more* powerful than the gods had been. And that thought was much more disturbing than a pantheon of imperfect deities.

"What about what Shaelis said?" she asked, thinking aloud. "Who was this Lothren he mentioned? Have you heard that name before?"

The council was at a loss.

"Was he an ascendant, you think?" asked Agren. "Someone high up, perhaps, who'd been working with Shaelis?"

Soril made a face. "Unlikely. I would've read about him."

"Okay..." breathed Agren. "So not *high* up. Perhaps, he held a more conservative title. A steward, for instance?"

Neranda turned to Kaycia. "Was there nothing else? You looked through all the papers?"

"I went through them. Well, skimmed them—what was in the desk. I could check again if you'd like. There were still more rooms."

"No," said Soril. "I think you're right. It's past time you went searching for Ashaira's palace."

Agren leaned forward. "You think it's accessible?"

"I believe so. Yes. Elyriel has already crossed the threshold—the one preventing access to the city. It seems doubtful a second barrier would be needed. Or even possible."

The younger man nodded thoughtfully.

Soril turned to Kaycia. "You didn't happen across it—the Palace of Ordination—during your search for the prison? Stained glass windows, shaped as diamonds? Peaked rooftops and gleaming, white ramparts?"

"I don't think so," she said, searching her memory. If she'd seen the place, it no longer looked the same. After centuries of disrepair, it was difficult to find anything gleaming or white. "But I remember where it is—where the maps say it's supposed to be."

"Good. Good. In the meantime, I'll make a request for the old census records and see what we dig up on this...Lothren."

He slid a blank parchment across the desk toward her. "Could you write the name down using the exact characters you saw?"

As Kaycia obeyed, Neranda groaned. The woman clearly thought this a waste of time.

And maybe it was. If this 'Lothren' hadn't held an important position or been registered as an ascendant, his involvement might've been entirely incidental.

Kaycia shrugged. "He seemed important to Shaelis," she said as though to answer Neranda's unspoken question.

Soril looked up from the name she'd written. When his eyes locked with hers, there was a surprising weight behind them.

"Do you have nothing else to report?"

Only then did she remember their talk from before, asking for signs of the child goddess. He wasn't asking for anything specific, as this wasn't the time nor place to continue that conversation.

"Ah... No... Not that I could tell."

To her surprise, she found her feelings were mixed. It should've delighted her to report her suspicions were right. That the legend of Irisea was nothing more than a story.

Kaycia had walked the streets of Ahman, and she'd chanced across...nothing. No smoke from cook fires. No areas cleaned of dust. No footprints besides her own.

Wasn't that proof enough? If this goddess, supposedly, had spent the last *three hundred years* living amongst those ruins, how could she possibly have not left a mark?

And yet, Kaycia's pleasure felt unusually hollow.

It wasn't that she'd believed Soril's words. After everything he'd said, she was as convinced as ever it was all a sham—a pleasant lie for people to cope with desperation.

And yet, despite her unbelief, for the first time ever, something had changed. It was because of Elyriel. And Soril's ridiculous suggestion that, even now, she might be healed.

Kaycia should've known better. She *did* know better. And she was more determined than ever to not give in to false hope.

Soril pressed his lips together and gave a brief nod. "Make your way to Ashaira's palace. There's a lot to this we might never understand. All the more reason to keep an open mind. And an open heart. Don't you agree?"

Kaycia could no longer meet the man's eyes.

If anything, his persistence only made her angry.

She didn't know what to think. Only that it might be better Soril keep his mouth shut.

Chapter 25
THE SHATTERED WORLD

Bright clouds streaked the heavens across a backdrop burning deep, lustrous, and blue.

The roof must've caved in, Nesil thought, blinking himself awake. His head was groggy, and he couldn't remember where he was or how he'd gotten there.

Nesil stared up into the late morning light, feeling something hard dig into his shoulder and lower back. With a little concentration, he encouraged his slow, aching fingers to move. Then his toes.

A breeze entered the room, tousling his hair and stirring up a cloud of thin, brown dust. Nesil was thrown into a fit of coughing, and it wasn't until the air cleared that he realized what he was seeing.

There were blurry silhouettes floating above him in midair, blotting out the sky. Stones, in fact, still stacked and mortared upon each other in the shape of the walls they once had formed but with nothing remaining to hold them aloft.

This was Silverwater Castle. But it was as though entire fragments of architecture had forgotten to collapse. As though gravity, on a whim, had allowed multiple exceptions.

An old dusty portrait of Nesil's great-great-grandfather hung upon a ten-foot segment with crumbling edges. In the air to his right, he saw a partial oaken table with two missing legs—but rather than falling over, it remained upright and level atop an invisible floor.

Only then did he remember the statue—the demonic Ashaira bursting apart. There was no sign of her now. Not a single fragment of her aeisric effigy—but shouldn't that have made the illusions disappear?

They clearly hadn't. Instead, they'd all gone to hell.

His head began to throb, and he considered the possibility he'd received a concussion.

Additional memories surfaced—his wedding to a nefarious bride. The raging, blistering inferno.

...His grandfather's screams.

But he pushed those thoughts aside. Nothing productive could come from such feelings. For the moment, it was more important to determine he hadn't gone insane.

He sat up and gave himself a cursory inspection. Aside from a few scrapes and a film of stone dust, he appeared to have survived the worst of it. His arms ached as he stretched them forward, then backward.

Twisting around, he found a huge gash through his vest but no wound underneath. Just an angry line of red skin that throbbed mildly.

The hell?

The final pieces coalesced—the unmistakable agony and the wound that should've killed him.

So what was going on? Hadn't the knife been real?

And if it wasn't, then why was there a hole in his shirt?

Nesil brushed the dust off his clothing and looked around the room. Searching for anything to help him understand.

Parts of the floor were missing as well, with the largest chasm sundering the room in two. Crawling toward it on hands and knees, Nesil could see it was over ten feet across—which made no sense.

Hadn't he reached the ground floor? Even if the roof had fallen in—a fact he still couldn't determine to be illusion or reality—it wouldn't have been enough to justify this damage. Not to the building's foundation.

Nesil reached down, expecting to run into something solid, but his hand found only air. Lying on his chest, his arm continued into the hole as far as it would go.

So maybe he'd been wrong. Perhaps, there'd been a cellar beneath this wing he hadn't known about. An unlikely cellar, so dark, it didn't appear to have a bottom.

He worked his mouth and watched as his spittle fell into nothingness. No matter what this was, he'd been lucky, at least, to have awoken on solid ground.

There was a large man on the other side of the hole, lying dead or unconscious. With a bald head, grizzled beard, and a mismatched arraignment of leather armor, he wasn't anyone Nesil recognized. Certainly not one of his Seldoran soldiers.

Brach, then?

Nesil stood up slowly and quietly, fearing the monster might've also survived.

There wasn't, however, a way across—to reach the man before he woke...and slit his throat. Even after Nesil left the room and explored the adjacent corridors, he couldn't find an easy way around.

His only choice was to return where he started and take a second look. Now that he was calm—feeling assured that Brach couldn't reach *him*—he saw that it wouldn't have mattered anyway.

Squinting his eyes, he saw Brach's neck bent at an odd angle. There wasn't any blood on the stone floor, but he could make out red spots seeping through leather seams. Brach's armor had retained it inside, like a plum, ripe to bursting.

Nesil exhaled, relieved to have one victory, at least.

To add to his luck, he discovered Brach's knife on his own side of the hole. He reached down to pick it up, to have something to defend himself.

But the tips of his fingers collided with stone and missed the hilt entirely.

Embarrassed, he tried again but found his coordination wasn't the problem. His hand was in the right spot, but he couldn't so much as knock the hilt out of place.

Something was off. Even if the blade wasn't real, he should've been able to pick it up. But after trying a few times, he couldn't get a grasp of it.

His hands went to his back, to the wound that should've killed him. Was this the reason why? That somehow, against all odds, this knife was less than typical?

Or was there another explanation? Unforeseeable changes to the rules, only made possible when the statue shattered to pieces? Had his plan given rise to unlikely side effects?

Perhaps, his initial hope—that the illusions would cease to exist—had been flawed. Perhaps, without the statue, the illusions had simply been rendered...less tangible? If that was true, then last night would prove a monumental victory, despite everything his people had lost.

But Nesil couldn't cling to unfounded hope. A single knife wasn't proof. He needed to learn more.

"Is there anyone here?" he shouted, feeling more confident because Brach was dead.

His voice didn't echo. It didn't make the sound of an enclosed room but made him feel like he was outside, with real air pouring through the gaps in the walls.

No one responded.

Upon further reflection, there should've been people here. At the very least, the six men from the armory would've come looking. So where were they? Why hadn't they found him hours ago?

And why wasn't there smoke in the sky?

Taking a deep breath, he realized he needed to take one step at a time.

He decided to start with the wall.

Nesil approached the nearest place where several large blocks were suspended, impossibly, above two feet of air.

He reached out to touch them before stopping to wonder: what if they fell? What if this hovering was a freak accident? And a small touch upset the balance, reminding the rocks they were *supposed* to fall?

Nesil, however, was too curious to wait. He didn't want to be the kind of king who'd endanger others as if his life was less expendable than theirs.

So, instead, he glanced behind him—determining the safest direction to run—before stretching his hand to the precarious wall.

It proved remarkably solid, even after he levered his weight against it.

All right, then. So the stones were real.

He bent down to inspect the gap underneath, expecting some illusion had turned that part invisible.

Except...eerily, his hands encountered nothing—just like the hole in the ground. He needed a moment to run his hand beneath the entire length to convince himself no supports held it up.

Damn.

His prior assessment might've been wrong. What if, instead of becoming less, the illusions had become *more* tangible? Or, even more frightening, what if it was all random? Before the explosion, it'd been possible to make sense of the rules. But what if that was no longer the case?

Nesil refused to believe it. Whatever the change, the world might've become more dangerous—the answers more difficult to discern. But he would find them. He would fix this.

As Nesil hurried from the room, he saw the castle with new eyes. He stared in amazement at the tons of rock suspended overhead—some nearly a hundred feet up. It wasn't just the treasury. As he passed from one corridor to the next, he saw the explosion had torn through wall after wall, as though they were paper.

Entire rooms were left hanging in the sky, with no way to reach them. All too often, he'd reach the end of a hallway and look out across an enormous divide. He'd see the rest of the building in jagged cross-section, with no way across.

"Hello?" he yelled.

To his surprise, a woman appeared from around a corner, wearing a long woolen dress covered in soot.

"Thank heavens!" he breathed, "I thought I'd never find—"

The woman didn't see him but turned to ascend an invisible staircase. Not a real person after all, but one of the shambling folk. The mindless wanderers.

As Nesil pushed ahead, he came across them more often. He'd see arms sticking from the rubble—still moving. He saw lifeless bodies floating in the sky.

He did his best to ignore them, trying not to think what this might mean.

But he couldn't keep his heart from sinking. Their continued presence proved his victory was incomplete. Because if they'd survived, it was only natural to conclude the high aeisr had as well.

Fortunately, it wasn't all bad news. As he made for higher ground, he saw confirmation there were still men out there. People had survived.

He saw it in the smoke.

From this vantage, he saw the wind had driven the plumes southward—that's why he hadn't seen them before. Miles of smoke drowned the valley beyond. Dark, enormous columns that rose so high, they appeared nearly motionless at the top.

On one side, however, the smoke was thinner. Rather than deep gray, it was white. Not smoke but steam. And that's how he knew his people were there, fighting the flames.

With renewed determination, Nesil pushed on.

After ten more minutes exploring the maze, he had yet to see a platform deviate or drop from the sky. So, rather than avoid them, he began experimenting with how well the floating rocks could support his weight.

He was surprised to discover even the smallest block had no trouble staying aloft. It didn't tremble when he struck it but proved immovable, as though supported by the sections gone missing.

After multiple tests, just to be certain, Nesil began to take small risks. As holes became more frequent, he began to jump for the nearest rocks.

He felt sick every time, certain *this* rock would be the exception. *This* platform would prove as intangible as Brach's knife had been. But then he'd land, grasp the firm stone with his hands, and prepare his launch for the next.

After scaling a wall face and preparing to jump to a nearby roof, he saw two soldiers at the far end of a chasm. He did a double-take to make sure they were real and not aeisr who happened to resemble his men.

"Hey!" Nesil shouted, climbing faster.

The soldiers didn't hear.

He reached the top of the wall and perched himself carefully—before he realized the men weren't watching the drop-off.

"Stop!" he yelled.

But the men continued onward, over the edge, as though walking on air.

With a frown, Nesil could only think of two possibilities.

One: the men weren't real after all. They were designed to trick him into crossing the hole himself.

Or two: these men saw something Nesil didn't. Which seemed ridiculous since illusions had never worked that way. Whatever one man saw would be the same for everyone.

His sense of dread returned. He hated not knowing. There were too many variables. Too many risks.

"Over here!" he yelled again, rising to his feet. He made the jump to the nearby roof.

The vaulting proved sturdy, but the tiles weren't.

Nesil slid, knocking tiles free as he scrambled to slow his descent.

His hand caught something wooden—a part of the roof's underlying structure. He dangled in place, heart thumping madly.

The tiles careened off the edge but didn't crash into the ground. An eerie silence followed as though the tiles would keep falling forever.

He cursed himself for not learning his lesson the night before. Falling once from a roof was once too many.

"Did you see that?" asked a man. This was followed by a rush of footsteps.

Nesil looked down, but the edge blocked his view.

"I'm up here!" he yelled, hoping, this time, they might hear—but fearing they wouldn't.

"They went right through the ground!"

"The hell you talking about?" asked the other.

"The tiles. Off the roof."

"Your point? Happens all the time. Place like this."

Nesil didn't understand. Was some illusion interfering with his voice?

He crawled upward, double-checking each handhold as he went.

In a flash of insight, he pulled another tile free—a fragment too small to cause serious injury—and sent it skittering down.

"There!" said the first. "Tell me you saw that."

This time, when Nesil looked down the roof, the men came into sight. They'd walked away from the building to view the top.

The soldiers were standing in midair. They were looking right at him, but something was wrong. Something prevented them from seeing him properly.

"Hey...!" he shouted, the despondency clear in his tone.

Nesil prised up another tile.

"Move!" stammered the first. "Get going!"

"Damn it!" Nesil shouted. "Stop! It's me!"

But they didn't hear. And they didn't stop.

Nesil had seen that look before. It was the same fear inspired by the aeisr.

And Nesil was overcome with a new worry: what if *no one* could see him?

Or, more confusing, what if only some people could, while others couldn't?

No, no, no. He needed to stop guessing. Instead of leaping to ridiculous conclusions, it was better to keep moving and wait for real explanations.

This had to be another of the aeisr's tricks. Was she here, somewhere, following him? Laughing at his inner turmoil?

"Sefina?" he yelled. But that wasn't her name.

"Aeisr!" he hissed as though it were a curse.

Knowing better than to chase after the men, he finished crossing the roof and dropped down to an adjacent balcony.

He considered testing the air where the soldiers walked to see if it might be real. But there wasn't an easy way to get there. Not without jumping and risking being wrong.

Instead, he focused on getting out of this place alive.

It took half an hour to reach the outer wall, but eventually, the journey became easier. The castle itself had been utterly ravaged, but the explosion hadn't extended far into the city beyond. That was good. For a while, he'd begun to fear the entire world had gone to shit, and he'd be jumping and climbing the rest of his life.

Once outside, he began to run faster, doing his best to remember holes or other dangers.

With the fires burning out of control, Nesil was forced to take the long way around. The neighborhoods he passed were no longer familiar. Doors and windows hung open. Clothes and other possessions were scattered across the street, dropped in haste or neglect.

They painted a picture of the events he'd missed. Rather than preserve what remained of the town itself, the ascendants had directed the survivors toward the outskirts. More specifically, they'd prioritized the defense of their granaries and food stores.

As long as those remained safe, the rest could burn.

A pair of soldiers emerged from a doorway. A patrol, perhaps, searching for stragglers. Their faces were tired, their armor blackened, but their eyes were alert and determined.

"Please!" he shouted as loud as he could. "It's me, your king! Heed my words!"

He didn't expect a response, and he didn't get one.

Crestfallen, he ran in front and waved his hands. But they didn't stop and nearly ran him over.

In desperation, he risked touching a man's back. He did so carefully, prepared to evade the man's reaction.

But his hand felt only air.

Panicked, he thrust out his arm, and it passed through the man's body. As though these men, Seldoran soldiers, were now a part of the aeisr's army.

As Nesil stood there considering, an alternative explanation sprouted in his mind—one that filled him with sickening dread.

What if these soldiers weren't fake, but Nesil himself had changed?

These men weren't there when the statue exploded, but Nesil was. He'd been caught in the middle, watching in horror as eerie light crashed through the room. He'd felt a deafening unquiet pass through his body, like luminescent tendrils. Or ghostly hands.

But none of that had been *real*...

Of all the ideas he'd considered thus far, this one seemed too preposterous—too outlandish—to possibly be true.

He'd lifted the roof tiles, hadn't he?

Nesil dashed to the side of the road, deciding to pick up anything to get these soldier's attention. Not because he thought he could communicate but out of the simple necessity to affirm his own existence. Even if these men ran away in horror, it would at least confirm Nesil was still here. That he could still touch the world.

But the bushes melted through his fingers. The dry planks of discarded wood refused to budge. And the door remained silent, as his banging was reduced to awkward swings of his arms.

"NO!" he shouted. It was a trick! The aeisr must've lured him into an empty field—that's why he couldn't feel anything!

He closed his eyes and began to run, keeping in one direction. Better to collide with something. Trip over something. Come into contact with *anything* than admit he'd been transformed into the thing he hated most.

But as the seconds stretched, he went on, unhindered. Free as a ghost.

When he opened his eyes, he found himself inside a building. He'd passed through the wall without feeling a thing. Moreover, there was an old wooden table cutting through his stomach.

Unnerved by the picture, he stepped out to the side.

"Damn it!" he yelled, slamming his fists into the floor and surprising himself when they passed right through. He had to scramble backward with his knees to prevent himself from falling through the earth.

Slow and steady, he thought, feeling his heart pound in his chest. The ground had supported his weight until now, and there was no reason for it to stop.

Nesil rolled onto his back and closed his eyes. Was this all a dream? A living nightmare?

He supposed it might be better to return to the castle—back to the shattered world, where the rules had been different. At least there, near the explosion, he could interact with objects. Maybe not everything, but there were things he could manipulate. Other illusions.

He could try, perhaps, to write messages on the walls. To tell the soldiers he was still alive. That he hadn't abandoned them.

Nesil, however, didn't feel like standing up. The castle wasn't going anywhere. So instead, he lay there. Trying not to feel like shit.

After several long minutes, a new consideration surfaced. As he stared up at the rotted ceiling, he wondered if his invisibility wasn't all bad news. If the soldiers couldn't see him, then maybe *all* the illusions outside the castle were invisible.

If that were true, then destroying the statue had been worthwhile after all. The Seldoran people, at last, might be free from the aeisr. And their chances of survival would increase exponentially.

So long as they withstood the fire.

It was this thought alone that brought Nesil to his feet. No matter what might be happening with him, he was more concerned for the fate of his people.

Nesil approached the door, pretended to open it, and walked on through.

With the dark column towering overhead, it would've been easy to take the most direct route. If he wanted, Nesil could make a straight line through the buildings, but he didn't.

He felt more comfortable taking the usual streets, not only to make sure he didn't get lost but also to see the city for himself. He wanted to visit these neighborhoods while their memory was still fresh.

In a few areas, the fires raged so hot, he deliberately chose to take detours instead. He told himself it was because of the smoke. He needed to go around to preserve his vision. But, deep down, he knew the truth—that though the fires couldn't hurt him, they still filled him with terror.

He kept imagining what it was like for the people who'd been here. Far too often, he stumbled across bodies beneath the cinder and ash. Each one seared a picture into his mind—a woman trapped while rescuing her child, or a man caught unawares by an invisible, blistering embrace.

Nesil felt guilty for not being here—for not suffering the pains he'd failed to prevent. But, perhaps, he could still do something. If he blocked the path of an invisible fire, could he cancel the illusion and make it visible again?

For a few minutes, he entertained this idea—of becoming a silent protector of his people. If any illusions lingered, like the ones at the castle, Nesil was the only person who could help.

These thoughts of heroism, however, weren't only pathetic, they were proven unreasonable, and worse, unnecessary.

It soon became clear only regular flames remained. There were no illusions for Nesil to face. And, if he were being honest, he would've lacked the courage, anyway.

His thoughts turned inward, feeling numb. For the first time in a long while, he stopped searching for a plan.

When he finally stumbled across the survivors' camp, he was surprised by how few were present. Between the tents of blankets and the people boarded up in nearby buildings, he couldn't see them all. But if he had to make a guess, only a hundred or so remained.

There should've been closer to a thousand.

He supposed there were many still out there. They'd gotten away from the flames, but in their panic, they hadn't followed the ascendants' plan. They'd either been too far away to hear, or they'd been forced to split up by the fires' unpredictable movements.

Some would be rescued, while others would not.

The majority were women and soot-covered children, with the men needed elsewhere to fight the flames. There were crying babies and the moans of burn victims. But most were quiet, too sullen and tired to do more than rest.

Nesil approached the tent where they were handing out rations.

"I have three children!" cried the large woman in front. "And this is what you give us?"

"You *had* three children!" scowled the woman next to her. "Now shove off! We're all starving!"

"You *dare* suggest my boys are dead?!"

"Go fetch them, why don't you? They can stand in line like the rest of us!"

Nesil might've heard more but was distracted by a person running toward him. Someone he recognized.

Alerisa wore the same red dress from the night before, but her hair was a mess, with her makeup running in streaks down her face. Her eyes were bloodshot from lack of sleep and a refusal to be consoled.

It took only a second, however, to realize she wasn't running to *him* but to the soldiers behind him who'd recently arrived.

"Jeros?!" she yelled. "Where is he? Do you know if he's still out there?"

"Who? ...You mean Ascendant Jeros. I'm deeply sorry, ma'am. I haven't seen him since last night."

"What?! But you were with him! Please! If something's happened, you'd tell me, wouldn't you?"

"I..." The man appeared uncomfortable. "There are a lot of people missing. I'm sorry, but these things take time."

Nesil's heart began to break. He remembered all too well what'd happened to her husband, though he couldn't bring himself to speak it out loud.

In a way, it made him glad Alerisa couldn't see him. She had no way of seeing the guilt on his face and no way to force out his confession.

By now, her husband's ashes would be impossible to recognize. And, for the rest of her life, she'd wonder what'd happened.

Nesil felt a desire to leave.

To properly assess their survival, he should find the ascendants. He should know how his men fared against the flames.

But before he could go, he spotted a pair of guards outside a large, heavy door. By their rank, he inferred there'd be officers inside. Possibly, Ascendant General Corvan himself.

A few days earlier, these men would've turned Nesil away, insistent he provide good reason for interfering—or his grandfather would hear of it. Now, however...

As he walked through the door, no one spared him a second glance. Or a first, for that matter.

Inside, a team of secretaries were rummaging through ledgers and scrolls. From the looks on their faces, they were having trouble prioritizing which records were needed and which could be left behind.

They ignored the argument from deeper within—the voices Nesil found curious because he happened to recognize them.

To his surprise, he found the ascendant general speaking with none other than Terak, the prince's close friend. While Nesil was overjoyed to discover they'd survived, he was also confused by the debate in progress.

Terak's voice was rising. "Isn't that why you called me here? To provide information on the prince?"

"What information? These are half-baked theories!"

"You saw him, didn't you? I know you did—the way he stood there, at the center of the firestorm."

"I'll admit, I saw something that *looked* like Nesil, but—"

"That's it, exactly!" said Terak. "It wasn't him! It *couldn't* have been him, or he'd have died right then. Same as the king. And then how would you explain what happened at the castle?"

"Wait!" said Nesil, though neither could hear him. "You know of the explosion? *You know I was there*?"

The only people who knew that were the ones from the armory—confirming, at least, one had made it back.

But, if that was the case, why had they left him there? Though he realized they couldn't see him—not in his present state—he would've expected the search to go on. He understood that most soldiers needed to help with the fires, but surely they could've spared *more than two men*! It was almost as though they didn't want him to be found.

"The prince was clearly involved with the aeisr," said Corvan. "At the start of the ceremony, he was there, on the dais, alongside the king. Of that, there can be no doubt. And the way I see it, he couldn't possibly have escaped unless the aeisr *wanted* him alive."

"I can think of several reasons why he—"

"Speculation," interrupted Corvan. "Ultimately, it boils down to the fact that the prince knew something but told no one. And now, despite whatever good you may think of him, our king is dead."

Terak's face was incredulous. "Are you suggesting Nesil had something to do with that?"

"He *obviously* had something to do with it! Now don't get me wrong. I'm not putting the blame on him. The murders of last night rest squarely on the aeisr. But I can't ignore that our prince did nothing."

"How can you say that? Nesil loved his grandfather! He couldn't have known what the aeisr was planning. He was tricked along with everyone else!"

"Tricked into what? Not asking for help? He might not have known specifics, but he should've warned us—before the fire started."

Terak shook his head. "Nesil's smart. He would've had good reason to—"

"Speculation."

"No!" shouted Terak. "*Not* speculation! Come on—you can't be this willfully stupid!"

Nesil winced, worried his friend was taking this too far. While he appreciated the young man's defense and felt deeply honored, it was also misinformed. Nesil *had* known what was happening, and he *hadn't* been smart.

"Care to try that again?" asked the general, holding back his anger.

"You're treating him like a traitor!"

"I never said that."

Terak threw up his hands in irritation. "And yet, you do nothing to defend him! To preserve his honor!"

"I'm sorry you see it that way. However, if the prince were here, I believe he would agree with me. We can't afford to risk the lives of more men."

"I'm not asking for more. I'll go by myself!"

"Go where?" asked Nesil, suddenly concerned. "The castle's not safe. Please, don't go!"

"I'll find proof," explained Terak. "I'll figure out what Nesil did, so no one has to wonder."

"The answer is no. The Silverwater's getting worse. You can see that from here."

"Which is why it must be now! If we wait any longer, we won't get another chance."

"I understand your concern—and, believe me, I want answers as much as you do."

"Like *hell* you do!"

"The only difference here is how much I hold *your* life in esteem. I won't let you die. Not for this. We'll need everyone we can get to face what's coming. Or is *that* not important to you? Is the survival of our people not worth your attention?"

The young man scowled but didn't argue.

"Listen to him," said Nesil, stretching a hand to Terak's shoulder but stopping himself short. "This isn't worth it."

Corvan swallowed. "Do you remember now? The problems we faced *before* the aeisr?"

Terak looked up with eyes of defeat.

"You remember the creatures—the invisible beasts? Because *that's* where we need to turn our attention. *That's* why I can't afford to lose more men. If we don't stand prepared, the memory of Seldor—including our memory of the prince—isn't going to matter."

The young man nodded somberly.

"The last two men I sent to the castle—they went, knowing they'd be the last. Maybe they'll find the answers you're hoping for and maybe not. They'll make a final attempt to retrieve the bodies but have orders to retreat at the first sign of trouble."

Nesil stood there, stunned. From the way the general spoke, he was unlikely referring to the bodies of soldiers. While, ideally, they'd want to recover them all—to honor each and every man who'd sacrificed for their nation—there were too many corpses. Far more than could be assigned to a pair of men.

Which meant what? Did he mean Sefina's body?

"Will I get the chance to see him?" asked Terak, his composure slipping near the end. "If they make it back..."

Corvan sighed heavily. "You heard the report—how they discovered his body... It won't help you heal in the way you think."

"No, no, no!" The words escaped Nesil's mouth. "You're not talking about *me*?! I'm standing right here! Corvan, I'm right next to you!"

Terak closed his eyes. "I don't care. I want to see him."

"It's a fake!" shouted Nesil. "Someone else *disguised to look like me!*"

He spoke this knowing his own words were bullshit. Even if the aeisr was still capable of her tricks, she wouldn't expend her remaining strength on something so meaningless.

But Nesil didn't care. He refused to believe that this was the explanation—that they stopped searching because he'd been found.

"I'm not dead!" shouted Nesil—though only mostly convinced. He couldn't be dead, or how else did he explain the roof tiles?

The general sighed. "We can decide this later. But promise me, you won't do anything drastic. I don't want reports that you've suddenly vanished despite my clear instructions."

Terak hesitated.

"Why don't we compromise?" suggested Corvan. "Just this once, I'll make an exception and allow you to speak at the prince's memorial. You can share your theories and tell everyone about the hero Nesil was."

"I'll tell them myself!" shouted Nesil. "There won't be a funeral. Just hold on! Give me time to figure this out!"

"You'd let me do that?" asked Terak.

"You'll be expected to state, in clear terms, that nothing can be proven—but I think it's a good idea. Why shouldn't the people believe in heroes? Right at the moment we need them most."

Nesil fled the room, unwilling to stomach one more word. He didn't care whether they thought him a hero or traitor. It didn't matter how they remembered him because he wasn't gone!

"I'm still here!" he said to the people outside. But if there was a way to make them notice—to make them care—it eluded his grasp.

He was a stranger to them now. An outcast. A memory.

"I'll come up with a plan," he muttered to no one in particular. Even to him, the words sounded empty and hollow. They disappeared into the wind and became as nothing.

He didn't have a plan, and it left him terrified. He'd run out of options with nowhere left to go.

He could only say he wasn't dead, without any certainty that it made a real difference.

Chapter 26
LOST CONNECTION

Elyriel was not in the place Kaycia left her.

She opened her eyes to a cathedral of sorts, with cracked stone walls overgrown with ivy, and the remnants of stained glass windows glittering with color. There were splintered benches, blackened with mold, and scattered tiles from where the ceiling had caved in. The impact had caused the floor to collapse, leaving a large hole at the opposite end of the room. Revealing a shadowed chamber underneath, of which Kaycia could only see the slightest part.

"Damn it, Elle...!" she muttered, though more angry at herself for allowing this to happen. "No..."

She ran to the nearest window, more worried about the light than anything else. The sky was no longer blue but the bright golds and oranges of sunset.

To her relief, the shadows were still not so dark as she'd feared. While Elyriel's curiosity might've caused her to wander, she hadn't strayed far enough to put them in danger. Not so far that Kaycia couldn't fix this.

She'd always known something like this would happen, as Elyriel couldn't be expected to sleep every time she left. No amount of exhaustion could restrain her forever.

The girl was restless—anxious—and undoubtedly confused by where she'd awakened. Of course, she'd wander, if for no greater reason than to seek out her sister.

The thought gave Kaycia pause. She couldn't imagine what might be going through Elyriel's head. Did the girl feel lost and afraid? Was she possibly despondent, thinking Kaycia had abandoned her? Or was her mind at ease? Relieved to be free from people—free to be herself?

To Kaycia's dismay, the buildings outside the window were entirely unfamiliar.

They were as discolored and forlorn as every other ruin in this godsforsaken place.

In the warped glass, she caught a glimpse of Elyriel's reflection, though it wasn't the same face from recent days. The eyes that stared back weren't blank and hollow but filled with intensity and unusual pity.

As she looked back at herself, she saw a girl who was lost. And something else as well. A twisted curve to the corners of her lips. Menacing. Accusatory.

They seemed to say, *This is no more than you deserve.*

In rising panic, Kaycia searched for a way to get higher, knowing how important it was to regain her bearings. She couldn't think of anything worse than being caught off guard and not knowing where to run. Or how to get out.

Suspecting no stairs would reach as far as the roof, she looked up at the vines—the thickest crowded around the collapsed rooftop, where they had access to the most light. The growth hanging from the center was exceptionally dense, where she realized the vines had overtaken a chandelier.

Kaycia approached it from underneath, wondering if the chain would support her weight. She'd likely need her conviction to avoid undue strain on the debilitated roof.

As she crossed the room, however, the light dimmed, and she felt a chill.

At first, she thought nothing of it, thinking the sun had merely shifted as before. But this was no shadow.

Her eyes began to droop, suddenly drowsy. This, too, might've seemed perfectly natural, were she not reminded this was Elyriel's body. And while, yes, the girl did get tired, it never happened so abruptly or without recognizable cause.

What was more, the strength she usually felt was no longer there.

Kaycia froze in her tracks, realizing something was wrong. She couldn't identify the reason but could only guess it had something to do with her location. The sensation only started when she crossed the room—as she'd drawn closer to that yawning hole.

As she considered it now, there was something...off...about that area. The vines nearest the gap weren't merely overshadowed—they appeared dark and slimy. Glittering with hoarfrost.

Kaycia took a step back, intending to go the other way.

At the slightest movement of her head, however, the room began to spin. Her stomach clenched with nausea, and it took enormous effort to stay on her feet. She dropped a hand to a knee, feeling the urge to vomit, and she squeezed her other arm around her middle.

Beneath her, the stone undulated like the surface of the sea—though she suspected this was only in her mind. She was losing control as though at the mercy of some powerful narcotic.

"Help…" she rasped, surprised by the effort required to speak. Her breath was visible in the frigid air.

Whatever this was—this force or entity—it was unlike anything she'd ever encountered. It sapped away her warmth and her will to escape.

She took one step.

Then another.

The room shifted, and her head smacked hard against the floor.

Her vision clouded. The world pulsed and darkened with every heartbeat. The golden windows lost their color, glowing bright silver and seeming impossibly far away.

She twisted and crawled, thinking her own dizziness was causing the floor to teeter.

But then the ground itself began to tilt.

Her body slid the wrong direction—not away from the hole but toward it.

"Help!" she screamed. Or tried to. Even if the town hadn't been empty of people, her voice was too frail to be heard by anyone.

She grabbed the leg of a nearby bench, but the wood came away like frozen mush in her hand.

When she tried a second time, her fingers brushed against a vine that snaked across the floor—the brief contact causing her muscles to constrict in agony.

She didn't understand. As she looked at the vines through tear-filled eyes, they seemed somehow different. The colors were all wrong—with broad leaves not unlike human skin.

Her descent was slow, but she could do nothing to stop it. Her mind was too unfocused to draw on her conviction.

The vines didn't move, but she felt a pressure envelop every part of her body. It was like she were wrestling against dozens of hands—twisting her muscles and chilling her bones.

Her foot passed the edge and dangled free.

Then her hips.

She was falling, and…

K aycia screamed.

"What is it?" asked a girl's voice beside her.

It was such a surprise, she jerked back in fear. And sent pillows scattering across the floor.

Was this her bed? What was she doing here?

For a moment, she did nothing but lay there confused. It wasn't unlike waking from a dream—from a nightmare—and realizing none of it had been real, except…

It had been real. She knew it was real. And...

"Bloody heavens!" she breathed, bringing a hand to her mouth. "Elle?"

"Did something happen?" asked Chesandril, full of concern. "Is she okay?"

"I..." Kaycia looked up at the young girl. "I don't know."

This, of course, wasn't the whole truth. She *did* know. While she might be hazy about the details and couldn't say what was happening right then, it was undoubtedly horrific.

And it was all her fault.

"Should I get someone?" asked the girl. "Perhaps, Soril will know—"

"Don't," she responded with a groan of despair. "How's he going to help?"

Chesandril gaped. She clearly wanted to do something but was at a loss.

"I need you," said Kaycia. "Don't go anywhere!"

"You're going back?"

"Of course, I'm going back!" she snapped. "I have to try!"

Chesandril nodded and regathered the pillows.

"Don't mention this to anyone... At least, not yet."

Kaycia repositioned her body and attempted to relax.

This, of course, proved impossible.

She couldn't avoid the thought of her sister lying there, tangled in a web of writhing vines.

If the pain was anything like her brief contact with one of them, it was no wonder the connection between their minds had been severed. The trauma was too much for their bond to handle.

Kaycia reached for her sister in the hope against hope she might get through. Perhaps, if she anticipated the pain, she'd be more prepared to hold onto that connection and not be forced out a second time.

But as she searched for Elyriel, nothing happened.

It made her wonder if her fears were part of the problem—which, of course, only caused them to multiply.

She was terrified of those things—those vines—or whatever they'd been. She'd never heard of a force that could inflict such pain. She could only observe the similarities it shared with the current.

Their auras seemed to work in the exact same way—except, this time, it wasn't her hearing that was affected but her strength and well-being. In mere seconds, it had stripped away her power and control.

And worse, as Kaycia lay there on the bed—chest heaving and heart racing—she felt certain her greatest fear had come true. That, in proceeding with this investigation, she'd lost the very thing that mattered most.

"Damn it..." she moaned as tears escaped her eyes and dampened her pillow.

Chesandril took her hand. "Could you...try again?" she asked, with a hope that was both quiet and pitiful. The softness of her touch brought Kaycia some comfort.

"I..." Her voice cracked, and she nodded her head. "I'll try all night if I have to."

K aycia awoke to a new sensation, unaware of how much time had passed. The pain had returned—a sickening throb—threatening to pull her under all over again. But it was different, somehow.

Her arms slunk down like worn-out rags as she felt herself being lifted into the air.

For a long moment, she didn't know what this was. Her mind refused to make sense of it, and she could only stare in wonder as the light above grew steadily larger.

She couldn't turn her neck to see what was happening. She could only feel something cradling her back—a kind of rising platform. Her legs were dangling, tugged by gravity, with her toes pointed back down the hole.

And then she remembered her conversation with Chess. Her desperation to reconnect with her sister.

At some point, it must've worked! She couldn't remember how long she'd lain there, tossing in bed, wanting to scream in frustration—but something, eventually, must've clicked. It was the only explanation that made any sense. She was back in Elyriel's body, and...

It was *not* the result of anything she'd done.

She'd only returned because of this *thing*—whatever it was—slowly lifting her up to the roof.

Even now, as she gained distance from those festering vines, she felt the world shift into focus. The pain was squeezed from her muscles, leaving her empty and raw.

Kaycia should've been afraid. After being helpless for so long, like an insect in a web, it wasn't difficult to imagine the spider had come for her.

There was no doubt in her mind she'd been liberated from one fate only to face another. But that terror was still nothing when compared to her relief.

She'd been given another chance.

Her sister hadn't been lost to some unknown fate. And while she wasn't out of danger and still might meet some horrifying end, she couldn't help but feel that this was better.

At least, this way, they'd face it together.

She couldn't imagine a worse feeling—lying there, unable to do anything. The worst was the not knowing—of having idea after idea pop into her head, coalescing into a mass of shapeless fears.

In comparison to that, the fear of death was...manageable.

Kaycia was lifted outside before the thing supporting her gave a sudden tilt.

Unable to catch herself, her body rolled forward, and she was deposited onto the near-horizontal rooftop. She landed on her side, facing back the way she came. Her arms smacked the weathered clay tiles, with her head tilted down across one shoulder.

She was turned the wrong way, unable to see what else was on the roof. But she *could* see the thing that'd lifted her up, just for a moment, before it shrank away.

And it filled her with hope.

It wasn't a monster but a thin, wiry support. It was the same porous material as the bridge from before and the spikes that'd skewered those monsters in the forest.

She had no guarantees the creator wasn't dangerous—that he wasn't worse than a pack of abyssal creatures. But if the man was human, there was a chance he'd listen. Though they might not be on the same side or from the same nation, they could, at least, act in a civilized manner.

"Hello...?" she inquired. Her voice was feeble but loud enough for an ascendant to hear. "Someone there?"

No response.

She got the impression that this was deliberate. Though she was too weak to turn and see for herself, she could *sense* the man's presence. She could feel his eyes on her back, regarding her with calculated interest.

Was it possible they didn't speak the same language? As a Navaran, that wouldn't make sense, but perhaps he'd come from somewhere else—from further away.

His steps were so soft as he moved across the roof, she almost didn't realize he was walking away.

"Please don't go!" she said, suddenly desperate. It wasn't just the awful thing waiting in the basement—it was this entire place. It was knowing how close she'd been to losing Elyriel. And the dawning realization she didn't know enough—she wasn't *prepared* enough—to keep her safe.

To hell with Soril's plan. Knowing him, the older ascendant would've insisted she be quiet and let the stranger leave. That way, she'd still be following orders.

But Kaycia didn't care about that now. She found it hard to view the creator as her enemy—not after he'd saved her life.

When she finally recovered the strength to turn around, her breath caught in her throat.

She recognized the penetrating eyes and scaled eyelids, but in the light of the sun, she saw he wasn't a man but a child.

A small boy, no older than twelve.

His face was still hidden beneath dark folds, but his difference in size began to make sense.

Did she have it wrong, then? Her first thought was that *this* was the god-child—but Irisea was supposed to be a girl. Of that, the tales were perfectly clear.

She supposed the stories might be mistaken, but this still made no sense. Irisea had been conceived by Shaelis and Ashaira. This boy, on the other hand, was incontestably the product of Creation—of the goddess, Meileen. What was more, Irisea had been born centuries ago and wouldn't likely appear a child at all.

So no. It only took a moment to realize this boy was something else.

A *transcendent*, she reminded herself. The twelve-year-old product of illegal experimentation.

In stark contrast to the boy's overwhelming power, his steely eyes were wide and wary. He had no desire to stay and appeared to be waiting for provocation—for any excuse at all—to leave her alone on this roof.

"What's your name?" she asked, trying her best not to remember the forest—how easily this child had impaled those creatures.

The boy didn't move as though inwardly conflicted.

Had she been in her own body—that of an adult—it could've easily been worse. But, even at sixteen, Elyriel was a fair bit taller than the boy. And the fact she was a girl might be intimidating in its own right.

"I'm Kaycia," she offered. "Kaycia Eldren. I want to thank you for—"

"Just stop," he said in a raspy voice. "I did what I did because..." He shook his head in resignation. "This was a mistake."

"I don't think it was."

The boy groaned. "Can you just tell me you're all right? Are you seeing straight?"

"How did you find me?" she asked, fearing he'd have reason to leave if she answered his question.

"You were making a lot of noise."

"No. I wasn't."

The boy made a face, and Kaycia thought she might be wrong. For all she knew, Elyriel might've screamed and screamed.

But, ultimately, he shrugged this off as unimportant.

"Were you...following me?" she asked.

"There's nothing wrong with your speech—I think you'll live."

He turned to go.

"But...!" Kaycia wasn't sure what to say. "What if I need you again? I... I don't know anything about this place!"

"Then you shouldn't be here," he said without bothering to turn around. "Try not to land yourself in more trouble. No one will get you out."

It wasn't the sort of thing she'd expect a child to say.

"What do you want?" she asked. "Perhaps, we could help each other?"

As he continued away, he said, "I want you to leave."

By this point, she'd regained enough strength to rise to a knee.

But before she could take a step, a thin line of spikes burst up through the tiles.

She shrieked and stumbled back. It took a second to realize they weren't pushing her down the hole. This wasn't the monster's attempt to reclaim her but the boy's intervention to stop her from following.

He hadn't needed to wave his hands or close his eyes to concentrate. He'd sensed her approach and reacted on instinct.

"You're right," she said, grasping for anything that might keep the boy here. "I shouldn't have come."

To her relief, the boy paused.

"So..." she lied, "if you could help me this once—if you could get me to the exit—I'll leave you be. You won't see me again."

His brow furrowed as he turned to face her. "That easy, huh? Why should I believe you?"

She exhaled softly. "Because I mean it. I just... I don't want my—" She nearly said 'sister.' "Because I'm scared."

This much, at least, was true.

The boy's expression didn't change, unmoved by compassion. But he stood quiet a moment as he considered his options.

Kaycia was tempted to say more—to appeal to the boy's sense of honor—or whatever it was that'd driven him to save her. He clearly wanted to do what was right—but he also didn't like being told what to do.

"You'll leave Ahman?" he asked. "And never return? I need you to think about this. Things around here are about to get...dangerous."

These words were spoken in an ominous tone, but that didn't detract her from his question.

She *did* mean to leave, if only for a while. She'd learn from the histories and be better prepared to face these dangers. After the Navaran was gone, she could sneak back in and finish what she started.

The plan was good, in theory—but something in his warning was difficult to ignore. A part of her wanted to listen. To keep her sister away from this place and avoid all risk.

She'd regret not reaching Ashaira's palace and losing her chance to participate in these discoveries. But couldn't the boy do all that? While he hadn't admitted to anything, he was here for a reason. And if the Navaran Empire uncovered these answers, rather than Carheim, would that really be so bad?

There was a lot to consider, but there'd be time enough later to change her mind.

"I'm sure," she said in feigned resignation. "Just get me out, and I'll be on my way."

The spikes lowered, and the boy gave a nod.

Relief washed over her. "This means a lot to me."

He shrugged and led the way across the roof.

"What should I call you?" she asked as she trailed after him.

No response.

"I can't just call you *boy...*"

His face suggested she certainly could. But, at last, he relented. "If you must, you can call me Aico."

"Aico..." she repeated. "I like that name."

The boy didn't seem to care.

At the edge of the roof, there wasn't a bridge. Rather, a flat surface had risen up from the ground floor, waiting to carry them down.

"We'll take the waterways," he announced. "They tend to be safer and not move around so much."

Kaycia nodded without admitting she hadn't known this detail. It made her curious, however, of what else he might know about Ahman and the abyssal current. He didn't seem afraid of that thing in the basement, and he'd offhandedly suggested that things would worsen.

Was that merely an observation? Or was he planning to do something to stoke the fire?

As their platform descended, she studied the rough gray skin of his slender hands. She'd been told the infliction was a constant torment—spreading through muscle and making it difficult to move. Especially after waking up in the morning.

"You can stop staring," he said, causing her to blush.

"I... Of course," she replied, not knowing what else to say.

After an awkward pause, he added, "It's really not so bad. I've had it since I was born. It's just part of who I am."

She forced herself not to gawk. The fact he'd been a transcendent from birth wasn't the sort of detail she'd expect him to reveal, considering how tight-lipped he was about everything else. But, she supposed it wasn't much of a secret, as he obviously hadn't received his rites in the proper fashion.

There was a story here, but she knew better than to press him further. If she seemed too interested, he'd likely close up and say nothing for the rest of their time together.

After they reached the bottom, it was only a short walk to the edge of the water. But, rather than make a bridge as she'd expected, Aico fashioned a small boat.

The arrangement was simple, with only two seats and not even the presence of oars to propel them. The boat, however, wasn't like the structures he'd made before. It wasn't crude or porous but made of smooth, white wood.

She supposed this made sense, as even small holes would interfere with its purpose, but she got the impression there was more going on. It was all in the details—how the prow was perfectly curved and etched with small vines and flowers. Even the wooden seats had been beveled, raising the craftsmanship to a near artisan level.

This exceeded the requirements for this short, simple trip—and they suggested a desire to be noticed. Why else would Aico have taken such care if not for her benefit?

The boat rocked steadily as she took her seat.

As he followed, appearing aloof as ever, her impression of him changed. At such a young age, he'd learned that the appearance of showing off would come across as arrogant. So, instead, he went through pains to make it seem he didn't care.

Ordinarily, this would've made her all the more critical, but it didn't. Perhaps, if he'd been older, she'd have been worried of false motives. But, being the child he was, she found his attempts to impress her slightly endearing.

Without a word, the boat sliced the mirror surface. The craft seemed to know exactly where to go, even with Aico facing the wrong way.

And yet, he didn't use this freedom to meet Kaycia's gaze. If anything, he made a point of feigning disinterest.

Until he asked, "When was the last you ate?"

She looked down and noticed her pack was missing. Had she lost it in the basement, discarded among the vines? She didn't think so. In fact, as she thought back, she didn't remember carrying the bag at the cathedral. She must've lost it before. Or rather, Elyriel had lost it.

"That's alright," she said. "I can eat when I get back. There's no reason for you to share—"

To her surprise, as if from nowhere, the boy produced a bright red apple. And she realized it *had* come from nowhere.

"You...can do that?" she asked.

For a brief second, she glimpsed a hidden smile.

As she thought back to her studies, she'd never heard of a creator capable of making food—*real* food that the body could digest. She could only imagine how many problems it might solve. There had to be a catch.

Already, as she reached for the fruit, she noticed differences from the real thing. Its shape, for one, was overly symmetrical and round to the point of exaggeration. As she turned it over, its bottom was completely smooth, uninterrupted by core or stamen.

"Don't worry," he said. "It's perfectly safe."

"It's not that. I... I've just never seen this before."

"It's an apple."

"No. It isn't."

The boy became defensive. "Give it back, then. I haven't had time to get it right."

"What if I don't want to give it back?" she asked, hoping to sound playful.

Aico merely shrugged.

As she bit into it, she found its texture more akin to a raw potato. It even left a grainy feel in her mouth that was quite distracting. But the taste was sweet, with a faint trace of honey.

"What do you think?" he asked with measured interest.

"Well, that depends. Do I have to worry about this apple disappearing from my stomach?"

Aico shook his head but didn't elaborate.

She had no choice but to take him at his word. If she had to guess, it likely had to do with the apple's complexity. It went far beyond that of a bridge or a boat—where the only purpose was to mimic structural integrity. The composition of food would require extra attention—enough, perhaps, to add a degree of permanence to its existence.

The thought, however, had her inspecting the fruit more closely. She almost expected to discover minuscule pores in the surface, like a smaller version of what she'd seen before. She needn't have worried, however, as the surface was smooth. Almost impossibly smooth.

She smiled. "I think it's wonderful. The taste could use some work, but that's hardly a setback if your people don't go hungry."

At this, his expression became uncomfortable.

Kaycia couldn't tell why. Did he feel guilty, perhaps, for not taking this obvious initiative? Or was there another reason the idea was untenable? Perhaps he'd only made the apple's creation appear effortless when, in truth, it was quite demanding.

How was she supposed to know if he wouldn't talk?

"This is truly amazing," she confessed, taking another bite. "What else can you do? I imagine you've tried lots of things."

She caught the beginnings of a smile before he stopped himself.

"Aico... You've got nothing to be afraid of. I'm just trying to talk—one person to another. We can keep this between the two of us if that's what's bothering you. I won't tell my leaders. I won't tell anyone."

His gaze locked with hers longer than before, but he wasn't convinced.

She licked her lips. "What if I told you something about me? That'd be fair, wouldn't it?"

This caught him by surprise. "I... I'm not used to this."

"Giving rides to strangers...or talking to girls?"

His cheeks flushed red.

"I'm teasing!" she said. "Aico... I'm sorry. I shouldn't have said that. But look at it this way—if you're feeling uncomfortable, you only need practice. So here's your chance. Ask me something."

He paused for several seconds, thinking it over.

Still embarrassed, he said, "I...don't know."

"That's alright. But I won't let you give up so easily. Just take more time. You'll get there."

"Could you give me some ideas?"

"Maybe to start."

But as she considered what to say, she felt self-conscious. It wasn't just a matter of offering advice so he'd know the right questions. It was the simultaneous awareness she'd have to answer those questions.

"Okay... With a little observation, you might discern people's interests. They might dress a certain way. Men enjoy talking about their scars. Am I making sense?"

"So...I might ask about your knives?"

"Perfect."

"But what if I'm not interested in those things?"

She tried not to feel offended. "Well... That's a different skill you'll have to pick up. People won't talk if you're insincere."

Aico looked confused. "Then why are *you* still talking?"

"I'm trying to help."

The boy shook his head. "People only notice me because they want something from me. Even you. And I'm tired of it."

Kaycia felt hurt but also a bit guilty.

"Can you blame them?" she asked. "The things you do—they're part of who you are. A big part. If you want people to notice something else—to see more than your abilities—that's something you have to show them. If you run away and—"

"I didn't run away!"

"I never said you did. Bad choice of words. What I'm saying is not to *push* them away. While there may be some—a lot of people—who only want to take advantage—that isn't true of everyone. I promise. But you have to give them a chance. Once you close yourself off, it's no longer their fault. It's yours."

He looked away as though ready to end the conversation.

She took another bite, resisting the urge to pry further. She didn't want to make it seem she only wanted something from him.

After a while, though, she felt silly—because *all* relationships were based on give and take. People came together because they needed each other. No exceptions.

Aico's problem stemmed from his belief that he didn't need anyone. He'd found it possible to do most anything by himself. He didn't appreciate the costs of being alone.

Kaycia let it drop, getting the sense he wasn't open to advice. Instead, she made use of what time was left.

"Aico... During your explorations of this place, you haven't come across other people, have you?"

He looked at her as though she were crazy.

"Well... I thought you might've noticed signs—footprints, or... I don't know what I'm saying."

"Is that why you came? You followed me in here to look for someone else?"

She looked at him askance. "I thought we were respecting each other's secrets."

"You're right," he said. "I shouldn't have asked."

"It's all right. Aren't you interested?"

His brow furrowed in consternation. "It's just that... I need to be certain you won't come back. You can't be here right now. Ahman's about to go through significant changes."

"You mentioned that before. What do you mean?"

He closed his mouth, unwilling to say.

"Nothing?" she asked. "I'm not asking a full explanation or for anything confidential."

"I've already said too much."

"No. You haven't. You said the place was changing, but it's *always* changing!"

To her annoyance, he shrugged his shoulders.

"Could you, at least, say when? Will it be today? Tomorrow?"

"Probably not. I haven't decided. But what difference will it make if you're not coming back?"

Kaycia didn't have an answer. From the way he was talking, she was more and more tempted not to come back for a while. In comparison to this boy, she was practically useless. And if he thought it was dangerous, she should probably listen.

 AUSTIN LYNN CLARK

Her main problem was not knowing how to deal with Soril.

The boat neared the water's edge, and she could already see the enormous stone arches of Hin Gelnida. From here, it was a few minutes walk to the cave.

"Kaycia Eldren, of Carheim. I'll hold you to your word. You're to leave this place and tell no one you saw me. I'll not help again, just so we're clear."

"Aico..." she said, pausing a moment, not knowing what to say. Not wanting to lie or promise anything. "...You'll be careful, won't you?"

The boy merely shrugged and walked away.

Chapter 27
FALLING

A thin stream of water fell sideways through the air, crossing the street and blocking Nesil's path.

Four feet off the ground, it battered against an old cobbler's workshop, piling upward and outward. Some poured through broken windows, some flowed off the roof, with the rest cascading away on either side. From there, it continued sideways toward depths unknown.

Not truly an obstacle, Nesil could've ducked beneath the stream without a second thought. He could've braced himself and walked straight through, if he didn't mind getting wet. But it was an anomaly too intriguing to pass up. Unlike his new existence, this recalcitrant waterfall was a mystery he could investigate now. So he decided to follow it to its origin.

More often than not, the stream would cling to one wall of the blackened alley, giving him plenty of space to walk astride its current. But the alleys weren't straight, changing directions frequently, and the stream would leap from one side to the other. Nesil would be forced to duck or crawl and shield his face from spattering droplets. He followed it through a burned-out theater and storage room. And after a few more turns, to his disappointment, he remembered where he was.

It wasn't the same fountain from the church—the one presently lost to the impenetrable smoke and blistering embers—but it was a fountain of the same sinister design. If Nesil's memory served correctly, no one had set foot in this district for the past three years.

It was among the first neighborhoods to burn, back before anyone understood what was happening—before appropriate precautions took over. To his knowledge, it was one of the few districts not to produce a single survivor. And no one had mustered the courage to bury the dead.

The burned-out structures still stood, surrounding the marble fountain on all sides. The walls were blackened husks. The homes gutted and littered with bones and ash.

Despite all this, the water remained crystal clear. It continued to pour from the brass dish of the fountain's upper tier. The vessel, however, had fallen onto its edge, half submerged. Thus—a waterfall pointed sideways.

There, on the fountain's rim, sat Sefina.

Facing inward, her feet dipped into the reflective shallows. Her head was bowed, and she sat atop her hands, hiding them beneath her immaculate white skirt.

Nesil froze, uncertain what to feel. Moments earlier, he'd been racking his skull for any confirmation he was still alive. But testing *her*—checking if *she* could see him—this wasn't what he'd had in mind.

He had no plans for this. No words to mollify her inevitable outburst.

As quietly as possible, he backed the way he came—but it didn't matter. Perhaps it was her acute sense of hearing, or maybe she'd sensed his presence.

"You..." she breathed, with forlorn impassivity.

He should've been more careful. He should've never gotten this close.

"I—! I'll come back later," he lied before turning away.

"No. Wait!"

He broke into a run.

"You can see me?" she called out. "Stop!"

A wall of stone appeared before him, cutting off the alley in a dead end.

Without slowing down, he turned his shoulder into it, as though charging a wooden door.

The impact drove the air from his lungs. He bounced backward, and the world went out of focus. He was suddenly on the ground, feeling a sharp pain across his forehead, his knees, and his ribs.

He heard a high-pitched gasp. It was followed by swift footsteps and a stifled giggle.

Drawing a painful breath, he tried not to lose hope. A part of him realized, however, that the game had changed. The lessons he'd learned the night before—that only illusions could push back other illusions—took on a whole new meaning.

Sefina stood over him, her face filled with amusement and intrigue.

"Something's different," she observed, without making it a question. Reaching down to brush his face with her hand, she sat upon his stomach, straddling him with her legs. Her weight made it difficult to breathe.

Sefina pulled her fingers back in shock. "Damn..." she said, both confused and amazed. Then her brows lowered in accusation. "What did you do?"

"Get off!" he demanded.

A new sort of fear took hold of his mind. In the past, he'd been afraid of the things he couldn't see. Of the dangers obscured by the illusions—not the illusions themselves.

But, if Sefina were to surround him with flames at that moment, even on a whim, they might prove fatal...

She grabbed his jaw and raised her chin. "Tell me!" she said as though confronting a petulant child.

Arching his back, he threw her off. With his escape blocked by the wall, he made a break for the fountain.

A second wall appeared, blocking the alley from both ends.

Without thinking, he turned toward the black wooden buildings at his sides. As he'd suspected, the real walls posed no obstacle.

He found himself inside a crumbling apartment. But as he ran toward the decrepit hallway, the door slammed shut on its own.

He turned left, but Sefina materialized from thin air. Her arms were folded, and she was shaking her head.

Nesil spun and ran through a wine cabinet, but Sefina was also in the kitchen.

She was also in the foyer. And the study.

The next wall he tried proved solid.

"Calm down," she said.

He ran to a window, only to find it replaced by uninterrupted wall. One by one, the other windows disappeared, dropping the study into shadow.

"Let me out!" he yelled.

"Don't be such a baby."

Nesil's thoughts turned to the floor, but when he tried to pound his fists through it, the wood banged loud and hard, jarring his arms with the impact.

Sefina was learning, and she was blocking every exit.

The broken ceiling began to knit itself together. Only tiny slivers of white sunlight remained, coming in through dozens of slender cracks between rafters and boards.

Until even those filled in—every single one.

Spots drifted across his vision—afterimages of a world he could no longer see.

A small hand shoved him back against the wall and held him in place.

"Don't touch me!" he said, swinging out with his arm.

She easily caught his wrist and pinned it to the side.

Before he could move his other, she caught it with a *third* hand. This was so surprising, he had to count them again.

From the darkness came two more palms, soft and cool, grasping tightly onto his ankles. He felt himself lifted off the ground and sliding up the wall. Each of her five grips was small and delicate, but try as he might, he couldn't move more than an inch in any direction.

As he tried imagining the scene, he wondered if these extra limbs were independent. Were they conjured from the air, floating by themselves? Or did they protrude from her slim torso—like a deformed human spider?

Then, as though he were lying on the ground and not pressed against a wall, he felt her knees straddle his sides once more. She sat atop him, as she'd done in the alley outside, holding him down—well...sideways. And he couldn't help but wonder what kept them from falling.

"Don't waste your energy," said Sefina, her body trembling with exertion and restrained laughter. He could feel her breath against his face, mere inches away. It filled his nostrils with the sweetness of jasmine and ash.

"What do you want with me?" he demanded. As close as she was, Nesil should've been able to see her, but he couldn't. It was like being trapped in a sealed crypt. A mausoleum.

"Do you have to ask? I've never done this before. Not to anyone..." She smacked her lips. "I think I like it..."

With a surge of strength, he wrenched an arm free. He took a swing, found her neck, and tried shoving her away.

But it was as though she had arms coming out of her back. His wrist was caught a second time and slammed against the wall—so hard, the wood cracked. Yet more hands took hold of his elbows, shoulders, and knees. Their combined tension was so tight, he could barely move.

"Damn it!" he yelled. "You can't keep me here!" He knew his ravings were unlikely to sway her, but he didn't care. "Get the hell off!"

Her voice remained calm. "I can keep you as long as I want."

"Why in the gods' names would you want that?! I hate you! I HATE YOU! I—"

Soft fingers closed across his mouth. He struggled back, but yet another fist grabbed a handful of his hair. He tried biting fingers but failed.

"Now you listen to me," she said, her tone becoming menacing. Her head came close, filling his face with her hair. Her body pressed against his, and she spoke into his ear. "This is far less than you deserve, little boy..."

Nesil tried to yell through her grip, but her hand squeezed tighter. Instead of anything intelligible, he barely managed a whimper.

He clenched his eyes tight and sent tears down his face, wetting Sefina's hair and her clutched fingers.

"Stop it," she said.

Ordinarily, Nesil would've done just that. He'd push the grief aside and hold it in for later. Until now, he'd needed to stay strong. To think through the next problem. To plan his next move.

But now... Now...

"We're going to try this again," she said. "But only if you promise not to yell. You'll be a good boy, won't you?"

Nesil was tempted to lay there dumbly and refuse to take part in her game. He was worried, though, how Sefina might respond—to what lengths she might go to compel cooperation.

So he forced himself to nod.

"Now then..." she said, letting go of his mouth. "You should count yourself lucky. It's against my nature to be so...lenient. But heed my warning: my patience and mercy won't last forever."

There was an edge in her voice as sharp as death. It sent a shiver down his spine but also something else.

To his surprise, he felt satisfaction. He wanted her to be angry as proof he'd done something right.

"So it's true?" he asked. "What you said outside—no one can see you?"

Over a dozen hands grew taut at once. They stretched the limbs from his sockets, causing him to cry out in pain. But, just as quickly, she relaxed and exhaled in frustration.

In a voice barely controlled, she demanded, "Tell me what happened."

Nesil's chest was heaving, bewildered by how quickly—how easily—she handled him.

"Tell me!" she hissed.

He didn't know where to begin—until a new set of fingers began to close around his throat.

"It was the statue!" he choked. "Ashaira's statue! At the castle. It blew apart. It—"

Her hair swung against his face as she shook her head. "That couldn't have been you."

"I was there! I'm telling you—"

"But how could...?" Her voice died away as something clicked in her mind. And, in defeat, she breathed, "...Brach."

Nesil was grateful for the momentary respite, but he was also surprised she'd figured it out so quickly.

"That imbecile!" she screamed. "He knew better than to go anywhere near that place! I swear when I find him—!"

"There's no need."

"...He's dead?" She paused before reaching another conclusion. "You *killed* him?"

To his surprise, however, she didn't sound disappointed—or even skeptical. If anything, she seemed impressed.

Her reactions were confusing. She was sulking, yes, but he'd been waiting for more. When she recognized her loss—that her precious statue was gone—she should've peeled off his skin! She'd melt him into slag!

But she didn't.

She was angry, yes, but not nearly enough.

"My, my..." she said. "I never knew you had it in you."

Her voice, however, hadn't come from in front. Instead, it was as though a second Sefina, like a ghost in the wall, had materialized behind him. Her arms hooked beneath his in a gentle embrace, and she laid her head across his shoulder.

"What are you doing?" he asked.

She began to play with his hair. "What did you think would happen? It's just the two of us now. You...and me...and all the time in the world."

Nesil wanted to struggle—to demand she get off—but he felt strangely paralyzed.

In part, it was due to his overwhelming exhaustion. She was too damn strong, and he didn't have it in him to fight forever.

But there was also something else. A stir of memories—private daydreams he'd nearly forgotten. They weren't gentlemanly thoughts or ones he was proud of—but they'd been centered around her. Not the aeisr but the girl she was impersonating. The girl he'd loved.

"You're too worked up," she soothed, brushing his face with her fingertips. "We're on our honeymoon, remember?"

"No!" he said as his reserves kicked in. "You aren't her! Damn it—! She's dead because of you!"

Her bodies stiffened against him. "Does it matter?" they asked in unison. "You didn't marry her. You're married to us!" said one, while the other said, "Me."

"That's not how marriage works!" he groaned in disgust.

"But it is," said the one behind.

"It's the only reason you're still alive," said the other.

At first, Nesil took this as a threat—that she'd kill him if he didn't give in to her whims. But that seemed too petty, even for the aeisr.

Soft fingers caressed his back, poking through the tear in his shirt and finding the knife wound that should've spelled his death.

Only then did he understand. When the aeisr spoke about marriage, she was referring to the ceremony—the process of aligning souls.

She was suggesting Nesil's aspect had been changed, and he was now bonded to Aviathas, the god of Innovation. He'd become like her, and it'd saved his life.

"No!" he insisted as the blood drained from his face. "We're not the same!"

"We're more alike than you think." The two girls leaned their heads against his. "Willing to do anything to get what we want. Lie. Pretend. ...Even kill."

He tried again to break away, but they only pressed closer.

Nesil sensed he was missing something and needed to stop momentarily to figure out her angle. While teasing him with seduction wasn't unexpected—and certainly not beneath the aeisr's character—why was she doing so now?

As if reading his mind, they said, "You're overthinking this. I know you're still hurting—and our fight is far from over. But there'll be time for that later. This isn't about love but unwinding for a second."

"So you admit this isn't real?"

"Most things aren't, Nesil—when you think about it. But they don't need to be real to possess a purpose. After last night, we could both use a moment to recover, don't you think?"

Nesil disagreed. While there was sense in her words, he couldn't help but suspect she was after something else. She didn't stand to gain anything from keeping him here or stalling him a while—so what did she want?

He made his best guess. "I think you're frightened. You've just realized you have *no one*. And you're desperate for reasons to keep me around—even ones that don't make sense."

"Oh sure..." they said, acting annoyed. "I'm terrified of losing you—a stupid little boy."

The anger in her tone caught him off guard.

"Gods, Nesil—you're smarter than this! Or are you so full of yourself? You think *you* have what it takes to keep us satisfied?"

His cheeks flushed red. "Well...no... But I'm not talking about that. There are more basic needs. It's not about losing me—specifically—but about you, being alone...again."

Nesil had nearly forgotten their earlier conversation—back before the night fell apart. Though it was easier to view the aeisr as an unfeeling monster—she *did* possess emotion. For a brief moment, after learning of Kadrek's death, Nesil had even found empathy for what she felt against his grandfather.

"You speak like I've given you a choice!" she hissed. "You don't think I can keep you?

That I can't force you to do anything I want?"

Nesil was hesitant to contradict her—afraid, out of spite, she'd make good on her threats. But his confidence was rising.

"That isn't what you want. If you were after a plaything, you could make one from air. You could have anything you wanted—but you'd still be unsatisfied. Your illusions bore you and can't possess more meaning than what *you* put into them. That's why you need someone like me—to mix things up and challenge your decisions."

Nesil lifted his chin. "It's the one thing you love about me the most—and *hate* the most! Because I use my agency to reject you."

He expected her to laugh, but she didn't.

For a long moment, the two Sefinas said nothing.

Then, one by one, her hands let go. The girl melted back into the wall while the other stood and retreated across the floor.

Strangely, Nesil's body didn't fall. Somehow, he felt like he was lying on the ground, and it was Sefina, instead, walking up the wall away from him.

Lights appeared around the room. Tiny red flames flickered atop a multitude of candles adorning the floor. Even more rested atop blackened tables and decrepit wooden shelves.

Sefina had gone back to two arms and legs. From the way her hair and dress hung normally—toward the actual floor—she was not experiencing the same gravity as he.

"You leave me no choice but to do this the hard way," she said, her voice forlorn.

When she turned around, her eyes were empty sockets, spilling blood down her front. "I've never shown aversion to destroying my toys—you should know that after what's become of Seldor. A broken prince, after all, beats no prince at all."

Nesil realized he might not have thought this through.

The candle flames lengthened, rising around her.

"Care to make a bet?" she asked. "How long you'll take before coming around? Because I've seen your mettle—how easily you break."

"Are you insane?!"

She cocked her head. "Sort of?"

Nesil didn't know what to say. If the girl was really off her rocker, he'd only succeeded in digging his own grave.

"Before long," she continued, "you'll be begging me to stay. You'll be a sniveling wreck whose only desire is to please."

"I don't doubt it," he admitted. "I know I'll break. My threshold for pain is guaranteed to disappoint."

Her lips curled into a snarl—but the fires' movement slowed as though trapped in thick air.

He pushed on. "See? You don't even know what you want anymore! For so long, you thought killing Renat was the answer—and maybe it helped, but not like you'd hoped. Your sadness lingers—and you know what? Taking your frustrations out on me *won't* be any different."

When she didn't respond, Nesil felt certain he'd made a mistake. He'd been grasping at straws, and even if there was a lick of truth to what he said, the aeisr was too prideful to confess a damn thing.

Eventually, however, her expression grew hard.

With a turn of her head that was almost imperceptible, the side wall exploded. Daylight flooded in as the shattered timbers burst outward, leaving a hole twice the size of an average doorway.

As easy as that, she was setting him free.

She'd forgotten his momentary disagreement with gravity—but he didn't feel like pointing this out. He'd rather climb the sides of buildings—and risk falling sideways forever—than give her the chance to change her mind.

"Just go," she said, devoid of emotion.

Nesil shouldn't have cared. He wouldn't have cared, except...

Something still bothered him. If her feelings were authentic—if she was so terrified of being alone, then why wasn't she more upset about the statue?

It didn't make sense. For someone whose existence depended on that artifact—who couldn't talk to anyone, who couldn't play with anyone—shouldn't *that* have been her focus?

Or was the change so monumental—so unfathomable—she hadn't had the chance to process what it meant?

That didn't seem likely.

No. The only reason for her to act this way—as a disgruntled version of her playful self—was if she *wasn't* concerned.

She wasn't bothered about losing anything. She wasn't worried about the statue because...

...Because the statue was incomplete.

He felt suddenly stupid, wondering why he hadn't seen it before. From the beginning, Ashaira had been comprised of a chest, a head, and an arm.

Where was the rest of her?

It was only a guess, but Nesil believed he was onto something. And without a shift in tactics—if he chose this moment to sever ties with the aeisr—he might forever lose his chance to finish what he'd started.

Shoulders slumped, Sefina walked away.

"Wait!" he said, trying to think. There was no way to apologize without sounding insincere.

Her eyes were still bleeding, but she, at least, stopped to listen.

"Perhaps there's another way—we don't need to decide now. Maybe there *is* something between us—I won't call it friendship—but this is happening too fast. We should think before—"

She scowled in irritation. "Take all the time you need." And she turned away again.

"What do you want from me?" he asked. "Am I supposed to pretend you didn't kill everyone I know? That you didn't try to kill *me* on more than one occasion?"

Her face was confused. "*This* is how you argue for me to stay?"

"No! I just want you to understand—this is hard for both of us." He realized his words weren't helping. "I don't know what I'm asking... Maybe a truce?"

"A truce?"

"Provisionally. Long enough to find certainty. While I know I don't like you, I *don't* know if being alone would be better."

It was a feeling she'd identify—and it might also hold truth for himself.

Sefina eyed him with suspicion. "And what would we do with more time together?"

"Most likely? ...We'll argue. But we can keep it civil. We can settle on a place we both want to go. And, before we do anything, we should both give consent."

The aeisr groaned. "You obviously have somewhere in mind. Out with it, then."

Nesil paused, uncertain he'd been obvious about anything.

He knew better, however, than to mention the place she'd come from—the most likely home for the rest of the statue. If he didn't do this carefully, she'd guess his intentions.

"Well..." he began. "Since you don't know what you want, we could try something else. Didn't you say Kadrek wanted something? Some kind of key? You mentioned it before—but he never got it because of my grandfather's failure?"

She was angered by the reminder but also intrigued. "Why would you give a damn about Kadrek?"

"Not him, specifically. But it'd help me understand what this was all about—why Seldor got involved. If it was even worth it."

"None of this was worth it."

"Maybe not for you. *Definitely* not for me. But Kadrek thought it was. To the point he was willing to sacrifice his life."

Sefina still didn't bite. If anything, she seemed poised to strike—unwilling to confront such painful memories.

"You don't want to think about it—I get that," said Nesil. "It's easier to blame his death on Renat—end of story. But there's more to it than that. You know there is."

"Some stupid key?"

Nesil raised his hands. "You're right. It might not even be there anymore. But that's not the point. What happened between you is still unresolved. This might be the 'key' to restoring your sense of peace."

Sefina was unamused by the pun.

Eventually, however, she sighed. "It's not that easy. From the beginning, Kadrek needed help from another person. As an ordinator, he needed someone from this world. Someone physical—which excludes the two of us. It's the whole reason your grandfather was there—to reach the Nightmare Throne and bring back the prize."

"So?" asked Nesil. "We wait. We might not find someone tomorrow or even this year—but someone *has* to show up, eventually, right?"

Nesil waited for her objection—to say the plan was impossible. They'd never find anyone because no one could see them. After the statue's destruction, it wasn't an option.

So, when Sefina said nothing, it was as good a confirmation as any.

Part of the statue remained.

Nesil felt both relieved and dismayed. The cycle, very nearly, had started all over again. The aeisr would've found a new victim—a new people to destroy—and Nesil wouldn't have known.

He'd been *this close* to throwing the game. But, out of sheer luck, he'd still be at the aeisr's side. He'd follow her home to where it all started.

Sefina eyed him thoughtfully. "I guess we have a deal."

"We do?" he asked, trying not to seem excited.

She smiled. "I know you've got your reasons. You weren't trying to cheer me up—but this helps... Thanks."

After a moment of awkward silence, he asked, "So what now?"

"We can go."

"Right this moment?"

With a loud crack, the wall behind him shuddered and broke apart.

He fell backward through the air, shielding his eyes from the sudden brightness and the shower of wooden splinters.

Ten feet later, he landed in a heap against the building across the alley.

"Perhaps a warning next time?" he said through the hole above.

He brushed dust from his clothing and awkwardly stood up.

The world, however, did nothing to correct itself. He stood sideways against the brick wall, surrounded by shattered timbers.

"Sefina?" he called out, warily.

When she didn't come down, his curiosity took him to the building's edge. He leaned with caution as though peering off a cliff. The sight was dizzying, with the street going straight down half a mile or so.

Before he could react, Sefina was behind him.

"Boo!" she said with a slight push.

He tumbled off the edge, head over heels, passing building after building in a terrifying blur.

With gaining speed, he reached the end of the straightway, where an old library rushed to greet him.

Nesil screamed, but there was no impact. The rooms flew by so quickly, he couldn't make sense of them.

He burst out the other side—outdoors, once again. He traversed another building. Another. Another.

"Sefina!" he shouted. "This isn't what I meant!"

The city ended, and he found himself surrounded by trees and open air.

"Sefina!!" he shouted again.

But he kept on falling, with no end in sight.

Chapter 28
CRUMBLING FOUNDATIONS

"Tell me more about these vines."

The question came from someone new—a man Kaycia had never seen on the council. He had a wide, iron beard and a freckled scalp. His thick robe bore testament to some high office and was suggestive of Carheim's noble gentry.

"You remember Sir Laurus Cairn?" asked Soril in a careful tone. "I mentioned his arrival when you came in this morning."

It was only then that Kaycia recognized the problem. Due to her recent troubles, she'd failed to make her scheduled report. And since Soril didn't know the entire story, nor how long she'd spent reestablishing contact with her sister, he'd simply assumed she'd lost track of time. Regardless, Soril had lied on her behalf, so this new official wouldn't doubt her professionalism.

"Of course..." she said, somewhat convincingly—while refraining to ask the obvious question, *Why was the man here?*

Laurus smiled primly. "We have much to discuss. But, first, indulge me. Did the vines move in truth or only in seeming?"

The question took her by surprise, as she had yet to describe the horrific experience. It could only mean he'd seen such vines before or had heard tale from someone who had.

"A hallucinogenic," she replied. "Induced by spores. The effect inhibits motor functions and creates the perception of motion, as you say. But it's merely a snare. Of the most insidious and painful variety."

"Yet, here you stand. Completely unharmed."

Kaycia said nothing. It wasn't that she feared reprisal for her actions—for making contact with Aico—but she'd rather keep things simple. She had no way of knowing how the council would respond. She didn't understand her feelings for the boy.

When she was silent too long, Soril vouched for her. "Our Miss Eldren is being modest. It should be plain, however, that what's impossible for others is not the same when applied to transcendents."

Neranda sat back in her seat and rolled her eyes. Thankfully, she had enough respect for Soril not to interfere.

"Ah," said Laurus. "So you got out in the nick of time?"

He was dubious, but Kaycia chose to treat this as a statement, not a question. Rather than lie, she turned it around. "If these vines have appeared outside Ahman, why hasn't the public been warned?"

"They've been warned—when necessary. Our rangers, for instance, have been thoroughly briefed. In the city, however, it would only fuel people's nightmares and stir unrest. These are the dragons and tigers of the untamed forests—of the depths of the sea—so far removed from civilization, they might as well not exist."

Kaycia wasn't sure she agreed with this, but she was grateful, at least, the knowledge wasn't held hostage.

"All right," she said. "So what warning can you give me? How have your people escaped in the past?"

"Usually? They don't." His tone was inexpressive. "Which was why I was hoping you might tell us more."

Kaycia did what she could to hide her disappointment. Hoping to move things along, she asked, "How much do you know?"

"Not much, I'm afraid. The vines are similar to the abyss we've been facing till now—but also different. So categorically different an associate of mine has given them their own designation."

She raised a brow in question.

"For our usual creatures," the man continued, "the ones with silencing auras—he's coined the term *Isolation*. It's the way they hunt, catching you by yourself and hindering your senses. These vines, on the other hand, hinder your strengths. They ensnare and disable. And are thusly called *Subjugation*."

Just hearing the two names sent a chill down her spine.

The man made a face. "Personally, I disagree with the nomenclature—as it generates misunderstanding. The abyssal layers are so dissimilar to our aspects, they shouldn't be made to sound as such. But that's neither here nor there. The names are useful if nothing else."

"Are there only two?" she asked. "Abyssal layers?"

The man scratched his head. "Difficult to say. It's tempting to put names on what we don't understand. There are places that induce paranoia or forgetfulness. But just because phenomena can't be explained, doesn't mean they're the result of the abyssal current. Not all the time, anyway."

Kaycia nodded.

"Now it's your turn," said Laurus. "I want to know how you escaped."

Once again, Kaycia faced a decision—but, for some reason, she still couldn't talk about Aico. It made her feel guilty, as she wanted to regain Soril's trust.

Except... This stranger had come in and taken over leadership. For some reason, Soril had taken a back seat, and she couldn't ignore her rising misgivings.

"I... I just got lucky. I sensed something was wrong. A single step closer and I might've never made it out."

The man was irritated. "Is there something you're not telling us? You appear rather frightened."

"Of course, I'm frightened! Before today, I didn't know these things existed!"

"But now that you do, could you do it again? Can you elude their trap?"

"It's not just the vines," she said, remembering Aico's warning. "The city keeps changing. Becoming increasingly dangerous."

Laurus' smile was woefully condescending. "Master Soril's reassured me you're one of our best. That you not only survived an encounter with this rogue transcendent, but that you tracked him down in the middle of battle."

She stared at Soril, wondering what else the commander might've shared.

"I'll just get to the point," said Laurus, leaning forward in his seat. "I need reassurance you can finish the job."

"Which one?" she asked, with growing frustration. "I apologize, but I thought Master Soril was in charge of this investigation."

Laurus raised a brow, while Soril gave her a significant look, urging her to show more respect.

But Kaycia would have none of it. Though she had only herself to blame, she was tired of this posturing. "Who is this man?"

"I thought you knew," said Laurus, without blinking. "I'm the man offering a full pardon for your sister. Contingent, of course, on your willingness to cooperate."

She stood there, stunned, unable—or unwilling—to grasp what he was saying. What the hell did he know about Elyriel? And what office did he hold to lobby such promises?

It was altogether possible he didn't have the details. Or that this pardon was for something else—that Soril had modified her story to protect her.

Otherwise, she feared she'd made a grave mistake.

"Oh good," said Laurus. "I've gotten your attention."

She studied Soril's face, but the commander merely shook his head as though in apology. He didn't try to reassure her or correct her apparent misapprehensions.

"Could you be more specific?" she asked, returning to Laurus.

"Your confusion is warranted. I've sat in judgment for cases like yours—heretics, illegitimates, and the like. None of them good."

"I see," she said, swallowing hard. "You...represent the church."

"The state. But I don't think the difference should matter to you. In matters of ascension, Carheim's position is famously inflexible. And under any other circumstance, you wouldn't be spared."

It was still too much for Kaycia to believe. In all her experience, it was unheard of for the church to make exceptions for anyone.

But then she saw it—the sullen mood that'd pervaded the tent since her arrival. The way no one was speaking or arguing with Laurus.

Something had happened.

Something terrible.

"What I'm about to tell you stays in this tent. Do I have your solemn vow?"

Kaycia licked her lips and nodded.

"Carheim's in danger."

Her breath caught in her throat. "...We're under attack?"

"Not exactly. It's more the result of gradual change. The city won't fall today or a month from today—probably... But it's hanging on an edge."

She didn't know what to say. From the somber look on Soril's face, it had to be true.

The man continued. "It has to do with the changes to the land. You're already familiar with how that works—how the terrain shifts when nobody's around?"

She struggled to keep a straight face. In comparison to Ahman, where entire streets could move when you faced the wrong direction, the changes to the countryside were relatively harmless.

"It's getting worse?" she asked. "Around Carheim?"

"That's one way of putting it," the man said dryly.

"But how? There are people there! Over twenty thousand people!"

Laurus shook his head. "I'm not talking of the surroundings. It's one thing to look down at a map and see the abyssal line draw nearer our walls. If that were all we had to worry about, I'd be happy as a peach. But the unfortunate truth is that the world is *not* represented by only two dimensions."

She frowned, struggling to see what he was getting at. Until it dawned on her.

"There've been changes...beneath the city?"

It was such a frightening thought, she hoped she was wrong.

But Laurus smiled thinly and didn't correct her.

"About a month ago, two priests emerged from the catacombs, reporting a collapse. Happens all the time, particularly on the lower levels. The place is ancient, and we don't have the manpower to keep it in good repair.

"Nonetheless, we sent a team to investigate—but, by the time they arrived, it'd gotten worse. It wasn't just the ceiling that caved in—but the floor."

Kaycia envisioned a dark tunnel disappearing into the ground. After her experience beneath the monastery, she could imagine it perfectly.

It made sense, didn't it? No matter how many people lived in the city proper, hardly anyone spent much time below. It was the perfect place for the current to manifest and for the creatures to sneak in beneath their noses.

"Do the people know of this?"

"I'm afraid not. If word got out, we'd have a riot on our hands. Too many would make a run for it, and we'd have no way of protecting them."

Kaycia groaned and tried to see the whole picture. "So let me get this straight. You want me to come back with you? You think if I fight these creatures, it'd put Carheim on my side?"

He shook his head. "While an attack is possible, it isn't our chief concern. There's no reason for the creatures to mount an offensive."

"What do you mean?"

"They won't have to." Laurus' gaze bore into her own. "The city's sinking, Kaycia, and I'm not speaking metaphorically."

Only then did she realize she wasn't thinking big enough.

He went on. "We're not talking a single tunnel. We've sent companies of men to assess the damage—only to find enormous caverns previously absent. They extend like tendrils beneath the city walls. And they keep growing larger, every day."

"How enormous?"

"There are already cracks in the city's foundation."

To Kaycia, it felt like her world was crashing down. While her memories of Carheim were far from pleasant, due to the rising refugees gathered within its walls—it'd always been home. Everyone she'd known had put up with the filth and risk of disease because...well...there was no safer place.

The city had been an impenetrable fortress. It'd stood as their nation's final refuge—meant to outlast the smaller villages. In her mind, it was the place where everything ended. Where, despite it all, she'd return when the world fell to pieces.

If it was destroyed now, then... Where else was there to go? The garrisons weren't large enough to house that many people. They'd have to flee to other lands despite knowing nowhere was safe. And no one had the resources to support outsiders.

They'd be turned away to fend for themselves in the countryside.

"So that's it? You think Carheim will let my sister live so long as we help the evacuation?"

He shook his head. "If what Soril tells me is true, the answer's right here."

She was about to protest—but she got the impression he wasn't talking of Irisea. But what, then? He couldn't be referring to Ahman, either. Though the ruins offered shelter, the people would never cross the barrier.

"Dark heavens..." she breathed. "You're talking about—" She nearly spoke his name. "...the Navaran."

Laurus narrowed his gaze over steepled fingers.

Kaycia might've thought of it herself—of using creation to save their home. After seeing what Aico could do, he could replace the missing substructure with spikes or pillars, or...

But she also saw the problem. While the boy might be capable of generating the material, the solution was impermanent. It boiled down to a matter of scale. It was one thing for the boy to make an apple that would last and quite another to perpetuate tons upon tons of solid rock. At the moment he left town, it'd all disappear.

Which meant...the boy needed to stay. They wanted him to fix Carheim's problem and never be allowed to leave.

"It won't work," she said. "Even if I found him—even if I asked—he'd never come!"

Laurus' voice was forlorn. "It was never my intention to give him a choice."

"There has to be another way!" she insisted. "We can evacuate! We can go somewhere else—"

"No," intoned Laurus. "We can't. Just listen to yourself. Do you have any idea what that would take? We're talking twenty-four and a half thousand people! Do you have a plan to keep them safe?"

Kaycia turned on Soril. "And you're okay with this? Kidnapping a—?"

She was about to say child, but they didn't have that information.

"A what?" asked Laurus. "Finish the question."

She shook her head, refusing to excuse them. Even if the plan was to enslave a grown man—it was beyond horrendous.

"I can't do this! Even if I went back, I don't have the power to stop another transcendent—to detain him! You've seen what he can do!"

The judge sighed. "It's not so complicated. A small trace of poison. So long as you're careful, he won't see it coming."

Kaycia gaped. "You're serious? All of you?"

Since she'd first met Soril, he'd always exhibited a perfect moral character. He made the right choice, even when it was hard—to the point of aggravation. And yet, he chose this moment to stop doing so?

She swallowed. "You have family, don't you? Living in Carheim?"

None of the council needed to answer.

When it all came down to it, the decision was more complicated than enslaving a single boy. While it might be easier to believe in a moral high ground—that kidnapping Aico was simply not an option—it'd be equally wrong not to do anything. If they chose another path, the deaths of thousands of people would be on their hands.

Laurus sighed. "What about you? Don't you have someone?"

Kaycia didn't want to talk about her mother. While she loved the woman, there was a separation between them beyond physical distance.

She couldn't balance Aico's life against her mother's. It wasn't even a comparison between one person and twenty thousand.

No matter how horrible she might feel doing anything to Aico, it couldn't surpass the guilt she already possessed—her obligation to her sister.

Soril licked his lips in hesitation. "Of course, there's one possibility we haven't yet discussed."

"What do you mean?" she asked, without much hope. "If you had a better solution, you would've brought it up earlier."

Neranda leaned forward.

Even Laurus was confused. "What's this about?"

"I said *possibility*," clarified the commander. "Not solution... Right now, the Navaran is our surest bet. We know where he is and know he can help. I only hesitate because of how you might respond."

"Just tell me," said Kaycia.

"We wouldn't need the Navaran if someone else could help instead."

"Like who?" asked Laurus.

But Kaycia already knew who Soril meant, and it was all she could do not to curse in frustration.

She was sick of his promises—the false hope that Irisea might heal her sister. And, now, the goddess was going to fix this, too?

He raised his brows, at a loss.

"I *have* been looking," said Kaycia, not knowing if she was more angry at him or at herself for listening. "But I haven't seen signs of the Navaran's presence, let alone that of anyone else."

"Like who?" repeated Laurus.

Neither Kaycia nor Soril spoke a word to clarify.

Her anger cooled, and she forced herself back to their original discussion.

"If I agree to this...and fail. If the Navaran slips through my fingers and makes a break for it—what then? Will you have mercy on Elyriel?"

"I will," said Laurus without hesitation. "So long as you make an honest effort, I guarantee Carheim will have your back."

"We're on your side," added Soril. "With everything coming, it'd be a travesty if the judges can't see that. We need you, Kay. Even without the Navaran—or anyone else—we still need *you*."

His plea wasn't necessary, as she realized her mind was already made up.

But there was nothing they could say to make her feel good about it.

Chapter 29
DEEP WATER

The world fell away in a sickening blur.

As Nesil crashed through evergreens above the forest floor, he took control of his spin and pointed his feet downward—or rather, in the direction he was traveling. This made it difficult to see his eastern trajectory—or was it southeast?—but he felt more comfortable having the world rush toward his feet rather than his head. In the end, he was less concerned with where he was going and only knew he'd left Seldor far, far behind.

He should've felt liberated. He'd spent years yearning for this moment—to escape his besieged kingdom and see the great outdoors. But he felt no relief, and he didn't feel free. Even without his overturning stomach, he would've still felt sick—he was sure of it.

Looking up, he caught sight of Sefina gaining on him.

Her body was arched in a perfect swan dive, pressing her face into the wind, trailing her arms and legs behind. The white hem of her dress was a flutter of movement, snapping like a sail. It was the same with her light hair, fanning out to glisten and shine. Her eyes were closed, as serene as they were fearless.

"You're gonna get us killed!" he called out above the rush of air.

She pretended not to hear, though the corners of her lips might've stretched up a little.

"This is crazy!" he continued. "What's the hurry? We've got nothing but time—you said so yourself!"

Opening her eyes, she brought her head close to his—only upside down. "It's not like you could've said your goodbyes. Or maybe you wanted to pack a bedroll? An extra pair of boots? Some cooking supplies?"

He supposed she had a point. No matter the length of their journey, they didn't need physical preparations—only mental ones.

The trees disappeared, and he was falling through empty space. Instead of rocks and fields, there were nothing but clouds and endless sky.

When he turned, he saw a rippling sheet of glass extending beside him like an infinite plane. And he looked up just in time to see the shoreline shrink away, up into the distance.

"We're crossing the sea? I never agreed to this!"

Her expression became one of pity. "Must you always be so negative? Most humans dream of flying—or am I wrong?"

"Flying?" he echoed incredulously. "This isn't flying!"

She shook her head in disappointment. "What would you call it, then? Falling? Let me show you the difference."

There wasn't time to scream before the waves gave a tilt.

Nesil's body skipped across the water in a mad tumble. Each impact had the force to break bones—the back of his shoulder, his opposite hip. White water sprayed his face as his heel cut the surface and whipped him around.

He plunged under, and the icy depths slowed his spin.

Bubbles escaped his nose as he looked up at the sunlight, glittering through the surface. Through the shimmer, he saw Sefina descend and land gently atop the waves with the balls of her feet.

He'd just begun to swim toward her when something grabbed his leg. He looked down as dark figures rose from the depths—men and women with ragged clothing and stained teeth.

In panic, he kicked hard, stretching a hand upward. He called for help, but a flurry of bubbles muted his voice. He choked on saltwater.

"Oh, *do* calm down." Her voice wasn't distorted as he'd expect but crisp and clear as though standing beside him. "What are you so afraid of? Drowning?"

Nesil continued to thrash—despite knowing she was right.

"It's okay," she cooed as her body swam into view from behind him—as though she'd been there all along. She glided effortlessly before his face as the light cast a web across her billowing hair and slender form. "Go on. Take a breath."

He hesitated, unwilling to be tricked.

"Or not," she continued. "Your takeaway from this is that *you don't need to breathe.* At least, not like you used to."

She spoke as though oblivious to the woman climbing his legs.

"That's not the problem!" he tried to say—with the last air from his lungs. His voice still sounded fifteen feet underwater.

He pushed down with his hands, catching the intruder by the head.

There were more of them now, floating up through the water—people, he realized, who were oddly familiar.

And he realized he'd seen them before. This elderly woman, with iron hair and threadbare clothing—he'd seen her at the market on more than one occasion.

As though bored, Sefina waved her hand, and the woman let go. She didn't disappear but floated to the side, joining the mass of drifting bodies.

When Nesil discovered he still had air, he wanted to yell. He wanted to scream at the aeisr for the indelicate landing. She'd known what he'd meant, not wanting to fly. But she could never resist her need for amusement.

Even now, his mind struggled to accept where he was. After taking a few breaths—entirely on accident and entirely painless—it was still unbearably difficult to breathe. Though he knew his body remained in one piece, it did nothing to soothe his burning muscles.

But rather than yell, as she'd expect him to do, he tried to think of something else.

"What are they doing here?" he asked. His voice was distorted, but she still understood.

With a shrug, she said, "No matter where I go, there's always a few."

"But that's not— These aren't just wanderers—they're the exact same ones! I recognize that woman!"

Sefina raised her brow as though awaiting his point.

"Are they tied to you somehow? How else could they get here so fast?"

She frowned in consideration, but after looking once at the woman he'd singled out, she quickly lost interest.

"I've never really thought about it, I suppose."

Nesil was so appalled, it became easier to forget he was talking underwater. "You mean to tell me you don't know what these things are?"

"Well... It's not like I know *nothing*. There was a time I used to follow them and watch what they did."

Nesil was surprised. On many occasions, he'd done the exact same thing—shadowing them out of sheer curiosity. He'd done so carefully, being mindful of traps, but he'd always been amazed by how lifelike they seemed.

"In some ways, they're family," she continued. "They were all I had when I was on my own. Without them, I might've never learned what it's like to be human."

"From *them*? You're serious?"

"Why not?"

"Because humans aren't fake! These things are just going through the motions—"

She shook her head, causing her hair to float in a shimmering halo. "And you should know, right? Because none of you humans 'go through the motions.' You know exactly what everyone's feeling, and it's *never* an act." Her eyes bore into his, pointing out his hypocrisy.

"You know what I mean..." he muttered.

"No, Nesil. I don't think *you* know what you mean."

Without giving him the chance to argue, she pressed on. "Honestly, I don't see your problem. To the outside observer, there's hardly a difference. These 'fakes,' as you call them—they fight about money and enjoy sleeping late. They feel insecure about their bodies and hold grudges against their colleagues. And when they're done, they go home to their wives—or their neighbors' wives—and they—"

"I get it," he interrupted.

Nesil couldn't argue, having witnessed these idiosyncrasies for himself—but he'd always passed them off as complex redirection. They'd been part of the aeisr's grand scheme, to keep his kingdom distracted while the noose tightened.

Now, she was saying this wasn't the case at all. The High Aeisr wasn't in charge, and they'd been doing these things long before she came around.

They aren't alive, he wanted to say—but he could guess her response. She'd question if some humans were alive in the truest sense. Or worse, she'd turn it on him and ask if *he* was alive after losing his body.

Sefina surprised him, then, by volunteering a detail he'd been missing. "If you had time to follow them longer, you'd uncover the biggest difference. When real humans die, they don't start at the beginning and repeat the cycle."

"Wait..." said Nesil. "These things are caught in a loop?"

"When they deviate, it's due to my interference—like now, for example. I can instruct them to perform menial tasks—make them follow you around. But invariably, they'll get back on track and resume their routine."

She smiled weakly. "It gets boring, after a while—watching them repeat their lives, over and over."

He wasn't sure which disturbed him more—that their routines went on for so long, or the fact the aeisr was so ancient, she'd seen the sequence more than once.

"How could you watch them all these years and still not know where they came from? You didn't investigate?"

"Of course I did," she said, turning away.

"But...?" he coaxed.

Her expression was evasive—which, of course, was utter bullshit. She was either pressing him to ask because she wanted to tell him—or she was after something else. For all he knew, this was a test to gauge his reactions—to see where his true interests lie.

Feigning reluctance, she went on. "There's only one explanation that makes any sense."

He grew impatient. "Which is?"

"Well... The statue of course."

And there it was, like an open invitation.

Nesil considered his next words carefully. While he was glad he hadn't broached the topic himself, he couldn't pretend *not* to be interested. That'd be nearly as suspicious as asking where it was and how he might destroy it.

"You say 'of course,' but I don't get it. Isn't the statue's function to make them visible—so regular people can see them—see *us*? What does Ashaira have to do with them repeating themselves?"

She gave him a look. "You're not even thinking. You mention 'Ashaira' and 'the statue' in a single breath without consideration for how they're related."

Nesil turned his head in confusion.

"You've never wondered why it's *her*? If the statue's only purpose was to empower our aspect, wouldn't the likeness of Aviathas be more appropriate?"

Her question stirred up memories—conversations he'd overheard when the siege had begun. But, even back then, the question had been easy to dismiss.

"Because it's Ashaira," he said, with a touch of doubt. "The betrayer."

Sefina smirked. "Spoken like a true idiot. And how, pray tell, did Ashaira betray anyone?"

"You know I can't answer that." His tone became excited. "But *you* know what happened?"

Her smile thinned. "I've been around a long time—but not that long."

He couldn't hide his disappointment. "So nobody knows."

"I know there aren't grounds to accuse her of anything. But your people don't care so long as someone's to blame."

"Can we step back a bit? You were saying she had something to do with the statue. So where's the connection?"

She sighed. "I have to spell everything out, don't I?"

"I'm missing information!" he said defensively.

"You have enough."

His mouth gaped.

"Didn't you pay attention at school? Tell me, Nesil, what role does Ordination hold? What's it supposed to do?"

The question caught him off guard. While she was right—he *had* learned this—it was a topic he'd never probed in depth. Since the Ordinators were gone, without hope of coming back, none of his teachers had given them much importance.

"Come on," she said, drifting up toward the surface. "Time for an object lesson."

Nesil watched as she shot through the water. She didn't swim with her arms but was propelled by some mechanism he didn't understand.

Left with no choice, he swam clumsily after her.

Twenty seconds later, his head burst above the waves. He spat out seawater and sucked in large gulps of air—more for his comfort than any real need. It felt good to breathe, and no one could tell him otherwise.

Sefina, however, hadn't merely reached the surface. Once again, she stood upon the waves, bobbing up and down, dripping water from her skirt. Her blond hair was plastered to her neck, glistening wet in the sun. Her dress clung so tight, it didn't hide—

Nesil turned away, feeling his face flush red.

She was doing it again. Pretending to be innocent, with her carefree smile—while her every move was a calculated tease.

The ocean grew dark.

Still treading water, he looked down in alarm as something large rose from the depths. It didn't writhe like a creature but steadily grew to the size of a city block.

His feet found purchase as it pushed through the surface, spilling water in every direction. The force of the current would've dragged him with it, but Sefina grabbed his shoulder and held him like a vice.

As the water receded, it revealed dark basalt underneath, smooth and jagged. There were clumps of brown seaweed and clustered barnacles.

They were standing on a beach. Somewhere in the middle of the ocean, they were *standing on a beach.*

Sefina gazed past the water's edge to where a second island waited, over a hundred yards distant.

"Perhaps you'll remember this from school," she said. "A group of ascendants came to the water's edge, but the bridge had been destroyed. How did each cross?"

"What?"

Shivering, he gazed across the water. He noticed a few light fragments beneath the surface—all that was left of the bridge she'd mentioned.

"Oh, come on, Nesil! I know you've heard this before."

He had—but the experience of it all made it difficult to think. The breeze tore through his clothing, and his nostrils burned of salt.

"I'll start you off. The creator fashions a bridge of his own and walks the distance."

Nesil made a face, wanting to protest. Her words seemed a gross oversimplification. From what he understood of creators, it would require hours—if not days—to shape anything on the scale of a bridge. It made more sense to fashion a small boat instead.

But, for the purposes of the illustration, it hardly mattered.

"All right," said Nesil, ignoring the cold. "The transfigurer has some options. He can add energy to his momentum and leap the gap. Or, alternatively, he can draw energy from the water and freeze the surface."

She nodded curtly. "Next?"

"The convictor alters the tensile strength of its surface—"

"The *what*?" she asked, wrinkling her nose.

"He makes the water *want* to hold him up."

She didn't look convinced—despite the fact she'd been doing something similar only minutes ago—but she accepted the answer.

"The founder has it easiest of all. He makes it as though the water isn't there and makes the crossing in a single step.

"The equilibrist is nearly as fast. He falls the distance as if the island were beneath him."

"And the devoter..." He smiled as though reaching the punchline of a joke. "With a binding, compels the fish to carry him across."

Sefina didn't laugh but continued to wait. "All right. Next?"

Nesil paused, confused. In the illustration, there were usually only six ascendants.

With a smirk, he added, "The innovator crashes into the water's surface, dragged against his will by a maniacal—"

She stopped him with a hand. "Nice try. But you're not an innovator."

"I'm not?"

Sefina scowled. "Honestly?"

Nesil didn't see the problem. Not too long ago, she'd made such a big deal he was just like her.

She shook her head. "That's like saying by marrying an ascendant, you'd gain her abilities. It doesn't work that way, does it?"

He conceded her point—and tried not to feel stupid.

"Okay..." he said. "The innovator glides across the water while she drags along a helpless—"

"Just skip Innovation. We can walk, fly—we can literally do anything you can think of. It's what the word *means*. We could walk across the bottom of the sea if we wanted."

"So...what's next? Stratum?"

"Skip that one, too. Stratists *made* the layers and the laws that define them. As such, they have more options than we do. I'm waiting for Ordination."

"But that's what I don't know! Wasn't that the reason for this whole demonstration?"

"Sure. But you have to give yourself more credit. If you gave it some thought, I bet you could figure it out."

Was that true? Ordination seemed to defy commentary. It was open to varied interpretations, since there were no living examples.

In some ways, it was purported to be similar to Conviction in the way it dealt with an object's purpose. But while Conviction was more flexible, allowing the ascendant to produce most effects he could think of, Ordination was governed by a different set of rules.

Ordination dealt with the object's *original* purpose. As such, it was tied to the object's history—to what it'd been ordained to do.

Only then did he remember one more detail—a part of this hypothetical situation his teachers left out.

"The ordinator..." he began, putting it together. "He restores the bridge that was there. It goes back to how it was meant to be before it was destroyed."

Sefina beamed. "See? I knew you had it in you."

Nesil shook his head in frustration. "The bridge part, maybe. But it's more complicated than that."

"How so?"

"Because the effects of Ordination are temporary—just like the other aspects. It doesn't change the past. Once the man's across, the bridge falls apart."

"So? The objective wasn't to fix the bridge. Once he's made it across, he can stay there—with or without the continued use of Ordination. That isn't temporary."

"I'm not arguing that. But I'm well past the bridge and talking about the statue. That's where this is going, right? Everyone knows Innovation was destroyed, along with its people. But what you're saying—if I'm hearing this right—is that Ashaira, somehow, reversed all that?"

Sefina was impressed. "Crude, but you're in the right direction."

"Am I? Because the way I see it, Innovation was *gone*. It ceased to exist, and that can't be changed. Even Ashaira—the goddess herself—couldn't fix that. Not permanently. If she brought the aspect back, it'd just disappear when she relinquished her power."

"Good points—but you're skipping details. You talk about restoring Innovation, but that's not what happened—not in the way you describe. Had our aspect truly gone back to how it was, we'd both have bodies—real ones. We could go anywhere in the world. Interact with anyone."

Nesil frowned in consideration. He thought of the lesser aeisr—dim echoes reenacting a semblance of their lives. An odd immortality—a gift from Ordination. A *curse* from Ordination, dooming them forever to repeat the same mistakes.

"Not a full restoration, then. Even so—"

"Not even *close* to a restoration. The statue creates an aura like an ascendant's. It changes the world—but only for people within close proximity."

This made a strange sense—much more than he thought it would—and his mind had difficulty keeping up.

She went on. "It does this, *not* by restoring Innovation but Aviathas, directly."

"He's dead."

"Doesn't matter. Aviathas is the *bridge*. So long as we're across, it can fall back apart."

Nesil's head was beginning to hurt.

She still wasn't done. "Whoever designed the statue was a bloody genius. It isn't comprised of a single aspect but *three*."

"Three?" asked Nesil. "Ordination and which others?"

"Innovation's one."

Nesil was unsure if this inclusion was redundant or a downright paradox. How could Innovation be part of the statue if its power couldn't exist without it?

But as he thought it over, he knew she was right. The statue didn't exist in a physical sense—otherwise, it would've been easy to destroy.

"And the third?" he asked.

She worked her mouth. "This one's more difficult."

"You don't know?" he asked doubtfully.

"I do—but it doesn't make sense... The evidence clearly points to Stratum, though Shaelis wasn't part of the statue's creation."

"Clearly? How is that clear?"

"Somehow, the statue can segregate an area and make it inaccessible from the outside world."

"I've never seen it do that."

"Not in Seldor. No."

Unfortunately, Nesil's experience was limited to his homeland. He knew Renat had acquired the statue someplace else, but Nesil had never learned where from.

She eyed him steadily. "It's the entire reason Ahman disappeared."

"Wait—what? You mean *the* Ahman? The one near Carheim?"

"You know a different one?"

"But—! You're telling me grandfather went there? The lost city of the gods?"

Sefina smiled in amusement but said nothing.

"So wait... Back up a moment. It was the statue, then, that cut off the city? Barring the gods' entry, so they couldn't save the world?"

"More or less."

"So I was right! Ashaira *was* at the heart of it. She betrayed the gods when she made the statue."

"Not necessarily."

"But you just said—!"

"She was involved, yes. But I don't think the statue was created for that purpose."

"Then why hide it? I'm unsure about the details, but I know she was hiding something. It's how Shaelis justified putting her on trial."

Sefina nodded. "You're right. But just because an object's dangerous, doesn't mean Ashaira meant to use it for evil."

Nesil scoffed. "Still, you defend her?"

"I'm looking at the facts. When Ashaira was home, the statue's use was limited. It cut off a single courtyard and nothing more. It wasn't until later—while she wasn't there, mind you—someone else made the change. Someone else made it target the city as a whole."

"But who could do that? No one else could get inside!"

"That we know of."

"So who—?"

She shook her head. "The question of the ages."

Once again, Nesil staunched his disappointment.

He found it difficult to think of *another* betrayer. An unidentified variable skulking in the shadows. It was all too much—a mountain of information in a scant few minutes. He had to fight not to feel overwhelmed.

Even more disturbing was how forthcoming Sefina had been about everything. It was a notable departure from her usual secrecy—so she was either lying about something, or she was after something else.

Why else would she divulge so much about the statue? From these simple revelations, he'd not only learned the statue's role but its historical significance. More importantly, he'd learned how dependent she was on its continued existence.

That was the kicker. Sefina, in effect, had told him that if the statue were destroyed—and destroyed completely—it wouldn't just prevent others from seeing them. It would undo the powers that enabled their existence.

She'd laid her weakness out in the open—letting him know, in no uncertain terms, that by destroying the statue, she'd be gone forever.

Both of them would.

This wasn't exactly a deal-breaker, as he'd never expected to live very long. He liked to believe he was willing to do anything—to pay any cost—if it meant ridding the world of the aeisric threat.

Was it possible Sefina had known this about him? Why else would she have told him so much—to clarify what his actions might cost?

"Did I say something wrong?" asked Sefina. "I lost you just now."

"Sorry. I'm just thinking..."

But Nesil didn't know what to think. Because, somehow, when confronted with the greater picture, a new question had overtaken his thoughts:

Why, dear gods, was he so hesitant to die?

Chapter 30
CONVERGENCE

Above all other stories, there was a type Kaycia hated most. It was the idea that god was supposed to fix everything. It wasn't that she doubted the gods' capabilities—if they *could* have fixed everything. Her problem was with man's arrogance to insist they should.

She'd seen it in plays and read it in books. How people wound up in the worst situations. An enemy horde was descending on the town—most characters were dead or beyond all hope. But somehow, the gods would intervene and end their suffering.

It was so misguided and simplistic, Kaycia had difficulty believing Soril bought into it. He called it faith—his hope that Irisea might come to their rescue—not only solving their problems but the ones the gods themselves had been unable to solve! It was a pleasant notion but baseless and juvenile.

It was nearly enough to make her want to poison Aico. He wasn't a god but a regular person. More importantly, she knew firsthand that he was real.

And yet...she couldn't help but feel it was nearly the same thing. They were pinning their hopes on a single person. They were still depending on the gods—on the talents they'd given him. If anything, the plan was worse because it required poison and coercion.

No matter how she looked at it, she couldn't win. Finding Aico—confronting Aico—would be problem enough, but he wasn't the only reason she'd left this place.

Even without his warnings, this place frightened her. The vines were proof of the current's influence—from at least two layers. She'd faced the possibility of losing Elyriel, and she'd sworn to herself it wouldn't happen again.

...Yet, here she was.

The barren streets were just as she remembered—though slightly more damp and a bit less colorful. There were no thin bridges crossing overhead. No moving platforms. No boat at the water's edge.

A faint mist had settled over the ruins, clinging to mildewed corners and the hidden recesses of her mind.

"We don't have a choice," she muttered to her sister. "I keep asking myself, what would you do in this situation? After seeing you barefoot in that circle to save me—I'd like to think this would be your choice. That you'd want to save our mother and our neighbors from what's coming."

Her hands went to the ring on her finger—the one Laurus had provided, concealing a potent toxin within. She twisted it idly, trying not to think of what it meant.

"But I'm not heroic. Not like you. If this doesn't work, I'm getting you out. I made it clear to the council I won't leave you alone—not for a second. No reports this time. We go in together, we go out together—that was the deal. Even if it means losing our home. Does that make me a coward?"

Elyriel, of course, didn't respond. The poison, itself, was answer enough.

The hours ticked by without signs of the boy. This either indicated she was searching the wrong areas or he was actively avoiding her.

In either case, she considered it a blessing. It allowed her to focus on the street and ensure the sun remained overhead. It gave her time to think about both physical dangers and ethical ones.

She was still convincing herself of her choices when, entirely on accident, she stumbled across Ashaira's palace. Its steepled, slate rooftop pierced the sky, a few stories higher than the buildings around it. Most of the windows were broken, but Kaycia recognized the layout from the maps.

Unable to believe her luck, she started toward it—and was dismayed when the sky darkened.

"Really?" she asked, to no one in particular. "Here, of all places?"

She debated turning back and finding another way. But there was nothing to guarantee she'd find the place again—or that next time, the sky wouldn't be even darker.

And besides—what if Aico was here? She'd sooner find the boy and get the mission over with. Then she could leave and breathe easily again.

Kaycia pressed forward, keeping an eye on the sky. She could tolerate the sun's descent—just a little—but if it got too near the horizon, she'd abandon the plan and make escape her priority.

The palace interior was much like everything else—tumbledown walls that let in sunlight. Creeping vines speckled with dust. The entire western wing was tilted and sinking into the adjacent water channel. But fortunately, the arboretum lay in the opposite direction.

As she neared her destination, she had to quell her disappointment. Once again, the dust was undisturbed, with no signs that Aico—or anyone else—had been through here in a very long time. So she set those feelings aside and hoped, at the very least, the answers she found would be worth the trouble.

The palace opened up into an enormous, wild garden—not a conservatory for music but the archaic variety for preserving nature. An enormous glass canopy stretched overhead, some twenty feet off the ground, making the place into a sort of greenhouse. Most of the windows were cracked—many shattered—seeding the overgrowth with menacing shards. The remaining glass was opaque with grime, tinting the trees with a dull, bronze glow.

Taking care where she stepped, she followed the path toward the center. It was difficult to see clearly with so many trees, and she often had to duck beneath untrimmed branches. Thus far, however, she hadn't noticed anything dangerous. The daylight appeared to be late in the afternoon, and a rainbow shimmer caught her eye.

As the trees opened up to a furnished patio—with cabinets, dressers, and moldy chairs—she couldn't tell, at first, where the colors were coming from. It wasn't until she looked up and back the way she came that she noticed the elaborate stained glass window. It bore a floral design of colorful petals. She marveled to find it mostly intact—mostly still clean—and glittering in the evening light.

She turned back to the deck and began to wonder what she was looking for. From what she remembered, Aviathas had been hiding in this place—but nothing stood out or grabbed her attention. There were no corpses or evidence of animal sacrifice. No symbols on the floor or signs of a ritual.

Instead, she found a few dusty hammocks and some overgrown tables. There were broken bottles and scattered trinkets—but nothing that announced the end of the world.

Was she searching the wrong place? After everything she'd read at the prison, she'd expected to find something worth hiding—something of such importance that it warranted Ashaira's incarceration. But if there'd been anything else besides Aviathas himself, Kaycia feared it was no longer here.

Around the tables and toward the back of the deck was a stone alcove that might've held something important.

At first, she wasn't certain what it was. Near the ground, the stone rippled and folded into a shape like a tree trunk, ending at a height above her waist. The sculpted lines, however, were too smooth to be bark—and, upon closer inspection, she found something that might've been a stone hand near the top.

Only then did it make sense. She was looking at the remains of what'd once been a statue. The folds made up the lower part of a dress, but everything above—the torso and head—was missing.

She would've recognized it sooner had the rest of the stone woman simply fallen to the ground, but the pieces weren't there. There were no fragments behind the statue or leaning to one side.

Kaycia kept looking, on the off-chance someone had left some notes or a diary behind. But, unlike the prison, this place had faced severe exposure to the elements. If any such things had once existed, they were long gone.

So what now? she thought. *Does the trail just stop without answers for anyone?*

She considered going for help and asking Soril for ideas—but she knew that was stupid. She'd already taken a risk, letting the sun go down. She wasn't about to give Elyriel the chance to wander more and get them into trouble.

She should leave while it was safe. Though this was a dead end, it didn't mean there weren't other things to find.

For some reason, however, she couldn't bring herself to move. This confused her for a moment until she realized why.

It was the reason she'd avoided the rooftops. She needed the trail to keep going—to keep searching for answers because... Because it was *so much easier* than looking for Aico. When it all came down to it, that was the problem. She didn't want to find him because she didn't want to poison him.

As long as she had something else to do, she still had options. It even meant she might find Irisea—no matter how unlikely that seemed. She'd rather go against her beliefs and hope for that outcome, if it spared her the need to compromise her honor.

She laughed bitterly to herself as she seriously considered the act of prayer—despite the fact that prayer was meaningless. That, for centuries, people had prayed for help they'd never receive.

And yet...Kaycia felt so helpless, she felt she could understand why they prayed anyway. Why people needed that power greater than themselves. Because their own capabilities were never enough. And, without something more, what remained but darkness? But defeat?

Damn it! she wanted to scream. *What am I supposed to do?!* It wasn't as though she could see the future. *Are there any gods listening?!*

Irisea, are you there?

Her head shot up as the stained glass shattered.

There was a resounding crash as thousands of multifaceted shards filled the space above, scattering the premature twilight into a deadly rainbow. She averted her eyes, shielding her face from the glittering knives...that never fell.

Not a single fragment hit the ground, and after a few seconds, she gathered the courage to look up again.

The spray of glass hung in the air as though the explosion had slowed to a crawl. The particles drifted, descending through a fiery morass, gleaming with the blinding vestiges of sunset.

At the center of the prismatic maelstrom, there floated a person—no...*two* people: a boy and a girl.

Before they could see her, Kaycia ducked behind a nearby cabinet. She stilled the air around her, masking the sounds of her movement, her breathing, and her beating heart.

She'd seen enough of the boy to know he wasn't Aico. This newcomer seemed closer to Elyriel's age—not so old to appear dangerous, but Kaycia wasn't so foolish to go off appearances.

These strangers had literally flown through the window! And, considering where this was, that meant they were transcendents. The world was somehow swimming in them, though *no* transcendents were supposed to exist!

"You could've warned me first!" said the boy.

"Why? Are you hurt?"

He groaned. "Bloody heavens... Where is this?"

The smile in the girl's voice was plain, though she was outside Kaycia's view. "Now you're just pretending to be dense. What were you expecting?"

Boots crunched over glass. "I wasn't expecting much of anything—but these ruins... They're just... I don't know."

She giggled. "What? Because this place belonged to the gods? Are the rocks supposed to glow or something? They're *ruins*, Nesil. They're supposed to be like this."

The boy sighed. "If you say so."

Their casual tone put Kaycia at ease, but she still didn't reveal herself. Were these people also Navarans? If they were friends of Aico, it'd explain why the girl seemed familiar with the place. It also suggested her response would be similar—unwilling to trust a stranger from Carheim.

"We didn't drop in anywhere," she continued. "This palace is the place where Ashaira kept him hidden."

Kaycia nearly choked.

The boy—Nesil, as the girl called him—didn't sound surprised. "That's what I don't get—why would Ashaira care what the pantheon knew? I mean, I'd think they'd be glad to know he was alive."

"Some of them, maybe."

"...The gods *wanted* him dead?"

The girl sighed. "Why else do you think they locked her up? It wasn't so much about punishing *her*. They needed her gone—out of the picture—so when he died again, she couldn't bring him back."

As the youths crossed the patio, Kaycia circled the furniture to stay out of sight. She waited for the right moment, then left the deck entirely to hide more effectively under the cover of trees.

"Why couldn't she?" asked Nesil. "Going back to the example of the bridge, it shouldn't matter how much time has passed."

"Well, no... But only because all the pieces were still there. Imagine if they weren't— if a strong storm had carried a few blocks deeper into the ocean. Farther than ascendancy's limited range."

"But...?! Then Ordination would *never* work. There'd always be something missing."

"Oh, it works. The bridge would still come together—only missing those blocks."

"Wouldn't that make it fall?"

"That entirely depends. The more blocks missing, the more drain on the ascendant."

Kaycia quietly reflected on her own experience—the rope's determination to follow her intent despite its lack of durability. The girl's words carried a semblance of truth— and kindled her curiosity.

Peering through the leaves, she studied the stranger. She had straight blond hair and was much younger than Kaycia expected. This would've been shocking had she not already met Aico, who was still younger than this girl by a year or so.

"Okay," continued Nesil. "But this is Ashaira we're talking about—not any ascendant. I'd bet half the bridge could be gone, and she'd hold it together without breaking a sweat."

"She might at that... But we weren't talking about a bridge, now, were we?"

He shrugged. "She gets out of prison and finds all the pieces."

"Body parts."

"Whatever. As long as she gets most of them—"

"She'd get a reanimated corpse. It's not the same thing. He wouldn't come back to life."

Nesil paused. "Because something's still missing."

"It's the closest we've come to proving the soul exists—or something to that effect. At the moment of death, a certain time frame must be kept. If you're quick—and lucky— you can snag that *something* before it becomes irretrievable. Otherwise, it's gone—beyond even the reach of Ashaira herself."

The boy went silent, considering what this meant.

Kaycia, however, had her doubts. Bringing the dead back to life? It was all she could do to keep herself hidden and not challenge the girl how she knew these things. Had the girl already searched this place and found evidence for her claims? Or was she like Kaycia's old professors, who'd adopted the habit of stating their opinions as fact?

In the end, there was no way to tell—not without knowing who this girl was. She carried herself with unwavering confidence—with even more poise than most adults. It almost made Kaycia want to believe her, despite her youthful appearance.

Or was that just a trick? Perhaps, like Elyriel, she had the body of a child but was possessed by an adult. Kaycia didn't believe Aico was pretending, but this newcomer didn't act thirteen.

"So, what you're saying," he continued, "is that Aviathas is gone—permanently, this time."

"They're *all* gone, Nesil. You knew that."

"But I mean *gone* gone. Ordination doesn't stand a chance at saving them. Not even a little."

"Did you think it did?"

"Well, no…"

"We didn't come here for them. We came here for *us*—to finish what Kadrek started. Wasn't that your idea?"

The boy shrugged.

Despite Kaycia's reservations—and not knowing who this 'Kadrek' was—she was beginning to like this girl.

Hadn't she been praying for this very thing—to uncover more options? This was strangely perfect—as she no longer had to choose between unfounded faith and kidnapping a child.

While this girl might not be Irisea, she had the potential to be even better. And though that didn't mean Kaycia was willing to trust her, it gave her a reason to stay and watch.

"*You look like you want to say something*," said Sefina. Nesil would've responded, but there was a problem. Moments earlier, as he'd sat down on the dusty hammock, he'd noticed a pair of eyes hiding in the trees. At first, he'd thought it was only a wanderer, but the gaze was too cautious. Too…deliberate.

Sefina studied his face. "*It's all right. Just press your teeth together—like back at the party—and only I will hear.*" Her lips didn't move.

This was a relief, except... It also made him realize he didn't need to say anything. Her words indicated she was aware of the stranger. She'd likely known since they arrived—if not before.

And yet, she'd done nothing to hide their conversation. She'd let him speak of Aviathas as though the topic were mundane. As though to see how the stranger would respond. She'd known about this person for two whole minutes, and *already* she was handing out tests?

"What're you so worried about? You think she'll sneak up on us? Slit our throats while we sleep?"

Nesil shook his head in frustration. *"She?"*

"Nearly your height. Slim. Blond hair—a few shades darker than mine. Light freckles. I'd say she's about fourteen."

He didn't know what to say.

If he expressed concern for their visitor—of Sefina doing something to *her*—he might prompt the very thing he hoped to avoid.

Of course, there was no guarantee she wouldn't harm her anyway.

"I thought you said there'd be no one here."

"Is that a problem? Because YOU said you WANTED to find a helper—for what we need to do."

"I..."

He couldn't deny it, but after hearing her stories, he'd expected to wait *years* before someone showed up.

"Did you know someone would be here?"

"Honestly? I'm as surprised as you are," she said with a wordless smile. *"But it'd seem your grandfather's not the only one to have figured it out."*

Nesil refused to believe this a coincidence. Considering everything the aeisr had been through, she had reasons for contingencies. After finally escaping this place, she must've left clues or sent messages, somehow, to make it easier to find.

"Should we talk to her?" he asked.

"In a moment..."

Without further warning, the sea of glass dust lifted off the ground. The particles revolved in a glittering vortex, with Sefina at their axis, before they shot toward the ceiling and reknit themselves back into the stained glass window.

That wasn't all—the repairs kept going, replacing the missing roof fragments. The weather-beaten glass traveled backward in time, as though each nick and crack had never occurred. Decades of calcification melted away, making the glass transparent, smooth, and sparkling.

AUSTIN LYNN CLARK

At least in appearance.

This was nothing more than an extravagant display of Sefina's vanity. And it made Nesil uncomfortable, knowing their visitor would get the wrong impression.

Out loud, he asked, "Is this necessary?"

"You preferred the way it was?" she asked innocently. "After wallowing in Seldor so long, you *enjoy* the stench of dust?"

"You know what I mean," he said without hiding his irritation. Clenching his teeth, he added, *"It's not like we're breathing any of this."*

"But SHE is, Nesil. Don't you want her to feel welcome?"

Only then did he recognize another problem. While sprucing up the place seemed harmless enough, there were other reasons for Sefina to remodel.

He had no doubt the statue was somewhere nearby. Without it, Kaycia wouldn't be able to see them.

But though he'd carefully pretended not to search for it, he'd been too slow. By now, it was likely already invisible. Obscured behind this elaborate spectacle. As always, Sefina was one step ahead.

Of course, it might not have mattered anyway. It'd been in her power to hide the statue prior to their arrival. And even if he'd caught a glimpse where it was—even that might've been a trick to throw him off track.

Nesil swallowed, having accepted long ago this wouldn't be easy. He kept his face straight as though oblivious to her scheme.

"Is this for her benefit...or yours?" he asked. *"You're just showing off. It's not like any of this helps her. Not in a way that matters."*

"That depends on how you look at it. You should listen to her heartbeat—she's loving this! Every little bit!"

"But that's because she doesn't know who you are—or that none of this is real!"

Sefina merely smiled.

"So...you're not going to tell her?"

"Now, honestly, Nesil... Where would the fun be in that?"

Chapter 31
DANGEROUS PARTNERS

Kaycia gaped in silent wonder.

Without so much as a wave of her hand, the girl cleared away large swathes of vines. The weathered limestone regained its orange hue, shedding years of dust and brightening in the light of the setting sun.

Small chips and fragments clicked into place—the cracks working backward, smaller and thinner until erased from existence. The wooden furniture regained its strength, shine, and scent of polish. Cloth tapestries mended and straightened along the walls. Budding plants sprang up from the cultivated earth.

And Kaycia's tree—behind which she was hiding—abruptly untwisted and left her exposed.

The miracles slowed, and the girl in the white dress gave a startled gasp.

Kaycia swallowed in horror, realizing how she must look. Instead of sneaking away while she had the chance, she'd been caught like a spy. Either that or a frightened teenager hiding in the trees.

"I..."

She didn't know what to say. Any hope of behaving professionally—of approaching this transcendent with a diplomatic proposal—it all came crashing down.

The girl recovered with a smirk. "Did I unearth a hidden prize?"

"I—I'm sorry... I didn't think anyone would be here."

"You can come on out. I don't bite. Tell her, Nesil."

Strangely, the boy had to think of his answer.

Kaycia stepped around the tree.

"Ohhh!" exclaimed the girl. "And she's a pretty one, too!"

The comment made Kaycia blush in surprise.

"Don't mind her," said Nesil, reassuringly. "Sefina's always like this—saying anything to get a reaction."

The girl pouted. "Really? You don't think she's pretty?"

Nesil smiled uncomfortably. "See what I mean?"

While Kaycia felt relieved by their amiable exchange, she struggled to keep up. The girl's antics were peculiar, but her eyes were gentle—without hints of madness. Even her body was intact and free from the twisted scars of ascendancy.

"What's your name?" asked Sefina, rushing toward her.

"...Kaycia."

The girl sighed in delight before throwing her arms around her.

Kaycia turned to Nesil for help. "She's *always* like this?"

His face was apologetic. "Typically. When she wants something from you."

Not knowing what else to do, she tried returning the embrace—but not before Sefina slipped away.

The girl beamed. "I can already tell we'll be the best of friends!"

"That's...wonderful. But you know nothing about me."

Sefina smiled deviously. "What do you think, Nesil? Aren't I a good judge of character?"

"Don't make me a part of this."

The girl shrugged and appraised Kaycia as though taking on a challenge.

"By the lilt in your accent and style of your leather, I can tell you're from Carheim."

Kaycia nodded appreciatively.

"From the dust in your hair and dried-up sweat, I know you've been here at least a few days. That tells me you're dedicated and fearless...to a degree.

"But more than that, you still smell good—letting me know you take pride in yourself. You wash your face regularly and tend to your hair. You insist on being your best self, though there's been no one around to see you."

Kaycia bit her lip but accepted these points without argument. In truth, she gave Elyriel's body more attention than she'd ever given herself—a habit she'd adopted more from guilt than pride. But there was no reason to explain this to a complete stranger.

Sefina went on. "You bear the chains of Conviction, though they're fairly new. Your armor, on the other hand, has seen more battles—by someone not so small as you. A family heirloom, perhaps? You won't grow into it, having reached your full height."

"I'm impressed," said Kaycia, with a self-conscious smile.

But Sefina wasn't finished.

"Your stomach is growling, though you've got food in your pack. Most likely, you haven't eaten because you don't want to pee. You've been holding it for hours, but the stress of this place has you worried. With your moonblood only days away, you dread the possibility it might come early."

Heat rushed to her face.

The girl continued to regard her, deadly serious.

"You pretend you're not afraid, but my words unsettle you. It's more than the anxiety of meeting a stranger. Since our arrival, your heart has born the rhythm of hope—of something you wish to ask me. But you hesitate from fear. Because the last thing you want is my refusal—risking something you value more than life itself."

Kaycia's mouth ran dry, wanting nothing more than to deny these words. "Like what?" she asked.

"A loved one? Your sense of honor, perhaps? I can only go off the clues you've given me—and like you said...I know *nothing* about you."

Kaycia licked her lips—reminded of her first encounter with Aico. In comparison to these...children, she was out of her depth. She could only play at transcendence without ever knowing what it meant.

She considered it fortunate, then, that the girl was different from Aico—making Kaycia feel she could approach her and not be in danger of an instant death.

"It's all right," said Sefina. "You don't have to say anything... I can wait here while you go behind those trees and attend to your needs. No need to rush. When you're up to it, we'll talk. We'll share a bite to eat and come to an arrangement."

Kaycia turned to Nesil for help.

Oddly, the boy had nothing to say.

And so she walked away, trying to quell her confusion between dread and hope.

*"**I**'m surprised by you, Nesil. I thought, for sure, you'd be getting in my way. You're not going to warn her? Tell her what it means to enter an agreement with me?"*

"The thought crossed my mind," he admitted. He swung out his legs and was pleased when the hammock—or rather, its illusion—moved with him. *"Should I be worried?"*

"I don't know. Aren't you?"

"You might be insane, but I know you're not stupid. As long as you need something, you won't put her in danger. And even then, it's not like Kaycia's done anything to earn your wrath."

"I suppose," she said, turning toward the trees where Kaycia disappeared.

Nesil wasn't bothered. Even if events went horribly wrong, he intended to sort this out long before then. Though he needed more time to destroy the statue, he could at least ensure it stayed where it was. As long as it never left this place, the aeisr would stay put—and other lands would be spared Seldor's fate.

He laid back on the hammock and clenched his teeth. "*...Suppose I HAD warned her. Just curious—what would you have done?*"

"*Stopped you.*"

"*Obviously. But how? You'd put a gag in my mouth?*"

"*Not a visible one.*"

"*Still seems suspicious. You're not worried she'd think something was off?*"

"*You know me better than that. She'd only see what I wanted her to see.*"

Nesil, however, wasn't so sure. While he didn't doubt for a second that Sefina could overpower him, he'd noticed something these past few days.

The difference was subtle. The mechanisms she used to keep him in line—they were all *external*. Admittedly, that extended to nearly everything—including gravity—but it was all a detraction from the single illusion outside her control:

Nesil himself.

He was an entirely different beast from her wandering constructs. His body was his own and his mind unpredictable. And while she pretended to enjoy the challenge he represented, she must've been worried he'd foul something up.

He'd already done so once, hadn't he?

Of course, if absolute control ever became her goal, she'd only need to lock him in a cell and put a doppelganger in his place. He suspected, however, she'd only do this as a last resort. She enjoyed the game and wasn't about to ruin it unless pushed too hard.

It became Nesil's goal, then, to play a game of his own and seek out the limitations of his freedom. He'd be careful to ensure she never felt threatened, but a little aggravation could go a long way.

When Kaycia returned, he made a point of speaking first.

"Awfully curious—how much did Sefina get right?"

The young woman was uneasy as she looked for a place to sit. "More than expected... I'm not sure what you're asking."

"Considering you made it here at all, I'm not questioning your ascendancy. You'll have to forgive my rudeness...but did you have a family member teach you? I've never been to Carheim, but I was sure there was a minimum age for their academies."

He expected Kaycia to go on the defensive, but she didn't. "Is that *her* excuse?" she asked, nodding toward Sefina. "Family privilege?"

Nesil shook his head. "She's older than she looks."

Kaycia settled down on the grass beside the patio, in a place he remembered to have been covered in mud. She didn't appear surprised by his comment, but her eyes flicked toward Sefina as though searching for something she'd missed.

"If you don't want to say, that's fine by me," he continued. "We all have our secrets. But I'd feel better knowing you've received formal training. Not to scare you, but my grandfather nearly died in this place. You sure you know what you're doing?"

"Nesil!" scolded Sefina.

"What?" he asked, with a touch of defiance. "Kaycia wants our help—and *we* need to know what she can handle."

Their visitor lifted a brow. "You need *me* for something?"

"Let's not get ahead of ourselves," said Sefina, giving Nesil a cold stare.

"Whatever," he said, rising to his feet. "I'll let the two of you hash this out."

Kaycia appeared concerned, as though blaming herself for his sudden departure.

"*What are you doing*?" hissed Sefina.

"I won't go far," he explained—not to her but to their guest. "It's been a long day, and *she's* the one you want to talk to."

This had been his plan all along—not only to give Kaycia an indirect warning but to provide himself an excuse to leave.

The conversation itself wouldn't be that interesting, as nothing he said would change the outcome. Alternatively, there were things he could do while the aeisr was distracted.

"Don't mind him," said Sefina as he stepped off the patio. "He gets jealous sometimes."

Nesil resisted the urge to turn back.

When Kaycia said nothing, Sefina went on. "He's not used to sharing me with other people. We were just married, you see, a few days back."

"Really?" asked the girl, sounding impressed. "Well...congratulations? You're not joking, are you?"

"Honest truth. And thank you. Don't you worry—you're not in the way. Our marriage is one of mutual respect. And personal space. Isn't that right, Nesil?"

He pushed through the trees and gave no response. While he intended to stay close and hear them talk, he couldn't dismiss the odd feeling the statue was nearby.

He wasn't sure what gave him this idea. While, yes, this was Ashaira's palace, and, yes, the statue had been made in her image—there was more to it than that. The fact both Kaycia and Sefina had been drawn to the same location—even that might've been a coincidence.

He couldn't put his finger on it, but he was sure it was here. Perhaps, after forming a personal bond with the aeisr, it became something he could sense on an instinctual level.

Or maybe it was nothing more than wishful thinking.

Behind him, Sefina said, "Some might consider this a personal failing, but I refuse to talk to anyone on an empty stomach."

"A failing?" asked Kaycia, a smile in her voice. "To me, that's practical sense."

"Is it? I mean, you're not anxious? You don't mind waiting?"

Kaycia laughed. "If anything, I need something to calm my stomach. This is nice—having someone around... Or are you one of those people who takes hours to eat?"

Nesil rolled his eyes, not wanting to think of what tricks the aeisr had in store. There was another reason, after all, he was avoiding Kaycia. In all likelihood, she wouldn't live that long.

Unfortunately, as he returned his attention to his search, there wasn't much to see. He'd been hoping to find something like a dried-up fountain, a clearing of trees, or a circular walkway where you'd expect a stone pedestal. But there was nothing of the sort. Besides the scattering of furniture—which he couldn't open and was ill-suited to hide large statues—he only found more bushes.

He decided to wait a bit longer before trying his luck. It was possible these plants weren't here a moment ago. But he was reluctant to plow through before Sefina was more engaged with present company.

Then, if she still tried to stop him...wouldn't that prove he was on the right track?

K aycia didn't know what to make of Sefina.

She'd always been cautious when people seemed too friendly, but something about this girl put her at ease. Sefina didn't put on airs like your typical con artist, whose sense of enthusiasm was only skin deep. Though she obviously had ulterior motives, her playful disposition was wholly genuine.

With a mischievous grin, Sefina said, "Look in your bag."

Kaycia hesitated before bringing her satchel out in front—the one Soril had given her to replace the one she'd lost. To her surprise, the bag appeared different—less frayed around the edges, as though the leather had been renewed and freshly oiled.

When she looked up with suspicion, Sefina nodded insistently.

So she opened it. And froze.

"But...!"

Warm steam hit her face, filling her with the scent of freshly baked muffins laced with bright red fruit.

"Are these...strawberries?" she asked, lifting one out. It was hot, sticky, and glistening with glaze. It was a far cry from the stale bread she'd been forced to deal with—the small loaves that'd stocked her pack until a minute ago.

"You made this?" she asked, bringing it to her eyes. Even up close, she couldn't see any flaws. Each yellow crumb—the crust of crystallized sugar—was all so perfect, just like the real thing.

"Are you just going to stare? I promised it's not poisoned."

Kaycia paled, worried she'd caused offense. Then took a bite.

Closing her eyes, she moaned in delight.

"These are amazing!" she gushed after she'd swallowed. She didn't need to lie to win the girl over. It was the honest truth. "No wonder he married you."

Sefina beamed and bit into her own—which seemed to have materialized from nowhere. Her muffin was identical, so neither had to share.

With a grin, the girl said, "Yeah... I've got him snagged forever."

Kaycia scanned the trees but couldn't see where Nesil had gone. She didn't understand why he'd been upset with Sefina, but she supposed he'd be back if he ever got hungry. The girl didn't seem concerned, which likely meant they'd known each other a long time. A very long time if he was no longer fazed by the things she could do.

Try as she might, she couldn't place a finger on *what* the girl was doing. Early on, with the restoration of the glass ceiling, she'd felt certain she was watching the lost aspect of Ordination. But now, with these muffins—far more complex than those apples from before...

It was an unfair comparison. Aico, after all, was only twelve. And though Sefina appeared young—the result, perhaps, of being preserved by transcendency—she'd had a lot more time to hone her talents. Someday, Aico would be just as good. Maybe even better.

Sefina, however, hadn't just created them. She'd *transfigured* them from the bread in Kaycia's pack. She could also fly—like the masters of equilibrium. So where did that leave her?

Kaycia supposed this was the difference of transcendency. Perhaps, after reaching a certain level, there were paths that'd been lost since the age of the gods.

It was the only explanation. Otherwise, she'd have to consider Sefina to hail from Stratum—the aspect of Shaelis himself. It'd mean this girl, in fact, was Irisea in the flesh. And Kaycia wasn't ready to make that leap.

The girl didn't act like the child goddess. And Nesil didn't treat her like the child goddess.

"Well then," began Sefina when they'd both had their fill. "Judging where we are, I imagine you need help finding something?"

"Not exactly," said Kaycia, using the grass to clean the stickiness from her fingers. As she searched for the right words, she was dismayed to find the muffins hadn't helped. If anything, her stomach felt more sick than before. "I came here searching... How should I say this—? I need someone like you to assist with a problem."

It was Sefina's turn to act confused. "Someone...like me... ... And Ahman was the first place you checked?"

Heat flushed through her face. "I know how this sounds—and no, it's not the reason I came—not initially."

"It's all right. Just tell me. I'm good with secrets if that's what worries you. You can trust me."

Kaycia forced a smile, grateful for the reassurance. Wanting the reassurance. Except, nothing about this was normal at all.

They might act like friends, but that was no guarantee of an honest relationship. If anything, it was more reason to stay on her guard and suspect Sefina would want more than she asked for.

But she kept these reservations from appearing on her face.

"Earlier, you mentioned Seldor... Is that where you're from?"

Sefina cocked her head. "Does that matter?"

"Well..."

The girl suddenly nodded. "Your problem, then, isn't personal? But something for your people?"

"That's...exactly right. I might as well say it. Our troubles aren't just from outside but below. The bedrock's crumbling away—replaced by holes and caverns. The city, itself, is on the verge of collapse."

"I see..." said Sefina, turning her eyes down.

This wasn't the reaction Kaycia had hoped for. But it wasn't unexpected.

For a while, the girl said nothing at all.

"I don't know what I'm asking," continued Kaycia. "I just saw what you did with this place, and..." She felt like an idiot.

"And you hoped for a miracle."

"I was hoping for your input. I thought you'd know better what our options might be. If it can't be reversed, then maybe it can be slowed. Or, maybe we need a place to take us in."

At this point, Kaycia felt even worse. She remembered that Seldor had its own share of problems—even with Sefina on their side. The girl, after all, was just one person.

"Okay," said Sefina, leaning back. "You ask a lot, but we might be able to help each other."

Kaycia's breath stuck in her throat. "...R—really?"

"Just so we're clear—I can't offer an immediate solution. From what it sounds like, you've got a lot to rebuild. And I can't do anything to speed that up. We're talking months. Years. I don't deal in miracles."

"Of course," said Kaycia, hiding her embarrassment. But she was also swayed by the girl's approach. Straight to the point, without smoothing any edges.

"I can't guarantee how much can be saved—if any, at all. I haven't seen the damage and have no grasp of Carheim's resources. But I *can* offer exactly what you asked—a way to slow it down. A way to push the current back so your workers stand a chance."

"That's...more than I could've hoped for! You can really do that? How would you—?"

"It's not so different from what I did for Seldor."

"You mean...? I heard about the siege..."

The girl raised a brow. "Did you, now? Well, there you have it. Proof I can hold my side of the bargain."

"But how?" asked Kaycia. "What did you do?"

Sefina shook her head. "I can't share all my secrets. And, right now, it won't mean a thing if you can't offer what I want in return."

"Of course," said Kaycia.

She'd known all along there had to be a catch. But she couldn't keep her excitement down. It was hard to believe this was actually working out. She'd barely met this girl—this wonderful, unlikely girl!—and the future no longer felt so impossible.

"What do you need?" asked Kaycia. "I can't speak for the elders, but I promise they'll do what they can to repay you."

"I'm sure they will—commensurate with how long my skills are needed. But that's not what I meant. There's something I need from you right now."

"Me?" asked Kaycia.

The girl smiled in an attempt to be comforting. "A favor is all."

But Kaycia wasn't comforted. What was it Nesil said? He asked about her training—not only what she could handle but how much she could handle *in this place*.

"It's enough that you're here," continued Sefina. "Enough you were able to enter Ahman—something many would consider a miracle in its own right. So, in that sense, I consider this an even exchange. Something only I can do for you, for something only you can do for me."

When she put it like that, it made a sort of sense. No matter what was involved, it'd be a small price to pay for what Sefina was offering—even if it meant staying longer than she liked.

But what sort of help might that be? Sefina was the most powerful person Kaycia knew of. And, if *she* needed help, the obstacles must be nearly insurmountable.

Kaycia took a deep breath. "...You need someone to watch your back?"

"Is that a problem?"

"I... I can try, but I'm not sure I'm the person you want."

Sefina's face scrunched together. "You're the only one here."

That wasn't entirely true. When compared to Kaycia, the boy Aico was far more capable. He'd been born a real transcendent, where Elyriel was an accident.

However, if Kaycia so much as mentioned his name, the deal, most assuredly, would be off. Sefina would have no obligation toward Kaycia—and wasn't that exactly what she needed? Wasn't that worth the risk?

"You're having doubts," the girl observed. "But I'm really not asking anything difficult. We'll be back within a day—two at most. I mainly need someone to come along with me—someone *not* from Seldor, which leaves Nesil out."

"Doing what, though? Coming back from where?"

"That's the best part. I don't need you to do anything—only act as a witness. So if we *do* find something, it'll be easier to avoid an international incident. So people won't think our King is pushing his own agenda. Or trying to claim the bones of Shaelis for himself."

Kaycia gawked. "The bones—!"

Sefina bit back a chuckle. "That's only an example. I don't know what we're going to find."

"But you must know *something*! You've been here before, obviously."

The girl didn't answer but gave a tantalizing smile.

"You don't get lost?"

Sefina beamed. "See? Don't look at it as though you're helping me. We'll be doing this together, with me as your guide."

More than anything else, it was Sefina's confidence that swayed her. She didn't seem the sort of girl who wanted to die, and if she thought they'd be safe, who was Kaycia to argue?

Most likely, Kaycia wouldn't be the one watching Sefina, but the other way around. If they encountered anything unexpected, the girl would handle it. Wouldn't she?

She hesitated a moment, wondering if it'd be polite to probe the girl's past. She felt embarrassed to admit, after everything she'd seen, she still hadn't identified Sefina's aspect. Any other ascendant with years of experience would've figured it out by now.

In the end, it was this fear of looking stupid that kept her mouth shut.

Sefina raised two stemmed glasses with a shimmering russet liquid. "From the moment I found you in this historic location, I knew you were special."

Kaycia didn't think she deserved such praise but accepted the drink with keen interest.

"Careful!" warned Sefina. "The crystal's delicate. Try not to squeeze."

"Of course. You're very kind."

Kaycia swirled the curious liquid and detected the floral scent of berries. Without need for encouragement, she sipped its sweetness and was surprised by how smoothly it slid down her throat.

Sefina smiled at her reaction.

"But now," the girl continued, "let's move away from where it started. Our concern goes beyond how Ahman vanished to what happened after. We seek now for the moment it was attacked, with only Shaelis and Ashaira to hold back the tide.

"We go to the end, where the gods met their death."

Nesil had just left the bushes when he spied a stone alcove, and he couldn't believe his eyes.

What was left of the statue wasn't hidden or invisible. It was simply there. Unlike the rest of the garden, the statue hadn't been restored. It was nothing more than the lower half of Ashaira's dress, whisking the pavement—but that didn't diminish its sinister presence.

He hadn't forgotten what this statue had cost him, and his mind pieced together what it once had looked like—how Ashaira must've been in all her glory.

Could it really be so easy?

Though it might've been a decoy, he felt something from this area that couldn't be faked. At least, it seemed unlikely.

So...what, then? A trap? Was the aeisr waiting to see what he'd do—if he'd reveal his stupidity while she was a mere thirty feet away?

Nesil took a step back, unwilling to take the risk. No—there had to be a better way. A smarter way.

Perhaps, after leaving, while they were making their way to the Nightmare Throne, Nesil could make a run for it. Sefina was fast, yes, but she couldn't search everywhere. More importantly, she'd need to stay with Kaycia. He could wait for his chance and make his way back here.

Except...his feet wouldn't move.

Looking down, he found vines poking from the ground, wrapping his ankles, and holding him in place.

"*Are you proud of yourself?*" asked Sefina.

His heart began to race. "*Did something happen? I stopped listening a few minutes ago.*"

"*You found something more interesting?*"

"Well...yes. But I wasn't going to DO anything with it."

"Your heart says otherwise."

Nesil scoffed in disbelief. *"Nice try—but you can't make me feel guilty. I've done nothing wrong, and you know it."*

He didn't point his words in a specific direction, as Sefina's body wasn't here. No doubt, she was still sitting with Kaycia.

"...You sound defensive."

"Do I? Perhaps I don't like being tied up!"

"Oh, you mean like this?"

Dark vines shot from the trees at his sides, seizing his wrists and stretching him out like a scarecrow. Before Nesil could yell, a vine snaked across his mouth like a gag.

Despite the commotion, he was certain Kaycia heard none of it—so close by, yet oblivious to his predicament.

"So let me get this straight," said the aeisr's disembodied voice. *"All this time, you hoped I'd look the other way? Perhaps you thought Kaycia and I would head off alone, so you could stay and what? Take care of what's left?"*

He shook his head—refusing to confess anything. He'd made some mistakes, yes, but she had no way of proving the plans in his head.

The sad truth, however, was that it might not make a difference. As long as she believed he was up to no good, what could he possibly say to convince her otherwise?

"Don't act surprised. I know what it's like to hate someone so thoroughly—so perfectly—it consumes your every thought. Your desire for vengeance isn't so different from mine. Except, you're not going after a murderer. You're trying to kill ME.

"You want it so badly, you're willing to die yourself. No doubt, you've made it out as some noble sacrifice! But don't fool yourself, Nesil. How can anything be noble if you're willing to pay with innocent blood?"

Through the vine, he tried to protest, *"Hmmgghh!"*

"Oh? You didn't think that far ahead? You'd watch Kaycia leave, knowing, full well, you'd be leaving her defenseless? You think she'll make it out without my assistance?"

Nesil snorted. To his surprise, the vine retracted and allowed him to speak.

"She's only going because of YOU! Because YOU'VE been hiding the truth." He said this with confidence, having heard the most important parts of their discussion. *"Did you even mention the Nightmare Throne? You don't think a name like that might affect her decision?"*

"Right. You argue that I'm a selfish liar— I already know that! You, on the other hand—you just don't see it. If the statue's destroyed and Kaycia dies...that's entirely on YOU."

In truth, Nesil *had* considered this. He realized his plan would put the girl in danger—but she was already in danger. If Kaycia knew everything, she'd take his side—he was sure of it!

...And even if she didn't, she was only one person. What was one life in comparison to the *thousands* saved once the aeisr was dead? All things considered, it was an acceptable risk.

"You disappoint me, Nesil. All your talk of what it means to be human—and still, you stoop to anything to get what you want."

He shook his head before insisting, *"I didn't do anything."*

There was a long pause. *"No... I suppose you didn't. But here's the thing—I've lost my taste for taking chances. It was fun for a while, but I won't have Kaycia run off because YOU can't keep your mouth shut."*

He strained his arms against the vines, but they were as strong as steel cords. *"How's this fair?"*

"Come on, Nesil! Why in the gods' names would I ever play fair?"

"You can't leave me here!"

He couldn't believe this! After the pains he'd gone through to be more careful—it'd amounted to nothing. No matter how he struggled, Kaycia had no chance of seeing the trembling vines. And when he tried to scream, only silence escaped.

"We'll be back. Don't worry. Meanwhile, I hope you use this opportunity to think—and think real hard. You've no business anywhere near that statue. I don't care how strongly you feel about this—just stop it. Stop it right now."

"I wasn't DOING ANYTH—!"

Once again, a vine constricted across his mouth.

"And, just so we're clear—I'm not saying your revenge is misguided. I KNOW you hate me. You'll probably hate me for all eternity—and I'm fine with that. I am.

"But just quit it already. There's no point in trying because you'll never succeed."

Invisible hands caressed his cheeks. Even her tone became gentle.

"I know it. You know it. I'll stop you every time."

Chapter 32
THE DESCENT

Sefina led the way, and Kaycia followed.

Their route wasn't one she could've ever anticipated—or even remembered. The girl seemed to guess how the city would change. She never got lost and never had to backtrack.

Even then, Kaycia couldn't make sense of it.

They'd enter an alley strewn with ashes and weeds, turn around, and find everything different. The trees would change color, or it'd start raining—ordinary rain with actual water.

Sefina never paused, unconcerned by the sun's movements or how overshadowed the world became. She simply knew where to go, with a confidence that was comforting. And a little unsettling.

It was a constant reminder of Kaycia's reliance. Of how helpless she'd be if anything went wrong. Somehow, in a matter of minutes, she'd put her life in the hands of a stranger. An accomplished stranger but a stranger, all the same.

"I still don't understand why Nesil stayed behind," said Kaycia, when they'd stepped into an apartment so small, it was practically a closet.

"Oh, he's not the adventuring type. He's happier keeping an eye on our camp—knowing I'll find it easier to keep track of one person rather than two."

This wasn't enough to ease her worries. "Could you, maybe, explain what you're doing? To me, this dwelling's no different from the others. Why are we here?"

Sefina hesitated, perhaps wondering if they had time for this discussion.

"The ins and outs of Ahman isn't like other cities," she began. "Don't think of it like a map, where places are linked by orientation and proximity. It's less about where you turn left or right—but when you take a step and why. It has to do with perception and association."

To Kaycia, this made no sense at all. "So, you're drawing connections? Between what?"

"The memories of Ahman."

"You mean...its history?"

"Even cities have a life of their own—shaped by the people who gave them purpose. But no. I don't mean events as they actually transpired. More often than not, memories and truth are *not* the same thing."

When Kaycia was slow to respond, the girl beckoned her closer.

Putting an arm around her shoulders, Sefina pointed at the table near the center of the room, moldy and covered in cobwebs.

At first, she saw nothing of interest, until Sefina caressed some marks on the wood— the worn indentation from years of rolling dough.

"But what does that have to do with—?"

Her breath caught in her throat because she *did* see something. It was faint, like a shade, in the hunched shape of a woman. Her hair was short, and her eyes were sad.

"Don't ask me her name," said Sefina. "But when her mother fell ill, she started making bread. It was the least she could do for the caretakers at the abbey, who took her mother in when no one else would. She couldn't spare any money, you see. And so she delivered the bread herself—not just once but every week for fifteen years, even after her mother died."

Still leading her by the shoulder, Sefina took her out the door—except it didn't go outside. Instead, they were standing in a large stone vestibule, with arches so high, they disappeared into the night.

"An abbey...?" Kaycia echoed in disbelief. "But, how'd you know it'd be here?"

"Trial and error," the girl said with a smile. "You'd figure it out, too, if you had more time."

Kaycia disagreed. While Sefina appeared quite young, this wasn't something you could learn in days or months. With a few marks, the girl had unraveled a story. And all Kaycia had seen was the shape of a woman.

"What now?" she asked. "Is this building important?"

"It isn't the abbey we've come for but the caretakers I spoke of. Not all of them were kind and generous. One nurse in particular had a penchant for stealing blood while no one was looking."

"Stealing...blood?" asked Kaycia, feeling her stomach turn sour. "To what end? And why does that interest us?"

"Kaycia... To reach the place we're going, we must go *down*. It isn't possible to see the depths while keeping your head above water."

She found herself holding her breath. Down? But a part of her had already known this. She'd known they'd be facing the current—she just hadn't realized that 'down' was more than a direction.

"You haven't told me where we're going."

"Well... It isn't a place in the usual sense. I'm not sure I could explain it."

"Or you don't *want* to explain it."

"To be honest, I'd rather focus on keeping you safe. We made a deal, remember? You help me with my problem, I help you with yours?"

Kaycia didn't like this. She wasn't even sure how much she trusted this girl. It was only their agreement—the promise of helping Carheim and, through that, her sister—that persuaded her to keep going a little while longer.

From that moment on, Sefina took Kaycia down the roads of blood—the murderers and miscreants who'd operated in secret. While some had been caught and imprisoned, it wasn't possible to expunge all evil—not even from the City of the Gods.

Most had been cautious and made sure not to steal from the deities themselves. Instead, it was those who were careless—the ordinary folk caught alone in the night—who fell victim to their schemes.

Upon mention of underground rituals and profane worship, Kaycia suspected this might've contributed to the origin of the current—but Sefina just laughed. Mere mortals were incapable of creating the dark. Instead, it was man who succumbed to its sickness.

These memories were shadows—windows to a place that was already there.

With each horrific tale, Kaycia saw changes to the buildings around her. The darkness didn't simply overtake the sky but the gaps between planks, where the wood didn't align. In some places, the colorless boards became splintered, and a frigid breeze slipped through the crevices.

"Take care where you step," warned Sefina. "Some of these holes don't lead anywhere."

The floor creaked under Kaycia's feet. "Like a bottomless pit?"

"Stay on the wood, and you won't have to worry."

Kaycia did her best to follow that advice, but after a few more doorways, the path became progressively worse. Entire walls went missing, granting a view of black space, like staring off a cliff on a starless night.

She kept her distance and went no nearer the edge than the path required—but, sometimes, there'd be drops on both sides. It was like a bridge of slanted, uneven floorboards, without anything discernible holding it up.

She heard the sounds of creatures, scrambling in the dark. Somehow, Sefina could tell where they were and the unique dangers that each represented. There were the usual varieties—ones that dampened sound and the vines that sapped away strength. But there were also ones that Kaycia had never heard of. Creatures that made movement slow to a crawl. Creatures that hindered wakefulness. Others that hindered memory.

But to Kaycia's dismay, Sefina was reluctant to share many details. And she only answered questions as they pertained to their ongoing progress.

"The deeper we go, the path becomes more...fragmented," explained Sefina. "The associations more stretched and harder to follow. Moreover, there's a tendency to start seeing things that aren't there."

Kaycia couldn't tell if the girl was joking. "Does that matter? None of this is supposed to be here anyway."

"Maybe not, but you can still interact with what's in this room. Take this chair, for example," said Sefina, brushing her fingers along the back of a worn, bleached rocker. "I don't know where it came from or why it's here—but if you take a seat, it'll support your weight."

Kaycia frowned. "Other chairs won't?"

"Chairs, rooms... People. What you need to remember is that these events happened in the past. Besides us, there's no one else here. You might see other people, but they won't see you. They won't *hurt* you, understand?"

"Like the woman from earlier?"

"Worse."

"And they're here—why? The city's memory?"

"You're thinking too hard," said Sefina. "But I suppose I should tell you. It'll make things easier. What we're dealing with isn't some abstract memory—the twisted workings of natural cause. It's more specific than that. For the most part, they're the memories of a single individual—albeit someone powerful enough to give them shape."

"Is that supposed to mean something?"

"I speak of Aviathas. He's dead, of course, but his mind...lingers. He's here, somewhere—an echo of what he was. But he's the reason this place has become what it is, without your typical rhyme or logic. He makes no distinction between living or dead, which is why we need to proceed with caution."

"Aviathas...?" Kaycia paused, remembering what she'd learned of Ashaira and how the goddess had fought to keep him alive. "So what you're saying is that he makes ideas real? That's what Innovation does? He makes illusions or something?"

Sefina smiled. "I knew you'd understand. And don't worry, I've passed through here before. I'll warn you before we face any danger."

"...Thanks."

"In fact, last time, I brought some tools to help—some special armbands. They made things easier."

"Really? What made them special?"

"Think of them as a lifeline. You put one on, and it gives me something to track—to find your location."

This made sense. While Kaycia had no intention of getting lost, she had no defense against illusions.

"It's just a precaution," the girl added. "And the best part? One of the bands is still down here. We're nearly there."

To Kaycia, this was a detail that should've come up earlier. But Sefina spoke very little about their plan—either because Kaycia wouldn't understand or she'd be too frightened if she knew what was coming.

They forged ahead, and Kaycia saw more and more shapes—floating rooms overhead or twisting staircases Sefina chose to ignore. The girl hardly made a sound, moving on bare feet, and it was all Kaycia could do to keep up.

Eventually, an enormous mass appeared in the distance—a floating tower of multi-tiered rooftops and boarded-up windows. The path became straighter and easier to manage.

By the time they reached the end of the bridge, however, and they stood facing two large open doors, Sefina had become...different.

"Something wrong?" asked Kaycia.

The girl stopped twenty feet from the threshold and wouldn't come closer. Her cheerfulness evaporated, and she became quiet. Forlorn.

"The armband's inside," she muttered. "Right through there."

"Aren't you coming?"

"I... I can't."

Kaycia couldn't believe it. "What's the problem? You never said I'd go anywhere by myself!"

"It's just this once. I promise. Then I'll be with you the rest of the way."

Kaycia shook her head. While she wanted to be helpful—and show she was brave—she couldn't help but feel this was a trap. If something was capable of frightening Sefina, why should Kaycia face it alone?

The girl's face was apologetic. "I hate to do this to you, but it's out of my control. It's...different for me. Although you can see me, we're *not* in the same place. For you, there's a path with an open doorway. But for me..."

This confused Kaycia even more, and after several seconds, it seemed the girl wouldn't finish the sentence.

"For me, there's nothing but painful memories..." Her face became stolid, revealing nothing. "I... I lost someone. I hope you understand."

"Like hell I do! You're saying it's dangerous? That *isn't* comforting!"

"We've been through this," groaned Sefina. "It happened in the past. The events back then can't harm you now. For you, it's just an empty building."

Kaycia wasn't so sure. At this point, Sefina might say anything to compel cooperation.

But if she refused, then what? Sefina didn't seem the sort of person who'd leave a companion to die merely out of spite. She'd have to realize Kaycia had never agreed to this. She'd have to show her the way out.

"It gets easier," the girl promised. "We get the band, and I'll keep you safe."

Kaycia eyed the black doorway with a look of suspicion. From only a few feet away, she couldn't see past the threshold.

Sefina spoke as though it were settled. "No need to worry. I'll be waiting right here."

S truggling only caused the vines to dig deeper.

Whenever Nesil tried to scream, breathing became difficult, and saliva would dribble around the vine and down his chin. His face burned hot with pent-up rage.

By the gods—how he hated her! He hated the way she asserted control—to not only stop him but leave him humiliated. To remind him he was at her constant mercy.

Ultimately, he had no choice but to relax and dangle in place. There was little doubt Sefina would've left if there remained the slightest possibility of his breaking free.

Even so, he could only hope. Perhaps, when she was far enough away, her control might slacken? The possibility was slim, but he decided he'd wait fifteen minutes before making another go.

The worst part was being so near the statue. It was right there in front of him— rough granite edges with traces of bright moss. Sefina had been smart not to trust him, but he saw this as proof he'd been on the right track.

Why else tie him up if she wasn't concerned? While he, himself, doubted he could finish the task—she, apparently, believed he could.

Fool the aeisr once, shame on him. Fool her twice...

He slumped in dejection, feeling the vines tear into his wrists. Is this what awaited him the rest of his life—he, a puppet with vines for strings? He needed to believe this wasn't the case. Sooner or later, she'd make a mistake. He just needed to wait.

After fifteen minutes, the vines were stronger than ever.

It was the same after thirty.

After an hour.

He was preparing himself to try again when he heard a noise.

"Bak alwedy?" he tried to say. He knew Sefina would understand. She always did.

Straining his ears, he thought he detected light footsteps, but he couldn't turn around to see who it was. Perhaps it was an animal—or Sefina's idea of a joke? He wouldn't put it past her to try and frighten him.

The noise stopped a moment before moving to the other side of the garden. Besides that, there was only the sound of trickling water.

Finally, after several long minutes, the newcomer came into view—gazing around as though searching for something.

It was a child wrapped in black cloth.

He was thin as a reed—not at all the sort of person you'd expect to find in Ahman. An apparition, then? One of Sefina's devotees? But even that made no sense. Her illusions were meant to be convincing, and there was nothing plausible behind the way this boy looked.

"Hmmgghh!" spat Nesil—hoping the child could be trusted but not caring either way.

The boy must've heard because he turned his gaze on the tangle of vines.

His eyes were dark but expressed mild curiosity. His arms were folded across his black shirt. Without so much as a shrug, he turned to face the other way.

Nesil was appalled. Had this *child* just ignored him? A tied-up victim in clear need of help?

Of course, considering the nature of aeisric illusions, the boy might not have been able to do anything. But he hadn't even tried!

Instead, the boy turned his attention to the statue as though in recognition—as though it were the reason he'd come in the first place.

Nesil cried out in alarm. "Waathh et!" he tried to say, but it came out as a strangled moan. "Ith noth seff!"

To his surprise, the boy smirked. "I'll be fine."

"Yohh...undahthand?"

The boy sighed and turned to face him once more. "You're different from the others."

"Othas?"

"I'm familiar with your kind. You wander these grounds like an infestation—but none have ever spoken to me. Not directly, anyway." He cocked his head in consideration. "You're the one who arrived with *her*, aren't you?"

"Thefinah?"

The boy frowned as though not understanding this last part. After a moment's hesitation, he came forward and picked up a sharp stick. He prepared to swing at the vine near Nesil's mouth.

"Thass nah gonna—"

To his surprise, the slice was clean.

Nesil spat out the end, still dripping with saliva, and worked his jaw from side to side. "How did you—?"

The boy raised the stick as though in explanation. It was nothing more than a branch, freshly fallen from a tree. Except...Nesil knew this was wrong. It only *appeared* to be fresh after Sefina's handiwork.

Somehow, the stranger had identified it as having both physical and illusory traits. Or he'd just been lucky.

"Sefina?" asked the boy. "That's her name?"

"Well... I never learned her real name. She's just...the aeisr. The high aeisr. Sefina's what I call her."

"What's an aeisr? Aren't you one of them?"

"Not by choice."

The boy didn't care for the distinction.

"I'm Nesil," he offered. "And what should I call you?"

Another pause. "Aico."

"Thank you, Aico... Could you please cut me down?"

The boy looked at Nesil's wrists but didn't come closer. "Always a trick, isn't there? That's what your kind does."

Nesil groaned. "Not me! I'm telling you—I'm not with her! Why do you think I'm tied up? Does it look like she trusts me?"

"Perhaps... Or, maybe you're stalling. Keeping me off course."

Nesil stiffened, thinking of the statue. Did he dare hope they might want the same thing? After all his efforts to see it destroyed—and this perfect opportunity, with Sefina absent—was it finally coming true?

"You'll need my help. The statue's different from the rest. That stick of yours won't do anything against stone."

Aico's face screwed together. "You think I'd use a stick?"

"I'm saying it won't matter. Nothing will work. Just...let me down! She could be back at any moment."

"You know where she went?"

"That's..." Nesil didn't have time for that story. Even mentioning the throne would invite unwanted questions. Moreover, he didn't want to think of Kaycia and what might

AUSTIN LYNN CLARK

happen to her.

"I'll explain later. We need to use this chance, or we won't get another. Trust me, you don't want her getting in the way."

The boy wasn't concerned. "For all I know, you *are* her—in disguise."

"You're serious? If I was her, why would I want the statue destroyed?"

Aico's confusion returned. "You think I came all this way just to destroy it?"

Nesil's heart sank. Though he had no idea what the boy was after, this was not a good sign.

At that moment, however, Aico froze. His eyes darted across the trees with a look of suspicion—raising a hand to deter further questions.

Nesil strained his neck but saw nothing unusual. And when he turned back, Aico was gone.

"Someone's been naughty..." said a familiar, feminine voice.

Nesil was at a loss for words. He hadn't really thought she'd be back so soon, but his luck had been on a losing streak.

Had she already reached the throne and was just now returning? Or had something gone wrong...and Kaycia was dead?

More confusing, he hadn't seen where Aico had gone. Perhaps he was skilled at hiding...or maybe he hadn't been real to begin with.

When he examined the evidence—the arrival of an unlikely child capable of cutting through Sefina's vines—it didn't look good. And Nesil realized what he'd just confessed to the boy—his real intentions regarding the statue.

A pair of arms came from behind, slipping around his middle in a gentle embrace.

"You're back..." he said over his shoulder.

"I felt bad leaving you like this." Ducking beneath his arm, she circled in front. "Just a quick visit. To make sure you're okay."

He shook his head, hoping for a more sensible explanation. "Did you forget something?"

"Oh no," she intoned, lifting what remained of the vine and inspecting its severed end. "I know what you've been doing, and I *never* forget."

Then her smile disappeared—having noticed the cut wasn't made by teeth. Her eyes came up sharply, meeting his.

And she spun at the moment Aico attacked.

For a moment, Nesil wasn't sure what he was seeing. The ground heaved as a surge of stone erupted beneath the boy's feet. It carried him forward like a wave, knocking trees sideways and adding more force to his swung pole than his small body could produce.

Sefina stood her ground—perhaps expecting the weapon to pass through her. With a grunt and a clang, she was sent sprawling back, tumbling over dirt.

Nesil gaped—having never thought he'd see the day. The pole must've come from a nearby wall hanging—infused with illusion she had created. Of course, he knew better than to think she was hurt.

As she rose to her feet, her dress was streaked with black dirt. There were scrapes on her arms and legs, and blood dripped from her forehead.

Without losing momentum, Aico leaped into the air—using the swell of a column to propel him upward—before he plunged the pole straight down through her chest. It tore through her arched back and planted deep into the ground, propping her up on her feet like a tattered flag.

Sefina's head slumped back, swinging her hair inches off the ground. Her arms dangled at her sides, and she coughed up blood.

Aico retreated a step, with eyes uncertain. He'd likely expected to meet more resistance. Or he was repulsed by the sight of so much blood, sluicing down her front, to soak into the earth.

"*Who's your friend?*" she asked, not out loud but to Nesil alone. Her tone lacked concern, as they both knew she was in no real danger.

When Aico turned his direction, Nesil shook his head in apology. "You should probably get out of here."

The boy's face screwed together, and he turned back to Sefina. Perhaps he was wondering if there was more he could do—a way to worsen her injuries.

But he needn't have bothered. Blood began to drain from her eyes and seep into her hair. It erupted from her throat and coiled down her arms.

It burst from the trees like crimson sap.

Aico paled, confused by Sefina's love for the excessive. His expression was less disturbed than it was disgusted.

Her toes left the ground as her ribcage jerked upward. In a wet, sickly grind, she slid up the pole.

"What are you waiting for?!" urged Nesil. He'd watched ascendants fight the aeisr before—it never ended well.

To his horror, the boy merely steeled himself. "She's nothing I can't handle."

"What?!"

With a grisly pop, she cleared the pole and hovered midair.

Black clouds filled the sky, dropping the trees into shadow. Sefina's white dress— now gray—stood out, in contrast, like a floating spectress. Her eyes were dark pits, leaking blood. And the corner of her lips turned up in a smirk.

"Didn't your mother teach you to be more courteous?"

The boy raised his chin in defiance without a hint of regret.

"Ah, but that's right," she continued. "You've never met your mother, have you?"

For the first time, Aico's expression faltered.

"You're surprised? You didn't think I'd heard of you—the aberration of Navara? The boy who *would* have been god, had the emperor's experiments gone as planned?"

Nesil wasn't sure what was happening. This went beyond Sefina's reading of Kaycia. No—the aeisr actually knew of this boy, as though she'd been to Navara, unseen and unnoticed.

"You're wrong," said Aico. "My father was a revolutionary—there's no one else like me in the entire world!"

"And yet...the Empire stands on the brink. You weren't born a savior. Instead, you ran away, eager to escape the emperor's shadow—and disappointment. How has that helped your people?"

Aico grit his teeth. "I didn't run away."

"Is that why you're here?" she pestered. "In some misguided attempt to prove yourself?"

He blew out his breath but didn't argue.

Sefina leered down at him. "Instead...you picked a fight that you cannot win."

As one, the trees bowed inward. Hundreds of angry branches, now defoliated, bent their points earthward, seeking blood.

Aico didn't run. He didn't cower or flinch. His eyes never left hers as he was pierced and skewered and made a bleeding ruin.

It wasn't real, of course, but Nesil knew it must hurt. In his own experience, the aeisric suggestion of pain was often worse than the real thing.

Somehow, Aico stood his ground. His eyes glistened as each wooden knot passed through his ribs—but he didn't falter.

In a strained voice, barely audible, he asked, "Is that...the best...you can do?"

Sefina scowled. This was far from the reaction she was used to seeing.

The earth surged once again, launching Aico at Sefina. The branches exploded, protruding from his chest like pins in a cushion. Caught within the splintered tangle, Aico's attack turned into a serrated storm—with Sefina bearing its full brunt.

There was so much wood and debris, Nesil couldn't make sense of it. Moreover, he didn't see the point. Why were they fighting when neither could harm the other? Wasn't this a stalemate?

The world began to spin—a tactic Nesil recognized. The aeisr shifted everything to throw Aico off her trail. It became difficult to remember where the true dangers lie, putting the boy at risk of hurting himself.

With a sound like thunder, the trees holding Nesil were torn from the ground. The earth heaved as his vines stretched taut, snapped, and set him free.

Without hesitation, he broke into a run. Shielding his face from the shower of rocks, he hoped the confusion would obscure his movements.

Unfortunately, as he leaped across an earthen chasm—where an uprooted tree had been—his legs were seized from behind. His jump was pulled short, slamming his face against the edge.

He kicked with fury as he slid down the hole, trying to escape. But it was no use. The vines snaked up his legs—no, not vines—they were dozens of slithering hands. Elongated and dirt-stained, they protruded from the earth and pulled him under.

"Let him go!" shouted Aico.

Dirt fell into the hole, and there wasn't anything Nesil could do. He squirmed, trying to get the dirt off his face, but his arms were held down by innumerable fingers. As more dirt fell, he could no longer see. He could no longer breathe.

So it surprised him to discover he could still hear Aico—speaking so loud, it shook the earth.

"I WON'T ASK AGAIN!"

In the silence that followed, the ground seemed to thrum with the beat of his heart. It throbbed with the weight constricting his chest, filling the darkness with his will to survive.

He wanted to tell Aico to save his breath. Sefina wasn't one to surrender control. Her reaction to resistance was to squeeze even tighter.

The hands held him in a loving embrace. Gentle but tenacious. With an obsession meant to hold him forever.

Until suddenly, to his astonishment, they dragged him upward, back toward the light.

Nesil knew better than to think she'd been swayed. Likely, she was only flaunting her control. Teasing her enemy.

However, as he emerged from the ground and the dirt fell from his eyes, the scene in the garden had drastically changed.

The fighting had stopped. Sefina and Aico stood facing each other, each covered in dirt, with neither backing down.

Nesil didn't understand until his eyes turned skyward.

An enormous monolith—several tons of porous rock—had materialized from nothing. It hovered midair—cutting a hole through the glass ceiling—directly above the remnants of Ashaira's statue.

It wasn't clear, at first, why this would change anything. Nesil knew from experience that this wouldn't harm the aeisr—not in a permanent way. He'd even told Aico as much.

But... If the statue was reduced to its illusory form, without anything physical for outsiders to touch—then it couldn't be moved. It'd become stuck in place, like the one in Seldor's treasury.

"Do it!" shouted Nesil, embracing the idea.

Sefina shot him a withering look.

Aico, however, grit his teeth. His face was strained as though it cost enormous effort to keep the stone from falling.

Nesil tried to understand but was unable to guess why Aico would hesitate. What could he possibly want? What reason was there to leave the statue intact?

"I'm going to set this down," began Aico, "nice and gentle. And then we're going to talk, understand? If you try anything funny, we'll be back to square one—and you don't want that."

"Talk? Sure," said Sefina, her voice almost bored. "But...could we, maybe, hold off a few minutes? This is awkward, but you caught me at rather a bad moment."

Aico didn't blink, convinced this was another of the aeisr's tricks.

She forged ahead, anyway. "You see, there's this...person I've been caring for. A real person—a girl. It was never my intention to leave her this long. But then *you* showed up, and—"

His face became concerned. "What girl?"

"You know Kaycia?" she asked, arching a brow.

"I... I saved her life once. She's new to this place. She didn't know about the vines—the paralyzing ones that inflict pain."

Nesil didn't know what he was talking about, but Sefina did.

The boy shook his head. "They frightened her off. I watched her leave!"

"You did, did you?"

Aico rounded on Nesil. "You knew she was in danger? And you didn't say anything?"

Nesil was speechless. He could only imagine what the boy was thinking—wondering why Nesil might want the statue destroyed, knowing it'd leave Kaycia to fend for herself.

"You left her alone?" asked Aico, his face becoming hard. "Where?"

F
ifteen feet off the floor was a dangling corpse. It was wrapped in a web of iron cords, suspended from the ceiling by a dozen hooks. Its position was all wrong, twisting its arms and feet upward, with the chest and one shoulder drooping to the

ground.

The flesh was emaciated, like brittle leather, but enough remained to show it'd been a man. He seemed to wear tattered clothing—but upon closer inspection, the dark smears weren't fabric but faded blood.

Repulsed, Kaycia turned away but only momentarily, having spotted a detail she couldn't ignore. A single loop around the left arm, high near the shoulder, differed from the rest. It didn't form part of the bindings or contribute in any way to his contorted demise.

In the dim lighting of the lofty tower windows, it reflected the brushed finish of bronze, only slightly tarnished after all these years.

"Damn it, Sefina!" she mumbled to herself. It was just like her to omit how she'd find the armband. *Oh, by the way, be on the lookout for a deadman...*

It was nearly enough to make her turn around, as it was obvious why the girl had left this out. After all her excuses, her explanation didn't add up. If the armband was meant for protection, what good was it if it failed to save this man?

Kaycia couldn't imagine what'd possibly done this. This wasn't a trap or something he'd stumbled into on accident. He'd been murdered and left to rot.

But...if Sefina had been as close to him as she pretended, why hadn't she come back? And what of Nesil's father—or had it been his grandfather? Had he left, too? Or was he guilty of something worse?

Kaycia's breathing became troubled, wondering what she knew of this mysterious girl. Was it possible the man had been lured to this place through similar promises made by Sefina?

Licking her lips, Kaycia looked around the spacious chamber. There were plenty of areas to hide an ambush. There were overturned tables and dark doorways, all of which were seemingly empty.

She shook her head, feeling foolish. It made no sense for Sefina to go through all this trouble if she'd just wanted to kill her. As powerful as she was, she could've done it outside without the help of an accomplice.

As Kaycia reinspected the scene, the manner of death was more characteristic of abyssal killings—from creatures that held no regard for their prey. The most likely explanation was that their group had been attacked, and they'd fled the tower out of fear for their lives.

Either way, she didn't feel any better. She was back where she started, facing something even Sefina couldn't handle—that'd left her so traumatized, she wouldn't come inside.

All the more reason to hurry.

Unfortunately, the corpse was too high to reach. Her chains were long enough to hook a blade beneath the band, but doing so might pull off the arm as well. Out of respect for the dead, it was in her best interest to opt for a gentler approach.

Should she cut him down? The wires looked tough, but they weren't indestructible. Perhaps, if she put the man to rest with some semblance of dignity, she might win over Sefina. She'd feel a whole lot better if the two of them were friends.

Something dark dripped to the floor, directly beneath the corpse.

She stared in confusion as fresh blood seemed to well from ancient wounds. It snaked down his body and joined the puddle underneath.

The blood, however, didn't come from the man. It ran down the cords from higher above. Stray droplets fell through the open windows, speckling the ground in a grisly spray.

The rain, she thought. Nothing more than that. It was an eventuality that couldn't be avoided. She should consider herself lucky not to have seen it before—not once since entering Ahman.

Still, she didn't move. Her reaction seemed perfectly natural. Who wouldn't be unnerved, alone in the dark with a mangled corpse?

"*...Wh—where isss it?*" came a whisper, seemingly from nowhere.

Kaycia spun but saw no one in the room.

The voice was one she didn't recognize—so raspy, she couldn't tell if it was male or female. Its accent, however, was most peculiar—using an outdated slur from centuries gone.

"Someone there?" she asked.

She couldn't help but remember what Sefina had said—that she'd start seeing things. Did that extend to voices as well? Murmurs from the past?

"*Th—the k—ey... G—give it to m—eeeee...*"

Kaycia swallowed, knowing nothing of a key. According to Sefina, however, there'd be no point in making sense of the words. If anything, the distraction was slowing her down.

She took a step forward, and the puddle bulged.

It began as a blister, rising steadily. The curdled surface stretched like a red sheet draped over a crystal ball—except the shape it concealed wasn't spherical. It was bowed forward—the curved spine of a man—straightening as it rose.

She stifled a gasp as something touched her leg. Looking down, there were smaller puddles, appearing more quickly than the rain could account for. An elongated hand protruded from one, and she jerked herself away.

It's not real, she told herself. Or, if it *had* been real, it was a distant echo. Wasn't that what Sefina said? A retelling of events? Perhaps, of the creature that had bled this man dry?

"Y—you c—cannot h—ide it. D—don't resissssst."

Kaycia spun to make sure nothing was sneaking up on her, then she pulled on her chains. They slid easily from her body, uncoiling like serpents, ready to strike.

It didn't matter if this thing couldn't harm her; she wanted to be ready to harm it back—just in case.

Keeping one chain on the defensive, she brandished the other like a whip and targeted the armband. Aiming wasn't necessary. She told her blade what to do, and it slid into place at the corpse's shoulder.

Nothing interfered. The swelling puddles now numbered in the dozens, with various shapes lurking beneath the surface—but nothing got in her way.

From the middle, the manlike thing had nearly emerged, wading in blood only up to its knees. The blood-soaked cloth completely covered its head, sagging inward at precise indentations—two sockets for eyes and the nose cavity of a skull. A second cloth was tied around its waist, leaving the rest of him naked. The blood parted to reveal pale muscles underneath—flesh that was dead but not lacking in strength.

With a hard yank, Kaycia pulled the band free. It slid off easily, slick with fresh blood. Working her fingers, she caught it in her hand without losing hold of her heavy chain.

"Is this what you're after? Your key?" she asked, holding up the trinket. If this thing were a memory, it wouldn't answer—but that wasn't the only thing wrong with this picture.

His voice wasn't human. When she'd first heard it, she hadn't been sure—but all doubt was gone. Though abyssal creatures weren't known to speak, this one was different.

The dripping cloth swayed from side to side as he shook his head.

It couldn't be a coincidence. Though Kaycia wanted to believe that Sefina was right and that this thing was an illusion—a projection from Aviathas—how else did she explain this?

"Y—you know what I w—ant..."

It paused. Then added, *"...Kay...ciaaa..."*

Her heart lurched in horror. But rather than make sense of it, she fled from the room. Her chains obediently wrapped up her arms.

"Sefina!" she yelled as she weaved past obstacles, desperate to get outside.

She expected the creature to cry in fury—but it held its silence, unbothered by her escape.

In truth, a part of her didn't want to run. She was far from defenseless, and it was in her nature to fight. In normal situations, the act of running—of turning your back on the enemy—was an easy way to get killed.

But nothing about this was normal. It couldn't be a memory if it knew her name. Which meant it *wasn't* an illusion. This *wasn't* Aviathas but something worse. Something *intelligent*.

She reached the bridge outside and found it empty.

"Sefina?!" she shouted, spinning around.

By then, the wooden planks were sodden with blood. What had started as a drizzle was gaining in strength. It stung her eyes and soaked through her hair. It ran down her neck and under her shirt.

Red sheets poured down the tower walls. But no matter where she looked along the hovering pathways, the girl wasn't there.

"*Y—ou cannot essscape...*"

The voice came from behind, where a protrusion was again rising from the blood.

"Who are you?!" she asked. "I don't have your frigging key!"

Cadaverous hands broke through the surface—only a few for now, but enough to worry her.

"*...LIESSS!*"

She stepped away and took a giant leap backward.

Across the gap was a dripping staircase suspended in the air. She didn't know where it went, but that didn't matter. She needed to reach a place where that thing couldn't follow.

She'd ascended two flights before remembering the band. It was still clutched in her fingers, tight against her chain.

It wouldn't hurt to try.

Getting it on her arm, however, took a little work. She wrapped her chains somewhere else, then focused her conviction into her left shoulder. The buckles came loose of their own accord, allowing the sleeve to be removed and the band to slide up her bare skin. Perhaps, when she had more time, she'd find a way to affix her armor on top.

"Sefina?!" she shouted, hoping, this time, the girl might hear.

Still no response.

The steps reached an open platform, and the hooded man was there, waiting patiently.

"I can't help you!" she insisted, keeping her eyes on the scattered, sickly hands, not wanting to get surrounded.

Her words, however, weren't making a difference. And she was left to communicate the only way she knew how.

Her chains lashed out and found their targets—slicing the fingers and arms nearest to her. They recoiled and writhed but didn't retreat.

The man didn't react or change in posture. Even without armor, he couldn't be bothered to take a defensive stance.

Kaycia didn't let this dissuade her—she threw her blades. With a squelch, they plunged deep into its head. Against all expectations, it didn't block the attack. It barely staggered from the impact. Even now, it did nothing to pull the blades free.

Instead, it grabbed hold of the chains and pulled her in.

"Oh, shit!"

She tried to resist, but its strength was overwhelming. She was so terrified of getting close to the creature that she nearly let go. At the last moment, she leaped sideways and allowed its strength to pull her past and far behind it.

Hands reached from the ground and tried to grab her, but she landed clear. With some slack on her chains, she whipped a paired undulation back at her opponent.

The chains formed a loop around each of its wrists, and she yanked on them savagely. They cut through flesh—nearly severing its arms—but it wasn't enough.

"Let go!" she screamed, whipping her chains again.

When the creature complied, she lost her footing and slipped backward over blood. She righted herself quickly, uncertain if she'd succeeded on her own or if it'd freed her on purpose.

Either way, her best chance was to end this quickly.

She circled her weapons, warding off the hands straying too close, before she crossed the chains in front and struck a 'V' across its neck.

To her amazement, it still didn't resist. Even as her chains wrapped the bloody cloth and locked around its neck, it reached with its hands to pull her in.

Its single-mindedness pleased her because, this time, she didn't care what it did. As long as she stayed out of its reach and put all her effort into this act, it was a matter of time before its head came free.

It didn't cry in pain or try to break free, but her strategy was working. She knew this because the rain itself had increased to a downpour.

Gritting her teeth, she blinked away blood and felt her weapons constrict, closing the circle.

Through the rancid curtains, she couldn't see what happened next, but her chains went slack. Something fell to the floor and rolled near its feet.

Breathing heavily, she turned to make sure nothing was behind her.

Overall, the task had been easier than the nightmaiden—but that was thanks to these impressive chains. Without proper weapons, there was no way she could've lasted this long.

"Sefina?" she called out, letting the rain wash over her.

In response, a flash of red lightning split the sky.

The sudden brightness was painful—illuminating a sea of twisted platforms as far as the eye could see.

The next moment, she was blind, with an afterimage of the figure shambling toward her.

"...*Kkkkkk... ...K—keeeeyy...*"

She stumbled backward in shock. Perhaps, this time, if she ran...?

Hands locked around her ankles and sent her sprawling to the ground. She kicked in horror and managed to break free—but new ones took their place.

Worst of all, she still couldn't see—caught completely off guard by the brilliant flash.

Sensing the creature's approach, she lashed out wildly. Out of habit, she went for its head—and was amazed when her blades swerved to the side, finding the lump that'd fallen to the floor.

Breathing frantically, she yanked them back, hoping to catch the creature before it was too late.

Lightning crashed again.

A second image was seared into her mind—one Kaycia would never forget.

Above the headless creature...there were bodies in the sky.

Like a distant flock of birds, they darkened the heavens, naked and writhing in tortured agony.

The source of the rain, she thought, in abject horror.

As the world went dark, she scrambled away, kicking in desperation.

Hands seized her legs and sent pain up her body. Blistering pain. Familiar pain—the same she'd experienced from the vines before.

She choked on blood. She spasmed to the side, but...

Instead of wood, she was laying on something soft.

"Kaycia?" It was a young girl's voice—but not Sefina's.

And she realized where she was.

"Damn it!" she shrieked with a surge of nausea. "Not now!"

"What?" asked Chesandril. "Again?"

She wanted to scream, having no desire to explain where she'd been. She needed to go back! She couldn't allow Elyriel one more second with that thing!

But as she reached with her mind, there was nothing there.

Her sister was in a place that shouldn't exist.

Chesandril asked no questions but stooped down to recover the scattered pillows.

Kaycia squeezed her eyes shut and sent tears down her face.

Not like this! she thought, squirming in frustration. *Why won't it work*?!

She could only imagine the scene. The creature—whatever the hell it'd been—was already too close. Even if she reached her sister now, she'd be too late.

There was no damn way! This had to be a dream!

After everything she'd done—listening to Sefina and entering their agreement—Elyriel was supposed to live. It was supposed to solve everything!

She had to keep trying. Gathering her strength—and her love for her sister—she put everything into finding Elyriel again.

But the minutes stretched out, seemingly eternal.

In the end, it didn't matter. Elyriel was gone.

Part 5
The Princess of Oblivion

In darkness, you shall find me,
The usefulness of fear—
Not only for preservation,
But of self-revelation,
That momentary spark
Of unencumbered identity.
So let the darkness drown
Let it show you who you are.
Lay my burdens upon you,
And never fear again.
-Confessions of Irisea
(year unknown)

Chapter 33
CROSSED BOUNDARIES

Nesil wasn't a bad person, so why did he always feel like one?

At no point had he harbored ill feelings toward Kaycia. He hadn't wanted her in danger but had merely accepted the inevitable outcome. He wasn't yet in a position to challenge the aeisr, so he'd chosen to focus on getting there first.

It made him a realist, anxiously waiting for his moment to arrive. It made him a pragmatist who'd done what he could to give Kaycia warning—not an explicit one, but a warning, nonetheless. Which was still more than Aico could claim.

The other boy, in contrast, had sent her away! If Aico cared so much, he should've prepared her. He should've protected her. And yet, it was *Nesil's* fault she wound up in danger? Not the aeisr's. Not Aico's. But the boy without any power of his own?

Maybe that was the problem. Nesil wasn't terrible from a moral standpoint—he was terrible in the sense of being utterly useless. He hadn't tried to do anything because he couldn't do anything. Which was worse, perhaps, than being a coward.

Even now, his presence was slowing them down. He couldn't match the aeisr's pace as she skirted gaps in the floorboards. And Aico wouldn't allow her to cover them up—as illusions put the real boy in danger. So, instead, they waited patiently for Nesil to catch up.

He moved as quickly as he could, but though his body wasn't real, his fear of falling *was*. No one explained where he'd end up if he lost his footing. No one explained why this darkness was here.

The sensible solution would be to leave him behind, but neither Sefina nor Aico wanted to be alone with the other. As such, Nesil had defaulted to the role of mediator—and, even in this, he was failing miserably.

"What now?" asked Aico. "Why did you stop?"

Rather than answer, she spoke to Nesil. "*You tell him.*"

"Tell him what?" he asked in irritation. He shielded his face from the blistering heat. "Shouldn't *he* be the one worried about the fire?"

"What fire?" asked Aico.

Nesil didn't understand. "Is that a joke?"

As they journeyed through the dark and countless platforms, these fires served as a blazing beacon. They'd cast the floating rooms in an orange glow—one Nesil had seen from miles away. Filling him with dread as they drew ever closer.

But Aico didn't share his fear. Though his body was shrouded from head to foot, he didn't appear hot. His hands weren't sweating.

"So...? You really don't see them?" asked Nesil.

This made no sense. Even if the flames were a kind of illusion, they would've had the same effect on everyone. They'd be visible to everyone.

"*It was the same for Kaycia,*" Sefina explained. "*To her, this was nothing but an empty bridge.*"

"Bloody heavens..." muttered Nesil. "So tell that to him!"

"*If it comes from me, he'll think it's a trick.*"

"What's she saying?" asked Aico.

Nesil groaned. "That Kaycia couldn't see the fires, either."

Aico looked down the bridge, oblivious to the firestorm.

For Nesil, the scene stirred up painful memories. And though his eyes confirmed the boy was unharmed, it was difficult not to yell and tell him to run.

"They're everywhere," said Nesil. "You're almost standing in them."

The boy took a step backward but didn't appear afraid.

Nesil turned to Sefina. "Can't you make some water? Clear a path?"

She responded with a face that made him feel stupid. If it'd been so simple, she would've done it by now.

"So what's the plan?" asked Aico. "Do I go in alone?"

"...I guess so," said Nesil, seeing no way around the barrier.

He turned to the aeisr, but she avoided his gaze.

It was only then that he realized the girl was embarrassed. For all her power and all her skill, it was the first obstacle they'd encountered that she couldn't cross. It was no wonder she wasn't willing to speak this out loud.

"What is this?" asked Nesil. "Why are these here?"

She sighed. "*There's a lot about Ahman that doesn't make sense. Some nightmares surpass my own capabilities.*"

"Nightmares?"

"It's just a word. If I had to guess, these flames were produced by Aviathas himself."

He frowned in confusion. Was she suggesting the god—in his partially restored state—was somewhere nearby? And these were random flickers of his dying intellect?

"All right," said Aico. "Suppose I believe you. You can't go inside. How do you know she's still in there?"

This time, Sefina gave her answer: "I just do, okay? Under a quarter mile that way. You can't miss her."

"Not good enough."

Nesil was embarrassed for not questioning this himself. At some point, he'd stopped wondering how the aeisr knew things she shouldn't.

She tried to explain. "We came here because I needed Kaycia to get something. It was a precaution—an armband to keep tabs on her location."

The boy cocked his head.

"A band?" asked Nesil. "Like my grandfather's?"

She stepped closer to Aico and pointed at her shoulder. Where it'd once been bare, there was now a band of finely crafted metal. "Perhaps you've seen one. You know what this is?"

The boy hesitated. "A band of Devotion... And Kaycia agreed to this? Knowing the two of you would be connected?"

"It worked, didn't it? It led us straight here."

Nesil was still uncertain of many details. Even after seeing his grandfather's band—and knowing how it helped control his ascension—he'd never gotten more explanation than that.

Aico, on the other hand, wasn't confused. And his concern for Kaycia outweighed his questions.

"This isn't over," he said, backing away.

Her smile was thin. "Just bring her back. Don't go anywhere else, or I'll know."

The boy smirked and said nothing more. Then he turned and disappeared into the flames.

Nesil squinted but could barely see anything against the raging brightness.

Not ten seconds later, Sefina muttered, *"Something's not right."*

"Could you be more specific?"

"Just a feeling. Something I'm getting from Kaycia."

"From—? You mean...through the band?" he asked, thinking back to his wedding and the glimpses he'd seen of the aeisr's past. *"You can see her thoughts? Her memo-*

ries?"

She considered this a moment before shaking her head. *"Nothing so explicit—but the idea's similar. Historically, these bands were a supplement to wedding vows, adding strength to Devotion. They let you know your spouse was okay, even from afar. These days, however, they're so difficult to make, you hardly see them anymore. They're incredibly valuable."*

"How did you get them?"

"From Kadrek."

She looked up at the wall of flame, and her eyes grew distant.

"It's like I'm going through it all over again. We reached this spot, and I couldn't go in. I waited right here, but I could feel what Kadrek and Renat were going through. The helpless wandering and bouts of fear. I was with them—but my hands were tied. I couldn't send warning when Renat's feelings shifted to betrayal."

Nesil didn't know what to say.

"It was horrible," she continued. *"You think I'm lying, but you don't know what I experienced. Back then, I had a fondness for your grandfather. I trusted him. And to sense his turmoil—struggling against an act he knew to be wrong... I can still feel it so clear in memory. His blistering guilt, as he left Kadrek to die."*

Nesil thought he understood, but it also made him wonder. If the two had been connected, how long had it lasted? Had she been privy to Renat's feelings these past few years? Providing insight as she mounted her offense?

Were they connected at the end? So intimately, she'd know he'd suffered enough?

He pushed those thoughts away, deciding to stay on topic.

"But what about now? What's wrong with Kaycia?"

She frowned. *"I... I'm not sure. I only sense flickers, but...they don't feel like her."*

Nesil raised a brow. *"Is she hurt?"*

"It... It's more like she's half-awake. And can't make sense of her feelings. If she'd bumped her head, I'd feel that, too."

"I don't follow. She's daydreaming?"

"There's a possibility the person with the band ISN'T Kaycia."

"But then...?"

"I don't know! There's no one else down here!"

Nesil couldn't contain himself. *"And you didn't warn him? Aico went in there, and you didn't say a thing!"*

"Like what? I don't know what's wrong! He'll see the truth before I do!"

"Unless he walks into a trap."

She grinned. *"I'll try not to get my hopes up."*

Nesil forced himself to breathe. He'd been through this enough times to know she wouldn't change. What was done was done. And he hoped Aico was prepared to handle surprises.

He almost asked the first question that came to mind: 'Why do you hate him so much?' Except...playing games like this wasn't really hate—not for Sefina. So, instead, he asked, "*What's his deal, anyway? You know what he's after?*"

"*Of course. Don't you?*"

"*The statue. Apparently. But he wants it intact. It makes no sense.*"

She raised a brow.

Nesil tried to recover. "*I mean, what benefit does he gain?*"

"*That, too, is obvious. He seeks to make Navara the new capital of the world.*"

When Nesil didn't understand, she asked, "*When you look at Ahman, what do you see?*"

"*Besides a ruin?*"

"*Look past the surface. What does the place mean?*"

"*I'm tired,*" he said, shaking his head. "*Just tell me.*"

"*Tranquility. Security... From the start, Ahman has been separate—placed, as it were, on a pedestal. The gods gained distance and vantage above mankind. And you know what? The place still has that! People have spent centuries trying to get in, and no one can. They can't even find the entrance.*"

"*So... That's what he wants? For Navara? To hoard his resources and keep his empire safe from vagrants and refugees?*"

"*Not just people.*"

Only then did he remember what his grandfather said—how the statue shielded their kingdom from the current.

He shook his head. "*Statue's broken. We've seen the creatures. They're all over the place.*"

"*No,*" she insisted. "*NOT all over. The city's become fragmented, mirrored, and replicated to the point it can't all be covered. But if you limit your view to the actual township—the original buildings—you won't find a trace of shadow. It's perfect, really. A closed utopia.*"

"*I suppose...*" he conceded—concealing his opinion that the aeisr was worse than any abyssal creature. Seldor was proof.

Sefina guessed his thoughts. "*Don't worry. He hasn't forgotten me. He intends to— what do you call it? When you cleanse evil spirits? ...An exorcism?*"

Nesil was incredulous. "*But...! We aren't—!*"

"*Then choose a different word. He knows what I can do and plans to be rid of me.*"

"*He can do that?*"

She tossed her hair casually and turned to the tower where Aico disappeared. "*Not a chance.*"

Her tone was confident, as usual. She was prepared for everything—even Aico, with his inhuman power.

But despite Nesil's efforts, he couldn't guess her plan. She always had another trick—another *twist* to get ahead. It was only a matter of time before she became unstoppable.

Since Aico couldn't see that, Nesil needed to be ready. He'd make his move—whether it was wanted or not.

His goal, after all, wasn't to be liked. He didn't care for Aico's opinion or even being a good person. So long as the aeisr was put down, he'd rest in peace.

"*You're sure about this?*" he asked, hoping she might just give him a clue. "*You expect an attack?*"

She spun on her heel and flashed a beautiful smile. "*Just wait and see.*"

Kaycia felt numb.

She couldn't speak. She could barely breathe.

Almost an hour had passed and still...nothing.

It was different from the first time when Aico came for her. Even then, she hadn't deserved to be saved. She'd made a horrible mistake and had only gotten free out of sheer dumb luck.

Apparently, the experience had taught her nothing. She'd rolled the dice again, and why? Because the value of the prize had increased. She'd been tempted by the chance to do something heroic. But that didn't matter. When the odds were stacked against her, a loss was still a loss.

Kaycia didn't know what had gone wrong. Sefina had said she would stay. She'd made a promise! But a lot of what she'd said wasn't exactly the truth.

With the abyssal current involved, it might not have been on purpose, but, in the end, she wasn't there. That was the part Kaycia couldn't forgive. It didn't matter if the threat was beyond the girl's power—it was her fault Elyriel had gone inside in the first place. In turn, it was on her to see her out.

There was a part of Kaycia—so stubborn and so stupid—that clung to the hope of that still happening. A lot of time had passed—too much if she was being honest—but Sefina remained the only person who could help. Her only hope was a girl who couldn't be trusted.

There came a knock at the door.

Kaycia dropped her hands and looked up from where she sat.

Outside the carriage window, the sun hung low in the sky. Was it going down already? ...Or coming up? The fact she couldn't tell—or even remember East from West—was a good indication of how lost she felt. A few days in Ahman had been murder to her rhythms.

Chesandril eyed the door but made no move toward it. She was waiting for Kaycia to say it was okay, not wanting to do anything that might cause distress.

Poor girl, she thought, knowing how confusing this must be. Hour after hour, unable to do anything. The girl couldn't even leave to get herself food.

As Kaycia considered this, she relaxed, realizing it was likely a servant with Chesandril's dinner. ... Or was it breakfast? She still couldn't tell.

Sure enough, the opened door brought the fragrance of food. Unfortunately, the person with the tray was none other than Soril.

"Oh, hell..." she muttered, regretting not first looking out the window.

"Good. I didn't know you were awake." Handing the tray to Chesandril, he stepped inside.

"Get out," she said, trying not to yell. "I can't deal with you right now."

He bit his lip. "Is this because of Laurus? Or has something else happened?"

His concerned tone didn't make her feel better. If anything, it reminded her of what little he could do—the little *anyone* could do to fix this mess.

"I said, *Get out*! I..."

He'd just begun to leave when an impulse struck her.

"...Hold on."

The man paused but didn't face her.

"Can I ask you something?"

When he didn't move, she took this as a form of acceptance.

"How much do you know of the abyssal rain?"

He turned, working his mouth uncomfortably. Even Chesandril was surprised by the shift in topic.

She did her best to clarify. "It's basic, I know... But has anyone seen where it comes from? The source of the blood?"

"I'm sorry. What's this about?"

Unwilling to mention Elyriel, she said. "I'm curious, is all. There's a rumor that's started to bother me. I'd nearly forgotten till now."

"You'll have to be more specific."

"That the blood isn't, well... It doesn't just look like blood. It's *actual* blood. Not animal, either—but human."

He sighed. "You know better than to believe—"

"It isn't just the rain," she pressed. "The creatures themselves exhibit human characteristics. Body parts. Mannerisms. I used to believe it was to frighten their prey—so we'd lose focus. But there's more to it, isn't there? I'm not saying I believe all the stories, but I've been wondering what sorts of things you've seen."

"Such as?"

"Anything exceptionally odd... Has a creature—I don't know—ever tried to communicate? You know...with words?"

"A fear tactic," he said, shaking his head in disgust. "They've been known, from time to time, to imitate sounds—things they've picked up while observing us. But it's mere diversion. You mustn't drop your guard because you think—"

"I know that. I'm not talking about mimicry. For most of them, I agree—they react to our tone without making sense of what we say—but aren't *some* smarter? Have you ever heard one talk?"

"Personally? Never." He was almost irritated.

It was too late, however, for Kaycia to back down. "Okay, then. What of your comrades? Someone you trust? Have you ever felt doubt for no greater reason than the rumor's source?"

Soril hesitated and asked, "What's this about? Don't give me this garbage of a rumor you heard. I can see it in your face. Something's wrong, and it happened recently."

"That isn't...! Please don't be upset with me. I know your feelings about sharing everything—but I can't go into it now. I just..."

She felt herself begin to break down. It'd been a mistake to attempt a normal conversation. If Soril saw through her when she was at her best, what chance did she have of succeeding now?

His expression showed that he was annoyed but not as angry as she would've feared—perhaps in reaction to her distress.

"Kaycia..." he breathed. "I *want* to help. I truly do. However... I need to know if you've chanced across an Abyssal Lord."

She blinked in genuine surprise. "Why would you think...?"

He looked at her askance. "Human speech? Unusual intelligence?"

"Yes, but—! I didn't mean—"

"You mentioned the rain as well. The victims of Praxys."

"I..." She immediately thought of the bodies she'd seen, bleeding in the sky. "I've never heard that name before."

She really hadn't and was able to say this with enough conviction, there was a good chance he'd believe her. Which was important because if the man knew anything—and it was obvious he did—these were precisely the details she needed to know.

Unfortunately, the mere mention of a lord had thrown her emotions into turmoil. The control of her features was beginning to slip. And so she kept talking, focusing on the mystery and less on the horror her sister was experiencing.

"Praxys...?" she repeated, testing the word. "Is that another name for them?"

"Not them. *Him*. Nobody's certain where the name comes from or if 'Praxys' is even his rightful designation."

"But we know he's real? One of them, at least? A lord?"

"No one's actually seen him—no one living, that is. It's been so long, people think they went away for a reason. Possibly, that the lords lost their interest in mortals."

"And you believe that?"

"Well..." He took a deep breath. "I can't fathom what thoughts might occupy such a being, but..." He lowered his voice. "It'd be foolish to drop our guard."

An unease fell over the carriage.

Chesandril sat back, uncertain she should be listening.

"Supposing he's still around," continued Kaycia, "what've you heard?"

Soril's eyes fell out of focus as he consulted his thoughts. "The Extractor, some call him. From the ancient tongue—roughly translated—we get something like the Strangler. But it's not a reference to air or typical asphyxiation. The title that appears most often, by far, marks him as the Harvester of Blood."

This struck a nerve, and it was all Kaycia could do to avoid her memories—the fall of heavy rain and the twisted hands.

"Okay..." She swallowed. "And this Harvester...he's been known to speak...? With actual words?"

"Nothing's been confirmed, but that's what they say. About *all* the lords. The problem, of course, is lack of evidence—as no witnesses are known to survive these encounters. We can't even say how many lords there are."

"But then...?"

"It's the same reason no one speaks of Irisea. The only records are apocrypha and discredited by the church."

She drooped her shoulders. It all came back to their earlier discussion—the reports she'd tried so hard to dismiss.

The problem was their source. As far as anyone could prove, no witnesses from that day were supposed to exist.

The City of Ahman had been off limits—beyond the reach of men and gods. By some miracle, Shaelis and Ashaira got back inside with a few trusted generals. But that was it. When they were killed, no one else could get inside. And word of what happened could not get out.

The only information to surface afterward—including all mention of the child goddess—came from a source that couldn't be trusted.

It was rare for a Velthr to survive past infancy. These peculiar people—if they could be called people—were exempt from the gods' blessings. They were the tragic offspring of incest, fornication, and adultery—from parents who hadn't been properly wed. Without a unified aspect, the Velthr were born with none.

In nearly every case, this ended in death—usually in the form of a merciful killing—to prevent an outcome far more gruesome. The scarce few to reach adolescence lived in constant fear of unseen threats. They didn't live in the same world as everyone else. And this unique existence—being both in the world and outside—made it feasible for a few to enter Ahman that day.

Highly improbable but not impossible.

Soril licked his lips. "There was a girl—Jaleina. I've read her transcripts before—several times, to be honest. But after our recent discoveries, I was drawn to them again.

"She was only seven. Most of what she said was an unintelligible mess. The scribes had to stop repeatedly to calm her down. But they captured the experience in surprising detail—down to the syllables they couldn't understand.

"If there's time in the future, you can read it yourself. She talks a lot about Shaelis, recounting what he said. As such, it's comprised mostly of commands—ordering his troops to one front or another. But more than once, she references two distinct sounds: Lah and Ren."

Kaycia thought back to the prison memo. "Lothren?" she asked.

He smirked. "Right? Until now, the meaning was unclear. Most have speculated she was talking of a place—that this 'Lah Ren' was where the monsters came from. A location that came and went without explanation."

Kaycia frowned at the picture this created in her mind.

"But if Lothren was a person," Soril continued, "he was undoubtedly related to the current somehow. The way Jaleina speaks... She might've been referring to a ritual. Or a summoning.

"'The skies weep!' she said. 'Endless screams from the sea of the dying! Lord Praxys shall reap, and none shall abide the wrath of his coming!'"

Kaycia narrowed her eyes. "That's not unintelligible. Nor sound like a child."

"There are moments, yes. She babbles one minute, then quotes entire passages verbatim. It's been a point of conflict all these years. As though the words were...*given* to her. Planted in her mind. By a source, some claim to be entirely malicious."

This explained a lot to Kaycia. She'd often wondered at the fuss surrounding these documents. If it all was fake, then everyone should be allowed to see it for themselves.

There should've been no reason for the church to get involved.

But if more was going on—some hidden agenda... If a fiend intended to break people's spirits, there were methods even worse than filling them with dread. Like hope, for example. To mix in the invention of a false savior. A beguiling future, brittle as glass.

For much the same reason, Kaycia had been too afraid to seek the documents herself. And, now, to discover her fears might be justified...

Soril clearly didn't share this worry. Despite the strangeness of Jaleina's speech, he favored other explanations.

He went on. "There's a specific passage: 'I've come to tear down the masters and set us free.'"

"I've heard that one," she said with a frown. From the corner of her eye, Chesandril nodded as well. "Shaelis, right?"

"I'd be surprised if you hadn't. It's been repeated by priests—many who don't know where the quote originated. And it's easy to see why. It's a powerful image—of our god defying death until the bitter end."

He took a deep breath. "I... I studied it again... And it's possible we've been reading it wrong. It might not have been Shaelis who said it at all."

"If not him... Lothren?"

"That's my fear."

"But then...? If he was the one summoning the lords...what was the point? Did he mistakenly believe he could bring them down and end them permanently?"

Soril frowned. "I hadn't considered that—but I fear your assessment is overly optimistic. I don't believe he was addressing the lords at all. He was crying defiance against Shaelis. And the rest of the pantheon."

Kaycia swallowed.

He went on. "I think Jaleina herself was confused. Much of what she said can be reliably attributed to the King of the Gods. But it's all mixed together—and far from complete. If half the dialogue was Lothren's, it starts to read like a heated debate. As though there was an argument between them."

"But who was he?" she asked, so deeply intrigued she almost forgot the distress she'd been feeling. "Why have we never heard of this man?"

"...I don't know."

"Is there any truth to what he said? Do we have reason to believe the gods were unjust? That man needed to be saved from their rule?"

Soril's eyes grew angry.

"I'm not taking his side!" she said quickly. "What Lothren did was horrible. I just want to understand. What if he honestly believed he had no choice? In a world where the gods held absolute control, if anyone disagreed, what could they possibly do?"

"There were systems for petitioning—"

"And when those didn't work? No one stood a chance in actual combat. You couldn't start a revolution. It should go without saying why Lothren was desperate."

"Lothren was wrong."

"Even so... He might've fashioned himself a hero—the only one with the courage to do what was necessary."

Soril took a deep breath. "I think you're giving him too much credit."

"I'm just trying to figure this out. What else did you learn? Was there anything else in Jaleina's file?"

There was a glint in Soril's eye. "That all depends. If you're willing to hear it."

She'd known this was coming—but, this time around, she was genuinely curious about Irisea.

Soril waited for her nod before he continued.

"Toward the end, there's a marked shift in tone. 'Even in death, the gods are restless!' says Jaleina. 'Their pawns lay havoc to the world of the living. But all is not lost.

"'The heavens will yet stand while one god remains.

"'A child! A miracle! Asleep within Ashaira. Awaiting her destiny.

"'Take this key, and set her free.'"

S omething had indeed happened to Kaycia.

It took Nesil a moment to get past the blood—to convince himself that it wasn't hers. But he saw something in her eyes as she emerged from the flames. Her pupils shifted with unfocused fury—even toward Aico. She kept pulling back, having clearly resisted the entire way.

"Kaycia?" cried Sefina, rushing forward. "What...? What did you do to her?"

The boy was furious. "That's for me to ask *you*! She was like this when I found her!"

For a moment, Kaycia's eyes paused on Nesil, but she didn't display any hint of recognition. In fact, her efforts to break away redoubled now that she faced three people rather than one.

"She hasn't talked?" asked Sefina. "Did you see anything else? Was she in any danger?"

"Only from herself... I found her screaming at some vines."

"Vines?"

Aico was in no mood to explain. "I'm taking her out of here."

"You can't!"

"Just try and stop me."

Their shouting did nothing to calm the girl's mood. Saliva trailed from her mouth, thick from exertion. Her lips curled into a snarl.

"Kay?" asked Nesil. "What's gotten into you?"

She lunged at him so forcefully, Aico lost his grip.

Nesil's reaction was to flinch, even as her fingers clawed through him.

Meeting no resistance, she was thrown off balance and smacked hard on the wooden planks. A second later, she was back on her feet, hair spinning, and eying him with utter bewilderment.

"It's me!" he yelled. "Nesil! ...You know me!"

Her eyes blazed with hatred. Spittle seethed through her teeth.

She attacked again—only this time, she went for Sefina. Her hands raked through her dress, over and over, undeterred by her inability to connect.

The aeisr's gaze never left Aico's.

"These vines..." said Sefina. "They were causing her pain?"

Aico shook his head. "She wasn't touching them."

"But they're the same ones?" she asked. "The ones that burn?"

Nesil had never heard of such a thing and wondered if the fires might have something to do with it.

Instead of answering, Aico brought Kaycia under control. He did so easily despite her arms being slick with blood. And Nesil noticed stone-like tendrils snaking from his sleeves, holding her in place.

As Aico dragged her away, the aeisr shouted, "We haven't agreed on anything!"

"Look around! This is no place for her! She needs help!"

"We don't know what's causing this! No one outside will have a solution!"

Nesil realized he should say something. If Aico stormed off, there was no telling what he'd do. He might even take the statue without regard for the consequences.

"She's right," he said. "Just a few minutes. We can talk this out."

Aico turned on Nesil. "What do you care? If memory serves, you were fully content to leave Kaycia here!"

"That wasn't what I—!"

But the boy had stopped listening. He looked past Nesil with odd concern.

"What's she doing?"

When Nesil turned around, Sefina's eyes were closed. Her arms were at her sides. Her chest rose and fell, though more slowly than before.

"I don't know," he said, frustrated their discussion had gotten off track. It only took one look, however, to see something was wrong.

Her nose scrunched together, and her eyelids squeezed tight. Her face gave a twitch of forceful concentration.

"Make her stop," said Aico.

Nesil, however, didn't know what to do. "Even if I—!"

"Quiet!" said Sefina, with eyes still closed. "I almost have her…"

Aico hesitated. Beside him, Kaycia had stopped pulling away. Both girls stood in the same position, across from each other. They breathed steadily, in perfect unison.

"Damn it…!" said Aico, as his eyes went to the band.

"Don't touch it!" she said. "She's still in there. Just give me a moment to—"

The boy wouldn't listen. He reached for the band and only stopped when Kaycia's eyes snapped into focus.

Her expression was strange, like a person waking from deep sleep.

"Kaycia?" he asked timidly.

She didn't seem to hear. She raised a bloody hand to her face and studied it curiously.

He snapped his fingers, and she turned, startled.

"Aico?" she asked. "What's going on? Where are we?"

"You don't remember…? We came to your rescue. Does anything hurt? Can you tell us what happened?"

Nesil was afraid it was just a trick. The aeisr made it seem like Kaycia was talking. But if that was the case, Aico should've known and wouldn't be responding the way he was.

Which meant, what, exactly? That Kaycia was back? She'd miraculously healed of her mental injuries without a drawn-out recovery? And it was thanks to Sefina?

That couldn't be right.

Kaycia's face squeezed together. "What are you doing?" she asked. "Let go of me."

The boy released her and took a step back. "I'm sorry. I was taking you outside. I was going for help."

"Thanks…but that isn't necessary."

"We really ought to have you checked."

"I'm fine," she insisted. She tried to smile, but something about her features was off.

Nesil couldn't put his finger on it, but her behavior was unusual. After everything she'd been through, he didn't expect her to act normal—at least, not immediately. But she was too indifferent. And not nearly so frightened as she should've been.

There was another problem, besides: since the moment she awoke, the aeisr hadn't moved. Her eyes were still closed, though not so tense as before.

"*Sefina?*" he asked, but no sound came out. His voice was blocked, though he'd deliberately avoided clenching his teeth.

"*What is this?*" he hissed. "*Did you really help, or...?*"

"I thought you left," said Aico, still focused on Kaycia. "I watched you leave!"

"I... I changed my mind."

"I don't believe that." He turned to the aeisr. "This has got your stench all over it. What have you done to her?"

A sickening dread stirred within Nesil. He hadn't believed this was the aeisr's doing—that she'd somehow seized possession of Kaycia. The acting wasn't good enough. If she'd wanted them to think the girl had returned, it was entirely within her skill to do so convincingly.

Unless, of course, she didn't *want* to be convincing.

Aico stepped toward Sefina, full of suspicion.

"*Watch out!*" shouted Nesil, but the boy didn't hear. He didn't see Nesil open his mouth or waving his arms.

And he didn't see Kaycia twist the ring on her hand.

Nesil rushed forward—despite the fact he could do nothing to stop her.

Aico spun and flinched away, but it was already too late. A fine cloud of powder landed on his face, and it didn't matter how much he blinked or rubbed it away.

If anything, the cloth around his skin made it worse, absorbing the tears from his deep, dark eyes. And preventing any chance of removing the agent.

With eyes squeezed shut, he wasn't watching her approach, but spikes burst from the ground to block her path. *Stunted* spikes that rose a few inches before crumbling to dust beneath Kaycia's feet.

"Y—you aren't... Kaycia would n—never..."

"She'd never what?" asked the girl, twisting the ring closed. She wiped her hands clean on Aico's shirt. "You think she meant to use this on me? She already had this with her since before we met. Who else would it be for, if not you?"

"She's lying!" said Nesil, surprised his voice was working again—but also dismayed. It could only mean that the aeisr had won, and he could do nothing to make this right. "Kaycia *wouldn't* want to kill you. So that stuff isn't deadly. It can't be!"

With renewed strength, Aico reached for her shoulder and the band that was there.

But Sefina was faster. Even in a body that wasn't her own, she seized his wrist and looked down into his face with utter contempt.

Aico slumped and leaned his weight into her. His eyes were still closed—but his wits weren't gone.

Nesil knew this because of what the boy did next.

His objective hadn't been the band at all. Rather, he wanted her to grab him so he could pull her in.

...And cough in her face.

She twisted away in sudden fury. She landed a kick to his groin and sent him sprawling to the ground.

That's it! thought Nesil. He could've blessed the boy for his quick thinking. Though the sedative wouldn't have affected Sefina, it *would* work on Kaycia. Even at a fraction of the dosage.

She stumbled backward and covered her nose.

"You...asshole!" she shouted, as her eyes lost focus.

Aico grinned, with losing strength. He fell onto his back and promptly passed out.

It took longer for Kaycia to follow suit. "I... I can still...!"

She lowered to the ground. "Just... Need a moment..."

Nesil came forward as the girl rested her head on an arm, lying on her side.

While this outcome was far from ideal, it was certainly better than what'd almost happened.

Just thinking about it made Nesil cringe—the thought of the aeisr having a body. The havoc she could cause. The people she could kill.

Bloody heavens... With a body of her own, she wouldn't need any help. She'd break out of Ahman, and he'd be powerless to stop her.

His first thought, naturally, was to make a break for the statue. He'd leave them sleeping, and... And what? He was far from confident he could retrace their steps. After everything he'd seen, it was one in a thousand he'd find the way in time. More likely, he'd get lost and be no help to anyone when she eventually woke up.

Of this, of course, he had no doubt. The aeisr would wake up. And there would be a reckoning.

"Damn it...!" he hissed, searching for options.

He started toward Aico, wondering what it'd take to wake him up. The boy had received a full blast of the powder, but with enough provocation...

Instead, he crouched over the sleeping girl.

"Kaycia!" he shouted. "Are you in there...somewhere? Kaycia, it's me! You have to wake up!"

He tried shaking her shoulder—which didn't do much. He could only hope the girl might feel it and do the rest herself.

To his surprise, her eyelids twitched.

"Kaycia?" he asked, with sudden hope. "Can you hear me? I...! It's hard to explain, but I need your help! You need to push through this!"

She let out a moan.

"Good!" he said. "There's not much time, but we have to stop her! We can kill Sefina!

There's a statue in the garden where we—"

Her lips began to move.

"Huh? You have to speak up!"

He leaned in closer and made out a single word.

"K-kill...?" she asked.

Nesil drew a deep breath. "I know. It's extreme. You have to trust me on this. You don't know her like I do. It's kill or be killed."

Her eyes snapped open and locked on his.

"...Kay?" he asked, jerking back.

When her lips stretched, the smile was painfully familiar.

"I told you," she said, somewhat slowly. "I just...needed a moment."

Nesil's mouth stammered but not out of shame. He didn't give a damn what the aeisr had heard. He was just frustrated Kaycia wasn't there.

"You can't...!" he said. "This isn't right! You can't just take another person's body!"

She scowled. "I'll give it back. Eventually."

For some reason, he had trouble believing her.

"Kay? Are you there? You have to fight this!"

Her face twisted in disparagement. "Save your breath. It's just me in here. Since I first took over, she hasn't resisted. Not once. If anything, her mind was laid open. Like a vacant inn room. She *wanted* me in."

"No one would want that."

She shrugged her shoulders and sat herself up. Her eyes drew inward, and she licked her lips slowly as though savoring the sensation. Or the taste of dried blood.

She worked her mouth as though suppressing a smile. Pushing up onto a knee, she drew a knife from her hip.

The blood drained from Nesil's face. "You can't! What are you doing?!"

"Wasn't that what you said? Kill or be killed?"

"That's not what I...! No!"

Her eyes widened in feigned innocence. "I'm just defending myself. Defending *her*, even."

"It's not the same at all! Aico's never tried to *kill* you!"

"Not directly, no. But now he's motivated."

"He isn't like that. He's angry, sure, but—!"

"But nothing. And don't pretend you know him at all. He might be a kid, but he isn't stupid. He knows I'm a threat. Now, more than ever."

"That doesn't mean—!"

"You've seen what he can do, Nesil. And if you think I'd risk fighting *that* again, then you don't know me, either."

The aeisr had a point. That ring had been Kaycia's only advantage. Without it, neither stood a chance against Aico.

Which was precisely why Nesil needed him alive.

It didn't matter how he felt about the boy—how he hated Aico's arrogance and the way he pretended to be in control of everything. It didn't matter that the boy thought so little of Nesil.

"Use her chains!" he suggested. "Tie him up so he won't come after you!"

Her disdain reappeared.

Nesil sensed he was grasping at straws, but he was desperate for a way to talk her out of this.

"I…! I promise to cooperate!"

She raised a brow in amusement. "Like you have a choice?"

"Isn't this better? I'll keep my mouth shut! You won't have to force me, because you'll have leverage. Something for me to lose."

She weighed this over but didn't look convinced. "All this for a boy you barely met?"

"Not for me," said Nesil. "His country needs him."

Her expression said she didn't care.

She raised the knife, and he held his breath.

"Have it your way," she said as she returned it to its sheath. "Just because I like you…

"But don't come crying to me later. There's only one place I'll leave him, and I doubt he'll be grateful."

Chapter 34

THE DOORS OF HEAVEN

Simple chains wouldn't do—not for someone like Aico.

After carrying him back to the city, beneath the light of the stars, Sefina dropped him down a hole. He landed atop some vines and promptly began to thrash with convulsions.

Nesil couldn't speak, weighed down with guilt. He couldn't help but feel that dying would be better, and his meddling had led to this horrific fate.

To make things worse, Sefina laced the basement with a multitude of illusions. In the event that Aico regained a semblance of awareness—through the fog of pain—it'd be all but impossible to find the way out.

Eventually, the boy would die anyway—from hunger, fatigue, or an addled brain. Nesil had done nothing but extend his suffering.

But still, this wasn't the time for regrets. And he swore to himself he'd make this all count for something.

With Aico out of the way, Sefina's attention returned to Kaycia, intent on performing a more thorough examination and ensuring she hadn't sustained any injuries.

"Oh my..." she breathed, standing ankle-deep in water. "This is....amazing! I mean, I've always had sensitivities. I've felt just about everything...but this?"

She gave a twirl, looking down at herself. "You never told me it was like this—having a body. A *real* body. I can't explain it. It's so...tactile! So—!"

"Real?" he suggested.

She didn't seem to hear—as though captivated by the sensation of running her fingers down her arms, scaled with dried blood.

"So *intense*! I've got to hand it to you. It's no wonder you humans are so...sensual.

So ensnared by desire—and your appetites!"

She swept her hands through her matted hair, grazing the sides of her neck and stomach and crossing down to her thighs.

Nesil turned away, feeling his face flush red.

He wasn't usually offended by Sefina's brash and impetuous nature, but it was so much worse in another person's body. It was a violation of privacy and common decency.

When she undressed to bathe, he found a safe place to hide.

He knew better than to leave. He couldn't risk the girl running off by herself, or he might never find her again. Now that she was free, she didn't need him anymore. At least not in the way she used to.

So, instead, he pressed his back against a rock and listened carefully to the sounds of her splashing. He ignored her invitations and false claims she didn't have a clue what she was doing. Luckily, she didn't push him very long. She must've sensed his change of mood and how deeply he'd been affected by Aico's predicament.

After several long minutes, lost in thought, he almost didn't notice when Kaycia spoke up.

"I... I'm... ... Holy shit..."

He sat up, unsure how to take this comment. Even her tone was different. It didn't feel like another of Sefina's traps, as though he'd suddenly grow careless and drop his guard.

"Kaycia?" he asked, without disguising his skepticism. "That you?"

There was a long pause, making him wonder if it was just a fluke—if he'd somehow imagined it.

"Nesil...? Dear gods. Yes, I'm here! I don't know how, but—! What are you doing back there?"

Her voice sounded normal enough. She wasn't bashful or shy, lending reassurance Sefina had, at least, gotten her clothes back on. Even so, he crept out with caution, on the off-chance he was wrong, and Kaycia had been too distracted to notice such details.

Luckily, he found her standing at the water's edge in the simple, tight clothing that went beneath her armor. Her leather gear had been left out to dry along the stone-brick dock, only slightly more clean than it'd been before.

"How did we get here?"

"It's really you...?" he asked, coming a few steps closer. "How are you feeling? We didn't know what was wrong."

"I bet..." she said, unexpectedly unsurprised. She shivered and wrapped her arms across her chest. "But...why were you hiding?"

Her confusion was genuine, having no recollection of being possessed.

"*Be very careful what you say,*" said the aeisr's disembodied voice. "*We don't want her frightened, got that?*"

He groaned inwardly but remembered their agreement. "*I won't mention Aico. But shouldn't she know what you did? What you can do? It's her body we're talking about.*"

Kaycia, of course, didn't hear this exchange. She came closer and studied Nesil with a worried expression.

"*You'd only cause problems,*" added the aeisr. "*For her, I mean.*"

"Something wrong?" asked Kaycia.

Sefina appeared at the top of the muddy bank. "He's embarrassed, is all."

Kaycia stiffened.

"You feeling okay?" asked Sefina, with sincerity. "Glad to see you talking again."

"Me, too... Why's my hair wet?"

"I—" The girl's mouth opened and closed. "I washed it, remember?"

Kaycia's face went through a series of expressions as she took into account the rest of her body—and the thoroughness of Sefina's care.

"You were a complete disaster. You wouldn't answer our questions or tell us what was wrong. So I brought you somewhere safe. I inspected you myself. And, Nesil—well... He's acting strange because he might've seen a bit more than he should."

His face went hot because this simply wasn't true. He'd kept his distance and averted his eyes—but what else could he say? He *was* acting strangely—so much it'd be hard to make a convincing denial.

"It was perfectly innocent," explained Sefina. "We were frightened by your behavior. His involvement was strictly professional. The perfect gentleman."

For the moment, Kaycia didn't seem to care about that. Her eyes were trained on Sefina with a look of confusion. "Forgive me. But how did I get back? When...? The last I remember, you'd completely abandoned me. You weren't at the tower—you weren't anywhere!"

"And for that, I feel terrible—honest! You have my deepest apologies. If you recall, I warned you of this possibility—that the geography can twist quite unexpectedly."

This only added to Kaycia's anger. "Which is why I told you we shouldn't split up!"

"It's not my fault the barrier was—!" Sefina blew out her breath in clear frustration. "I found you, didn't I? In the end, I upheld my part! I *saved* you!"

"Then explain it to me. I was about to die—! How did you reach me? Did you drive him away?"

"Drive who away?"

"The man—! Dead flesh and a hood over his face? What happened to him?"

Nesil began to feel deeply uncomfortable. He didn't know what she'd been through, but it was obvious he should've been there with her. Sefina, too. Everything would have been different had he not been so fixated on the statue.

The aeisr raised a brow. "Kaycia... When we found you, there wasn't anyone else. You were alone. Talking nonsense."

"I was?"

"Nothing coherent. You really don't remember? We've been with you these past few hours. Is this...normal? Have you experienced gaps before?"

"I..." the girl began to stammer. "You need to listen to me! This wasn't a hallucination. Or glimpse of the past."

"I didn't say it was."

"But you're thinking it, aren't you? And I get it. I... I haven't been myself."

"Of course, I believe you. The current is filled with dangers. And not just the sort that'll mess with your head."

"It's more than that! This man was part of the blood. He—he knew my name!"

Sefina paused, appearing uncertain.

Kaycia pressed further. "You've heard of Praxys? The Harvester of Blood?"

"...You mean it *looked* like—"

"I know what I saw! Bloody heavens—! It was all I could do to fight him off!"

"Just think what you're saying. If you'd truly encountered an abyssal lord, then why aren't you dead?"

Kaycia looked about to scream. "...This isn't going to work! I'm sorry for what you've been through—for making you take care of me—but I've heard enough."

"What?"

"That's it. I'm out."

She was obviously terrified, but Nesil was more afraid of what would happen next. Because if Kaycia's reaction could be considered inevitable, so too would Sefina's.

"Why now?" asked the aeisr, shaking her head. "This is so stupid! I mean—we just got the band! We can finish and not worry about—"

"The *band*?!" shouted Kaycia, as though it was a curse. "The one I found on a dangling corpse?"

"A corpse...?" asked Nesil. When she didn't respond, he turned to Sefina. "She means Kadrek, right? So it was his band she found? Beyond those flames?"

"It's too late," said Kaycia. "I don't care anymore—who this Kadrek was or why the band didn't save him. Show me the way out. You can have this back."

She raised a hand to remove it, and Sefina cried, "Don't!"

Nesil stiffened. In a split second, the aeisr could seize control, if only to ensure the band stayed on.

"Look," said Kaycia, dropping her hand. "You can give it to someone else. I'm not the only one in Ahman. There was a boy here—more powerful than I. It should be him helping you."

Nesil averted his gaze.

"...You've seen him?"

"We've met," said Sefina. "But Aico's not an option. He's already left."

Kaycia gaped a moment, but her face remained hard.

Nesil studied her expression before dropping his eyes to the band on her shoulder. Only then did he realize a way he might help.

"Can I say something?"

Her gaze was defiant, as though determined nothing would change her mind.

"We've all faced horrors, and I understand why you don't want to work with Sefina. She can be a real bitch. But there's more to all this. Including something for you."

She raised a skeptical brow.

So he dove right in. "For three years, my grandfather wore a band like that. To be honest, I didn't know much about it—or that it came from this place—not till recently.

"The important part is that it *helped* him. Before then, he'd always been a great leader—with more talent in ascendancy than anyone I've known."

"A transcendent?" asked Kaycia, with unexpected interest.

"Some said he was. He could do things most people said were impossible—but it came at a cost, as you well know. It made him harder, stronger, and utterly ruthless. He was so effective at fighting the current, people turned a blind eye to his...other indiscretions."

She nodded knowingly. "Did he kill anyone?"

Nesil grimaced. "...He might've. But what I'm saying is that all of that changed. When he came back with that band, he was a different man. He wasn't perfect by any means. He still had outbursts—but they were no worse than a regular person's. He went back to how he was before ascendancy."

She shrugged indifferently. "I've been wearing this a while, and—according to you—I was still speaking gibberish."

"I was wondering that, too—until I looked more closely. See here," he said, stepping forward to point at an indentation. "My grandfather's had a white gemstone in this slot."

He turned to Sefina. "I'm right, aren't I? This band is incomplete?"

"...Oh, is it my turn to talk now?"

Kaycia groaned.

"Okay!" said Sefina in exasperation. "I was going to get to all this—"

"When?" he demanded.

"When it became necessary."

Nesil was out of patience. "Can't you see what I'm doing? Is the band able to help her or not?"

Sefina pretended to pout, but it was only an act—he could see that now. She'd likely caught on to his plan when he'd first brought it up, and it was simply in her nature to be as difficult as possible. To stretch anticipation to the point of breaking.

She smiled thinly at Kaycia. "I didn't tell you of the gemstone because I couldn't risk you using it early. Don't look at me like that! I trust you—but it was the same with Renat. He seemed honest at first. Until he ruined everything."

"Renat...? You mean the King of Seldor? *He's* your grandfather?"

Nesil couldn't meet her gaze. It wasn't just from shame, but the fact he still couldn't process his feelings. Renat had openly confessed to being a coward but not necessarily a murderer.

"Who else did you think?" asked Sefina. "Nesil just told you how powerful he was. But it didn't matter. Renat still betrayed us. At the first sign of trouble, he used the stone to escape—even after promising he wouldn't."

"Escape?" asked Kaycia, with narrowed brows.

Sefina's eyes twinkled. "That's what they're for. We knew the risks we'd face. The abyssal current is always in motion—and the depths are worse. Our greatest fear wasn't the darkness at the bottom, but that the undertow would make our retreat impossible."

"Undertow?" echoed Kaycia. She took a deep breath. "So these gems—? Do they point the way out? Like how you found me?"

"Even better. Once inserted, the effect is instantaneous. They *remove* you from Ahman. Allow me to explain:

"You mustn't confuse the bands and stones—the principles behind each are wholly separate. The bands were formed on the basis of Devotion, meant only to provide access to a person's aspect. Luckily, this provides a few additional benefits—such as linking yours to mine, which is why I could find you."

It was also how Sefina had possessed her body—a secret making Nesil increasingly uncomfortable.

The aeisr went on. "We needed our aspects available to the stones. They're the crux to everything—not infused with Devotion but *Ordination*."

"But that's...! How did...?"

"You'd have to ask Kadrek. He already had the stones with him. He's who you saw down in that tower."

Sefina's voice became distant. "Kadrek was special. He was the first...and only Ordinator I've met. Without him, none of us would be here. Ahman would've remained cut off—out of your reach. As well as Aico's. And Renat's."

"What about you?" asked Kaycia. "You make it sound as though you were already here."

Nesil grew nervous, but Sefina sidestepped the issue.

"There's a lot to explain. But before I get to the rest of your questions, let me finish the one you already made: how Ordination was supposed to help us escape."

Kaycia appeared flustered and then embarrassed. In the end, she adopted a more patient expression.

Only then did Sefina continue. "What Kadrek did, in a sense, was open the door. But only for a few. As you know, it takes a special kind of person to enter Ahman. For everyone else, it doesn't exist. Do you see where I'm going with this?"

Kaycia scrunched her nose. "Not really?"

"With Ordination, you revert to the person you were before you came inside. Make no mistake, it doesn't turn back time or make you any younger. Rather, it restores you to the person you were intended to be—your most natural self—a version unable to exist inside Ahman. Therefore, you're removed."

"I'll just appear outside?"

"More or less."

There was fire in Kaycia's eyes when she turned to Nesil. "Let me get this straight. When you said your grandfather changed, this is why? The stones—what they do—they revert your aspect? He didn't just become kinder. His mind was healed because his ascension was *gone*?"

Nesil didn't know how to read her excitement. He could understand why an ascendant might fear losing her abilities, but he didn't think Kaycia was afraid.

He smiled gently. "I thought you might be interested. After seeing you—the way you were..."

She gaped a moment. "How big a change are we talking about? Three years, you said, and you didn't notice any scarring? Nothing unusual in the way he acted?"

"It was as though he'd never ascended to begin with."

"What of his memories?"

"He remembered everything. And continued to blame himself for every misdeed. It made him better, I think. He became all the more determined to make up for his wrongs."

"I... I need to sit down."

Nesil should've felt pleased. He'd expected this reaction, knowing the band would do everything he said. The only problem, however, was that none of it would matter if Sefina had other plans.

"*You've convinced her,*" said the aeisr, only to him. "*I didn't expect you to be such a great help, but thank you.*"

"*I didn't do it for you.*"

"*I know. But it's enough for now. I'll take it from here.*"

"*What?*" he asked, more annoyed than fearful. "*I've done everything you asked! I didn't mention anything that—!*"

"*And I thanked you, didn't I? For now, sit tight and keep your mouth shut.*"

Kaycia sat on the dock, utterly stunned. She was still overwhelmed by the fact she was here—that, against all odds, she'd returned to her sister. But, after all that, to learn Elyriel might also be healed? She couldn't believe it. She was too scared to believe it.

She'd never considered the idea of reversing ascension, but, according to Nesil, it wasn't just theoretically possible. He'd witnessed the miracle with his own two eyes.

A lump caught in her throat. She tried to imagine it—Elyriel, back to the way she'd been. The innocent girl she was meant to be. It was too good to be true. She had to be missing something.

"Where's the gemstone?" she asked, looking up at Sefina.

The girl merely laughed. "Slow down. Like I said. Not till the end."

"No. I want to see it now. I need proof it's here—that it actually works."

"You have my word."

"Just let me see it—and use it briefly. Let me go outside and have a chance to breathe. Give me this reassurance, and I swear you'll have my complete cooperation. I'll come back in and do whatever you want."

Sefina shook her head. "You misunderstand. It doesn't work that way. The stones will only work the first time. Once they're inserted, they can't be removed."

"What do you mean? It goes on the band. I'll take the thing off."

"Well…yes, you could. It won't stick to your skin or anything like that. But it'll only form its connection once. If your only intention was to escape, you could use it for that purpose and throw the band away. But it won't work again—that's what I'm saying. When you put it back on, the stone will be useless."

Kaycia turned to Nesil—whom she realized now to be *Prince* Nesil. "What of your grandfather? For him, it wasn't temporary."

His face was sympathetic, but he made no denial.

It was Sefina who explained. "He never took it off."

"But that's absurd! He just abandoned the fight for his kingdom? He watched idly as the current battered its walls?"

The girl sighed. "No one thought less of him for it. He'd already given so much. In the end, his people didn't need another general. They needed a *father*—someone they could trust."

Nesil grew suddenly angry but, curiously, kept his thoughts to himself.

Kaycia's eyes locked with his as though to ask what was wrong, but he merely shook his head.

"This is your chance," said Sefina. "If this is something you want—and it seems like it is—you'll just have to wait. The gem's not here, anyway. If you want to see it, we have to go down."

"And what? I'm just supposed to take you on your word?"

Sefina sighed. "What more do you want? I've told you everything."

"No. You haven't. You still haven't told me who you are. I don't even know what we're doing down here! You keep saying you want to reach the bottom—that there's something you want to find. But you keep hiding what that is!"

"I..." Sefina took a deep breath. "It isn't a secret. The problem is—and I apologize for not saying this sooner—I don't know what to expect when we reach the bottom."

"No idea at all?"

"Kadrek was the one with the answers. He was on a mission of sorts. It sounded important, so I decided to help."

Kaycia was incredulous. "You just went along and didn't ask questions?"

"Of course, I asked! And he did everything he could to explain along the way. But he died so quickly, no one saw it coming. If there are parts I don't remember, that's my fault—not his."

"But you do remember some of it?"

"Not word for word. Our primary objective, however, which he repeated more than once, was to retrieve a particular key."

Kaycia felt a chill run down her spine. Here it was again, so soon after her conversation with Soril. Back in the carriage, as they finished their discussion, Kaycia had wondered this very thing—if Sefina's goal was related to this mysterious key. But to learn it was true was still quite a shock.

"You know about that...?" she asked. "Do you know what it is? What else did he say?"

Sefina's face was uneasy. "It was central, somehow, in the death of the gods. He didn't mention where it came from or even what it looked like. But he said we'd find it where the battle took place. He made it sound as though Shaelis had it with him."

"But what's it *for*? What does it do?"

"I have a few theories. I remember Kadrek speaking of a doorway—but it didn't make sense. It was somehow connected to the gods' immortality. Almost as though it were a doorway to heaven."

Kaycia puzzled this over. "So, if someone wanted the gods dead, they'd need to—what? Get the door open? Seal it shut? Destroy it altogether?"

"The explanation should be simple. And maybe it is. All Kadrek said was that we needed the key. He didn't talk about using it. Just bringing it out."

Kaycia's mind returned to her encounter with Praxys. She was bothered by the memory, still desperate to know how she'd gotten away.

"The Lord I saw—the Harvester of Blood—was also looking for the key. He kept asking about it. He seemed to think I had it."

Sefina lowered her brows as though trying to believe what Kaycia was saying.

"What if that's the reason?" Kaycia suggested. "He let me go because he thought I was hiding it. If he'd chosen to kill me, he'd risk losing the truth."

"So he let you go?"

"Sounds crazy, but I can't think of another explanation. He was *real*, Sefina. Believe me, I wish I were making this up, but—!"

"All right, all right. I believe you, okay? We'll be careful moving forward, I promise."

"That's all you have to say? An Abyssal Lord is on our tail—so we'll be *careful*?"

"Don't look at me like that. I know perfectly well how dangerous he is."

"You do? You've seen him before?"

"I have."

"Did you fight him?"

"Look. I already told you I'd keep you safe, haven't I?"

"Yes, but...! Bloody heavens... ... How?!"

The girl gave a prim smile.

Kaycia was dumbstruck. She'd already been suspicious of Sefina's abilities—unable to understand just what the girl did. Even back in the garden, she'd sensed something was off. Her command of her surroundings seemed too perfect—the strawberry muffins too delicious to be real.

But if it wasn't real—if it was all an illusion—Kaycia couldn't explain the rest. Sefina had successfully carried her to safety. She'd overpowered Elyriel and brought her here.

On an impulse, Kaycia ran her fingers through her hair. It was silly, but she needed to be sure it was clean—and not just on the surface.

"Be straight with me," she said. "If anyone like you were living in Seldor, I would've known."

Sefina shook her head. "Obviously, you didn't."

"Stop dodging the issue. Where did you come from?"

The girl didn't answer.

"So that's it?" asked Kaycia, her face growing hot. "You *refuse* to tell me?"

"I'm asking you to trust me. I have my reasons, okay?"

"You're hiding something!"

"So what if I am? Are you going to tell me you don't want to come? You'll walk away from this chance and forget about your sister?"

Kaycia stared in disbelief.

"Oh? Did I guess correctly? I suspected something was off when your consciousness reappeared. It was nothing close to a typical recovery. You came from a completely different place—from another person's mind."

Kaycia was speechless.

"But you know what?" asked Sefina. "I don't even care. You can keep your secrets—so long as I can keep mine."

"I thought we were working together."

"And so we are."

"So what's the problem? I'm not going to judge you. I'd find it easier to count on you if I only understood—"

"We're done with this conversation. If you don't want to come, I'd sooner look for another partner."

Kaycia swallowed her anger. She didn't understand why this was such a big deal. By insisting on hiding such a simple thing, the girl was setting them up for failure.

And unfortunately, Kaycia would go along with it. She'd take those odds because they were the *only* odds that included a future for Elyriel.

She sighed in defeat. "Of course, I'll go."

Sefina's smile was pretty but oh-so-irritating. "Don't look so glum. If there's one thing you should know about me, it's that I never lose. Isn't that right, Nesil? She has nothing to worry about."

The boy didn't answer. He didn't even nod.

As they renewed their descent, Nesil grit his teeth. "*I always knew you were evil, but this...?*"

"*I haven't forced her to do anything. Not recently, anyway.*"

"*She thinks you'll keep her safe!*"

"*And I will.*"

"*Against visions and dreams. What of the rest?*"

"That isn't your problem. Let me handle it."

"What about the gemstone? There's just the one, right? Back in Seldor, you implied Renat took it from Kadrek."

"Two stones. He ran away with both."

"But that doesn't make sense! If he only needed one, then—?"

"Kadrek and Renat got split up. He was supposed to return it, but Renat decided to run instead."

Nesil's jaw was beginning to hurt. *"You didn't say that to Kaycia! How's she supposed to find it if Renat took it to Seldor?"*

"It's not in Seldor. Trust me. I searched everywhere. Literally, everywhere."

"So you don't know where it is."

"I've narrowed it down. There aren't many places I haven't checked."

It didn't take long to puzzle this out. *"You think he left it past the barrier—the wall of fire? Otherwise, you'd know."*

Sefina didn't answer, but he sensed she was angry.

He sighed. *"Even if you only have a guess, she should know that much."*

"This isn't up for discussion. If you've got nothing useful to say, then hold your tongue."

Nesil knew, deep down, there was nothing he could do. And he was more and more frustrated with his diminishing freedoms.

"If you won't let me do anything or SAY anything—why not leave me here?"

Sefina smirked. *"Don't lie. You're just saying that so you can go back to Aico."*

There was no point in hiding it. *"Would that be so bad? Or are you actually worried I'll help get him out?"*

She considered this a moment.

"Come on," he insisted. *"It's obvious you don't want me getting in the way. You'll have a better chance of keeping her safe if I'm not distracting you."*

He expected a refusal—that she'd invent a reason to keep him around, if only for her amusement. But she didn't.

"You'll keep an eye on him, then? If you think this will help you feel better...it won't."

"Perhaps not. But it might. If he happens to wake up, he won't be alone."

"I guess that's true."

Nesil wasn't sure how to take this. While she seemed to be showing concern for Aico, she might just want to take his mind off Kaycia.

Either way, it didn't matter. He couldn't help either of them—not Aico nor Kaycia—so long as the aeisr was watching. In the end, this wasn't about returning to the other boy. He mainly needed to get away from her.

She turned to Kaycia. "Could you give us a moment? I'll be back in two minutes."

"*Why?*" he asked. "*What's going on?*"

"*I'm taking you to Aico, silly. And making sure you stay there.*"

He groaned. "*Is that necessary? I wasn't even THINKING of the statue if that's what you're worried about.*"

"*Of course, I'm not worried. You're getting better—that's for sure. But let's not play games. I know you, Nesil. Like I know myself.*"

"*How can I prove myself if you won't give me a choice?*"

"*Baby steps, Nesil... Baby steps.*"

Chapter 35
SINGULARITY

Kaycia was finding it difficult to concentrate.

Once more, she was surrounded by floating staircases and endless dark—but her head was swimming with thoughts of her sister. Of being with her again, alive and well.

But even that wasn't enough to hold her attention. Her mind was filled with too many worries. And her daydreams were interrupted by a single phrase: "Take this key, and set her free."

Her... The child goddess.

She'd meant to bring it up with Sefina, but their discussion had derailed a bit prematurely. And though this seemed to have been the other girl's fault, there was a possibility—a slight possibility—Sefina had good reason to act as she did.

Kaycia found it difficult to trust other people and wondered if she might approach this relationship differently. Under ordinary circumstances, the two might be friends. And, with effort, some damage might be undone.

"I've been wondering something," she said conversationally.

They were traversing a stone walkway that seemed, at some point, to have been part of a courtyard. It branched into a network of paths, but the space between was absent of vegetation. Rather than trees and earth, there was empty void.

When Sefina didn't respond, she asked, "During your time in this place—or, perhaps, in your talks with Kadrek—did you ever learn anything about the child goddess? You know, Irisea?"

The girl searched around as though looking for danger. If anything, she seemed to be avoiding Kaycia. "...What about her?"

"Anything, really. To everyone I've met, she's nothing but a story. I just thought, after everything you've been through...?"

Sefina rolled her eyes and closed her mouth.

"Look," said Kaycia. "I apologize for earlier. I don't mean to pry. If you'd rather talk of something else, I'm open to suggestions. I only brought her up because of something I heard. Perhaps you've heard it, too—how this key might be needed to set her free."

Still no response.

Rather than get frustrated, Kaycia decided to give her some space. They still had a long way to go, and there'd be more opportunities to bring it up later.

A few minutes, however, was all the time Sefina needed.

"...I've never put much stock in the legend," she said. "I've heard what people say—how they pin their hopes on a single person. A child born against all odds in the wake of the greatest tragedy this world has known. It's damn absurd, is what I think."

Kaycia was surprised.

"What?" asked Sefina. "Not the answer you were looking for?"

"No. It's just that...I entirely agree."

"You do?"

"Everyone's searching for the easy way out. I understand the world's a dangerous place, but too many use the goddess as an excuse to sit back. And they hide their indolence by calling it 'faith.'"

Sefina smirked. "But not you?"

"I do what I can. I won't pretend it's much or that my way's better. I'm constantly reminded of what I *can't* do on my own. But I feel better in the end. Sometimes, I do. Knowing I've tried."

"So let me get this straight. You *don't* believe in her?"

"I didn't say that, either. I simply refuse to believe she's the answer to everything. If she *does* exist and can make a difference—even a small one—we'd be stupid not to take it."

Sefina frowned. "That's... I'd say that sounds reasonable—if you had the slightest clue what you were talking about."

Kaycia might've been offended, but she was far more curious. "So you *do* know something?"

When the girl hesitated, she added, "Come on—is she real or not?"

"Oh, she's real all right. But I wouldn't count on her to do much of anything."

"Why not? Is she trapped, somehow?"

"In a manner of speaking. But it's not the sort of thing any key will fix."

"But...Shaelis said—"

"I know what he said. But—god or no—he was clueless about a great many things."

Sefina's eyes grew focused, and Kaycia turned to find the scenery had changed. Or, rather, it was changing.

In the distant dark, where she could barely discern the shapes of bridges, everything was on the move. The floating rooms revolved in steady circles, connecting to one passage for a moment and then another. The orbiting paths were in constant conflict, with walls that'd sweep her off the edge if she got careless.

"Keep close, and do everything I tell you."

They were already side-by-side, but Kaycia drew so close she could wrap an arm around Sefina if she thought it'd help.

"Focus on the path. Don't look them in the eye."

"Who?" she asked, unable to see anyone. Though she knew Sefina was talking of shadows, they were either too far ahead or too faint to see.

She began to hear screams. They came in bursts—fading into silence after a few short seconds. Fading downward—like a person falling through infinite space.

"Where are we?" asked Kaycia.

"This way," said Sefina, taking her elbow and directing her toward an approaching staircase. At its current trajectory, the bottom step wouldn't reach their walkway but fall short a few feet.

"Now," said the girl before the moment disappeared.

Kaycia leapt the gap, trying not to think about what might happen if she fell. Though she knew she could trust Elyriel's balance, it wouldn't matter if she froze at the wrong moment.

With the stairs still moving, Kaycia resorted to using her hands. She kept her center of gravity low, crawling after Sefina.

They emerged through the floor of a dusty classroom with chairs and tables sized for children. After exiting the back door and crossing a narrow corridor, they jumped out a window onto a drifting rooftop fifteen feet below.

Crouched low against the tiles, Sefina paused. She eyed the space ahead, waiting for their building to reach its destination.

Kaycia couldn't help but feel intimidated. The girl was fearless and never seemed lost. Not only did she move with perfect confidence, she did so barefoot while wearing a dress.

"See that?" Sefina asked.

Kaycia turned where she was facing—but saw only darkness. It wasn't until she broadened her focus that she thought she understood.

Though the bridges moved in separate directions, they were hiding a pattern. There was a space in the middle that none of them crossed. Instead, their paths curved in varied ellipses, as though the center was the fulcrum to all this chaos.

It reminded her of something.

"That day—when Ahman disappeared," she began. "Piece by piece, from around Ashaira's palace... That's not what this is, is it? I mean, if this was here, all this time—?"

"You're right. What we're seeing is more a distorted memory. Everything here is a matter of perception—of those still living and those who've gone."

Kaycia held her breath.

On occasion, the paths of two structures would converge. There'd be a violent collision as stone smashed, wood twisted, and broke away in new directions.

There were other moments, however, when the buildings passed through one another. The shape of one would blur like an afterimage, and she'd see multiple worlds in a single moment.

"Where now?"

"Watch my direction, then follow me."

The girl raced down the rooftop and leaped into darkness.

As the girl disappeared, Kaycia followed. She used the angle of Sefina's jump to intuit a sense of distance. Her step faltered, however, when an enormous black tree rose up in her path.

"*Don't slow*!" said Sefina's voice as though still beside her. "*It won't touch you. Go through!*"

Making the leap wasn't easy, and her footwork was sloppy, but Kaycia chose to stay committed.

Even so, she couldn't stop her hands from shielding her face. The jumbled branches blocked everything, and she almost missed the rooftop where Sefina had landed.

The awkward leap had thrown Kaycia off track. She passed the other girl, and her feet slid dangerously close to the edge.

"Sefina!" she shouted, grabbing for her arm—and missed.

Instead, she fell backward. She flailed in confusion—feeling certain she *couldn't* have missed. She reached for the edge, but it was already too late.

Her stomach rose in her throat as Sefina's building disappeared above her. There wasn't time to scream. She had to fight against her hair as she swerved, searching for anything below.

"*There's an apartment coming up on your right. Use your chains! Now!*"

Kaycia spun, saw her target, and sent her blades flying. Consequently, she was pushed in the opposite direction, and for a brief moment, she wondered if their reach would be long enough.

Their tips buried into stone and held fast like anchors. At the other end, she was whipped around in a circle. But, as she started moving back toward safety, the cracked blocks gave a jolt and broke free from the wall.

Kaycia cursed, overcome with rage.

She was falling again and, this time, attached to a hunk of dead weight.

"Whip it around!" said Sefina. *"Go north, or you'll—! Oh, bloody hell!"*

This wasn't the encouragement Kaycia needed, but she found herself doing as the girl instructed. She wasn't sure which way was north, but her head snapped around as though drawn instinctively toward solid ground.

Her hands moved on their own, fueled by her desperate need to survive. The chains pulled taut in a complex vertical maneuver she didn't understand. It launched her in an upward arc, not toward the platform, but—

It didn't make sense. Her blades detached from the stone without waiting for her permission. Even her arms pulled inward, accelerating her spin when she wanted to slow.

She was accustomed to her conviction making choices for her—to do what was necessary to meet her instructions. But this was different.

Her body turned, and her feet connected with a wall—one she hadn't even realized was there. She wasn't given a chance to take in her surroundings before she leaped away again into boundless dark.

She *wasn't* in control, and she was bothered that Sefina hadn't spoken for a while.

"What's happening?" she shouted.

"Stop resisting!" the girl shouted back.

Consequently, they slammed into an edge, and neither could grasp hold of anything.

Kaycia couldn't breathe, and she started sliding backward.

"Are you trying to die?" demanded Sefina.

The girl was trying to help, but if Kaycia was getting in her way, she didn't know how. And she didn't have time to figure it out.

She scrambled with her hands, desperate to avoid another fall.

"Let go!" said Sefina.

Kaycia was too frightened even to consider it. She knew there was likely a building below. Otherwise, the girl wouldn't have made the suggestion. But Kaycia couldn't trust herself to make another landing—not while her body was behaving unpredictably.

Her arms began to tremble—more than she'd expect from holding herself up. Rather, her muscles worked against themselves, as though trying to hold on and let go simultaneously.

In the end, it didn't matter. Gravity won.

She lost sight of the edge and couldn't orient herself in the tumble that followed. She couldn't even tell up from down.

Once again, her torso shifted, all on its own—not against her movement but a redirection so slight, it was nearly imperceptible. It happened so fast, there wasn't time to resist.

It was a good thing she didn't, as it lined her lower body into the collision. Her legs and back slammed into the roof and tore a hole into the lower room. Timbers and tiles crashed down around her, and, luckily, her head was spared the worst of the damage.

She writhed on the floor, feeling the painful urge to cough away dust, but her lungs were too weak. Her vision faded, and it became too dark to see.

Though she knew she'd landed on solid ground, it still felt like she was falling. Falling forever into peaceful oblivion.

And she lost all consciousness.

When Kaycia woke, she was in a different place.

At first, this didn't bother her, as she was used to Elyriel wandering around. Kaycia often assumed control of a walking position or some other task, and it never really felt like waking from sleep.

Only, this time, Kaycia hadn't come from the carriage. She hadn't shifted from one alert mind to another but came to her senses slowly and groggily.

She vaguely recalled Sefina taking control, and she suspected it was she, not her sister, who'd brought them to this place.

Gone were the bridges and floating buildings. There were no man-made structures at all. It was as though they'd left Ahman entirely and were walking along a sandy lakeshore.

For the moment, she forgot her anger and asked, "Where is this place? How long was I out?"

"Yay... You're back," said Sefina dryly, walking up from behind. Her hair and dress flapped lightly in the wind.

Kaycia knew this was wrong—the girl's body hadn't been there two seconds ago. But she had more pressing questions. "What happened to Ahman? Did we...? Did we get out?"

"You're still coming to your senses. You'll put it together."

She took this to mean the answer was obvious—of course, they were out. But that, too, was wrong. If they'd left, the sky would be dark. Instead, it shimmered in a silvery overcast—with clouds that rolled a bit too quickly.

The lake was the same as the one she remembered—from outside the cave—but it was also different. There were more trees in the distance. More plants and foliage. Hearkening back to the time before the blood rains came.

"Another memory?" she asked.

"These roads connect by association. Consider this more in terms of a narrative."

"But why? You said Aviathas was making these illusions, but—"

"Not him specifically. But the same powers that brought him back to life. That've restored, along with him, echoes of the past. In the form of shadows and dim recollections. They don't have a name, but the Seldorans took to calling them the 'aeisr.'"

"The aeisr?" asked Kaycia, wondering at the word. "So this place...is what came after? The survivors of Ahman wound up here?"

Looking around, she began to see them—or, more precisely, *feel* them. There was nothing concrete, like facial features, but she perceived their confusion. Some were angry. The images swirled a moment and quickly faded.

Kaycia wanted to see more and hear what they were saying—but it was enough, for the moment, to know they weren't a threat.

She rounded on Sefina. "I know you've been controlling me, and I want to know how."

Sefina groaned and smiled in derision. "You're welcome."

"No! This isn't happening again! Why should I be grateful? I wouldn't have fallen were it not for you!"

"Kay, I can't control what—"

"I know what I saw! I landed on that roof, and my hand passed through you!"

Before the girl could deny it, Kaycia lunged forward.

Sefina was quicker and sidestepped away.

"Come on!" said Kaycia in bitter frustration. "I'm not going to hurt you. I just need your arm. Or does that pose a problem?"

The girl's eyes blazed in defiance, but she ultimately gave in. She thrust out her hand and looked the other way.

"Thank you," said Kaycia, stepping close once again.

The wrist was slender and perfectly smooth. It felt solid, at first, held within Kaycia's cut and scraped fingers. It resisted pressure when she squeezed.

If she hadn't known better, she might've been convinced. But the tension she felt was also wrong—as though something was telling her fingers not to squeeze. It wasn't a physical barrier but a mental one. And with the proper resolve, she crossed some threshold.

"Could you let go, now?"

Kaycia didn't. She stared in awe at her hand—because, even then, everything appeared natural. Her fingers hadn't broken through skin, and Sefina's wrist didn't compress beneath her tightening grip. Even after Kaycia closed her fist, leaving no space inside—her fingers appeared to have stopped, maintaining a handhold perfectly relaxed.

"What are you?" she breathed.

Sefina extricated her hand with surprising ease—even though Kaycia hadn't let go.

"It's hard to explain."

"I'm in no hurry." To make her point, she sat down on a smooth length of driftwood and crossed her legs. "We're not going anywhere till I get some answers."

The girl's voice became menacing. "I wouldn't be so sure about that."

"Is that a threat? You'll retake control? *Permanently*? Instead of talking this out, you'll force compliance?"

"It's tempting. Sure."

Kaycia took a deep breath and tried to make sense of her situation. It only took a moment to remember the band—the one that operated, of all things, on the basis of devotion. She'd been too flustered to consider it sooner, but the connection wasn't difficult to make.

With renewed determination, she grabbed her shoulder and pulled it off.

Or rather, she *tried* to pull it off. Her hand went slack, as though paralyzed, and fell away from the metal.

"Stop it!" she said. "It's *my* arm, and I want the thing off!"

"We can discuss that later."

"It comes off, now!"

Kaycia grit her teeth and forced her fingers to move.

She didn't get far.

She tried moving them sideways to avoid Sefina's direct opposition, but the girl adjusted quickly. The hand jerked around aimlessly and got no closer to removing the band.

"I need you to calm down," Sefina intoned. "I've got nothing against you staying in control. It's better for you and easier for me. But the band stays on. It's for your protection."

"My...? Bloody heavens! I can protect myself!"

Sefina closed her mouth and turned to face across the water.

This only added to Kaycia's frustration because they both knew her argument amounted to little. It wasn't the first time her efforts had failed to keep her safe.

She groaned out loud, wanting nothing more than to deny this simple truth. But, deep down, she knew it wasn't a matter of experience. Even with better training, there was no way she could've replicated what Sefina had done—spinning through the dark with preternatural ease. It was more than skill. The girl possessed an awareness that bordered on the impossible. And she'd forged a solution despite Kaycia's resistance.

In the end, Elyriel had survived the fall—which, undoubtedly, was the best solution for everyone. She couldn't fault Sefina for her intervention and didn't wish the past undone.

But if Kaycia was supposed to be grateful, she couldn't muster it. She refused to accept that this was her fate. That every time she faced challenges beyond her abilities, this girl—this *stranger*—could deny her the opportunity. Deny her the growth and the chance to fail.

It seemed stupid, sure, as it shouldn't matter who saved her sister so long as she survived. Elyriel's life was more important than feelings of jealousy or Kaycia's need to prove her self-worth. If she truly cared for her sister, the choice should be simple.

And, perhaps, it would be if Sefina possessed something more than skill. Though the girl was undoubtedly the best in terms of survival, that was far from being what was best for Elyriel.

"Look," said Sefina. I know you're upset, but nothing needs to change. I asked you to come down here, and that's all that interests me. It was never my intention to get between you and your sister. You can keep your privacy and personal freedoms. Let's go after the key and forget this happened."

"...So long as I keep the band on."

"As I said, for reasons entirely practical."

"And after that...? You said she'd have to wear this the rest of her life! That's rather convenient, don't you think? What's to stop you from taking control whenever you desire?"

It took a while for Sefina to answer. "I'm certain it won't work that way."

"What do you mean?"

"This connection between us—it isn't natural. It isn't what the bands were intended to do. The only reason this works, I suspect, is entirely dependent on whatever *you* did. Were it not for this bond you share with your sister—"

"You're saying this is *my* fault?"

"I didn't say that. I don't even care how you managed it at all. The only thing that matters is that it'll be reversed. *Completely* reversed. Don't you get it? Once we have the gemstone and your sister's healed—*she'll* be in control. Not you. Not me. All of this will be over. Isn't that what you want?"

"...It is."

"Good. Because, right now, we're after the same thing."

Kaycia wanted to believe this but feared she couldn't. Sefina had never inspired much trust. She hid too many secrets and was too aggressive in pursuing her interests.

She met the girl's eyes. "So let's have it. I've seen your illusions—some of them, at least. There's no point in hiding what you are. I'm willing to go on—to ignore the problems your lies have caused—but we need to get past this."

The girl groaned.

"It's Innovation, isn't it?" she pressed. "I know about Aviathas—how he came back to life. Were you one of his ascendants? You could at least say that much."

Sefina, however, refused even that.

"Why is this so difficult?!"

The girl finally burst. "Because it doesn't matter!"

"...What doesn't matter?"

"All of it! Learning about me wasn't part of our agreement!"

"You don't think so? Remind me then. Can you even remember *what* we agreed on?"

Sefina's anger faltered.

"Because now, I'm having doubts. Tell me, Sefina, how are illusions going to help my city? You don't think a small detail—like who you are—impacts your side of the deal? Did you ever intend to save Carheim at all?"

"Well...no."

Kaycia gawked. "So you admit it?!"

"Is there any point in pretending otherwise? Like I said, *it doesn't matter*. You needed a push in the garden, so I gave you one. But since that time, our agreement has changed."

"That's not for you to decide!"

"Isn't it? I think it's a fair trade—your help in exchange for the life of your sister? Or is that not enough? I was sure you'd agree, even if the terms weren't spoken out loud."

Kaycia grit her teeth. "How can I agree, when you keep going back on everything you say?"

"Not everything."

"Even this gemstone might be a lie! What's to stop you from seizing control *before* Elyriel's healed?"

"Is that your sister's name?"

"Answer the question!"

Sefina sighed. "It's rather obvious. If she doesn't get healed, then she doesn't escape. How do I benefit if she ends up dead?"

Kaycia couldn't believe it. Despite the girl's logic, there were too many variables and too much that could go wrong. If Sefina wanted Elyriel to herself, there was little doubt she had ways to make it happen.

"I want to trust you," said Kaycia. "I want this to work, for all our sake. But, to be blunt, you're not making this easy."

"You want to call it off?"

"Right... As if you'd let me go. You've proven you can force me to do just about anything. After coming this far, I'm supposed to believe you'll give up?"

"...I won't give up."

Kaycia scoffed.

"You asked for honesty, so let's be honest."

"This is utter bullshit, and you know it! You won't get anywhere without my cooperation! I'll actively resist your every step!"

"If that's what you want. Of course, you'll just get us killed."

"That's right," agreed Kaycia, doing her best not to falter. "The question is: Is that what *you* want? You pretend this key is all that matters, yet you refuse to find a workable solution. Go on, then! Use force and aggression! Let's see how close you get to your precious key!"

Sefina's face was unreadable. "My, my. Such flair for the dramatic... But I don't believe you. You care too much for her."

"You're damned right, I care! I don't want her to die! I want her the chance at a normal life! But, now, I can't be sure that was ever your intention. You make these promises as though you were planning to cheat from the start! And, if there's a chance—any chance at all—of you stealing Elyriel for yourself and putting her through something *worse* than death... By all means, keep believing I won't stop you!"

"This is all quite pointless. I have no interest in your sister."

"You need to convince me!"

Sefina turned away as though the matter was settled.

"We aren't finished!" said Kaycia. She stood up and brushed the sand from her boots.

The other girl, however, wasn't ignoring her but had fixated on a point near the water's edge. "...Do you see that?"

Kaycia gaped, feeling certain this was just an excuse—some ill attempt to avoid the argument.

Sefina's expression had lost its hardness but stared forward with marked intensity—not fearful, per se, but something between curiosity and amazement.

"I... I'll answer everything. Just look!"

Kaycia turned, but there was nothing there.

"What am I supposed to see?"

"They're standing right there! Shaelis and Ashaira—or, at least, an echo of them. They must've come here, too, after it happened."

There was a twist in the air. Kaycia thought it was a ripple on the lake, but it was much closer.

She walked forward, convinced it was an illusion. The timing, after all, was just too convenient. For Shaelis, himself, to appear? At the precise moment Sefina was in want for distraction?

Unfortunately, Kaycia couldn't discount the phenomenon. Of all the players Sefina could've picked, she'd chosen wisely.

"Has this happened before?" Kaycia asked. "Have you seen these memories? Seen *him*?"

"Not memories. Aeisr. And, no, I haven't. I never made it this far down."

Kaycia grew frustrated. The air blurred and shifted but didn't coalesce into sensible shapes. "What are they saying?"

"They're arguing. Can't you hear?"

To Kaycia's surprise, she *did* hear something—a groan of frustration. It was a woman's voice—an ordinary voice that could've been human.

It defied expectations, and Kaycia knew why. She'd seen a god, herself, if only once—the blistering visage when Telarien took her sister. But that had been different. That was a god in the throes of undying.

In comparison, there was nothing spectacular about Shaelis' appearance. She could see him now, clear as day. When the god was alive, he seemed rather mundane—an ordinary guise concealing an extraordinary fate.

He was shorter than expected, and his hair wasn't white, as depicted in the murals. Instead, it bore the hue of iron with a silvery finish. His eyes were the same, set deep in a face Kaycia knew well. And they blazed with a strength she'd never seen in anyone.

Ashaira's eyes had it, too, burning like sapphires. Her hair flowed like molten bronze, laced with gold. Her dress, on the other hand, was rough-spun and common. Not the dress of a goddess but that of a prisoner.

Her arms were folded as she tapped a finger against her elbow. "You think I planned this?" Her face scrunched together. "You think I *wanted* this?"

"How did you get out?"

"You're asking how I escaped a crumbling prison?"

"Crumbling because your man was behind it. This Lothren you've been hiding. He went into your garden. He knew about your sister's statue. How to *alter* her statue. Look around, Ashaira! Look where we are!"

She shook her head in anger. "And why do you think he was able to do that?"

"You still deny it? He told me everything!"

The goddess sneered. "Of course, he did."

Shaelis didn't falter. "I didn't recognize him at first, but then I remembered. That day, over a hundred years back, when Retria died—when Aviathas was supposed to die—that man was there, too. Looking the same now as he did back then. And you want to claim you're not responsible? That it wasn't your aspect keeping him alive? Keeping *both* of them alive behind my back?"

There was too much for Kaycia to unpack at once. "Retria?" she asked, turning to Sefina. "Is that her sister's name? I've never heard of her."

"I haven't, either."

She did her best to remember this word for word, hoping Soril might know something of help. At the very least, she'd confirmed that his guess was correct—the destruction of Ahman had been caused by a mortal. An unusually long-lived mortal.

By using the statue? Kaycia wished she could ask for clarification and not be at the mercy of this awkward illusion. This otherwise private conversation, rippling through time.

Ashaira's face was like ice, unwilling to say anything. Merely waiting for the god to finish his piece.

Shaelis shook his head. "You knew what Lothren was. How much he *hated* us after we—"

"No," she interrupted, with eyebrows raised. "No!"

"What do you mean, no?"

"Exactly that. I did more than roll back Lothren's life. I rolled back his memories to before that day. So no, he *doesn't* hate us. He has no reason to."

"Obviously, he does. You took a risk, Ashaira. You needed someone capable of watching Aviathas. To protect your secret. And you chose poorly."

"Asshole..." she muttered, turning away.

"Me?" he asked.

"You don't see it, do you? Even now, after losing our city, you don't realize what you've done."

She huffed with restrained, bitter laughter. Then turned her scowl across the lake, eyes glistening, unable to so much as look at Shaelis.

For a moment, the god was at a loss for words. His brow furrowed as though the back of her head might explain how any of this was actually his fault.

She exhaled sharply and spun around. "Lothren *couldn't* have done anything. Even if he remembered. Even if he thought he could reach the statue. I made *sure* of that."

Shaelis made a face to remind her that recent events proved otherwise.

"Come on! I've been in prison for *months*! And during all that time, did Lothren do anything? No, he didn't. You know why? There was always one god standing in his way. Making sure the man stayed in line."

The god's eyes narrowed, still confused. But only for a moment. He blinked in surprise, and his mouth fell open in utter shock.

"That's right," said Ashaira, with a menacing tone. "Lothren came to you. He told you everything—precisely because he knew how you'd respond. That you'd be jealous enough—*angry enough*—to ensure Aviathas died again. This time, for good. He was the only god on that side of the barrier, and now *none of us* can get through!"

Shaelis scowled, unwilling to accept his part in this. "How was I supposed to know that?"

"That killing Aviathas was the wrong decision?

"It was his life or Retria's."

"The first time! A hundred years ago!" Her eyes were wide. "But even back then, he didn't deserve it. And you didn't kill him now because you thought she'd come back. You did it out of spite! Because you wish it'd been him rather than her!"

Kaycia was getting frustrated. "But who was she?" she asked, knowing the gods wouldn't hear her question.

"Believe me," said Ashaira. "I wish I'd been able to save them both. I miss her, too, you know! I would've done anything to get her back. Anything! Except for letting Aviathas die. You were wrong to ask it of me."

His jaw was clenched, but after a moment, he relaxed a little. "We're wasting time. We need to get back in."

By the look on her face, there was more she wanted to say, but she also recognized their present urgency. "I never told him, Shaelis. If Lothren knows about the throne—"

"Never mind how he learned it. He's been in there for hours. We have to assume he knows about the key."

Kaycia's breath caught in her throat.

Ashaira sighed. "That was my fear as well... But have you thought this through? If I change us back, even for a moment—"

"I know what I'm asking." His face became hard and stoic. "If Lothren succeeds in opening that door, this world will lose more than the two of us."

She nodded gravely and touched his arm. "We'll take him by surprise. He won't be expecting us. He can't. We'll fix this. And make sure it never happens again."

"I hope you're right."

The memory faded.

Kaycia was so overwhelmed, she forgot her lingering resentments toward Sefina.

"Change themselves back?" she asked. "That's how they got in? But how does that even work? Change back into what?"

Sefina looked troubled. "Your guess is as good as mine."

"There's something else bothering me. Not something they said, but something they didn't."

"Just one?" The girl smiled wryly.

Kaycia ignored this. "From the way they were arguing, they didn't seem like a couple about to have a baby. So what's that about? Neither spoke a word of her pregnancy. We've nearly reached the battle—so, shouldn't Irisea have been conceived by now?"

"I suppose."

"But...? You're telling me Ashaira didn't know?"

"I suppose she didn't. Why does that matter?"

"Because...! It means they *didn't* figure it out. After thousands of years, unable to have children, it means Irisea was born by *chance*?"

Sefina sighed. "Once again, you're making the same mistake as everyone."

"And what's that?"

"Believing Irisea is somehow special."

Kaycia gaped, and all her frustrations came tumbling back. She was furious Sefina kept hiding what she knew.

"Relax," said the girl. "We're nearly to the end—at least, I think we are. We'll find our answers together."

"If you know what happened, just tell me!"

"I— I will... If we get down there and the answers aren't laid out, I'll tell you what I know—or what I think I know."

Kaycia groaned. "Why? Why can't you tell me now?"

"Because...I hope I'm wrong. I can't prove any of it, at least, not yet."

"Prove what? What can be worse than the deaths of the gods? What are you so scared of?"

"Hopefully, nothing. But we've been here too long. The narrative link won't last forever."

Chapter 36
THE THRONE

There was something wrong with the memory.

Kaycia couldn't explain it. The dark walls and figures melted into fog, going in and out of focus of their own accord.

She saw enough to know it was a place she didn't recognize—a palace of sorts, of foreign construction. Rather than stone, the walls were forged of metal—dull, oxidized, and unrefined. It was unlike anything she'd seen in Ahman. But whether that was her perception—darkened by the current—or because they'd left the city, she couldn't say.

At the center of the room was an immense throne—forged from the same red ore as the floors and ceiling. It was so massive, with a back stretching over twenty feet high— Kaycia couldn't help but wonder why no one had mentioned it all these years.

"Stay back!" came a shout, echoing loudly. "Not a step closer! You want her to die?"

Kaycia thought she saw soldiers along the edge of the room, but they were so indistinct, she couldn't make out the shape of their armor.

There were three exceptions—three key figures, more visible than the rest. Two whom she recognized and one she didn't.

The man was leaning forward from his seat on the throne. At his feet sat Ashaira, clearly unconscious, with a knife to her throat.

Ten feet shy of the dais, Shaelis feigned indifference. "She's immortal, Lothren. Don't be foolish."

Kaycia stepped closer for a better look, but it was as they'd said—Lothren was just a man. With short brown hair and a chiseled beard, there was nothing remarkable to his appearance, demeanor, or size. She never would've guessed he'd lived longer than a century.

"You think she'll heal?" He rested an elbow over one knee. "Without her godhood?"

Kaycia didn't understand. Was this because of their recent reversion? Or had the gods already lost their divinity?

But no—that made no sense. Shaelis was still in his right mind. Lothren might have been referring to something else. A nullifying aura that existed in the past? Either way, it didn't hinder Kaycia's conviction now.

"Just put the knife down. Tell us what you want."

"Patience, patience... Do I need repeat myself? I said, *stand back!*"

Shaelis grit his teeth but didn't come closer. At the same time, he didn't move away.

As the vision continued to materialize, Kaycia saw a large stone doorway some thirty feet to the right of the throne. It stood over twice her height and had intricate patterns carved into its surface.

The Doors of Heaven, she thought. They weren't set into a wall but stood apart on their own. Even so, they opened to a different location.

But to where? she wondered. And how long had they been open?

The dark room through the frame was difficult to see, but it was unlike the red place she was standing in now. The flagstones were brown and polished smooth.

"Is that why you're here?" asked Shaelis. "To become like us? You seek to be a god?"

Lothren's face screwed together in disgust. "Quite the opposite. I've come to do away with your unjust rule. To tear down the masters and end our slavery once and for all!"

Kaycia knew those words but was still surprised. She looked around, wondering if Jaleina was there.

Shaelis shook his head. "We saved the world, and you call it slavery?"

"If every soul must contribute their strength to your aspects—? If every man, woman, and child must bow to your will, then, aye, it is! Your entire existence, Shaelis, is wholly unnatural. It always has been."

The god groaned. "If not for us, this world will fall."

"Or so you tell us. One more lie to keep us in line."

"Let's skip all this. You clearly aren't listening. So where is this going...? Even if you kill Ashaira, you can't get away. We have you surrounded."

The man sneered. "Ah. Straight to the point. But it isn't *me* you should be worried about."

Shaelis grit his teeth and looked around the room.

Kaycia saw them, too—the shadows that crept from the darkened corners. Indistinct, like the soldiers. Filling the room with the echoes of fighting.

Lothren chuckled, and the god barked orders, rearranging his men to handle the threat.

But when Shaelis moved to join the defense, Lothren tsked.

"Not you!" he said, adjusting his grip on the knife. "Didn't I say, be patient?"

Shaelis paled, and his eyes flicked to the doorway. His hands were twitching as though in need of a weapon. His ax, however, lay on the floor—cast aside, no doubt, out of fear for Ashaira's life.

"Do you know what's in there?" asked Kaycia, approaching the hazy figures guarding the door—curious to know what they meant by heaven.

"From what it sounds like? The source of the gods' power."

"But what does that even mean?"

Kaycia stepped around the men and was about to stick her head inside when Sefina stopped her.

"You can't," she said. "It isn't part of this memory. There's no telling where you'd go—but it won't be the place you're seeing now. Not if the door is closed at present."

Even so, Kaycia peered into the dark chamber. Everything was sealed, without windows or open doors, but she could just make out what appeared to be a worship circle. The first, perhaps, of all such circles. With statues more lifelike than any she'd encountered.

It was all so curious, she almost didn't hear the shouts.

The men were spreading out and looking at the ceiling directly above Kaycia's head.

She dove to the side as the beast dropped—a lion-shaped mass of human heads and arms. Her reaction was late, but it didn't matter. The limbs thrashed the ground but did her no harm.

"No!" shouted Shaelis. "Don't let it get inside!"

Kaycia spun as the men thrust their spears—passing straight through her.

The creature's many heads phased in and out of view—over a dozen, howling with twisted, tortured expressions. They were surrounded by a mane of blood-matted fur—behind which thrashed innumerable arms, batting aside the soldier's weapons and reaching for throats.

So desperate was Shaelis, he broke into a run—an ordinary run, unaided by divinity. It confirmed what Lothren said. The world didn't reform or reshape to the god's will, but rather, Shaelis was subjected to a higher law.

As such, he didn't make it in time.

Despite the spears embedded in its flesh, the beast turned and squeezed through the portal.

Only moments before the doors slammed shut.

"Oops!" said Lothren, holding up something in his hand, tight against the hilt of his knife. Kaycia couldn't see from this distance, but she suspected it must be the key they were after. How else could he control the gate without being near it?

Shaelis slammed a fist against solid stone.

"What's this?" Lothren scoffed. "If I didn't know better, I'd say you were frightened, Shaelis! You—who call yourselves gods! Eternal! Infallible!" He shook his head in pity. "How can one measly creature unman you so? You're completely invulnerable—unconquerable—isn't that what you taught us?"

Shaelis grit his teeth.

Though she couldn't be sure, Kaycia sensed this was the turning point. It had only taken a single creature—to what? Destroy those statues? Whatever it was doing, it would eventually affect the gods themselves.

So, then—? Kaycia was incredulous. "Why's he standing there? The key's right in front of him! He should be rushing Lothren!"

But Shaelis did nothing, controlled by the knife, once again, at Ashaira's throat.

"This is ridiculous!" insisted Kaycia. "She's going to die anyway!"

Sefina shook her head. "It isn't *her* he's worried about."

"What do you mean?"

"Just look at his eyes. He's been watching her belly from the very start."

"...But?!"

The ground trembled to the break of thunder.

Though the throne was indoors, blood began to fall from the distant ceiling. It started as drops, spattering the red floor a darker shade.

Lothren gazed up in wonder as it dotted his face. He began to laugh. "And so it begins! None shall abide the wrath of their coming!"

"The Lords?" asked Shaelis. "*They* are the ones who deserve your fear!"

Ashaira stirred and began to scream. The shrill scream of a person who didn't understand the state they were in. She struggled against the knife, but Lothren wrestled her under control.

As he'd said from the start, she had no abilities. Not here, anyway. And, now, it was worse because her mind was gone.

Kaycia knew that look. The mania that consumed Ashaira's expression—made all the more complete by her prison garb. Some vital component had already been lost. Already been destroyed.

But how? she wondered. Had she missed it? After waiting so long for this moment, she couldn't see past those doors. She vaguely understood what Lothren had done, but the picture was incomplete.

When Ashaira began to thrash, he struck her head with the knife's pommel. She screamed and wailed—but with faltering strength as he struck her again.

He grimaced at Shaelis. "Your composure is admirable! Waiting for the end... Counting the seconds for your turn to come up."

The god's hands were shaking, but Kaycia could see that Sefina was right. He was only holding back out of fear for the child.

"Let her go!" he demanded. "Take me instead!"

"I'll pass," said Lothren. "You're about to die, anyway. And our current arrangement suits me just fine."

Shaelis clenched his teeth, unsure what to do.

Lothren sneered. "Wanna know a secret...? I already know of your precious child."

Kaycia blanched.

The god's face revealed nothing—perhaps, in the hope the man was bluffing.

But there could be no doubt. In the next moment, Lothren lowered the knife from Ashaira's throat to her womb.

Shaelis blew out his breath.

"Don't deny it," said Lothren. "She told me, herself, begging for mercy...before I cracked her skull. Otherwise, the story's a bit hard to swallow—what, with the trial and drama between the two of you? I'm curious, though... Did you do it in her cell? Did you *force* her?"

Shaelis didn't answer.

"Doubtful... Because that would imply some passion was involved. I bet it was the opposite. As though making a child were an act of duty. A contingency to avoid the annihilation of your race."

The god still said nothing.

"Since time immemorial, you feed us these falsehoods. You claim to be sterile and incapable of progeny—but that falls shy of the mark. It's a simple limitation of power. Only a certain number of gods can exist.

Lothren sighed in contemplation. "I wonder... Were you really the first? Or were there more gods before you? Ones you replaced when their rule reached its end?"

"Speak plain!" said Shaelis. "What are you after?"

"I thought that was clear. I want the same thing you do..." Lothren smiled. "I want the cycle to continue—but, this time, without your evil machinations. This child will grow without your interference."

Shaelis' eyes widened. "She's to live, then...? As your puppet?"

Lothren shook his head. "We've been through this. If your men don't kill me, those creatures will."

The god groaned. "And the child? They'll kill her, too!"

"Well, that depends, now, doesn't it?"

Shaelis reddened, thoroughly confused.

Lothren grinned. "I'm honestly surprised that you're still alive. Still in your right mind—the last of the pantheon. But it doesn't matter. The question if the babe lives or dies...is entirely up to you."

"To me?"

"Is that not how this works? Your daughter can't ascend while you yet live. So I ask—will you not relinquish your mantle? Give up your godhood and die before me? By your own hand?"

The god clenched his jaw.

"What's the problem, Shaelis? One last chance to give your death some meaning! Is the trade not fair? Your immortality for hers?"

The man raised the knife.

"No!"

"Choose!"

The knife plunged downward, and Shaelis howled. It stabbed deep into Ashaira's pelvis, over and over, until the goddess' dress was a bloody ruin.

Kaycia stared in horror. It was all more ghastly than she could've imagined. It couldn't end like this!

Shaelis roared and lunged forward.

Lothren ducked to the side, using the throne for cover, but he wasn't fast enough.

The god went for the knife, slamming the man's wrist against the oxidized floor. Shaelis' movements were slow and clumsy, unaided by the divinity he was accustomed to, but they proved sufficient. With a few more slams, the blade skittered away from Lothren's hand.

"W—wait!" the man whimpered.

But the god didn't listen. With both hands, he dragged the man's shirt in the opposite direction—away from the weapon and away from Ashaira.

He then beat his face into a bloody pulp.

Kaycia, however, was only dimly aware of this. She rushed toward the bleeding goddess on the floor, needing to see for herself that Ashaira still lived.

The woman was breathing, ragged and feeble, and her eyes were rolled back into her head. There was too much blood spreading on the floor.

Kaycia knew it was pointless. Everything she saw had happened in the past. It was already a memory and couldn't be changed.

"Is there nothing we can do?" she asked Sefina.

The other girl, however, had her attention on Shaelis—who'd ripped the chain from Lothren's throat—on which hung the key.

Bringing his rage under control, the god returned to Ashaira.

Even without his abilities, he was incredibly strong. He took her gently in his arms and hurriedly carried her toward the open doorway.

Lothren tried to laugh, but it was more of a sputter. "The ch—child's dead, you fool!"

Kaycia was equally confused. Was it because the doors led to a different place? Far enough away, the god's divinity might function again?

Ashaira's, at any rate.

She couldn't shake the doubts Sefina had given her. That Irisea was unable to help. Was this the reason? Because she'd died a mortal? Having lost the chance to ascend, in truth?

At the threshold, the god lovingly laid his wife on the floor. A few soldiers rushed past him with orders to destroy the creature inside.

"It won't make a difference!" Lothren cackled. "You won't keep the Lords out! They'll break through the stone!"

Shaelis ignored him.

To everyone's surprise, he didn't close the doors. He didn't even wait for his men to return. Rather, he lifted his ax off the floor and struck a powerful blow to the frame itself.

The world, opposite, shifted and wavered.

"Heh...!" muttered Lothren. "But you're still too late! You deprived the babe of her only chance!"

Shaelis didn't answer. His repeated strikes drove cracks through the stone. Until, at last, the massive slabs tumbled to the ground, and all signs of Ashaira vanished into oblivion.

Only then did he stop and regain his breath.

Lothren watched him, propped up against the base of the throne. Despite his injuries, he smiled through bloody teeth.

"Couldn't do it, could you? Not even to save her life. I shouldn't be surprised... "

"You're wrong," said Shaelis in a dispassionate tone. "The child may yet live."

"...May?" asked Lothren in disbelief. Then he frowned. "Why not? One more lie to add to your legacy. But even you can't believe it. The souls of men don't linger long—not like a god's. If you'd done as I said...? But no. You made your choice. It was *you* who deprived her a proper ascension."

"That would be true..." admitted Shaelis, "if I were the father."

Kaycia's heart skipped a beat. She didn't know what this meant, but he seemed to be suggesting there was still some hope.

Lothren wasn't impressed. "Now you're pushing it. You think anyone will believe that?"

"Matters not what they believe. It's the simple truth."

"She's been locked in a cell! With no one else! It's been months!"

"I'm telling what I saw—what I sensed within her. The child isn't mine."

Lothren was aghast. "She hasn't been with Aviathas s—since... Since..."

Aviathas? wondered Kaycia, piecing it together. She'd long suspected there was something between him and the goddess, considering what she'd endured to save his life. But...if he was the father...

Kaycia's eyes shot toward Sefina with unreserved suspicion.

When the girl looked away, there could be no doubt.

Here was the princess they'd all been searching for. Not the daughter of Stratum— but Innovation!

The girl had known all along—even warning Kaycia she wouldn't like what she'd find. And she'd insisted Irisea was unable to help.

But she was worse than unable. And worse than dead.

Sefina was *unwilling*. She was downright selfish!

Shaelis sighed. "You seem surprised—but you shouldn't be. This is Ashaira, remember? She could always restore what was meant to be. Reverting our bodies to enter this place. Reverting his seed. Time is of no import. She knew that Aviathas had—"

"I'd be touched," interrupted Lothren, "but this is utterly meaningless! The child's a captive of her undying mother's womb! Locked in a tomb that can't be reopened! Just admit it, Shaelis—you've gained nothing!"

"Today, we've all lost something—more than your pitiful existence can fathom. But we haven't lost *everything*—and that makes the difference."

Kaycia was speechless. A few minutes earlier, she would've given anything to hear these words—to know Shaelis, himself, hadn't given up.

But now, hearing the hope in his tone and the trust he was placing in the unborn child—the girl who'd grow to reject her destiny—Kaycia couldn't take it.

She rounded on Sefina. "How long have you known?"

Sefina scoffed and shook her head.

Kaycia was furious. "Don't ignore me! Or treat me like I don't understand!"

The girl's eyes widened. "Really? What do you expect of me? You heard what happened!" She pointed an angry finger at Shaelis. "What right does he have to decide my fate? He who murdered my father *again*?!"

Kaycia didn't back down. "You don't have to agree with him! You can curse his name till the end of time! But you're behaving like a child! You care nothing for the people who are counting on you!"

Sefina groaned. "You're one to judge. Even you couldn't stomach the fate you were given. Bloody heavens! You sacrificed your sister to defy their decision!"

"That...wasn't my choice... But that's beside the point. No one cares about *me*!"

"Oh, right. *I* was singled out, so I don't get a say. Condemned to waste my existence, saving a world that can't be saved."

Kaycia swallowed, empathizing with the girl's sense of futility.

"You think I haven't tried?" Sefina asked. "You don't know what I've done! How much I struggled to accept it. To do anything I could—but nothing makes a difference."

"It does. Maybe not in the end. Maybe, no matter how hard you try, it'll all fall to shit. But that doesn't mean—!"

"What?" asked Sefina, her cold eyes glistening. "That I can't help someone today? Don't be so naive! I can only make it worse. Each day this world goes on is one of pain and fear. Would you have me suffer to add false hope to the list? That isn't mercy, that's *cruel*!"

"It isn't," said Kaycia. "And you're wrong. Because, despite the suffering, there are people out there who find reasons to live. Who find moments of joy—small though they are. That's why they believe in you."

"I never asked them to!"

"And yet, they still do. Because all of us are trapped. Not just you."

Sefina grit her teeth as though swallowing a scream.

Only then did Kaycia notice the fight surrounding them—continuing to unfold despite her inattention. No longer did the men defend the perimeter; they'd been driven toward the center of the room.

Though the scene was still hazy, the monsters had become more than indistinct shadows. She caught glimpses of snapping teeth and mutilated skin. She could hear them screech and smell the viscera.

Even Shaelis was fighting, going toe to toe against a new arrival—a creature that seemed more man than beast.

Over its cadaverous flesh, it wore something like a cloak. The material was black, threadbare, and matted with blood—but it was clearly being worn.

At some point, the god had been clawed, with gaping cuts across his tunic and face. But he couldn't be stopped. He hacked at the creature with relentless abandon until nothing remained but a pile of limbs.

Taking a deep breath, the god spoke.

They were the same words Kaycia had heard from the stories, but they surprised her all the same. Not for the message contained but the fact the god's eyes were looking straight at her.

"Irisea shall be born of grief and blood, and all the world shall know her name!"

Kaycia looked around, but there was no one else whom the god could be talking to. He seemed to know she was watching, though her presence was more than three hundred years late.

The blood rain continued, blanketing the floor from wall to wall.

Most drops went straight through Kaycia, but a few didn't. They speckled her armor, already dark with stains. She didn't get the chance to worry this over as Shaelis' eyes demanded her attention.

"She mustn't be left to stand alone. She'll need your support. Your encouragement. Your fealty. For only then will she be free to walk the abyss."

He placed the key atop the seat of the throne.

Without thinking, Kaycia reached toward it...and the image changed.

The key faded and darkened but didn't disappear. After three hundred years, it remained on the chair, worn, weathered, and layered with dust.

Even in her hands, she had difficulty believing it was real. But, no matter how hard she squeezed, the key remained firm.

"But, the door's gone!" she cried, her heart hammering in her chest. "What am I to do with this?"

The god raised his ax to ward off a new threat.

"Take it!" he yelled. "Get out of here!"

There was so much urgency in his tone, her eyes were drawn back to the figure on the floor—the one Shaelis had so savagely butchered.

It didn't seem possible.

As though pulled together by invisible wire, its limbs reconverged. The effect was slow and mostly hidden beneath cloth, but there could be no mistake. It was still alive.

Sinew and bone popped and twisted. The black, severed threads writhed like the legs of a centipede. The weave tightened back together, and the creature regained its feet.

No. This wasn't a mere creature. She'd been too distracted earlier to see what it was. But now, with a cloak drenched in bright red blood—and a hood that wasn't facing Shaelis or the army of creatures but directed at *her*—Kaycia knew.

"Praxys..." she breathed, stumbling back involuntarily.

As it continued to rise, Shaelis tried to stop it.

His ax, however, passed through it like mist.

"Sefina?" cried Kaycia over the rise of her heartbeat. "Make it stop! It's an aeisr, right? That's what you called them?"

"I'll try...!"

The scene wavered for a moment. The light thrummed as the creatures faded and folded back into memory.

All except the lord.

Its form remained the same, though its appearance changed. Its flesh was no longer slick with slime but dry and crackled. White flakes peeled off its deformed muscles, like withered scales—but it was more or less the same. It shambled toward her with insatiable bloodlust.

"Gggggg—!" Shaelis' voice was distorted. "Ggggooo!"

Kaycia turned, but her feet wouldn't move.

"*What are you waiting for?*" asked Sefina.

"I—! I can't—!"

The air was thick, as though her body were suspended in honey. She fell into a slow, backward stumble but knew she wouldn't get away in time.

"*Come on!*" urged Sefina.

A lance flew through the air and impaled the creature. It was followed by a second. A third. A fourth.

The lord missed a step and howled in pain, but it couldn't be stopped.

...Because the weapons weren't real.

Kaycia recognized them as projections of Sefina's power—doing everything she could to buy more time.

The girl let out a yell, and the ceiling collapsed, burying the beast beneath enormous metal slabs.

Drawing on her conviction, Kaycia moved faster. She leaped over a fallen corpse, and by the time she hit the ground—several long seconds later—she'd gained momentum.

The lord kept coming, pushing through debris and the torrent of wind that blocked its path.

By then, Kaycia was out the door and moving through a columned patio at near-regular speed.

She passed an enormous gate and found the district outside impossible to recognize.

The corroded, black cobbles were riddled with corpses—both human and otherwise. Dark, rolling clouds stretched across the sky, pulsating with a deep, red glow like the beat of a heart.

"*See that chapel up ahead?*" asked Sefina. "*We need to go through and up past the loft.*"

"Chapel...? Is the gemstone there?"

The girl didn't answer.

"Come on, Sefina! Where is it?"

"We need to backtrack some more. To the tower. Maybe less."

"You don't know?"

"It's hard to explain. We need to find another memory."

"Then why, dear gods, didn't we do that before?"

"The fires, remember? The ones you couldn't see? I couldn't get past them. But together—!"

Kaycia couldn't believe it. When they'd discussed this earlier, Sefina hadn't known possessing her was possible. So she was either full of shit, or she'd never had a reliable way to get the gem in the first place.

There wasn't time, however, for Kaycia to be angry. She burst through the heavy doors, ran up the steps, and crossed through a chamber that vaguely resembled a loft.

It transitioned into a sort of cave, but the walls were made of a slick, pink substance. They were encrusted in red pustules and a sickly slime.

The walls were moving, swaying in and out like a slovenly drunkard.

"Left!" said Sefina. *"Squeeze through there."*

Kaycia obeyed, putting all her trust in the girl's sense of direction. Were it not for this, she suspected, they wouldn't have outstripped the lord's pursuit.

"Whose memory are we searching for? Kadrek's? Or was it Renat who had the stones?" Kaycia knew this was a sensitive subject, but there wasn't time to tiptoe around it.

"Kay...?" asked Sefina in a pensive tone. *"Can I ask you something?"*

She swallowed in annoyance. "Will it get us where we need to go?"

"I've been trying to figure out what happened back there—the way Shaelis spoke to you. How he gave you the key."

Kaycia huffed. "It's confusing, I know—but can't we figure that out later?"

"Don't you get it? You somehow interacted with the memory! You changed what—"

"No. We didn't change anything." Kaycia paused, trying to figure out the best way to explain. "If we had, it'd imply the memory was different before we arrived. But it wasn't. We saw everything exactly as it happened. Shaelis *knew* we'd be there—somehow. He was so sure of it, he set down the key and trusted us to keep it safe."

"But that—! Stop! Take those stairs."

Kaycia switched directions and asked, "Remember when I told you of Praxys? How he was after me because he thought I had it? This is why! *He saw me take it!* Because there's only one version of events, and it can't be changed."

Sefina went quiet, thinking this over.

Kaycia had no choice but to keep on running. She could only hope the girl would warn her if she went the wrong way.

"*I want to try something,*" Sefina announced. "*You won't approve, but I... I have to do this.*"

Kaycia's heart sank, suspecting, at once, what the girl was after. It didn't take much thought to identify which of these memories she'd hope to change.

"Sefina... I'm sorry, but there's nothing we can do. Kadrek's dead. I saw his body strung from the ceiling."

"*I... I understand that... ... But...*"

"Where's the gem, Sefina?"

"*That's just it! We have to take it from Renat. He used the first and hid the second. But I don't see the point of waiting till then. Why not take them from an earlier memory—before Renat makes his move? We use one for ourselves and give the other to Kadrek!*"

"That's a bad idea."

"*How's it different from taking the key?*"

"It's completely different!"

"*I'm supposed to save people, right? Isn't that what this whole Irisea thing's about? Don't you see why I need this? Why I need to try?*"

Of course, thought Kaycia. Even in this, the girl was determined to use her destiny in the most selfish way possible. Even at the cost of reason.

When they reached the next fork, Elyriel's body went left, though Kaycia hadn't decided to do so.

"Damn it!" she shouted. "Just because we disagree, doesn't mean you can—!"

"*Don't resist me, Kay. Go back to your own body!*"

Kaycia wanted to scream. She didn't care whether Sefina was a goddess, because the girl certainly wasn't acting like one. In fact, when Shaelis asked her to help Irisea, she was certain he didn't mean her to stand aside and validate the girl's reckless impulses.

However, she was more worried about what might happen if she *did* resist. With an abyssal lord on their tail, they couldn't afford a repeat of their earlier fall, even if that meant surrendering control.

It made her furious! Why was *she* the only one who cared for Elyriel? Why didn't the other girl realize how her irresponsible actions put them all at risk?

But the question was stupid because she knew the answer. Were their situations reversed and it were Elyriel strung up in that ruined tower, it was doubtful Kaycia would give up so easily.

Sefina was doing this out of sheer desperation. It was just as much for Kadrek as it was for herself. And though Kaycia felt bad for opposing such heroism, she felt even worse, knowing how it would end.

"*Look! There he is!*" said Sefina.

Kaycia was confused because the area was nothing like where she'd seen him before. Instead of colorless walkways suspended in darkness, it was more like a forest of endless pillars.

"*Don't you see him? He's by himself. It's perfect!*"

As usual, it took a while before Kaycia saw anything—though both were looking through the same pair of eyes.

"Kadrek?" Sefina cried through Elyriel's mouth. "Can you see me?"

The shadow coalesced, giving Kaycia a view of a middle-aged man with deep gray eyes and a clean-shaven face. His dark hair hung just past his shoulders.

"Look at me!" she pleaded. "I need to warn you of something!"

But the man didn't turn. He was walking through the pillars—no—he was walking down a *hallway* and inspecting each door, one by one.

"Kadrek...? Kadrek!!"

Kaycia felt horrible. "I told you this wouldn't—"

The man cocked his head.

"*He sees us! It's working!*"

Kadrek furrowed his brow. "You...aren't one of them. What are you doing down here?"

"I know you don't recognize me," explained Sefina, "but there isn't much time. Your life is in danger."

The man's lips pressed together, and his brow lowered. His eye, however, flicked to the chain at her neck.

She seized the opportunity and held out the key. "This is what you came for, right? You know what this is?"

When he stretched his hand forward, Kaycia wanted to pull back. It wasn't that she mistrusted Kadrek but that Shaelis had specifically given the key to her.

The man, however, made no move to grab it. A single touch convinced him it was real and that he should take her words more seriously.

"See?" she asked. "There's no reason to stay! We need to move quickly if you want to live through this!"

"What's the problem?"

"The man you're with—Renat—he means to betray you."

"He...? How do you know about either of us?"

"Look. I can't explain right now, but he intends to leave you trapped. And take the gemstones for himself."

"Renat? He'd never—!" Realization dawned in Kadrek's eyes. His hand disappeared into his pocket, and he searched around.

Sefina panicked. "You still have them, right? Both of them?"

"Yes," he said, relaxing visibly. "They're here."

When Elyriel sighed, Kaycia got a physical sense of Sefina's relief. If she was being honest, she, too, was relieved. That stone, after all, was more than the surest way out—it was the only way to get Praxys off their trail.

"Come on," he said. "This way."

"We should use them now!"

"Not here. It's your turn to trust me."

The nearest stone wall burst into white flakes and dust. It scattered like hail, only to slow into sludge beneath the torrent of blood that entered from outside.

"Go!" shouted Kadrek. "Run!"

To Kaycia's astonishment, the previous explosion played in reverse, with the blood drawing together and rising through the air. The bricks and shards rolled backward before leaping into their original positions, blocking the path of the enraged lord.

It was much like the scene she'd witnessed in the garden, except this had been real—at the time of this memory. Unlike Sefina, who'd merely restored appearance, Kadrek had drawn upon the might of Ordination.

"Don't just stand there! I'll catch up! I promise!"

The wall burst a second time, and the blocks caught themselves after only a few feet. They stitched back together—less perfect than before.

Kaycia ran, uncertain if this was her own volition or Sefina's.

They'd both seen what was happening—how, in spite of Kadrek's efforts, a small amount of blood had remained on the floor. It wasn't yet enough to give the lord an entry point, but Kadrek was only delaying the inevitable.

"*See?*" asked Sefina, so only she would hear. "*It wasn't like this before. The memories* can *be changed!*"

Kaycia wasn't convinced but decided not to argue. After all, what was the point? If this was all predetermined to end in misery, the girl would soon see it for herself.

At the same time, however, a part of Kaycia hoped for a miracle. Though it didn't make sense, what if Sefina was right, and there were exceptions? What if the laws were different when applied to gods? Or if this key, somehow, might cause them to bend?

It was this, more than anything, that swayed her doubts. The key was an enigma she couldn't explain. Somehow, it possessed importance beyond opening a single door. Why else would the gods have been so protective, were it not meant to open something more?

To open possibilities? To open potential?

It seemed a stretch, but Kaycia was desperate. Desperate enough to think the unthinkable.

Except...as Kadrek caught up, she recognized the place where he was taking them. Sefina recognized it, too.

"No!" she cried. "We can't go in there!"

Kadrek grit his teeth. "It's the safest place! We have no choice!"

"But...!"

He pushed her through the door into the tower.

When compared with her memory, there were certain differences. The walls were newer and less worn with age.

The man closed the door and lowered an iron bar into place.

"There! That should hold him a while." He searched through his pocket before holding out the gemstone.

Sefina didn't take it. "Where's yours?"

Something hard slammed into the door, causing both of them to jump. But these walls were superior to the hallways they left behind.

"What's the problem?" asked Sefina. "We have them both!"

"...No. We don't."

The blood drained from Elyriel's face.

"I'm sorry," said Kadrek. "I lied."

"What?!" she demanded, her face squeezing taut. She took a step back, and her vision blurred.

The man raised his brows. "If I told you earlier, you wouldn't have come. You would've gone after Renat, and I couldn't let that happen."

Sefina gaped. "You led me here so *he* could get away?"

"His escape was always part of the plan. He's done nothing wrong."

"No. I won't accept that! I'm going back! I'll find an earlier memory!"

"You mustn't! Why are you so hellbent on Renat's death?"

"Because *you* need to live! I— I need you to—!"

"You still don't get it. It isn't Renat I'm trying to save—but *you*."

Both Kaycia and Sefina were at a loss for words.

The man forced a smile. "I've known who you were since the moment I saw you—both in this stranger's body and before when I arrived in Ahman. Please forgive me for not saying so, but it was all for the best."

Sefina still said nothing, though Kaycia sensed her raging turmoil. What did he possibly mean? He wasn't talking of Sefina's disguise but something more. Something deeper.

As an Ordinator, this was a part of who he was—not seeing the world as it stood before him but details as they were meant to be. People as they were ordained to be.

"Ixeya…" he continued, reaching for her hand and squeezing it tight. "You're better than this."

Her voice cracked. "Wh—what does that even mean? What are you talking about?"

When Kadrek shook his head, it was painful to watch. "The Ixeya I know would've never done these things. She wouldn't condemn an innocent man to die or act out of vengeance. Or compel the cooperation from a random stranger."

Kaycia swallowed and had the strange impression he was looking at her. Though he was talking to Sefina, he saw them both.

"I did it to save you!"

"I know why you did it. I'm grateful you care and for the love in your heart. But god-hood is *not* about getting what you want. You see that, don't you?"

"I don't give a fuck what it's about! I need you so much!"

"I know how this hurts. If there was any other way—"

"Then—!"

Kadrek grit his teeth and looked away. "We're wasting time. There's only one gem-stone, and we both know who it's for."

From beyond the door, the thrashing continued—a frenzied pounding that would eventually break through.

"Kadrek…! I—!"

She grabbed the back of his head and pulled him into a kiss.

Startled and horrified, Kaycia pushed away.

Sefina let her go.

Her back hit the wall, and she watched the couple pull together in a loving embrace.

Except…Sefina was no longer a thin, blond teenager. Her wavy hair was a glistening auburn and hung past her knees.

Though Kaycia had never seen her, she *did* look familiar. There were certain charac-teristics she shared with Ashaira. Her beauty was stunning despite her tightly clenched eyes and tear-stained cheeks.

The kiss continued, long enough for Kaycia to turn away in discomfort.

Kadrek pushed away and held up the gem.

"Here," said Sefina, pushing his hand toward Kaycia and looking into her eyes. "Get out of here. Save your sister."

Wordlessly, Kaycia stretched her hand forward, overwhelmed by the power the stone represented: salvation for Elyriel and for Kaycia as well.

"Go on! Before I change my mind!"

Kaycia snatched it and took a step back. She knew exactly what the girl was thinking—that *Kadrek* should be the one to be given the key. That he should escape, and she should die.

The man, however, placed his hand on Sefina's shoulder, and the young goddess turned to face him.

"Is any of it true?" she asked.

"The gemstone?"

"I mean Irisea! They're all counting on me to fulfill their dreams! To set things right! But I don't—!"

Kadrek shook his head. "I can only see you as you're *meant* to be—not the person you'll become. There's a difference."

The girl clearly didn't like this answer.

He turned to Kaycia. "You need to go—but, please, listen. It won't be easy. I beg of you—find it in your heart to forgive Ixeya. You've already done so much, and for that, I'm grateful. It'd be perfectly in your rights to walk away from all this. But I'm afraid, if you do, she'll buckle beneath the weight. She can't do this on her own. No one's that strong."

Kaycia could only nod.

She didn't trust Sefina or expect her to change—at least, not immediately—but she recognized the hope he was placing in them both. It was the same desperation she'd seen in Shaelis.

She turned to Sefina. "You coming?"

"...Not just yet. Go on without me."

"But—!"

"You don't have to worry about me. That thing can't harm me, remember?"

"Not your body, but—"

"Kay, listen! I know I can't save him. You tried to tell me—and I get it now. I really do. But I also can't leave him. Do you understand? Just..." She blinked away tears. "I'll come find you. Later. I promise."

Kaycia felt guilty leaving by herself, knowing what pain was in store for the girl. She kept hearing the words that Kadrek had spoken, *She can't do this on her own.*

But she saw something else in Sefina's eyes—a determination that hadn't been there before. She still meant to fight—to use all her strength to keep Kadrek safe, if only a moment longer.

The door flew off its hinges in an earsplitting crash.

"You need to go!" he shouted.

Sefina took her position and drove the lord back with a sea of fire.

An enraged squealing came from outside as the tower itself was engulfed in flame. A blazing barrier—as Sefina had told her. The same one that'd kept her from entering before.

With this final reassurance, Kaycia nodded.

"Thank you," she breathed. "The both of you."

Then she inserted the stone, and the world disappeared.

Chapter 37
THE IMPOSSIBLE

Kaycia lay in bed, coming to terms with everything that'd happened.

Irisea was real.

She was broken, yes, and horribly twisted—but undeniably real.

Tragically real.

Strangely, she supposed Kadrek was real, too—taking part in events that affected the present. Kaycia didn't even try to understand. It had something to do with indeterminate geographies and a place wrenched apart from time.

As such, it might be possible for Sefina to find Kadrek again in another memory—or, perhaps, to relive the same event all over again.

But no matter the possibilities, the outcome wouldn't change. Though Kaycia understood why Sefina might want to stay, the overall benefits were bound to turn sour. And she could only hope the girl knew what she was doing.

Bright light streamed through the carriage windows.

All was quiet, and it took her a moment to find Chesandril asleep against the door. She had a book nearby, fallen from her hands.

"Chess?" she asked as she propped herself up. This took more effort than expected, having neglected this body for far too long. She'd remembered to eat and expend her bowels but had done little more. It'd been over a week since last she bathed.

When the girl didn't wake, she tossed a pillow.

"Huh...? What's wrong?"

"Get Agren—hurry!"

Chesandril's eyes widened. "Elyriel? Is she hurt?"

"No," said Kaycia, unable to keep from smiling. "This time, she's fine. Better than fine."

The girl was confused but came to her senses. Rising to her feet, she did as she was told.

Kaycia swung her legs off the edge and tried to make herself presentable. Her hair, strangely, was already brushed. Chesandril must've done it during moments of boredom.

More than anything, it was her mind that needed preparation. She closed her eyes and controlled her breathing, assuring herself it'd all be okay. But no matter what she did, her emotions wouldn't be satisfied—not until she saw Elyriel with her own two eyes.

"What's happened?" asked Agren, and she nearly jumped.

She looked up. "Perfect. I need to go to the cave. Now!"

He sensed her urgency and withheld his questions. "I'll need to ask Soril. You know how it is."

"But—!" But he was already gone.

Kaycia was unable to suppress her anxiety. Only a few minutes had passed, but she didn't like Elyriel being alone. With her powers gone, she'd be defenseless against anything that chanced her way.

It felt like an eternity before Agren returned, bringing with him a disgruntled Soril.

"What's this about?"

By then, she was sure the worst had transpired. Though Elyriel had no reason to remove the armband, it couldn't be guaranteed. Even if Kaycia had instilled the band with the last of her conviction—to secure it in place—the effect would've ended and accomplished nothing.

"I'll explain when we're there," she said, rising to her feet. She took Agren's hand. "Just get us to the cave!"

Another endless second, and Soril nodded.

Everything went dark.

At first, Kaycia thought something had gone wrong—until she realized she was standing in ankle-deep water.

Without the aid of ascendancy, she couldn't see a thing.

"What's this about?" asked Soril, his voice echoing loudly.

Kaycia panicked. "You don't see her?"

She'd been counting on the others to see through the dark. The cave wasn't big enough to hide an extra person.

A voice moaned.

The clear voice of a girl. The most blessed voice in the entire world.

Soril took a step back. "Is that...?"

"Yes!" exclaimed Kaycia, unable to contain her excitement. "Elle? Where are you? I can't see!"

The man cursed in apology, and a blade ignited in his outstretched hand. The glowing dagger was much smaller than his sword, but it was enough to set the cave walls glistening, with projections dancing off the rippling pool.

The shadows were so deep, Kaycia didn't immediately spot the thin, crouched figure. She emerged from behind a pair of stalagmites, shielding her eyes from the sudden brightness.

Those eyes. It wasn't just the intelligence behind them, it was the look of recognition—the confirmation Elyriel knew who she was. Such a small thing—but it'd been missing now, for what? A month? It felt much longer.

Kaycia was at a loss for words. She stood there, doing everything in her power to keep from trembling.

"What am I doing here?" asked Elyriel.

It was such a simple question, but something inside Kaycia broke. Hearing her sister speak—with actual words—she splashed forward and pulled the girl into a tight embrace.

Elyriel laughed but was unable to match Kaycia's joy. Her limbs were tense and her expression confused. As though entirely convinced something awful had transpired.

While this was true—it had definitely been awful—it was also true it was over now. Kaycia could see it in Elyriel's face and the way she was acting. Her emotions might be negative, but they were normal. Perfectly normal.

"How are you feeling?" she asked, pushing the girl's wet hair away from her face.

"A little cold."

"Here," said Soril, stepping forward to share the heat from his blade.

The girl backed away and tried to hide behind Kaycia.

"It's all right, Elle," she said, giving Soril a look of apology. "He's a friend. Don't you remember anything?"

The girl didn't answer.

Kaycia couldn't guess what she was thinking or how lost she must feel.

"Perhaps we should head back to camp," he suggested. "A few blankets? Some warm tea while you explain how this happened?"

Finding her sister's reaction to be less than favorable, Kaycia said, "Not just yet. It's quieter here. Could you...maybe...give us a moment?"

The man nodded reluctantly. "In that case, we'll bring the blankets here."

In a few minutes, he did a bit more than that. A wooden bench was brought in so they could sit above the water. A few braziers provided a balance of light and heat, and the blankets made the cave feel downright cozy.

Elyriel sat by her side, holding a warm cup between her hands. She was eerily quiet and hadn't taken a sip—but her eyes gradually lost their edge.

Soril, on the other hand, was losing his patience. He made a point of hiding it and to come across as a good-natured host, but Kaycia could tell he was waiting for answers.

She tried to calm him with a sympathetic look, adding hope to her expression and imploring him to wait a little longer.

He swallowed in annoyance. "Shout if you need anything."

His feelings, however, ranked low on her priorities.

She had to stretch her mental faculties to find a way to approach her sister. Now that they were alone, all words escaped her. Her desire to be comforting was weighed down by guilt. There was too much to say and for which to apologize.

It was nearly half a minute before she forced out the question, "...Are you okay?" It made her feel pathetic.

Elyriel didn't lift her eyes. "I... I don't know... I feel like I want to throw up."

"Like you're sick?"

The girl shook her head. "I keep seeing things flashing through my mind. But none of it makes sense!"

Kaycia pulled her into another embrace.

Her sister didn't resist but also didn't reciprocate.

Kaycia knew she should say something—to explain that none of this was Elyriel's fault—but the words wouldn't come. Instead, she took the cowardly approach and kept her silence. As though a simple hug might set things right.

She knew, deep down, the problem wouldn't fix itself. But she seemed to be hoping for exactly that—for the pieces to come together in Elyriel's head. For the pain to disappear without the help of a salve.

The girl studied herself. "...This is your armor."

"It is."

"I don't understand. Since when—? What have I been doing?"

Kaycia took a deep breath. "What's the last you remember? We left Wern's Hold with Marien—you remember that?"

"I... I do, but..." The girl's face squeezed tight before her eyes widened in shock. "Weren't we attacked? There was a—! Is Marien okay?"

"She..." Kaycia swallowed hard. "Marien's dead."

Elyriel went quiet.

After several long seconds, Kaycia asked, "What else do you remember?"

The girl didn't answer.

Kaycia was dying to know what Elyriel was thinking, but she worried what might happen if she pressed too hard. As though her sister were glass.

Out of habit, she stroked Elyriel's hair.

A glistening tear ran down the girl's cheek.

After a moment, Elyriel blinked it away. "What—? What's this?"

"Oh," said Kaycia, looking down at the ring. "It was just a precaution. Something Soril gave us."

"Soril?"

"That man who was here. The ascendant."

Elyriel nodded and raised her hand closer to see. "I... I *remember* this."

"...You do?"

"Look. Right here, you just have to—"

"Elle! No!"

She twisted it open. "Empty, see?"

Kaycia nearly snatched the ring off Elyriel's finger, but the girl was right. Not a single trace of poison remained.

Her relief, however, paled when compared to the implications.

"What else do you remember? Was it like this all along?"

Her sister didn't answer.

"Did the contents fall out? How did you know about this?"

"I—! I don't...!"

Kaycia groaned and took a moment to regain her composure. "I'm sorry. I'll be quiet a moment."

On the inside, however, she was far from quiet. It wasn't just the poison that had her on edge, but the fact it'd been used without her knowledge. She should've remembered everything that happened to her sister—it was her job to know! To be aware of what she did and keep her safe!

But she couldn't even manage to help with her memories. The girl knew more than she was willing to say, and Kaycia could only stare in silence.

"It's hard to remember faces," Elyriel began. "I... I don't know these people. All I can say is we were somewhere dark. Completely and terrifyingly dark. I remember a girl."

"A blonde? In a white dress?"

Her sister looked up in surprise.

"She goes by Sefina."

Elyriel didn't react. Her eyes were drawn inward, examining her thoughts. "She was angry with someone. This boy was holding onto my arm. He was... Dear gods, I don't understand anything!"

"You're doing great," said Kaycia. "Just breathe. We'll make sense of this together. Tell me of this boy. Was he an older teenager? Was it Nesil?"

Elyriel turned her head. "I don't... ... He was strong. I mean, *really* strong. I kept trying to escape, but he wouldn't let go."

To Kaycia, this didn't match Nesil at all. If he was anything like Sefina, he shouldn't even have a body. But if Elyriel was remembering a different moment—a different person—Kaycia couldn't pinpoint a time frame.

The girl might have been simply confused. Considering her state of mind, her memory was unreliable, with multiple events bleeding together.

"Aico..." said the girl. "That was his name."

Kaycia blinked in surprise. "But then—! That must've been earlier. You're saying he was there, along with Sefina...? At the same time?"

"That's right. They were arguing with each other. Aico wanted to leave and take me with him, but Sefina wouldn't hear of it."

Only then did the image start to come together. A believable scenario from the hours she'd missed.

"And?"

Elyriel froze, narrowing her eyes.

"Come on, Elle! What happened next?"

"It— It was then that I... I..."

Kaycia swallowed, watching the girl's face fill with anguish.

"It's not your fault."

"It is! I poisoned him, Kay!"

"Look at me! I know this doesn't make sense, but it wasn't you. Otherwise, you wouldn't be confused. Your memories would be clear. But *none of this* was you. You weren't in control."

"Then who—? What the hell does that even mean?"

Kaycia grimaced. "It's hard to explain... I don't mean to be insensitive, but I need you to think. The poison wouldn't kill him—not by itself. So what did they do to him?"

The girl stammered in shock but understood how important this was. "I was *going* to kill him. I had my knife out and everything, but another boy—possibly the teenager you mentioned—convinced me not to."

Kaycia breathed a sigh of relief, both for Aico's benefit and Sefina's.

"We dropped him off somewhere," Elyriel continued. "A place he'd be trapped."

"Like where? ...That doesn't make sense."

"We were worried— *They* were worried of what he might do."

"No. Aico only wanted you safe. He'd have no reason to—"

"They thought he'd be angry. And go after Sefina."

Kaycia almost laughed. "So what? He couldn't possibly harm her."

Elyriel was confused.

"I'll explain later," said Kaycia. "But, trust me. Sefina will be fine. She... She's a *goddess*, Elle."

This did nothing to diminish her sister's concern.

Kaycia smiled in reassurance. "I know how this sounds, but I swear on my life—it's *her*, Elle. The child from the stories. Irisea."

The girl's face screwed together. "I thought you didn't believe in any of that."

"That's because I didn't. Not until recently."

Elyriel studied her eyes, trying to gauge Kaycia's sincerity. In their late-night discussions, Elyriel had always supported Irisea. It was the reason she'd condemned Ashaira's failure as a mother.

The girl's amazement, however, in Kaycia's change of heart was soon stymied by another concern.

"...Sefina, though?"

"I know," said Kaycia with a laugh. "She's nothing like anyone expected. Half the time, she's an absolute bitch. Utterly ruthless to get what she wants—but she isn't all bad. At least, we have to hope she isn't."

Elyriel's smile, however, was short-lived.

"Kay... They want to kill her."

"Aico?"

"Him and the other one. They were talking about it."

"You mean they were frustrated. They want to be rid of her."

"They want her *dead*. Erased from existence."

At first, Kaycia was incredulous. Nesil was supposed to be Sefina's husband. Their relationship, however, was far from ordinary. And even without their story, it wasn't difficult to imagine reasons for wanting Sefina gone.

Kaycia fell back on her earlier argument. "She doesn't have a body. She can't be killed."

"He seemed to know what he was saying—the older one. Something about a statue? He was serious, Kay. I know what I heard."

She didn't want to believe it, but Aico's involvement worried her.

"That's all he said? A statue?"

"No one bothered to explain! From the way he was talking, they all knew what it was. *Where* it was." After a pause, the girl added, "He wants it destroyed."

This wasn't much information, but it gave her a rough idea. Innovation, after all, wasn't supposed to exist. And it was possible Ashaira's solution wasn't perfect or irreversible.

She drew a deep breath, not knowing what to do. It might've been different if she were still in Ahman, but she wasn't. Now that her sister was back to normal, they could only wait and watch from the sidelines.

"Do you think he's still there?" Kaycia asked. "Aico, I mean? Wherever they put him."

Elyriel nodded. "They seemed certain he wouldn't get out. It was a strange place. Scary. A temple of vines."

"They—!"

Kaycia felt sick. It was the exact sort of thing Sefina was likely to do. To ensure no one got in her way.

And yet, Kaycia also knew something of Aico. No matter how much he suffered, he was bound to get out. He had experience with those vines. And he'd be all the more angry. All the more determined.

Enough for murder? As unlikely as that seemed, she couldn't discount what Elyriel had seen. There weren't many ways to deal with Sefina. If she was interfering with his plans for his people, her elimination might be his only choice.

"Bloody heavens...!" she muttered, wondering if they might already be too late. "If we could only talk to him!"

Elyriel gawked. "What?"

"I've spoken with him before. He's just a kid, Elle. He'll listen to me."

She said this with more confidence than she felt. Though Aico might look like a child, he didn't tend to listen to anyone.

"What's the problem?" asked her sister. "You've been there, right? You know how to get there?"

Kaycia groaned, debating whether she should start at the beginning. Her sense of urgency, however, prevented her from doing so.

"Get up," she said. "Come over to this wall."

It was a desperate move—grasping at straws—but what choice did they have? She could only hope there was another way in. That it wasn't transcendency that let her inside but something else about her. Some unknown qualification.

But as the girls faced the stone, nothing happened.

"What do I do?" asked Elyriel.

Kaycia slapped the rock with her palm and fought the urge to scream.

"Do you see anything?"

"Like what?"

"Anything at all? ...Indentations? Patterns?"

When her sister was slow to respond, Kaycia grabbed the girl's wrist and placed her hand against the wall. "Right here. The door's supposed to be right here."

With a doubtful expression, Elyriel followed her eyes. She stepped closer to the wall for a better look.

Seconds passed, and she was clearly only doing this for Kaycia's benefit. She didn't see a thing and wouldn't see a thing no matter how hard she tried.

"The key!" she exclaimed, suddenly hopeful. "On your neck! Get it out!"

As the girl pulled out the chain, it was obvious she hadn't realized it was there.

"What's it for?"

"Hand it here."

Elyriel obeyed.

It wasn't, however, an ordinary key. Though the metal was shaped like one, it was only intended to convey the idea. The prongs weren't designed to turn actual cylinders.

As such, Kaycia didn't know what to do with it.

She touched it to the stone wall. She tried turning it as though unlocking a door. She tried thinking really hard, using the strength of her will to open a path.

Nothing worked.

"You try," she told Elyriel.

Still no results.

"What's it for?" the girl repeated.

"...We don't even know," she said with a sigh. "There was another set of doors—the Doors of Heaven. It opened those. For all we know, that's all it does."

Perhaps, with more clues, she might've found a way to divine its purpose. In all likelihood, however, it shared no connection with their current problem. It didn't respond to wishes, and they were wasting time.

Eventually, they had no choice but to put the key away.

Her sister tried to be helpful. "Don't you think, maybe, we're overreacting? You said this was Irisea, right? If there's any truth to that, she'll know what to do!"

Kaycia bit her lip. "Maybe. If she knew of the danger. But she's...occupied at the moment. Aico's got to be the last thing on her mind."

"Could we send her a warning?"

"She's further than Aico! It's not like we can—"

Kaycia paused. Once again, she was acting in desperation but didn't want to rule out any possibility.

"This band," she said, touching Elyriel's shoulder. "It was our link to her. At least, it was before we—"

She shook her head, trying to rid herself of doubt. Deep down, however, she knew it wouldn't work. The whole point of the gemstone was to revert Elyriel to normal. It changed everything. Sefina even said their bond would go away.

"We might as well try," said Kaycia with forced optimism. "I don't know. Maybe close your eyes? Try to think out the words as loud as you can. Tell her Aico's getting out, and she needs to be careful."

Elyriel, the good sister that she was, didn't question her. Not out loud, at any rate. She squeezed her eyes and mouthed the words.

This went on for several seconds, but Kaycia knew it made no difference.

But what else were they supposed to do? There was no way in! After centuries of attempts to enter Ahman, they finally knew the reason. Only transcendents could enter, and there weren't any left!

Very briefly, she had another crazy idea. What if they repeated the ceremony and made another transcendent? But even as she thought this, she knew it was absurd. The process would take too long, and they didn't have the bones.

She couldn't be sure when Aico would wake up. She couldn't be sure he'd go through with his plan. But she hated this feeling—knowing something awful was going to happen and not being able to do a damned thing about it.

Elyriel opened her eyes. "Should I feel a response?"

Kaycia exhaled. "You did your best. There's nothing we can do."

Once again, the girl clung to hope. "Come on, Kay. This is Irisea we're talking about. Isn't she *destined* to survive?"

"Don't be naive."

"What of the legends? If she was meant to do all these incredible things, she has to get through this, doesn't she?"

These words, however, didn't feel right. If anything, they made Kaycia feel worse.

Irisea, after all, wasn't anything like the stories. She was brash, irresponsible, and hopelessly selfish. What was worse, she didn't want to improve.

There was no guarantee she'd fix anything.

In the end, perhaps, it was better this way. Sefina *should* be the one to save herself. And if it didn't work out, and Aico killed her, the girl would only be getting what she deserved.

The legends were wrong. Shaelis was wrong.

Was Kaycia prepared to risk their lives for *that*? Even if they could get inside, it'd probably end in disaster. They'd get hopelessly lost or, worse, killed. It'd been danger-ous enough with transcendency on her side, but even that was gone. And that was a good thing, wasn't it?

Getting Elyriel back was the best outcome she could've hoped for. It was the miracle of a lifetime and more than she deserved.

If they just walked away, no one would blame her. They'd go back to how things were. Two sisters surviving. In spite of the darkness.

Isn't that what she wanted?

To await the inevitable?

...Because nothing could stop it.

Not even destiny.

"Elle...?" she breathed, so softly, she wasn't certain her sister would hear. She had to repeat herself, with forced determination, "Elle?"

The girl backed to arm's length. "What is it?"

Kaycia opened her mouth but found herself unable to speak.

"Kay?"

"I... Bloody heavens... I can't do this."

Elyriel's eyes narrowed. "Do what? What's this about?"

An enormous pressure rose in Kaycia's chest, like a heavy balloon, making it difficult to breathe.

"Kay... You're scaring me."

"...There *is* one more option."

Elyriel said nothing, but her face went white.

Just seeing this was enough to change Kaycia's mind. "Forget it. It's unthinkable... I'd never."

"Never *what*?!"

She shook her head and wiped a tear from her cheek. "We'll find another way."

Elyriel, of course, didn't understand. "Just tell me what it is! What's bothering you, Kay?"

"*Nothing's* bothering me. We're not going to do it!"

"Don't *I* get a say?"

Kaycia couldn't take it.

"No!" she screamed. "If you remembered *half* of what's happened, you'd never forgive me! You'd be begging to leave! To never go back! You'd be terrified, Elle! And you should be! No one should remember the things you've been through!"

The girl stammered, and her voice cracked. "Y-you're right. I *am* terrified."

Kaycia studied her eyes, wondering how much the girl remembered.

"But you're also wrong," Elyriel continued. "Because I *do* forgive you. I don't remember all of it. Maybe not half. But enough to understand."

Her words were a knife in Kaycia's gut. They twisted inside her and made her want to vomit.

"Out of everything, you know what I remember most? It was *you*, Kay. No matter how bad things got, you were always there. Watching over me. Only *you* could make the darkness bearable."

"Elle, stop! I'd never forgive myself if—!"

"I know. No one should have to ask this. Especially now. Now that you've *finally* begun to believe..." The girl began to tremble. "Which is why I'm not making you ask."

"I said no! We'll find another option!"

"When? A month from now? Ten years from now?!" Elyriel squeezed her eyes shut and sent tears down her cheeks. "Even if the goddess didn't need us this instant, what good are we to anyone in our current state?"

"We're not having this discussion."

The girl shook her head. "If you want another way, then find another gemstone! You brought me back once. You can do it again."

Kaycia gaped. "What if there aren't more?"

"Then... ... Just remember... This wasn't your fault."

The girl reached for the armband, but Kaycia stopped her. She grabbed Elyriel's wrist and pushed her up against the wall.

"No!" shouted Kaycia. "I won't lose you again!"

She couldn't afford to be gentle. She overpowered her sister, keeping her hand away from her opposite shoulder.

The last thing she expected was for Elyriel to hit her.

Her vision flashed as her nose felt the brunt of the girl's forehead.

She retreated a step, tasting blood on her lips.

"You—!" Kaycia was so startled, she couldn't even speak.

"I'm sorry!" cried Elyriel. "I didn't mean to!"

Pushing through the pain, Kaycia wrestled for control of her sister's arm.

"I'm sorry!" the girl repeated over and over. "I'm sorry! I...! I love you, Kay!"

And then it was over.

Amid their skirmish, the band fell free and plopped into the water.

"NO!!!" she wailed, ignoring the blood that streamed from her nose.

She snatched up the band and slid it up the girl's arm.

Elyriel's eyes, however, had lost their focus.

"What's going on?" asked a voice from behind. "I heard shouting."

Kaycia couldn't face him. She couldn't face anyone.

She didn't even wait for her body to fall. With Elyriel's hands, she pushed through the door.

The darkness welcomed her like a protective blanket. It provided an escape, a way to flee from what had happened.

But despite all her strength and inhuman speed, Kaycia found breathing near impossible.

The weight was unbearable. The pain was too much.

Yelling didn't help. Or cursing the gods.

She punched the walls with her fists and sent cracks through the stone. She pounded and pounded until her knuckles bled. But even that was nothing against the agony she felt.

She could only run and keep on running.

She needed to reach Sefina and make the girl pay.

To prove she was worth it.

Conviction flowed through Elyriel's veins.

Like a fountain overflowing, it flooded the city before her.

She faced the empty streets and caused them to move.

Chapter 38
ECHOES OF DIVINITY

After hours of struggle, Nesil was finally free.

For too long, he'd focused on the vines themselves. He'd pull and pull until his arms were wrenched from their sockets. He'd try to find a weakness in the hopes the vines would stretch and eventually slacken. But that never happened. The vines weren't real.

That was the part that frustrated him the most. He knew he was fighting a patch of air—an ethereal nothingness that adhered to its own rules. He wasn't fighting constraints but the *idea* of constraints, and he didn't have the tools to defeat an idea.

For a while, he thought the solution might rest in his mind. So he tried to change how he perceived the vines. He reasoned that if Sefina could create them with her imagination, he might affect them in a similar fashion.

He tried everything, and nothing worked.

Nesil wasn't an ascendant, just as she'd told him. He was a regular person—or the aeisric equivalent—and lacked the power to change the world.

Everything around him was Sefina's domain—the vines, the trees...the sky, itself. And for him to fight that was utterly ridiculous.

It was this realization that changed everything. Sefina could make him invisible and silence his voice, but she couldn't control his actual person. Otherwise, these vines wouldn't have been necessary.

His objective, then, was to change the way he thought of himself. He'd done it before, as they crossed the Melorian Sea—convincing his brain he didn't need to breathe. It hadn't been easy, coming face to face with his self-image and a lifetime of habit. But, for a fleeting moment, he'd altered his body. He'd become a person who didn't need air.

After considering what other conversions might be possible, his first attempts were too ambitious. Though he could picture his arms becoming thin as noodles, it was a different thing entirely to make himself believe it. No amount of reassurances—repeating to himself that his body wasn't real—was enough to produce an actual change.

He only gained ground by trying something basic. He pulled against the vines until his arms hurt—then forced himself further. He convinced himself that the pain didn't matter, and there'd be no permanent damage to the joints in his shoulders.

Though he could not make his bones disappear, he tried to make them flexible. These smaller changes were easier to swallow. They were far from painless, but he didn't lose focus. He closed his eyes and imagined himself bending free.

More than five minutes later, his arms felt like jelly and burned with agony, but the vines slipped free and flopped to his sides.

He nearly made a run for it as though the vines might retaliate and ensnare him again—but that was stupid. And he wasn't the only one trapped in this place.

Sefina had been true to her word, bringing Nesil to the cathedral overlooking Aico's prison. She'd left him on the roof, where he'd have a clear view of the boy below—while being far enough away that conversation was impossible.

At first, this arrangement had made Nesil angry. He was certain she'd done this to piss him off. Now, however, he wasn't so sure. As he grabbed hold of the vines and shimmied down the chamber walls, he realized something he hadn't before.

Though Nesil might be illusion, he wasn't immune to the effects of the current. A sickening pain began to churn in his stomach, making it increasingly difficult not to let go and fall the remaining distance. By the time he reached the ground floor, he wanted to throw up.

By leaving him on the roof, Sefina had done him a courtesy. If he'd faced such pain while seeking the solution, it was possible he wouldn't have escaped at all,

And Nesil was only halfway to the basement.

Aico's moans had ceased over an hour back. But he wasn't unconscious, and he wasn't dead.

There was a time, early on, when he'd tried to climb free, but the vines had taken their toll on his senses. They'd stripped him of reason and his ability to discern illusion from reality. And so he'd propped himself up into a seated position, folded his legs, and withdrawn inside himself in forced meditation.

"Aico?" shouted Nesil. "Up here! Can you hear me?"

The boy didn't respond, and Nesil became worried he'd have to descend further. This was worrisome, not only because he'd crumple beneath the pain but because of the illusions Sefina had left down below. There were floating reflections and drifting barriers. Even the vines didn't match their truthful positions, writhing in unpredictable directions. And though Nesil could see Aico from up top, it was the only angle that provided such advantage.

If Nesil started downward, he'd wind up more lost than Aico himself.

"Come on!" he yelled. "I'll lead you out of this! Just follow my voice!"

Still no answer.

The boy had closed himself off from the world, ignoring the pain and the rest of his faculties. It was a valiant display of superhuman resilience, but it brought him no closer to actual freedom.

Nesil took a deep breath and prepared to jump when he noticed Aico shift position. The movement was slight—nearly imperceptible—but it almost seemed like the boy was closer. He hadn't drifted to either side but was rising off the ground.

A small, stony shape coalesced underneath him and lifted the boy upward.

"That's it!" cried Nesil. "Keep coming toward me!"

But it wasn't so easy. The illusions reacted and redoubled their confusion. It wasn't just a matter of deceptive obstacles but distortions in gravity, fouling his sense of direction.

"Over here! To me!"

When Aico changed course, it was still the wrong way.

Nesil realized something was twisting sound, making his voice seem to come from elsewhere.

"Never mind. Move to your left... Tilt yourself forward. A little more... Stop. Now up."

Through all these instructions, Aico's eyes remained closed. His face contorted with exertion, needing to concentrate on the shape holding him aloft.

"Good!" said Nesil. "A little higher..."

The shape was so malformed and feebly thin, Nesil feared it might break at any moment. If that happened, it wouldn't only be a matter of starting over, Aico would need time to recover. And their following attempt would be all the more difficult.

Lucky for them, the boy's strength persevered, bearing him out through the storm of tendrils.

As the vines came closer, Nesil stepped in to fend them off. They were painful to touch but not so bad as the real ones they imitated.

"Forward... Forward... Good! You're here!"

The boy's eyes cracked open—just barely—before he collapsed onto the stone floor. The twisted shape, supporting him, dispersed into nonexistence. The vines withdrew, and Aico fell asleep.

Nesil sighed, regretting they hadn't made it out of the cathedral, but he could stomach the discomfort for a little while longer.

"You're unbelievable," he said to the unconscious boy. "Truly. One of a kind."

His sense of relief, however, didn't last long. As the minutes stretched by, he became more and more worried they were running out of time.

The longer they took getting back to the statue, the more likely it became that Sefina would return.

A part of him was tempted to leave Aico here. As long as the boy stayed asleep, he'd be safe from danger. Probably.

Nesil, on the other hand, would be free to attempt what he could with the statue. He'd have no control over its physical material, but he wasn't certain this mattered. While the tangible stone was necessary for relocation, it wasn't essential for its primary function. Back in Seldor, the illusions had persisted, even after the stone was gone.

It was possible, then, that only the illusory component needed to be destroyed. It would explain why Sefina hadn't taken the risk—why she'd tied him up and prevented him from getting close.

But Nesil was unable to bring himself to leave. He worried about the boy tossing in his sleep and falling down the hole. He was worried about facing Sefina alone.

And so he waited. For almost an hour.

"Thank you," said Aico as his eyes regained focus.

"...It was nothing. How are you feeling? Can you stand?"

"Saving my life isn't nothing. I'm in your debt."

Nesil smiled modestly, but this was precisely the reaction he'd hoped for. He needed the boy's help but didn't have much to offer in return.

"How much have I missed?" asked Aico. "Is Kaycia awake? The *real* Kaycia?"

"She is. She *was*. I'm sorry, but I haven't seen them for a while. They left. Just the two of them."

As the boy thought this over, Nesil spoke his mind.

"Look. You might want to go after her, but even if we found them—which is unlikely by itself—we can't be sure how Sefina will respond. Everything's changed. You know that, right? If the aeisr has control of a body—a real body..."

Aico looked offended. "I can handle her."

"I'm not saying you can't. But wouldn't it be better to be sure? We can split the two up. We can make sure that Kaycia is actually Kaycia. And we can do it from here."

The boy shook his head. "We're not destroying the statue."

"It's our best option! You know it is—not just for us but also for her!"

Aico wasn't convinced.

AUSTIN LYNN CLARK

Nesil pressed further. "You were just telling me you owe me a life debt! Well...this is all I ask. Simple. Easy."

"I won't do it!" he said, growing angry.

Nesil gaped. "Why not? She almost killed you, Aico! She had the knife out and everything!"

"Perhaps, but my decision hasn't changed. I'm not looking for an easy way out. I told you before, I need it intact."

"Why? So you can put Navara at the aeisr's mercy? How will that save anyone?"

"I won't let that happen. You have your doubts—"

"You're damn right, I do! She's surprised you once, and she'll do it again! There's no room for half-measures. Not against her."

The boy took a deep breath. "You might be right. But you're missing the point. No matter how destructive your aeisr might be, she doesn't hold a candle to the abyssal current. That's my concern. And anything less than a functional statue *is* a half-measure."

Nesil grit his teeth but realized arguing wouldn't get him anywhere.

Aico would never understand because he hadn't lived it. The boy was overconfident because he didn't know Sefina—not like Nesil did.

As a result, she'd find a way to trick him. She'd slip through any plan meant to fend her off. And his people would pay the price.

Against the current or the aeisr, dead was dead.

Nesil pressed his lips together and feigned resignation.

Though he'd made a mistake, waiting for the boy to wake up, it wasn't too late to set things right. When compared to the aeisr, Aico was little more than an inconvenience. And it'd be easy to make a move behind the boy's back.

Without another word, he followed Aico into the streets.

When they reached the garden, it was still a mess. The trees were tilted away from the center. Their roots twisted up into the air, exposing rotted earth and gaping holes. The metal rod was still stuck in the dirt, streaked with Sefina's dark, dried blood.

Nesil approached it, knowing it possessed an illusory quality—something he could touch. He didn't fool himself into thinking he could move it—not the physical part, anyway—but he widened his stance and grasped the pole with his hands.

At first, it refused to budge. Despite his greatest efforts, it was as though the rod were fused into stone.

Had the illusion been different—created by Sefina to withstand his meddling—he wouldn't have bothered. But the pole had been left here, loose in the dirt. As such, he wasn't fighting against her will but at the link that merged realities together.

The link was strong, but that didn't mean he couldn't be stronger. That his muscles—which weren't real to begin with—couldn't develop into something greater than he'd possessed in life.

The illusion tore apart.

Instead of one, there were two metal rods. One was old and corroded, jutting from the ground. While the other was smooth, shiny, and caked with blood.

It was a meaningless victory—to anyone but himself.

Nesil set his jaw and clenched his new weapon.

But, before he could use it, the statue lurched. The ground trembled, and an enormous mass materialized beneath its base.

"No!" he shouted, running toward it.

The column lifted the statue skyward, growing in the way of Aico's creations.

Nesil tried to grab hold, but his hands passed through. Without the makings of illusion, there was nothing he could climb.

"You're making a mistake!" he shouted to Aico.

The boy merely shrugged as he rose into the air. "I'm sorry, but I don't see it that way."

Kaycia's path didn't lead to the garden, but she found the statue, all the same. It slid across the sky upon a narrow bridge—a palanquin without servants or entourage.

Her heart skipped a beat, realizing how much she'd already missed. If Aico had wanted the statue destroyed, she would've been too late. Sefina would be gone, and Kaycia would have nothing to show for her loss.

For some reason, however, the statue was here, which was almost as bad. She didn't know how the thing worked but guessed it had something to do with proximity. The statue needed to stay within range of Sefina—or Aviathas. The particulars were complicated, but Kaycia's objective wasn't.

She swallowed her despair and raised her voice. "Aico! We need to talk."

The bridge slowed, and a face peered down over the edge.

At the same time, Nesil came out from beneath the bridge, using a pole like a walking staff. He regarded her with an expression between suspicion and hatred.

"It's me!" she said defensively. "I don't want to fight."

"It's all right," said Aico, descending a flight of materializing steps. "It's really her this time. And she's alone."

Nesil narrowed his gaze, less than convinced.

Aico reached the ground and studied her from a distance. "It's good to see you,

Kaycia, but this isn't a good time. You need to leave. Like I told you before, it's about to get dangerous."

"But that's just it," she insisted. "The statue needs to stay."

His surprise was replaced with amused curiosity. "And why's that?"

"It's...complicated. You have to believe me. The statue won't help you push back the current."

He lowered his brows. "Did Sefina put you up to this?"

"What? No! Just think for a moment! What's more important—a hunk of rock left behind by the gods or the power of the gods themselves? The statue, on its own, isn't the answer. Not without *her*."

When Aico paused, she added softly, "Sefina isn't who you think she is. When I was down there, I saw—"

He stopped her with a hand. "Doesn't matter what you saw—or what you *think* you saw. You should be grateful for getting out. That she *let* you out."

Kaycia groaned. "I get it. You don't trust her. Bloody heavens—! *I* don't trust her!"

Nesil came forward and pointed at her band. "I see you got the gem. She lied about that, too? You failed to escape?"

She grit her teeth. "It wasn't a lie. We got out. The stone healed my sister, but... Maybe now you'll understand. We didn't have a choice! When we realized you were going to—!"

"Wait... You removed the band because of *us*?"

"That's what I've been saying! It's that important!"

Nesil gaped in disbelief. "I'm sorry, but you shouldn't have returned. Sefina's fate's been decided."

Aico took a deep breath. "I might as well hear your reasons. Has she threatened you? What's she done this time?"

"It's not what she's done but what she still needs to do. Aico... Nesil... When I was down there, I saw a memory of Shaelis. Don't look at me like that. He wasn't an illusion!"

Aico shook his head. "By definition, the aeisr are all—"

"You know what I mean!"

She was initially tempted to show them the key—the physical proof that she wasn't lying. But as she thought about it, she realized she should've left it behind. Because if Aico decided he wanted to take it, she wouldn't be able to stop him.

"He spoke of the prophecy," she said instead. "About the child of rumor—the successor to the gods. You know, Irisea?"

The boy narrowed his brows but didn't speak.

"It's *her*," she declared. "Sounds crazy, but—!"

Nesil shook his head.

"Listen!" she insisted. "Haven't you ever wondered where Sefina came from? Why her story started here, of all places?"

"I've considered it, yes. But it doesn't matter. Even if she is this girl of legend, she has to die. She's more than earned it."

Kaycia was shocked by the venom in his voice. "You're not giving her a chance!"

Nesil seethed. "You just don't get it! Sefina's a *murderer*! It goes deeper than madness or loss of self-control. She's downright evil."

"She might seem that way, but—!"

He shook his head, unwilling to listen.

Kaycia pushed on. "Whatever she's done—however she's hurt you—could you let it go? At least, for a while?"

"Can you even imagine what it's like to have your family murdered?"

She blinked in surprise. "That's a strange question."

"She killed my mother, Kaycia. Just last week. My grandfather, too. The King of Seldor."

For a brief moment, Kaycia was confused. She understood Sefina's reasons for wanting Renat dead, but the man had escaped less than an hour back.

Nesil, however, wasn't talking about that. He was referring to something that happened much later after Renat returned home.

And the boy wasn't finished. "On that same day, she killed my betrothed. You know, the girl she's impersonating? The blond teenager—the *original* Sefina? The aeisr *killed* her and has been gallivanting in her body ever since."

Kaycia stammered, trying to come up with an explanation. It wasn't the sort of thing the boy would make up—or could've been duped into thinking was true. And if it actually happened, it wasn't something she could easily ignore.

Nesil went on. "She destroyed my kingdom. *Thousands* of people. Over the past three years, she's besieged us with—"

"Wait," interrupted Kaycia. "You're saying that was her? The siege—the one I've been hearing about—that was Sefina? All by herself?"

"That isn't her name."

"Fine. Irisea, then."

He raised his brows. "You think I'm exaggerating. I wish I were. But I've been living this nightmare for years. And after all that time and a fair amount of luck, I finally stopped her. I destroyed the fragment—the part of this statue that was brought into Seldor. Were it not for that, she'd still be there, finishing us off. Every last one."

Kaycia buried her face in her hands.

Dear gods—what mess had she gotten herself into? She'd been prepared to deal with Sefina's eccentricities—the peculiar nature that made her so dangerous. But she'd clearly been missing crucial information.

What was worse, she'd fully committed herself to this path. She'd lost her sister again—and for what? To pin all their hopes on a mass murderer?

The girl, herself, had warned her of this. Sefina wasn't the savior type.

"I agree with Nesil," said Aico. "She isn't worth the risk. Even if she is Irisea—and this isn't some deception she'd have us believe—what has she done to prove her worth?"

Kaycia opened her mouth but didn't have an answer—not a good one, anyway.

It was difficult to express what she'd seen near the end. It wasn't Sefina, after all, who'd clung to hope, but Kadrek who'd brought out the best in her. He'd seen something inside—some hidden potential—and it'd inspired the girl to start trying again.

It was a single moment. A surge of emotion that'd come and gone. And yet, it was the only proof Kaycia had. That drove her to believe there was purpose behind this.

But Kaycia couldn't say it. She wouldn't admit her answer boiled down to faith—the flimsy excuse she'd so often scorned.

Aico started back up the steps. Without turning, he said, "Go home, Kaycia."

"I'm not done talking!"

Nesil gave a sympathetic shrug as though nothing she did could make a difference.

Her voice caught in her throat. "The world *needs* a savior... Don't you see that?"

Aico paused on the steps. "I honestly do. Sadly, that girl isn't it."

"You don't know that!"

He sighed and continued his way to the top.

"I won't let you do this!"

She grit her teeth, trying to hide her embarrassment. She knew full well she was no match for Aico, but she refused to walk away.

She was unable, however, to come up with a plan. And, for the longest moment, she could do nothing but stare helplessly as the statue renewed its earlier course.

She stood there, paralyzed, counting the seconds. She'd been hoping Aico would give her a chance—to talk this out a little longer.

But her options had run out. And she could no longer afford to hesitate.

Ordinary ground would've resisted her efforts. It would've demanded the strength of a workforce equal to men and horses—and everything you'd expect to move tons upon tons of earth and stone. Without anything at hand to supply such energy, the task exceeded Elyriel's capabilities.

In this place, however, Kaycia did not need to move physical substances. The landscape of Ahman was already twisted and prone to drift. As such, she only needed to tell the streets to diverge and send the ground beneath the pillars in opposite directions.

The air split with a resounding crack. The bridge, once solid, broke apart. Amid a shower of shards, the statue fell.

In sudden panic, Kaycia moved a rooftop underneath it and heard the crash after only a few feet. The solution was inelegant but, at least, bought her time.

She bolted into an alley, trying to hide.

The boy, however, was already ahead of her.

A surge of spikes erupted from the ground, sundering the stonework and blocking her escape.

Were it not for her conviction, her momentum would've driven her straight onto them, leaving her impaled like the creatures outside.

Aico's intent, however, wasn't to kill. She knew this, as the spikes had come at her from a distance.

His voice echoed from the rooftop above. "This is pointless, Kaycia. I see this means a lot to you, but you must let it go."

She turned the other way and found yet more spikes blocking her in. They exploded through the walls, spraying her with dust and shattered brick.

She prepared to jump, but more slanted down from the buildings above.

Had she been anywhere else, she would've known when to quit.

Instead, she twisted the world and found a version of the alley where the spikes weren't there.

Kaycia ran through a mist, pierced by morning sun. Even the walls were different, fringed with bright green moss. It was eerily quiet, without signs of Aico.

She was tempted to keep running but couldn't bring herself to leave the statue behind. If she could close the distance, she might get the chance to twist the rooftop away. She could take it somewhere else, where Aico couldn't follow.

It seemed like a stretch. There was no doubt in her mind he'd anticipate this approach. He'd learn from his mistakes and stop holding back. If left without a choice, he could still kill her. That much hadn't changed.

But what else could she do?

It'd be impossible to go to Sefina for help. Even if Kaycia got down there in time, without getting lost, she hadn't forgotten the Abyssal Lord. In comparison to Aico, he was far more deadly. After everything it'd cost to escape him once, there was no way in hell she'd face him again.

So, where did that leave her?

Sefina! she shouted within her mind. *I don't know if you can hear me, but I need you now! Aico's taking the statue, and we have to stop him!*

No response came.

She tried again, only this time without words. She focused her emotions and converted them into an expression of need. If anything, it almost felt like a prayer. And, considering there was a goddess on the receiving end, it might be the first true prayer she'd made in her life.

Come on, Sefina... Irisea...!

Kaycia kept moving. She twisted the world back so Aico wouldn't think she'd abandoned the game. Her only plan at the moment was to stay alive—long enough, hopefully, to come up with something better.

Nesil charged up the stairs, two at a time, making sure his pole didn't bump the walls.

He'd been quick to take advantage of Kaycia's distraction, but he was far too angry to feel gratitude toward her.

It was embarrassing to admit he'd once felt sorry for her—he'd even felt guilty for putting her life in danger. He'd clearly misjudged her.

No upright person could've possibly believed all the bullshit she'd spouted. He'd seen it in her face, the way she faltered when he told her the aeisr's sins. Kaycia had known all along of Sefina's vile nature, but she was too damn stubborn to relinquish the deception.

She'd overlook anything, even murder, if it validated the course she'd chosen for herself. And while she hadn't committed the crimes themselves, to Nesil, this was tantamount to open endorsement.

In the end, it was all up to him. If neither Kaycia nor Aico dared to stand against the aeisr, Nesil would have to do it himself.

Life, as usual.

At the top of the stairs, he crept out the door. Luckily, Aico wasn't waiting on the roof. For the moment, the boy was more concerned with Kaycia, giving Nesil an opportunity that might never come again.

There was no time for hesitation or second thoughts. He charged at the statue and swung his weapon.

In the process, he put all his focus into his arms. It wasn't the statue that mattered or the pole itself—his primary influence flowed from his center. He wasn't bound by his muscles or the force they could generate. His only limitation was his strength of will.

The metal clanged and nearly jumped from his hands. The vibrations wrenched against his arms and rattled his skull. But he held on tight and swung again.

Though he refrained from yelling, the racket was bound to draw Aico's attention. As such, Nesil didn't bother to check the damage he'd caused. He kept swinging, imagining each successive blow to be more powerful than the last.

He tried to recall what he'd seen in his soldiers—the way they placed their feet and committed their weight into each attack. He'd never done it himself, but it was the idea that mattered. The manifestation of violence.

Even so, his arms grew weary in less than ten blows.

Through all that time, the statue didn't give an inch. It didn't fracture or crumble as he'd desperately hoped. Instead, his greatest efforts yielded nothing more than a hairline crack near the remnants of Ashaira's hand.

And it was possible that crack had been there from the start. Created at the moment it landed on the roof.

But rather than lose hope, he considered himself lucky Aico hadn't returned. The boy was either too far away or too busy to investigate.

So Nesil kept trying.

Ignoring the pain in his arms, he imagined himself built of something stronger than flesh. That his bones were wrought from iron, and his muscles had a density to rival the statue's stone.

In his mind, he fashioned himself as a sculptor, striking at the crack with unerring precision. And though his actual skills fell short of the mark, his vision started to bleed into reality.

"My, my..." said a voice. "This was not what I expected."

His heart sank, and he forced all his rage into his next strike, fearing it would be his last. The metal clanged and sent his ears ringing.

He spun away from the rebound and aimed his pole at Sefina's head.

She caught it effortlessly in the palm of her hand.

In an instant, the humming metal was silenced and went perfectly still.

"I thought we were through this. Must you insist on ending your existence? You need this statue as much as I do."

Nesil blinked in surprise. He hadn't exactly forgotten this detail, so much as he'd painstakingly avoided the thought. He'd pushed it completely from his mind so it wouldn't weaken his strikes.

For this same reason, he avoided her question.

"How did you win her over? Kaycia, I mean. I never thought she could be this blind—not without you offering something in return."

His pole dematerialized, and she lowered her hand.

"What can I say? She likes me. Get over it."

He swallowed in annoyance. "I want a real answer. Why does she think you're the daughter of the gods?"

Sefina licked her lips and looked at him sideways. "What do you want from me, Nesil? To deny it...? Fine. It was all a lie. Am I the one to blame if she's so damn gullible?"

Nesil groaned. He knew better than to expect a straight answer from her. It made every conversation a waste of time.

"Now," she continued, "if you'll excuse me a moment, my girl needs some help. You'll be a good boy, won't you? And stop causing trouble?"

Before he could blink, Sefina vanished.

He stood there in shock, unable to believe she'd leave him unattended.

But when he tried to move, he found that he couldn't.

There were no vines this time or iron chains. The air itself seemed to hold him prisoner—as though he were encased in solid crystal.

It was enough to make him fear the worst—that Sefina had the power to control him all along. She'd simply let him believe he still held some strings.

Nesil tried to scream, but his jaw wouldn't move. No matter how he flexed, he couldn't move a muscle. Even his chest felt compressed and made breathing difficult.

His sense of claustrophobia took him by surprise.

Until he realized he hadn't lost all control. He could still move his lungs and still move his eyes. These details might've otherwise seemed insignificant, but they were enough to tell him that nothing had changed.

Despite all appearances, she wasn't controlling his body. She'd simply tied him up with invisible constraints. The problem was more complex but ultimately the same. And if he'd broken out once, he could do so again.

He only hoped he'd be fast enough.

Because, in his momentary struggle, he'd noticed something important.

His eyes had fallen on the nearby statue. On the hairline crack near Ashaira's hand.

It wasn't his imagination—he was sure of it.

After his final strike, the crack had gotten larger.

Kaycia threw herself sideways, and the courthouse burst apart. As the world turned over, she sprang off the ground with her hands and tumbled over a cracked roof section. She then veered left, using her conviction to weave through rocks and debris.

She landed in a different version of the street and adjusted her eyes to a moonlit night—but the spikes pursued her. They erupted through the cobbles and allowed her no rest.

For the past few minutes, Aico had stayed on her trail. It didn't matter where she went or how she twisted the world—he'd quickly learned how to follow her anywhere.

At first, she hadn't allowed this to bother her. She'd been surprised when the boy followed her into a snowstorm, but she'd also understood the extent of his abilities. Without access to conviction, the boy couldn't make the changes himself but was forced to close in on the windows she created.

So she tried to lose him. She leaped to the rooftops and slid somewhere else. She passed through version after version, trying to create more distance. She'd throw buildings in his path to block his pursuit.

But there was nothing she could do that Aico couldn't see. He perceived every feint and could break every obstacle. Even when the boy fell behind, it only took one spike to hold the window open.

"*Ooooh!*" said a voice. "*This looks fun.*"

It came just as Kaycia was flying out a window and had to focus on redirecting herself onto the roof.

"Sefina?" she asked when she caught her breath.

"*...Did you miss me?*"

There was a crash as the roof buckled and fell from under her.

Kaycia's body twisted on its own, and she didn't resist.

Rather than escape the hole, Sefina drove her downward and took hold of her chains.

Aico leaped back in surprise and formed a defensive wall.

She threw her blades, not in an attack, but to throw her momentum sideways and slide across the floor into an adjacent room.

"Oops!" she taunted, "Did I scare you, boy?"

Spikes burst through the walls but somehow couldn't reach her.

Kaycia didn't understand—until she saw the walls moving away. In a fashion similar to splitting the bridge, Sefina had sundered the building in two.

She fell down the chasm, tumbling head over heels, with her chains still spinning. The circular momentum curved her backward through the building and up through the floor, right behind Aico.

The boy didn't turn, but new spikes managed to block her blades.

Sefina, however, hadn't meant to harm him. Her chains had thrown her body in reverse, out through a window, as the building split again.

Kaycia flipped away from the collapse. She landed on her feet, skidding backward, just as the cloud of dust overtook her.

It stung her eyes and made it impossible to see. The tremors, however, left no room for doubt. She heard the roof collapse—the same moment the boy's creations blocked him inside.

"Give it a rest, already!" Sefina shouted through the dust. "Believe it or not, I don't want to kill you."

Before Kaycia knew what was happening, her body twisted evasively. She could hear the spikes, though she couldn't see them.

Sefina laughed. "Go ahead. Get it all out. I can see you're not used to this—missing your target. But I can wait. When you're ready to talk—"

The dust split as an enormous boulder fell from the sky.

Aico's voice was deafening. "I've had enough of your tricks!"

Kaycia wanted to run, but Sefina reined her in.

They stood their ground together as the boulder crashed, no doubt, in a different version of the street.

"Is that the way of it?" she asked. "You avoid discussion, just as you've run from everything else?"

"Let Kaycia go. Then, we'll talk."

She laughed again. "You've got it all wrong. Did it not occur to you that maybe she wants my help? That she's given herself freely because she trusts me?"

"Trust in a murderer?"

"She knows what I am. She doesn't agree with all of it—well, most of it, really—but right now, you're the one who's trying to kill her."

The dust died down, revealing a protective cage of spikes beneath the rubble.

Aico wasn't there.

For a long moment, he gave no answer.

Sefina shrugged her shoulders. "I mean, she gets it, of course. Your fight isn't personal. But you *would* let her die to deprive me of this body."

Somehow, his voice seemed to come from everywhere. "That isn't true! Kaycia, listen! Can't you see how she is? The way she operates?"

Kaycia tried to speak and met no resistance. "Aico! I do! But this is exactly what the abyss wants from us! For us to fight each other!"

Another pause.

"You don't have to forgive her!" she continued. "You don't have to agree to anything. Not right away. Just—"

"Just what?" he interrupted. "Leave the statue alone? Nice try, Sefina."

Kaycia felt an unexpected twinge of urgency. Her mouth opened on its own. "Damn it!" she hissed. "It's Nesil!"

And without further explanation, she felt Sefina leave.

"Nesil?" asked Aico, stepping out from behind a rock. "Is this another trick?"

Kaycia gaped. She waited a moment for Sefina to return, but the girl was gone. "I...! She left! I don't know why!"

Aico shook his head. "She wants me to think the statue's in danger. As though Nesil could destroy it with his bare hands. I'm not falling for it."

Kaycia took a step back. "I'm telling the truth!"

"All right," he said without slowing his approach. "If she's gone, prove it to me."

"What? How?"

"...Take off the band."

"The—?" She paused a moment, thinking it over.

"I'll make this easier for you. If it doesn't come off in five seconds, I'll know you're lying. And I'll attack with everything I got."

"But that's not—!"

"Three seconds."

"You have to believe me!"

Her problem wasn't with taking it off—it would prove her innocence and cost her nothing. But she was more afraid of Aico's intentions, convinced he'd destroy the thing. Which wouldn't only affect Sefina, it would negate Elyriel's chance of being healed in the future.

Aico lunged forward.

On instinct, Kaycia crossed realms—but she wasn't fast enough.

A surge of rock swept her legs out from under her, with more than enough force to break a regular person's bones.

She rolled sideways onto snow and rose to her knees—as something slammed the back of her head.

Stars sprayed across her vision, and she tasted blood. The ground disappeared, and she tumbled without seeing. Something crashed against her ribs, knocking the wind from her lungs. Something else smacked her hip.

It was different than before. The attacks were coming so fast it couldn't be a test. Aico was venting his frustrations. A twelve-year-old boy, losing control. No longer interested in sparing her life.

Somehow, a chain was still in her hand. Before she knew what was happening, she gave it a tug and whipped herself around.

When her body moved, diving between spikes, the feeling was familiar.

"Sefina?" she asked, in sudden alarm. "Were you able to—?"

"*Not now.*"

Kaycia was dizzy, unable to make sense of the rocks whizzing past her head. Instead, she let Sefina do the work—ducking, twisting, and sliding past obstacles.

Aico didn't relent—emboldened, perhaps, to have been proven right. He pressed the attack—right to the moment an explosion split the sky.

Glimmering colors shook the heavens, so bright, Kaycia was forced to turn away.

Looking back, she saw Aico's face dawning with regret.

"It's not possible..." he breathed.

He broke into a run toward the blinding light.

"Shouldn't you go, too?" asked Kaycia, worried for the statue but afraid it was too late.

Sefina stood beside her, shaking her head.

Kaycia was stunned. "But...!"

She didn't understand why Sefina came back. To save her, yes, but at what cost? Of all the times to betray her selfish nature, why change now?

"If it's destroyed, how will you—?"

"*It'll be all right,*" said the girl. "*Aico will be angry, but he'll let you go. There's no reason to hold you.*"

"But what about you?"

Sefina shrugged helplessly. "*I think... Maybe Nesil was right. After everything I've done, I don't deserve redemption.*"

Kaycia refused to believe this was the end. Could it possibly be a trick? An extreme illusion to throw Aico off their trail?

Otherwise, there'd be no point to this. They'd thrown the dice and come up wanting.

An urgency overtook Sefina's eyes. She looked deep into Kaycia's, ignoring the thundering colors above.

"*Maybe the world doesn't need Irisea.*"

She touched the key around Kaycia's neck.

"*Her legacy can go on... Through you.*"

With her other hand cupping Kaycia's cheek, the girl forced a smile.

And, then, disappeared.

A MATTER OF TRUST

Nesil closed his eyes and waited for the end.

He could imagine it perfectly—the shattered realities and blistering light. It was just as he remembered, back in Seldor.

Against all odds, he'd done it again. He'd convinced his body to escape the aeisr's clutches—not by breaking his bonds but by passing through them. He'd made himself immaterial—or, at least, a different material that didn't align with his momentary prison.

After that, it was easy. With his fists, he'd attacked the stone with maniacal fury. The chain reaction sent cracks through every inch of Ashaira, leaving not so much as a trace behind.

He was surprised, then—and more than a little worried—when the world stopped shaking. The noise died away, and for reasons unexplainable, Nesil was still alive.

He opened his eyes.

As expected, there were broken buildings and crumbled walls, but the damage was nothing out of the ordinary. There were no floating rocks or bottomless chasms. It could all be explained by Aico's fight with Kaycia.

So what was going on? If there were no illusions, why did Nesil remain?

"I should kill you right now," said the other boy from behind him.

Nesil turned, feeling something like shame. It wasn't regret, as he couldn't feel guilty for doing what was necessary. Even so, he didn't like being the focus of such unbridled loathing.

"Are you expecting an apology?" he asked. "Because you know my fight was never with you. If anything, I was helping. Saving you from her."

Aico scrunched his face in disgust as if to say he'd had everything under control. The boy, however, resisted the impulse to continue their argument, perhaps recognizing that what was done was done.

Instead, he held up a tiny shard. "Do you know what this is?"

As he turned it in the light, it looked like a finger or part of a hand. The edges were sharp, as though it'd been chipped from the statue. By some miraculous stroke of luck, the piece had escaped consumption, perhaps flying free mere moments before detonation.

Whether this was good luck or bad, he was yet to determine.

Nesil swallowed hard. "Is she...? Is she still alive?"

Aico exhaled slowly and shook his head.

"You're sure? You're absolutely certain? I mean, look! If I'm still here, then—!"

"Be quiet," said Aico, thoroughly out of patience, "and try to pay attention... This was the only fragment I managed to secure. Perhaps, if I'd gotten here a moment sooner, I could've saved more."

Nesil didn't know what to think. He should've felt relieved—perhaps even grateful—that the boy had the insight to save his life. But, instead, he felt overwhelming anxiety.

Aico had no trouble guessing why.

"Just stay right there," said the boy. "I need to show you something."

He turned to walk away. Slowly.

This was so unexpected, Nesil soon fell into frustration.

Except, after Aico had gone a mere ten paces, Nesil began to feel lightheaded. A prickling sensation enveloped his body, like losing circulation from sitting the wrong way. He felt it everywhere, like a thousand needles.

Looking down at his hands, he was able to see through them. His body became semi-transparent, and it only got worse as Aico moved away.

"Do you see what I mean?" asked the boy. "Or should I walk even further?"

Nesil forcefully shook his head. At fifteen paces, the unpleasant sensation had escalated to agony, as though his body were being stretched into a million threads.

"This shard," said Aico, walking back, "is the only reason you're alive. You and only you. Got that?"

Nesil needed a moment to catch his breath. "...But how can you be sure?"

"If Sefina were nearby, I'd know. Trust me."

A part of Nesil wanted to believe him—to celebrate his hard-won victory and miraculous survival. The proof was right in front of him—the single shard to which he owed his life.

Even so, it wasn't enough.

Nesil shook his head and steeled himself. "You should destroy it."

"What?" asked Aico, at a loss.

"Please. It's the only way to be sure."

The boy was speechless.

"Come on!" he pressed. "I can see it in your face—the way you hate me! I went behind your back! I deprived your people of their only chance!"

Sure enough, his words struck a nerve. Aico's grip tightened around the fragment as though preparing to crush it.

Nesil's heart pounded, feeling he was close.

"Just do it already! Why are you standing there?"

But the seconds dragged out, long and tortuous.

"Why?" asked Nesil. "Is it because of me? Because I saved your life? I'm telling you that you've got it backward! I *want* you to destroy it! *That's* how you repay me!"

Aico grit his teeth. "You're a real asshole, you know that?"

The insult took Nesil completely by surprise.

Aico went on. "Playing the part of the tragic hero—prepared to sacrifice it all in some noble gesture? But you know what? No one gives two shits if you die today. Because your death would be meaningless. A cowardly escape and not much else."

"You don't understand," Nesil pleaded. "I have to finish what I started! My entire life has been building to this moment!"

"You're sure about that?" Aico raised his chin, unwilling to back down. "Your existence amounts to a single purpose? To destroy the aeisr and nothing more?"

"Someone has to do it!"

"Maybe," said Aico, groaning with disgust. "But now, I think, that's just an excuse. Because if you truly had honor, you wouldn't give up. You'd find a new purpose. Something greater."

Nesil's face grew red, unable to bear being lectured by a child. Though he knew, deep down, that Aico was right, he didn't have the strength for self-introspection. He didn't have the courage.

Aico took a deep breath. "I don't have time to sit and grovel. And you shouldn't, either. If you're done feeling sorry for yourself, there might be a way for you to make this up to me."

Nesil didn't bother to look up.

"Look," said the boy, "I'm finding it very hard not to be angry. If it's a fight you're after, I'll set this down. You can stay right here and figure things out for the rest of eternity."

A part of Nesil wanted just that. If the boy was unwilling to finish the deed, Nesil could destroy the shard himself.

But another part was curious to know more.

He met Aico's eyes. "Why do you even care?"

The boy shrugged. "Perhaps I'm loathe to walk away empty-handed. I came to this place in search of help."

Nesil grunted. "So you'll take me, instead?"

"Just think about it. Even if you've only just become one, you're the last aeisr in the entire world. And that means something, I think. There are talents you can offer like nobody else."

"Like walking through walls?"

"Why not? Espionage. Reconnaissance. Missions that range deep into the current—the ones that mean death for a regular person. You could be there. You could stare our true enemy right in the face and be certain to walk away with the intelligence we need."

"Aren't you forgetting something?" asked Nesil, gesturing toward the shard.

"You wouldn't be alone, of course. Someone in the group would know your secret and carry the fragment where you need to go."

Nesil frowned. "I thought you said it would be dangerous."

"And I meant it. I'm not going to lie. There's a chance only you would survive the mission. But that's the difference. If the others die, their deaths would mean something because you would retain the answers discovered."

Nesil sighed, surprised his interest was actually piqued. It was more than a new purpose—it was the prospect of facing a new set of challenges. Of saving a group of people doomed from the start.

Anything less wouldn't be worth his time.

"So, are you coming or not?" asked Aico.

Nesil worked his mouth. "I could always change my mind later... I just have one question."

Aico eyed him sideways. "You still think I'm wrong. About Sefina."

He reddened with embarrassment. "I'm that easy to read?"

"Look," said Aico. "When your mind's been set, nothing I say will make a difference. But shouldn't you ask yourself—if she did get away, by some freak accident... If it isn't the shard keeping her alive, what good would it do to destroy it now?"

The boy had a point. For Nesil to believe in one impossibility, he needed to be open to others as well.

Nesil held back a laugh, feeling utterly stupid.

When it all came down to it, nothing was certain.

Especially if he decided to give up now.

"**K**ay?" asked Chesandril. "Everything all right?"

"I...think so... How did I get here?"

The girl scrunched her face in confusion.

"My body," clarified Kaycia. Then, she sighed, unable to blame Chesandril for what she did or didn't know.

The girl sat down on the bed beside her. "Agren brought you back from some cave. They said something about Elyriel. That she was better or something? He wasn't very clear."

Kaycia didn't want to remember. "Where's Soril now?"

"Well... He's... You don't know?"

"Know what? Just tell me, Chess!"

"The whole camp's been talking—how Ahman's returned. The entire city. Out by the lake."

Kaycia swallowed, surprised at herself for not putting this together—for not remembering the statue's primary function. She could only imagine the heightened emotion—particularly from Soril.

"Did all of them go? The ascendants?"

"Most of them, I think. He was worried about you—Elyriel, I mean."

This made sense. But it didn't explain why Kaycia was here. There was no reason for being expelled from Elyriel's mind. No physical danger. No mental trauma.

But before she could lie down and reach for her sister, Agren stepped into the carriage.

He snapped his fingers in triumph. "I told them you'd be here."

Kaycia sat up. "What are you talking about?"

He pressed his hands together with a look of apology. "We went into Ahman. You know that, right...? But when we found your sister—"

"Thank the gods!" she exclaimed, swinging her feet off the bed.

There was something in his face that betrayed uncertainty.

"What's happened?" she demanded. "She's not hurt, is she?"

"No," he added quickly. "It's not that at all. But... Maybe you should come see for yourself."

He made it seem like he was hiding a surprise—and not the sort that should have her worried.

Even so, she knew better than to raise her hopes.

They left a rather disappointed Chesandril behind and stepped out onto an empty field. Another few steps and they were surrounded by birch and cedar.

And then they were there, walking amid the ruined buildings Kaycia knew well. Several worse for wear after her recent battle.

Being here in her own body felt strange—keenly aware of Aico's warning. With the statue gone, the city wasn't safe. And it was a matter of time before the abyssal creatures claimed the land for their own.

For now, her life was in Agren's hands.

As well as in Soril's, who'd just stepped from a doorway.

And behind him...

Elyriel's appearance was...absolutely normal. A few scrapes on her face and tangles in her hair—but her eyes were focused and free from mania.

Kaycia refused to feel relief. After everything that'd happened, she couldn't put stock in miracles without cause.

Sure enough, a voice spoke into her ear.

"Please don't be upset. I didn't mean for this to happen."

Kaycia closed her eyes and nodded to herself. To her surprise, she wasn't terribly disappointed. She was glad Sefina had made it out alive and couldn't blame the girl for this unexpected outcome. But her relief was tainted, nonetheless.

"Can I have a moment?" she asked Soril, as she reached for Elyriel's hand.

He kept his body between them. "I've made that mistake once already."

She stifled a groan. "Thirty seconds," she said. "Over there, where you can see us... Please?"

For a moment, she was worried he wouldn't back down. His jaw tightened in disapproval, but Soril was unusually fond of second chances. And third ones. And fourths.

She scrunched her face in apology and tried to be quick.

"Don't speak," said Sefina. *"I can't hide your voice with the statue gone. No illusions at all. But you can still hear me because of our bond."*

Kaycia paused a moment, somewhat disappointed. It was hard to think of Sefina without her abilities. But that couldn't be helped after recent events.

She had to think about her questions, knowing Soril was likely listening.

Luckily, Sefina had already thought this through.

"I know this is hard," said her disembodied voice. She didn't move her lips, but her face appeared genuinely sorry. *"I wouldn't want to do it either—to act and pretend as though I'm your sister. But think about it. If word gets out—how long will it take before Aico hears?"*

Kaycia groaned. She'd anticipated a request along these lines. It was more than just Aico. It was difficult to predict how anyone would respond to hearing Irisea was alive and real.

For the majority, such news would be met with skepticism. A few would find hope—even if the goddess fell short of expectations. But there would also be those who'd react with fear. Who'd feel threatened or upset by her sacrilegious claim.

Keeping it secret, however, brought its own set of difficulties. Acting as though her sister was better when she wasn't? Kaycia wasn't convinced she could pull it off.

"You finished?" asked Soril.

She closed her eyes and nodded reluctantly. She didn't want to push him longer than needed.

"You're going to tell me everything," he said. "How the city's returned. What's become of the Navaran. But first, you're going to tell me about her." He raised his brows toward the girl at her side.

She worked her mouth, trying to hide her discomfort. None of these subjects were easy to explain, and Elyriel was undoubtedly the worst of all.

Soril sighed in disgust. "And this time, can we skip the lies?"

"Perhaps I should explain," said Elyriel, stepping forward.

Soril narrowed his eyes at the girl.

"You see," she continued. "Kaycia wasn't here for part of the picture. Not like I was."

Kaycia kept quiet, unsurprised by Sefina's knack for lying but grateful all the same.

"Tell me," said Elyriel, meeting the man's gaze, "how much have you heard of the Goddess of Creation?"

"Meileen? What does she have to do with this."

The girl shook her head. "She doesn't. Not directly. I'm asking about her body. Are you aware of what became of her after the Navarans put her away?"

Soril paled and looked at Kaycia.

Kaycia merely shrugged, as she'd never spoken of these matters with her sister or Sefina. The girl, on her own, knew exactly what it'd take to divert the conversation.

Soril turned toward Agren—who was smart enough to leave and allow them some privacy.

"Speak plain," he told Elyriel. "How do you know about this?"

The girl pretended not to hear the threat in his tone. "I know Emperor Mahod was personally involved. Intimately, some might say. He visited the goddess frequently, in her vault beneath the capitol."

Kaycia was shocked, with no way of knowing how much of this was true.

She didn't have to guess what Soril was thinking, remembering his mention of illegal experiments.

"Again—how do you know this?"

Elyriel's face remained innocent. "He told me."

Soril was far from convinced. "The emperor was here?"

She shook her head in apology. "Not Mahod. His son."

Kaycia was speechless. This was either an elaborate attempt to cover the truth, or Sefina was referring to—

"Aico?" she asked. "That's who you mean?"

The girl kept her gaze trained on Soril. "You asked me how I recovered my mind. Well, here's your answer. The boy... He... He did something to me. I think it was an accident. He might not be aware of doing anything at all."

This part was obviously untrue, but it was the closest thing Soril was likely to believe. At least Kaycia would never produce a more convincing lie.

So she lent her support. "I met him, too. It sounds wild, but you've seen what he can do. The way he culled the abyss, out in the forest. It's the same person. Turns out, I was chasing a twelve-year-old boy."

Until that moment, Soril had seemed ready to argue. He kept opening his mouth, trying to cut a word in edgewise—but his expression changed.

"Twelve years?" he asked, lost in thought.

Kaycia assumed he was consulting the timeline—to explain how Mahod had kept the child a secret. At the same time, however, she was missing something vital—how an experiment could produce such formidable power.

Except...

Sefina had already dropped enough hints.

It wasn't that Aico was the son of Mahod but the fact he was also the son of Meileen. Or, at least, what remained of her body. Of her womb.

It changed how Kaycia thought of illegal experiments.

Soril licked his lips, having reached this same conclusion. "And this boy... It was *him* who saved you? You're sure about that?"

Kaycia shrugged. "As sure as we can be. If this sounds confusing, that's because it is. But what else could explain this?"

Soril grimaced. "Doesn't matter what I think. You haven't said anything that will help with your trial. You can't build a case on conjecture and theories."

"Trial?" asked Elyriel.

"I'll explain later," said Kaycia, keeping her eyes on Soril. "But what of everything else? The City of Ahman has returned—we have witnesses! The judges can't suggest we're making this up. Not all of it."

The man shook his head. "It's not that simple. If anything, Ahman only makes it worse. They'll want to comb through everything. And if the details don't add up, you might be imprisoned for a very long time."

"What trial?" repeated Elyriel.

Kaycia didn't blame her. A close examination, after all, had to be the farthest thing from Sefina's mind. How could she protect her secrets when placed beneath the scrutiny of a panel of judges?

"We'll figure something out," Kaycia said. "We'll prove to them we're not a liability. More than that, they can count on our help when they need it the most."

Soril shook his head. "That might not be enough. I know these men—the way they think. They're loathe to trust what they don't understand."

Kaycia knew he was right. And worse, she was starting to feel guilty.

Though Soril hadn't come out and said it, he was clearly holding onto his reservations. And why shouldn't he when she continued to lie at every opportunity?

It never changed—her desperate need to cover something up. Even when it distanced the people closest to her. She found it exhausting.

So, in that moment, she made a decision.

"Soril... I know how hard it is to trust me. Since the moment we met, I've always had reasons to hide the truth."

He worked his mouth but said nothing.

"Well...it doesn't matter how good my reasons have been—if I was protecting myself or anyone else."

"*What are you doing?*" asked Sefina in sudden alarm.

"Just trust me on this," she spoke beneath her breath.

"*Come on, Kay! You aren't thinking!*"

"Maybe not," she hissed. "But Soril's a good man. If we want his help, he deserves the truth."

Soril was confused but also intrigued. Rather than suspect this to be another trap, he was inclined to believe she was finally being honest.

And it was this, most of all, that cemented the deal. It was his trust in Kaycia—despite her bullshit—that made her want to reciprocate confidence.

"*No,*" said Sefina, without moving Elyriel's lips. "*I don't know this man! Even if he doesn't betray us, he'll make a mistake!*"

"Sometimes..." breathed Kaycia. "Sometimes, you just have to act on a feeling."

"What's this about?" Soril asked.

She drew a deep breath. "Aico didn't heal Elyriel. In fact, this isn't my sister at all."

He barely kept his expression in check. "I don't understand."

Kaycia tightened her smile. "I apologize, but I need your solemn promise. What I'm

AUSTIN LYNN CLARK

about to say needs to stay between the three of us."

By the look on his face, he was clearly reluctant.

"Trust me," she said. "This is one secret you'll want to keep."

END OF BOOK ONE

Acknowledgements

I'd like to first thank my wife, Erika Marlene Clark, without whose support none of this would have been possible. This project has been demanding, both in years and in sanity, and there's no one else in the world I'd rather have by my side.

Next comes my editor, Jonathan Smith, who hasn't only invested his time and skills, he's been a great advisor, confidant, gamer, and friend.

Some of my earliest support came from my old writing group, including Tina Sims Gifford and Marcus Varner. My alpha readers soon followed: Caleb Anderson, Jane Lawson, Josh Michaelson, and Halle Sherwood,

Beta readers include: Mike Anderson, Charles Bailey, Peter Jones, Brian Leavitt, Josh Morrey, Jeanette Nunnery, and John Wilson.

Additional readers and listeners include: Colton Bailey, Erin Anadon Beauchamp, Jeffrey Burke, Katie Burke, Brenna Bushman, Sinuhe Celaya, Freyja Lynn Clark, Henedine (Nanette) Hernando Clark Crawford, Kevin Lynn Clark, Andrew Corenejo, Jarvis Giles, Heather Goring Jensen, Alex Harrington, Kara, Crys Knell, Kelsey Leinbach, Jay Maldonado, Julia Rogers, Kevin Rothert, Kylie Sabol, Lacy Schumann, Miranda Tavares, and Randi Tolman.

About the Author

Austin Lynn Clark is an American author of dark epic fantasy, living in El Paso, Texas. He was born in Livermore, California and received his BA in English at Brigham Young University with an emphasis in Creative Writing.

He is married to Erika Marlene Clark. They have one daughter.

www.austinlynnclark.com

9 781969 055027